Weird Vampire Tales

Weird Vampire Tales

30 Blood-Chilling Stories from the Weird Fiction Pulps

Edited by
ROBERT WEINBERG
STEFAN R. DZIEMIANOWICZ
and
MARTIN H. GREENBERG

Introduction by Stefan R. Dziemianowicz

GRAMERCY BOOKS
New York • Avenel, New Jersey

First published in 1992 by Gramercy Books, distributed by Outlet Book Company, Inc., a Random House Company, 40 Engelhard Avenue, Avenel, New Jersey 07001.

Artwork copyright © 1945 by *Weird Tales*®. Reprinted by permission of Weird Tales, Ltd.

Printed and bound in the United States of America
Library of Congress Cataloging-in-Publication Data
Weird vampire tales : 30 blood-chilling stories from the weird fiction
    pulps / edited by Robert Weinberg, Stefan R. Dziemianowicz & Martin
    H. Greenberg ; introduction by Stefan R. Dziemianowicz.
        p.   cm.
    ISBN 0-517-06018-3
        1. Vampires—Fiction. 2. Horror tales, American. 3. American
fiction—20th century. I. Weinberg, Robert E. II. Dziemianowicz,
Stefan R. III. Greenberg, Martin Harry.
PS648.V35W44   1992
813'.0873808375—dc20   92-1113
                                                              CIP

8 7 6 5 4 3 2 1

ACKNOWLEDGMENTS

The Man Who Cast No Shadow by Seabury Quinn—Copyright 1927 by Weird Tales. Reprinted by permission of the Scott Meredith Literary Agency, Inc., 845 Third Ave., New York, NY 10022.

The Wolf Woman by Bassett Morgan—Copyright 1927 by Weird Tales. Reprinted by permission of Weird Tales Ltd.

The Canal by Everil Worrell—Copyright 1927 by Weird Tales. Reprinted by permission of Jeanne E. Murphy.

A Rendezvous in Averoigne by Clark Ashton Smith—Copyright 1931 by Weird Tales. Reprinted by permission of the Scott Meredith Literary Agency, Inc., 845 Third Avenue, New York, NY 10022.

Placide's Wife by Kirk Mashburn—Copyright 1931 by Weird Tales. Reprinted by permission of Weird Tales Ltd.

The Horror from the Mound by Robert E. Howard—Copyright 1932 by Popular Publishing Co. Reprinted by permission of Glenn Lord, agent for the heir to Robert E. Howard.

Vampire Village by Edmond Hamilton—Copyright 1932 by Weird Tales. Reprinted by permission of the Spectrum Literary Agency.

Revelations in Black by Carl Jacobi—Copyright 1933 by Popular Publishing Co. Reprinted by permission of the author's agent, R. Dixon Smith.

Shambleau by C. L. Moore—Copyright 1933; renewed © 1962 by C. L. Moore. Reprinted by permission of Don Congdon Associates, Inc.

Return to Death by J. Wesley Rosenquist—Copyright 1936 by Popular Publications, Inc. Reprinted by permission of Weird Tales Ltd.

Isle of the Undead by Lloyd Arthur Eshbach—Copyright 1936 by Popular Publishing Co. Copyright renewed © 1964 by Lloyd Arthur Eshbach. Reprinted by permission of the author and the author's agent, James Allen.

Doom of the House of Duryea by Earl Pierce, Jr.—Copyright 1936 by Popular Publishing Co. Reprinted by permission of Weird Tales Ltd.

I, the Vampire by Henry Kuttner—Copyright 1937; renewed © 1965 by the Estate of Henry Kuttner. Reprinted by permission of Don Congdon Associates, Inc.

The Silver Coffin by Robert Barbour Johnson—Copyright 1939 by Popular Publications. Reprinted by permission of Weird Tales Ltd.

Cross of Fire by Lester del Rey—Copyright 1939; copyright renewed © 1967 by Lester del Rey. Reprinted by permission of the Scott Meredith Literary Agency, Inc., 845 Third Avenue, New York, NY 10022.

CONTENTS

Weird Tales

Astounding Science-Fiction

Strange Tales of Mystery and Terror

Terror Tales

Horror Stories

Unknown/Unknown Worlds

INTRODUCTION

His face was strong—a very strong—aquiline, with high bridge of the thin nose and peculiarly arched nostrils; with lofty, domed forehead and hair growing scantily around the temples, but profusely elsewhere. His eyebrows were very massive, almost meeting over the nose, and with bushy hair that seemed to curl in its profusion. The mouth, so far as I could see it under the heavy moustache, was fixed and rather cruel-looking, with peculiarly sharp white teeth; these protruded over the lips, whose ruddiness showed astonishing vitality in a man of his years. For the rest, his ears were pale and at the top extremely pointed; the chin was broad and strong and the cheeks firm and thin. The general effect was one of extraordinary pallor.

The passage above, from the opening chapters of Bram Stoker's 1897 novel *Dracula*, has for nearly a century defined the image of the fictional vampire. When Stoker's novel was adapted none-too-scrupulously for the screen by Tod Browning in 1931, Bela Lugosi's portrayal of Transylvania's most famous native helped etch some of these features permanently on the consciousness of horror lovers around the world.

Dracula was not the first work of popular vampire fiction. A number of successful vampire stories preceded it into print, among them J. Sheridan Le Fanu's famous short novel *Carmilla*. But Stoker's novel was unique in its exhaustive cataloguing of myths and legends concerned with the origin and nature of vampires, and it quickly became the standard by which all subsequent vampire tales were measured. The peculiar habits of Count Dracula still serve as the prototype for the vampires of contemporary fiction, film and stage: Immortal (or at least "undead") he sleeps by day in his coffin and drinks the blood of his victims by night; he casts no shadow or image in a mirror and has hair on the palms of his hands; he can assume the shape of a bat, a wolf, or a dog and can make packs of rats and wolves do his bidding; he cannot cross a stream of running water on his own, but he can be transported over the ocean in a coffin filled with the soil of his native land; he must be invited to cross a threshold, and he can be repelled by garlic and the image of the cross; he cannot reproduce, but ultimately those whose blood he drains become vampires themselves; he is powerless when exposed to daylight and can be killed by a wooden stake driven through his heart. After his death those victims who have not been killed by his bite regain their health.

Though we credit Stoker with creating one of the most durable archetypes of horror fiction, *adapting* would be the more appropriate term. His imaginative embellishments notwithstanding, *Dracula* was a reshaping of four centuries of folk legends that had accreted around the historical Walachian warlord Prince Vlad Tepes ("the Impaler") into a Victorian morality tale. By its enormous success, Stoker's novel demonstrated how the vampire owed its immortality—in

11

the literary sense—to its ability to take the imprint of each age's fears and dreads.

It was in the pages of the pulp fiction magazines that the vampire story made the transition from the Victorian to the modern age and became a staple of supernatural horror fiction. Created in 1896, the pulp magazine was the immediate successor to the nineteenth-century penny dreadful and dime novel, a new vehicle for delivering escapist thrills, chills and adventures to middle- and working-class readers. Though the first pulps were general fiction magazines that did not discriminate between the different kinds of story they published, early in the twentieth century they gave way to magazines which specialized in specific fiction genres. Among these were a generous selection of mystery, fantasy, horror, and science fiction pulps in which the vampire was given room to evolve from Stoker's object of Victorian fear and loathing into the complex and intriguing figure it is today.

Weird Tales (1923–1954), the first pulp magazine devoted exclusively to weird fiction, was an important early market for the vampire story. Though it published fantastic fiction of all sorts, vampires were the theme of about ninety stories, and thus appeared in the magazine on an average of once in every three of its 279 issues. Virtually every one of *Weird Tales'*s most distinguished contributors—H.P. Lovecraft, Clark Ashton Smith, Robert E. Howard, Robert Bloch, Henry Kuttner, C.L. Moore, Manly Wade Wellman—at some time wrote a vampire story for the magazine.

Not surprisingly, the earliest vampire stories in *Weird Tales* echoed Stoker's classic. At the time, Stoker was still a formidable presence in the horror field— *Weird Tales* alone reprinted six of his short stories between 1927 and 1937—and his influence was reinforced by the immense popularity of the film *Dracula* and its sequel *Dracula's Daughter* in 1936. Indeed, it should be pointed out that until 1945 and the dawn of the nuclear age, weird fiction writers were closer in time, and probably temperament, to Stoker's era than the current one.

Yet the vampire stories in *Weird Tales* were not mere imitations. In "The Man Who Cast No Shadow," Seabury Quinn's vampire is of Transylvanian descent and revealed by the same hairy palms and absent mirror image that gave away Count Dracula. But by importing his evil Count Czerny to Harrisonville, New Jersey, home of intrepid psychic investigator Jules de Grandin, Quinn wrote one of the first vampire stories set on American soil and thus helped to expand the legacy of the literary vampire. Bassett Morgan gave the vampire maiden of "The Wolf Woman" the same command over a wolf army as Dracula had but made her the last of a vampiric race that walked the earth before the freezing of the ice caps. In "Vampire Village," Edmond Hamilton sent two Americans traipsing through Transylvania on the Feast of St. George, the same day as Jonathan Harker's ill-fated assignation at Castle Dracula, but Hamilton had them stumble upon an extinct vampire town magically brought to life on that day every year. Though anyone who had read *Dracula* would recognize the origins of these motifs, the considerable differences that distinguish these stories from one another show that *Weird Tales* writers were more determined to distance themselves from Stoker's novel than they were to evoke its memory.

No one formula determined how *Weird Tales*'s many variations on the vampire theme would be told, but early in the magazine's life distinct storytelling patterns emerged. In its first vampire tale, Victor Rowan's "Four Wooden Stakes," the protagonist discovers that the disfigured monster who visits him nightly is a vampirized member of his family. A number of writers followed Rowan's lead and depicted the vampire purely as a ruthless, physically intimidating monster. In "The Horror from the Mound," for example, Robert E. Howard kept his vampire offstage until the denouement and choreographed the climax like a brutal barroom brawl. Both Lloyd Arthur Eshbach's "Isle of the Undead" and Frank Belknap Long and Otis Adelbert Kline's "Return of the Undead" presented their vampires as little more than walking appetites. In these stories, development of the vampire's unique character took a backseat to action-packed adventure.

But many more pulp writers recognized, as Stoker had, that what makes the vampire so frightening is its close resemblance to ordinary human beings. In even the crudest pulp stories, vampires tend to display an enviable sophistication and urbanity—character traits that make their primitive blood lust more inexplicable and terrifying. More importantly, the pulp vampire was frequently portrayed as an object of romantic fascination. Elaborating on ideas left implicit in Stoker's Victorian novel, *Weird Tales* writes imagined vampires who used their imperishable beauty and seductive guile to snare victims.

Though he clearly preferred innocent women, Count Dracula had been indiscriminate in his choice of prey, looking on men and women alike as cattle for the slaughter. In deference to the prevailing values of the pulp era, though, *Weird Tales* writers usually paired vampire and victim in one of two standard relationships: older male vampire and young woman, or young female vampire and young man. Indeed, Clark Ashton Smith took this idea to its limit in his 1933 tale, "A Rendezvous in Averoigne," creating a vampire lord and lady who waylaid trysting lovers.

A number of vampire stories founded upon such relationships were little more than standard pulp romances in which the unnatural desires of both predator and prey spiced the tales with an acceptable illicitness. More often, though, writers treated romantic passion toward the vampire as a mark of human frailty manipulated by shrewd and uncanny intelligences. In Everil Worrell's "The Canal," for example, a jaded young man mistakes the willful behavior of his vampire lover as free-spiritedness and gladly helps her to cross the stream separating her from his helpless town. Similarly, in Kirk Mashburn's "Placide's Wife," a vampire woman counts on the loneliness of laborers in the Louisiana bayous to help her gain access to their camp. In Carl Jacobi's "Revelations in Black," a man is so smitten by a female vampire that he finds himself emotionally incapable of withdrawing from what his rational self recognizes is a suicidal relationship. From stories such as these, it's only a short hop to Henry Kuttner's "I, the Vampire,'' in which the hero's romantic obsession with a female victim conflicts with his instinctive drives and leads to his undoing. Kuttner's portrait of the vampire as a tragic figure anticipates the attitude of much contemporary vampire fiction, and led inevitably in *Weird Tales* to stories like Greye La Spina's ''Antimacassar,'' in which a child vampire is a sympathetic character as deserving of our pity as our fear.

As proof of the endless number of variations to which the vampire theme lent itself, many *Weird Tales* writers eschewed romance altogether to concentrate on inventive new renderings of superstitions in the vampire canon. Lester del Rey, in ''Cross of Fire,'' wondered how we might view vampirism were it explained as a symptom of a split personality that could eventually be brought under the control of the well-integrated self. In ''The Doom of the House of Duryea,'' Earl Peirce, Jr., replaced the traditional origins of vampirism with a family curse passed down through the generations. J. Wesley Rosenquist in ''Return to Death'' saw irony in a situation where a perfectly normal man might be mistaken for a vampire, and Robert Barbour Johnson proposed a seemingly foolproof and sanitary means for disposing of the Undead in ''The Silver Coffin.'' But probably the most ingenious approach to vampires and vampirism is found in the fiction of C.L. Moore. In ''Shambleau,'' ''Black Thirst,'' and other installments in the saga of her hero, Northwest Smith, Moore proposed the existence of extraterrestrial civilizations that had served as the basis for Earth's vampire myths. Devoid of any artifacts of traditional vampire lore, her stories epitomize the imaginative extremes to which *Weird Tales* pursued the vampire theme.

Because it lasted only seven issues, *Strange Tales of Mystery and Terror* (1931–1933), which was conceived as a direct competitor of *Weird Tales,* had little opportunity to make an impact on the vampire (or any other type of) tale. However, its four contributions to the pulp vampire legacy were motivated by the same inventive spirit one finds in *Weird Tales* fiction. Marion Brandon's ''The Dark Castle'' was a conventional tale of Transylvanian vampires that contrasted sharply with Philip Hazleton's ''After Sunset,'' a very different story narrated by a first-person vampire right up through death by staking. Of greater significance were Hugh Cave's two vampire tales. ''Stragella'' reworked an episode from Stoker into a suspense classic by installing a nest of vampires in a derelict ship chanced upon by the survivors of a shipwreck. ''Murgunstrumm'' used its rural Southern setting to create a mood of unrelievable creepiness; it is recognized today as a quintessential American vampire tale.

With its cast of cannibal dwarfs and bloodsucking lotharios, ''Murgunstrumm'' is a more restrained version of the type of story Cave wrote regularly for the ''shudder'' pulps. A unique species of weird fiction magazine, the shudder pulp, represented most faithfully by *Horror Stories* (1935–1941) and *Terror Tales* (1934–1941), offered readers tales of sadistic indignities and tortures inflicted upon hapless victims—usually beautiful women and their completely ineffectual boyfriends—by mad scientists and psychotic crooks masquerading as model citizens. Nearly every shudder pulp story involves a threat so outrageous that supernatural possibilities have to be entertained. Ultimately, though, the menace proves the handiwork of devious human beings involved in conspiracies so farfetched they make the supernatural look rational by comparison.

The *suggestion* that bizarre events are the work of a vampire before a more logical explanation emerges is a gimmick of many regular pulp stories, the most famous being Robert Bloch's *Weird Tales* opus, "The Bogeyman Will Get You," in which a werewolf covers its tracks by pretending to be a vampire. In the shudder pulps, though, it was assumed from the outset that the mock-supernatural premise of a story be explained away entirely by the end. For every tale like Raymond Whetstone's "The Thirsty Dead," which leaves ambiguous whether the narrator has been victimized by a vampire or merely driven mad by his ordeal, there were many more tales like Nat Schachner's "Thirst of the Ancients" and John H. Knox's "Men Without Blood," in which maniacs hypnotize their victims into believing that they must drink blood in order to live, or Arthur J. Burks's "Murder Brides," which rationalizes an elaborate stratagem to explain the vampiric immortality of a seemingly indestructible woman. Even when the vampire is genuine, as in Cornell Woolrich's "Vampire's Honeymoon," shudder pulp stories were more interesting for their perceptions of human gullibility and familiarity with vampire lore than for their efforts to suspend reader disbelief in the supernatural.

Indirectly, and certainly unintentionally, the shudder pulps proved a point now taken for granted in weird fiction writing: that a creature of such grotesque and exaggerated proportions as the vampire is as exploitable for humor as for horror. In this regard, Robert Bloch's "The Cloak" from *Unknown Worlds* (1939–1943) was a fantasy breakthrough. Bloch suggested that rather than fitting comfortably into the modern American environment as so many pulp vampires did, the average vampire might find it difficult to satisfy his unique appetite in a socially acceptable way. In so doing Bloch helped to perfect humorous horror, a subgenre that grew noticeably in the postwar years, when the serious horror story seemed to lose its relevance. August Derleth's "Who Shall I Say is Calling?" a 1952 story from *The Magazine of Fantasy and Science Fiction* (1949–   ) in which the vampiric behavior of a pair of cocktail party crashers offers a wry critique of middle-class social rituals, is a direct extension of Bloch's achievement.

Unknown Worlds published much humorous fantasy, though not entirely by design. Frustrated by the stock theatrics of so much "serious" supernatural fiction, editor John W. Campbell asked his writers to strip away the Gothic cliches, dispense with the histrionics, and reconceive their themes for the same logical world that is the audience for science fiction. Writers who focused on the incongruity of the supernatural erupting into such a world produced whimsical stories like Bloch's. Others created realistic scenarios in which the supernatural seems to fit unobtrusively. *Unknown Worlds* published only four vampire stories in its thirty-nine issues, but two by Manly Wade Wellman are good examples of the latter approach. In "When It Was Moonlight," he answered the tiresome question so often asked of horror writers, "Where do you get your ideas," by extrapolating a vampiric influence on some writings of Edgar Allan Poe. In "The Devil is Not Mocked," he pitted two versions of the devil incarnate against each other, Count Dracula and Adolf Hitler, and achieved the singular feat of making Dracula end up a hero.

Campbell also edited *Astounding Science-Fiction* (1930–   ), the most important science fiction pulp and a magazine whose scientifically enlightened attitude toward the fantastic all but excluded the vampire as a potential theme. Nevertheless, in "Asylum," A.E. van Vogt explored the same ground C.L. Moore had covered a decade before by proposing a race of intergalactic vampires as just one of several extraterrestrial species with designs on the planet Earth. Van Vogt so skillfully used the vampire to reinforce science fiction's sense of wonder at the vastness of what lies beyond our solar system that even Campbell must have forgiven him for naming his vampires Dreeghs, a subtle tip of the hat to Dracula.

With science fiction's growing popularity in the postwar years, the horror market began to dwindle, and many writers with good ideas for vampire tales suddenly found themselves in want of an outlet. *Beyond Fantasy Fiction* (1953–1954) continued in the same vein as *Unknown Worlds,* publishing Jerome Bixby and Joe E. Dean's "Share Alike," the tale of a cat-and-mouse game between a vampire and his quarry claustrophobically confined to a drifting rowboat. But *Beyond's* ten issues could only accommodate so many stories, and many horror writers began looking to the science fiction magazines as a potential market. Vampires had actually appeared infrequently in science fiction magazines as early as 1929, but by the 1950s sophisticated readers would no longer tolerate them as simply toothier versions of space opera's traditional bug-eyed monsters. As a result, writers were forced to reinvent the vampire as a fit creature for the atomic age.

In *Fantastic Universe* (1953–1960), William Tenn's "She Only Goes Out at Night" argued for peaceful coexistence between vampires and mortals achieved through the wonders of biotechnology. The majority of postwar vampire tales were not so optimistic, though, presenting instead vampires who found new niches in the new climate of progressive technology to practice their old ways. Cyril M. Kornbluth's "The Mindworm," from the first issue of *Worlds Beyond* (1950–1951), offered the most original vampire variant: a creature created in the human womb from radioactive exposure whose nourishment is the thoughts and emotions of those around him.

Though vastly different from Kornbluth's tale in their resurrection of the classic vampire, Joe L. Hensley's "And Not Quite Human" from *Beyond* and Charles Beaumont's "Place of Meeting" from *Orbit Science Fiction* (1953–1954) arrive at virtually the same conclusion: No matter how advanced humankind becomes it will always instinctively fear death; and in any future where death is feared, there will always be a place for the Undead.

Though the stories in *Weird Vampire Tales* were written within thirty years, for a handful of pulp fiction magazines, they cover a vast amount of territory, ranging in time from the prehistory to centuries in the future, and in settings from the backwash of Transylvania to the far reaches of outer space. Each was chosen to demonstrate the unlimited richness of the vampire theme, and to illustrate how the vampire has lodged so snugly in the imagination for the last century of horror readers and writers. There may be no such things as vampires—but, as these stories show, that does not make them any less entertaining or worthy of our attention.

—Stefan Dziemianowicz

New York, 1992

THE MAN WHO CAST NO SHADOW

SEABURY QUINN

Seabury Quinn was Weird Tales's *most prolific author, and psychic sleuth Jules de Grandin Quinn's most popular character. Without question, de Grandin's most common nemesis was the vampire, which appeared in some form in more than a half dozen of his ninety-three adventures. Quinn's stories frequently told of virtuous young women imperiled by sinister older men, a scenario that lent itself well to his first vampire tale, "The Man Who Cast No Shadow."*

1

"BUT NO, MY FRIEND, Jules de Grandin shook his sleek, blond head decidedly and grinned across the breakfast table at me, "we will go to this so kind Madame Norman's tea, of a certainty. Yes."

"But hang it all," I replied, giving Mrs. Norman's note an irritable shove with my coffee spoon, "I don't want to go to a confounded tea party! I'm too old and too sensible to dress up in a tall hat and a long coat and listen to the vaporings of a flock of silly flappers. I—"

"*Mordieu*, hear the savage!" de Grandin chuckled delightedly. "Always does he find excuses for not giving pleasure to others, and always does he frame those excuses to make him more important in his own eyes. Enough of this, Friend Trowbridge; let us go to the kind Madame Norman's party. Always there is something of interest to be seen if one but knows where to look for it."

"H'm, maybe," I replied grudgingly, "but you've better sight than I think you have if you can find anything worth seeing at an afternoon reception."

The reception was in full blast when we arrived at the Norman mansion in Tuscarora Avenue that afternoon in 192–. The air was heavy with the commingled odors of half a hundred different perfumes and the scent of hot jasmine tea, while the clatter of cup on saucer, laughter, and buzzing conversation filled the wide hall and dining room. In the long double parlors the rugs had been rolled back and young men in frock coats glided over the polished parquetry in company with girls in provocatively short skirts to the belching melody of a saxophone and the drumming rhythm of a piano.

"Pardieu," de Grandin murmured as he viewed the dancers a moment, "your American youth take their pleasures with seriousness, Friend Trowbridge. Behold their faces. Never a smile, never a laugh. They might be recruits on their first parade for all the joy they show—ah!" He broke off abruptly, gazing with startled, almost horrified, eyes after a couple whirling in the mazes of a foxtrot at the farther end of the room. *"Nom d'un fromage,"* he murmured softly to himself, "this matter will bear investigating, I think!"

"Eh, what's that?" I asked, piloting him toward our hostess.

"Nothing, nothing, I do assure you," he answered as we greeted Mrs. Norman and passed toward the dining room. But I noticed his round blue eyes strayed more than once toward the parlors as we drank our tea and exchanged amiable nothings with a pair of elderly ladies.

"Pardon," de Grandin bowed stiffly from the hips to his conversational partner and turned toward the rear drawing room, "there is a gentleman here I desire to meet, if you do not mind—that tall, distinguished one, with the young girl in pink."

"Oh, I guess you mean Count Czerny," a young man laden with an ice in one hand and a glass of non-Volstead punch in the other paused on his way from the dining room. "He's a rare bird, all right. I knew him back in '13 when the Balkan allies were polishing off the Turks. Queer-lookin' duck, ain't he? First-class fightin' man, though. Why, I saw him lead a bayonet charge right into the Turkish lines one day, and when he'd shot his pistol empty he went at the enemy with his teeth! Yes, sir, he grabbed a Turk with both hands and bit his throat out, hanged if he didn't."

"Czerny," de Grandin repeated musingly. "He is a Pole, perhaps?"

His informant laughed a bit shamefacedly. "Can't say," he confessed. "The Serbs weren't asking embarrassing questions about volunteers' nationalities those days, and it wasn't considered healthful for any of us to do so, either. I got the impression he was a Hungarian refugee from Austrian vengeance, but that's only hearsay. Come along, I'll introduce you, if you wish."

I saw de Grandin clasp hands with the foreigner and stand talking with him for a time, and, in spite of myself, I could not forbear a smile at the contrast they made.

The Frenchman was a bare five feet four inches in height, slender as a girl, and, like a girl, possessed of almost laughably small hands and feet. His light hair and fair skin, coupled with his trimly waxed diminutive blond mustache and round unwinking blue eyes, gave him a curiously misleading appearance of mildness. His companion was at least six feet tall, swarthy-skinned and black-haired, with bristling black mustaches and fierce, slate-gray eyes set beneath beetling black brows. His large nose was like the predatory beak of some bird of prey, and the tilt of his long, pointed jaw bore out the uncompromising ferocity of the rest of his visage. Across his left cheek, extending upward over the temple and into his hair, was a knife- or saber-scar, a streak of white showing the trail of the steel in his scalp, and shining like silver inlaid in onyx against the blue-black of his smoothly pomaded locks.

What they said was, of course, beyond reach of my ears, but I saw de Grandin's quick, impish smile flicker across his keen face more than once, to be answered by a slow, languorous smile on the other's dark countenance.

At length the count bowed formally to my friend and whirled away with a wisp of a girl, while de Grandin returned to me. At the door he paused a moment, inclining his shoulders in a salute as a couple of debutantes brushed past him. Something—I know not what—drew my attention to the tall foreigner a moment, and a sudden chill rippled up my spine at what I saw. Above the georgette-clad shoulder of his dancing partner the count's slate-gray eyes were fixed on de Grandin's trim back, and in them I read all the cold, malevolent fury with which a caged tiger regards its keeper as he passes the bars.

"What on earth did you say to that fellow?" I asked as the little Frenchman rejoined me. "He looked as if he would like to murder you."

"Ha?" he gave a questioning, single-syllabled laugh. "Did he so? Obey the noble Washington's injunction, and avoid foreign entanglements, Friend Trow-bridge; it is better so, I think."

"But look here," I began, nettled by his manner, "what—"

"Non, non," he interrupted, "you must be advised by me, my friend. I think it would be better if we dismissed the incident from our minds. But stay—perhaps you had better meet that gentleman, after all. I will have the good Madame Norman introduce you."

More puzzled than ever, I followed him to our hostess and waited while he requested her to present me to the count.

In a lull in the dancing she complied with his request, and the foreigner acknowledged the introduction with a brief handclasp and an almost churlish nod, then turned his back on me, continuing an animated conversation with the large-eyed young woman in an abbreviated party frock.

"And did you shake his hand?" de Grandin asked as we descended the Norman's steps to my waiting car.

"Yes, of course," I replied.

"Ah? Tell me, my friend, did you notice anything—ah—peculiar, in his grip?"

"H'm." I wrinkled my brow a moment in concentrated thought. "Yes, I believe I did."

"So? What was it?"

"Hanged if I can say, exactly," I admitted, "but—well, it seemed—this sounds absurd, I know—but it seemed as though his hand had two backs—no palm at all—if that means anything to you."

"It means much, my friend; it means a very great deal," he answered with such a solemn nod that I burst into a fit of laughter. "Believe me, it means much more than you suspect."

It must have been some two weeks later that I chanced a remark to de Grandin, "I saw your friend, Count Czerny, in New York yesterday."

"Indeed?" he answered with what seemed like more than necessary interest. "And how did he impress you at the time?"

"Oh, I just happened to pass him on Fifth Avenue," I replied. "I'd been up to see an acquaintance in Fifty-ninth Street and was turning into the avenue when I saw him driving away from the Plaza. He was with some ladies."

"No doubt," de Grandin responded dryly. "Did you notice him particularly?"

"Can't say that I did, especially," I answered, "but it seems to me he looked older than the day we met him at Mrs. Norman's."

"Yes?" the Frenchman leaned forward eagerly. "Older, do you say? *Parbleu,* this is of interest; I suspected as much!"

"Why—" I began, but he turned away with an impatient shrug. "Pah!" he exclaimed petulantly. "Friend Trowbridge, I fear Jules de Grandin is a fool, he entertains all sorts of strange notions."

I had known the little Frenchman long enough to realize that he was as full of moods as a prima donna, but his erratic, unrelated remarks were getting on my nerves. "See here, de Grandin," I began testily, "what's all this nonsense—"

The sudden shrill clatter of my office telephone bell cut me short. "Dr. Trowbridge," an agitated voice asked over the wire, "can you come right over, please? This is Mrs. Norman speaking."

"Yes, of course," I answered, reaching for my medicine case. "What is it—who's ill?"

"It's—it's Guy Eckhart, he's been taken with a fainting fit, and we don't seem to be able to rouse him."

"Very well," I promised, "Dr. de Grandin and I will be right over.

"Come on, de Grandin," I called as I shoved my hat down over my ears and shrugged into my overcoat, "one of Mrs. Norman's house guests has been taken ill; I told her we were coming."

"*Mais oui,*" he agreed, hurrying into his outdoors clothes. "Is it a man or a woman, this sick one?"

"It's a man," I replied, "Guy Eckhart."

"A man," he echoed incredulously. "A man, do you say? No, no, my friend, that is not likely."

"Likely or not," I rejoined sharply, "Mrs. Norman says he's been seized with a fainting fit, and I give the lady credit for knowing what she's talking about."

"Eh bien." He drummed nervously on the cushions of the automobile-seat. "Perhaps Jules de Grandin really is a fool. After all, it is not impossible."

"It certainly isn't," I agreed fervently to myself as I set the car in motion.

Young Eckhart had recovered consciousness when we arrived, but looked like a man just emerging from a lingering fever. Attempts to get a statement from him met with no response, for he replied slowly, almost incoherently, and seemed to have no idea concerning the cause of his illness.

Mrs. Norman was little more specific. "My son Ferdinand found him lying on the floor of his bath with the shower going and the window wide open, just before dinner," she explained. "He was totally unconscious, and remained so till just a few minutes ago."

"Ha, is it so?" de Grandin murmured half heedlessly, as he made a rapid inspection of the patient.

"Friend Trowbridge," he called me to the window, "what do you make of those objective symptoms: a soft, frequent pulse, a fluttering heart, suffused eyes, a hot, dry skin and a flushed, hectic face?"

"Sounds like an arterial hemorrhage," I answered promptly, "but there's been no trace of blood on the boy's floor, nor any evidence of a stain on his clothing. Sure you've checked the signs over?"

"Absolutely," he replied with a vigorous double nod. Then to the young man: "Now, *mon enfant,* we shall inspect you, if you please."

Quickly he examined the boy's face, scalp, throat, wrists and calves, finding no evidence of even a pinprick, let alone a wound capable of causing syncope.

"Mon Dieu, this is strange," he muttered; "of a surety, it has the queerness of the devil! Perhaps the bleeding is internal, but—ah, *regardez vous,* Friend Trowbridge!"

He had turned down the collar of the youngster's pajama jacket, more in idle routine than in hope of discovering anything tangible, but the livid spot to which he pointed seemed the key to our mystery's outer door. Against the smooth, white flesh of the young man's left breast there showed a red, angry patch, such as might have resulted from a vacuum cup being held some time against the skin, and in the center of the discoloration was a double row of tiny punctures scarcely larger than needle pricks, arranged in horizontal divergent arcs, like a pair of parentheses laid sidewise.

"You see?" he asked simply, as though the queer, blood-infused spot explained everything.

"But he couldn't have bled much through that," I protested. "Why, the man seems almost drained dry, and these wounds wouldn't have yielded more than a cubic centimeter of blood, at most."

He nodded gravely. "Blood is not entirely colloidal, my friend," he responded. "It will penetrate the tissues to some extent, especially if sufficient force is applied."

"But it would have required a powerful suction—" I replied, when his rejoinder cut me short:

"Ha, you have said it, my friend. Suction—that is the word!"

"But what could have sucked a man's blood like this?" I was in a near-stupor of mystification.

"What, indeed?" he replied gravely. "That is for us to find out. Meantime, we are here as physicians. A quarter-grain morphine injection is indicated here, I think. You will administer the dose; I have no license in America."

When I returned from my round of afternoon calls next day I found de Grandin seated on my front steps in close conference with Indian John.

Indian John was a town character of doubtful lineage who performed odd jobs of snow shoveling, furnace tending and grass cutting, according to season, and interspersed his manual labors with brief incursions into the mercantile field when he peddled fresh vegetables from door to door. He also peddled neighborhood gossip and retailed local lore to all who would listen, his claim to being a hundred years old giving him the standing of an indisputable authority in all matters antedating living memory.

"*Pardieu,* but you have told me much, *mon vieux,*" de Grandin declared as I came up the porch steps. He handed the old rascal a handful of silver and rose to accompany me into the house.

"Friend Trowbridge," he accused as we finished dinner that night, "you had not told me that this town grew up on the site of an early Swedish settlement."

"Never knew you wanted to know," I defended with a grin.

"You know the ancient Swedish church, perhaps," he persisted.

"Yes, that's old Christ Church," I answered. "It's down in the east end of town; don't suppose it has a hundred communicants today. Our population has made some big changes, both in complexion and creed, since the days when the Dutch and Swedes fought for possession of New Jersey."

"You will drive me to that church, right away, at once, immediately?" he demanded eagerly.

"I guess so," I agreed. "What's the matter now; Indian John been telling you a lot of fairy tales?"

"Perhaps," he replied, regarding me with one of his steady, unwinking stares. "Not all fairy tales are pleasant, you know. Do you recall those of *Chaperon Rouge*—how do you say it, Red Riding Hood?—and Bluebeard?"

"Huh!" I scoffed; "they're both as true as any of John's stories, I'll bet."

"Undoubtlessly," he agreed with a quick nod. "The story of Bluebeard, for instance, is unfortunately a very true tale indeed. But come, let us hasten; I would see that church tonight, if I may."

Christ Church, the old Swedish place of worship, was a combined demonstration of how firmly adzhewn pine and walnut can resist the ravages of time and how nearly three hundred years of weather can demolish any structure erected by man. Its rough-painted walls and short, firm-based spire shone ghostly and pallid in the early spring moonlight, and the cluster of broken and weather-worn tombstones which staggered up from its unkempt burying ground were like soiled white chicks seeking shelter from a soiled white hen.

Dismounting from a car at the wicket gate of the churchyard, we made our
way over the level graves, I in a maze of wonderment, de Grandin with an
eagerness almost childish. Occasionally he flashed the beam from his electric
torch on some monument of an early settler, bent to decipher the worn inscription, then turned away with a sigh of disappointment.

I paused to light a cigar, but dropped my half-burned match in astonishment
as my companion gave vent to a cry of excited pleasure, *"Triomphe!"* he
exclaimed delightedly. "Come and behold. Friend Trowbridge. Thus far your
lying friend, the Indian man has told the truth. *Regardez!"*

He was standing beside an old, weather-gnawed tombstone, once marble,
perhaps, but appearing more like brown sandstone under the ray of his flashlight.
Across its upper end was deeply cut the one word:

SARAH

while below the name appeared a verse of half-obliterated doggerel:

Let nonne difturb her deathleffe fleepe
Abote ye tombe wilde garlick keepe
For if fhee wake much woe will boaft
Prayfe Faither, Sonne & Holie Goaft.

"Did you bring me out here to study the orthographical eccentricities of the
early settlers?" I demanded in disgust.

"Ah bah!" he returned. "Let us consult the *ecclesiastique*. He, perhaps, will
ask no fool's questions."

"No, you'll do that," I answered tartly as we knocked at the rectory door.

"Pardon, Monsieur," de Grandin apologized as the white-haired old minister
appeared in answer to our summons, "we do not wish to disturb you thus, but
there is a matter of great import on which we would consult you. I would that you
tell us what you can, if anything, concerning a certain grave in your churchyard.
A grave marked 'Sarah' if you please."

"Why"—the elderly cleric was plainly taken aback—"I don't think there is
anything I can tell you about it, sir. There is some mention in the early parish
records, I believe, of a woman believed to have been a murderess being buried
in that grave, but it seems the poor creature was more sinned against than
sinning. Several children in the neighborhood died mysteriously—some epidemic the ignorant physicians failed to understand, no doubt—and Sarah, whatever the poor woman's surname may have been, was accused of killing them by
witchcraft. At any rate, one of the bereft mothers took vengeance into her own
hands, and strangled poor Sarah with a noose of well-rope. The witchcraft belief
must have been quite prevalent, too, for there is some nonsense verse on the
tombstone concerning her 'deathless sleep' and an allusion to her waking from
it, also some mention of wild garlic being planted about her."

He laughed somewhat ruefully. "I wish they hadn't said that," he added,

"for, do you know, there are garlic shoots growing about the grave to this very
day. Old Christian, our sexton, declares that he can't get rid of it, no matter how
much he grubs it up. It spreads to the surrounding lawn, too," he added sadly.

"*Cordieu!*" de Grandin gasped. "This is of the importance, sir!"

The old man smiled gently at the little Frenchman's impetuosity.

"It's an odd thing," he commented, "there was another gentleman asking
about the same tomb a few weeks ago; a—pardon the expression—a foreigner."

"So?" de Grandin's little waxed mustache twitched like the whiskers of a
nervous tomcat. "A foreigner, do you say? A tall, rawboned, fleshless living
skeleton of a man with a scar on his face and a white streak in his hair?"

"I wouldn't be quite so severe in my description," the other answered with
a smile. "He certainly was a thin gentleman, and I believe he had a scar on his
face, too, though I can't be certain of that, he was so very wrinkled. No, his hair
was entirely white, there was no white streak in it, sir. In fact, I should have said
he was very advanced in age, judging from his hair and face and the manner in
which he walked. He seemed very weak and feeble. It was really quite pitiable."

"*Sacre nom d'un fromage vert!*" de Grandin almost snarled. "Pitiable, do
you say, Monsieur? *Pardieu,* it is damnable, nothing less!"

He bowed to the clergyman and turned to me. "Come, Friend Trowbridge,
come away," he cried. "We must go to Madame Norman's at once, right away,
immediately."

"What's behind all this mystery?" I demanded as we left the parsonage door.

He elevated his slender shoulders in an eloquent shrug. "I only wish I knew,"
he replied. "Someone is working the devil's business, of that I am sure, but what
the game is, or what the next move will be, only the good God can tell, my
friend."

I turned the car through Tunlaw Street to effect a shortcut, and as we drove
past an Italian greengrocer's, de Grandin seized my arm. "Stop a moment,
Friend Trowbridge," he asked, "I would make a purchase at this shop.

"We desire some fresh garlic," he informed the proprietor as we entered the
little store, "a considerable amount, if you have it."

The Italian spread his hands in a deprecating gesture. "We have it not,
Signor," he declared. "It was only yesterday morning that we sold our entire
supply." His little black eyes snapped happily at the memory of an unexpected
bargain.

"Eh, what is this?" de Grandin demanded. "Do you say you sold your
supply? How is that?"

"I know not," the other replied. "Yesterday morning a rich gentleman came
to my shop in an automobile, and called me from my store. He desired all the
garlic I had in stock—at my own price, *Signor,* at once. I was to deliver it to his
address in Rupleysville the same day."

"Ah?" de Grandin's face assumed the expression of a crossword fiend as he
begins to see the solution of his puzzle. "And this liberal purchaser, what did he
look like?"

The Italian showed his white even teeth in a wide grin. "It was funny," he confessed. "He did not look like one of our people, nor like one who would eat much garlic. He was old, very old and thin, with a much-wrinkled face and white hair. He—"

"*Nom d'un chat!*" the Frenchman cried, then burst into a flood of torrential Italian.

The shopkeeper listened at first with suspicion, then incredulity, finally in abject terror. "No, no," he exclaimed. "No, *Signor, santissima Madonna,* you do make the joke!"

"Do I so?" de Grandin replied. "Wait and see, foolish one."

"*Santo Dio* forbid!" The other crossed himself piously, then bent his thumb across his palm, circling it with his second and third fingers and extending the fore and little fingers in the form of a pair of horns.

The Frenchman turned toward the waiting car with a grunt of inarticulate disgust.

"What now?" I asked as we got under way once more. "What did that man make the sign of the evil eye for, de Grandin?"

"Later, my friend, I will tell you later," he answered. "You would but laugh if I told you what I suspect. He is of the Latin blood and can appreciate my fears." Nor would he utter another word till we reached the Norman house.

"Dr. Trowbridge—Dr. de Grandin!"—Mrs. Norman met us in the hall— "you must have heard my prayers. I've been phoning your office for the last hour, and they said you were out and couldn't be reached."

"What's up?" I asked.

"It's Mr. Eckhart again. He's been seized with another fainting fit. He seemed so well this afternoon, and I sent a big dinner up to him at 8 o'clock, but when the maid went in, she found him unconscious, and she declares she saw something in his room—"

"Ha?" de Grandin interrupted. "Where is she, this servant? I would speak with her."

"Wait a moment," Mrs. Norman answered; "I'll send for her."

The girl, an ungainly young Southern woman, came into the front hall, sullen dissatisfaction written large upon her face.

"Now, then," de Grandin bent his steady, unwinking gaze on her, "what is it you say about seeing someone in the young Monsieur Eckhart's room, *hein?*"

"Ah did see sumpin', too," the girl replied stubbornly. "Ah don' care who says Ah didn't see nothin', Ah says Ah did. Ah'd just toted a tray o' vittles up to Mistuh Eckart's room, an' when Ah opened de do', dere wuz a woman—dere wuz a woman—yas, sar, a skinny, black-eyed white woman—a-bendin' ober 'um an'—an'—"

"And what, if you please?" de Grandin asked breathlessly.

"A-bitin' 'um!" the girl replied defiantly. "Ah don' car whut Mis' Norman says, she wuz a-bitin' 'um. Ah seen her. Ah knows whut she wuz. Ah done hyeah tell erbout dat ol' Sarah woman what come up out 'er grave wid a long rope erbout her neck and go 'round bitin' folks. Yas, sar; an' she wuz a-bitin' 'um, too. Ah seen her!''

"Nonsense," Mrs. Norman commented in an annoyed whisper over de Grandin's shoulder.

"*Grand Dieu,* is it so?" de Grandin explained, and turning abruptly, leaped up the stairs toward the sick man's room, two steps at a time.

"See, see, Friend Trowbridge," he ordered fiercely when I joined him at the patient's bedside. "Behold, it is the mark!" Turning back Eckhart's pajama collar, he displayed two incised horizontal arcs on the young man's flesh. There was no room for dispute, they were undoubtedly the marks of human teeth, and from the fresh wounds the blood was flowing freely.

As quickly as possible we staunched the flow and applied restoratives to the patient, both of us working in silence, for my brain was too much in a whirl to permit the formation of intelligent questions, while de Grandin remained dumb as an oyster.

"Now," he ordered as we completed our ministrations, "we must get back to that cemetery, Friend Trowbridge, and once there, we must do the thing which must be done!"

"What the devil's that?" I asked as we left the sickroom.

"*Non, non,* you shall see," he promised as we entered my car and drove down the street.

"Quick, the crank-handle," he demanded as we descended from the car at the cemetery gate, "it will make a serviceable hammer." He was prying a hemlock paling from the graveyard fence as he spoke.

We crossed the unkempt cemetery lawn again and finally paused beside the tombstone of the unknown Sarah.

"Attend me, Friend Trowbridge," de Grandin commanded, "hold the searchlight, if you please." He pressed his pocket flash into my hand. "Now—" He knelt beside the grave, pointing the stick he had wrenched from the fence straight downward into the turf. With the crank of my motor he began hammering the wood into the earth.

Farther and farther the rough stake sank into the sod, de Grandin's blows falling faster and faster as the wood drove home. Finally, when there was less than six inches of the wicket projecting from the grave's top, he raised the iron high over his head and drove downward with all his might.

The short hair at the back of my neck suddenly started upward, and little thrills of horripilation chased each other up my spine as the wood sank suddenly, as though driven from clay into sand, and a low hopeless moan, like the wailing of a frozen wind through an ice cave, wafted up to us from the depths of the grave.

"Good God, what's that?" I asked, aghast.

For answer he leaned forward, seized the stake in both hands and drew suddenly up on it. At his second tug the wood came away. "See," he ordered curtly, flashing the pocket lamp on the tip of the stave. For the distance of a foot or so from its pointed end the wood was stained a deep, dull red. It was wet with blood.

"And now forever," he hissed between his teeth, driving the wood into the grave once more, and sinking it a full foot below the surface of the grass by thrusting the crank-handle into the earth. "Come, Friend Trowbridge, we have done a good work this night. I doubt not the young Eckhart will soon recover from his malady."

His assumption was justified. Eckhart's condition improved steadily. Within a week, save for a slight pallor, he was, to all appearances, as well as ever.

The pressure of the usual early crop of influenza and pneumonia kept me busily on my rounds, and I gradually gave up hope of getting any information from de Grandin, for a shrug of the shoulders was all the answer he vouchsafed to my questions. I relegated Eckhart's inexplicable hemorrhages and the blood-stained stake to the limbo of never-to-be-solved mysteries. But—

<h1 style="text-align:center">2</h1>

"GOOD MORNIN', gentlemen," Detective Sergeant Costello greeted as he followed Nora, my household factotum, into the breakfast room, "it's sorry I am to be disturbin' your meal, but there's a little case puzzlin' th' department that I'd like to talk over with Dr. de Grandin, if you don't mind."

He looked expectantly at the little Frenchman as he finished speaking, his lips parted to launch open a detailed description of the case.

"*Parbleu*," de Grandin laughed, "it is fortunate for me that I have completed my breakfast, *cher Sergent,* for a riddle of crime detection is to me like a red rag to a bullfrog—I must needs snap at it, whether I have been fed or no. Speak on, my friend, I beseech you; I am like Balaam's ass, all ears."

The big Irishman seated himself on the extreme edge of one of my Heppelwhite chairs and gazed deprecatingly at the derby he held firmly between his knees. "It's like this," he began. " 'Tis one o' them mysterious disappearance cases, gentlemen, an' whilst I'm thinkin' th' young lady knows exactly where she's at an' why she's there, I hate to tell her folks about it.

"All th' high-hat folks ain't like you two gentlemen, askin' your pardon, sors—they mostly seems to think that a harness bull's unyform is sumpin' like a livery—like a shofur's or a footman's or sumpin', an' that a plainclothes man is just a sort o' inferior servant. They don't give th' police credit for no brains, y'see, an' when one o' their darters gits giddy an' runs off th' reservation, if we tells 'em th' gurrl's run away of her own free will an' accord they say we're a lot o' lazy, good-fer-nothin' bums who are tryin' to dodge our laygitimate jooties by castin' mud on th' young ladies' char-ac-ters, d'ye see? So, when this Miss Esther Norman disappears in broad daylight—leastwise, in th' twilight—o' th' day before her dance, we suspects right away that th' gurrl's gone her own ways into th' best o' intentions, y'see; but we dasn't tell her folks as much, or they'll be hollerin' to th' commissioner fer to git a bran' new set o' detectives down to headquarters, so they will.

"Now, mind ye, I'm not sayin' th' young lady *mightn't* o' been kidnaped, y'understand, gentlemen, but I do be sayin' 'tis most unlikely. I've been on th' force, man an' boy, in unyform and in plain clothes fer th' last twenty-five years, an' th' number of laygitimate kidnapin's o' young women over ten years of age I've seen can be counted on th' little finger o' me left hand, an' I ain't got none there, at all, at all."

He held the member up for our inspection, revealing the fact that the little finger had been amputated close to the knuckle.

De Grandin, elbows on the table, pointed chin cupped in his hands, was puffing furiously at a vile-smelling French cigarette, alternately sucking down great drafts of its acrid smoke and expelling clouds of fumes in double jets from his narrow, aristocratic nostrils.

"What is it you say?" he demanded, removing the cigarette from his lips. "Is it the so lovely Mademoiselle Esther, daughter of that kind Madame Tuscarora Avenue Norman, who is missing?"

"Yes, sor," Costello answered, " 'tis th' same young lady's flew the coop, accordin' to my way o' thinkin'."

"Mordieu!" The Frenchman gave the ends of his blond mustache a savage twist. "You intrigue me, my friend. Say on, how did it happen, and when?"

" 'Twas about midnight last night th' alarm came into headquarters," the detective replied. "Accordin' to th' facts as we have 'em, th' young lady went downtown in th' Norman car to do some errands. We've checked her movements up, an' here they are."

He drew a black leather memorandum book from his pocket and consulted it.

"At 2:45 or thereabouts, she left th' house, arrivin' at th' Ocean Trust Company at 2:55, five minutes before th' instytootion closed for th' day. She drew out three hundred an' thirty dollars an' sixty-five cents, an' left th' bank, goin' to Madame Gerard's, where she tried on a party dress for th' dance which was bein' given at her house that night.

"She left Madame Gerard's at 4:02, leavin' orders for th' dress to be delivered to her house immeejately, an' dismissed her sho-fur at th' corner o' Dean an' Tunlaw Streets, sayin' she was goin' to deliver some vegytables an' what-not to a pore family she an' some o' her friends was keepin' till their old man gits let out o' jail—'twas meself an' Clancey, me buddy, that put him there when we caught him red-handed in a job o' housebreakin', too.

"Well, to return to th' young lady, she stopped at Pete Bacigalupo's store in Tunlaw Street an' bought a basket o' fruit an' canned things, at 4:30, an'—" He clamped his long-suffering derby between his knees and spread his hands emptily before us.

"Yes, 'and'—?" de Grandin prompted, dropping the glowing end of his cigarette into his coffee cup.

THE MAN WHO CAST NO SHADOW

"An' that's all," responded the Irishman. "She just walked off, an' no one ain't seen her since, sor."

"But—*cordieu!*—such things do not occur, my friend," de Grandin protested. "Somewhere you have overlooked a factor in this puzzle. You say no one saw her later? Have you nothing whatever to add to the tale?"

"Well"—the detective grinned at him—"there are one or two little incidents, but they ain't of any importance in th' case, as far as I can see. Just as she left Pete's store an old gink tried to 'make' her, but she give him th' air, an' he went off an' didn't bother her no more.

"I'd a' liked to seen th' old boy, at that. Day before yesterday there was an old felly hangin' 'round by the silk mills, annoyin' th' gurrls as they come off from work. Clancey, me mate, saw 'im an' started to take 'im up, an' darned if th' old rummy wasn't strong as a bull. D'ye know, he broke clean away from Clancey an' darn near broke his arm, in th' bargain? Belike 'twas th' same man accosted Miss Norman outside Pete's store."

"Ah?" de Grandin's slender, white fingers began beating a devil's tattoo on the tablecloth. "And who was it saw this old man annoy the lady, *hein?*"

Costello grinned widely, " 'Twas Pete Bacigalupo himself, sor," he answered. "Pete swore he recognized th' old geezer as havin' come to his store a month or so ago in an autymobile an bought up all his entire stock o' garlic. Huh! Th' fool said he wouldn't a gone after th felly' for a hundred dollars—said he had th' pink-eye, or th' evil eye, or some such thing. That sure do burn me up!"

"Dieu et le diable!" De Grandin leaped up, oversetting his chair in his mad haste. "And we sit here like three *poissons d'avril*—like poor fish—while he works his devilish will on her! Quick, Sergeant! Quick, Friend Trowbridge! Your hats, your coats; the motor! Oh, make haste, my friends, fly, fly, I implore you; even now it may be too late!"

As though all the fiends of pandemonium were at his heels he raced from the breakfast room up the stairs three steps at a stride and down the upper hall toward his bedroom. Nor did he cease his shouted demands for haste throughout his wild flight.

"Cuckoo?" The sergeant tapped his forehead significantly.

I shook my head as I hastened to the hall for my driving clothes. "No," I answered, shrugging into my topcoat, "he's got a reason for everything he does; but you and I can't always see it, Sergeant."

"You said a mouthful that time, doc," he agreed, pulling his hat down over his ears. "He's the darndest, craziest Frog I ever seen, but, at that, he's got more sense than nine men out o'ten."

"To Rupleysville, Friend Trowbridge," de Grandin shouted as he leaped into the seat beside me. "Make haste, I do implore you. Oh, Jules de Grandin, your grandfather was an imbecile and all your ancestors were idiots, but you are the greatest zany in the family. Why, oh, why, do you require a sunstroke before you can see the light, foolish one?"

I swung the machine down the pike at highest legal speed, but the little

Frenchman kept urging greater haste. *"Sang de Dieu, sang de Saint Denis, sang du diable!"* he wailed despairingly. "Can you not make this abominable car go faster, Friend Trowbridge? Oh, ah, *helas,* if we are too late! I shall hate myself, I shall loathe myself—*pardieu,* I shall become a Carmelite friar and eat fish and abstain from swearing!"

We took scarcely twenty minutes to cover the ten-mile stretch to the aggregation of tumbledown houses which was Rupleysville, but my companion was almost frothing at the mouth when I drew up before the local apology for a hotel.

"Tell me, Monsieur," de Grandin cried as he thrust the hostelry's door open with his foot and brandished his slender ebony cane before the astonished proprietor's eyes, "tell me of *un vieillard*—an old, old man with snow-white hair and an evil face, who has lately come to this so detestable place. I would know where to find him, right away, immediately, at once!"

"Say," the boniface demanded truculently, "where d'ye git that stuff? Who are you to be askin'—"

"That'll do"—Costello shouldered his way past de Grandin and displayed his badge—"you answer this gentleman's questions, an' answer 'em quick an' accurate, or I'll run you in, see?"

The innkeeper's defiant attitude melted before the detective's show of authority like frost before the sunrise. "Guess you must mean Mr. Zerny," he replied sullenly. "He come here about a month ago an' rented the Hazelton house, down th' road about a mile. Comes up to town for provisions every day or two, and stops in here sometimes for a—" He halted abruptly, his face suffused with a dull flush.

"Yeah?" Costello replied: "Go on an' say it; we all know what he stops here for. Now listen, buddy"—he stabbed the air two inches before the man's face with a blunt forefinger—"I don't know whether this here Zerny felly's got a tellyphone or not, but if he has, you just lay off tellin' 'im we're comin'; git me? If anyone's tipped him off when we git to his place I'm comin' back here and plaster more padlocks on this place o' yours than Sousa's got medals on his blouse. Savvy?"

"Come away, *Sergent;* come away, Friend Trowbridge," de Grandin besought almost tearfully. "Bandy not words with the *cancre;* we have work to do!"

Down the road we raced in the direction indicated by the hotelkeeper, till the picket fence and broken shutters of the Hazelton house showed among a rank copse of second-growth pines at the bend of the highway.

The shrewd wind of early spring was moaning and soughing among the black boughs of the pine trees as we ran toward the house, and though it was bright with sunshine on the road, there was chill and shadow about us as we climbed the sagging steps of the old building's ruined piazza and paused breathlessly before the paintless front door.

"Shall I knock?" Costello asked dubiously, involuntarily sinking his voice to a whisper.

"But no," de Grandin answered in a low voice, "what we have to do here must be done quietly, my friends."

He leaned forward and tried the doorknob with a light, tentative touch. The door gave under his hand, swinging inward on protesting hinges, and we tiptoed into a dark, dust-carpeted hall. A shaft of sunlight, slanting downward from a chink in one of the window shutters, showed innumerable dust motes flying lazily in the air, and laid a bright oval of light against the warped floor-boards.

"Huh, empty as a pork butcher's in Jerusalem," Costello commented disgustedly, looking about the unfurnished rooms, but de Grandin seized him by the elbow with one hand while he pointed toward the floor with the ferrule of his slender ebony walking stick.

"Empty, perhaps," he conceded in a low, vibrant whisper, "but not recently, *mon ami*." Where the sunbeam splashed on the uneven floor there showed distinctly the mark of a booted foot, two marks—a trail of them leading toward the rear of the house.

"Right y'are," the detective agreed. "Someone's left his track here, an' no mistake."

"Ha!" De Grandin bent forward till it seemed the tip of his highbridged nose would impinge on the tracks. "Gentlemen," he rose and pointed forward into the gloom with a dramatic flourish of his cane, "they are here! Let us go!"

Through the gloomy hall we followed the trail by the aid of Costello's flashlight, stepping carefully to avoid creaking boards as much as possible. At length the marks stopped abruptly in the center of what had formerly been the kitchen. A disturbance in the dust told where the walker had doubled on his tracks in a short circle, and a ringbolt in the floor gave notice that we stood above a trapdoor of some sort.

"Careful, Friend Costello," de Grandin warned, "have ready your flashlight when I fling back the trap. Ready? *Un—deux—trois!*"

He bent, seized the rusty ringbolt and heaved the trapdoor back so violently that it flew back with a thundering crash on the floor beyond.

The cavern had originally been a cellar for the storage of food, it seemed, and was brick walled and earth floored, without window or ventilation opening of any sort. A dank, musty odor assaulted our nostrils as we leaned forward, but further impressions were blotted out by the sight directly beneath us.

White as a figurine of carven alabaster, the slender, bare body of a girl lay in sharp reverse silhouette against the darkness of the cavern floor, her ankles crossed and firmly lashed to a stake in the earth, one hand doubled behind her back in the position of a wrestler's hammer-lock grip, and made firm to a peg in the floor, while the left arm was extended straight outward, its wrist pinioned to another stake. Her luxuriant fair hair had been knotted together at the ends, then staked to the ground, so that her head was drawn far back, exposing her rounded throat to its fullest extent, and on the earth beneath her left breast and beside her throat stood two porcelain bowls.

Crouched over her was the relic of a man, an old, old, hideously wrinkled witch-husband, with matted white hair and beard. In one hand he held a long, gleaming, double-edged dirk, while with the other he caressed the girl's smooth throat with gloating strokes of his skeleton fingers.

"Howly Mither!" Costello's County Galway brogue broke through his American accent at the horrid sight below us.

"My God!" I exclaimed, all the breath in my lungs suddenly seeming to freeze in my throat.

"Bonjour, Monsieur le Vampire!" Jules de Grandin greeted nonchalantly, leaping to the earth beside the pinioned girl and waving his walking stick airily. "By the horns of the devil, but you have led us a merry chase, Baron Lajos Czuczron of Transylvania!"

The crouching creature emitted a bellow of fury and leaped toward de Grandin, brandishing his knife.

The Frenchman gave ground with a quick, catlike leap and grasped his slender cane in both hands near the top. Next instant he had ripped the lower part of the stick away, displaying a fine, three-edged blade set in the cane's handle, and swung his point toward the frothing-mouthed thing which mouthed and gibbered like a beast at bay. "A-ah?" he cried with a mocking, upward-lilting accent. "You did not expect this, eh, Friend Blood-drinker? I give you the party-of-surprise, *n'est-ce-pas?* The centuries have been long, *mon vieux;* but the reckoning has come at last. Say, now will you die by the steel, or by starvation?"

The aged monster fairly champed his gleaming teeth in fury. His eyes seemed larger, rounder, to gleam like the eyes of a dog in the firelight, as he launched himself toward the little Frenchman.

"Sa-ha!" the Frenchman sank backward on one foot, then straightened suddenly forward, stiffening his sword-arm and plunging his point directly into the charging beastman's distended, red mouth. A scream of mingled rage and pain filled the cavern with deafening shrillness, and the monster half turned, as though on an invisible pivot, clawed with horrid impotence at the wire-fine blade of de Grandin's rapier, then sank slowly to the earth, his death cry stilled to a sickening gurgle as his throat filled with blood.

"Fini!" de Grandin commented laconically, drawing out his handkerchief and wiping his blade with meticulous care, then cutting the unconscious girl's bonds with his pocket-knife. "Drop down your overcoat, Friend Trowbridge," he added, "that we may cover the poor child's nudity until we can piece out a wardrobe for her.

"Now, then"—as he raised her to meet the hands Costello and I extended into the pit—"if we clothe her in the motor rug, your jacket, *Sergent,* Friend Trowbridge's topcoat and my shoes, she will be safe from the chill. *Parbleu,* I have seen women refugees from the *Boche* who could not boast so complete a toilette!"

With Esther Norman, hastily clothed in her patchwork assortment of garments, wedged in the front seat between de Grandin and me, we began our triumphant journey home.

"An' would ye mind tellin' me how ye knew where to look for th' young lady, Dr. de Grandin, sor?" Detective Sergeant Costello asked respectfully, leaning forward from the rear seat of the car.

"Wait, wait, my friend," de Grandin replied with a smile. "When our duties are all performed I shall tell you such a tale as shall make your two eyes to pop outward like a snail's. First, however, you must go with us to restore this *pauvre enfant* to her mother's arms; then to the headquarters to report the death of that *sale bête*. Friend Trowbridge will stay with the young lady for so long as he deems necessary, and I shall remain with him to help. Then, this evening—with your consent, Friend Trowbridge—you will dine with us, *Sergent,* and I shall tell you all, everything, in total. Death of my life, what a tale it is! *Parbleu,* but you shall call me a liar many times before it is finished!"

Jules de Grandin placed his demitasse on the tabouret and refilled his liqueur glass. "My friends," he began, turning his quick, elfish smile first on Costello, then on me, "I have promised you a remarkable tale. Very well, then, to begin."

He flicked a wholly imaginary fleck of dust from his dinner jacket sleeve and crossed his slender, womanishly small feet on the hearth rug.

"Do you recall, Friend Trowbridge, how we went, you and I, to the tea given by the good Madame Norman? Yes? Perhaps, then, you will recall how at the entrance of the ballroom I stopped with a look of astonishment on my face. Very good. At that moment I saw that which made me disbelieve the evidence of my own two eyes. As the gentleman we later met as Count Czerny danced past a mirror on the wall I beheld—*parbleu!* what do you supposed?—the reflection only of his dancing partner! It was as if the man had been nonexistent, and the young lady had danced past the mirror by herself.

"Now, such a thing was not likely, I admit; you, *Sergent,* and you, too, Friend Trowbridge, will say it was not possible; but such is not the case. In certain circumstances it is possible for that which we see with our eyes to cast no shadow in a mirror. Let that point wait a moment; we have other evidence to consider first.

"When the young man told us of the count's prowess in battle, of his incomparable ferocity, I began to believe that which I had at first disbelieved, and when he told us the count was a Hungarian, I began to believe more than ever.

"I met the count, as you will remember, and I took his hand in mine. *Parbleu,* it was like a hand with no palm—it had hairs on both sides of it! You, too, Friend Trowbridge, remarked on that phenomenon.

"While I talked with him I managed to maneuver him before a mirror. *Morbleu,* the man was as if he had not been; I could see my own face smiling at me where I knew I should have seen the reflection of his shoulder!

"Now, attend me, the *Sûreté General*—what you call the police headquarters—of Paris is not like your English and American bureaus. All facts, no matter however seemingly absurd, which come to that office are carefully noted down for future reference. Among other histories I have read in the archives of that office was that of one Baron Lajos Czuczron of Transylvania, whose actions had once been watched by our secret agents.

"This man was rich and favored beyond the common run of Hungarian petty nobles, but he was far from beloved by his peasantry. He was known as cruel, wicked and implacable, and no one could be found who had ever one kind word to say for him.

"Half the countryside suspected him of being a *loup-garou,* or werewolf, the others credited a local legend that a woman of his family had once in the olden days taken a demon to husband and that he was the offspring of that unholy union. According to the story, the progeny of this wicked woman lived like an ordinary man for one hundred years, then died on the stroke of the century *unless his vitality was renewed by drinking the blood of a slaughtered virgin!*

"Absurd? Possibly. An English intelligence office would have said 'bally nonsense' if one of its agents had sent in such a report. An American bureau would have labeled the report as being the sauce-of-the-apple, but consider this fact: in six hundred years there was no single record of a Baron Czuczron having died. Barons grew old—old to the point of death—but always there came along a new baron, a man in the prime of life, not a youth, to take the old baron's place, nor could any say when the old baron had died or where his body had been laid.

"Now, I had been told that a man under a curse—the werewolf, the vampire, or any other thing in man's shape who lives more than his allotted time by virtue of wickedness—cannot cast a shadow in a mirror; also that those accursed ones have hair in the palms of their hands. *Eh bien,* with this foreknowledge, I engaged this man who called himself Count Czerny in conversation concerning Transylvania. *Parbleu,* the fellow denied all knowledge of the country. He denied it with more force than was necessary. 'You are a liar, *Monsieur le Comte,*' I tell him, but I say it to myself. Even yet, however, I do not think what I think later.

"Then came the case of the young Eckhart. He loses blood, he cannot say how or why, but Friend Trowbridge and I find a queer mark on his body. I think to me, 'if, perhaps, a vampire—a member of that accursed tribe who leave their graves by night and suck the blood of the living—were here, that would account for this young man's condition. But where would such a being come from? It is not likely.'

"Then I meet the old man, the one you call Indian John. He tells me much of the history of this town in the early days, and he tells me something more. He tells of a man, an old, old man, who has paid him much money to go to a certain grave—the grave of a reputed witch—in the old cemetery and dig from about it a growth of wild garlic. Garlic, I know, is a plant intolerable to the vampire. He cannot abide it. If it is planted on his grave he cannot pass it.

"I ask myself, 'Who would want such a thing to be, and why?' But I have no answer; only, I know, if a vampire have been confined to that grave by planted garlic, then liberated when that garlic is taken away, it would account for the young Eckhart's strange sickness.

"*Tiens,* Friend Trowbridge and I visit that grave, and on its tombstone we read a verse which makes me believe the tenant of that grave may be a vampire. We interview the good minister of the church and learn that another man, an old, old man, have also inquired about that strange grave. 'Who have done this?' I ask me; but even yet I have no definite answer to my question.

"As we rush to the Norman house to see young Eckhart I stop at an Italian greengrocer's and ask for fresh garlic, for I think perhaps we can use it to protect the young Eckhart if it really is a vampire which is troubling him. *Parbleu,* some man, an old, old man, have what you Americans call 'cornered' the available supply of garlic. *'Cordieu,'* I tell me, 'this old man, he constantly crosses our trail! Also he is a very great nuisance.'

"The Italian tell me the garlic was sent to a house in Rupleysville, so I have an idea where this interfering old rascal may abide. But at that moment I have greater need to see our friend Eckhart than to ask further questions of the Italian. Before I go, however, I tell that shopkeeper that his garlic customer has the evil eye. *Parbleu,* Monsieur Garlic-Buyer you will have no more dealings with that Italian! He knows what he knows.

"When we arrive at the Norman house we find young Eckhart in great trouble, and a black serving maid tells of a strange-looking woman who bit him. Also, we find toothmarks on his breast. 'The vampire woman, Sarah, is, in very truth, at large,' I tell me, and so I hasten to the cemetery to make her fast to her grave with a wooden stake, for, once he is staked down, the vampire can no longer roam. He is finished.

"Friend Trowbridge will testify he saw blood on the stake driven into a grave dug nearly three hundred years ago. Is it not so, *mon ami*?''

I nodded assent, and he took up his narrative:

"Why this old man should wish to liberate the vampire-woman, I know not; certain it is, one of that grisly guild, or one closely associated with it, as this 'Count Czerny' undoubtedly was, can tell when another of the company is in the vicinity, and I doubt not he did this deed for pure malice and deviltry.

"However that may be, Friend Trowbridge tells me he have seen the count, and that he seems to have aged greatly. The man who visited the clergyman and the man who bought the garlic was also much older than the count as we knew him. 'Ah ha, he is coming to the end of his century,' I tell me; 'now look out for devilment, Jules de Grandin. Certainly, it is sure to come.'

"And then, my Sergeant, come you with your tale of Mademoiselle Norman's disappearance, and I, too, think perhaps she has run away from home voluntarily, of her own free will, until you say the Italian shopkeeper recognized the old man who accosted her as one who has the evil eye. Now what old man, save the one who bought the garlic and who lives at Rupleysville, would that Italian accuse of the evil eye? *Pardieu,* has he not already told you the same man once bought his garlic? But yes. The case is complete.

"The girl has disappeared, an old, old man has accosted her; an old, old man who was so strong he could overcome a policeman; the count is nearing his century mark when he must die like other men unless he can secure the blood of a virgin to revivify him. I am more than certain that he count and baron are one and the same, and that they both dwell as Rupleysville. *Volià*, we go to Rupleysville, and we arrive there not one little minute too soon. *N'est-ce-pas, mes amis?*"

"Sure," Costello agreed, rising and holding out his hand in farewell, "you've got th' goods, doc. No mistake about it."

To me, as I helped him with his coat in the hall, the detective confided, "An' he only had one shot o'licker all evenin'! Gosh, doc, if one drink could fix me up like that I wouldn't care how much Prohibition we had!"

THE WOLF WOMAN

BASSETT MORGAN

Bassett Morgan is known to Weird Tales *aficionados as the writer obsessed with brain transplants, the theme of nearly half of her thirteen contributions to the magazine. Although Morgan also favored South Sea settings for her stories, she chose the icy wastes of Alaska for her 1927 vampire story "Wolf Woman." In so doing, she merged the vampire tale with another favorite pulp fiction type, the tale of arctic adventure, to produce a story in which men engage in a struggle for survival with nature as well as the supernatural.*

B EATEN BACK BY fogs and blizzards of the heights, the Stamwell party was camped in a sun-warmed valley at the base of Mount Logan, which lifts its ice-capped head in eternal solitude and awful silence above the most intensely glaciated region of the world.

Three years before, in an attempt to follow MacCarthy, who first ascended Logan, the intrepid mountain-climber Morsey had fallen into a crevasse; and Professor Stamwell was now attempting to recover his body from the glacier and by a process of his own experimentation restore it to life.

His assistant, Lieutenant Cressey, who had been more intrigued by the adventure of the climb than by Stamwell's sanguinary hope of resuscitating flesh entombed and even perfectly preserved in the ice, was reluctant to admit failure. Nevertheless, he enjoyed the sun-warmth of the valley after the terrific frost-fangs and ice-claws of the heights. Along the shores of a little river whose source lay in the glaciers, the dogs romped, catching fish with the dexterity of the husky breed and gorging themselves.

Baptiste, the big part Indian Canadian guide who looked after the comforts of the men, had been roving all day. At supper time he returned, tossing his cap in the air and yelling excitedly.

"*M'sieus*," he shouted, "I have find wan funny mans what makes t'ings of ivory. You come an' see. You lak heem ver' much."

Nothing loath to leave the discussion of their defeat, Stamwell and Cressey followed the exuberant Baptiste for a mile or two along the river to a stoutly timbered cabin beside which an old man watched his supper cooking over a fire outside. At sight of him, Cressey laughed, while Baptiste explained his new acquaintance.

"Hees name ees Jo. He ess half Indian, half Eskimo. An' I savvy hees talk ver' fine."

While Baptiste talked in tribal jargon, Cressey's amusement mounted. The old man was toothless and wrinkled. A beaded band kept the lank hair from obscuring his sight, and as his jaw wagged constantly on a quid of chewing tobacco, two knobbed knucklebones of seals thrust through slits in his cheeks gave the appearance of tusks. Ragged, wolf-skin trousers and elk-hide moccasins completed his attire, but he smiled grotesquely as he led the way inside the cabin. There he lighted a wick floating on a dish of oil, threw wide a window shutter and let in sunlight, which revealed a collection of carved ivory objects on shelves about the walls.

Baptiste was even more eager than the carver to display his skill. He handed Stamwell a figure copied from comic supplements of newspapers and familiar in homes from the Arctic Circle to the Florida Keys. A moment later he brought forth its mate. Stamwell held in his hands cleverly chiseled likenesses of Mutt and Jeff. Flattered by the interest of these white men, Jo showed them the source of his inspiration, a sheaf of old newspapers from the pages of which he took his ivory models. Baptiste, convulsed with mirth, laid in Cressey's hand a figure which brought a responsive laugh.

"She got bellyache!" he shouted. Even Professor Stamwell chuckled at his description of a lovely little "September Morn."

They spent a good deal of time with the contents of the shelf before Jo took up the oil dish and threw a flickering light on a recumbent figure in the cabin corner. Stamwell went on his knees, and Cressey gasped at the beauty of a woman carved in ivory lying as if asleep with one arm under her head and her long hair draped over her shoulder. The figure was almost life-size, and the ivory block showed no seam or joint. Stamwell touched the slender leg with gentle fingers, then looked at Cressey.

"Cressey, this ivory is of different texture from the small figurines. I should say it was fossilized, but where on earth would the old fellow obtain such a huge block of material?"

"And the woman-model!" exclaimed Cressey. "A white woman, undoubtedly. Look at the sensitive nostrils and straight nose, and the rounded cheeks. No Kogmollyc or Indian woman posed for this. The old fellow didn't create her, either. He couldn't. You can see he has only a great skill in imitating and copying. Baptiste, ask Jo where he saw such a woman asleep.''

Baptiste's conversation with the old man occupied some time, and before it ended the big guide was fingering his scapular.

"Jo, he say dees woman froze een ice. He git dees big chunk ivory from ver' beeg land-whale, also froze een ice.''

"A land-whale! Cressey, he means a mammoth. We've come across real treasure. Baptiste, tell Jo we would like to see this land-whale.''

Baptiste interpreted. The ivory-carver nodded good-naturedly and started at once to lead them to the source of his art material.

"Jo, he say,'' offered Baptiste when the dogs were harnessed and food on the sled in case of an overnight trip, "he say dees womans ees froze een ice long tam. Maybe dis summer fetch her out. She come down ver' fast. Long tam ago, Jo see her ver' high up. Jo say more as hunderd snows when he first see her.''

"Frozen in the glacier more than a hundred years ago! Preposterous! The old fellow exaggerates.'' Stamwell waved aside Jo's veracity. "We've evidently stumbled on a tragedy. Snow madness makes its victims strip naked, usually, which would account of her nudity, and Jo looks aged, but I don't credit his hundred-year memory.''

"Her hair must have touched the ground, Professor. That dates her pretty far back.''

For some hours the ice trail, steep though not perilous, claimed their attention. The sun swung down to the horizon for the brief moments of northern midnight, then began its upward arc. They found that Jo had cut steps on the glacial river which wound down from the grim sides of Mount Logan. Mounting steadily, they reached a terrace which led to lofty pinnacles of ice so clearly blue it was like a fairy palace, where steps led to an outstanding archway and natural grotto of rock that had been broken from its base and carried down.

Inside the grotto the light was weirdly blue, the ice underfoot clear as glass. Jo pointed and Cressey knelt, and a moment later his cry echoed from the grotto walls. Under the crystal shell lay the carver's model, more beautiful than the carved ivory, a woman, young, lovely, golden hair half robing her form, tawny eyelashes on her rounded cheeks. Near by, as if they had lain down to sleep and been caught by instant and painless death, were seven large hounds or wolves, with snow-white pelts.

Baptiste, plagued by superstitious fear, gazed long and earnestly, then leaped from the cave with a wild cry and ran down the steps which led to the broken end of the lower terrace. Cressey and Stamwell, engrossed by the sight beneath their feet, did not miss Baptiste until he returned, holding his nose and grimacing.

"Name of a Name! She smell ver' dead, dat land-whale!''

They followed him to the terrace, below which lay the enormous carcass of a hairy mammoth in advanced stages of putrefaction, smelling, as Baptiste had said, "very dead.''

One great tusk lay on the tundra, the other had been sawn off, proving Jo's assertion about the source of his ivory. Cressey was staring at the mass below in absorbed silence, when Stamwell clutched his arm and exclaimed: "Cressey, we did not find Morsey. But we've found this woman. By heaven, we'll take her and the dogs from their ice tomb!"

"But—but what a pity!" cried Cressey. "The air will finish them in no time, like that mammoth. And she is beautiful in death!"

"Another summer would bring her down to that finish anyway," argued Stamwell. "And what if it isn't death? What about its being merely suspended animation? Here is our chance to test my discovery. I meant to try it on Morsey. We can't do that for him, but what a triumph to bring this woman back to life after, God alone knows how many years of sleep; a Diana of eld and her hunting pack!"

"But aren't you interested in this mammoth at all, Stamwell?"

"What is a mammoth, decayed at that?" Stamwell's eyes burned with the passion of a zealot. "Mammoths have been found everywhere, their skeletons mounted and their existence traced. We shouldn't have even the satisfaction of originality. But to carry out a living woman who has been buried in the ice, no one can say how long—Cressey, look at those hounds!" Stamwell was hurrying to the cave and growing more excited every moment. "Do you know of a living breed of dogs like them? They are true wolf, even larger than the timber wolves. And albinos. It is stupendous, staggering, the antiquity revealed under this shell of ice. And to think, if we had been a year later this superb discovery would have moved down with the glacier and broken off at the terrace, the prey of wild animals, the bones scattered. That will happen next year unless we rescue her!"

Cressey did not answer. The idea of taking this frozen beauty from the ice and restoring her to life sounded like the talk of a man demented. Yet, as he heard the calculating plan of Stamwell unfold, Cressey admitted to himself that it was a new and alluring adventure. At Stamwell's succinct commands, he accompanied Baptiste to the valley camp to bring back their packs and establish a camp in the grotto which penetrated the floe for a hundred feet or more and would serve admirably as a shelter.

By the time Baptiste had made beds of pine boughs and started a fire with wood hauled from below, Cressey found that Stamwell had made remarkable progress in chipping the ice from the entombed woman and her dogs. The guide cooked breakfast. The cave had assumed an appearance of comfort exceeding their valley tents, and after a meal of flapjacks they slept.

Cressey was wakened by the noise of Stamwell's pick on the ice.

"What if that hammering should start an avalanche?" he asked.

"There isn't much danger. The sun warmth melting the ice also welds it, and the floe is less crisp here than in higher altitudes. Don't think up discouragements, Cressey. Get busy and help me."

They worked all day, cutting a rectangular space which included the entire group. Baptiste and the guides had slept huddled in parkas, in the tents erected outside the grotto, which they refused to enter except to carry out the broken ice. It was apparent to both Stamwell and Cressey that their men regarded this disturbance of the ice-entombed woman as a sacrilege that would brew trouble, and Baptiste solemnly voiced prophetic warning.

"Dogs!" he snorted. "Who ever see dogs lak dem? Dey look more lak ghost-wolf, the *loup-garou*. Me, I don' lak dees bisniss. I come for to climb mountain, not dig up dead womans." Nor would he gaze into the deepening hole where Stamwell and Cressey labored until only a thin shell of ice covered the bodies of the woman and hounds. Then Stamwell called a halt.

"We must prepare things for her resuscitation, Cressey. Help me with these packs."

They toiled until Cressey reeled with weariness, preparing ice slabs covered with furs, arranging apparatus, pulmonary respirators, hypodermics, bottles of precious distillations known only to Professor Stamwell, blankets and kettles of hot water.

"If you should be tempted to give an account of this to the world, Cressey, I trust you will guard the secret of my process," said Stamwell that night.

"Obviously," answered Cressey, "since I haven't the faintest idea of success in such a preposterous attempt to cheat death."

Buoyed up by excitement, Stamwell seemed unwearied, but Cressey was glad to lie down, and it seemed only a few moments of sleep when again he was awakened by Stamwell's chipping ice in the task of extricating one of the white hounds. By noontime, they were lifting it from the hole and placing it on a fur-covered slab of ice to roll in blankets and be gradually warmed with hot water cans until the nine-inch length of fur fell wet and limp as it thawed.

It was some time before the flesh grew pliable, for the beast measured eleven feet from snout to tail-tip and was all the two men could manage. With sweat pouring down his face, Cressey obeyed the crisp commands of Stamwell with trained military precision while the professor applied one after another of his processes and both took turns in expanding and contracting the great fur-clad chest by sheer strength, and manipulating the hypodermic of fluid which started heart action. Then Cressey felt a twitching of the body muscles and saw the legs jerk. He could scarcely credit his sight as Stamwell poured small doses of prepared broth down the dog's throat, and it swallowed them with a faint, gurgling whimper. Stamwell's cry held triumph.

In vain Baptiste announced mealtime. The sun had dipped and begun another day before the great hound was swathed in blankets and furs and the two white men took the hot coffee they sorely needed.

"Eureka!" shouted Stamwell, beside himself with joy.

"And now that the beast is alive, what will we do with him?" was Cressey's rejoinder.

"Take excellent care of him. Take him down to the valley as soon as possible, where Baptiste can feed and look after him."

After a brief three hours of sleep, Stamwell roused Cressey and they exhumed another hound, going through the same laborious work as before, to be rewarded eventually by a whimpering whine and the signs of recurring animation. By that time the first hound was able to take boiled meat and showed ravenous greed, and after the meal it attempted to struggle to its feet but was still weak. In three days it left the blankets and took a few staggering steps, then lifted its magnificent head and howled mournfully again and again, a sound at which Baptiste made the sign of the cross and muttered Chippewan incantations against evil.

When ten days were gone, Baptiste was delegated to escort a pack of seven white hounds, for which stout leather collars and light chains were provided, to the valley. With him went all the guides except one who remained to cook for the white men in the grotto. Baptiste had orders to hunt game and feed the hounds and keep the sled dogs on leash at the cabin of the ivory-carver for greater safety.

With the grotto cleared of the dogs, Stamwell turned his attention to the central block of ice. The hypodermic needles were carefully sterilized, and the greatest care and precautions taken as they lifted the crystal casket from the hole and carefully thawed the ice embedding the woman. Sweat poured off both men while they worked, and their breaths came in sharp hisses long before the first sign of life was evinced in a whispered sigh from the pale lips.

Stamwell's eyes were shadowed to the cheekbones and he seemed to have aged years when the muscular twitching of her slender legs began and a sigh of agony quivered into the silence.

"If you've had your flesh frozen and thawed, you will understand the pain she feels," said Stamwell. "I almost regret inflicting this suffering upon her, but when she pulls through and realizes that she is alive, then, Cressey, I shall be repaid."

Cressey's thoughts denied that potential gratitude. Suppose this woman had been dead any great length of time and found none of her own generation alive in the world, would she thank them? Cressey doubted it, but she was so lovely that he lost all sense of dread and felt only a vast pity in his heart for the beautiful creature lying in the red blankets, her golden hair spread like a silken veil on the colored wool.

It was almost midnight when her eyelids fluttered open and the two men saw eyes of purple softness which moved slowly as she seemed aware of the two men and firelight illuminating the dark ice of the cave. The blueness left her finger-nails and color returned to her lips as she was fed hot milk and broth; then her eyelids closed and her body relaxed in sleep. Stamwell was like a man insane with fear until he applied a stethoscope to her breast.

"Thank God, it is sleep!" he cried. "But there will be no peace for me until she is out of danger. While I watch her, you had better rest. Cressey, do you realize that I have brought the dead to life?"

To Cressey his cry was a challenge, a sacrilege. He felt something of the same uncanny fear which Baptiste had displayed at Stamwell's assumption of super-natural power, and wondered if it were beneficence or crime to restore that lovely creature to life after her long sleep.

His sleep was troubled because in the valley the great hounds howled all night. Dozing, waking to curse them, he saw Stamwell beside the woman's couch, and rising he bade the professor sleep while he watched. He made coffee and carried a steaming cup to his seat beside the sleeping beauty, sipping it as he gazed at the sun-gold creeping down the glacier to the grotto door. A sigh roused him. A white hand touched his wrist. Turning, Cressey was aware that the violet eyes of the woman gazed at him and she smiled, then her fingers touched the tin cup he held as if she was thirsty.

"I can't give you that," he found himself telling her as if she understood his talk. He reached for a bowl of broth simmering on the alcohol stove, heavy with meat juices and nourishing tonic medicines, and fed her. Color tinted her throat and cheeks. She seemed momentarily to gain strength. Cressey was thrilled and awed by the miracle happening before his eyes, and shocked at the languorous coquetry of her glance and the white fingers clinging to his hand.

Again he fed her, aware that she was ravenously hungry, until the broth was finished. He thought she was again asleep until her hand lifted her golden hair and trailed it across his face and a low-toned, throaty laugh startled him. Feeling helpless in face of a crisis, he replaced the golden tress on the couch and felt his fingers tingling as from a light galvanic shock at its touch. He leaned forward and instantly his neck was circled by her arms and she pressed her face against his throat. Cressey was so astonished that he did not try to draw back, and an instant later he felt her teeth on the flesh of his neck.

Alarm and swift revulsion seized him. He was afraid to tear her arms away for fear of bruising the tender skin. He knew her heart beat under the forced stimulation of Stamwell's drugs and feared a sudden shock might halt its action, then while he hesitated a strange drowsiness clouded his senses and stole over his body. He felt no pain where her teeth pierced the skin of his throat; her arms were satin-smooth, the warmth of her lips tempted him to rest in the alluring embrace.

Then a cry from Stamwell roused Cressey from drowsiness that nearly swung into blissful unconsciousness. He was wrenched from her arms and felt the sting of flesh her teeth released. Glancing at her, he saw her lips moist and crimson-stained, and she was struggling in the clutch of Stamwell.

"Fill that hypo with the medicine in the third bottle, quickly, Cressey. She is so strong I can scarcely control her."

Cressey obeyed, even to inserting the needle into the skin of her arm. Her scream was piercing as she fought Stamwell, who held her until the drug took effect and she sank back, relaxed. Then Stamwell turned to Cressey.

"Good God, man, I trusted you to stay awake and watch."

Cressey did not reply. Stamwell was disinfecting the wound on his neck to which he applied a pad of cotton gauze and adhesive tape. Cressey could not even smile, nor would he tell Stamwell how she had coquetted with him before catching him in her arms.

A few minutes later they saw Baptiste toiling up the glacial drift, and from outside the grotto door he called to them.

"*M'sieus*, I cannot hold dose dog, dey grow so beeg, so strong, an' my men ees scare' dey break dem chain. I am ver' scare' of dose dog my own self. Me, I am good dogman, but not dat kind of dog. I feed heem nineteen rabbit, seven coyote, wan elk and much fish in wan week. All my men do ees hunt for feed dose dog. Me, I am 'bout ready quit my job. I tak sled dogs an' tie heem across rivaire cause eef dose white dog git loose—well, we walk back outside."

"Cressey, the white hounds must not kill our sled dogs and Baptiste must be pacified, for if he deserted we should never get our menagerie out alive. I think we can take the woman down to the valley by tomorrow. Suppose you go down now and look after the camp."

Following Baptiste down the ice trail, Cressey saw the ivory-carver industriously sawing off the remaining tusk of the mammoth, and watching him a moment, he slipped and fell headlong. He was only slightly stunned, but a worse calamity had befallen, for in extricating his foot from a small fissure, he felt the snapping of bone and a dull pain. Cressey cursed.

"Baptiste, I've snapped a bone!" The warm-hearted Baptiste lifted him to his shoulder and made his way down to the valley, where their arrival started a terrific din of howling dogs and answering yelps of the sled huskies leashed across the river. Baptiste muttered oaths.

"Eef dose white dog git loose, dey swallow my dog lak I swallow loche liver without chew heem," he commented and grumbled his distaste of the whole business of the grotto miracle. Baptiste was about ready to desert, and it occurred to Cressey that he had better summon Stamwell at once. The great white hounds leaped the length of their chains and the sturdy pine trees were swaying and jerking from the lunge of their powerful bodies.

"Baptiste, you had better fetch Professor Stamwell and his packs down at once, and we'll made a start outside," he said. Again Baptiste took the trail to the grotto, while Cressey soaked his foot in hot water, then bound it with wet moss and cotton. The cook was preparing supper, the other men had gone to assist old Jo to fetch his big mammoth tusk to his cabin, then they all came to where Cressey sat and one of the guides translated Jo's talk.

"*M'sieu*, he say eet ees not good to stay where devils come to life. Dees white wolf ees devil-wolf. Dis woman ees devil-woman. Jo, he say we better froze de dogs and womans again and go out, queeck."

"He's a timid, superstitious old man," said Cressey. "The dogs are savage but the woman can not harm anyone."

Yet as he spoke Cressey felt uneasy. The gauze pad on his neck was a reminder of his personal experience with the woman. He ate supper and waited impatiently for the coming of Stamwell, but it was nearly midnight when he saw Baptiste coming down swiftly, alone. The big guide broke into excited cries as he ran toward Cressey.

"*M'sieu! Le professeur* ees dead, an' *la femme*, she ees gone!"

"Gone! Stamwell dead!" echoed Cressey. Baptiste crossed himself and muttered broken snatches of Chippewan mingled with Roman Catholic prayers, looking apprehensively at the hounds. The dogs stood silent but alert, ears stiffly pointed, and sniffing the wind.

"*M'sieu,* een de cave ev'ting toss dees way an' dat. *Le professeur* he ees lay on floor and hees t'roat ees got bite. Hees hands dey look lak dey soak in water long tam."

Like a blow from a bludgeon the explanation crashed on Cressey. When Stamwell dozed, the woman had caught him as she seized Cressey, possibly drained his blood like vampire bats of southern caves, and with renewed strength had left the grotto. He remembered that she was unclad and the air of the ice fields bitterly cold. With his injured foot he was hampered in reaching the glacier, and nothing he could say or do would persuade Baptiste and his men to search and bring the woman to the valley.

Stamwell's death had come so suddenly he could not yet realize the tragedy. Then he noticed that the dogs were rousing to uncanny excitement, whining and growling, tugging strenuously at their chains. Cressey began to regret bitterly what had been done and longed to break camp and escape from the weird influences loosed by Stamwell and himself. Baptiste saw him look toward the ivory-carver's cabin.

"Good, *M'sieu.* We camp tonight een Jo's house. Eet ees not good to be here. *Non!*"

Under Baptiste's commands the men toiled to carry everything to the cabin, then they set about strengthening it with a barricade of young firs quickly cut down and heaped about the log walls.

"The good priest, he say all trees ees made by *le bon Dieu,*" explained Baptiste, "an', Name of a Name! we need Heem dis night to keep us safe." Cressey could only nod assent, for as he dropped on a couch of freshly cut pine branches, he was aware that stealing over him was that same blissful unrest he had felt in the arms of the death-delivered woman of the glacier. He felt possessed of a wild desire to find her and thrill again to the touch of her satin arms and her mouth warm on his flesh. He knew it for an evil thing, a worse craving than whiskey or dope, and found himself battling the weakness of flesh with arguments prompted by reason which his lips betrayed to Baptiste.

"It is cruel to let the woman wander alone on the ice. If you do not go and find her, Baptiste, I will."

The guide's dark face was grim with dogged determination.

"*M'sieu,* you do not leave dis cabin, not eef we must chain you lak wan dog. Me, I t'ink you have evil curse on you!"

And Baptiste barred both door and window of the cabin which held eight men, until within an hour of midnight the air had grown hot and foul and Cressey demanded fresh air. Reluctantly, Baptiste threw open the window-shutter and admitted a bar of diminishing sunlight. The white hounds were giving tongue in unearthly howlings, mournful as dog-wailings which to the superstitious folk announce death, and the blood of Cressey was leaping as at the cry of a hunting pack. He hobbled to the window and looked toward the glacier where Stamwell lay. Even now he could scarcely realize that his friend was dead, and again he urged Baptiste to open the door.

"No, for my life, *M'sieu*. Look!" There in the river of slow-moving ice stood the huntress, poised daintily on her toes as if in a dance, her arms uplifted to cup her hands at her lips, her long golden hair blowing about a body as softly rounded as a young girl. And on the midnight silence came a clear, ringing cry.

Instantly pandemonium broke loose among the white hounds. Their howls were deafening and the clank of chains made wild, metallic music, and they leaped, and fell back, and leaped again. With their heads thrust through the window opening, Baptiste and Cressey watched, leaning back against men crowded behind them, as one of the hounds snapped his chain and raced like a white cloud in great, swift bounds toward the glacier.

Within a few moments they were all free and flying to the heights, where they leaped about the woman with joyous yelps until she was hidden by a frenzied tumult of gigantic hounds. Then, seemingly at her command, their yelps ceased and they were squatted on their haunches at her feet, pink eyes shining like rubies in the soft twilight, red tongues lolling and quivering from white-fanged jaws. Again she cupped hands to her lips and sent out her hunting cry. At the sound, Cressey shivered. In every nerve he felt the piercing lure of that wail. She was calling him forth, and some hell-born desire to answer and go to her was fighting every prompting of reason. Again came her call, and Cressey plunged from the window toward the door. Baptiste was too quick for him and thrust his own great bulk against the timbers, flinging Cressey aside.

"*Non! M'sieu,* are you crazee? Look!" Baptiste had snatched a small silver crucifix from inside his shirt and clamped it against Cressey's forehead. He felt it searing his skin, like white-hot metal, and he sank to the pine couch, shuddering, sweat breaking out on his face. At Baptiste's command the men held Cressey down, and again. Baptiste flattened the crucifix over his breast and repeated bits of prayers strangely mixed with the incantations of his Chippewan mother's teachings. The sweat grew clammy on his body before Baptiste released him and gave him whisky from an emergency flask.

A somber group of men waited in the cabin until the sun was sailing high and the last faint howling of the white hounds had dwindled to silence. Cressey slept and wakened to see the door open and feel the warm wind blowing through the cabin, then Baptiste brought him coffee and flapjacks hot from the pan.

"*M'sieu,* I say to Jo that we use wan sled to carry out hees beeg tusk. We have sled to spare now we don' carry out medicine packs. Today we break camp."

Cressey considered in silence, his mind quite clear, the horror of the night-frenzy vanished with the sunlight. He could not, would not go outside and leave Stamwell's body without decent burial and said so.

"*M'sieu,* what happen hees body makes no nev' mind. Me, Baptiste, say you do not go to dat cave no more. Eet ees *la Chasse du Diable!*"

"Call it what you will, Baptiste. I do not leave here without placing the body of my friend out of reach of wolves. Perhaps already the white hounds have found it. If so, I shall be haunted for life."

"Me, I t'ink dat ees happen already, *M'sieu,*" commented Baptiste, "but now dey are gone, maybe we go fetch down *le professeur.*" Baptiste had clashed wills with Cressey before, and met defeat, yet when they dragged Cressey up the ice trail on a sled the guide wore crucifix and scapular in full view on his breast and every man did likewise.

They found no trace of the hounds, not even pad-marks on the snow. The grotto showed signs of a struggle, but fortunately Stamwell had packed his medicines and instruments. His body lay on the couch, relaxed before rigor mortis set in, and his face had even the semblance of a smile, but on his throat was an ominous white mark of strong, even teeth, and the visible skin was puckered as if his veins were empty. Otherwise the corpse was unmolested, at which Cressey marveled until he remembered that the white hounds had been supplied with meat by the men. The gaping ice hole presented a solution of a temporary tomb, and Professor Stamwell, blanket wrapped, was laid deep, the broken ice shoveled in, and heated water poured until the grave was filled and already freezing, safe against depredation.

It was while that task engrossed him that Cressey felt the force of the tragedy and a growing desire to avenge the murder of Stamwell, and he forgot the weird spell of the night in which the untombed woman had tempted him to follow her by the memory of her beauty and blissful languor of her caress. It was cowardly to run away now, nor had he any proof of the tale he must tell of Stamwell's death when he was again outside. Then he remembered that since the conquest of Mount Logan by MacCarthy, other parties had set out, and he knew approximately the location of three groups headed for that ascent, all hard-headed mountain climbers and scientists. Giving orders to Baptiste to dispatch men in search of these expedition groups, he started up the glacier in spite of the vehement protests of the guide, who, just before leaving on the valley trail, tossed over Cressey's head the deerskin thong holding the crucifix.

"Wan ver' good priest bless it, *M'sieu.* You take care of heem for Baptiste."

Irreligious himself, Cressey respected the faiths of other men and humored Baptiste. Then, drawn on a sled by two men, he adventured the heights, watching for a glimpse of the woman.

They had traversed a considerable distance, had seen ptarmigan tame as chickens, and edelweiss growing through the snow. Halting to pluck one of these brave little blooms, Cressey saw something glittering over a flower that seemed withered in first unfolding, and he picked from it a long, glistening thread of golden hair that curled, by some attraction of warm blood, about his fingers.

The snow-glare was blinding, the wind whistled keen as whiplashes, and to eat their meal sheltered from its cutting blast, Cressey ordered a detour toward a group of ice-spires which on closer inspection proved a labyrinthine entrance of shining columns leading to a second grotto. Leaning on a stout fir branch used as a cane, he limped down the passage, then halted in alarm. Low, menacing growls and clanking metal told of the hounds within, and a moment later they had leaped forth, a cloud of white death!

Cressey turned to run, knowing how meager was his chance for life. His revolver was in his hand, but as shots rang out, the hounds circled past him, apparently untouched, while he reeled in shocked amazement that he had missed a hit at such close range. Screams from the ice entrance brought his heart to his throat, cries of the two men that were drowned in the bay of wolves on the kill. Cressey stood paralyzed, unable to prevent the dreadful carnage, unable to save his men even while he pumped lead into that swirling, milling cloud of destruction now fighting fiercely over the mangled remains of their victims.

Weakly, he leaned against the ice wall, his senses reeling as he reloaded his revolver with trembling fingers, knowing lead was impotent against those ghost-wolves. For he knew them, now, to be more than flesh and blood. They were some infernal incarnation invulnerable to man-dealt destruction.

A high-pitched, ringing call, clear as a bugle, brought his gaze to the grotto and he saw the woman standing against the blue gloom, golden hair wind-blown, posed on her toes. She glided, dazzlingly lovely, toward him with arms outstretched, and in his last moment of reason Cressey threw one wrist up to shield his eyes from that dread allure. Then again he felt the fierce desire of her and flung out his arms. She came within five feet of him and halted, a puzzled expression on her features, her hands sweeping and weaving as if she tried to tear from between them some barrier invisible to Cressey. When he tried to seize her, she retreated, still fighting at the space separating them until man and woman reached the entrance to the ice passage, where the dogs leaped back from too close a contact, and with a gesture of despair she turned and ran, calling in her ringing voice and leading her pack to the heights. Cressey fell on his knees beside the gnawed bones of his men and heard his own cries imploring her to return.

Sweat rained from his face, his body quivered; he was a man corroded by the poison of an evil desire. After a long time his head lifted and he clutched at the crucifix on his breast, then reason gradually conquered and as he pressed it to his head and lips he felt the sun-warmth and cool wind and knew he was himself. Slowly, painfully, he retraced his trail down the glacier and found Baptiste had reached the lower grotto and was searching for him, frantic with fear.

"The two men are dead, eaten by the white hounds," he told Baptiste, and shuddered at the guide's cry of horror. "Take me down and bind me in the cabin, Baptiste. I am a man accursed."

"Help will come wit' dose men I send out, M'sieu," comforted Baptiste.

But they waited for three days, seeing nothing of the white hounds and woman, until one man returned, a trapper old on the trails, and with chattering teeth told a tale of horror.

"White wolves broke into the first camp I git to, M'sieu, an' I find only wan man alive. He tell me of La Chasse du Diable, then he die. M'sieu, am ver' old man. But I hear when I was babee, of this Chasse du Diable, from my gran'-gran'-père, an' hees gran'-père tell heem."

*   *   *

For a week they waited the return of the second man sent out, then one morning Baptiste reported men coming up the valley, and Cressey hobbled to meet them.

"Thank God you've come!" he cried. "My name is Cressey. My companion, Professor Stamwell, is dead, and I have a tale to tell almost beyond belief."

"I'm Johnson," said the leader of the newcomers, "and I think I know something of your story. Your man told us a little and we found the Stillwell camp ravaged—a terrible sight. I'm worried about another party toward the west, for we had a friendly wager as to who would first climb Logan. But I am amazed at the hunger of wolves in summer, that they attack men."

"These are more than wolves, Johnson, as Baptiste will tell you." Cressey began to relate his adventures, omitting nothing, not even his own accursed desire which had recurred each night and which Baptiste fought with incantation and holy symbol.

"Laugh if you will. To me it is horrible," he ended.

"I'm not even smiling. Your face shows the strain, Cressey. But have you nerve enough to accompany me and the men to the grotto again?"

"Of course. Waiting here is hell."

Johnson and Baptiste held weighty consultations while Cressey lay on the grass, too pain-racked to take part. His lips twisted in a sneer when the men made rude crosses of wood and gathered a blanket full of windflowers, those pale blooms which Indian converts say "spring up where angels' tears have fallen," and loaded sleds. Cressey was oblivious to everything but the fact that he was returning to the grotto where he had seen the huntress, and with a low cunning that shamed him he was plotting a meeting with her that should cradle him in her arms.

They threaded the passageway of ice turrets, carrying pine torches which gave smoky light to the blueness of the grotto as Johnson examined it, then flung himself on the ice floor with a cry.

"Cressey, for God's sake, look! Here's a mammoth, as I'm alive! And other beasts. Lord, man, some mighty convulsion of nature must have herded your huntress, her wolves, and other denizens of her long-departed era into close quarters and caught them. Good heavens, if your secret process will restore the woman and wolves, why not try it on bigger game?"

Cressey laughed. The evil spell of the place had caught Johnson, and if he could be persuaded to carry out this wild scheme of digging up this frozen mammoth, there would be time . . . time to seek again his huntress and find the Lethe of her embrace.

Through ensuing talk, Cressey was enthusiastic. The men were sent to bring the packs from the first grotto, and the digging began. About the cave entrance, the wooden crosses were arranged with arms touching and draped with windflowers that were also scattered on the ice trail. Cressey's own men and Baptiste refused to assist the ice-digging. Jo, the ivory-carver, was still below in his cabin. Nothing would persuade him to take part.

"Old Jo declares this woman and her dogs are evil, yet he seems unafraid,'' Cressey remarked one day.

"Jo,'' interrupted Baptiste, "he say he too old, an' have not much blood. He say he make charm een hees ivory womans. When dis hunter-womans come, he pick up ax and smash ivory womans, an' the ghost-womans go 'way an' nev' come back.''

"Oddly enough, the natives of the south seas and Africa have the same belief,'' said Johnson. "They make an image of some enemy and either burn it or put it in water to rot, and the object of their venom sickens and dies. The world, Cressey, is small.''

That night, as the sun sank lower, came the howling of wolves, and Cressey felt the prickling of his scalp and leap of blood. Although toil-weary, the men were awake, and guns in hand they watched the great white hounds streaking down the glacier, led by the flying huntress. Cressey started for the ice-passage, but Baptiste leaped and bore him down, his great weight pressing the breath from the smaller man as he struggled and fought in sudden rage. Subsiding, he laughed, but the sound of his laughter was unpleasant even to his own hearing.

It seemed as if the party had small chance of defense against those ghastly, ravening death-wolves, but to the amazement of every man, the pack halted abruptly beyond the wooden crosses, and the huntress stood there twisting her white hands as if baffled. The crosses and blessed windflowers had turned the hunt, but there began hours of fearful waiting until the pack circled the pinnacles, even leaping over the grotto arch and howling from behind the fence of crosses over the cave entrance. The sun was well above the horizon when they drifted away.

Night after night the diabolic chase returned only to retreat, baffled by barriers they could not break down. By day the men slaved to unearth the frozen beasts belonging to an era when the north was tropic swale. Baptiste, who hunted in the valley for fresh meat, reported that Jo was carving a second figure of the hunt-ress, standing upright, extremely lifelike, and that he scarcely left his work to eat or sleep.

At last the great hairy mammoth lay clear of ice, and because they had no means of lifting its immense weight from the hole, Cressey and Johnson built fires about it, shielded from the carcass by screens of flattened oil-cans until it was thawed and restoratives from Stamwell's stores applied. Blankets and fur robes were shoved under it by leverage of cut pine sticks, and all hands rubbed the gigantic limbs and trunk with rough pads of twigs bound together by coarse grass. It was a Herculean task and the men were exhausted before the monster shuddered, stirred his mighty body, strained ponderously, while everyone scram-bled out of the ice-hole. Then, heaving himself to his knees, the mammoth staggered slowly to his feet. As the puny humans fled from his path, he crushed the ice under his forefeet, burst the ropes with which he had been bound, and lumbered out of his tomb, his tusks crashing down the ice-pinnacles of the passage and scattering the protecting crosses, then he lunged to the glacial river and went tottering to the valley.

Cressey, white-faced and shaking as he realized the titanic grimness of the thing he and Johnson had loosed, ordered the trek to begin immediately down the ice floe to the valley. At the same time he realized that, working with pick and shovel, concentrating on the healthful task of manual labor, he had liberated his mind and body from the huntress' evil sway. He no longer paid attention to the midnight *Chasse du Diable,* and he slept soundly through the baying of ghost-wolves. He breathed deep drafts of the balsam-laden valley warmth as they approached Jo's cabin, reverently thankful for his release.

"Baptiste," he said gently, "you have looked after me and I am grateful. I have been caught in the power of hell, but it is gone."

Baptiste caught him by the arms and looked deep into his eyes.

"Oui, M'sieu. No more I can see dat woman-shape in your eyeball. All dees time, eet was dere an' I know you are een her power. Now, eet ees gone!"

Cressey felt a tremor of apprehension. He had not known that the image of the huntress was photographed on the retinas of his eyes until Baptiste spoke of it. He held out his hand and the breed gripped it in solemnity of silence that was like prayer, then he pointed to the almost finished figure at which Jo worked assiduously, never lifting his hands from the task. The delicacy of his skill was never so apparent as now. From the ivory base still shrouding her feet, the huntress seemed to dance, wind-blown hair, curving limbs, round young breasts so perfect that it seemed a pity he could not, like Pygmalion of old, breathe life into this Galatea. Cressey put out a hand to touch it but Jo waved him aside and yelped a warning.

"He say you mus' not touch her, or you have devil in your liver some more," translated Baptiste.

"Tell him I shall buy her and pay well," said Cressey, but Baptiste returned a disconcerting negative.

"Jo say, he keep her for to lay curse you have loos' een dees world. No, *M'sieu,* we go outside."

But this time it was Jo who demurred at departure. His harangue, interpreted by Baptiste, told Cressey that he was responsible for releasing the powers of darkness in the valley and it was no longer safe to be caught on the trail at night until the evil was overcome. This simple acceptance by the old ivory-carver of the presence of terrifying supernatural powers did more to persuade Johnson than all Cressey's talk.

"They're merely flesh and blood animals," he argued. "We may have to take precautions as we would with any wild beasts, but I mean to follow that mammoth and herd him into some museum."

In the sun-warmed valley, where fires and cooking spread the comfort of commonplace occurrences, it was easier to lay aside superstitious fears, but when Baptiste's convictions were strengthened by Jo's calm acceptance of peril, Cressey realized he would better bow to their opinion that they take the river instead of land trails on their way out, and for this purpose Baptiste was already cutting timber to make rafts, which were the quickest and most serviceable solution of their need.

The long day passed and night closed in again. The crosses, carried down by the careful Baptiste, stood like a fence about the cabin, draped with fresh wind-flowers, with one gap left by which the men went to and fro on the way to logs they rolled to the river for the raft.

Johnson fell into heavy sleep and Cressey lay near him, smoking a last pipe. The old ivory-carver worked by the light of his oil lamp in the corner, although sunlight still shone in at the open window. The sled dogs had been brought and leashed inside the encircling crosses, but Cressey had scarcely dozed off when he heard their whimperings. Rising, he went outside.

From far off came the baying of the chase, and he saw the huntress flying down the ice, followed by her hounds. Johnson came from the cabin and both men stood in that twilight which had grown longer in the waning of summer which would soon give way to winter. A pale crescent moon danced on one silver toe, a fit companion for that lovely Diana dancing on the ice.

"Even now," said Johnson. "I can't believe but that she is a flesh and blood woman. Cressey, I'd like to clasp her hand and know for myself."

Cressey did not reply. The huntress was coming nearer, the baying of the hounds grew louder. He looked to see that the crosses were in place and did not observe that Johnson had stepped past them until he heard the cry of Baptiste. Then he saw the dark figure of the man, the radiant white fire of the huntress' beauty, and they melted into each other's arms. With a yell, Cressey leaped the barrier of crosses and raced to where the two stood swaying in close embrace.

As if the hounds sensed the symbol on Cressey's breast, they fell back as he approached. He had a swift wonder at their timidity until his hands seized Johnson, who screamed and writhed at his touch and fought being rescued as the huntress' head lifted from his shoulder and she slowly retreated, step by step, her moistened red lips parted, showing her strong white teeth in almost a snarl of hatred.

Cressey fought to draw Johnson to safety, and as he came nearer the cabin, the huntress advanced, hands reaching, weaving, tearing at the space separating her from her victim, unable to brush aside or combat the force for good protect-ing him. Slowly the hounds advanced with her, and the cries of the sled dogs made the night hideous, when suddenly the huntress threw back her head and shrilled her wild call.

Once inside the barrier of crosses, Cressey dropped the half-crazed Johnson into Baptiste's arms, then he stared into the brightening light of dawn on the mountains. There were sounds from far off, of crashing brush and thunderingly ominous tread, and into their view loomed the giant of the ancient world, lum-bering forward with incredible speed until it reached the woman's side, a dread-ful menace which only for the frail barrier could have crushed the cabin and scattered the last vestige of men and dogs.

The howling of sled dogs and cries of men were terror-muted for a few moments. Then they were alert. Guns cracked in sharp fusillade, but the ghost-beasts neither quivered nor showed signs of a wound. The huntress was screaming at her beasts and waving white arms to urge them on, but they slunk aside until she howled at the mammoth, who caught her in his trunk and swung her to his broad head. There she stood, ethereally lovely and evil, her lips stained by the interrupted draft of human life, while the night waned and the blessed sun shot from the curving breasts of snow on Mount Logan. A cry as of frenzied despair came from her. The mammoth turned, the hounds leaped ahead, and the whole cavalcade vanished in the direction of the icefields.

Cressey turned to find Johnson as mad as he himself had been.

"You cur," he howled, "to come between me and my woman! You've had your day and now you begrudge me my hour of happiness."

"Johnson, she killed Stamwell, drained his body of life. She almost killed me. Left me like a maniac, as she will leave you. Here, this trinket of Baptiste's protected me; you shall wear it."

He dropped the thong of the crucifix over Johnson's head and heard his cry of pain. Cressey knew the white-hot searing of that symbol on flesh accursed and felt only pity for the man. All that day Johnson moaned, watched over by Cressey, while Baptiste directed the men in their task of making the raft.

"No ghost can pass running water," he said, and that night the logs were lashed together and the rafts moored to shore trees, and the barrier of crosses was strengthened.

Meanwhile, working ceaselessly, Jo had cut the ivory from the feet of the huntress he was carving, and was chiseling her pretty toes with their filbert-shaped nails. He had truly caught the grace of her dancing poise in the slender ankles, and she stood like a fairy molded of mellow gold when the sun touched the far horizon and brief night began in violet-tinted twilight.

Cressey was fascinated by the figure. "Tell Jo that I must have it. I will pay well, five hundred dollars, even a thousand. I will take her out with me."

Reluctantly Baptiste interpreted his demand and for the first time the old ivory-carver showed emotion. Fire leaped in his eyes as he wrathfully waved Cressey aside and refused to consider even so great a sum of money for his statue of the woman.

Cressey did not argue, but in his heart he determined to obtain the ivory figure, and fell asleep planning a means to that end. He slept lightly, dreaming of the huntress, and muttering in his sleep. His broken talk wakened Johnson, who looked toward Cressey with hatred in his eyes, which changed to cunning.

Johnson cautiously slipped the thong of the crucifix from his neck and it dropped on the floor. Then for a time he lay still except for the convulsive twitching of his body and the rolling of his tortured eyes.

At midnight came the whimpering of the sled dogs and baying of white hounds from afar. Immediately every man in the cabin was alert. They grabbed guns and plunged outside, waiting that dread visitation. The moon was fuller and gave silver light pricked out by velvet dark blotches of the trees. The glacial river gleamed like pearl. Another day and the party would have escaped, afloat on rafts carried by the swift-running stream, but this one night must be endured.

The huntress was not alone with her dogs, for she stood on the head of the mammoth which thundered into the plain cleared by his voracious feeding, and about them raced the white hounds. The hearts of the men were seized by icy fingers of fear even while they poured volley after volley of shots at the advancing horror and realized as they pulled the triggers that no man-invented mode of death could halt them.

The old ivory-carver, Jo, alone seemed fearless or careless of those terrific ghouls of eld, for he came leisurely from the cabin, toddling toward the barrier fence of wooden crosses and peering as if to feast his sight on the vision he had foregone during those nights he toiled at the ivory figure of the woman.

Cressey stepped to Jo's side. He had forgotten Johnson in the cabin. There was none to see Johnson spring from the couch and with the desperation of a madman seize the ivory huntress in his arms and rush from the door on shoeless feet that made no sound.

Cressey's first glimpse of him came when Johnson leaped the barrier of crosses and headed for the river raft. But the huntress had also seen that plunging human and her cry rang like the long-drawn note of a silver horn. The mammoth lunged forward, the hounds leaped in white arcs of flying fur, and Johnson's scream stabbed through the din of animal howls.

They saw the huntress leap from her titanic steed to catch Johnson in her arms; saw the ivory figure knocked from his grasp. The golden hair of the huntress enveloped him like a ruddy silk mantel and her mouth was pressed to his throat.

But a greater tragedy was imminent. As if the scent of human blood maddened it, the mammoth plunged forward, his great tusks lunging between the leaping hounds to stab his human enemy; and the hounds closed in with unearthly yelpings.

Transfixed by the sight, the men at the cabin stared at the calamity they were powerless to avert, until there came a loud crunch as the mammoth's foot trod on the ivory figure of the huntress which Johnson had dropped.

Then, as if at a signal, the ghost-beasts seemed frozen in their tracks, and from them came a glistening white mist which swayed to and fro as it rose and drifted across the face of the young moon, and the watchers saw, like a frail cloud, the shining form of that lovely, hell-born huntress, as it blew away on the wind of dawn.

Light grew swiftly. The sun came up and shone on a mountainous mass of hairy mammoth flesh and long-furred hounds lying on the tundra.

As they stood, chained to the spot by paralysis of horror, every nerve taut, the men at the cabin saw that mound of flesh subside to pulp, and a dreadful stench arose in a smoky steam. By noon there was a gelatinous mass, which by nightfall had soaked into the earth, leaving only the skeletons. A clean, cold wind from the snows sweetened the air where Jo prodded the bones with a stick to recover all that was left of his ivory huntress, a head on which the features faithfully depicted her inscrutable smile, with lips and teeth slightly parted.

Cressey did not offer to buy it, and the head still hangs above Jo's cabin door.

THE WOLF WOMAN   57

One glance at that lovely face had power to recall all too vividly the fate of Stamwell and Johnson, for whom crosses were erected in the valley and lop-sticks nearby carved with their names. Cressey did not smile nor dispute the assertion of Baptiste that he should never return to that valley.

"M'sieu," said Baptiste, "dat devil-womans have dreenk your blood wan time, an' eef some day she come back, she catch you again because all womans ees jealous, an' eef a womans git jealous eet open doors of ver' bad hells. You do what Baptiste say, you wear a li'l crucifix all time." And though not a religious man, Cressey has never since been without that symbol.

THE CANAL

EVERIL WORRELL

Everil Worrell's twenty-eight-year relationship with Weird Tales *was one of the magazine's longest, and included her oft-reprinted vampire tale "The Canal." Its premise, that a vampire can be thwarted by a stream of running water, derives from traditional vampire lore. The modern relationship that develops between the vampire and her unsuspecting male victim was Worrell's own invention. The story was later adapted for Rod Serling's television program "Night Gallery."*

Past the sleeping city the river sweeps; along its left bank the old canal creeps.

I did not intend that to be poetry, although the scene is poetic—somberly, gruesomely poetic, like the poems of Poe. Too well I know it—too often have I walked over the grass-grown path beside the reflections of black trees and tumbledown shacks and distant factory chimneys in the sluggish waters that moved so slowly, and ceased to move at all.

I shall be called mad, and I shall be a suicide. I shall take no pains to cover up my trail, or to hide the thing that I shall do. What will it matter, afterward, what they say of me? If they knew the truth—if they could vision, even dimly, the beings with whom I have consorted—if the faintest realization might be theirs of the thing I am becoming, and of the fate from which I am saving their city—then they would call me a great hero. But it does not matter what they call me, as I have said before. Let me write down the things I am about to write down, and let them be taken, as they will be taken, for the last ravings of a madman. The city will be in mourning for the thing I shall have done—but its

mourning will be of no consequence beside that other fate from which I shall
have saved it.

I have always had a taste for nocturnal prowling. We as a race have grown too
intelligent to take seriously any of the old, instinctive fears that preserved us
through preceding generations. Our sole remaining salvation, then, has come to
be our tendency to travel in herds. We wander at night—but our objective is
somewhere on the brightly lighted streets, or still somewhere where men do not
go alone. When we travel far afield, it is in company. Few of my acquaintance,
few in the whole city here, would care to ramble at midnight over the grass-
grown path I have spoken of, not because they would fear to do so, but because
such things are not being done.

Well, it is dangerous to differ individually from one's fellows. It is dangerous
to wander from the beaten road. And the fears that guarded the race in the dawn
of time and through the centuries were real fears, founded on reality.

A month ago, I was a stranger here. I had just taken my first position—I was
graduated from college only three months before, in the spring. I was lonely, and
likely to remain so for some time, for I have always been of a solitary nature,
making friends slowly.

I had received one invitation out—to visit the camp of a fellow employee in
the firm for which I worked, a camp which was located on the farther side of the
wide river—the side across from the city and the canal, where the bank was high
and steep and heavily wooded, and little tents blossomed all along the water's
edge. At night these camps were a string of sparkling lights and tiny, leaping
campfires, and the tinkle of music carried faintly far across the calmly flowing
water. That far bank of the river was no place for an eccentric, solitary man to
love. But the near bank, which would have been an eyesore to the campers had
not the river been so wide—the near bank attracted me from my first glimpse
of it.

We embarked in a motorboat at some distance downstream, and swept up
along the near bank, and then out and across the current. I turned my eyes
backward. The murk of stagnant water that was the canal, the jumble of low
buildings beyond it, the lonely, low-lying waste of the narrow strip of land
between canal and river, the dark, scattered trees growing there—I intended to
see more of these things.

That weekend bored me, but I repaid myself no later than Monday evening,
the first evening when I was back in the city, alone and free. I ate a solitary
dinner immediately after leaving the office. I went to my room and slept from
seven until nearly midnight. I wakened naturally, then, for my whole heart was
set on exploring the alluring solitude I had discovered. I dressed, slipped out of
the house and into the street, started the motor in my roadster and drove through
the lighted streets.

I left behind that part of town which was thick with vehicles carrying people
home from their evening engagements, and began to thread my way through
darker and narrower streets. Once I had to back out of a cul-de-sac, and once I

had to detour around a closed block. This part of town was not alluring, even to me. It was dismal without being solitary.

But when I had parked my car on a rough, cobbled street that ran directly down into the inky waters of the canal, and crossed a narrow bridge, I was repaid. A few minutes set my feet on the old towpath where mules had drawn riverboats up and down only a year or so ago. Across the canal now, as I walked upstream at a swinging pace, the miserable shacks where miserable people lived seemed to march with me, and then fell behind. They looked like places in which murders might be committed, every one of them.

The bridge I had crossed was near the end of the city going north, as the canal marked its western extremity. Then minutes of walking, and the dismal shacks were quite a distance behind, the river was farther away and the strip of waste land much wider and more wooded, and tall trees across the canal marched with me as the evil-looking houses had done before. Far and faint, the sound of a bell in the city reached my ears. It was midnight.

I stopped, enjoying the desolation around me. It had the savor I had expected and hoped for. I stood for some time looking up at the sky, watching the low drift of heavy clouds, which were visible in the dull reflected glow from distant lights in the heart of the city, so that they appeared to have a lurid phosphorescence of their own. The ground under my feet, on the contrary, was utterly devoid of light. I had felt my way carefully, knowing the edge of the canal partly by instinct, partly by the even more perfect blackness of the water in it, and even holding fairly well to the path, because it was perceptibly sunken below the ground beside it.

Now as I stood motionless in this spot, my eyes upcast, my mind adrift with strange fancies, suddenly my feelings of satisfaction and well-being gave way to something different. Fear was an emotion unknown to me—for those things which make men fear, I had always loved. A graveyard at night was to me a charming place for a stroll and meditation. But now the roots of my hair seemed to move upright on my head, and along all the length of my spine I was conscious of a prickling, tingling sensation—such as my forefathers may have felt in the jungle when the hair on their backs stood up as the hair of my head was doing now. Also, I was afraid to move, and I knew that there were eyes upon me, and that that was why I was afraid to move. I was afraid of those eyes—afraid to see them, to look into them.

All this while, I stood perfectly still, my face uptilted toward the sky. But after a terrible mental effort, I mastered myself.

Slowly, slowly, with an attempt to propitiate the owner of the unseen eyes by my casual manner, I lowered my own. I looked straight ahead—at the softly swaying silhouette of the treetops across the canal as they moved gently in the cool night wind; at the mass of blackness that was those trees, and the opposite shore; at the shiny blackness where the reflections of the clouds glinted vaguely and disappeared that was the canal. And again I raised my eyes a little, for just across the canal where the shadows massed most heavily, there was that at which I must look more closely. And now, as I grew accustomed to the greater blackness and my pupils expanded, I dimly discerned the contours of an old boat or barge, half sunken in water. An old, abandoned canal-boat. But was I dreaming, or was there a white-clad figure seated on the roof of the low cabin aft, a pale, heart-shaped face gleaming strangely at me from the darkness, the glow of two eyes seeming to light up the face, and to detach it from the darkness?

Surely, there could be no doubt as to the eyes. They shone as the eyes of animals shine in the dark, with a phosphorescent gleam, and a glimmer of red! Well, I had heard that some human eyes have that quality at night.

But what a place for a human being to be—a girl, too, I was sure. That daintily heart-shaped face was the face of a girl, surely; I was seeing it clearer and clearer, either because my eyes were growing more accustomed to peering into the deeper shadows, or because of that phosphorescence in the eyes that stared back at me.

I raised my voice softly, not to break too much the stillness of the night.

"Hello! who's there? Are you lost, or marooned, and can I help?"

There was a little pause. I was conscious of a soft lapping at my feet. A stronger night wind had sprung up, was ruffling the dark waters. I had been over-warm, and where it struck me the perspiration turned cold on my body, so that I shivered uncontrollably.

"You can stay—and talk a while, if you will. I am lonely, but not lost. I—I live here."

I could hardly believe my ears. The voice was little more than a whisper, but it had carried clearly—a girl's voice, sure enough. And she lived *there*—in an old, abandoned canal-boat, half submerged in the stagnant water.

"You are not *alone* there?"

"No, not alone. My father lives here with me, but he is deaf—and he sleeps soundly."

Did the night wind blow still colder, as though it came to us from some unseen, frozen sea—or was there something in her tone that chilled me, even as a strange attraction drew me toward her? I wanted to draw near to her, to see closely the pale, heart-shaped face, to lose myself in the bright eyes that I had seen shining in the darkness. I wanted—I wanted to hold her in my arms, to find her mouth with mine, to kiss it. . . .

With a start, I realized the nature of my thoughts, and for an instant lost all thought in surprise. Never in my twenty-two years had I felt love before. My fancies had been otherwise directed—a moss-grown, fallen gravestone was a dearer thing to me to contemplate than the fairest face in all the world. Yet, surely, what I felt now was love!

I took a reckless step nearer the edge of the bank.

"Could I come over to you?" I begged. "It's warm, and I don't mind a wetting. It's late, I know—but I would give a great deal to sit beside you and talk, if only for a few minutes before I got back to town. It's a lonely place here for a girl like you to live—your father should not mind if you exchange a few words with someone occasionally."

Was it the unconventionality of my request that made her next words sound like a long-drawn shudder of protest? There was a strangeness in the tones of her voice that held me wondering, every time she spoke.

"No, no. Oh, no! *You must not swim across.*"

"Then—could I come tomorrow, or some day soon, in the daytime; and would you let me come on board then—or would you come on shore and talk to me, perhaps?"

"Not in the daytime—*never* in the daytime!"

Again the intensity of her low-toned negation held me spellbound.

It was not her sense of the impropriety of the hour, then, that had dictated her manner. For surely, any girl with the slightest sense of the fitness of things would rather have a tryst by daytime than after midnight—yet there was an inference in her last words that if I came again it should be again at night.

Still feeling the spell that had enthralled me, as one does not forget the presence of a drug in the air that is stealing one's senses, even when those senses begin to wander and to busy themselves with other things, I yet spoke shortly.

"Why do you say, 'Never in the daytime'? Do you mean that I may come more than this once at night, though now you won't let me cross the canal to you at the expense of my own clothes, and you won't put down your plank or drawbridge or whatever you come on shore with, and talk to me here for only a moment? I'll come again, if you'll let me talk to you instead of calling across the water. I'll come again, any time you will let me—day or night, I don't care. I want to come to you. But I only ask you to explain. If I came in the daytime and met your father, wouldn't that be the best thing to do? Then we could be really acquainted—we could be friends."

"In the nighttime, my father sleeps. In the daytime, *I* sleep. How could I talk to you, or introduce you to my father then? If you came on board this boat in the daytime, you would find my father—and you would be sorry. As for me, I would be sleeping. I could never introduce you to my father, do you see?"

"You sleep soundly, you and your father." Again there was pique in my voice.

"Yes, we sleep soundly."

"And always at different times?"

"Always at different times. We are on guard—one of us is always on guard. We have been hardly used, down there in your city. And we have taken refuge here. And we are always—always—on guard."

The resentment vanished from my breast, and I felt my heart go out to her anew. She was so pale, so pitiful in the night. My eyes were learning better and better how to pierce the darkness; they were giving me a more definite picture of my companion—if I could think of her as a companion, between myself and whom stretched the black water.

The sadness of the lonely scene, the perfection of the solitude itself, these things contributed to her pitifulness. Then there was the strangeness of atmosphere of which, even yet, I had only partly taken note. There was the strange, shivering chill, which yet did not seem like the healthful chill of a cool evening. In fact, it did not prevent me from feeling the oppression of the night, which was unusually sultry. It was like a little breath of deadly cold that came and went, and yet did not alter the temperature of the air itself, as the small ripples on the surface of the water do not concern the water even a foot down.

And even that was not all. There was an unwholesome smell about the night—a dank, moldy smell that might have been the very breath of death and decay. Even I, the connoisseur in all things dismal and unwholesome, tried to keep my mind from dwelling overmuch upon that smell. What it must be to live breathing it constantly in, I could not think. But no doubt the girl and her father were used to it; and no doubt it came from the stagnant water of the canal and from the rotting wood of the old, half-sunken boat that was their refuge.

My heart throbbed with pity again. Their refuge—what a place! And my clearer vision of the girl showed me that she was pitifully thin, even though possessed of the strange face that drew me to her. Her clothes hung around her like old rags, but hers was no scarecrow aspect. Although little flesh clothed her bones, her very bones were beautiful. I was sure the little pale, heart-shaped face would be more beautiful still, if I could only see it closely. I must see it closely—I must establish some claim to consideration as a friend of the strange, lonely crew of the half-sunken wreck.

"This is a poor place to call a refuge," I said finally. "One might have very little money, and yet do somewhat better. Perhaps I might help you—I am sure I could. If your ill-treatment in the city was because of poverty—I am not rich, but I could help that. I could help you a little with money, if you would let me; or, in any case, I could find a position for you. I'm sure I could do that."

The eyes that shone fitfully toward me like two small pools of water inter-mittently lit by a cloud-swept sky seemed to glow more brightly. She had been half crouching, half sitting on top of the cabin; now she leaped to her feet with one quick, sinuous, abrupt motion, and took a few rapid, restless steps to and fro before she answered.

When she spoke, her voice was little more than a whisper; yet surely rage was in its shrill sibilance.

"Fool! Do you think you would be helping me, to tie me to a desk, to shut me behind doors, away from freedom, away from the delight of doing my own will, of seeking my own way? Never, never would I let you do that. Rather this old boat, rather a deserted grave under the stars, for my home!"

A boundless surprise swept over me, and a positive feeling of kinship with this strange being, whose face I had hardly seen, possessed me. So I myself might have spoken, so I had often felt, though I had never dreamed of putting my thoughts so definitely, so forcibly. My regularized daytime life was a thing I thought little of; I really lived only in my nocturnal prowlings. Why, this girl was right! All of life should be free, and spent in places that interested and attracted.

How little, how little I knew, that night, that dread forces were tugging at my soul, were finding entrance to it and easy access through the morbid weakness of my nature! How little I knew at what a cost I deviated so radically from my kind, who herd in cities and love well-lit ways and the sight of man, and sweet and wholesome places to be solitary in, when the desire for solitude comes over them!

That night it seemed to me that there was but one important thing in life—to allay the angry passion my unfortunate words had aroused in the breast of my beloved, and to win from her some answering feeling.

"I understand—much better than you think," I whispered tremulously. "What I want is to see you again, to come to know you, and to serve you in any way that I may. Surely, there must be something in which I can be of use to you. All you have to do from tonight on forever, is to command me. I swear it!"

"You swear *that*—you do swear it?"

Delighted at the eagerness of her words, I lifted my hand toward the dark heavens.

"I swear it. From this night on, forever—I swear it."

"Then listen. Tonight you may not come to me, nor I to you. I do not want you to board this boat—not tonight, not any night. And most of all, not any day. But do not look so sad. I will come to you. No, not tonight, perhaps not for many nights—yet before very long. I will come to you there, on the bank of the canal, when the water in the canal ceases to flow."

I must have made a gesture of impatience, or of despair. It sounded like a way of saying never—for why should the water in the canal cease to flow? She read my thoughts in some way, for she answered them.

"You do not understand. I am speaking seriously—I am promising to meet you there on the bank, and soon. For the water within these banks is moving slower, always slower. Higher up, I have heard that the canal has been drained. Between these lower locks, the water still seeps in and drops slowly, slowly downstream. But there will come a night when it will be quite, quite stagnant—and on that night I will come to you. And when I come, I will ask of you a favor. And you will keep your oath."

It was all the assurance I could get that night. She had come back to the side of the cabin where she had sat crouched before, and she resumed again that posture and sat still and silent, watching me. Sometimes I could see her eyes upon me, and sometimes not. But I felt that their gaze was unwavering. The little cold breeze, which I had finally forgotten while I was talking with her, was blowing again, and the unwholesome smell of decay grew heavier before the dawn.

She would not speak again, nor answer me when I spoke to her, and I grew nervous, and strangely ill at ease.

At last I went away. And in the first faint light of dawn I slipped up the stairs of my rooming house, and into my own room.

I was deadly tired at the office next day. And day after day slipped away and I grew more and more weary; for a man cannot wake day and night without suffering, especially in hot weather, and that was what I was doing. I haunted the old towpath and waited, night after night, on the bank opposite the sunken boat. Sometimes I saw my lady of the darkness, and sometimes not. When I saw her, she spoke little; but sometimes she sat there on the top of the cabin and let me watch her till the dawn, or until the strange uneasiness that was like fright drove me from her and back to my room, where I tossed restlessly in the heat and dreamed strange dreams, half waking, till the sun shone in on my forehead and I tumbled into my clothes and down to the office again.

Once I asked her why she had made the fanciful condition that she would not come ashore to meet me until the waters of the canal had ceased to run. (How eagerly I studied those waters! How I stole away at noontime more than once, not to approach the old boat, but to watch the almost imperceptible downdrift of bubbles, bits of straw, twigs, rubbish!)

My questioning displeased her, and I asked her that no more. It was enough that she chose to be whimsical. My part was to wait.

It was more than a week later that I questioned her again, this time on a different subject. And after that, I curbed my curiosity relentlessly.

"Never speak to me of things you do not understand about me. Never again, or I will not show myself to you again. And when I walk on the path yonder, it will not be with you."

I had asked her what form of persecution she and her father had suffered in the city, that had driven them out to this lonely place, and where in the city they had lived.

Frightened seriously lest I lose the ground I was sure I had gained with her, I was about to speak of something else. But before I could find the words, her low voice came to me again.

"It was horrible, horrible! Those little houses below the bridge, those houses along the canal—tell me, are they not worse than my boat? Life there was shut in, and furtive. I was not free as I am now—and the freedom I will soon have will make me forget the things I have not yet forgotten. The screaming, the reviling and cursing! Fear and flight! As you pass back by those houses, think how you would like to be shut in one of them, and in fear of your life. And then think of them no more; for I would forget them, and I will never speak of them again."

I dared not answer her. I was surprised that she had vouchsafed me so much. But surely her words meant this: that before she had come to live on the decaying, water-rotted old boat, she had lived in one of those horrible houses I passed by on my way to her. Those houses, each of which looked like the predestined scene of a murder!

As I left her that night, I felt that I was very daring.

"One or two nights more and you will walk beside me," I called to her. "I have watched the water at noon, and it hardly moves at all. I threw a scrap of paper into the canal, and it whirled and swung a little where a thin skim of oil lay on the water down there—oil from the big, dirty city you are well out of. But though I watched and watched, I could not see it move downward at all. Perhaps tomorrow night, or the night after, you will walk on the bank with me. I hope it will be clear and moonlit, and I will be near enough to see you clearly—as well as you seem always to see me in darkness or moonlight, equally well. And perhaps I will kiss you—but not unless you let me."

And yet, the next day, for the first time my thoughts were definitely troubled. I had been living in a dream—I began to speculate concerning the end of the path on which my feet were set.

I had conceived, from the first, such a horror of those old houses by the canal! They were well enough to walk past, nursing gruesome thoughts for a midnight treat. But, much as I loved all that was weird and eery about the girl I was wooing so strangely, it was a little too much for my fancy that she had come from them.

By this time, I had become decidedly unpopular in my place of business. Not that I had made enemies, but that my peculiar ways had caused too much adverse comment. It would have taken very little, I think, to have made the entire office force decide that I was mad. After the events of the next twenty-four hours, and after this letter is found and read, they will be sure that they knew it all along! At this time, however, they were punctiliously polite to me, and merely let me alone as much as possible—which suited me perfectly. I dragged wearily through day after day, exhausted from lack of sleep, conscious of their speculative glances, living only for the night to come.

But on this day, I approached the man who had invited me to the camp across the river, who had unknowingly shown me the way that led to my love.

"Have you ever noticed the row of tumble-down houses along the canal on the city side?" I asked him.

He gave me an odd look. I suppose he sensed the significance of my breaking silence after so long to speak of *them*—sensed that in some way I had a deep interest in them.

"You have odd tastes, Morton," he said after a moment. "I suppose you wander into strange places sometimes—I've heard you speak of an enthusiasm for graveyards at night. But my advice to you is to keep away from those houses. They're unsavory, and their reputation is unsavory. Positively, I think you'd be in danger of your life, if you go poking around there. They have been the scene of several murders, and a dope den or two has been cleaned out of them. Why in the world you should want to investigate them—"

"I don't expect to investigate them," I said testily. "I was merely interested in them—from the outside. To tell you the truth, I'd heard a story, a rumor— never mind where. But you say there have been murders there—I suppose this rumor I heard may have had to do with an attempted one. There was a girl who lived there with her father once, and they were set upon there, or something of the sort, and had to run away. Did you ever hear *that* story?"

Barrett gave me an odd look such as one gives in speaking of a past horror so dreadful that the mere speaking of it makes it live terribly again.

"What you say reminds me of a horrible thing that was said to have happened down there once," he said. "It was in all the papers. A little child disappeared in one of those houses, and a couple of poor lodgers who lived there, a girl and her father, were accused of having made away with it. They were accused—they were accused—oh, well, I don't like to talk about such things. It was too dreadful. The child's body was found—*part* of it was found. It was mutilated, and the people in the house seemed to believe it had been mutilated in order to conceal the manner of its death; there was an ugly wound in the throat, it finally came out, and it seemed as if the child might have been bled to death. It was found in the girl's room, hidden away. The old man and his daughter escaped, before the police were called. The countryside was scoured, but they were never found. Why, you must have read it in the papers, several years ago.''

I nodded with a heavy heart. I *had* read it in the papers, I remembered now. And again, a terrible questioning came over me. Who was this girl, *what* was this girl, who seemed to have my heart in her keeping?

Why did not a merciful God let me die then?

Befogged with exhaustion, bemused in a dire enchantment, my mind was incapable of thought. And yet, some soul process akin to that which saves the sleepwalker poised at perilous heights sounded its warning now.

My mind was filled with doleful images. There were women—I had heard and read—who slew to satisfy a blood lust. There were ghosts, specters—call them what you will, their names have been legion in the dark pages of that lore which dates back to the infancy of the races of the earth—who retained even in death this blood lust. Vampires—they had been called that. I had read of them. Corpses by day, spirits of evil by night, roaming abroad in their own forms or in the forms of bats or unclean beasts, killing body and soul of their victims—for whoever dies of the repeated ''kiss'' of the vampire, which leaves its mark on the throat and draws the blood from the body, becomes a vampire also—of such beings I had read.

And, horror of horrors! In that last cursed day at the office, I remembered reading of these vampires—these undead—that in their nocturnal flights they had one limitation—*they could not cross running water.*

That night I went my usual nightly way with tears of weakness on my face— for my weakness was supreme, and I recognized fully at last the misery of being the victim of an enchantment stronger than my feeble will. But I went.

I approached the neighborhood of the canal-boat as the distant city clock chimed the first stroke of twelve. It was the dark of the moon and the sky was overcast. Heat-lightning flickered low in the sky, seeming to come from every point of the compass and circumscribe the horizon, as if unseen fires burned behind the rim of the world. By its fitful glimmer, I saw a new thing: between the old boat and the canal bank stretched a long, slim, solid-looking shadow—a plank had been let down! In that moment, I realized that I had been playing with powers of evil which had no intent now to let me go, which were indeed about to lay hold upon me with an inexorable grasp. Why had I come tonight? Why, but that the spell of the enchantment laid upon me was a thing more potent, and far more unbreakable, than any wholesome spell of love? The creature I sought out—oh, I remembered now, with the cold perspiration beading my brow, the lore hidden away between the covers of the dark old book which I had read so many years ago and half forgotten—until dim memories of it stirred within me, this last day and night.

My lady of the night! No woman of wholesome flesh and blood and odd perverted tastes that matched my own, but one of the undead! In that moment, I knew it, and knew that the vampires of old legends polluted still, in these latter days, the fair surface of the earth.

And on the instant, behind me in the darkness there was the crackle of a twig, and something brushed against my arm.

This, then, was the fulfillment of my dream. I knew, without turning my head, that the pale, dainty face with its glowing eyes was near my own—that I had only to stretch out my arm to touch the slender grace of the girl I had so longed to draw near. I knew, and should have felt the rapture I had anticipated. Instead, the roots of my hair prickled coldly, unendurably, as they had on the night when I had first sighted the old boat. The miasmic odors of the night, heavy and oppressive with heat and unrelieved by a breath of air, all but overcame me, and I fought with myself to prevent my teeth clicking in my head. The little waves of coldness I had felt often in this spot were chasing over my body, yet they were not from any breeze; the leaves on the trees hung down motionless, as though they were actually wilting on their branches.

With an effort, I turned my head.

Two hands caught me around my neck. The pale face was so near that I felt the warm breath from its nostrils fanning my cheek.

And, suddenly, all that was wholesome in my perverted nature rose uppermost. I longed for the touch of the red mouth, like a dark flower opening before me in the night. I longed for it—and yet more I dreaded it. I shrank back, catching in a powerful grip the fragile wrists of the hands that strove to hold me. I must not—I must not yield to the faintness that I felt stealing over me.

I was facing down the path toward the city. A low rumble of thunder—the first—broke the torrid hush of the summer night. A glare of lightning seemed to tear the night asunder, to light up the universe. Overhead, the clouds were careering madly in fantastic shapes, driven by a wind that swept the upper heavens without causing even a trembling in the air lower down. And far down the canal, that baleful glare seemed to play around and hover over the little row of shanties—murder-cursed, and haunted by the ghost of a dead child.

My gaze was fixed on them, while I held away from me the pallid face and fought off the embrace that sought to overcome my resisting will. And so a long moment passed. The glare faded out of the sky, and a greater darkness took the world. But there was a near, more menacing glare fastened upon my face—the glare of two eyes that watched mine, that had watched me as I, unthinking, stared down at the dark houses.

This girl—this woman who had come to me at my own importunate requests, did not love me, since I had shrunk from her. She did not love me—but it was not only that. She had watched me as I gazed down at the houses that held her dark past, and I was sure that she divined my thoughts. She knew my horror of those houses—she knew my newborn horror of *her*. And she hated me for it, hated me more malignantly than I had believed a human being could hate.

And at that point in my thoughts, I felt my skin prickle and my scalp rise again: Could a *human being* cherish such hatred as I read, trembling more and more, in those glowing fires lit with what seemed to me more like the fires of hell than any light that ought to shine in a woman's eyes?

And through all this, not a word had passed between us!

So far I have written calmly. I wish that I could write on so, to the end. If I could do that, there might be one or two of those who will regard this as the document of a maniac, who would believe the horrors of which I am about to write.

But I am only flesh and blood. At this point in the happenings of the awful night, my calmness deserted me—at this point I felt that I had been drawn into the midst of a horrible nightmare from which there was no escape, no waking! As I write, this feeling again overwhelms me, until I can hardly write at all— until, were it not for the thing which I must do, I would rush out into the street and run, screaming, until I was caught and dragged away, to be put behind strong iron bars. Perhaps I would feel safe there—perhaps!

I know that, terrified at the hate I saw confronting me in those redly gleaming eyes, I would have slunk away. The two thin hands that caught my arm again were strong enough to prevent that, however. I had been spared her kiss, but I was not to escape from the oath I had taken to serve her.

"You promised, you swore," she hissed in my ear. "And tonight you are to keep your oath."

I felt my senses reel. My oath—yes, I had an oath to keep. I had lifted my hand toward the dark heavens, and sworn to serve her in any way she chose. Freely, and of my own volition, I had sworn.

I sought to evade her.

"Let me help you back to your boat," I begged. "You have no kindly feeling for me, and—you have seen it—I love you no longer. I will go back to the city—you can go back to your father, and forget that I broke your peace."

The laughter that greeted my speech I shall never forget—not in the depths under the scummy surface of the canal—not in the empty places between the worlds, where my tortured soul may wander.

"So you do not love me, and I hate you! Fool! Have I waited these weary months for the water to stop, only to go back now? After my father and I returned here and found the old boat rotting in the drained canal, and took refuge in it; when the water was turned into the canal while I slept, so that I could never escape until its flow should cease, *because of the thing that I am*—even then I dreamed of tonight.

"When the imprisonment we still shared ceased to matter to my father—come on board the deserted boat tomorrow, and see why, if you dare!—still I dreamed on, of tonight!

"I have been lonely, desolate, starving—now the whole world shall be mine! And by *your* help!"

I asked her, somehow, what she wanted of me, and a madness overcame me so that I hardly heard her reply. Yet somehow, I knew that there was that on the opposite shore of the great river where the pleasure camps were, that she wanted to find. In the madness of my terror, she made me understand and obey her. I must carry her in my arms across the long bridge over the river, deserted in the small hours of the night.

The way back to the city was long tonight—long. She walked behind me, and I turned my eyes neither to right nor left. Only as I passed the tumble-down houses, I saw their reflection in the canal and trembled so that I could have fallen to the ground, at the thoughts of the little child this woman had been accused of slaying there, and at the certainty I felt that she was reading my thoughts.

And now the horror that engulfed me darkened my brain.

I know that we set our feet upon the long, wide bridge that spanned the river. I know the storm broke there, so that I battled for my footing, almost for my life it seemed, against the pelting deluge. And the horror I had invoked was in my arms, clinging to me, burying its head upon my shoulder. So increasingly dreadful had my pale-faced companion become to me, that I hardly thought of her now as a woman at all—only as a demon of the night.

The tempest raged still as she leaped down out of my arms on the other shore. And again I walked with her against my will, while the trees lashed their branches around me, showing the pale under-sides of their leaves in the vivid frequent flashes that rent the heavens.

On and on we went, branches flying through the air and missing us by a miracle of ill fortune. Such as she and I are not slain by falling branches. The river was a welter of whitecaps, flattened down into strange shapes by the pounding rain. The clouds as we glimpsed them were like devils flying through the sky.

Past dark tent after dark tent we stole, and past a few where lights burned dimly behind their canvas walls. And at last we came to an old quarry. Into its artificial ravine she led me, and up to a crevice in the rock wall.

"Reach in your hand and pull out the loose stone you will feel," she whispered. "It closes an opening that leads into deep caverns. A human hand must remove that stone—your hand must move it!"

Why did I struggle so to disobey her? Why did I fail? It was as though I *knew*—but my failure was foreordained—I had taken oath!

If you who read have believed that I have set down the truth thus far, the little that is left you will call the ravings of a madman overtaken by his madness. Yet these things happened.

I stretched out my arm, driven by a compulsion I could not resist. At arm's length in the niche in the rock, I felt something move—the loose rock, a long, narrow fragment, much larger than I had expected. Yet it moved easily, seeming to swing on a natural pivot. Outward it swung, toppling toward me—a moment more and there was a swift rush of the ponderous weight I had loosened. I leaped aside and went down, my forehead grazed by the rock.

For a brief moment I must have been unconscious, but only for a moment. My

head a stabbing agony of pain, unreal lights flashing before my eyes, I yet knew
the reality of the storm that beat me down as I struggled to my feet. I knew the
reality of the dark, loathsome shapes that passed me in the dark, crawling out of
the orifice in the rock and flapping through the wild night, along the way that led
to the pleasure camps.

So the caverns I had laid open to the outer world were infested with bats. I had
been inside unlit caverns, and had heard there the squeaking of the things, felt
and heard the flapping of their wings—*but never in all my life before had I seen
bats as large as men and women!*

Sick and dizzy from the blow on my head, and from disgust, I crept along the
way they were going. If I touched one of them, I felt that I should die of horror.

Now, at last, the storm abated, and a heavy darkness made the whole world
seem like the inside of a tomb.

Where the tents stood in a long row, the number of the monster bats seemed
to diminish. It was as though—horrible thought!—they were creeping into the
tents, with their slumbering occupants.

At last I came to a lighted tent, and paused, crouching so that the dim radiance
which shone through the canvas did not touch me in the shadows. And there I
waited, but not for long. There was a dark form silhouetted against the tent; a
rustle and confusion, and the dark thing was again in silhouette—but with a
difference in the quality of the shadow. The dark thing was *inside* the tent now,
its bat wings extending across the entrance through which it had crept.

Fear held me spellbound. And as I looked, the shadow changed again, imperceptibly, so that I could not have told *how* it changed. But now it was not the
shadow of a bat, but of a woman.

"The storm, the storm! I am lost, exhausted! I crept in here, to beg for refuge
until the dawn!"

That low, thrilling, sibilant voice—too well I knew it!

Within the tent I heard a murmur of acquiescent voices. At last I began to
understand.

I knew the nature of the woman I had carried over the river in my arms, the
woman who would not even cross the canal until the water should have ceased
utterly to flow. I remembered books I had read—*Dracula*—other books and
stories. I knew they were true books and stories, now—I knew those horrors
existed for me.

I had indeed kept my oath to the creature of darkness—I had brought her to
her kind, under her guidance. I had let them loose in hordes upon the pleasure
camps. The campers were doomed—and through them, others. . . .

I forgot my fear. I rushed from my hiding place up to the tent door, and there
I screamed and called aloud.

"Don't take her in—don't let her stay—nor the others, that have crept into the
other tents! Wake all the campers—they will sleep on to their destruction! Drive
out the interlopers—drive them out quickly! *They are not human—no, and they
are not bats!* Do you hear me?—Do you understand?"

I was fairly howling, in a voice that was strange to me.

"She is a vampire. They are all vampires. *Vampires!*"

Inside the tent I heard a new voice.

"What can be the matter with that poor man?" the voice said. It was a woman's, and gentle.

"Crazy—somebody out of his senses, dear," a man's voice answered. "Don't be frightened."

And then the voice I knew so well—so well: "I saw a falling rock strike a man on the head in the storm. He staggered away, but I suppose it crazed him."

I waited for no more. I ran away madly through the night and back across the bridge to the city.

Next day—today—I boarded the sunken canal-boat. It is the abode of death—no woman could have lived there—only such a one as *she*. The old man's corpse was there—he must have died long, long ago. The smell of death and decay on the boat was dreadful.

Again, I felt that I understood. Back in those awful houses, she had committed the crime when first she became the thing she is. And he—her father—less sin-steeped, and less accursed, attempted to destroy the evidence of her crime, and fled with her, but died without becoming like her. She had said that one of those two was always on watch—did he indeed divide her vigil on the boat? What more fitting—the dead standing watch with the undead! And no wonder that she would not let me board the craft of death, even to carry her away.

And still I feel the old compulsion. I have been spared her kiss—but for a little while. Yet I will not let the power of my oath draw me back, till I enter the caverns with her and creep forth in the form of a bat to prey upon mankind. Before that can happen, I too will die.

Today in the city I heard that a horde of strange insects or small animals infested the pleasure camps last night. Some said, with horror-bated breath, that they perhaps were rats. None of them was seen; but in the morning nearly every camper had a strange, deep wound in his throat. I almost laughed aloud. They were so horrified at the idea of an army of rats, creeping into the tents and biting the sleeping occupants on their throats! If they had seen what I saw—if they knew that they are doomed to spread corruption. . . .

So my own death will not be enough. Today I bought supplies for blasting. Tonight I will set my train of dynamite, from the hole I made in the cliff where the vampires creep in and out, along the row of tents, as far as the last one—then I shall light my fuse. It will be done before the dawn. Tomorrow, the city will mourn its dead and execrate my name.

And then, at last, in the slime beneath the unmoving waters of the canal, I shall find peace! But perhaps it will not be peace—for I shall seek it midway between the old boat with its cargo of death and the row of dismal houses where a little child was done to death when first *she* became the thing she is. This is my expiation.

A RENDEZVOUS IN AVEROIGNE

CLARK ASHTON SMITH

One of Weird Tales'*s most inventive writers, Clark Ashton Smith was usually at his best when conjuring monstrosities uniquely suited to life in his imaginary lands Zothique, Hyperborea, and Xiccarph. Exceptions were his tales of the medieval French province of Averoigne, where unenlightened citizens feared most the monsters of traditional myth and legend. Vampires appeared in two of these tales, "The End of the Story" and "A Rendezvous in Averoigne."*

GERARD DE L'AUTOMNE was meditating the rimes of a new ballade in honor of Fleurette as he followed the leaf-arrassed pathway toward Vyones through the woodland of Averoigne. Since he was on his way to meet Fleurette, who had promised to keep a rendezvous among the oaks and beeches like any peasant girl, Gerard himself made better progress than the ballade. His love was at that stage which, even for a professional troubadour, is more productive of distraction than inspiration; and he was recurrently absorbed in a meditation upon other than merely verbal felicities.

The grass and trees had assumed the fresh enamel of a medieval May. The turf was figured with little blossoms of azure and white and yellow like an ornate broidery, and there was a pebbly stream that murmured beside the way, as if the voices of undines were parleying deliciously beneath its waters. The sun-lulled air was laden with a wafture of youth and romance, and the longing that welled from the heart of Gerard seemed to mingle mystically with the balsams of the wood.

Gerard was a *trouvère* whose scant years and many wanderings had brought him a certain renown. After the fashion of his kind he had roamed from court to court, from chateau to chateau; and he was now the guest of the Comte de la Frênaie, whose high castle held dominion over half the surrounding forest. Visiting one day that quaint cathedral town, Vyones, which lies so near to the ancient wood of Averoigne, Gerard had seen Fleurette, the daughter of a well-to-do mercer named Guillaume Cochin, and had become more sincerely enamored of her blond piquancy than was to be expected from one who had been so frequently susceptible in such matters. He had managed to make his feelings known to her. And, after a month of billets-doux, ballads and stolen interviews contrived by the help of a complaisant waiting woman, she had made his woodland tryst with him in the absence of her father from Vyones. Accompanied by her maid and a manservant, she was to leave the town early that afternoon and meet Gerard under a certain beech tree of enormous age and size. The servants would then withdraw discreetly, and the lovers, to all intents and purposes, would be alone. It was not likely that they would be seen or interrupted, for the gnarled and immemorial wood possessed an ill-repute among the peasantry. Somewhere in this wood there was the ruinous and haunted Chateau des Fausses-flammes, and, also, there was a double tomb, within which the Sieur Hugh du Malinbois and his chatelaine, who were notorious for sorcery in their time, had lain unconsecrated for more than two hundred years. Of these, and their phantoms, there were grisly tales. There were stories of loup-garous and goblins, of fays and devils and vampires that infested Averoigne. But to these tales Gerard had given little heed, considering it improbable that such creatures would fare abroad in open daylight. The madcap Fleurette had professed herself unafraid also, but it had been necessary to promise the servants a substantial *pourboire*, since they shared fully the local superstitions.

Gerard had wholly forgotten the legendry of Averoigne, as he hastened along the sun-flecked path. He was nearing the appointed beech tree, which a turn of the path would soon reveal, and his pulses quickened and became tremulous as he wondered if Fleurette had already reached the trysting place. He abandoned all effort to continue his ballade, which, in the three miles he had walked from La Frênaie, had not progressed beyond the middle of a tentative first stanza.

His thoughts were such as would befit an ardent and impatient lover. They were now interrupted by a shrill scream that rose to an unendurable pitch of fear and horror issuing from the green stillness of the pines beside the way. Startled, he peered at the thick branches, and as the scream fell back to silence, he heard the sound of dull and hurrying footfalls, and a scuffling as of several bodies. Again the scream arose. It was plainly the voice of a woman in some distressful peril. Loosening his dagger in its sheath and clutching more firmly a long hornbeam staff which he had brought with him as a protection against the vipers which were said to lurk in Averoigne, he plunged without hesitation or premeditation among the low-hanging boughs from which the voice had seemed to emerge.

In a small open space beyond the trees, he saw a woman who was struggling with three ruffians of exceptionally brutal and evil aspect. Even in the haste and vehemence of the moment, Gerard realized that he had never before seen such men or such a woman. The woman was clad in a gown of emerald green that matched her eyes. In her face was the pallor of dead things, together with a faery beauty, and her lips were dyed as with the scarlet of newly flowing blood. The men were dark as Moors, and their eyes were red slits of flame beneath oblique brows with animal-like bristles. There was something very peculiar in the shape of their feet, but Gerard did not realize the exact nature of the peculiarity till long afterward. Then he remembered that all of them were seemingly club-footed, though they were able to move with surpassing agility. Somehow, he could never recall what sort of clothing they had worn.

The woman turned a beseeching gaze upon Gerard as he sprang forth from amid the boughs. The men, however, did not seem to heed his coming; though one of them caught in a hairy clutch the hands which the woman sought to reach toward her rescuer.

Lifting his staff, Gerard rushed upon the ruffians. He struck a tremendous blow at the head of the nearest one—a blow that should have leveled the fellow to earth. But the staff came down on unresisting air, and Gerard staggered and almost fell headlong in trying to recover his equilibrium. Dazed and uncomprehending, he saw that the knot of struggling figures had vanished utterly. At least, the three men had vanished; but from the middle branches of a tall pine beyond the open space, the death-white features of the woman smiled upon him for a moment with faint, inscrutable guile ere they melted among the needles.

Gerard understood now, and he shivered as he crossed himself. He had been deluded by phantoms or demons, doubtless for no good purpose. He had been the gull of a questionable enchantment. Plainly there was something after all in the legends he had heard, in the ill-renown of the forest of Averoigne.

He retraced his way toward the path he had been following. But when he thought to reach again the spot from which he had heard that shrill unearthly scream, he saw that there was no longer a path, nor, indeed, any feature of the forest which he could remember or recognize. The foliage about him no longer displayed a brilliant verdure; it was sad and funereal, and the trees themselves were either cypresslike or were already sere with autumn or decay. In lieu of the purling brook there lay before him a tarn of waters that were dark and dull as clotting blood, and which gave back no reflection of the brown autumnal sedges that trailed therein like the hair of suicides, and the skeletons of rotting osiers that writhed above them.

Now, beyond all question, Gerard knew that he was the victim of an evil enchantment. In answering that beguileful cry for succor, he had exposed himself to the spell, had been lured within the circle of its power. He could not know what forces of wizardry or demonry had willed to draw him thus, but he knew that his situation was fraught with supernatural menace. He gripped the horn-beam staff more tightly in his hand, and prayed to all the saints he could remember as he peered about for some tangible bodily presence of ill.

The scene was utterly desolate and lifeless, like a place where cadavers might keep their tryst with demons. Nothing stirred, not even a dead leaf, and there was no whisper of dry grass or foliage, no song of birds nor murmuring of bees, no sigh nor chuckle of water. The corpse-gray heavens above seemed never to have held a sun, and the chill, unchanging light was without source or destination, without beams or shadows.

Gerard surveyed his environment with a cautious eye, and the more he looked the less he liked it for some new and disagreeable detail was manifest at every glance. There were moving lights in the wood that vanished if he eyed them intently; there were drowned faces in the tarn that came and went like livid bubbles before he could discern their features. And, peering across the lake, he wondered why he had not seen the many-turreted castle of hoary stone whose nearer walls were based in the dead waters. It was so gray and still and vasty, that it seemed to have stood for incomputable ages between the stagnant tarn and the equally stagnant heavens. It was ancienter than the world, it was older than the light: It was coeval with fear and darkness; and a horror dwelt upon it and crept unseen but palpable along its bastions.

There was no sign of life about the castle, and no banners flew above its turrets or its donjon. But Gerard knew, as surely as if a voice had spoken aloud to warn him, that here was the fountainhead of the sorcery by which he had been beguiled. A growing panic whispered in his brain, he seemed to hear the rustle of malignant plumes, the mutter of demoniac threats and plottings. He turned and fled among the funereal trees.

Amid his dismay and wilderment, even as he fled, he thought of Fleurette and wondered if she were awaiting him at their place of rendezvous, or if she and her companions had also been enticed and led astray in a realm of damnable unrealities. He renewed his prayers, and implored the saints for her safety as well as his own.

The forest through which he ran was a maze of bafflement and eeriness. There were no landmarks, there were no tracks of animals or men; and the swart cypresses and sere autumnal trees grew thicker and thicker as if some malevolent will were marshaling them against his progress. The boughs were like implacable arms that strove to retard him. He could have sworn that he felt them twine about him with the strength and suppleness of living things. He fought them, insanely, desperately, and seemed to hear a crackling of infernal laughter in their twigs as he fought. At last, with a sob of relief, he broke through into a sort of trail. Along this trail, in the mad hope of eventual escape, he ran like one whom a fiend pursues. After a short interval he came again to the shores of the tarn above whose motionless waters the high and hoary turrets of that time-forgotten castle were still dominant. Again he turned and fled, and once more, after similar wanderings and like struggles, he came back to the inevitable tarn.

With a leaden sinking of his heart, as into some ultimate slough of despair and terror, he resigned himself and made no further effort to escape. His very will was benumbed, was crushed down as by the incumbence of a superior volition that would no longer permit his puny recalcitrance. He was unable to resist when a strong and hateful compulsion drew his footsteps along the margent of the tarn toward the looming castle.

When he came nearer, he saw that the edifice was surrounded by a moat whose waters were stagnant as those of the lake, and were mantled with the iridescent scum of corruption. The drawbridge was down and the gates were open, as if to receive an expected guest. But still there was no sign of human occupancy, and the walls of the great gray building were silent as those of a sepulcher. And more tomblike even than the rest was the square and overtowering bulk of the mighty donjon.

Impelled by the same power that had drawn him along the lakeshore, Gerard crossed the drawbridge and passed beneath the frowning barbican into a vacant courtyard. Barred windows looked blankly down, and at the opposite end of the court a door stood mysteriously open, revealing a dark hall. As he approached the doorway, he saw that a man was standing on the threshold, though a moment previous he could have sworn that it was untenanted by any visible form.

Gerard had retained his hornbeam staff, and though his reason told him that such a weapon was futile against any supernatural foe, some obscure instinct prompted him to clasp it valiantly as he neared the waiting figure on the sill.

The man was inordinately tall and cadaverous, and was dressed in black garments of a superannuate mode. His lips were strangely red, amid his bluish beard and the mortuary whiteness of his face. They were like the lips of the woman who, with her assailants, had disappeard in a manner so dubious when Gerard had approached them. His eyes were pale and luminous as marsh lights, and Gerard shuddered at his gaze and at the cold, ironic smile of his scarlet lips that seemed to reserve a world of secrets all too dreadful and hideous to be disclosed.

"I am the Sieur du Malinbois," the man announced. His tones were both unctuous and hollow, and served to increase the repugnance felt by the young troubadour. And when his lips parted, Gerard had a glimpse of teeth that were unnaturally small and were pointed like the fangs of some fierce animal.

"Fortune has willed that you should become my guest," the man went on. "The hospitality which I can proffer you is rough and inadequate, and it may be that you will find my abode a trifle dismal. But at least I can assure you of a welcome no less ready than sincere."

"I thank you for your kind offer," said Gerard. "But I have an appointment with a friend, and I seem in some unaccountable manner to have lost my way. I should be profoundly grateful if you would direct me toward Vyones. There should be a path not far from here, and I have been so stupid as to stray from it."

The words rang empty and hopeless in his own ears even as he uttered them, and the name that his strange host had given—the Sieur du Malinbois—was haunting his mind like the funereal accents of a knell, though he could not recall at that moment the macabre and spectral ideas which the name tended to evoke.

"Unfortunately, there are no paths from my chateau to Vyones," the stranger replied. "As for your rendezvous, it will be kept in another manner, at another place than the one appointed. I must therefore insist that you accept my hospitality. Enter, I pray, but leave your hornbeam staff at the door. You will have no need of it any longer.''

Gerard thought that he made a move of distaste and aversion with his over-red lips as he spoke the last sentences, and that his eyes lingered on the staff with an obscure apprehensiveness. And the strange emphasis of his words and demeanor served to awaken other fantasmal and macabre thoughts in Gerard's brain, though he could not formulate them fully till afterward.

Somehow he was prompted to retain the weapon, no matter how useless it might be against an enemy of spectral or diabolic nature. So he said, ''I must crave your indulgence if I retain the staff. I have made a vow to carry it with me, in my right hand or never beyond arm's reach, till I have slain two vipers.''

''That is a queer vow,'' rejoined his host. ''However, bring it with you if you like. It is of no matter to me if you choose to encumber yourself with a wooden stick.''

He turned abruptly, motioning Gerard to follow him. The troubadour obeyed unwillingly, with one reward glance at the vacant heavens and the empty courtyard. He saw with no great surprise that a sudden and furtive darkness had closed in upon the chateau without moon or star, as if it had been merely waiting for him to enter before it descended. It was thick as the folds of a cerecloth; it was airless and stifling like the gloom of a sepulcher that has been sealed for ages. Gerard was aware of a veritable oppression, a corporeal and psychic difficulty in breathing, as he crossed the threshold.

He saw that cressets were now burning in the dim hall to which his host had admitted him, though he had not perceived the time and agency of their lighting. The illumination they afforded was singularly vague and indistinct, and the thronging shadows of the hall were unexplainably numerous and moved with a mysterious disquiet, though the flames themselves were still as tapers that burn for the dead in a windless vault.

At the end of the passage, the Sieur du Malinbois flung open a heavy door of dark and somber wood. Beyond, in what was plainly the eating room of the chateau, several people were seated about a long table by the light of cressets no less dreary and dismal than those in the hall. In the strange, uncertain glow, their faces were touched with a gloomy dubiety, with a lurid distortion; it seemed to Gerard that shadows hardly distinguishable from the figures were gathered around the board. But nevertheless he recognized the assembled company at a glance, with an overpowering shock of astonishment.

At one end of the board, there sat the woman in emerald green who had vanished in so doubtful a fashion amid the pines when Gerard answered her call for succor. At one side, looking very pale and forlorn and frightened, was Fleurette Cochin. At the lower end reserved for retainers and inferiors, there sat the maid and the manservant who had accompanied Fleurette to her rendezvous with Gerard.

The Sieur du Malinbois turned to the troubadour with a smile of sardonic amusement.

"I believe you have already met every one assembled," he observed. "But you have not yet been formally presented to my wife, Agathe, who is presiding over the board. Agathe, I bring to you Gerard de l'Automne, a young troubadour of much note and merit."

The woman nodded slightly, without speaking, and pointed to a chair opposite Fleurette. Gerard seated himself, and the Sieur du Malinbois assumed according to feudal custom a place at the head of the table beside his wife.

Now, for the first time, Gerard noticed that there were servitors who came and went in the room, setting upon the table various wines and viands. The servitors were preternaturally swift and noiseless, and somehow it was very difficult to be sure of their precise features or their costumes. They seemed to walk in an adumbration of sinister insoluble twilight. But the troubadour was disturbed by a feeling that they resembled the swart demoniac ruffians who had disappeared together with the woman in green when he approached them.

The meal that ensued was a weird and funereal affair. A sense of insuperable constraint, of smothering horror and hideous oppression, was upon Gerard, and though he wanted to ask Fleurette a hundred questions and also to demand an explanation of sundry matters from his host and hostess, he was totally unable to frame the words or to utter them. He could only look at Fleurette and read in her eyes a duplication of his own helpless bewilderment and nightmare thralldom. Nothing was said by the Sieur du Malinbois and his lady, who were exchanging glances of a secret and baleful intelligence all through the meal. Fleurette's maid and manservant were obviously paralyzed by terror, like birds beneath the hypnotic gaze of deadly serpents.

The foods were rich and of strange savor; the wines were fabulously old, and seemed to retain in their topaz or violet depths the unextinguished fire of buried centuries. But Gerard and Fleurette could barely touch them. They saw that the Sieur du Malinbois and his lady did not eat or drink at all. The gloom of the chamber deepened; the servitors became more furtive and spectral in their movements. The stifling air was laden with unformulable menace, was constrained by the spell of a black and lethal necromancy. Above the aromas of the rare foods, the bouquets of the antique wines, there crept forth the choking mustiness of hidden vaults and embalmed centurial corruption, together with the ghostly spice of a strange perfume that seemed to emanate from the person of the chatelaine. And now Gerard was remembering many tales from the legendry of Averoigne, which he had heard and disregarded, was recalling the story of a Sieur du Malinbois and his lady, the last of the name and the most evil, who had been buried somewhere in this forest hundreds of years ago, and whose tomb was shunned by the peasantry since they were said to continue their sorceries even in death. He wondered what influence had bedrugged his memory that he had not recalled it wholly when he had first heard the name. And he was remembering other things and other stories, all of which confirmed his instinctive belief regarding the nature of the people into whose hands he had fallen. Also, he recalled a folklore superstition concerning the use to which a wooden stake can be put, and realized why the Sieur du Malinbois had shown a peculiar interest in the hornbeam staff. Gerard had laid the staff beside his chair when he sat down, and he was reassured to find that it had not vanished. Very quietly and unobtrusively, he placed his foot upon it.

The uncanny meal came to an end, and the host and his chatelaine arose. "I shall now conduct you to your rooms," said the Sieur du Malinbois, including all of his guests in a dark, inscrutable glance. "Each of you can have a separate chamber, if you so desire or Fleurette Cochin and her maid Angelique can remain together and the manservant Raoul can sleep in the same room with Messire Gerard."

A preference for the latter procedure was voiced by Fleurette and the troubadour. The thoughts of uncompanioned solitude in the castle of timeless midnight and nameless mystery was abhorrent to an insupportable degree.

The four were now led to their respective chambers, on opposite sides of a hall whose length was but indeterminately revealed by the dismal lights. Fleurette and Gerard bade each other a dismayed and reluctant good-night beneath the constraining eye of their host. Their rendezvous was hardly the one which they had thought to keep, and both were overwhelmed by the supernatural situation amid whose dubious horrors and ineluctable sorceries they had somehow become involved. And no sooner had Gerard left Fleurette than he began to curse himself for a poltroon because he had not refused to part from her side. He marveled at the spell of druglike involition that had bedrowsed all his faculties. It seemed that his will was not for his own but had been thrust down and throttled by an alien power.

The room assigned to Gerard and Raoul was furnished with a couch and a great bed whose curtains were of antique fashion and fabric. It was lighted with tapers that had a funereal suggestion in their form and which burned dully in an air that was stagnant with the mustiness of dead years.

"May you sleep soundly," said the Sieur du Malinbois. The smile that accompanied and followed the words was no less unpleasant than the oily and sepulchral tone in which they were uttered.

The troubadour and the servant were conscious of profound relief when he went out and closed the leaden clanging door. And their relief was hardly diminished even when they heard the click of a key in the lock.

Gerard was now inspecting the room, and he went to the one window, through whose small and deep-set panes he could see only the pressing darkness of a night that was veritably solid, as if the whole place were buried beneath the earth and were closed in by clinging mold. Then, with an access of unsmothered rage at his separation from Fleurette, he ran to the door and hurled himself against it, he beat upon it with his clenched fists but in vain. Realizing his folly, and desisting at last, he turned to Raoul.

"Well, Raoul," he said, "what do you think of all this?"

Raoul crossed himself before he answered; and his face had assumed the vizard of a mortal fear.

"I think, Messire," he finally replied, "that we have all been decoyed by a malefic sorcery, and that you, myself, the demoiselle Fleurette, and the maid Angelique are all in deadly peril of both soul and body."

"That also is my thought," said Gerard. "And I believe it would be well that you and I should sleep only by turns, and that he who keeps vigil should retain in his hands my hornbeam staff, whose end I shall now sharpen with my dagger. I am sure that you know the manner in which it should be employed if there are any intruders, for if such should come, there would be no doubt as to their character and their intentions. We are in a castle which has no legitimate exist- ence, as the guests of people who have been dead, or supposedly dead, for more than two hundred years. And such people, when they stir abroad, are prone to habits which I need not specify."

"Yes, Messire." Raoul shuddered, but he watched the sharpening of the staff with considerable interest. Gerard whittled the hard wood to a lancelike point, and hid the shavings carefully. He even carved the outline of a little cross near the middle of the staff, thinking that this might increase its efficacy or save it from molestation. Then, with the staff in his hand, he sat down upon the bed, where he could survey the litten room from between the curtains.

"You can sleep first, Raoul." He indicated the couch, which was near the door.

The two conversed in a fitful manner for some minutes. After hearing Raoul's tale of how Fleurette, Angelique, and he had been led astray by the sobbing of a woman amid the pines and had been unable to retrace their way, the troubadour changed the theme. Henceforth he spoke idly and of matters remote from his real preoccupations to fight down his torturing concern for the safety of Fleurette. Suddenly he became aware that Raoul had ceased to reply, and saw that the servant had fallen asleep on the couch. At the same time an irresistible drowsi- ness surged upon Gerard himself in spite of all his volition, in spite of the eldritch terrors and forebodings that still murmured in his brain. He heard through his growing hebetude a whisper as of shadowy wings in the castle halls; he caught the sibilation of ominous voices, like those of familiars that respond to the summoning of wizards; and he seemed to hear, even in the vaults and towers and remote chambers, the tread of feet that were hurrying on malign and secret errands. But oblivion was around him like the meshes of a sable net, and it closed in relentlessly upon his troubled mind and drowned the alarms of his agitated senses.

When Gerard awoke at length, the tapers had burned to their sockets, and a sad and sunless daylight was filtering through the window. The staff was still in his hand, and though his senses were still dull with the strange slumber that had drugged them, he felt that he was unharmed. But peering between the curtains, he saw that Raoul was lying mortally pale and lifeless on the couch, with the air and look of an exhausted moribund.

He crossed the room and stooped above the servant. There was a small red wound on Raoul's neck and his pulses were slow and feeble, like those of one who has lost a great amount of blood. His very appearance was withered and vein-drawn. And a phantom spice arose from the couch—a lingering wraith of the perfume worn by the chatelaine Agathe.

Gerard succeeded at last in arousing the man, but Raoul was very weak and drowsy. He could remember nothing of what had happened during the night, and his horror was pitiful to behold when he realized the truth.

"It will be your turn next, Messire," he cried. "These vampires mean to hold us here amid their unhallowed necromancies till they have drained us of our last drop of blood. Their spells are like mandragora or the sleepy sirups of Cathay, and no man can keep awake in their despite."

Gerard was trying the door, and somewhat to his surprise he found it unlocked. The departing vampire had been careless in the lethargy of her repletion. The castle was very still, and it seemed to Gerard that the animating spirit of evil was now quiescent, that the shadowy wings of horror and malignity, the feet that had sped on baleful errands, the summoning sorcerers, the responding familiars, were all lulled in a temporary slumber.

He opened the door, he tiptoed along the deserted hall and knocked at the portal of the chamber allotted to Fleurette and her maid. Fleurette, fully dressed, answered his knock immediately, and he caught her in his arms without a word, searching her wan face with a tender anxiety. Over her shoulder he could see the maid Angelique, who was sitting listlessly on the bed with a mark on her white neck similar to the wound that had been suffered by Raoul. He knew, even before Fleurette began to speak, that the nocturnal experiences of the demoiselle and her maid had been identical with those of himself and the manservant.

While he tried to comfort Fleurette and reassure her, his thoughts were now busy with a rather curious problem. No one was abroad in the castle, and it was more than probable that the Sieur du Malinbois and his lady were both asleep after the nocturnal feats which they had undoubtedly enjoyed. Gerard pictured to himself the place and the fashion of their slumber, and he grew even more reflective as certain possibilities occurred to him.

"Be of good cheer, sweetheart," he said to Fleurette. "It is in my mind that we may soon escape from this abominable mesh of enchantments. But I must leave you for a little and speak again with Raoul, whose help I shall require in a certain matter."

He went back to his own chamber. The manservant was sitting on the couch and was crossing himself feebly and muttering prayers with a faint, hollow voice.

"Raoul," said the troubadour a little sternly, "you must gather all your strength and come with me. Amid the gloomy walls that surround us, the somber ancient halls, the high towers and the heavy bastions, there is but one thing that veritably exists, and all the rest is a fabric of illusion. We must find the reality whereof I speak, and deal with it like true and valiant Christians. Come, we will now search the castle ere the lord and chatelaine shall awaken from their vampire lethargy."

He led the way along the devious corridors with a swiftness that betokened much forethought. He had reconstructed in his mind the hoary pile of battlements and turrets as he had seen them on the previous day, and he felt that the great donjon, being the center and stronghold of the edifice, might well be the place which he sought. With the sharpened staff in his hand, with Raoul lagging bloodlessly at his heels, he passed the doors of many secret rooms, the many windows that gave on the blindness of an inner court, and came at last to the lower story of the donjon-keep.

It was a large, bare room, entirely built of stone and illumined only by narrow slits high up in the wall that had been designed for the use of archers. The place was very dim, but Gerard could see the glimmering outlines of an object not ordinarily to be looked for in such a situation, that arose from the middle of the floor. It was a tomb of marble, and stepping nearer, he saw that it was strangely weather-worn and was blotched by lichens of gray and yellow, such as flourish only within access of the sun. The slab that covered it was doubly broad and massive, and would require the full strength of two men to lift.

Raoul was staring stupidly at the tomb. "What now, Messire?" he queried.

"You and I, Raoul, are about to intrude upon the bedchamber of our host and hostess."

At his direction, Raoul seized one end of the slab, and he himself took the other. With a mighty effort that strained their bones and sinews to the cracking point, they sought to remove it, but the slab hardly stirred. At length, by grasping the same end in unison, they were able to tilt the slab, and it slid away and dropped to the floor with a thunderous crash. Within, there were two open coffins, one of which contained the Sieur Hugh du Malinbois and the other his lady Agathe. Both of them appeared to be slumbering peacefully as infants. A look of tranquil evil, of pacified malignity, was imprinted upon their features, and their lips were dyed with a fresher scarlet than before.

Without hesitation or delay, Gerard plunged the lancelike end of his staff into the bosom of the Sieur du Malinbois. The body crumbled as if it were wrought of ashes kneaded and painted to a human semblance. A slight odor as of age-old corruption arose to the nostrils of Gerard. Then the troubadour pierced in like manner the bosom of the chatelaine. And simultaneously with her dissolution, the walls and floor of the donjon seemed to dissolve like a sullen vapor, they rolled away on every side with a shock as of unheard thunder. With a sense of indescribable vertigo and confusion Gerard and Raoul saw that the whole chateau had vanished like the towers and battlements of a bygone storm, that the dead lake and its rotting shores no longer offered their malefical illusions to the eye. They were standing in a forest glade, in the full unshadowed light of the afternoon sun, and all that remained of the dismal castle was the lichen-mantled tomb that stood open beside them. Fleurette and her maid were a little distance away, and Gerard ran to the mercer's daughter and took her in his arms. She was dazed with wonderment, like one who emerges from the night-long labyrinth of an evil dream and finds that all is well.

"I think, sweetheart," said Gerard, "that our next rendezvous will not be interrupted by the Sieur du Malinbois and his chatelaine."

But Fleurette was still bemused with wonder and could only answer him with a kiss.

PLACIDE'S WIFE

KIRK MASHBURN

Long before movie studios struck box-office gold by combining the audience-drawing power of more than one monster in films like "Dracula Meets Franken-stein" and "Frankenstein Meets the Wolfman," weird-fiction writers thrilled readers with stories that supported the existence of an abundance of supernatural creatures. In his 1931 story "Placide's Wife," Kirk Mashburn pitted men in the Louisiana bayous against both werewolves and vampires. The tale proved popular enough with Weird Tales *readers to generate a self-explanatory sequel "The Last of Placide's Wife."*

FROM THE depths of the dank, moss-festooned woods, a long-drawn howl quavered upward to a cloaked and sullen moon. There was a sinister, unearthly quality about the ululation that set it apart from the orthodox lament of any random, mournful hound.

It startled us, gathered there in the temporary shack that served the road-building crew for office and commissary combined. The dull buzz of conversation stilled for a long minute. I saw more than one stolid Cajun farmer—road builder, *pro tem*—furtively sign the cross; chairs and packing boxes croaked under the sudden uneasy shifting of their burdens.

"Placide's wife . . ." I heard someone's perturbed mutter.

It was old Landry, gnarled and seamed and squat of body, ordinarily taciturn to the point of sourness. A half-dozen pairs of eyes flashed distrustfully in my direction, then settled in common focus upon the speaker. The rebuke and its intimation were plain: I was a State Highway Department engineer in 1931, an alien in their midst, and whatever old Landry had meant, it was one of those many things, ranging from the utterly trivial to the supremely tragic, of which no discussion is had with strangers. If one be a French-descended Cajun of the southwestern Louisiana parishes, suspicious of all unproved folk, one does not speak haphazardly concerning obscure local matters.

Landry withdrew even more deeply into his shell of taciturnity; there was an ineffectual attempt or two to resume talk, but a damper seemed to have been put upon any further desire for conversation. In twos and threes, but never singly, the members of the group drifted away to their bunks in close succession. I was left alone with Delacroix, the young commissary clerk and timekeeper for the road gang.

"What was there about what the old man said, to sour the balance of them so thoroughly?"

My companion hesitated about replying. He was of the locality, and even though of a finer breed than the teamsters and laborers of the crew, he possessed, in less degree, some of their instinctive clannishness. Still, when one is working one's way through engineering school of the state university, there is evidence therein of qualities superior to the inhibitions of simplicity. Delacroix shrugged. "There is a story behind it," he admitted.

"Tell it," I urged. It was still too early for bed.

Once more, before he could comply, that weird latration from the forest set the night a-quiver. We listened in silence until it ended.

"So!" observed Delacroix.

Then he told me of one, Placide, and of Placide's wife; and this is the substance of his story.

Placide Duboin [said Delacroix] spent thirty of his nearly fifty years of life peacefully upon one patch of bayou land. His paunch was kept satisfactorily heavy with beans and with rice which he grew more by the kindness of heaven than any great exertion of his own. Sometimes he wheezed down the bayou in an ancient oyster boat, with the running of which the indulgence of Providence may also have had a hand, judging by the neglected condition of its decrepit engine.

In the bay, Placide caught shrimps; in the winter, he sporadically trapped muskrats and shot ducks. Always, he had enough black perique for his pipe and a little wine to wash down his food. Rarely, he would go to town and get very drunk. For a man with no wants beyond his creature comforts, and a masterless, indolent existence, it was a good life.

Then the time came when oil was found in the neighborhood of Placide's quarter-section, and he sold the ground that he had homesteaded thirty years before, for more money than Placide had any business with. Some people said he got ten thousand dollars. The highest estimate placed the amount at five times as much. At any rate, it was enough to be Placide's undoing.

He moved to town. Now, Labranch is a village to you or even to me, a sleepy little town of some three thousand souls; but to this old one, it was a veritable city. Not that it made any difference: Placide could loaf as well as, or even better, in the town than on the bayou, and he held on to his money with tight fingers.

Placide loafed too well! Not content with a full belly and freedom, with no more burden upon his shoulders than holding fast to the wealth with which accident had endowed him, he had so much time on his hands that he filled it in by marrying a woman out of a visiting carnival troupe. Having lived womanless for nearly fifty years, this stupid one, this great clod, must marry a gypsy-looking wench from a street fair. A snake charmer! Eh!

True, she was young, and more than good to look at (so they say), with her olive skin and black hair, and dark, inviting eyes that turned upward a little at the corners. Nita, her name was; and though the women of Labranch snubbed her for the memory of her snakes, and for marrying old lazy Placide for his money—it *had* to be his money!—the men were friendly enough, behind their women's backs. Too friendly!

Placide, seeing his wife's flirtations, stolidly packed her off to another shack on another bayou where oil had not as yet been found, and where there were fewer men for her to dally with, beating her methodically when she rebelled. He had a certain respect for his own rights, Placide.

So Nita ate red beans and rice and was lucky to have a pair of shoes. . . . You have heard it said, that the way to keep a woman virtuous is to keep her barefooted? Well! And all the time, Placide's money rotted wherever it was buried in the ground. No banks for that one!

And Nita, having sold herself to Placide and been cheated of her purchase price, soured inside herself, hating Placide more with each dull day. Her only companion was a great black cat that had come with her to Labranch, along with the snakes, only, one supposes, Placide had objected to the snakes, if they did not belong to the carnival, anyway.

This cat of Nita's had yellow eyes, out of which it glared hate at all the world except its mistress. The cat hated Placide more even than Nita did: It would stare at him for minutes on end, its eyes smoldering. Or, sometimes, it would arch its back and yowl at him like a fiend.

The cat would spit, also, at Henry Lebaudy and the few others who sometimes hunted or fished with Placide. It scratched Lebaudy, for no reason whatever, so Lebaudy, not liking this—and not liking cats at all, and this one even less—gabbled at Placide to kill the *sale bete noir*.

Placide—he liked the idea, him! So he shoots the cat. That is, Lebaudy swears to this day that he did—shot it at least a dozen times, loading and reloading his shotgun. Placide was a crack shot, you comprehend, and grew angrier and more determined with each belch of his gun. He did not like to miss, especially this cat.

Finally, Placide begins to be afraid he is *not missing*—although the buckshot does not kill the beast, nor even seem to hurt it. Placide is very superstitious.

Probably his hand trembles, and he tells Lebaudy, *"Sale bete noir, yeh!—du diable!"* Dirty black beast, yes—of the Devil!

They look at each other—one pictures them. They look back at the cat. But the cat is gone, disappeared. Afterward, Lebaudy admits, they let it alone, and signed the cross whenever it came near—which, Henry says, the cat did not like, and would go howling and spitting away. Well!

So only Nita loved the cat, and the cat loved Nita: Both hated Placide. As for him, this dumb Placide, he grew more sullen and suspicious than ever, without knowing exactly why, but went about his dull affairs as usual.

Sometimes he still rattled down to the bay to catch shrimps. That meant a day and part of the night away from home, even if the engine in his boat gave no trouble—which was not always, nor even often. On one such day, a vagabond gypsy peddler drove his wagon along the bayou, and stopped eventually at Placide's house.

This peddler was a bright-eyed ruffian, with dark hair falling over his forehead; not unhandsome, in a sly, evil way. Pierre Abadie, who passed Placide's shanty twice during the day, and stopped once to ask for matches to light his pipe, said that Nita and the peddler spoke together in a strange, outlandish tongue, neither French nor English. The peddler's horse was unharnessed, and grazed about the place all through that day. Placide heard of it, and he beat Nita. Naturally!

The peddler set up a tent outside Labranch and mended pots and pans, and without doubt engaged in other less open practices. He seemed unconcerned, once, when Placide came by and stopped a moment in front of the tent saying nothing, but glowering sullenly. So, after a bit, Placide went on to the shack where yellow Marie sold vile bootleg whisky, and hatched viler schemes in her festering old brain.

This Marie—if she had any other name, none knew, nor cared—was a quadroon woman who had lived in a tumble-down hovel on the fringe of town for as long as most people remembered. Some of the oldest *habitants* said she had once been a wildly beautiful creature, much as a sleek, cruel, yellow tigress is beautiful, but now she was a wrinkled old hag, a dispenser of vicious liquor, a procuress when chance offered—and, so the blacks and the ignorant whites whispered, a witch. The people of Labranch would have liked to have packed her off elsewhere, but there she was.

Eh? Oh! The sheriff, among others, was one of those old men who had memories of Marie's golden days. . . . You comprehend! Then, too, this Marie was clever, discreet, you understand. Nobody knew anything against her except rumors—nobody, that is, who cared to tell. So Marie stayed on.

The old hag had no love for Placide, and he had less for her. But the one had liquor that was as cheap as it was powerful, and the other had a thirst which a perpetual regard for economy required him to quench with as little expense as might be.

Now, Placide ordinarily drank almost not at all, except reasonably of wine with his supper, but on this day, he had quarreled again with Nita, and beat her without afterward feeling the proper satisfaction. He felt that even when he knocked her half senseless, she was still the stronger of the two. His sullen spirits needed further outlet.

You have noticed, have you not, how a very little thing can set in train a whole series of events? Well! A little thing it was that Placide, the tight-fisted, should unreasonably insist upon old Marie taking drink for drink with him of her corrosive whisky. Even though Placide paid for it, it was almost as unreasonable for Marie to accept knowing as she did the truth about what she dispensed. That is what greed for money will do: I have many times remarked that it is not a good thing.

So Placide and Marie drank together, and, after a while, Placide's sullen tongue loosened enough to where he growled of his wife to the yellow woman. That was not a good thing, either. . . . But, then, what to expect, it being that Placide?

Marie, being a she-devil sober, and a more malicious she-devil in liquor, twitted him about the peddler and his suspicions of Nita, even in the hearing of the other customers who sought her aid in poisoning themselves.

"Why she doan' leave yo', dat's all Ah doan' onnerstan'," gibed the hag, in Cajun-English like Placide's own.

"Aho!" says Placide, speaking in the reasonably pure French of his fathers, "she hopes to find the money I have buried in the ground—and she's not going to find it, I can tell you that!"

Marie was all ears, now, and her eyes glittered like a spider's watching a fly. Money in the ground! She attempted to draw more from Placide, but her eagerness betrayed itself, and he shut up like one of those oysters, suspicious.

He had right to his suspicions for he caught her, the very next day, prowling around the woods near his cabin on the bayou. She was peering carefully at the ground, scratching and probing here and there with a pole she carried. Now, Placide had been dully angry because he thought the peddler wanted his woman, but this Marie was after his money—and that was something else altogether! The peddler got glares and sullen maledictions, but Marie got the beating of her life. Almost, Placide killed her; and she was just able, after a long time, to drag herself back toward town as far as the peddler's tent.

The peddler helped her as well as he could, while the hag cursed Placide and all his works. After a while she quieted, and talked long and earnestly with the gypsy, who listened more attentively as her talk went on.

Doubtless, Marie knew, as do all those who have a hand in such matters, that curses and spells and *gris-gris* charms work much better when the victim knows about it. (Maybe they would not work at all, otherwise!) She knew that Placide was very superstitious. So she was careful that it came to Placide's ears that she was going to put a *conjur* on him, and that it would be better for him to dig up his money and leave the parish. Nita, of course, would tell the peddler, in case her man took the warning to heart. She would know when Placide dug up his money. . . . After which, you speculate on the ending for yourself.

A queer thing is that Marie must have believed in her own *gris-gris* charms, especially as the peddler doubled it with a dreadful spell of his own. Doubtless they both believed in it, and it may be that they were right. Eh! Only, it may also be that they meddled with much more dangerous things than they knew; Marie especially. What the peddler thought or knew, only he could have told. At any rate, they did more than threaten Placide with a spell. They went about it, seriously.

Now, much of this story has to be surmised, and the gaps filled in between the fragments of known fact, which are fewer than they might be. But these people around here tell the whole story, when they tell it at all, with the sureness that comes of believing what one wishes to believe. . . . Very well! That is the way I am telling it to you.

One thing is known: This peddler bought a crucifix at Jules Froissard's store in Labranch, which was afterward seen in Placide's cabin. Froissard remembered it by its general shape and design, and particularly because there was a little of the end broken off one arm of the cross. The peddler got it cheaply for that reason. The crucifix later seen in Placide's shanty had this same shortened arm, but it had been painted black and changed in other ways. For one thing, a file had been used to change the Savior's face beyond recognition, and—good old Father Soulin wept bitterly when they showed him the blasphemy of it—a pair of tiny horns had been soldered to the head. The gypsy tinner's work that! (Well, he paid for it!)

There was a little red bag tied around the cross—that was Marie. Eh? Yes, certainly; it was full of queer charms to make a spell on Placide. *Gris-gris.*

Well, the peddler carried it to Placide's woman, and one supposes that they plotted much together. One believes that the peddler wanted Nita as much as he wanted Placide's money, and it may be that Nita desired the peddler, *then.* . . . Afterward . . .

The woman put the impious crucifix under the bed—and that is where she made a mistake. Placide had heard of the plot to put a spell upon him, only that day, and he was both angry and afraid. He had gone to Marie's place, but he found her absent, and the dive closed—which may have been well for Marie. At the peddler's tent, Placide found the gypsy sitting cross-legged on the ground; elaborately whetting an edge upon a most ferocious-looking butcher knife. So Placide, not unreasonably, left the peddler at peace until he went back and got his gun, or at least, until he could deal with him on even terms. In the meantime, he doubtless argued that he could go home and beat Nita.

On the way back to his cabin, Placide drank from a flask he carried. Meeting with Henry Lebaudy, he would have given Henry a drink, but the bottle was empty. So Henry must come to Placide's cabin, where there was a whole demi-john of good wine, waiting to be drunk. It was not far off, and they would get drunk together.

At the cabin, Placide reached under the bed for the demijohn, felt something else, and—brought out that crucifix!

Now, Placide was superstitious—not religious, you will comprehend, but superstitious. The mutilated crucifix was so awful and startling thing to him; but whether he would have understood that it was evilly designed toward himself without that little red bag tied to it, I do not know. The *gris-gris* he understood quite well. He went mad.

Lebaudy says he seized Nita as one might take a ten-pound sack of flour and flung her hard to the floor. He was a bull for strength, Placide.

Then, while she lay stunned on the floor, Placide flung the desecrated crucifix full at her smooth throat. The cross was flat and thin, and its ends were flattened and beat into a design something like a wedgeshaped cloverleaf. With Placide's great strength behind it, it is no wonder that it tore deep into Nita's round throat, where it stood upright. It wobbled drunkenly, sickening Lebaudy, while Nita quivered and twitched for a few moments. Then she was still. The blood welled slowly from the wound, impeded by the instrument that caused it.

Then that great black cat bounded out of a corner, leaping over the body of its mistress as if to attack Placide. The beast thought better of it, perhaps; at any rate it turned back to sit upon the woman's breast. Lebaudy says it sat there and howled like one of those fiends in hell, while its yellow eyes blazed red fire. Heu!

Then the monster crept upward to Nita's throat. It licked away the dark blood; after which it started yowling with more energy.

All this, you understand, in just a very few minutes; while that stupid Lebaudy stood there, one assumes, with his slack mouth hanging open wider even than usual.

Both men looked long at the body of the woman: that was all—just looked. Then Lebaudy began to look at Placide, too. Sideways, you know, like that. Placide, he began to worry. . . . Well! It was time for him to worry, one comprehends!

"*Now* what you going to do, eh, Placide?" Lebaudy wants to know.

"Well," says Placide, speaking French like Lebaudy, and slow and heavy like he always talks, "I'm going to put her in the ground and bury her." Then he turns round and looks hard at Lebaudy, who said, afterward, that there was a red light in Placide's eyes.

"You're going to help me bury her—*and you're going to keep quiet, all the rest of your life!* Ain't you, Henry?"

"Heh?" gulps Lebaudy.

"Heh?" Placide says, too; but he says it a different way, and the veins kind of swelled in his forehead. He moved a step closer to Lebaudy.

"Yeh!" agreed this Henry, swallowing hard; "I'm going to help you bury her." (Henry Lebaudy is a little man, and he knows it!)

"*And—you're—going—to—keep—quiet!*" grits Placide. Another step closer!

"I'm gong to keep quieter than that!" Lebaudy is trying to swallow his tongue by this time, one supposes.

So Placide got spades, and they carried his woman out into the bushes a way, off behind the shack, and dug a deep hole. The cat went along, too, and spit and howled, and tried to claw Placide's legs. It hopped back and forth across the hole, after they put Nita in it and were ready to shovel the dirt on top of her.

Try as he would and did, Placide couldn't kill it with his spade. . . . What? Why, because he couldn't hit it, certainly. It dodged, you understand. Lebaudy says it *faded* from under the tool—and then there it was again, quick as a flash, just out of reach. (Of course, Lebaudy is stupid. Likewise he does not always tell the truth! No, not even now that he is an old, old man, who should be thinking seriously of his sins. . . . However, I am telling you what he said, and his salvation is the priest's business—not mine!)

Well, they buried Nita, and left the cat sitting on her grave. Afterward, Placide sent Lebaudy on his way, first giving him two great cupsful of strong wine, and growling a few plain threats in his ear—both of which were to stiffen Henry's resolution. So Lebaudy went.

Placide, you see, was not really a murderer, only a poor oaf to whom the good God sent too much money, and the Devil a woman. If he had been a murderer, he would have tried to cover up his crime by killing Lebaudy, too. Even this stupid Placide must have known that one hangs but once, regardless of how many times one kills. Probably he thought Lebaudy would keep quiet for a little while, at least, and give him time to get his money and escape.

But Lebaudy did not keep quiet—not very long. He didn't know how! And he was also afraid.

So Lebaudy went straight to the sheriff; and the sheriff, being an old man, sent his deputy, Sostan LeBleu—no, not the one you know; this was a cousin—who talked only less than Lebaudy. And thus LeBleu told others, and several volunteered to go to Placide's place with him; and one or two saddled their horses and came along without even volunteering.

They passed by the peddler's on the way, and paused long enough to wake him and tell him where they were going, and why. The peddler climbed on his old nag without bothering to saddle it, and came with them.

Now, it is some miles from Labranch to Placide's old cabin, but it is not a long ride for men on horseback. LeBleu and his posse were soon there, demanding entrance.

There was a light inside the cabin, when LeBleu hammered on the door. After a moment, the door opened. LeBleu had his pistol in his hand, and it was a good thing it didn't have a hair trigger, because the deputy was so surprised when that door opened, he dropped the gun.

It wasn't Placide who opened—it was Nita!

"Wal," she says (Nita couldn't speak French), "w'at yo want?"

LeBleu, having come to arrest her murderer, now didn't really know what he wanted, any more than she did!

"Ain't Placide killed yo'?" he blurts out. Somebody laughed (which, you can understand, almost anyone *would!*), and LeBleu says, embarrassed, "I mean, where is Placide?"

"Inside," Nita tells him. "Come on in."

Placide was lying in the bed. He looked dully at LeBleu and the others, who noticed, without thinking too much about it, that there were several nasty marks on his face . . . like the claw marks of a beast, for instance . . . or a woman. . . .

There was a bandage around Nita's throat, also. That much, at least, of Lebaudy's story was true—Placide had hurled something at her throat. Well, they would doubtless be thinking, after Nita got up, she scratched his face: nothing strange about that! A man and his wife could fight if they wanted to, could they not? Naturally!

"Too much wine: 'e's dronk!" Nita snarls. " 'E got dronk wit' t'at Lebaudy, an' beat me." She shrugs her shoulders, which was to say: "What is there of newness in *that*?

"Oho!" LeBleu says, as if comprehending much. "So Lebaudy was drunk! I s'pose the walk to town sobered him up some, otherwise I'd have seen it for myself."

"I was not drunk," Lebaudy indignantly protests. "Placide gave me only two cups of wine before I left—two cups, no more!" He points to a big cup, which will hold about a pint.

Everybody shouts and laughs. Lebaudy is one of those unfortunates who can not take one drink without it affecting his already dizzy brain. So much is known to all.

Somebody notices the paleness of Placide. A pale souse. He must be very drunk, and be in the habit of drinking, very heavily, in secret. Everyone had thought differently. Ah, well!

So they decided to go back to town. You will see that there was little else they could do; and, besides, there was something about Nita that made them all uncomfortable. And uneasy. She seemed changed, in a way none of them could put a finger to; there were smoldering flames deep down in her slanting eyes, and there was something repulsive about the way she would run her red, thin tongue over her red, red lips, whenever she looked at them. More than one man caught himself making the sign of the cross, without at all knowing why. . . . Well, they say one can smell the Devil a long way off. So!

As they were going, someone saw Nita glide up to the peddler and make a swift motion with her fingers, while it seemed she hissed a few words in a tongue strange to all the rest of them. There was only one word that could be understood and remembered—no, I do not know what it was—but they say that it was afterward said by another gypsy who was asked, to mean *gold,* or *money.*

Later, too, one of those who saw, or heard of it, was inspired to show old yellow Marie, as well as he could remember, the sign he thought Nita made. And Marie, she laughed evilly. Being very drunk and in high humor, she finally gave a sly hint that it *might* mean something like *poison,* in a certain dark and secret sign language. (Have I told you it was said, by some, that Marie engaged in darker practices than the keeping of her dive?)

Afterward, Marie told Lebaudy that Nita probably was only fooling the peddler, so as not to frighten him. Placide, added this Marie, did not die of poisoning. More than that, she would not say a word.

One guess is as good as another; but they say there was a greedy look in the peddler's eyes as he listened to Nita. Perhaps there was a greedy look, likewise, in Nita's eyes. But not for gold, one thinks.

Whatever it was that Nita said to the peddler, he went with LeBleu and the others when they rode back to town. For three or four days afterward, this peddler was busy mending his horse's harness and greasing his wagon; and he offered his stock of tinware at such cheap prices that he soon disposed of it. Getting ready to move on, he said. The third or fourth night, the gypsy disappeared.

Nobody was sorry to see him go, nor felt slighted that he left without saying good-bye. Then, a trapper stopped at Placide's cabin and discovered that it was deserted except for Placide himself, who was dead and therefore could hardly be said to count. He had been dead for some days and, it being warm as to weather, he was beginning to be unpleasant about it.

There was a curious wound, or maybe several wounds, in Placide's throat: part of him looked to have been eaten by a beast! Well, they buried him quickly.

I do not know what the coroner said about it, but other people lifted their eyebrows or shrugged, saying, "Placide died, or maybe his woman killed him; and the woman has run away with the peddler—after getting Placide's money! Ah, well, we are rid of the three of them: the peddler, Placide, and Placide's wife. . . . None of them amounted to much!"

Oddly enough, the peddler's horse was soon afterward found dead and partly devoured in a spot deep in the woods. Eh! People wondered at that, naturally.

Then, one afternoon about a month after Lebaudy swore he saw Placide murder Nita, this same Lebaudy was back in the woods behind Placide's cabin, when he came upon a mound of freshly turned dirt that excited his curiosity.

The longer Lebaudy regarded the mound, the more excited he became. This looked suspiciously like a grave—and no human grave had the least right to be in that spot—that much he knew.

Now, it *was* a grave! When Lebaudy, with the aid of a shovel which he ran and fetched from Placide's old cabin, finally overcame his indecision and dug into the mound, he found a man's body! And whose do you suppose it was? *The peddler's!*

What? Indeed not! That is the curious part of it: this peddler's body was not at all decomposed! And there was the same sort of wound, or wounds, in his throat that Placide had—and they were half healed!

Lebaudy, one can imagine, was knocking about the knees. It was getting dusk, and that made things worse. He had reason enough to know that this body did not look as it ought to look, having been dead and covered with dirt. Whether it had been buried one day or ten, it looked too *fresh*. It surely wasn't breathing, it was dead, and yet—it looked as if there might be warm blood beneath its skin! And then—

Lebaudy leaned upon the wooden handle of the spade he had used, and which must have been cracked, already, for it snapped beneath his weight. He was thrown off balance, and, clutching the long handle of the spade tighter than ever, stumbled forward on the dry clods he had dug from the grave, and which rolled under his feet. He fell forward, you understand, with the spade handle thrust before him. And the sharp, broken end of the handle, with Lebaudy's weight behind it, pierced the breast of the corpse at his feet!

(Now, you will remember, this is Lebaudy's tale: I am only telling it for *him*! So!)

Well, this broken end of the spade handle, which was really a hardwood pole, was sharp and keen, and it penetrated the corpse about where its heart should be. And the corpse moved! The dead lips screamed!

Then, the eyes opened wide (Lebaudy swears to this, although if *you* ask him, he will deny it), with such hate in them that it was like a look into the mouth of hell. But the fury swiftly faded into a look of great *gladness,* like the eyes of a bird suddenly set free of a cage; the working features softened into a mask of peace and contentment; the eyes closed. While Lebaudy watched the body began to mortify!

Lebaudy ran, to get out of that forest, where it was getting darker with each second—ran, too, to get away from that horror he had come upon. While he ran, it seemed that there was a patter of swift feet not far behind. Fear lent wings to his feet, until he came to the banks of the bayou upon which Placide's cabin stood.

The woods did not come down quite to the bayou, where the land had been more or less cleared. It was lighter here, although the sun had sunk, and night was falling fast. Panting, Lebaudy stopped and looked back toward the trees. Running toward him from the forest was a woman, who slowed to a walk as he looked, too tired and shocked already to feel much fresh surprise at her appearance there. She came closer, so that he recognized her in the twilight.

It was Nita!

Lebaudy says she smiled at him; but it was the sort of smile that made new shivers crawl on that back of his.

"Good ev'nin'," he says, remembering that Nita did not speak French.

He wondered why Nita was licking her red lips with her redder tongue. (From the way he speaks of it, when he will, one understands that Lebaudy did not care for this, at all!) He felt uneasy, it was so queer, you comprehend, when Nita did not answer him. Not a word from her—just licking her lips, staring at him, with that strange smile.

Lebaudy, one assumes, was at a loss to understand this situation, the woman saying nothing, and looking at him in a way that he did not at all care for. Finally he tells her, "I t'ought yo' run off wit' t' peddler."

Nita laughed . . . Lebaudy says he shivered at the sound!

It was getting darker all this time, and Nita moved closer to him still not making a sound beyond that one hellish laugh. Lebaudy watched her with a funny feeling in his flat stomach, and then he let out a yell—or one assumes he did, knowing this Lebaudy!

He says that he was looking at the same eyes all the time (which one doubts, because he does not like to look people in the eyes!), but one minute they were the eyes of Nita—as he knew Nita—and the next minute they were the eyes of—well, what do you think? The eyes of a great bitch wolf! A great she-wolf with slavering jowls, and a red tongue running in and out between fangs that glinted faintly in the dusk!

The wolf (or whatever it was!) leaped at Lebaudy, who undoubtedly howled as much as any wolf as he also leaped—backward, into the bayou. Now, only a very stupid one, such as this one, would leap unthinking and unlooking when he knew he was standing on the bank of a bayou. Yet, it may be that this stupidity saved Lebaudy from death, or worse. He struggled in the water, while the wolf yowled and slavered on the bank. Lebaudy says its eyes were red as hell's fires by this time. Eh!

Well, one knows without being told, that a swamp rat like Lebaudy could swim and the farther bank was not very distant. He climbed up on it, and the wolf gave a last fiendish howl as Henry scampered off toward Labranch.

Wet and quaking, and feeling a certain need of stimulation, Lebaudy scurried in to old Marie's place, wet clothes and all. One drink, and Lebaudy would stand on his head. That is only an expression, you will understand, but it served well for this old one, as what few brains he had would run out his mouth when he drank—which is a misfortune that might, perhaps, happen to a rattlebrain who stood too long upon his head in fact! However, if you understand me, he talked much when he drank a little.

He talked to Marie, telling her of his finding the corpse that was so different from other corpses, and of his meeting with Nita, or the wolf (or both in one), or whatever it was, on the bank of the bayou. Then he went back and told her the whole story in detail, from the time he had seen Placide throw Nita to the floor and hurl that desecrated crucifix into her throat. Before he had finished, Marie was so shaken that she was drinking her own rotgut liquor, and pouring more for Henry—all without charge to him!

"Ay-e-e!" she moaned. "The black crucifix, the black cat jumping across her body in the grave, licking her blood. Moonlight in her eyes while she's lying in her grave! Oh, Placide! Stupid Placide! Why did you not drive a stake through her heart when you buried her?"

"Eh?" says Henry Lebaudy, "What's all this you're talking about?"

"*Loup-garou!*" snarls Marie who was raised among people who speak French much better than, and in preference to, English; and she had absorbed all the folk lore of those French-descended people. (Marie's white blood, one assumes, came from the same source as theirs.)

"*Loup-garou!*" shudders Lebaudy. (You comprehend that it is the French name for werewolf? So!) "I was afraid so, me!"

Marie brightens, after a minute.

"One good thing," she exults, "this Nita can't get off her island—and *I'm* not going *there!* Me, I don't intend to see her!"

Now, as you already know, Labranch bayou forks and flows into the bay in two separate streams, like a wishbone, making an island nearly fifteen miles long and about ten miles wide at the bay end. The point, you understand, is that the werewolf is supposed to be unable to cross running water. . . . What? The vampire, also? Exactly! This *loup-garou* which is, or was, Nita, is safely in a pen, unless she can get some one to carry her across the bayou in his arms— which I doubt!

There is only a little more to tell. Lebaudy, at Marie's urging, went with his tale to Father Soulin. Whether the good priest had a hand in it or not, I do not know: but the parish sexton (who, naturally enough, was not given to agitation in the presence of dead bodies) went into the woods and cut off the spade handle a little way above the peddler's body. After which he drove the end of the handle a little more firmly in the corpse, and then covered it up to rest in peace.

Now, of course, that left Placide to be looked after. The sexton sharpened the part of the spade handle (Placide's own spade handle!) that he had kept, and dealt with Placide as the peddler had been dealt with. And Placide's wounds had healed, although they had been greater by far than the peddler's; and he screamed and squirmed beneath the thrust of the stake, and settled back at peace, as the peddler had done. The sexton piled back the dirt on what had become, in a twinkling, a heap of bones and unpleasantness.

So (Delacroix concluded with a shrug of his shoulders), that is the tale as I have heard it. It happened, so they say, when I was a boy, and I did not live in this parish then. Father Soulin has been dead these four years past, so you can not ask him.

Me, I don't know. . . .

I drew on my pipe for a couple of minutes, considering Delacroix's tale the while. Finally, I asked, "What do you mean by saying you don't know? You don't believe any of that, do you?"

Delacroix merely gave repetition of his frequent and noncommital shrug; and I knew that, for all his better education and larger contact with the world, he would be as taciturn as any of his ilk when conversation took a turn he did not like.

I was sleepy, by this time, and smothered a yawn.

"All right," I laughed, "I'm gong on over to my tent and turn in, and I hope none of those werewolves who have to lie in their graves between sun-up and sun-down have come to life tonight, to catch me on the way, nor come uninvited into my tent."

"They can't enter a house without an invitation," Delacroix rejoined, in all seriousness, "and one supposes that will apply to a tent, likewise."

I was tempted to laugh at his earnestness, but I had no wish to wound his sensibilities, and so refrained.

"Perhaps, after all," he said, "it would be better if you were to sleep with me while you are here. . . . Yes?"

"No." I carelessly shook my head. "I'll go over. . ."

At this moment I broke off, as there came a light tapping upon the door of the shack.

To this day, I do not know why one of us did not say, "Come in." Instead Delacroix, who was sitting close to the door, merely reached out and lifted the latch, the poorly hung door swinging inward of its own accord. At that, surprise kept either one of us from speaking for a minute, although I had sufficient presence of mind to rise from my seat upon a cracker box and say, "Good evening."

Standing just outside the doorway, framed in the light from within, was one of the most beautiful women (she was, apparently, little more than a girl) that I have ever seen. She was clad in rough, serviceable corduroy riding breeches and flannel shirt, and I could see a laced boot on the one leg that the shadows failed to screen from my view.

Even though she was so clad—I write these next words with considerable deliberateness!—in garments that she could have obtained from any chance hunter in the swamps around us, provided he were of slight stature, even, I say, though she was clad in such garments, there was no hiding the alluring femininity of her.

Before I could find wits and voice to speak to this astonishing apparition, the girl smiled and herself spoke—dashing my illusions. Her words, although there was an additional odd inflection, were the words of any unlettered Cajun girl of the swamp country.

"Ma car," she informed us, "it's bogged down on de ot'er side de bayou; an' ma ankle, Ah sprained it tryin' t' gat out. . . . Will yo' gen'leman he'p me?"

However, if her words were crude, her voice was not, and there was a wistful note in it that touched me. I could see, now, that she was leaning heavily on a stick, and the boot had been removed from one stockingless foot. She moved the foot, as if to ease its pain, so that it was more in the light. Unshod feet that are beautiful are rarity in women. I had been out in the swamps with a road camp for two long months; and, Cajun or no Cajun, this was Woman—and a beautiful woman, at that. As Delacroix would put it: Well!

"Certainly we will help you!" I was very gallant about it, hoping she would not be too fastidious to overlook my two days' growth of beard. I had another thought: bold, but maybe. . . . "And," I said, "as I see you cannot stand upon that foot—I'll carry you back across the bridge!"

I stared at the look of wild exultation that leaped into the girls' wonderful eyes, enchanting with their vague suggestion of the Orient, before she dropped her gaze.

"No!" yelled Delacroix, to my utter astonishment and indignation. *"Carry her across running water?* No! Never!"

My anger was flaring swiftly, and then I caught sight of the girl. I stopped the hot rejoinder I had upon my tongue for Delacroix, appalled with doubt and something more.

There was a positively feral light in those glorious eyes, now; and that seductive mouth had ceased to be such.

"Landry!" Delacroix was yelling, "bring your gun, the one with the silver bullets—she's here!"

The girl leaped away toward the swamp growth—there was no sign of lameness in her going. I had a vague, confused impression that she looked oddly inhuman, and dropped to all fours as she reached the shelter of the forest!

Old Landry, he of the weathered face and gnarled hands who had first mentioned Placide's wife that night, came running up. That was a huge revolver in one of those knotted fists.

Delacroix spoke to him in the French *patois* of the region, of which I knew enough to get the gist.

"Yes, it was *she*—but you are too late! She has reached the woods and you dare not follow—she and her pack would have your throat open before you knew they were near!"

"Silver bullets," was all I could understand of Landry's answer, taut as it was with suppressed emotion. Then, hoarsely, in which occurred the words, "my son," he croaked something else.

Delacroix shook his head. "Avenge him, and all the others, when the odds are even. Wait until you have another chance in the open."

"Eleven years!" said Landry, quite distinctly. "For so long have I carried this gun loaded with silver bullets blessed by the good Father—the only kind that can kill *them*!—waiting to use it."

Again Delacroix shook his head.

"We will be five or six months getting the road across the island. There will be other chances: You have waited eleven years, and you can surely wait a few months longer."

Delacroix slowly shut the door; and Landry plodded back to resume his disturbed rest . . . perhaps.

"You will sleep here tonight." It was a statement, simply made.

I nodded, as simply. Then, once more, I felt a shiver run along my spine.

From the forest came again that fiendish ululation—the baffled howl of Placide's wife.

THE HORROR FROM THE MOUND

ROBERT E. HOWARD

Though considered one of the most important writers to emerge from the pages of
Weird Tales, Robert E. Howard was primarily a writer of adventure fiction. His
heroic fantasies of Conan the Cimmerian, King Kull of Valusia and Solomon Kane
are perhaps more interesting for their portrayal of swashbuckling warriors putting
the values of civilization to the test than for their low-key supernatural element.
Similarly, ''The Horror from the Mound'' and other stories set in Howard's native
southwest are as distinguished for their portrait of the American frontier as their
manifest supernatural content.

STEVE BRILL did not believe in ghosts or demons. Jaun Lopez did. But neither
the caution of the one nor the sturdy skepticism of the other was shield
against the horror that fell upon them—the horror forgotten by men for more than
three hundred years—a screaming fear monstrously resurrected from the black
lost ages.

Yet as Steve Brill sat on his sagging stoop that last evening, his thoughts were
as far from uncanny menaces as the thoughts of man can be. His ruminations
were bitter but materialistic. He surveyed his farmland and he swore. Brill was
tall, rangy, and tough as boot leather—true son of the iron-bodied pioneers who
wrenched West Texas from the wilderness. He was browned by the sun and
strong as a long-horned steer. His lean legs and the boots on them showed his
cowboy instincts, and now he cursed himself that he had ever climbed off the
hurricane deck of his crank-eyed mustang and turned to farming. He was no
farmer, the young puncher admitted profanely.

Yet his failure had not all been his fault. Plentiful rain in the winter—so rare in West Texas—had given promise of good crops. But as usual, things had happened. A late blizzard had destroyed all the budding fruit. The grain which had looked so promising was ripped to shreds and battered into the ground by terrific hailstorms just as it was turning yellow. A period of intense dryness, followed by another hailstorm, finished the corn.

Then the cotton, which had somehow struggled through, fell before a swarm of grasshoppers which stripped Brill's field almost over night. So Brill sat and swore that he would not renew his lease—he gave fervent thanks that he did not own the land on which he had wasted his sweat, and that there were still broad rolling ranges to the west where a strong young man could make his living riding and roping.

Now as Brill sat glumly, he was aware of the approaching form of his nearest neighbor, Jaun Lopez, a taciturn old Mexican who lived in a hut just out of sight over the hill across the creek, and grubbed for a living. At present he was clearing a strip of land on an adjoining farm, and in returning to his hut he crossed a corner of Brill's pasture.

Brill idly watched him climb through the barbed-wire fence and trudge along the path he had worn in the short dry grass. He had been working at his present job for over a month now, chopping down tough gnarly mesquite trees and digging up their incredibly long roots, and Brill knew that he always followed the same path home. And watching, Brill noted him swerving far aside, seemingly to avoid a low rounded hillock which jutted above the level of the pasture. Lopez went far around this knoll and Brill remembered that the old Mexican always circled it at a distance. And another thing came into Brill's idle mind—Lopez always increased his gait when he was passing the knoll, and he always managed to get by it before sundown—yet Mexican laborers generally worked from the first light of dawn to the last glint of twilight, especially at these grubbing jobs, when they were paid by the acre and not by the day. Brill's curiosity was aroused.

He rose, and sauntering down the slight slope on the crown of which his shack sat, hailed the plodding Mexican.

"Hey, Lopez, wait a minute."

Lopez halted, looked about, and remained motionless but unenthusiastic as the white man approached.

"Lopez," said Brill lazily, "it ain't none of my business, but I just wanted to ask you—how come you always go so far around that old Indian mound?"

"*No sabe,*" grunted Lopez shortly.

"You're a liar," responded Brill genially. "You savvy all right; you speak English as good as me. What's the matter—you think that mound's ha'nted or somethin'?"

Brill could speak Spanish himself and read it, too, but like most Anglo-Saxons he much preferred to speak his own language.

"It is not a good place, *no bueno,*" he muttered, avoiding Brill's eye. "Let hidden things rest."

"I reckon you're scared of ghosts," Brill bantered. "Shucks, if that is an Indian mound, them Indians been dead so long their ghosts 'ud be plumb wore out by now."

Brill knew that the illiterate Mexicans looked with superstitious aversion on the mounds that are found here and there through the Southwest—relics of a past and forgotten age, containing the moldering bones of chiefs and warriors of a lost race.

"Best not to disturb what is hidden in the earth," grunted Lopez.

"Bosh," said Brill. "Me and some boys busted into one of them mounds over in the Palo Pinto country and dug up pieces of a skeleton with some beads and flint arrowheads and the like. I kept some of the teeth a long time till I lost 'em, and I ain't never been ha'nted."

"Indians?" snorted Lopez unexpectedly. "Who spoke of Indians? There have been more than Indians in this country. In the old times strange things happened here. I have heard the tales of my people, handed down from generation to generation. And my people were here long before yours, Señor Brill."

"Yeah, you're right," admitted Steve. "First white men in this country was Spaniards, of course. Coronado passed along not very far from here, I hear-tell, and Hernando de Estrada's expedition came through here—away back yonder—I dunno how long ago."

"In 1545," said Lopez. "They pitched camp yonder where your corral stands now."

Brill turned to glance at his rail-fenced corral, inhabited now by his saddle-horse, a pair of workhorses and a scrawny cow.

"How come you know so much about it?" he asked curiously.

"One of my ancestors marched with de Estrada," answered Lopez. "A soldier, Porfirio Lopez; he told his son of that expedition, and he told *his* son, and so down the family line to me, who have no son to whom I can tell the tale."

"I didn't know you were so well connected," said Brill. "Maybe you know somethin' about the gold de Estrada was supposed to hid around here somewhere."

"There was no gold," growled Lopez. "De Estrada's soldiers bore only their arms, they fought their way through hostile country—many left their bones along the trail. Later—many years later—a mule train from Santa Fe was attacked not many miles from here by Comanches and they hid their gold and escaped; so the legends got mixed up. But even their gold is not here now, because Gringo buffalo hunters found it and dug it up."

Brill nodded abstractedly, hardly heeding. Of all the continent of North America there is no section so haunted by tales of lost or hidden treasure as is the Southwest. Uncounted wealth passed back and forth over the hills and plains of Texas and New Mexico in the old days when Spain owned the gold and silver mines of the New World and controlled the rich fur trade of the West, and echoes of that wealth linger on in tales of golden caches. Some such vagrant dream, born of failure and pressing poverty, rose in Brill's Mind.

Aloud he spoke: "Well, anyway, I got nothing' else to do and I believe I'll dig into that old mound and see what I can find."

The effect of that simple statement on Lopez was nothing short of shocking. He recoiled and his swarthy brown face went ashy; his black eyes flared and he threw up his arms in a gesture of intense expostulation.

"*Dios, no!*" he cried. "Don't do that, Señor Brill! There is a curse—my grandfather told me—"

"Told you what?" asked Brill.

Lopez lapsed into sullen silence.

"I cannot speak," he muttered. "I am sworn to silence. Only to an eldest son could I open my heart. But believe me when I say better had you cut your throat than to break into that accursed mound."

"Well," said Brill, impatient of Mexican superstitions, "if it's so bad why don't you tell me about it? Gimme a logical reason for not bustin' into it."

"I cannot speak!" cried the Mexican desperately. "I *know!*—but I swore to silence on the Holy Crucifix, just as every man of my family has sworn. It is a thing so dark, it is to risk damnation even to speak of it! Were I to tell you, I would blast the soul from your body. But I have sworn—and I have no son, so my lips are sealed for ever."

"Aw, well," said Brill sarcastically, "why don't you write it out?"

Lopez started, stared, and to Steven's surprise, caught at the suggestion.

"I will! *Dios* be thanked the good priest taught me to write when I was a child. My oath said nothing of writing. I only swore not to speak. I will write out the whole thing for you, if you will swear not to speak of it afterward, and to destroy the paper as soon a you have read it."

"Sure," said Brill, to humor him, and the old Mexican seemed much relieved.

"*Bueno!* I will go at once and write. Tomorrow as I go to work I will bring you the paper and you will understand why no one must open that accursed mound!"

And Lopez hurried along his homeward path, his stooped shoulders swaying with the effort of his unwonted haste. Steve grinned after him, shrugged his shoulders and turned back toward his own shack. Then he halted, gazing back at the low rounded mound with its grass-grown sides. It must be an Indian tomb, he decided, what with its symmetry and its similarity to other Indian mounds he had seen. He scowled as he tried to figure out the seeming connection between the mysterious knoll and the martial ancestors of Juan Lopez.

Brill gazed after the receding figure of the old Mexican. A shallow valley, cut by a half-dry creek, bordered with trees and underbrush, lay between Brill's pasture and the low sloping hill beyond which lay Lopez's shack. Among the trees along the creek bank the old Mexican was disappearing. And Brill came to a sudden decision.

Hurrying up the slight slope, he took a pick and a shovel from the tool shed built on to the back of his shack. The sun had not yet set and Brill believed he could open the mound deep enough to determine its nature before dark. If not, he could work by lanternlight. Steve, like most of his breed, lived mostly by impulse, and his present urge was to tear into that mysterious hillock and find what, if anything, was concealed therein. The thought of treasure came again to his mind, piqued by the evasive attitude of Lopez.

What if, after all, that grassy heap of brown earth hid riches—virgin ore from forgotten mines, or the minted coinage of old Spain? Was it not possible that the musketeers of de Estrada had themselves reared that pile above a treasure they could not bear away, molding it in the likeness of an Indian mound to fool seekers? Did old Lopez know that? It would not be strange if, knowing of treasure there, the old Mexican refrained from disturbing it. Ridden with grisly superstitious fears, he might well live out a life of barren toil rather than risk the wrath of lurking ghosts or devils—for the Mexicans say that hidden gold is always accursed, and surely there was supposed to be some especial doom resting on this mound. Well, Brill meditated, Latin-Indian devils had no terrors for the Anglo-Saxton, tormented by the demons of drouth and storm and crop failure.

Steve set to work with the savage energy characteristic of his breed. The task was no light one; the soil, baked by the fierce sun, was iron-hard, mixed with rocks and pebbles. Brill sweated profusely and grunted with his efforts, but the fire of the treasure hunter was on him. He shook the sweat out of his eyes and drove in the pick with mighty strokes that ripped and crumbled the close-packed dirt.

The sun went down, and in the long dreamy summer twilight he worked on, almost oblivious of time or space. He began to be convinced that the mound was a genuine Indian tomb, as he found traces of charcoal in the soil. The ancient people which reared these sepulchers had kept fires burning upon them for days, at some point in the building. All the mounds Steve had ever opened had contained a solid stratum of charcoal a short distance below the surface. But the charcoal traces he found now were scattered about through the soil.

His idea of a Spanish-built treasure-trove faded, but he persisted. Who knows? Perhaps that strange folk men now called Mound-Builders had treasure of their own which they laid away with the dead.

Then Steve yelped in exultation as his pick rang on a bit of metal. He snatched it up and held it close to his eyes, straining in the waning light. It was caked and corroded with rust, worn almost paper-thin, but he knew it for what it was—a spur-rowel, unmistakably Spanish with its long cruel points. And he halted completely bewildered. No Spaniard ever reared this mound, with its undeniable marks of aboriginal workmanship. Yet how came that relic of Spanish caballeros hidden deep in the packed soil?

Brill shook his head and set to work again. He knew that in the center of the mound, if it were indeed an aboriginal tomb, he would find a narrow chamber built of heavy stones, containing the bones of the chief for whom the mound had been reared and the victims sacrificed above it. And in the gathering darkness he felt his pick strike heavily against something granite-like and unyielding.

Examination, by sense of feel as well as by sight, proved it to be a solid block of stone, roughly hewn. Doubtless it formed one of the ends of the death-chamber. Useless to try to shatter it. Brill chipped and pecked about it, scraping the dirt and pebbles away from the corners until he felt that wrenching it out would be but a matter of sinking the pick-point underneath and levering it out.

But now he was suddenly aware that darkness had come on. In the young moon objects were dim and shadowy. His mustang nickered in the corral whence came the comfortable crunch of tired beasts' jaws on corn. A whippoorwill called eerily from the dark shadows of the narrow winding creek. Brill straightened reluctantly. Better get a lantern and continue his explorations by its light.

He felt in his pocket with some idea of wrenching out the stone and exploring the cavity by the aid of matches. Then he stiffened. Was it imagination that he heard a faint sinister rustling, which seemed to come from behind the blocking stone? Snakes! Doubtless they had holes somewhere about the base of the mound and there might be a dozen big diamond-backed rattlers coiled up in that cavelike interior waiting for him to put his hand among them. He shivered slightly at the thought and backed away out of the excavation he had made.

It wouldn't do to go poking about blindly into holes. And for the past few minutes, he realized, he had been aware of a faint foul odor exuding from interstices about the blocking stone—though he admitted that the smell suggested reptiles no more than it did any other menacing scent. It had a charnelhouse reek about it—gases formed in the chamber of death, no doubt, and dangerous to the living.

Steve laid down his pick and returned to the house, impatient of the necessary delay. Entering the dark building, he struck a match and located his kerosene lantern hanging on its nail on the wall. Shaking it, he satisfied himself that it was nearly full of coal oil, and lighted it. Then he fared forth again, for his eagerness would not allow him to pause long enough for a bit of food. The mere opening of the mound intrigued him, as it must always intrigue a man of imagination, and the discovery of the Spanish spur had whetted his curiosity.

He hurried from his shack, the swinging lantern casting long distorted shadows ahead of him and behind. He chuckled as he visualized Lopez's thoughts and actions when he learned, on the morrow, that the forbidden mound had been pried into. A good thing he opened it that evening, Brill reflected; Lopez might even have tried to prevent him meddling with it, had he known.

In the dreamy hush of the summer night, Brill reached the mound—lifted his lantern—swore bewilderedly. The lantern revealed his excavations, his tools lying carelessly where he had dropped them—and a black gaping aperture! The great blocking stone lay in the bottom of the excavation he had made, as if thrust carelessly aside. Warily he thrust the lantern forward and peered into the small cavelike chamber, expecting to see he knew not what. Nothing met his eyes except the bare rock sides of a long narrow cell, large enough to receive a man's body, which had apparently been built up of roughly hewn square-cut stones, cunningly and strongly joined together.

"Lopez!" exclaimed Steve furiously. "The dirty coyote! He's been watchin' me work—and when I went after the lantern, he snuck up and pried the rock out—and grabbed whatever was in there, I reckon. Blast his greasy hide, I'll fix him!"

Savagely he extinguished the lantern and glared across the shallow, brush-grown valley. And as he looked he stiffened. Over the corner of the hill, on the other side of which the shack of Lopez stood, a shadow moved. The slender moon was setting, the light dim and the play of the shadows baffling. But Steve's eyes were sharpened by the sun and winds of the wastelands, and he knew that it was some two-legged creature that was disappearing over the low shoulder of the mesquite-grown hill.

"Beatin' it to his shack," snarled Brill. "He's shore got somethin' or he wouldn't be travelin' at that speed."

Brill swallowed, wondering why a peculiar trembling had suddenly taken hold of him. What was there unusual about a thieving old greaser running home with his loot? Brill tried to drown the feeling that there was something peculiar about the gait of the dim shadow, which had seemed to move at a sort of slinking lope. There must have been need for swiftness when stocky old Juan Lopez elected to travel at such a strange pace.

"Whatever he found is as much mine as his," swore Brill, trying to get his mind off the abnormal aspect of the figure's flight. "I got this land leased and I done all the work diggin'. A curse, heck! No wonder he told me that stuff. Wanted me to leave it alone so he could get it hisself. It's a wonder he ain't dug it up long before this. But you can't never tell about them Spigs."

Brill, as he meditated thus, was striding down the gentle slope of the pasture which led down to the creekbed. He passed into the shadows of the trees and dense underbrush and walked across the dry creekbed, noting absently that neither whippoorwill nor hoot owl called in the darkness. There was a waiting, listening tenseness in the night that he did not like. The shadows in the creek bed seemed too thick, too breathless. He wished he had not blown out the lantern, which he still carried, and was glad he had brought the pick, gripped like a battle-ax in his right hand. He had an impulse to whistle, just to break the silence, then swore and dismissed the thought. Yet he was glad when he clambered up the low opposite bank and emerged into the starlight.

He walked up the slope and onto the hill, and looked down on the mesquite flat wherein stood Lopez's squalid hunt. A light showed at the one window.

"Packin' his things for a getaway, I reckon," grunted Steve. "Ow, what the—"

He staggered as from a physical impact as a frightful scream knifed the stillness. He wanted to clap his hands over his ears to shut out the horror of that cry, which rose unbearably and then broke in an abhorrent gurgle.

"Good God!" Steve felt the cold sweat spring out upon him. "Lopez—or somebody—"

Even as he gasped the words he was running down the hill as fast as his long legs could carry him. Some unspeakable horror was taking place in that lonely hut, but he was going to investigate if it meant facing the Devil himself. He tightened his grip on his pick-handle as he ran. Wandering prowlers, murdering old Lopez for the loot he had taken from the mound, Steve thought, and forgot his wrath. It would go hard for anyone he caught molesting the old scoundrel, thief though he might be.

He hit the flat, running hard. And then the light in the hut went out and Steve staggered in full flight, bringing up against a mesquite tree with an impact that jolted a grunt out of him and tore his hands on the thorns. Rebounding with a sobbed curse, he rushed for the shack, nerving himself for what he might see— his hair still standing on end at what he had already seen.

Brill tried the one door of the hut and found it bolted. He shouted to Lopez and received no answer. Yet utter silence did not reign. From within came a curious muffled worrying sound that ceased as Brill swung his pick crashing against the door. The flimsy portal splintered and Brill leaped into the dark hut, eyes blazing, pick swung high for a desperate onslaught. But no sound ruffled the grisly silence, and in the darkness nothing stirred, though Brill's chaotic imagination peopled the shadowed corners of the hut with shapes of horror.

With a hand damp with perspiration he found a match and struck it. Besides himself only old Lopez occupied the hunt—old Lopez, stark dead on the dirt floor, arms spread wide like a crucifix, mouth sagging open in a semblance of idiocy, eyes wide and staring with a horror Brill found intolerable. The one window gaped open, showing the method of the slayer's exit—possibly his entrance as well. Brill went to that window and gazed out warily. He saw only the sloping hillside on one hand and the mesquite flat on the other. He started—was that a hint of movement among the stunted shadows of the mesquites and chaparral—or had he but imagined he glimpsed a dim loping figure among the trees?

He turned back, as the match burned down to his fingers. He lit the old coal oil lamp on the rude table, cursing as he burned his hand. The globe of the lamp was very hot, as if it had been burning for hours.

Reluctantly he turned to the corpse on the floor. Whatever sort of death had come to Lopez, it had been horrible, but Brill, gingerly examining the dead man, found no wound—no mark of knife or bludgeon on him. Wait! There was a thin smear of blood on Brill's questing hand. Searching, he found the source—three or four tiny punctures in Lopez's throat, from which blood had oozed sluggishly. At first he thought they had been inflicted with a stiletto—a thin, round, edgeless dagger—then he shook his head. He had seen stiletto wounds—he had the scar of one on his own body. These wounds more resembled the bite of some animal. They looked like the marks of pointed fangs.

Yet Brill did not believe they were deep enough to have caused death, nor had much blood flowed from them. A belief, abhorrent with grisly speculations, rose up in the dark corners of his mind—that Lopez had died of fright, and that the wounds had been inflicted either simultaneously with his death, or an instant afterward.

And Steve noticed something else; scattered about on the floor lay a number of dingy leaves of paper, scrawled in the old Mexican's crude hand—he would write of the curse on the mound, he had said. There were the sheets on which he had written, there was the stump of a pencil on the floor, there was the hot lamp globe, all mute witnesses that the old Mexican had been seated at the rough-hewn table writing for hours. Then it was not he who opened the mound-chamber and stole the contents—but who was it, in God's name? And who or what was it that Brill had glimpsed loping over the shoulder of the hill?

Well, there was but one thing to do—saddle his mustang and ride the ten miles to Coyote Wells, the nearest town, and inform the sheriff of the murder.

Brill gathered up the papers. The last was crumpled in the old man's clutching hand and Brill secured it with some difficulty. Then as he turned to extinguish the light, he hesitated, and cursed himself for the crawling fear that lurked at the back of his mind—fear of the shadowy thing he had seen cross the window just before the light was extinguished in the hut. The long arm of the murderer, he thought, reaching for the lamp to put it out, no doubt. What had there been abnormal or inhuman about that vision, distorted though it must have been in the dim lamplight and shadow? As a man strives to remember the details of a nightmare dream, Steve tried to define in his mind some clear reason that would explain why that flying glimpse had unnerved him to the extent of blundering headlong into a tree, and why the mere vague remembrance of it now caused cold sweat to break out on him.

Cursing himself to keep up his courage, he lighted his lantern, blew out the lamp on the rough table, and resolutely set forth, grasping his pick like a weapon. After all, why should certain seemingly abnormal aspects about a sordid murder upset him? Such crimes were abhorrent, but common enough, especially among Mexicans, who cherished unguessed feuds.

Then as he stepped into the silent starflecked night he brought up short. From across the creek sounded the sudden soul-shaking scream of a horse in deadly terror—then a mad drumming of hoofs that receded in the distance. And Brill swore in rage and dismay. Was it a panther lurking in the hills—had a monster cat slain old Lopez? Then why was not the victim marked with the scars of fierce hooked talons? *And who extinguished the light in the hut?*

As he wondered, Brill was running swiftly toward the dark creek. Not lightly does a cowpuncher regard the stampeding of his stock. As he passed into the darkness of the brush along the dry creek, Brill found his tongue strangely dry. He kept swallowing, and he held the lantern high. It made but faint impression in the gloom, but seemed to accentuate the blackness of the crowding shadows. For some strange reason, the thought entered Brill's chaotic mind that though the land was new to the Anglo-Saxon, it was in reality very old. That broken and desecrated tomb was mute evidence that the land was ancient to man, and suddenly the night and the hills and the shadows bore on Brill with a sense of hideous antiquity. Here had long generations of men lived and died before Brill's ancestors ever heard of the land. In the night, in the shadows of this very creek, men had no doubt given up their ghosts in grisly ways. With these reflections Brill hurried through the shadows of the thick trees.

He breathed deeply in relief when he emerged from the trees on his own side. Hurrying up the gentle slope to the railed corral, he held up his lantern, investigating. The corral was empty; not even the placid cow was in sight. And the bars were down. That pointed to human agency, and the affair took on a newly sinister aspect. Someone did not intend that Brill should ride to Coyote Wells that night. It meant that the murderer intended making his getaway and wanted a good start on the law, or else—Brill grinned wryly. Far away across a mesquite flat he believed he could still catch the faint and faraway noise of running horses. What in God's name had given them such a fright? A cold finger of fear played shudderingly on Brill's spine.

Steve headed for the house. He did not enter boldly. He crept clear around the shack, peering shudderingly into the dark windows, listening with painful intensity for some sound to betray the presence of the lurking killer. At last he ventured to open a door and step in. He threw the door back against the wall to find if any one were hiding behind it, lifted the lantern high and stepped in, heart pounding, pick gripped fiercely, his feelings a mixture of fear and red rage. But no hidden assassin leaped upon him, and a wary exploration of the shack revealed nothing.

With a sigh of relief Brill locked the doors, made fast the windows and lighted his old coal oil lamp. The thought of old Lopez lying, a glassy-eyed corpse alone in the hut across the creek, made him wince and shiver, but he did not intend to start for town on foot in the night.

He drew from its hiding-place his reliable old Colt .45, spun the blue steel cylinder and grinned mirthlessly. Maybe the killer did not intend to leave any witnesses to his crime alive. Well, let him come! He—or they—would find a young cowpuncher with a six-shooter less easy prey than an old unarmed Mexican. And that reminded Brill of the papers he had brought from the hut. Taking care that he was not in line with a window through which a sudden bullet might come, he settled himself to read, with one ear alert for stealthy sounds.

And as he read the crude laborious script, a slow cold horror grew in his soul. It was a tale of fear that the old Mexican had scrawled—a tale handed down from generation to generation—a tale of ancient times.

And Brill read of the wanderings of the caballero Hernando de Estrada and his armored pikemen, who dared the deserts of the Southwest when all was strange and unknown. There were some forty-odd soldiers, servants, and masters, at the beginning, the manuscript ran. There was the captain, de Estrada, and the priest, and young Juan Zavilla, and Don Santiago de Valdez—a mysterious nobleman who had been taken off a helplessly floating ship in the Caribbean Sea—all the others of the crew and passengers had died of plague, he had said, and he had cast their bodies overboard. So de Estrada had taken him aboard the ship that was bearing the expedition from Spain, and de Valdez joined them in their explorations.

Brill read something of their wanderings, told in the crude style of old Lopez, as the old Mexican's ancestors had handed down the tale for over three hundred years. The bare written words dimly reflected the terrific hardships the explorers had encountered—drouth, thirst, floods, the desert sandstorms, the spears of hostile Indians. But it was of another peril that old Lopez told—a grisly lurking horror that fell upon the lonely caravan wandering through the immensity of the wild. Man by man they fell and no man knew the slayer. Fear and black suspicion ate at the heart of the expedition like a canker, and their leader knew not where to turn. This they all knew: Among them was a fiend in human form.

Men began to draw apart from each other, to scatter along the line of march, and this mutual suspicion, that sought security in solitude, made it easier for the fiend. The skeleton of the expedition staggered through the wilderness, lost, dazed, and helpless, and still the unseen horror hung on their flanks, dragging down the stragglers, preying on drowsing sentries and sleeping men. And on the throat of each was found the wounds of pointed fangs that bled the victim white; so that the living knew with what manner of evil they had to deal. Men reeled through the wild, calling on the saints, or blaspheming in their terror, fighting frenziedly against sleep, until they fell with exhaustion and sleep stole on them with horror and death.

Suspicion centered on a great black man, a cannibal slave from Calabar. And they put him in chains. But young Juan Zavilla went the way of the rest, and then the priest was taken. But the priest fought off his fiendish assailant and lived long enough to gasp the demon's name to de Estrada. And Brill, shuddering and wide-eyed, read:

"And now it was evident to de Estrada that the good priest had spoken the truth, and the slayer was Don Santiago de Valdez, who was a vampire, an undead fiend, subsisting on the blood of the living. And de Estrada called to mind a certain foul nobleman who had lurked in the mountains of Castile since the days of the Moors, feeding off the blood of helpless victims which lent him a ghastly immortality. This nobleman had been driven forth. None knew where he had fled, but it was evident that he and Don Santiago were the same man. He had fled Spain by ship, and de Estrada knew that the people of that ship had died, not by plague as the fiend had represented, but by the fangs of the vampire.

"De Estrada and the black man and the few soldiers who still lived went searching for him and found him stretched in bestial sleep in a clump of chaparral; full-gorged he was with human blood from his last victim. Now it is well known that a vampire, like a great serpent, when well gorged, falls into a deep sleep and may be taken without peril. But de Estrada was at a loss as to how to dispose of the monster, for how may the dead be slain? For a vampire is a man who has died long ago, yet is quick with a certain foul unlife.

"The men urged that the Caballero drive a stake through the fiend's heart and cut off his head, uttering the holy words that would crumple the long-dead body into dust, but the priest was dead and de Estrada feared that in the act the monster might waken.

"So they took Don Santiago, lifting him softly, and bore him to an old Indian mound near by. This they opened, taking forth the bones they found there, and they placed the vampire within and sealed up the mound—*Dios* grant until Judgment Day.

"It is a place accursed, and I wish I had starved elsewhere before I came into this part of the country seeking work—for I have known of the land and the creek and the mound with its terrible secret, ever since childhood; so you see, Señor Brill, why you must not open the mound and wake the fiend—''

There the manuscript ended with an erratic scratch of the pencil that tore the crumpled leaf.

Brill rose, his heart pounding wildly, his face bloodless, his tongue cleaving to his palate. He gagged and found words.

"That's why the spur was in the mound—one of them Spaniards dropped it while they was diggin'—and I mighta knowed it's been dug into before, the way the charcoal was scattered out—but, good God—''

Aghast he shrank from the black visions—an undead monster stirring in the gloom of his tomb, thrusting from within to push aside the stone loosened by the pick of ignorance—a shadowy shape loping over the hill toward a light that betokened a human prey—a frightful long arm that crossed a dim-lighted window. . . .

"It's madness!'' he gasped. "Lopez was plumb loco! They ain't no such things as vampires! If they is, why didn't he get me first, instead of Lopez—unless he was scoutin' around, makin' sure of everything before he pounced? Aw hell! It's all a pipedream—''

The words froze in his throat. At the window a face glared and gibbered soundlessly at him. Two icy eyes pierced his very soul. A shriek burst from his throat and that ghastly visage vanished. But the very air was permeated by the foul scent that had hung about the ancient mound. And now the door creaked—bent slowly inward. Brill backed up against the wall, his gun shaking in his hand. It did not occur to him to fire through the door; in his chaotic brain he had but one thought—that only that thin portal of wood separated him from some horror born out of the womb of night and gloom and the black past. His eyes were distended as he saw the door give, as he heard the staples of the bolt groan.

The door burst inward. Brill did not scream. His tongue was frozen to the roof of his mouth. His fear-glazed eyes took in the tall, vulturelike form—the icy eyes, the long black fingernails—the moldering garb, hideously ancient—the long spurred boot—the slouch hat with its crumbling feather—the flowing cloak that was falling to slow shreds. Framed in the black doorway crouched that abhorrent shape out of the past, and Brill's brain reeled. A savage cold radiated from the figure—the scent of moldering clay and charnelhouse refuse. And then the undead came at the living like a swooping vulture.

Brill fired pointblank and saw a shred of rotten cloth fly from the Thing's breast. The vampire reeled beneath the impact of the heavy ball, then righted himself and came on with frightful speed. Brill reeled back against the wall with a choking cry, the gun falling from his nerveless hand. The black legends were true then—human weapons were powerless—for may a man kill one already dead for long centuries, as mortals die?

Then the clawlike hands at his throat roused the young cowpuncher to a frenzy of madness. As his pioneer ancestors fought hand to hand against brain-shattering odds, Steve Brill fought the cold dead crawling thing that sought his life and his soul.

Of that ghastly battle Brill never remembered much. It was a blind chaos in which he screamed beastlike, tore and slugged and hammered, where long black nails like the talons of a panther tore at him, and pointed teeth snapped again and again at his throat. Rolling and tumbling about the room, both half enveloped by the musty folds of that ancient rotting cloak, they smote and tore at each other among the ruins of the shattered furniture, and the fury of the vampire was not more terrible than the fear-crazed desperation of his victim.

They crashed headlong into the table, knocking it down upon its side, and the coal oil lamp splintered on the floor, spraying the walls with sudden flame. Brill felt the bite of the burning oil that spattered him, but in the red frenzy of the fight he gave no heed. The black talons were tearing at him, the inhuman eyes burning icily into his soul; between his frantic fingers the withered flesh of the monster was hard as dry wood. And wave after wave of blind madness swept over Steve Brill. Like a man battling a nightmare he screamed and smote, while all about them the fire leaped up and caught at the walls and roof.

Through darting jets and licking tongues of flame they reeled and rolled like a demon and a mortal warring on the fire-lanced floors of hell. And in the growing tumult of the flames, Brill gathered himself for one last volcanic burst of frenzied strength. Breaking away and staggering up, gasping and bloody, he lunged blindly at the foul shape and caught it in a grip not even the vampire could break. And whirling his fiendish assailant bodily on high, he dashed him down across the uptilted edge of the fallen table as a man might break a stick of wood across his knee. Something cracked like a snapping branch and the vampire fell from Brill's grasp to writhe in a strange broken posture on the burning floor. Yet it was not dead, for its flaming eyes still burned on Brill with a ghastly hunger, and it strove to crawl toward him with its broken spine, as a dying snake crawls.

Brill, reeling and gasping, shook the blood from his eyes, and staggered blindly through the broken door. And as a man runs from the portals of hell, he ran stumblingly through the mesquite and chaparral until he fell from utter exhaustion. Looking back he saw the flame of the burning house and thanked God that it would burn until the very bones of Don Santiago de Valdez were utterly consumed and destroyed from the knowledge of men.

VAMPIRE VILLAGE

EDMOND HAMILTON (HUGH DAVIDSON)

Edmond Hamilton was best known to readers of Weird Tales *as the author of scores of science fantasies that mingled elements of fantasy, horror, and science fiction. Under the pen name of Hugh Davidson he wrote four straightforward horror stories, two concerned with vampires. In contrast to the short novel,* The Vampire Master, *about a vampire scourge ravaging a small town in the Catskill Mountains, "Vampire Village" is a costume drama set in the traditional environs of vampire legend.*

"KNOCK AGAIN," I told Croft. "There's always someone up in these village inns, and it's not midnight yet."

"I've almost hammered the door down already," he replied. "Either these Transylvanians sleep like the dead or—what the devil!"

"What's the matter?" I inquired. He was shaking his hand ruefully.

"Bruised my knuckles on something on the door," he said irritably. He detached it from the door, then passed it to me. I saw that it was a little wooden cross. "A mighty inconvenient way of expressing religious fervor!" exclaimed Croft, as he knocked again.

I looked up and down the white road, gleaming in the starlight. Along it were strung the score or so of high-peaked frame cottages that formed the village of Kranzak. Croft and I had counted, as we had swung through the Transylvanian hills all day and evening, on getting here for a late supper and lodging for the night.

But now Kranzak seemed to offer small prospect of either supper or bed, for from the shuttered windows of its houses showed no lights, and our hammering at the inn's door had produced no response. We had heard voices inside the inn as we had approached it but at our first knock they had become abruptly silent.

Croft, annoyed by hurting his hand on the cross, called out now in our defective Hungarian. "Let us in! This is an inn, isn't it?"

An elderly, tremulous voice answered. "It is the inn of Kranzak, yes, but it opens to no one tonight."

"Why not?" my companion demanded.

The same voice answered. "Because this is the night of vampires, sirs! The night of St. George, when all those who were in life vampires and servants of evil rise again to work evil until dawn. No door here in Kranzak will open until dawn."

"Night of the devil!" I exclaimed. "What kind of craziness in this?"

Croft laughed, turning from the door. "No use, Barton. We've run into their superstitions and it looks like no lodging for us tonight."

A different and shriller voice called from inside. "If you want lodging go on to Wieslant!" it told us, and was followed by a buzz of three or four voices within.

We stepped back into the road, baffled, looking along the village's houses. Each had some sort of cross at its door and each was still dark and without invitation.

"Well, it looks as if we go on to Wieslant, wherever it may be," I said.

"Wieslant—I don't remember it on the map," Croft said. "But these villages are all pretty close together, so it can't be far."

"Forward march, then," I ordered, and we started along the road in the starlight.

"The night of St. George—night of the vampires," I repeated, as we swung out of the village and on through the dark pine woods. "Was that whole village sitting behind locked doors in fear of that old vampire superstition, Croft?"

He nodded. "It's a very deep belief here in Transylvania. These Transylvanians believe implicitly that when people die who have sold themselves to evil they become, not dead, but undead—become vampires who rise from their tombs by night to suck blood and life from others."

"I've read something of the belief, of course," I said, "but I thought vampires could rise any night between sunset and dawn. I didn't know this St. George's night was the only night in the year in which they could rise."

Croft laughed. "There's a distinction between vampires, Barton. All vampires can rise from their graves each night until priests have carried out over their graves the binding and exorcising rites that prison them there. But on this one night each year, St. George's night, even these prisoned vampires, who far outnumber the others, can rise and work evil until dawn."

"Which is why St. George's night finds them locked up back there at Kranzak," I said, shaking my head. "And those crosses on the doors?" I asked, jerking a thumb toward the little wooden one Croft had passed me, which I had thrust into my breast pocket.

He smiled. "To protect them from the vampires tonight, of course. A cross is the one sure weapon against vampires, you know, the one thing they fear. It's all mighty interesting, this vampire superstition."

"And mighty inconvenient for us," I added. "If this Wieslant's people are as terrorized by vampires tonight as Kranzak's, we're out of luck for sure."

We hitched our knapsacks higher on our shoulders and bent to the steady task of walking. The white road wound through dense forests up a long slope that seemed a pass between the big hills ahead and to the right. There was no moon, but the thin starlight outlined the road clearly in its windings through the dark pine woods.

As we swung on for steady mile after mile it came to me that the very gloominess of this somber Transylvanian landscape must be at the bottom of its people's fearful beliefs. It would be easy to believe, I speculated, that in the midnight darkness of the hills about us supernatural beings of evil were moving, loosed this one night from the tomb.

We could see once or twice black flying shapes of considerable size moving in the starlight low over distant woods. And while it was apparent enough to Croft and me that these must be hawks or owls searching the night forests for prey, I could well see, I thought, how any Transylvanians seeing them would believe them vampires abroad on this, their night.

Croft's voice at last interrupted my speculations. "There are the lights of a village down there," he announced. "Wieslant's I suppose."

We had reached the rim of a bowl-shaped valley some miles across that was encircled by the hills. Down in the darkness at this bowl's center gleamed a little pattern of lights, with at one spot the redder glow of fires.

"Nothing shut up about Wieslant, apparently," I said with rising spirits. "We may get supper and a bed tonight, after all."

"Looks as though there's a chance of it, at any rate," Croft agreed.

We swung down into the bowl-like valley toward the village's lights. Wieslant, it was apparent as we entered it, was a place unusually ancient, for the houses along its little streets were more antique in appearance than any we had yet seen. They had the grotesquely carved scrollwork and odd-shaped doors and windows common to the houses of the section a few hundred years ago.

These houses were illuminated with yellow candlelight but we could see no occupants in them as we passed among them. The reason for this was explained when we neared the open green at the village's center, for large fires were burning there, swift, gay music was audible, and gathered round the fire-lit green and dancing to the music were the people of Wieslant.

As Croft and I approached we could see these people only as black shapes dancing between us and the glowing fires. Their dark forms spun with such swiftness that to us, with the light in our eyes, they seemed to leave the ground and whirl through the air in the mad rush of the dance. Croft and I drew nearer and stopped in the shadows outside the fire-lit green's circle, watching with astonishment.

A half-dozen fires spilled ruddy light across the green, and around each fire one of the strange dances was going on. The dancers were clad, the men in outlandish brilliant jackets and tight trousers, the women in similarly bright skirts and bodices, the festal attire of Transylvanian peasants. Yet these costumes were of an older and odder style than any others we had seen.

Around the green's edge in the firelight were a hundred or two villagers watching and applauding the dance. They were clad like the dancers, there being in fact no modern dress visible. At one place was a peasant orchestra of stringed instruments pouring out the wild, swift music. Beside this a tall, white-mustached and fierce-faced oldster was calling above the din to the dancers as they whirled and spun.

I had never seen such a strange picture of mad gaiety, and Croft and I watched marveling from back in the shadows. These anciently dressed villagers seemed flinging themselves into the merriment of the dance with utter abandon. The eyes of dancers and spectators alike glowed crimson, apparently from reflected fire-light.

Suddenly one of the spectators glimpsed Croft and me back in the dark. He uttered a stabbing cry, and instantly all of them were rushing toward us.

In our momentary stupefaction it almost seemed that they were hurtling through the air to attack us, a crowded vision of crimson eyes and white-gleaming teeth. But when almost upon Croft and me they stopped short as though struck back!

They encircled us, giving vent to a babble of excited cries in a Hungarian dialect that was almost beyond our understanding, while their excited, gleaming eyes held upon us. The din was immense.

"Excitable beggars, aren't they?" said Croft. "Can you make out what they're shouting about?"

"Not while they're all crying at once," I answered. "What's the matter with them? I thought for a moment they were attacking us."

"These Transylvanians are all an excitable bunch," he said. "This looks like the head man of the village coming, and he ought to be able to calm them down."

It was the tall, white-mustached oldster who had been calling to the dancers who now shouldered through the throng toward us. He was dressed like the rest in the brilliant ancient festal costume, which set off his tall figure well enough. He bowed to us, his eyes sharp upon ours.

"Welcome to Wieslant, sirs," he addressed us, in the oddly twisted dialect of the others. "We did not expect strangers here tonight."

"I'm sorry if we've intruded on your festal celebrations," Croft told him. "We didn't mean to do so."

The other waved the apology aside smilingly. "My people here—I am Mihai

Hallos, headman of Wieslant—see but few strangers and so are excited when any visit our little village.''

"Well, it's not by intention we came," Croft said. "Back at the last village, Kranzak, every one was locked up for fear of vampires. They must have been afraid we were vampires ourselves, for they wouldn't let us in but told us to go on to Wieslant.''

Hallos' smile deepened and a laugh ran through the crowd. "Kranzak's people are much afraid of vampires on this night, it is true," the headman said, "for not far from Kranzak was located the vampire village.''

"Vampire village?" Croft repeated interrogatively, but Hallos waved his hand. "It is a belief in this part of Transylvania—I will tell you the story later. It keeps many villages in fear on this night.''

"Well, I'm glad at any rate it doesn't keep you of Wieslant locked up," I remarked. "We didn't fancy walking all night.''

"You'll find excellent accommodations here at Wieslant," Hallos assured me. "Indeed, you could have come at no better time than tonight.''

Again the chuckling laugh ran through the crowd, though I could see nothing humorous in the words. These gleaming-eyed, strangely dressed villagers were making both Croft and myself rather uncomfortable by their staring at us from all sides, and Hallos must have seen this.

"Our inn is over there at the green's edge," he said. "May I not lead you there?''

We protested against his taking the trouble, but with true Transylvanian courtesy he waved our protests aside. Hallos motioned the villagers to make way for us and was turning again toward us when I bumped awkwardly into him face to face.

To my surprise he staggered and fell to his knees, his hand on his heart and his face contorted by a spasm of agony. He regained his feet, though, before we had time to help him up, and I apologized as best I could for my clumsiness.

"It was not your fault," he said with hand still on his breast, "but I have a weakness here and the thing in your breast pocket prodded me when we collided.''

I looked down and saw projecting from my breast-pocket the little wooden cross Croft had handed me at Kranzak, which I had forgotten. "I'm very sorry," I said. "It was stupid of me to run into you.''

Hallos smiled and shook his head, but I noticed as we started through the crowd toward the inn that he kept Croft between him and myself. Apparently he did not intend trusting himself again to my awkwardness.

And as we moved through the gaily dressed villagers who parted to allow us passage I even thought that they shrank rather farther away from me than from Croft. It was a little discomfiting to me.

Hallos talked on urbanely as he led us to the inn. The music behind us had recommenced and the villagers were again dancing by the time we came to the ancient-looking inn at the green's edge.

We followed the head man into the stone-paved, broad-beamed tavern room. A great fire flickered in a wall fireplace, and behind the small bar at the room's end the fat and white-haired innkeeper was serving bottles of queer, twisted shapes to a dozen gaily costumed men and women.

They had been engaged in wild talk and laughter as we entered but fell dead silent at sight of Hallos and ourselves, staring toward us. I was struck again by the trick of the firelight falling upon these people's faces to make their eyes seem somehow crimson-lit.

The fat innkeeper came forward and Hallos made introduction.

"This is Kallant, innkeeper of Wieslant and as excellent a one as can be found in Transylvania," he told us smilingly. "He will be glad to see you, for it is not often he lodges strangers."

"Not often," admitted the fat Kallant, laughing in a strange way. "In fact, it is not often that I have custom of any kind. You will wish two rooms, sirs?"

"Oh, one room will do for both of us," Croft answered. "We're more concerned about supper than the room, right now."

"If you will do us an honor," Hallos interjected. "Our Wieslant festivities on this feast-night continue all night, and some of us leading villagers always have supper here at two o'clock. You would honor us by joining us."

"We'll be honored to do so," Croft said. "It's almost two now, so Barton and I had better brush up a little."

"I will show you the room, sirs," said Kallant, turning with a candle toward the narrow stair that rose back in the shadows.

We were entering the dark stairway with him when Hallos's voice stopped us. He was gesturing with an amused smile toward the wooden cross that still projected from my breast-pocket.

"That emblem of piety were best left in your room, sir," he told me smilingly. "On this night piety is forgotten here and we think but of merriment."

Croft and I laughed. "It's not really mine," I told the head man, "but of course I'll leave it. I don't want to be the skeleton at your feast."

As we went up the dark narrow stairway after the fat Kallant I heard a sudden babble of wild voices break out in the tavern room we had just quitted. There cut across them and silenced them the sharp voice of Hallos, and I smiled at this evidence that our courtly host could play the tyrant over his simple subjects when so inclined.

The stair led up into a long hall dimly lit by one or two candles in wall sockets along it. There were doors but half visible in the shadows, and Kallant led us to one of these and opened it, gesturing inside as he placed his candle in a socket inside the door.

"This will suit you, sirs," he told us. "It's a little musty—we don't often have custom here—but should be comfortable enough."

"It's quite all right," we assured him. "Tell Hallos we'll be down in a few moments." He bowed and withdrew. We looked about us.

"Musty is right," I commented. "Looks as if it hadn't been used for centuries."

The room, in fact, was covered with dust that lay thick over the floor and furniture and old-fashioned wooden bed. Through the odd-shaped windows we could glimpse the green outside, where the fires still were burning and the dark shadows of the dancers whirling to the wild music.

Croft and I spruced up as well as possible and then left the room. When we emerged from the dark stairway into the inn's tavern room again we found the head man Hallos there with two dozen or more men and women. They were without exception dressed in the antique festal costumes to which we were now accustomed.

Hallos almost rushed to meet us as we entered the tavern room, his eyes alight. But a little from us he stopped, staring at my breast.

I looked down and saw that I had forgotten to discard the little wooden cross from that pocket. "Oh, I'm sorry," I said. "But I suppose having the thing doesn't really matter?"

"Of course not," he told me courteously. "Will you not meet some of our people? These are my own two daughters."

He made introductions and we chatted as best we could in our halting Hungarian with the gay groups. I was somewhat chagrined, I admit, to see that they tended to gather around Croft and to avoid me. Recalling the head man's words, I supposed they judged from the cross projecting from my pocket that I was some strict and serious devotee.

Croft saw my isolation and shot amused glances at me now and then, for he was making great progress with the two brilliant-cheeked beauties Hallos had introduced as his daughters. Hallos himself talked with me, though at a little distance, until the fat Kallant appeared from another room to announce that the supper was ready.

We passed into the candlelit dining hall, where a long table laden with Transylvanian dishes and wines awaited us. Hallos seated himself at the table's end with Croft and the younger daughter at his right, and me and the elder daughter at his left. But before I could address a word to this elder sister she pulled her chair as far as possible from me and turned her back upon me to talk to her other neighbor.

The supper was gay, and Croft and the younger sister opposite me were of the gayest, though I was feeling somewhat chagrined at the cold treatment these people accorded me. I made up for it by attacking the spicy foods and strong wines with vigor, nor was Croft much behind me, since we had not eaten for a dozen hours.

The food and wines were as delicious as I had ever tasted but seemed strangely lacking in filling qualities; in fact, after disposing of a half-dozen dishes and several glasses I felt really as hungry as on beginning. Yet though Croft too looked a little puzzled, the others at table seemed not to notice it.

The room rang with laughter, chatter and clink of glasses, with echoes now and then of the dance music from outside. Kallant hovered about to see that all were served, and at the table's end Hallos was the picture of a courteous host.

During a lull in the chatter of voices Croft addressed him. "You said you'd tell us about the vampire village located near Kranzak," he reminded. "I'd like to hear the story if the rest don't mind."

Hallos smiled and I saw suppressed mirth on the faces of our companions, Kallant grinning in the background. "Why, all here know it well," the head man said, "but if it would interest you—"

At our quick assurance he went on "We of Transylvania have for many centuries known that vampires do exist. We have known that men and women who sell themselves in life to the forces of evil do not when they die become dead, but undead, vampires. By day vampires lie as though dead in their graves, but by night rise as though living and suck blood and life from whatever unprotected people they encounter.

"We Transylvanians know also that against the cross vampires are powerless. So whenever a vampire's grave is detected in this country, priests perform over it ceremonies of the cross that bind the vampire in his grave. Yet even vampires so bound and prisoned can on one night of the year, the night of St. George, still rise and work until dawn.

"Almost two hundred and fifty years ago there was in this section of Transylvania a village located not far from Kranzak. And this village near Kranzak came to be haunted by vampires as no village had ever been before. The forces of evil worked there until in the graves of that village lay some hundreds of vampires who came forth each night!

"It was, then, a vampire village! The living people left in it fled to Kranzak and other places, but the vampires remained. Each day that village lay deserted and untenanted beneath the sun. But each night the vampires rose to move through and inhabit the village as though alive, venturing often to attack people in nearby villages.

"So at last the people of the surrounding section came with many priests to put an end to this vampire village. Over each grave the priests carried out their binding rites, prisoning each vampire thus. From then on, though no living people ever again inhabited it, the vampires came forth no more by night save on that one night each year, the night of St. George, when all vampires are freed. On that night the vampire village again swarms until dawn with its undead inhabitants."

"And since the night of St. George is tonight," Croft smiled, "they feared back in Kranzak that we two were from the vampire village?"

"That is so," said Hallos, also smiling, "for despite the centuries that have passed, they of Kranzak and the other villages still fear this night of the year when the vampire village wakes to life again."

"But you here in Wieslant tonight don't seem to have much fear of the village of vampires?" I said. They all laughed at that.

"It is because St. George is our patron, and so on his festal night we have his protection," Hallos explained, "and can give ourselves up to merrymaking without fear."

Croft shook his head. "Strange, the power of some of these beliefs," he said. "Yet they fit with your ancient houses and costumes, somehow."

The elder Hallos girl laughed. "These costumes we wear on this festal night, all of us, but they must seem very odd to you," she told Croft.

"They seem beautiful," he told her. "Yet they make me feel as though Barton and I had in some way strayed into the past."

"Our dances are ancient ones too on this night," she said. "Will you not come with my sister and me to watch them?"

Her invitation so pointedly excluded me that Croft shot a grinning glance at me as he accepted. "Coming along, Barton?" he asked as we all rose.

I shook my head. "I'm going upstairs and get some much-needed sleep," I told him. "It's almost morning, you know."

Our company passed back into the tavern room, Croft between the two sisters and I with Hallos at my side. It was evident to me that Croft had made an impression on the two gaily clad beauties, for their eyes and little white teeth gleamed alike as they laughed up to him, their hands tightening on his arms in a caressing and almost possessive manner.

"I'll be up shortly, Barton," Croft told me as they turned to the door. "I could stand some sleep myself, all right."

"Sleep—there is enough of sleep in the world!" exclaimed the younger sister. "Tonight is a festal night and not for sleep but for life—for life!"

She spoke with astounding vehemence and with eyes really fiery, rather startling Croft, and myself also. Hallos, his own eyes crimson, shot her a furious look, and at that she dropped her lashes demurely.

As Croft went out with them I gave him a meaningful glance telling him not to make a fool of himself over the two Transylvanian beauties. Most of the company followed them and I bade them a general good-night. To Hallos and Kallant, who remained, I added my thanks before starting up the stair.

As I went up the dark stairway I thought I heard a quick step below and turned, but there was no one beneath. I heard Hallos's voice hissing to someone, evidently Kallant—"Not yet, you fool, he has it still with him!"

Kallant's muttered answer was inaudible, but their dispute was apparently no affair of mine and I went on up to our room. In the dim candlelight the musty bed was unattractive, but I sat down, yawning, glancing out the dusty window. The fires on the green still glowed red, but the music had stopped and the dark shapes of the villagers seemed clustered round some object of interest.

I loosened my collar, tossing onto the table with a smile the wooden cross whose significance of piety had given the villagers such a distaste for me. I was tossing our fat little blue guidebook after it when it occurred to me to look up Wieslant's exact location in it.

Croft had said that Wieslant was not on the map and I found it to be so, there being no village at all marked there between that of Kranzak and the distant one of Holf. Somewhat puzzled, I turned to the book's text but found no description of Wieslant there either, and was giving up with disgust at the inefficiency of guidebook makers when the name "Wieslant" in a footnote caught my eye.

As I started to read this I was aware subconsciously of two things: of a rush and commotion among the dark crowd out on the village green, and of the rustling sound of someone moving in the hall outside my door. But had thunder detonated about me it could not have aroused in me the unutterable horror that was rising in me as I read the fine type of the footnote.

The words seemed dancing before my eyes—

"Wieslant . . . approximately midway between Kranzak and Holf . . . deserted entirely in 1683 through fear of vampires . . . still called in that section the vampire village . . . now almost wholly in—"

And even as the terrific truth smashed home to my reeling brain there thrust to my ears from the green outside an agonized scream in Croft's voice.

I leapt across the room and flung the door open. Hallos and Kallant stood outside it with eyes gleaming hell-crimson at me out of the faces of fiends. The two shot as one through the air toward me and as they bore me backward I felt their sharp fangs at my throat, felt in my face their breath like airs of cold corruption from the grave.

But as I reeled backward with those two hell-vampires upon me, my outflung hand touched the table, and something on the table that my fingers closed on instinctively and that I thrust against them. It was the little cross, and as it touched them it hurled them back across the room and against the wall as though titanic forces had smitten them.

With eyes red flames of hell, Hallos and Kallant glared from there at me as I swayed to the door, Croft's scream stabbing again and weaker to my ears. I was flinging myself down the dark stairway with the two black, fire-eyed shapes of Hallos and Kallant after me, the cross still clutched in my grasp. I was reeling out onto the green to hear again Croft's muffled cry.

Croft was down and the madly whirling, scarlet-eyed vampire throng was upon him, white teeth sucking his throat. Half of them were rushing toward me, black fiend-shapes against the fires that were dimming as a faint promise of light showed eastward, black vampire-shapes that were about me and separating me from Croft.

They recoiled and parted as I stumbled forward, extending the cross. They raged about me like mad shadow-shapes of hell, their baffled shrieks in my ears. I was at Croft's side, and those upon him recoiled as I dropped beside him with the cross. He seemed senseless, and I felt my own senses going and the cross dropping from my weakened fingers as around us raged the ghastly vampire horde.

They were closing upon us as the cross slipped from my nerveless hand—the fiend-faces of Hallos and his daughters and all the others spun closer in a mad vista of red eyes and avid lips and sharp white teeth—and then from the paling east struck a gray shaft of dawn. Instantly it was as though gray mist enveloped the vampire throng and all the village about us, a mist that darkened in my mind as I lost consciousness.

The dawnlight eastward had changed from gray to gold when I came back to consciousness. Croft was stirring weakly, and as he sat up I saw and picked from the ground beside me, automatically, a little wooden cross. We staggered to our feet and gazed dazedly about us.

Ancient, weed-grown ruins stretched in the golden light around us. There were broken masonry outlines of building foundations, and in one place an enclosure of half-visible, time-worn tombstones, but there was no standing house or structure, or any sign of life. Croft and I stared, wordlessly, wildly, all the world silent about us in the light of the morning sun.

REVELATIONS IN BLACK

CARL JACOBI

Bizarre adventures that begin with the discovery of a book of secret lore constitute an entire subgenre of weird fiction. Carl Jacobi was among the earliest writers to link the scholarly thirst for knowledge stimulated by such discoveries with the seductive allure of the vampire. One of the most popular vampire stories to appear in Weird Tales, *"Revelations in Black" served as the title story of Jacobi's first fiction collection in 1947.*

IT WAS A dreary, forlorn establishment way down on Harbor Street. An old sign announced the legend: "Giovanni Larla—Antiques," and a dingy window revealed a display half masked in dust.

Even as I crossed the threshold that cheerless September afternoon, driven from the sidewalk by a gust of rain and perhaps a fascination for all antiques, the gloominess fell upon me like a material pall. Inside were half darkness, piled boxes, and a monstrous tapestry, frayed with the warp showing in worn places. An Italian Renaissance wine cabinet shrank despondently in its corner and seemed to frown at me as I passed.

"Good afternoon, *Signor*. There is something you wish to buy? A picture, a ring, a vase perhaps?"

I peered at the squat, pudgy bulk of the Italian proprietor there in the shadows and hesitated.

"Just looking around," I said, turning my eyes to the jumble about me. "Nothing in particular. . . ."

The man's oily face moved in smile as though he had heard the remark a thousand times before. He sighed, stood there in thought a moment, the rain drumming and swishing against the outer pane. Then very deliberately he stepped to the shelves and glanced up and down them considering. I moved to his side, letting my eyes sweep across the stacked array of ancient oddities. At length he drew forth an object which I perceived to be a painted chalice.

"An authentic sixteenth century Tandart," he murmured. "A work of art, *Signor*."

I shook my head. "No pottery," I said. "Books perhaps, but no pottery."

He frowned slowly. "I have books too," he replied, "rare books which nobody sells but me, Giovanni Larla. But you must look at my other treasures too."

There was, I found, no hurrying the man. A quarter of an hour passed, during which I had to see a Glycon cameo brooch, a carved chair of some indeterminate style and period, and a muddle of yellowed statuettes, small oils and one or two dreary Portland vases. Several times I glanced at my watch impatiently, wondering how I might break away from this Italian and his gloomy shop. Already the fascination of its dust and shadows had begun to wear off, and I was anxious to reach the street.

But when he had conducted me well toward the rear of the shop, something caught my fancy. I drew then from the shelf the first book of horror. If I had but known the terrible events that were to follow, if I could only have had a foresight into the future that September day, I swear I would have avoided the book like a leprous thing, would have shunned that wretched antique store and the very street it stood on like places accursed. A thousand times I have wished my eyes had never rested on that cover in black. What writhings of the soul, what terrors, what unrest, what madness would have been spared me!

But never dreaming the hideous secret of its pages I fondled it casually and remarked:

"An unusual book. What is it?"

Larla glanced up and scowled.

"That is not for sale," he said quietly. "I don't know how it got on these shelves. It was my poor brother's."

The volume in my hand was indeed unusual in appearance. Measuring but four inches across and five inches in length and bound in black velvet with each outside corner protected with a triangle of ivory, it was the most beautiful piece of bookbinding I had ever seen. In the center of the cover was mounted a tiny piece of ivory intricately cut in the shape of a skull. But it was the title of the book that excited my interest. Embroidered in gold braid, the title read:

"Five Unicorns and a Pearl."

I looked at Larla. "How much?" I asked and reached for my wallet.

He shook his head. "No, it is not for sale. It is . . . it is the last work of my brother. He wrote it just before he died in the institution."

"The institution?" I queried.

Larla made no reply but stood staring at the book, his mind obviously drifting away in deep thought. A moment of silence dragged by. There was a strange gleam in his eyes when finally he spoke. And I thought I saw his fingers tremble slightly.

"My brother, Alessandro, was a fine man before he wrote that book," he said slowly. "He wrote beautifully, *Signor,* and he was strong and healthy. For hours I could sit while he read to me his poems. He was a dreamer, Alessandro; he loved everything beautiful, and the two of us were very happy.

"All . . . until that terrible night. Then he . . . but no . . . a year has passed now. It is best to forget." He passed his hand before his eyes and drew in his breath sharply.

"What happened?" I asked sympathetically, his words arousing my curiosity.

"Happened, *Signor*? I do not really know. It was all so confusing. He became suddenly ill, ill without reason. The flush of sunny Italy, which was always on his cheek, faded, and he grew white and drawn. His strength left him day by day. Doctors prescribed, gave medicines, but nothing helped. He grew steadily weaker until . . . until that night."

I looked at him curiously, impressed by his perturbation.

"And then—?" I urged.

Hands opening and closing, Larla seemed to sway unsteadily; his liquid eyes opened wide to the brows, and his voice was strained and tense as he continued:

"And then . . . oh, if I could but forget! It was horrible. Poor Alessandro came home screaming, sobbing, tearing his hair. He was . . . he was stark raving mad!

"They took him to the institution for the insane and said he needed a complete rest, that he had suffered from some terrific mental shock. He . . . died three weeks later with the crucifix on his lips."

For a moment I stood there in silence, staring out at the falling rain. Then I said:

"He wrote this book while confined to the institution?"

Larla nodded absently.

"Three books," he replied. "Two others exactly like the one you have in your hand. The bindings he made, of course, when he was quite well. It was his original intention, I believe, to pen in them by hand the verses of Marini. He was very clever at such work. But the wanderings of his mind which filled the pages now, I have never read. Nor do I intend to. I want to keep with me the memory of him when he was happy. This book has come on these shelves by mistake. I shall put it with his other possessions."

My desire to read the few pages bound in velvet increased a thousandfold when I found they were unobtainable. I have always had an interest in abnormal psychology and have gone through a number of books on the subject. Here was the work of a man confined in the asylum for the insane. Here was the unexpurgated writing of an educated brain gone mad. And unless my intuition failed me, here was a suggestion of some deep mystery. My mind was made up. I must have it.

I turned to Larla and chose my words carefully.

"I can well appreciate your wish to keep the book," I said, "and since you refuse to sell, may I ask if you would consider lending it to me for just one night? If I promised to return it in the morning?"

The Italian hesitated. He toyed undecidedly with a heavy gold watch chain.

"No. I am sorry. . . ."

"Ten dollars and back tomorrow unharmed."

Larla studied his shoe.

"Very well, *Signor,* I will trust you. But please, I ask you, please be sure and return it."

That night in the quiet of my apartment I opened the book. Immediately my attention was drawn to three lines scrawled in a feminine hand across the inside of the front cover, lines written in a faded red solution that looked more like blood than ink. They read:

"Revelations meant to destroy but only binding without the stake. Read, fool, and enter my field, for we are chained to the spot. Oh wo unto Larla."

I mused over these undecipherable sentences for some time without solving their meaning. At last, shrugging my shoulders, I turned to the first page and began the last work of Alessandro Larla, the strangest story I had ever in my years of browsing through old books, come upon.

"On the evening of the fifteenth of October I turned my steps into the cold and walked until I was tired. The roar of the present was in the distance when I came to twenty-six bluejays silently contemplating the ruins. Passing in the midst of them I wandered by the skeleton trees and seated myself where I could watch the leering fish. A child worshipped. Glass threw the moon at me. Grass sang a litany at my feet. And the pointed shadow moved slowly to the left.

"I walked along the silver gravel until I came to five unicorns galloping beside water of the past. Here I found a pearl, a magnificent pearl, a pearl beautiful but black. Like a flower it carried a rich perfume, and once I thought the odor was but a mask, but why should such a perfect creation need a mask?

"I sat between the leering fish and the five galloping unicorns, and I fell madly in love with the pearl. The past lost itself in drabness and—"

I laid the book down and sat watching the smoke-curls from my pipe eddy ceilingward. There was much more, but I could make no sense to any of it. All was in that strange style and completely incomprehensible. And yet it seemed the story was more than the mere wanderings of a madman. Behind it all seemed to lie a narrative cloaked in symbolism.

Something about the few sentences—just what I cannot say—had cast an immediate spell of depression over me. The vague lines weighed upon my mind, hung before my eyes like a design, and I felt myself slowly seized by a deep feeling of uneasiness.

The air of the room grew heavy and close. The open casement and the out-of-doors seemed to beckon to me. I walked to the window, thrust the curtain aside, stood there, smoking furiously. Let me say that regular habits have long been a part of my makeup. I am not addicted to nocturnal strolls or late mean-derings before seeking my bed; yet now, curiously enough, with the pages of the book still in my mind I suddenly experienced an indefinable urge to leave my apartment and walk the darkened streets.

I paced the room nervously, irritated that the sensation did not pass. The clock on the mantel pushed its ticks slowly through the quiet. And at length with a shrug I threw my pipe to the table, reached for my hat and coat and made for the door.

Ridiculous as it may sound, upon reaching the street I found that urge had increased to a distinct attraction. I felt that under no circumstances must I turn any direction but northward, and although this way led into a district quite unknown to me, I was in a moment pacing forward, choosing streets deliberately and heading without knowing why toward the outskirts of the city. It was a brilliant moonlit night in September. Summer had passed and already there was the smell of frosted vegetation in the air. The great chimes in Capitol tower were sounding midnight, and the buildings and shops and later the private houses were dark and silent as I passed.

Try as I would to erase from my memory the queer book which I had just read, the mystery of its pages hammered at me, arousing my curiosity, dampening my spirits. "Five Unicorns and a Pearl!" What did it all mean?

More and more I realized as I went on that a power other than my own will was leading my steps. It was absurd, and I tried to resist, to turn back. Yet once when I did momentarily come to a halt that attraction swept upon me as inex-orably as the desire for a narcotic.

It was far out on Easterly Street that I came upon a high stone wall flanking the sidewalk. Over its ornamented top I could see the shadows of a dark building set well back in the grounds. A wrought-iron gate in the wall opened upon a view of wild desertion and neglect. Swathed in the light of the moon, an old courtyard strewn with fountains, stone benches and statues lay tangled in rank weeds and undergrowth. The windows of the building, which evidently had once been a private dwelling, were boarded up, all except those on a little tower or cupola rising to a point in the front. And here the glass caught the blue-gray light and refracted it into the shadows.

Before that gate my feet stopped like dead things. The psychic power which had been leading me had now become a reality. Directly from the courtyard it emanated, drawing me toward it with an intensity that smothered all reluctance.

Strangely enough, the gate was unlocked; and feeling like a man in a trance I swung the creaking hinges and entered, making my way along a grass-grown path to one of the benches. It seemed that once inside the court the distant sounds of the city died away, leaving a hollow silence broken only by the wind rustling through the tall dead weeds. Rearing up before me, the building with its dark wings, cupola and facade oddly resembled a colossal hound, crouched and ready to spring.

There were several fountains, weatherbeaten and ornamented with curious figures, to which at the time I paid only casual attention. Farther on, half hidden by the underbrush, was the lifesize statue of a little child kneeling in position of prayer. Erosion on the soft stone had disfigured the face, and in the half-light the carved features presented an expression strangely grotesque and repelling.

How long I sat there in the quiet, I don't know. The surroundings under the moonlight blended harmoniously with my mood. But more than that I seemed physically unable to rouse myself and pass on.

It was with a suddenness that brought me electrified to my feet that I became aware of the real significance of the objects about me. Held motionless, I stood there running my eyes wildly from place to place, refusing to believe. Surely I must be dreaming. In the name of all that was unusual this . . . this absolutely couldn't be. And yet—

It was the fountain at my side that had caught my attention first. Across the top of the water basin were *five stone unicorns,* all identically carved, each seeming to follow the other in galloping procession. Looking farther, prompted now by a madly rising recollection, I saw that the cupola, towering high above the house, eclipsed the rays of the moon and threw *a long pointed shadow* across the ground *at my left.* The other fountain some distance away was ornamented with the figure of a stone fish, *a fish* whose empty eye-sockets *were leering* straight in my direction. And the climax of it all—the wall! At intervals of every three feet on the top of the street expanse were mounted crude carven stone shapes of birds. And counting them I saw that *those birds were twenty-six bluejays*.

Unquestionably—startling and impossible as it seemed—I was in the same setting as described in Larla's book! It was a staggering revelation, and my mind reeled at the thought of it. How strange, how odd that I should be drawn to a portion of the city I had never before frequented and thrown into the midst of a narrative written almost a year before!

I saw now that Alessandro Larla, writing as a patient in the institution for the insane, had seized isolated details but neglected to explain them. Here was a problem for the psychologist, the mad, the symbolic, the incredible story of the dead Italian. I was bewildered, confused, and I pondered for an answer.

As if to soothe my perturbation there stole into the court then a faint odor of perfume. Pleasantly it touched my nostrils, seemed to blend with the moonlight. I breathed it in deeply as I stood there by the curious fountain. But slowly that odor became more noticeable, grew stronger, a sickish sweet smell that began to creep down my lungs like smoke. And absently I recognized it. Heliotrope! The honeyed aroma blanketed the garden, thickened the air, seemed to fall upon me like a drug.

And then came my second surprise of the evening. Looking about to discover the source of the irritating fragrance I saw opposite me, seated on another stone bench, a woman. She was dressed entirely in black, and her face was hidden by a veil. She seemed unaware of my presence. Her head was slightly bowed, and her whole position suggested a person deep in contemplation.

I noticed also the thing that crouched by her side. It was a dog, a tremendous brute with a head strangely out of proportion and eyes as large as the ends of big spoons. For several moments I stood staring at the two of them. Although the air was quite chilly, the woman wore no over-jacket, only the black dress relieved solely by the whiteness of her throat.

With a sigh of regret at having my pleasant solitude thus disturbed I moved across the court until I stood at her side. Still she showed no recognition of my presence, and clearing my throat I said hesitatingly:

"I suppose you are the owner here. I . . . I really didn't know the place was occupied, and the gate . . . well, the gate was unlocked. I'm sorry I trespassed."

She made no reply to that, and the dog merely gazed at me in dumb silence. No graceful words of polite departure came to my lips, and I moved hesitatingly toward the gate.

"Please don't go," she said suddenly, looking up. "I'm lonely. Oh, if you but knew how lonely I am!" She moved to one side on the bench and motioned that I sit beside her. The dog continued to examine me with its big eyes.

Whether it was the nearness of that odor of heliotrope, the suddenness of it all, or perhaps the moonlight, I did not know, but at her words a thrill of pleasure ran through me, and I accepted the proffered seat.

There followed an interval of silence, during which I puzzled my brain for a means to start conversation. But abruptly she turned to the beast and said in German:

"Fort mit dir, Johann!"

The dog rose obediently to its feet and stole slowly off into the shadows. I watched it for a moment until it disappeared in the direction of the house. Then the woman said to me in English which was slightly stilted and marked with an accent:

"It has been ages since I have spoken to anyone. . . . We are strangers. I do not know you, and you do not know me. Yet . . . strangers sometimes find in each other a bond of interest. Supposing . . . supposing we forget customs and formality of introduction? Shall we?"

For some reason I felt my pulse quicken as she said that. "Please do," I replied. "A spot like this is enough introduction in itself. Tell me, do you live here?"

She made no answer for a moment, and I began to fear I had taken her suggestion too quickly. Then she began slowly:

"My name is Perle von Mauren, and I am really a stranger to your country, though I have been here now more than a year. My home is in Austria near what is now the Czechoslovakian frontier. You see, it was to find my only brother that I came to the United States. During the war he was a lieutenant under General Mackensen, but in 1916, in April I believe it was, he . . . he was reported missing.

"War is a cruel thing. It took our money; it took our castle on the Danube, and then—my brother. Those following years were horrible. We lived always in doubt, hoping against hope that he was still living.

"Then after the armistice a fellow officer claimed to have served next to him on grave-digging detail at a French prison camp near Monpré. And later came a thin rumor that he was in the United States. I gathered together as much money as I could and came here in search of him."

Her voice dwindled off, and she sat in silence staring at the brown weeds. When she resumed, her voice was low and wavering.

"I . . . found him . . . but would to God I hadn't! He . . . he was no longer living."

I stared at her. "Dead?" I asked.

The veil trembled as though moved by a shudder, as though her thoughts had exhumed some terrible event of the past. Unconscious of my interruption she went on:

"Tonight I came here—I don't know why—merely because the gate was unlocked, and there was a place of quiet within. Now have I bored you with my confidences and personal history?"

"Not at all," I replied. "I came here by chance myself. Probably the beauty of the place attracted me. I dabble in amateur photography occasionally and react strongly to unusual scenes. Tonight I went for a midnight stroll to relieve my mind from the bad effect of a book I was reading."

She made a strange reply to that, a reply away from our line of thought and which seemed an interjection that escaped her involuntarily.

"Books," she said, "are powerful things. They can fetter one more than the walls of a prison."

She caught my puzzled stare at the remark and added hastily: "It is odd that we should meet here."

For a moment I didn't answer. I was thinking of her heliotrope perfume, which for a woman of her apparent culture was applied in far too great a quantity to manifest good taste. The impression stole upon me that the perfume cloaked some secret, that if it were removed I should find . . . but what? It was ridiculous, and I tried to cast the feeling aside.

The hours passed, and still we sat there talking, enjoying each other's companionship. She did not remove her veil, and though I was burning with a desire to see her features, I had not dared ask her to. A strange nervousness had slowly seized me. The woman was a charming conversationalist, but there was about her an indefinable something which produced in me a distinct feeling of unease.

It was, I should judge, but a few moments before the first streaks of dawn when it happened. As I look back now, even with mundane objects and thoughts on every side, it is not difficult to realize the dire significance, the absolute baseness of that vision. But at the time my brain was too much in a whirl to understand.

A thin shadow moving across the garden attracted my gaze once again into the night about me. I looked up over the spire of the deserted house and stared as if struck by a blow. For a moment I thought I had seen a curious cloud formation racing low directly above me, a cloud black and impenetrable with two winglike ends strangely in the shape of a monstrous flying bat.

I blinked my eyes hard and looked again.

"That cloud!" I exclaimed, "that strange cloud! . . . Did you see—"

I stopped and stared dumbly.

The bench at my side was empty. The woman had disappeared.

During the next day I went about my professional duties in the law office with only half interest, and my business partner looked at me queerly several times when he came upon me mumbling to myself. The incidents of the evening before were rushing through my mind in grand turmoil. Questions unanswerable hammered at me. That I should have come upon the very details described by mad Larla in his strange book: the leering fish, the praying child, the twenty-six bluejays, the pointed shadow of the cupola—it was unexplainable; it was weird.

"Five Unicorns and a Pearl." The unicorns were the stone statues ornamenting the old fountain, yes—but the pearl? With a start I suddenly recalled the name of the woman in black: *Perle* von Mauren. The revelation climaxed my train of thought. What did it all mean?

Dinner had little attraction for me that evening. Earlier I had gone to the antique-dealer and begged him to loan me the sequel, the second volume of his brother Alessandro. When he had refused, objected because I had not yet returned the first book, my nerves had suddenly jumped on edge. I felt like a narcotic fiend faced with the realization that he could not procure the desired drug. In desperation, yet hardly knowing why, I offered the man money, more money, until at length I had come away, my powers of persuasion and my pocketbook successful.

The second volume was identical in outward respects to its predecessor except that it bore no title. But if I was expecting more disclosures in symbolism I was doomed to disappointment. Vague as "Five Unicorns and a Pearl" had been, the text of the sequel was even more wandering and was obviously only the ramblings of a mad brain. By watching the sentences closely I did gather that Alessandro Larla had made a second trip to his court of the twenty-six bluejays and met there again his "pearl."

There was a paragraph toward the end that puzzled me. It read:

"Can it possibly be? I pray that it is not. And yet I have seen it and heard it snarl. Oh, the loathsome creature! I will not, I will not believe it."

I closed the book with a snap and tried to divert my attention elsewhere by polishing the lens of my newest portable camera. But again, as before, that same urge stole upon me, that same desire to visit the garden. I confess that I had watched the intervening hours until I would meet the woman in black again; for strangely enough in spite of her abrupt exit before, I never doubted but that she would be there waiting for me. I wanted her to lift the veil. I wanted to talk with her. I wanted to throw myself once again into the narrative of Larla's book.

Yet the whole thing seemed preposterous, and I fought the sensation with every ounce of willpower I could call to mind. Then it suddenly occurred to me what a remarkable picture she would make, sitting there on the stone bench, clothed in black, with a classic background of the old courtyard. If I could but catch the scene on a photographic plate? . . .

I halted my polishing and mused a moment. With a new electric flash-lamp, that handy invention which has supplanted the old mussy flash-powder, I could illuminate the garden and snap the picture with ease. And if the result were satisfactory it would make a worthy contribution to the International Camera Contest at Geneva next month.

The idea appealed to me, and gathering together the necessary equipment I drew on an ulster (for it was a wet, chilly night) and slipped out of my rooms and headed northward. Mad, unseeing fool that I was! If only I had stopped then and there, returned the book to the antique-dealer and closed the incident! But the strange magnetic attraction had gripped me in earnest, and I rushed headlong into the horror.

A fall rain was drumming the pavement, and the streets were deserted. Off to the east, however, the heavy blanket of clouds glowed with a soft radiance where the moon was trying to break through, and a strong wind from the south gave promise of clearing the skies before long. With my coat collar turned well up at the throat I passed once again into the older section of the town and down forgotten Easterly Street. I found the gate to the grounds unlocked as before, and the garden a dripping place masked in shadow.

The woman was not there. Still the hour was early, and I did not for a moment doubt that she would appear later. Gripped now with the enthusiasm of my plan, I set the camera carefully on the stone fountain, training the lens as well as I could on the bench where we had sat the previous evening. The flash lamp with its battery handle I laid within easy reach.

Scarcely had I finished my arrangements when the crunch of gravel on the path caused me to turn. She was approaching the stone bench, heavily veiled as before and with the same sweeping black dress.

"You have come again," she said as I took my place beside her.

"Yes," I replied. "I could not stay away."

Our conversation that night gradually centered about her dead brother, although I thought several times that the woman tried to avoid the subject. He had been, it seemed, the black sheep of the family, had led more or less of a dissolute life and had been expelled from the University of Vienna not only because of his lack of respect for the pedagogues of the various sciences but also because of his queer unorthodox papers on philosophy. His sufferings in the war prison camp must have been intense. With a kind of grim delight she dwelt on his horrible experiences in the grave-digging detail which had been related to her by the fellow officer. But of the manner in which he had met his death she would say absolutely nothing.

Stronger than on the night before was the sweet smell of heliotrope. And again as the fumes crept nauseatingly down my lungs there came the same sense of nervousness, that same feeling that the perfume was hiding something I should know. The desire to see beneath the veil had become maddening by this time, but still I lacked the boldness to ask her to lift it.

Toward midnight the heavens cleared and the moon in splendid contrast shone high in the sky. The time had come for my picture.

"Sit where you are," I said. "I'll be back in a moment."

Stepping quickly to the fountain I grasped the flash-lamp, held it aloft for an instant and placed my finger on the shutter lever of the camera. The woman remained motionless on the bench, evidently puzzled as to the meaning of my movements. The range was perfect. A click, and a dazzling white light enveloped the courtyard about us. For a brief second she was outlined there against the old wall. Then the blue moonlight returned, and I was smiling in satisfaction.

"It ought to make a beautiful picture," I said.

She leaped to her feet.

"Fool!" she cried hoarsely. "Blundering fool! What have you done?"

Even though the veil was there to hide her face I got the instant impression that her eyes were glaring at me, smoldering with hatred. I gazed at her curiously a she stood erect, head thrown back, body apparently taut as wire, and a slow shudder crept down my spine. Then without warning she gathered up her dress and ran down the path toward the deserted house. A moment later she had disappeared somewhere in the shadows of the giant bushes.

I stood there by the fountain, staring after her in a daze. Suddenly, off in the umbra of the house's facade there rose a low animal snarl.

And then before I could move, a huge gray shape came hurtling through the long weeds, bounding in great leaps straight toward me. It was the woman's dog, which I had seen with her the night before. But no longer was it a beast passive and silent. Its face was contorted in diabolic fury, and its jaws were dripping slaver. Even in that moment of terror as I stood frozen before it, the sight of those white nostrils and those black hyalescent eyes emblazoned itself on my mind, never to be forgotten.

Then with a lunge it was upon me. I had only time to thrust the flash-lamp upward in half protection and throw my weight to the side. My arm jumped in recoil. The bulb exploded, and I could feel those teeth clamp down hard on the handle. Backward I fell, a scream gurgling to my lips, a terrific heaviness surging upon my body.

I struck out frantically, beat my fists into that growling face. My fingers groped blindly for its throat, sank deep into the hairy flesh. I could feel its very breath mingling with my own now, but desperately I hung on.

The pressure of my hands told. The dog coughed and fell back. And seizing that instant I struggled to my feet, jumped forward and planted a terrific kick straight into the brute's middle.

"Fort mit dir, Johann!" I cried, remembering the woman's German command.

It leaped back and, fangs bared, glared at me motionless for a moment. Then abruptly it turned and slunk off through the weeds.

Weak and trembling, I drew myself together, picked up my camera and passed through the gate toward home.

Three days passed. Those endless hours I spent confined to my apartment
suffering the tortures of the damned.

On the day following the night of my terrible experience with the dog I
realized I was in no condition to go to work. I drank two cups of strong black
coffee and then forced myself to sit quietly in a chair, hoping to soothe my
nerves. But the sight of the camera there on the table excited me to action. Five
minutes later I was in the dark room arranged as my studio, developing the
picture I had taken the night before. I worked feverishly, urged on by the thought
of what an unusual contribution it would make for the amateur contest next
month at Geneva, should the result be successful.

An exclamation burst from my lips as I stared at the still-wet print. There was
the old garden clear and sharp with the bushes, the statue of the child, the
fountain and the wall in the background, but the bench—the stone bench was
empty. There was no sign, not even a blur of the woman in black.

My brain in a whirl, I rushed the negative through a saturated solution of
mercuric chloride in water, then treated it with ferrous oxalate. But even after
this intensifying process the second print was like the first, focused in every
detail, the bench standing in the foreground in sharp relief, but no trace of the
woman.

I stared incredulously. She had been in plain view when I snapped the shutter.
Of that I was positive. And my camera was in perfect condition. What then was
wrong? Not until I had looked at the print hard in the daylight would I believe
my eyes. No explanation offered itself, none at all; and at length, confused unto
weakness, I returned to my bed and fell into a heavy sleep.

Straight through the day I slept. Hours later I seemed to wake from a vague
nightmare, and had not strength to rise from my pillow. A great physical faintness had overwhelmed me. My arms, my legs, lay like dead things. My heart
was fluttering weakly. All was quiet, so still that the clock on my bureau ticked
distinctly each passing second. The curtain billowed in the night breeze, though
I was positive I had closed the casement when I entered the room.

And then suddenly I threw back my head and screamed from the bottomest
depths of my soul! For slowly, slowly creeping down my lungs was that detestable odor of heliotrope!

Morning, and I found all was not a dream. My head was ringing, my hands
trembling, and I was so weak I could hardly stand. The doctor I called in looked
grave as he felt my pulse.

"You are on the verge of a complete collapse," he said. "If you do not allow
yourself a rest it may permanently affect your mind. Take things easy for a while.
And if you don't mind, I'll cauterize those two little cuts on your neck. They're
rather raw wounds. What caused them?"

I moved my fingers to my throat and drew them away again tipped with blood.

"I . . . I don't know," I faltered.

He busied himself with his medicines, and a few minutes later reached for
his hat.

"I advise that you don't leave your bed for a week at least," he said. "I'll give you a thorough examination then and see if there are any signs of anemia." But as he went out the door I thought I saw a puzzled look on his face.

Those subsequent hours allowed my thoughts to run wild once more. I vowed I would forget it all, go back to my work and never look upon the books again. But I knew I could not. The woman in black persisted in my mind, and each minute away from her became a torture. But more than that, if there had been a decided urge to continue my reading in the second book, the desire to see the third book, the last of the trilogy, was slowly increasing to an obsession. It gripped me, etched itself deep into my thoughts.

At length I could stand it no longer, and on the morning of the third day I took a cab to the antique store and tried to persuade Larla to give me the third volume of his brother. But the Italian was firm. I had already taken two books, neither of which I had returned. Until I brought them back he would not listen. Vainly I tried to explain that one was of no value without the sequel and that I wanted to read the entire narrative as a unit. He merely shrugged his shoulders and toyed with his watch chain.

Cold perspiration broke out on my forehead as I heard my desire disregarded. Like the blows of a bludgeon the thought beat upon me that I must have that book. I argued. I pleaded. But to no avail.

At length when Larla had turned the other way I gave in to desperation, seized the third book as I saw it lying on the shelf, slid it into my pocket and walked guiltily out. I make no apologies for my action. In the light of what developed later it may be considered a temptation inspired, for my will at the time was a conquered thing blanketed by that strange lure.

Back in my apartment I dropped into a chair and hastened to open the velvet cover. Here was the last chronicling of that strange series of events which had so completely become a part of my life during the past five days. Larla's volume three. Would all be explained in its pages? If so, what secret would be revealed?

With the light from a reading-lamp glaring full over my shoulder I opened the book, thumbed through it slowly, marveling again at the exquisite hand-printing. It seemed then as I sat there that an almost palpable cloud of intense quiet settled over me, a mental miasma muffling the distant sounds of the street. I was vaguely aware of an atmosphere, heavy and dense, in which objects other than the book lost their focus and became blurred in proportion.

For a moment I hesitated. Something psychic, something indefinable seemed to forbid me to read farther. Conscience, curiosity, that queer urge told me to go on. Slowly, like a man in a hypnotic trance wavering between two wills, I began to turn the pages, one at a time, from back to front.

Symbolism again. Vague wanderings with no sane meaning.

But suddenly my fingers stopped! My eyes had caught sight of the last paragraph on the last page, the final pennings of Alessandro Larla. I stared downward as a terrific shock ripped through me from head to foot. I read, re-read, and read again those words, those blasphemous words. I brought the book closer. I traced each word in the lamplight, slowly, carefully, letter for letter. I opened and closed my eyes. Then the horror of it burst like bomb within me.

"What shall I do? She has drained my blood and rotted my soul. My pearl is black, black as all evil. The curse be upon her brother, for it is he who made her thus. I pray the truth in these pages will destroy them forever.

"But my brain is hammering itself apart. Heaven help me, Perle von Mauren and her brother, Johann, are vampires!"

With a scream I leaped to my feet.

"Vampires!" I shrieked. "Vampires! Oh, my God!"

I clutched at the edge of the table and stood there swaying, the realization of it surging upon me like the blast of a furnace. Vampires! Those horrible creatures with a lust for human blood, fiends of hell, taking the shape of men, of bats, of dogs. I saw it all now, and my brain reeled at the horror of it.

Oh, why had I been such a fool? Why had I not looked beneath the surface, taken away the veil, gone farther than the perfume? That damnable heliotrope was a mask, a mask hiding all the unspeakable foulness of the grave.

My emotions burst out of control then. With a cry I swept the water glass, the books, the vase from the table, smote my fist down upon the flat surface again and again until a thousand little pains were stabbing my flesh.

"Vampires!" I screamed. "No, no—oh God, it isn't true!"

But I knew that it was. The events of the past days rose before me in all their horror now, and I could see the black significance of every detail.

The brother, Johann—some time since the war he had become a vampire. When the woman sought him out years later he had forced this terrible existence upon her too. Yes, that was it.

With the garden as their lair the two of them had entangled poor Alessandro Larla in their serpentine coils a year before. He had loved the woman, had worshipped her madly. And then he had found the truth, the awful truth that had sent him stumbling home, stark, raving mad.

Mad, yes, but not mad enough to keep him from writing the facts in his three velvet-bound books for the world to see. He had hoped the disclosures would dispatch the woman and her brother forever. But it was not enough.

Following my thoughts, I whipped the first book from the table stand and opened the front cover. There again I saw those scrawled lines which had meant nothing to me before.

"Revelations meant to destroy but only binding without the stake. Read, fool, and enter my field, for we are chained to the spot. Oh, wo unto Larla!"

Perle von Mauren had written that. Fool that I was, unseeing fool! The books had not put an end to the evil life of her or her brother. No, only one thing could do that. Yet the exposures had not been written in vain. They were recorded for mortal posterity to see.

Those books bound the two vampires, Perle von Mauren and her brother, Johann, to the old garden, kept them from roaming the night streets in search of victims. Only him who had once passed through the gate could they pursue and attack.

It was the old metaphysical law: evil shrinking in the face of truth.

Yet if the books had bound their power in chains they had also opened a new avenue for their attacks. Once immersed in the pages of the trilogy, the reader fell helplessly into their clutches. Those printed lines had become the outer reaches of their web. They were an entrapping net within which the power of the vampires always crouched.

That was why my life had blended so strangely with the story of Larla. The moment I had cast my eyes on the opening paragraph I had fallen into their coils to do with as they had done with Larla a year before. I had been lured, drawn relentlessly into the tentacles of the woman in black. Once I was past the garden gate the binding spell of the books was gone, and they were free to pursue me and to—

A giddy sensation rose within me. Now I saw why the scientific doctor had been puzzled. Now I saw the reason for my physical weakness. Oh, the foulness of it! She had been—feasting on my blood!

With a sobbing cry I flung the book to a far corner, turned and began madly pacing up and down the room. Cold perspiration oozed from every pore. My heart pounded like a runner's. My brain ran wild.

Was I to end as Larla had ended, another victim of this loathsome being's power? Was she to gorge herself further on my life and live on? Were others to be preyed upon and go down into the pits of despair? No, and again no! If Larla had been ignorant of the one and only way in which to dispose of such a creature, I was not. I had not vacationed in south Europe without learning something of these ancient evils.

Frantically I looked about the room, took in the objects about me. A chair, a table, a taboret, one of my cameras with its long tripod. I stared at the latter as in my terror-stricken mind a plan leaped into action. With a lunge I was across the floor, had seized one of the wooden legs of the tripod in my hands. I snapped it across my knee. Then, grasping the two broken pieces, both now with sharp splintered ends, I rushed hatless out of the door to the street.

A moment later I was racing northward in a cab bound for Easterly Street.

"Hurry!" I cried to the driver as I glanced at the westering sun. "Faster, do you hear?"

We shot along the crossstreets, into the old suburbs and toward the outskirts of town. Every traffic halt found me fuming at the delay. But at length we drew up before the wall of the garden.

Tossing the driver a bill, I swung the wrought-iron gate open and with the wooden pieces of the tripod still under my arm, rushed in. The courtyard was a place of reality in the daylight, but the moldering masonry and tangled weeds were steeped in silence as before.

Straight for the house I made, climbing the rotten steps to the front entrance. The door was boarded up and locked. Smothering an impulse to scream, I retraced my steps at a run and began to circle the south wall of the building. It was this direction I had seen the woman take when she had fled after I had tried to snap her picture. The twenty-six bluejays on the wall leered at me like a flock of harpies.

Well toward the rear of the building I reached a small half-open door leading to the cellar. For a moment I hesitated there, sick with the dread of what I knew lay before me. Then, clenching hard the two wooden tripod stakes, I entered.

Inside, cloaked in gloom, a narrow corridor stretched before me. The floor was littered with rubble and fallen masonry, the ceiling interlaced with a thousand cobwebs.

I stumbled forward, my eyes quickly accustoming themselves to the half-light from the almost opaque windows. A maddening urge to leave it all and flee back to the sunlight was welling up within me now. I fought it back. Failure would mean a continuation of the horrors—a lingering death—would leave the gate open for others.

At the end of the corridor a second door barred my passage. I thrust it open—and stood swaying there on the sill staring inward. A great loathing crept over me, a stifling sense of utter repulsion. Hot blood rushed to my head. The air seemed to move upward in palpable swirls.

Beyond was a small room, barely ten feet square, with a low-raftered ceiling. And by the light of the open door I saw side by side in the center of the floor—two white wood coffins.

How long I stood there leaning weakly against the stone wall I don't know. There was a silence so profound the beating of my heart pulsed through the passage like the blows of a mallet. And there was a slow penetrating odor drifting from out of that chamber that entered my nostrils and claimed instant recognition. Heliotrope! But heliotrope defiled by the rotting smell of an ancient grave.

Then suddenly with a determination born of despair I leaped forward, rushed to the nearest coffin, seized its cover and ripped it open.

Would to heaven I could forget the sight that met my eyes. There lay Perle von Mauren, the woman in black—unveiled.

That face—how can I describe it? It was divinely beautiful, the hair black as sable, the cheeks a classic white. But the lips—oh God! those lips! I grew suddenly sick as I looked upon them. They were scarlet, crimson . . . and sticky with human blood.

I moved like an automaton then. With a low sob I reached for one of the tripod stakes, seized a flagstone from the floor and with the pointed end of the wood resting directly over the woman's heart, struck a crashing blow. The stake jumped downward. A sickening crunch—and a violent contortion shook the coffin. Up to my face rushed a warm, nauseating breath of rot and decay.

I wheeled and hurled open the lid of her brother's coffin. With only a flashing glance at the young, masculine, Teutonic face I raised the other stake high in the air and brought it stabbing down with all the strength in my right arm. Red blood suddenly began to form a thick pool on the floor.

For an instant I stood rooted to the spot, the utter obscenity of it all searing its way into my brain like a hot sword. Even in that moment of stark horror I realized that not even the most subtle erasures of Time would be able to remove that blasphemous sight from my inner eye.

It was a scene so abysmally corrupt—I pray heaven my dreams will never find it and re-envision its unholy tableau. There before me, focused in the shaft of light that filtered through the open door like the miasma from a fever swamp, lay the two white caskets.

And within them now, staring up at me from eyeless sockets—two gray and moldering skeletons, each with its hideous leering head of death.

The rest is but a vague dream. I seem to remember rushing madly outside, along the path to the gate and down the street, down Easterly, away from that accursed garden of the jays.

At length, utterly exhausted, I reached my apartment, burst open the door and staggered in. Those mundane surroundings that confronted me were like balm to my burning eyes. But as if in mocking irony there centered into my gaze three objects lying where I had left them, the three volumes of Larla.

I moved across to them, picked them up and stared down vacantly upon their black sides. These were the hellish works that had caused it all. These were the pages that were responsible. . . .

With a low cry I turned to the grate on the other side of the room and flung the three of them onto the still glowing coals.

There was an instant hiss, and a line of yellow flame streaked upward and began eating into the velvet. I watched the fire grow higher . . . higher . . . and diminish slowly.

And as the last glowing spark died into a blackened ash there swept over me a mighty feeling of quiet and relief.

SHAMBLEAU

C. L. MOORE

As the first published story of Catherine L. Moore, "Shambleau" introduced Weird Tales *readers to an author who would write some of the most important science fiction written during the war years. The first of more than a dozen tales of the intergalactic gunslinger Northwest Smith, it is unabashed space opera, but also one of the first science fiction stories to explore a theme usually relegated to the horror medium. Few tales since have so marvelously captured what Moore refers to as the "rapture and revulsion" inspired by the vampire.*

M AN has conquered Space before. You may be sure of that. Somewhere beyond the Egyptians, in that dimness out of which come echoes of half-mythical names—Atlantis, Mu—somewhere back of history's first beginnings there must have been an age when mankind, like us today, built cities of steel to house its star-roving ships and knew the names of the planets in their own native tongues—heard Venus's people call their wet world "Sha-ardol" in that soft, sweet, slurring speech and mimicked Mars's guttural "Lakkdiz" from the harsh tongues of Mars's dryland dwellers. You may be sure of it. Man has conquered Space before, and out of that conquest faint, faint echoes run still through a world that has forgotten the very fact of a civilization which must have been as mighty as our own. There have been too many myths and legends for us to doubt it. The myth of the Medusa, for instance, can never have had its roots in the soil of Earth. That tale of the snake-haired Gorgon whose gaze turned the gazer to stone never originated about any creature that Earth nourished. And those *ancient Greeks who told the story must have remembered, dimly and half be-lieving, a tale of antiquity about some strange being from one of the outlying planets their remotest ancestors once trod.*

"SHAMBLEAU! Ha . . . Shambleau!"
     The wild hysteria of the mob rocketed from wall to wall of Lakkdarol's narrow streets and the storming of heavy boots over the slag-red pavement made an ominous undernote to that swelling bay, "Shambleau! Shambleau!"

Northwest Smith heard it coming and stepped into the nearest doorway, laying a wary hand on his heat-gun's grip, and his colorless eyes narrowed. Strange sounds were common enough in the streets of Earth's latest colony on Mars—a raw, red little town where anything might happen, and very often did. But Northwest Smith, whose name is known and respected in every dive and wild outpost on a dozen wild planets, was a cautious man, despite his reputation. He set his back against the wall and gripped his pistol, and heard the rising shout come nearer and nearer.

Then into his range of vision flashed a red running figure, dodging like a hunted hare from shelter to shelter in the narrow street. It was a girl—a berry-brown girl in a single tattered garment whose scarlet burnt the eyes with its brilliance. She ran wearily, and he could hear her gasping breath from where he stood. As she came into view he saw her hesitate and lean one hand against the wall for support, and glance wildly around for shelter. She must not have seen him in the depths of the doorway, for as the bay of the mob grew louder and the pounding of feet sounded almost at the corner she gave a despairing little moan and dodged into the recess at his very side.

When she saw him standing there, tall and leather-brown, hand on his heat-gun, she sobbed once, inarticulately, and collapsed at his feet, a huddle of burning scarlet and bare, brown limbs.

Smith had not seen her face, but she was a girl, and sweetly made and in danger; and though he had not the reputation of a chivalrous man, something in her hopeless huddle at his feet touched that chord of sympathy for the underdog that stirs in every Earthman, and he pushed her gently into the corner behind him and jerked out his gun, just as the first of the running mob rounded the corner.

It was a motley crowd, Earthmen and Martians and a sprinkling of Venusian swampmen and strange, nameless denizens of unnamed planets—a typical Lakk-darol mob. When the first of them turned the corner and saw the empty street before them there was a faltering in the rush and the foremost spread out and began to search the doorways on both sides of the street.

"Looking for something?" Smith's sardonic call sounded clear above the clamor of the mob.

They turned. The shouting died for a moment as they took in the scene before them—tall Earthman in the space-explorer's leathern garb, all one color from the burning of savage suns save for the sinister pallor of his no-colored eyes in a scarred and resolute face, gun in his steady hand and the scarlet girl crouched behind him, panting.

The foremost of the crowd—a burly Earthman in tattered leather from which the patrol insignia had been ripped away—stared for a moment with a strange expression of incredulity on his face overspreading the savage exultation of the chase. Then he let loose a deep-throated bellow, "Shambleau!" and lunged forward. Behind him the mob took up the cry again, "Shambleau! Shambleau! Shambleau!" and surged after.

Smith, lounging negligently against the wall, arms folded and gun-hand draped over his left forearm, looked incapable of swift motion, but at the leader's first forward step the pistol swept in a practised half-circle and the dazzle of blue-white heat leaping from its muzzle seared an arc in the slag pavement at his feet. It was an old gesture, and not a man in the crowd but understood it. The foremost recoiled swiftly against the surge of those in the rear, and for a moment there was confusion as the two tides met and struggled. Smith's mouth curled into a grim curve as he watched. The man in the mutilated patrol uniform lifted a threatening fist and stepped to the very edge of the deadline, while the crowd rocked to and fro behind him.

"Are you crossing that line?" queried Smith in an ominously gentle voice.

"We want that girl!"

"Come and get her!" Recklessly Smith grinned into his face. He saw danger there, but his defiance was not the foolhardy gesture it seemed. An expert psychologist of mobs from long experience, he sensed no murder here. Not a gun had appeared in any hand in the crowd. They desired the girl with an inexplicable bloodthirstiness he was at a loss to understand, but toward himself he sensed no such fury. A mauling he might expect, but his life was in no danger. Guns would have appeared before now if they were coming out at all. So he grinned in the man's angry face and leaned lazily against the wall.

Behind their self-appointed leader the crowd milled impatiently, and threatening voices began to rise again. Smith heard the girl moan at his feet.

"What do you want with her?" he demanded.

"She's Shambleau! Shambleau, you fool! Kick her out of there—we'll take care of her!"

"I'm taking care of her," drawled Smith.

"She's Shambleau, I tell you! Damn your hide, man, we never let those things live! Kick her out here!"

The repeated name had no meaning to him, but Smith's innate stubbornness rose defiantly as the crowd surged forward to the very edge of the arc, their clamor growing louder. "Shambleau! Kick her out here! Give us Shambleau! Shambleau!"

Smith dropped his indolent pose like a cloak and planted both feet wide, swinging up his gun threateningly. "Keep back!" he yelled. "She's mine! Keep back!"

He had no intention of using that heat-beam. He knew by now that they would not kill him unless he started the gun-play himself, and he did not mean to give up his life for any girl alive. But a severe mauling he expected, and he braced himself instinctively as the mob heaved within itself.

To his astonishment a thing happened then that he had never known to happen before. At his shouted defiance the foremost of the mob—those who had heard him clearly—drew back a little, not in alarm but evidently surprised. The ex-patrolman said, "Yours! She's *yours*?" in a voice from which puzzlement crowded out anger.

Smith spread his booted legs wide before the crouching figure and flourished his gun.

"Yes," he said. "And I'm keeping her! Stand back there!"

The man stared at him wordlessly, and horror and disgust and incredulity mingled on his weather-beaten face. The incredulity triumphed for a moment and he said again,

"Yours!"

Smith nodded defiance.

The man stepped back suddenly, unutterable contempt in his very pose. He waved an arm to the crowd and said loudly, "It's—his!" and the press melted away, gone silent, too, and the look of contempt spread from face to face.

The ex-patrolman spat on the slag-paved street and turned his back indifferently. "Keep her, then," he advised briefly over one shoulder. "But don't let her out again in this town!"

Smith stared in perplexity almost open-mouthed as the suddenly scornful mob began to break up. His mind was in a whirl. That such bloodthirsty animosity should vanish in a breath he could not believe. And the curious mingling of contempt and disgust on the faces he saw baffled him even more. Lakkdarol was anything but a puritan town—it did not enter his head for a moment that his claiming the brown girl as his own had caused that strangely shocked revulsion to spread through the crowd. No, it was something deeper-rooted than that. Instinctive, instant disgust had been in the faces he saw—they would have looked less so if he had admitted cannibalism or *Pharol*-worship.

And they were leaving his vicinity as swiftly as if whatever unknowing sin he had committed were contagious. The street was emptying as rapidly as it had filled. He saw a sleek Venusian glance back over his shoulder as he turned the corner and sneer, "Shambleau!" and the word awoke a new line of speculation in Smith's mind. Shambleau! Vaguely of French origin, it must be. And strange enough to hear it from the lips of Venusians and Martian drylanders, but it was their use of it that puzzled him more. "We never let those things live," the ex-patrolman had said. It reminded him dimly of something . . . an ancient line from some writing in his own tongue. . . . "Thou shalt not suffer a witch to live." He smiled to himself at the similarity, and simultaneously was aware of the girl at his elbow.

She had risen soundlessly. He turned to face her, sheathing his gun, and stared at first with curiosity and then in the entirely frank openness with which men regard that which is not wholly human. For she was not. He knew it at a glance, though the brown, sweet body was shaped like a woman's and she wore the garment of scarlet—he saw it was leather—with an ease that few unhuman beings achieve toward clothing. He knew it from the moment he looked into her eyes, and a shiver of unrest went over him as he met them. They were frankly green as young grass, with slit-like, feline pupils that pulsed unceasingly, and there was a look of dark, animal wisdom in their depths—that look of the beast which sees more than man.

There was no hair upon her face—neither brows nor lashes, and he would have sworn that the tight scarlet turban bound around her head covered baldness. She had three fingers and a thumb, and her feet had four digits apiece too, and all sixteen of them were tipped with round claws that sheathed back into the flesh like a cat's. She ran her tongue over her lips—a thin, pink, flat tongue as feline as her eyes—and spoke with difficulty. He felt that that throat and tongue had never been shaped for human speech.

"Not—afraid now," she said softly, and her little teeth were white and pointed as a kitten's.

"What did they want you for?" he asked her curiously. "What had you done? Shambleau . . . is that your name?"

"I—not talk your—speech," she demurred hesitantly.

"Well, try to—I want to know. Why were they chasing you? Will you be safe on the street now, or hadn't you better get indoors somewhere? They looked dangerous."

"I—go with you." She brought it out with difficulty.

"Say you!" Smith grinned. "What are you, anyhow? You look like a kitten to me."

"Shambleau." She said it somberly.

"Where d'you live? Are you a Martian?"

"I come from—from far—from long ago—far country—"

"Wait!" laughed Smith. "You're getting your wires crossed. You're not a Martian?"

She drew herself up very straight beside him, lifting the turbaned head, and there was something queenly in the poise of her.

"Martian?" she said scornfully. "My people—are—are—you have no word. Your speech—hard for me."

"What's yours? I might know it—try me."

She lifted her head and met his eyes squarely, and there was in hers a subtle amusement—he could have sworn it.

"Some day I—speak to you in—my own language," she promised, and the pink tongue flicked out over her lips, swiftly, hungrily.

Approaching footsteps on the red pavement interrupted Smith's reply. A dryland Martian came past, reeling a little and exuding an aroma of *segir*-whisky, the Venusian brand. When he caught the red flash of the girl's tatters he turned his head sharply, and as his *segir*-steeped brain took in the fact of her presence he lurched toward the recess unsteadily, bawling, "Shambleau, by *Pharol!* Shambleau!" and reached out a clutching hand.

Smith struck it aside contemptuously.

"On your way, drylander," he advised.

The man drew back and stared, blear-eyed.

"Yours, eh?" he croaked. "*Zut!* You're welcome to it!" And like the ex-patrolman before him he spat on the pavement and turned away, muttering harshly in the blasphemous tongue of the drylands.

Smith watched him shuffle off, and there was a crease between his colorless eyes, a nameless unease rising within him.

"Come on," he said abruptly to the girl. "If this sort of thing is going to happen we'd better get indoors. Where shall I take you?"

"With—you," she murmured.

He stared down into the flat green eyes. Those ceaselessly pulsing pupils disturbed him, but it seemed to him, vaguely, that behind the animal shallows of her gaze was a shutter—a closed barrier that might at any moment open to reveal the very deeps of that dark knowledge he sensed there.

Roughly he said again, "Come on, then," and stepped down into the street.

She pattered along a pace or two behind him, making no effort to keep up with his long strides, and though Smith—as men know from Venus to Jupiter's moons—walks as softly as a cat, even in spaceman's boots, the girl at his heels slid like a shadow over the rough pavement, making so little sound that even the lightness of his footsteps was loud in the empty street.

Smith chose the less frequented ways of Lakkdarol, and somewhat shame-facedly thanked his nameless gods that his lodgings were not far away, for the few pedestrians he met turned and stared after the two with that by now familiar mingling of horror and contempt which he was as far as ever from understanding.

The room he had engaged was a single cubicle in a lodging house on the edge of the city. Lakkdarol, raw camptown that it was in those days, could have furnished little better anywhere within its limits, and Smith's errand there was not one he wished to advertise. He had slept in worse places than this before, and knew that he would do so again.

There was no one in sight when he entered, and the girl slipped up the stairs at his heels and vanished through the door, shadowy, unseen by anyone in the house. Smith closed the door and leaned his broad shoulders against the panels, regarding her speculatively.

She took in what little the room had to offer in a glance—frowsy bed, rickety table, mirror hanging unevenly and cracked against the wall, unpainted chairs—a typical camptown room in an Earth settlement abroad. She accepted its poverty in that single glance, dismissed it, then crossed to the window and leaned out for a moment, gazing across the low rooftops toward the barren countryside beyond, red slag under the late afternoon sun.

"You can stay here," said Smith abruptly, "until I leave town. I'm waiting here for a friend to come in from Venus. Have you eaten?"

"Yes," said the girl quickly. "I shall—need no—food for—a while."

"Well—" Smith glanced around the room. "I'll be in sometime tonight. You can go or stay just as you please. Better lock the door behind me."

With no more formality than that he left her. The door closed and he heard the key turn, and smiled to himself. He did not expect, then, ever to see her again.

He went down the steps and out into the late-slanting sunlight with a mind so full of other matters that the brown girl receded very quickly into the background. Smith's errand in Lakkdarol, like most of his errands, is better not spoken of. Man lives as he must, and Smith's living was a perilous affair outside the law and ruled by the raygun only. It is enough to say that the shipping port and its cargoes outbound interested him deeply just now, and that the friend he awaited was Yarol the Venusian, in that swift little Edsel ship the *Maid* that can flash from world to world with a derisive speed that laughs at patrol boats and leaves pursuers floundering in the ether far behind. Smith and Yarol and the *Maid* were a trinity that had caused the patrol leaders much worry and many gray hairs in the past, and the future looked very bright to Smith himself that evening as he left his lodging house.

Lakkdarol roars by night, as Earthmen's camptowns have a way of doing on every planet where Earth's outposts are, and it was beginning lustily as Smith went down among the awakening lights toward the center of town. His business there does not concern us. He mingled with the crowds where the lights were brightest, and there was the click of ivory counters and the jingle of silver, and red *segir* gurgled invitingly from black Venusian bottles, and much later Smith strolled homeward under the moving moons of Mars, and if the street wavered a little under his feet now and then—why, that is only understandable. Not even Smith could drink red *segir* at every bar from the Martian Lamb to the New Chicago and remain entirely steady on his feet. But he found his way back with very little difficulty—considering—and spent a good five minutes hunting for his key before he remembered he had left it in the inner lock for the girl.

He knocked then, and there was no sound of footsteps from within, but in a few moments the latch clicked and the door swung open. She retreated soundlessly before him as he entered, and took up her favorite place against the window, leaning back on the sill and outlined against the starry sky beyond. The room was in darkness.

Smith flipped the switch by the door and then leaned back against the panels, steadying himself. The cool night air had sobered him a little, and his head was clear enough—liquor went to Smith's feet, not his head, or he would never have come this far along the lawless way he had chosen. He lounged against the door now and regarded the girl in the sudden glare of the bulbs, blinding a little, as much at the scarlet of her clothing as at the light.

"So you stayed," he said.

"I—waited," she answered softly, leaning farther back against the sill and clasping the rough wood with slim, three-fingered hands, pale brown against the darkness.

"Why?"

She did not answer that, but her mouth curved into a slow smile. On a woman it would have been reply enough—provocative, daring. On Shambleau there was something pitiful and horrible in it—so human on the face of one half-animal. And yet . . . that sweet brown body curving so softly from the tatters of scarlet leather—the velvety texture of that brownness—the white-flashing smile. . . . Smith was aware of a stirring excitement within him. After all—time would be hanging heavy now until Yarol came. . . . Speculatively he allowed the steel-pale eyes to wander over her, with a slow regard that missed nothing. And when he spoke he was aware that his voice had deepened a little. . . .

"Come here," he said.

She came forward slowly, on bare clawed feet that made no slightest sound on the floor, and stood before him with downcast eyes and mouth trembling in that pitifully human smile. He took her by the shoulders—velvety soft shoulders, of a creamy smoothness that was not the texture of human flesh. A little tremor went over her, perceptibly, at the contact of his hands. Northwest Smith caught his breath suddenly and dragged her to him . . . sweet, yielding brownness in the circle of his arms . . . heard her own breath catch and quicken as her velvety arms closed about his neck. And then he was looking down into her face, very near, and the green animal eyes met his with the pulsing pupils and the flicker of—something—deep behind their shallows—and through the rising clamor of his blood, even as he stooped his lips to hers, Smith felt something deep within him shudder away—inexplicable, instinctive, revolted. What it might be he had no words to tell, but the very touch of her was suddenly loathsome—so soft and velvet and unhuman—and it might have been an animal's face that lifted itself to his mouth—the dark knowledge looked hungrily—from the darkness of those slit pupils—and for a mad instant he knew that same wild, feverish revulsion he had seen in the faces of the mob. . . .

"God!" he gasped, a far more ancient invocation against evil than he realized, then or ever, and he ripped her arms from his neck, swung her away with such a force that she reeled half across the room. Smith fell back against the door, breathing heavily, and stared at her while the wild revolt died slowly within him.

She had fallen to the floor beneath the window, and as she lay there against the wall with bent head he saw, curiously, that her turban had slipped—the turban that he had been so sure covered baldness—and a lock of scarlet hair fell below the binding leather, hair as scarlet as her garment, as unhumanly red as her eyes were unhumanly green. He stared, and shook his head dizzily and stared again, for it seemed to him that the thick lock of crimson had moved, *squirmed* of itself against her cheek.

At the contact of it her hands flew up and she tucked it away with a very human gesture and then dropped her head again into her hands. And from the deep shadow of her fingers he thought she was staring up at him covertly.

Smith drew a deep breath and passed a hand across his forehead. The inexplicable moment had gone as quickly as it came—too swift for him to understand or analyze it. "Got to lay off the *segir*," he told himself unsteadily. Had he imagined that scarlet hair? After all, she was no more than a pretty brown girl-creature from one of the many half-human races peopling the planets. No more than that, after all. A pretty little thing, but animal. . . . He laughed a little shakily.

"No more of that," he said. "God knows I'm no angel, but there's got to be a limit somewhere. Here." He crossed to the bed and sorted out a pair of blankets from the untidy heap, tossing them to the far corner of the room. "You can sleep there."

Wordlessly she rose from the floor and began to rearrange the blankets, the uncomprehending resignation of the animal eloquent in every line of her.

Smith had a strange dream that night. He thought he had awakened to a room full of darkness and moonlight and moving shadows, for the nearer moon of Mars was racing through the sky and everything on the planet below her was endured with a restless life in the dark. And something . . . some nameless, unthinkable *thing* . . . was coiled about his throat . . . something like a soft snake, wet and warm. It lay loose and light about his neck . . . and it was moving gently, very gently, with a soft, caressive pressure that sent little thrills of delight through every nerve and fiber of him, a perilous delight—beyond physical pleasure, deeper than joy of the mind. That warm softness was caressing the very roots of his soul with a terrible intimacy. The ecstasy of it left him weak, and yet he knew—in a flash of knowledge born of this impossible dream—that the soul should not be handled. . . . And with that knowledge a horror broke upon him, turning the pleasure into a rapture of revulsion, hateful, horrible—but still most foully sweet. He tried to lift his hands and tear the dream-monstrosity from his throat—tried but half-heartedly; for though his soul was revolted to its very deeps, yet the delight of his body was so great that his hands all but refused the attempt. But when at last he tried to lift his arms a cold shock went over him and he found that he could not stir . . . his body lay stony as marble beneath the blankets, a living marble that shuddered with a dreadful delight through every rigid vein.

The revulsion grew strong upon him as he struggled against the paralyzing dream—a struggle of soul against sluggish body—titanically, until the moving dark was streaked with blankness that clouded and closed about him at last and he sank back into the oblivion from which he had awakened.

Next morning, when the bright sunlight shining through Mars's clear, thin air awakened him, Smith lay for a while trying to remember. The dream had been more vivid than reality, but he could not now quite recall . . . only that it had been more sweet and horrible than anything else in life. He lay puzzling for a while, until a soft sound from the corner aroused him from his thoughts and he sat up to see the girl lying in a catlike coil on her blankets, watching him with round, grave eyes. He regarded her somewhat ruefully.

"Morning," he said. "I've just had the devil of a dream. . . . Well, hungry?"

She shook her head silently, and he could have sworn there was a covert gleam of strange amusement in her eyes.

He stretched and yawned, dismissing the nightmare temporarily from his mind.

"What am I going to do with you?" he inquired, turning to more immediate matters. "I'm leaving here in a day or two and I can't take you along, you know. Where'd you come from in the first place?"

Again she shook her head.

"Not telling? Well, it's your own business. You can stay here until I give up the room. From then on you'll have to do your own worrying."

He swung his feet to the floor and reached for his clothes.

Ten minutes later, slipping the heat gun into its holster at his thigh, Smith turned to the girl. "There's food concentrate in that box on the table. It ought to hold you until I get back. And you'd better lock the door again after I've gone."

Her wide, unwavering stare was his only answer, and he was not sure she had understood, but at any rate the lock clicked after him as before, and he went down the steps with a faint grin on his lips.

The memory of last night's extraordinary dream was slipping from him, as such memories do, and by the time he had reached the street the girl and the dream and all of yesterday's happenings were blotted out by the sharp necessities of the present.

Again the intricate business that had brought him here claimed his attention. He went about it to the exclusion of all else, and there was a good reason behind everything he did from the moment he stepped out into the street until the time when he turned back again at evening; though had one chosen to follow him during the day his apparently aimless rambling through Lakkdarol would have seemed very pointless.

He must have spent two hours at the least idling by the space-port, watching with sleepy, colorless eyes the ships that came and went, the passengers, the vessels lying at wait, the cargoes—particularly the cargoes. He made the rounds of the town's saloons once more, consuming many glasses of varied liquors in the course of the day and engaging in idle conversation with men of all races and world, usually in their own languages, for Smith was a linguist of repute among his contemporaries. He heard the gossip of the spaceways, news from a dozen planets of a thousand different events; he heard the latest joke about the Venusian emperor and the latest report on the Chino-Aryan war and the latest song hot from the lips of Rose Robertson, whom every man on the civilized planets adored as "the Georgia Rose." He passed the day quite profitably, for his own purposes, which do not concern us now, and it was not until late evening, when he turned homeward again, that the thought of the brown girl in his room took definite shape in his mind, though it had been lurking there, formless and submerged, all day.

He had no idea what comprised her usual diet, but he bought a can of New York roast beef and one of Venusian frog-broth and a dozen fresh canal-apples and two pounds of that Earth lettuce that grows so vigorously in the fertile canal soil of Mars. He felt that she must surely find something to her liking in this broad variety of edibles, and—for his day had been very satisfactory—he hummed *The Green Hills of Earth* to himself in a surprisingly good baritone as he climbed the stairs.

The door was locked, as before, and he was reduced to kicking the lower panels gently with his boot, for his arms were full. She opened the door with that softness that was characteristic of her and stood regarding him in the semi-darkness as he stumbled to the table with his load. The room was unlit again.

"Why don't you turn on the lights?" he demanded irritably after he had barked his shin on the chair by the table in an effort to deposit his burden there.

"Light and—dark—they are alike—to me," she murmured.

"Cat eyes, eh? Well, you look the part. Here, I've brought you some dinner. Take your choice. Fond of roast beef? Or how about a little frog-broth?"

She shook her head and backed away a step.

"No," she said. "I cannot—eat your food."

Smith's brows wrinkled. "Didn't you have any of the food tablets?"

Again the red turban shook negatively.

"Then you haven't had anything for—why, more than twenty-four hours! You must be starved."

"Not hungry," she denied.

"What can I find for you to eat, then? There's time yet if I hurry. You've got to eat, child."

"I shall—eat," she said, softly. "Before long—I shall—feed. Have no—worry."

She turned away then and stood at the window, looking out over the moonlit landscape as if to end the conversation. Smith cast her a puzzled glance as he opened the can of roast beef. There had been an odd undernote in that assurance that, undefinably, he did not like. And the girl had teeth and tongue and pre-sumably a fairly human digestive system, to judge from her human form. It was nonsense for her to pretend that he could find nothing that she could eat. She must have had some of the food concentrate after all, he decided, prying up the Thermos lid of the inner container to release the long-sealed savor of the hot meat inside.

"Well, if you won't eat you won't," he observed philosophically as he poured hot broth and diced beef into the dishlike lid of the Thermos can and extracted the spoon from its hiding place between the inner and outer receptacles. She turned a little to watch him as he pulled up a rickety chair and sat down to the food, and after a while the realization that her green gaze was fixed so unwinkingly upon him made the man nervous, and he said between bites of creamy canal apple, "Why don't you try a little of this? It's good."

"The food—I eat is—better," her soft voice told him in its hesitant murmur, and again he felt rather than heard a faint undernote of unpleasantness in the words. A sudden suspicion struck him as he pondered on that last remark—some vague memory of horror tales told about campfires in the past—and he swung round in the chair to look at her, a tiny, creeping fear unaccountably arising. There had been that in her words—in her unspoken words, that menaced. . . .

She stood up beneath his gaze demurely, wide green eyes with their pulsing pupils meeting his without a falter. But her mouth was scarlet and her teeth were sharp. . . .

"What food do you eat?" he demanded. And then, after a pause, very softly, "Blood?"

She stared at him for a moment, uncomprehending; then something like amusement curled her lips and she said scornfully, "You think me—vampire, eh? No—I am Shambleau!"

Unmistakably there were scorn and amusement in her voice at the suggestion, but as unmistakably she knew what he meant—accepted it as a logical suspicion—vampires! Fairy tales—but fairy tales this unhuman, outland creature was most familiar with. Smith was not a credulous man, nor a superstitious one, but he had seen too many strange things himself to doubt that the wildest legend might have a basis of fact. And there was something namelessly strange about her. . . .

He puzzled over it for a while between deep bites of the canal apple. And though he wanted to question her about a great many things, he did not, for he knew how futile it would be.

He said nothing more until the meat was finished and another canal apple had followed the first, and he had cleared away the meal by the simple expedient of tossing the empty can out the window. Then he lay back in the chair and surveyed her from half-closed eyes, colorless in a face tanned like saddle-leather. And again he was conscious of the brown, soft curves of her, velvety—subtle arcs and planes of smooth flesh under the tatters of scarlet leather. Vampire she might be, unhuman she certainly was, but desirable beyond words as she sat submissive beneath his slow regard, her red-turbaned head bent, her clawed fingers lying in her lap. They sat very still for a while, and the silence throbbed between them.

She was so like a woman—an Earth woman—sweet and submissive and demure, and softer than soft fur, if he could forget the three-fingered claws and the pulsing eyes—and that deeper strangeness beyond words. . . . (Had he dreamed that red lock of hair that moved? Had it been *segir* that woke the wild revulsion he knew when he held her in his arms? Why had the mob so thirsted for her?) He sat and stared, and despite the mystery of her and the half-suspicions that thronged his mind—for she was so beautifully soft and curved under those revealing tatters—he slowly realized that his pulses were mounting, became aware of a kindling within . . . brown girl-creature with downcast eyes . . . and then the lids lifted and the green flatness of a cat's gaze met his, and last night's revulsion woke swiftly again, like a warning bell that clanged as their eyes met—animal, after all, too sleek and soft for humanity, and that inner strangeness. . . .

Smith shrugged and sat up. His failings were legion, but the weakness of the flesh was not among the major ones. He motioned the girl to her pallet of blankets in the corner and turned to his own bed.

From deeps of sound sleep he awoke, much later. He awoke suddenly and completely, and with that inner excitement that presages something momentous. He awoke to brilliant moonlight, turning the room so bright that he could see the scarlet of the girl's rags as she sat up on her pallet. She was awake, she was sitting with her shoulder half turned to him and her head bent, and some warning instinct crawled coldly up his spine as he watched what she was doing. And yet it was a very ordinary thing for a girl to do—any girl, anywhere. She was unbinding her turban. . . .

He watched, not breathing, a presentiment of something horrible stirring in his brain, inexplicably. . . . The red folds loosened, and—he knew then that he had not dreamed—again a scarlet lock swung down against her cheek . . . a hair, was it? a lock of a hair? . . . thick as a thick worm it fell, plumply, against that smooth cheek . . . more scarlet than blood and thick as a crawling worm . . . and like a worm it crawled.

Smith rose on an elbow, not realizing the motion, and fixed an unwinking stare, with a sort of sick, fascinated incredulity, on that—that lock of hair. He had not dreamed. Until now he had taken it for granted that it was the *segir* which had made it seem to move on that evening before. But now . . . it was lengthening, stretching, moving of itself. It must be hair, but it *crawled;* with a sickening life of its own it squirmed down against her cheek, caressingly, revoltingly, impossibly. . . . Wet, it was, and round and thick and shining. . . .

She unfastened the last fold and whipped the turban off. From what he saw then Smith would have turned his eyes away—and he had looked on dreadful things before, without flinching—but he could not stir. He could only lie there on his elbow staring at the mass of scarlet, squirming—worms, hairs, what?— that writhed over her head in a dreadful mockery of ringlets. And it was lengthening, falling, somehow growing before his eyes, down over her shoulders in a spilling cascade, a mass that even at the beginning could never have been hidden under the skull-tight turban she had worn. He was beyond wondering, but he realized that. And still it squirmed and lengthened and fell, and she shook it out in a horrible travesty of a woman shaking out her unbound hair—until the unspeakable tangle of it—twisting, writhing, obscenely scarlet—hung to her waist and beyond, and still lengthened, an endless mass of crawling horror that until now, somehow, impossibly, had been hidden under the tight-bound turban. It was like a nest of blind, restless red worms . . . it was—it was like naked entrails endowed with an unnatural aliveness, terrible beyond words.

Smith lay in the shadows, frozen without and within in a sick numbness that came of utter shock and revulsion.

She shook out the obscene, unspeakable tangle over her shoulders, and somehow he knew that she was going to turn in a moment and that he must meet her eyes. The thought of that meeting stopped his heart with dread, more awfully than anything else in this nightmare horror; for nightmare it must be, surely. But he knew without trying that he could not wrench his eyes away—the sickened fascination of that sight held him motionless, and somehow there was a certain beauty. . . .

Her head was turning. The crawling awfulness rippled and squirmed at the motion, writhing thick and wet and shining over the soft brown shoulders about which they fell now in obscene cascades that all but hid her body. Her head was turning. Smith lay numb. And very slowly he saw the round of her cheek foreshorten and her profile come into view, all the scarlet horrors twisting ominously, and the profile shortened in turn and her full face came slowly round toward the bed—moonlight shining brilliantly as day on the pretty girl-face, demure and sweet, framed in tangled obscenity that crawled. . . .

The green eyes met his. He felt a perceptible shock, and a shudder rippled down his paralyzed spine, leaving an icy numbness in its wake. He felt the gooseflesh rising. But that numbness and cold horror he scarcely realized, for the green eyes were locked with his in a long, long look that somehow presaged nameless things—not altogether unpleasant things—the voiceless voice of her mind assailing him with little murmurous promises. . . .

For a moment he went down into a blind abyss of submission; and then somehow the very sight of that obscenity in eyes that did not then realize they saw it, was dreadful enough to draw him out of the seductive darkness . . . the sight of her crawling and alive with unnamable horror.

She rose, and down about her in a cascade fell the squirming scarlet of—of what grew upon her head. It fell in a long, alive cloak to her bare feet on the floor, hiding her in a wave of dreadful, wet, writhing life. She put up her hands and like a swimmer she parted the waterfall of it, tossing the masses back over her shoulders to reveal her own brown body, sweetly curved. She smiled, exquisitely, and in starting waves back from her forehead and down about her in a hideous background writhed the snaky wetness of her living tresses. And Smith knew that he looked upon Medusa.

The knowledge of that—the realization of vast backgrounds reaching into misted history—shook him out of his frozen horror for a moment, and in that moment he met her eyes again, smiling, green as glass in the moonlight, half hooded under drooping lids. Through the twisting scarlet she held out her arms. And there was something soul-shakingly desirable about her, so that all the blood surged to his head suddenly and he stumbled to his feet like a sleeper in a dream as she swayed toward him, infinitely graceful, infinitely sweet in her cloak of living horror.

And somehow there was beauty in it, the wet scarlet writhings with moonlight sliding and shining along the thick, worm-round tresses and losing itself in the masses only to glint again and move silvery along writhing tendrils—an awful, shuddering beauty more dreadful than any ugliness could be.

But all this, again, he but half realized, for the insidious murmur was coiling again through his brain, promising, caressing, alluring, sweeter than honey; and the green eyes that held his were clear and burning like the depths of a jewel, and behind the pulsing slits of darkness he was staring into a greater dark that held all things. . . . He had known—dimly he had known when he first gazed into those flat animal shallows that behind them lay this—all beauty and terror, all horror and delight, in the infinite darkness upon which her eyes opened like windows, paned with emerald glass.

Her lips moved, and in a murmur that blended indistinguishably with the silence and the sway of her body and the dreadful sway of her—her hair—she whispered—very softly, very passionately, "I shall—speak to you now—in my own tongue—oh, beloved!"

And in her living cloak she swayed to him, the murmur swelling seductive and caressing in his innermost brain—promising, compelling, sweeter than sweet. His flesh crawled to the horror of her, but it was a perverted revulsion that clasped what it loathed. His arms slid round her under the sliding cloak, wet, wet and warm and hideously alive—and the sweet velvet body was clinging to his, her arms locked about his neck—and with a whisper and a rush of unspeakable horror closed about them both.

In nightmares until he died he remembered that moment when the living tresses of Shambleau first folded him in their embrace. A nauseous, smothering odor as the wetness shut around him—thick, pulsing worms clasping every inch of his body, sliding, writhing, their wetness and warmth striking through his garments as if he stood naked to their embrace.

All this in a graven instant—and after that a tangled flash of conflicting sensation before oblivion closed over him. For he remembered the dream—and knew it for nightmare reality now, and the sliding, gently moving caresses of those wet, warm worms upon his flesh was an ecstasy above words—that deeper ecstasy that strikes beyond the body and beyond the mind and tickles the very roots of the soul with unnatural delight. So he stood, rigid as marble, as helplessly stony as any of Medusa's victims in ancient legends were, while the terrible pleasure of Shambleau thrilled and shuddered through every fiber of him; through every atom of his body and the intangible atoms of what men call the soul, through all that was Smith the dreadful pleasure ran. And it was truly dreadful. Dimly he knew it, even as his body answered to the root-deep ecstasy, a foul and dreadful wooing from which his very soul shuddered away—and yet in the innermost depths of that soul some grinning traitor shivered with delight. But deeply, behind all this, he knew horror and revulsion and despair beyond telling, while the intimate caresses crawled obscenely in the secret places of his soul—knew that the soul should not be handled—and shook with the perilous pleasure through it all.

And this conflict and knowledge, this mingling of rapture and revulsion all took place in the flashing of a moment while the scarlet worms coiled and crawled upon him, sending deep, obscene tremors of that infinite pleasure into every atom that made up Smith. And he could not stir in that slimy, ecstatic embrace—and a weakness was flooding that grew deeper after each succeeding wave of intense delight, and the traitor in his soul strengthened and drowned out the revulsion—and something within him ceased to struggle as he sank wholly into a blazing darkness that was oblivion to all else but that devouring rapture. . . .

The young Venusian climbing the stairs to his friend's lodging room pulled out his key absent-mindedly, a pucker forming between his fine brows. He was slim, as all Venusians are, as fair and sleek as any of them, and as with most of his countrymen the look of cherubic innocence on his face was wholly deceptive. He had the face of a fallen angel, without Lucifer's majesty to redeem it; for a black devil grinned in his eyes and there were faint lines of ruthlessness and dissipation about his mouth to tell of the long years behind him that had run the gamut of experiences and made his name, next to Smith's, the most hated and the most respected in the records of the patrol.

He mounted the stairs now with a puzzled frown between his eyes. He had come into Lakkdarol on the noon liner—the *Maid* in her hold very skillfully disguised with paint and otherwise—to find in lamentable disorder the affairs he had expected to be settled. And cautious inquiry elicited the information that Smith had not been seen for three days. That was not like his friend—he had never failed before, and the two stood to lose not only a large sum of money but also their personal safety by the inexplicable lapse on the part of Smith. Yarol could think of one solution only: Fate had at last caught up with his friend. Nothing but physical disability could explain it.

Still puzzling, he fitted his key in the lock and swung the door open.

In that first moment, as the door opened, he sensed something very wrong. . . . The room was darkened, and for a while he could see nothing, but at the first breath he scented a strange, unnamable odor, half sickening, half sweet. And deep stirrings of ancestral memory awoke within him—ancient, swamp-born memories from Venusian ancestors far away and long ago. . . .

Yarol laid his hand on his gun, lightly, and opened the door wider. In the dimness all he could see at first was a curious mound in the far corner. . . . Then his eyes grew accustomed to the dark, and he saw it more clearly, a mound that somehow heaved and stirred within itself. . . . A mound of—he caught his breath sharply—a mound like a mass of entrails, living, moving, writhing with an unspeakable aliveness. Then a hot Venusian oath broke from his lips and he cleared the doorsill in a swift stride, slammed the door and set his back against it, gun ready in his hand, although his flesh crawled—for he *knew*. . . .

"Smith!" he said softly, in a voice thick with horror. "Northwest!"

The moving mass stirred—shuddered—sank back into crawling quiescence again.

"Smith! Smith!" The Venusian's voice was gentle and insistent, and it quivered a little with terror.

An impatient ripple went over the whole mass of aliveness in the corner. It stirred again, reluctantly, and then tendril by writhing tendril it began to part itself and fall aside, and very slowly the brown of a spaceman's leather appeared beneath it, all slimed and shining.

"Smith! Northwest!" Yarol's persistent whisper came again, urgently, and with a dreamlike slowness the leather garments moved . . . a man sat up in the midst of the writhing worms, a man who once, long ago, might have been Northwest Smith. From head to foot he was slimy from the embrace of the crawling horror about him. His face was that of some creature beyond humanity—dead-alive, fixed in a gray stare, and the look of terrible ecstasy that overspread it seemed to come from somewhere far within, a faint reflection from immeasurable distances beyond the flesh. And as there is mystery and magic in the moonlight which is after all but a reflection of the everyday sun, so in that gray face turned to the door was a terror unnamable and sweet, a reflection of ecstasy beyond the understanding of any who have known only earthly ecstasy themselves. And as he sat there turning a blank, eyeless face to Yarol the red worms writhed ceaselessly about him, very gently, with a soft, caressive motion that never slacked.

"Smith . . . come here! Smith . . . get up . . . Smith, Smith!" Yarol's whisper hissed in the silence, commanding, urgent—but he made no move to leave the door.

And with a dreadful slowness, like a dead man rising, Smith stood up in the nest of slimy scarlet. He swayed drunkenly on his feet, and two or three crimson tendrils came writhing up his legs to the knees and wound themselves there, supportingly, moving with a ceaseless caress that seemed to give him some hidden strength, for he said then, without inflection,

"Go away. Go away. Leave me alone." And the dead, ecstatic face never changed.

"Smith!" Yarol's voice was desperate. "Smith, listen! Smith, can't you hear me?"

"Go away," the monotonous voice said. "Go away. Go away. Go—"

"Not unless you come too. Can't you hear? Smith! Smith! I'll—"

He hushed in midphrase, and once more the ancestral prickle of race-memory shivered down his back, for the scarlet mass was moving again, violently, rising. . . .

Yarol pressed back against the door and gripped his gun, and the name of a god he had forgotten years ago rose to his lips unbidden. For he knew what was coming next, and the knowledge was more dreadful than any ignorance could have been.

The red, writhing mass rose higher, and the tendrils parted and a human face looked out—no, half human, with green cat-eyes that shone in that dimness like lighted jewels, compellingly. . . .

Yarol breathed "Shar!" again, and flung up an arm across his face, and the tingle of meeting that green gaze for even an instant went thrilling through him perilously.

"Smith!" he called in despair. "Smith, can't you hear me?"

"Go away," said that voice that was not Smith's. "Go away."

And somehow, although he dared not look, Yarol knew that the—the other— had parted those worm-thick tresses and stood there in all the human sweetness of the brown, curved woman's body, cloaked in living horror. And he felt the eyes upon him, and something was crying insistently in his brain to lower that shielding arm. . . . He was lost—he knew it, and the knowledge gave him that courage which comes from despair. The voice in his brain was growing, swelling, deafening him with a roaring command that all but swept him before it— command to lower that arm—to meet the eyes that opened upon darkness—to submit—and a promise, murmurous and sweet and evil beyond words, of pleasure to come. . . .

But somehow he kept his head—somehow, dizzily, he was gripping his gun in his upflung hand—somehow, incredibly, crossing the narrow room with averted face, groping for Smith's shoulder. There was a moment of blind fumbling in emptiness, and then he found it, and gripped the leather that was slimy and dreadful and wet—and simultaneously he felt something loop gently about his ankle and a shock of repulsive pleasure went through him, and then another coil, and another, wound about his feet. . . .

Yarol set his teeth and gripped the shoulder hard, and his hand shuddered of itself, for the feel of that leather was slimy as the worms about his ankles, and a faint tingle of obscene delight went through him from the contact.

That caressive pressure on his legs was all he could feel, and the voice in his brain drowned out all other sounds, and his body obeyed him reluctantly—but somehow he gave one heave of tremendous effort and swung Smith, stumbling, out of that nest of horror. The twining tendrils ripped loose with a little sucking sound, and the whole mass quivered and reached after, and then Yarol forgot his friend utterly and turned his whole being to the hopeless task of freeing himself. For only a part of him was fighting, now—only a part of him struggled against the twining obscenities, and in his innermost brain the sweet, seductive murmur sounded, and his body clamored to surrender. . . .

"*Shar! Shar y'danis . . . Shar mor'la rol*—" prayed Yarol, gasping and half unconscious that he spoke, boy's prayers that he had forgotten years ago, and with his back half turned to the central mass he kicked desperately with his heavy boots at the red, writhing worms about him. They gave back before him, quivering and curling themselves out of reach, and though he knew that more were reaching for his throat from behind, at least he could go on struggling until he was forced to meet those eyes. . . .

He stamped and kicked and stamped again, and for one instant he was free of the slimy grip as the bruised worms curled back from his heavy feet, and he lurched away dizzily, sick with revulsion and despair as he fought off the coils, and then he lifted his eyes and saw the cracked mirror on the wall. Dimly in its reflection he could see the writhing scarlet horror behind him, cat face peering out with its demure girl-smile, dreadfully human, and all the red tendrils reaching after him. And remembrance of something he had read long ago swept incongruously over him, and the gasp of relief and hope that he gave shook for a moment the grip of the command in his brain.

Without pausing for a breath he swung the gun over his shoulder, the reflected barrel in line with the reflected horror in the mirror, and flicked the catch.

In the mirror he saw its blue flame leap in a dazzling spate across the dimness, full into the midst of that squirming, reaching mass behind him. There was a hiss and a blaze and a high, thin scream of inhuman malice and despair—the flame cut a wide arc and went out as the gun fell from his hand, and Yarol pitched forward to the floor.

Northwest Smith opened his eyes to Martian sunlight streaming thinly through the dingy window. Something wet and cold was slapping his face, and the familiar fiery sting of *segir*-whisky burnt his throat.

"Smith!" Yarol's voice was saying from far away. "N. W.! Wake up, damn you! Wake up!'

"I'm—awake," Smith managed to articulate thickly. "Wha's matter?"

Then a cup-rim was thrust against his teeth and Yarol said irritably, "Drink it, you fool!"

Smith swallowed obediently and more of the fire-hot *segir* flowed down his grateful throat. It spread a warmth through his body that awakened him from the numbness that had gripped him until now, and helped a little toward driving out the all-devouring weakness he was becoming aware of, slowly. He lay still for a few minutes while the warmth of the whisky went through him, and memory sluggishly began to permeate his brain with the spread of the *segir*. Nightmare memories . . . sweet and terrible . . . memories of—

"God!" gasped Smith suddenly, and tried to sit up. Weakness smote him like a blow, and for an instant the room wheeled as he fell back against something firm and warm—Yarol's shoulder. The Venusian's arm supported him while the room steadied, and after a while he twisted a little and stared into the other's black gaze.

Yarol was holding him with one arm and finishing the mug of *segir* himself, and the black eyes met his over the rim and crinkled into sudden laughter, half hysterical after that terror that was passed.

"By *Pharol!*" gasped Yarol, choking into his mug. "By *Pharol,* N. W.! I'm never gonna let you forget this! Next time you have to drag me out of a mess I'll say—"

"Let it go," said Smith. "What's been going on? How—"

"Shambleau." Yarol's laughter died. "Shambleau! What were you doing with a thing like that?"

"What was it?" Smith asked soberly.

"Mean to say you didn't know? But where'd you find it? How—"

"Suppose you tell me first what you know," said Smith firmly. "And another swig of that *segir*, too, please. I need it."

"Can you hold the mug now? Feel better?"

"Yeah—some. I can hold it—thanks. Now go on."

"Well—I don't know just where to start. They call them Shambleau—"

"Good God, is there more than one?"

"It's a—a sort of race, I think, one of the very oldest. Where they come from nobody knows. The name sounds a little French, doesn't it? But it goes back beyond the start of history. There have always been Shambleau."

"I never heard of 'em."

"Not many people have. And those who know don't care to talk about it much."

"Well, half this town knows. I hadn't any idea what they were talking about, then. And I still don't understand, but—"

"Yes, it happens like this, sometimes. They'll appear, and the news will spread and the town will get together and hunt them down, and after that—well, the story doesn't get around very far. It's too—too unbelievable."

"But—my God, Yarol!—what was it? Where'd it come from? How—"

"Nobody knows just where they come from. Another planet—maybe some undiscovered one. Some say Venus—I know there are some rather awful legends of them handed down in our family—that's how I've heard about it. And the minute I opened the door, awhile back—I—I think I knew that smell. . . ."

"But—what *are* they?"

"God knows. Not human, though they have the human form. Or that may be only an illusion . . . or maybe I'm crazy. I don't know. They're a species of the vampire—or maybe the vampire is a species of—of them. Their normal form must be that—that mass, and in that form they draw their nourishment from the—I suppose the life-forces of men. And they take some form—usually a woman form, I think, and key you up to the highest pitch of emotion before they—begin. That's to work the life-force up to intensity so it'll be easier. . . . And they give, always, that horrible, foul pleasure as they—feed. There are some men who, if they survive the first experience, take to it like a drug—can't give it up—keep the thing with them all their lives—which isn't long—feeding it for that ghastly satisfaction. Worse than smoking *ming* or—or praying to *Pharol*."

"Yes," said Smith. "I'm beginning to understand why that crowd was so surprised and—and disgusted when I said—well, never mind. Go on."

"Did you get to talk to—to it?" asked Yarol.

"I tried to. It couldn't speak very well. I asked it where it came from and it said—'from far away and long ago'—something like that."

"I wonder. Possibly some unknown planet—but I think not. You know there are so many wild stories with some basis of fact to start from, that I've sometimes wondered—mightn't there be a lot more of even worse and wilder superstitions we've never even heard of? Things like this, blasphemous and foul, that those who know have to keep still about? Awful, fantastic things running around loose and we never hear rumors of at all!

"These things—they've been in existence for countless ages. No one knows when or where they first appeared. Those who've seen them, as we saw this one, don't talk about it. It's just one of those vague, misty rumors you find half hinted at in old books sometimes. . . . I believe they are an older race than man, spawned from ancient seed in times before ours, perhaps on planets that have gone to dust, and so horrible to man that when they are discovered the discoverers keep still about it—forget them again as quickly as they can.

"And they go back to time immemorial. I suppose you recognized the legend of Medusa? There isn't any question that the ancient Greeks knew of them. Does it mean that there have been civilizations before yours that set out from Earth and explored other planets? Or did one of the Shambleau somehow make its way into Greece three thousand yeas ago? If you think about it long enough you'll go off your head! I wonder how many other legends are based on things like this—things we don't suspect, things we'll never know.

"The Gorgon, Medusa, a beautiful woman with—with snakes for hair, and a gaze that turned men to stone, and Perseus finally killed her—I remembered this just by accident, N. W., and it saved your life and mine—Perseus killed her by using a mirror as he fought to reflect what he dared not look at directly. I wonder what the old Greek who first started that legend would have thought if he'd known that three thousand years later his story would save the lives of two men on another planet. I wonder what that Greek's own story was, and how he met the thing, and what happened. . . .

"Well, there's a lot we'll never know. Wouldn't the records of that race of—of *things,* whatever they are, be worth reading! Records of other planets and other ages and all the beginnings of mankind! But I don't suppose they've kept any records. I don't suppose they've even any place to keep them—from what little I know, or anyone knows about it, they're like the Wandering Jew, just bobbing up here and there at long intervals, and where they stay in the meantime, I'd give my eyes to know! But I don't believe that terribly hypnotic power they have indicates any superhuman intelligence. It's their means of getting food— just like a frog's long tongue or a carnivorous flower's odor. Those are physical because the frog and the flower eat physical food. The Shambleau uses a—a mental reach to get mental food. I don't quite know how to put it. And just as a beast that eats the bodies of other animals acquires with each meal greater power over the bodies of the rest, so the Shambleau, stoking itself up with the life-forces of men, increases its power over the minds and the souls of other men. But I'm talking about things I can't define—things I'm not sure exist.

"I only know that when I felt—when those tentacles closed around my legs—I didn't want to pull loose, I felt sensations that—that—oh, I'm fouled and filthy to the very deepest part of me by that—pleasure—and yet—"

"I know," said Smith slowly. The effect of the *segir* was beginning to wear off, and weakness was washing back over him in waves, and when he spoke he was half meditating in a low voice, scarcely realizing that Yarol listened. "I know it—much better than you do—and there's something so indescribably awful that the thing emanates, something so utterly at odds with everything human—there aren't any words to say it. For a while I was a part of it, literally, sharing its thoughts and memories and emotions and hungers, and—well, it's over now and I don't remember very clearly, but the only part left free was that part of me that was all but insane from the—the obscenity of the thing. And yet it was a pleasure so sweet—I think there must be some nucleus of utter evil in me—in everyone—that needs only the proper stimulus to get complete control; because even while I was sick all through from the touch of those—things—there was something in me that was—was simply gibbering with delight. . . . Because of that I saw things—and knew things—horrible, wild things I can't quite remember—visited unbelievable places, looked backward through the memory of that—creature—I was one with, and saw—God, I wish I could remember!''

"You ought to thank your God you can't," said Yarol soberly.

His voice roused Smith from the half-trance he had fallen into, and he rose on his elbow, swaying a little from weakness. The room was wavering before him, and he closed his eyes, not to see it, but he asked, "You say they—they don't turn up again? No way of finding—another?"

Yarol did not answer for a moment. He laid his hands on the other man's shoulders and pressed him back, and then sat staring down into the dark, ravaged face with a new, strange, undefinable look upon it that he had never seen there before—whose meaning he knew, too well.

"Smith," he said finally, and his black eyes for once were steady and serious, and the little grinning devil had vanished from behind them, "Smith, I've never asked your word on anything before, but I've—I've earned the right to do it now, and I'm asking you to promise me one thing."

Smith's colorless eyes met the black gaze unsteadily. Irresolution was in them, and a little fear of what that promise might be. And for just a moment Yarol was looking, not into his friend's familiar eyes, but into a wide gray blankness that held all horror and delight—a pale sea with unspeakable pleasures sunk beneath it. Then the wide stare focused again and Smith's eyes met his squarely and Smith's voice said, "Go ahead. I'll promise."

"That if you ever should meet a Shambleau again—ever, anywhere—you'll draw your gun and burn it to hell the instant you realize what it is. Will you promise me that?"

There was a long silence. Yarol's somber black eyes bored relentlessly into the colorless ones of Smith, not wavering. And the veins stood out on Smith's tanned forehead. He never broke his word—he had given it perhaps half a dozen times in his life, but once he had given it, he was incapable of breaking it. And once more the gray seas flooded in a dim tide of memories, sweet and horrible beyond dreams. Once more Yarol was staring into blankness that hid nameless things. The room was very still.

The gray tide ebbed. Smith's eyes, pale and resolute as steel, met Yarol's levelly.

"I'll—try," he said. And his voice wavered.

RETURN TO DEATH

J. WESLEY ROSENQUIST

In many vampire stories, the vampire manipulates the skepticism of the average character to his advantage. Of course, there are cultures where disbelief in vampires is the exception rather than the norm. In "Return to Death," J. Wesley Rosenquist speculates briefly on a horrifying mistake in a town still governed by superstition.

GREAT SADNESS reigned in the little Transylvanian village of Rotfernberg; Herr Feldenpflanz was dead. Here and there, as one walked in the cobblestoned streets, one saw a sudden dampness in the eyes of passersby as his name was mentioned. Everyone was talking about him, praising his virtues, lamenting his early death; and in the eyes of many a fräulein was more than a trace of tears. He was indeed well beloved by all the village.

"Poor Herr Feldenpflanz," said the tailor sadly, "a fine man, as honest as the day is long. And a learned man, too. He went to the University of Berlin for four years, and knew more than any other man in Rotfernberg. Yes indeed, a very fine man."

The tailor blew his nose with vigor, and his listeners did likewise.

"And poor Fräulein Feldenpflanz! She loved her brother very dearly. She has no one else in the world. What will she do now?"

The tailor and his listeners all shook their heads sadly.

"Even now she sits beside him. For two days she has watched him, lying like life, so calm, and prays for his soul. We all know how he drifted away from God.

Those wizard's things that he did in his big, white room! Tubes full of strange vapors and lights there were, and lightning in glass balls. He always said that it was not magic—as if we had not eyes!''

"Yes," said the grocer sadly but with vigor, "as if we had not eyes!"

The village priest sat there also, a little outside the group, with sorrow written on his face; and every time one of the townsmen spoke of poor Herr Feldenpflanz's obvious traffic with Lucifer, an expression of deep pain passed over his mild and benign countenance. He was a short, stout, dark-haired man, and wore the vestments of his calling. He sat very calm and still. At last he could no longer listen without speaking his mind.

"Please, please," he said softly, "say no more of our good friend. He is now, I hope, among the blessed saints, and we must speak only well of the dead. Remember, he was a good man; perhaps he strayed without knowing that he was ensnared by the Enemy's wiles. If that be so, there is salvation for him. Let us not speak of Herr Feldenpflanz; let us not use our human judgment; let us rather pray with the Fräulein Feldenpflanz, who even now prays beside her brother's coffin."

So saying, he got up from his chair and motioned to the men gathered there in the tailor's store to follow him. They did so: the grocer, the tailor, the blacksmith, the butcher and the mayor. They climbed the steep mountain path with energy and puffing, and said nothing. The evening dew lay heavy on the long, wild grass; and from overhead fell cool drops from the leaves of the thick, ancient oaks growing on the mountainside. That cool, calm, mountain hush had descended with the twilight. It was as though a great, blue, star-sprinkled bowl had been inverted and placed upon the earth, with the summit of the mountain touching its spangled center.

Suddenly the priest spoke to his companions.

"See, my friends, there lies the Feldenpflanz dwelling. When we enter let us conduct ourselves with fitting dignity and propriety. We must not speak to the bereaved fräulein when we enter, but gather around the coffin and pray with her. We must not disturb her."

So it was. The big house, white-painted and gabled and surrounded by gardens, lay just before them. Marring the pure, solid color of the walls and the big front door hung a significant black ribbon. The calm hush was very pronounced here. In a window near the front door there twinkled a single electric light, the only one in the town of Rotfernberg. The unschooled villagers had always been amazed by the electric fixtures and the apparatus in Feldenpflanz's home and laboratory.

All silent, the group of men reached the end of the path and tried the door. It was open, and quietly they entered, Father Josef in the lead. They passed through a long, dark hall, at the end of which was a door leading into the parlor. Light gleamed through the crack along the floor. As they approached they heard the muffled sound of low praying, mingled with sobs.

Father Josef opened the door carefully and tiptoed in, followed by the five other villagers. They crossed themselves in unison.

By a simple, black coffin of wood knelt Fräulein Feldenpflanz. Under her knees was a cushion to make possible long vigils. Her face was hidden by her long, black hair, and her head hung low over the bier. Her pale lips moved constantly. At the head of the coffin, in spite of the electric light, burned a candle; the whole coffin itself was covered with mountain blooms. The heavy, cloying odor peculiar to death did not hang in the air, however. The kneeling woman cast one vacant, tearful glance at the entering men and resumed her former attitude.

The six men came close to the coffin and gazed down upon its occupant. There lay Herr Feldenpflanz, calm and handsome and indeed very lifelike, dressed in a suit made by the tailor himself. They all knelt around the bier and prayed. . . .

As he lay there, Feldenpflanz, terrified by his predicament, could think of only one thing—escape. And one word echoed and re-echoed through his brain—catalepsy, catalepsy! . . .

For hours he had been forced to listen to his sister's prayers and tears; long hour after hour he heard his death mourned, and was unable to move. He felt his own heartbeat, very slow and very gentle so that no one would be able to detect it; but it sent the blood through his numbed brain, sustaining consciousness, so that, aware of all that went on, he could know the pangs of mortal fear and the bittersweet of faint hope. "Help! Help!" he tried to shout, but his mind alone formed the words; his lips defied his will.

An educated man, he knew the danger of his state. A chance existed that he might regain control of his limbs before he was buried—buried alive. Consciousness was a good sign, he knew. If now he could force his body to obey his will, the final stage of recovery from this dreadful malady, he would be saved; he would return to the world he loved, to life and living, to his sister Maria.

And then a terrifying thought flashed through his head. He realized that inevitably, if not soon, the air in his coffin would be exhausted! The oxygen of the air was slowly being used up; for although he did not move his chest, did not breathe, the air was entering and leaving his lungs by diffusion. If he could only move, a tap on the side of the box would attract attention and effect his release. Was he doomed to impotence and burial alive? The poor superstitious folk of Rotfernberg, including his sister, would probably flee in terror. It would be hopeless, then, even if he did recover the use of his limbs. They would leave him to struggle futiley in his flower-bedecked prison! Oh, why were these people not educated? Why must they confine themselves to a home and a mountainside?

Gradually he fell into a dreamy, reflective state, in which the first sharp agony of terror had dissolved away from sheer exhaustion; and only two hopes remained in his mind, like brilliant butterflies that rested for a brief moment on a withered flower. First, he must move; and second, his sister must not be afraid; she must set him free from his narrow prison. And these two hopes, bitter for their improbability and sweet for their possibility, were all for which he existed. . . .

To his ears still came the muffled voice of Maria, hoarse and weary from long use; through his eyelids the vigil-light shone. Suddenly he heard the sound of feet in the room where he was lying. He listened carefully; they were men, he calculated, about a half-dozen. Here was new hope! If he moved or made a sound, one of the men might have sense and courage enough to free him. Then his ears caught the sound of voices praying in unison. So now they too were praying for him!

Several minutes grew into an hour, and then the voices became still, including his sister's. A pang of apprehension ran through him like a red-hot sword. Were they going to leave him? But no. He heard the sound of scraping chairs and the rustle of clothing. They were sitting down. As he listened attentively, he heard a voice that was familiar, low-pitched though it was from respect for the dead, and muffled by the wooden walls that enclosed him. It was Father Josef.

"Please, Fräulein Feldenpflanz," he insisted gently, "you must go to bed now. You are very weary, and tomorrow you must rise early for your brother's funeral. Please sleep now."

There was no answer, but Feldenpflanz heard the sound of footsteps on the stairs. Maria was going upstairs, evidently.

"Let us hope," said Father Josef, "that our good friend has no need of our prayers. By now he is in Heaven or Hell. Be it not the latter."

The six men sat there quietly, nodding their heads.

"Or Purgatory," added the tailor, looking toward the priest for agreement.

The unmoving man in the coffin almost felt amused.

"After the burial the fräulein will no doubt destroy the unholy things in her brother's big, white room in the cellar," spoke up the blacksmith, who was a big man and who very seldom spoke. "I think," he continued, "that cellars should rightly hold only wines."

So they would like to see his laboratory destroyed! And after he was buried. . . . He made a desperate, mighty attempt to move, but could not. Was it imagination or was the air really growing bad? His head began to swim, and he thought he felt his heart beat a little faster.

"The whole village of Rotfernberg will come to see the Feldenpflanz funeral," said the mayor, a tall, thin man, "and I will lead the procession. He was one of my best friends, and hence it is only fitting that I do so. Ah, well I remember his cheerful 'Good morning' and his fine wines. He was a generous man, too, always giving alms, and he paid the highest taxes in town. No one was more honest, either. A very fine man."

The mayor blew his nose gently, as he was in the presence of the dead. All nodded their heads in agreement except Father Josef, who was absorbed in a prayerbook. His pale hands stood out against his black cassock, and his lips moved slightly; several minutes passed before he looked up.

"Dear God, dear God," prayed Feldenpflanz over and over as he felt the true death approaching. But what was this? He felt a tremor pass over his body. His heart beat faster, and a warm flush passed over his numbed limbs! Slowly, he felt his will creep down the sleeping nerves into his extremities. Very soon now, he hoped, freedom would be his.

"Let us go now," said the priest, and a pang of terror passed through the man in the coffin. He heard the scraping of chairs and the shuffling of feet. Now was the moment! Now he must move! The beating of his heart was tumultuous; his fingertips were tingling; his face felt hot and his head full of blood. He heard the footsteps cease; they had evidently paused over him. He heard the rustle of clothing as they rubbed against the coffin. Then the butcher spoke, in a strained tone.

"How very lifelike indeed! His face flushes with blood!"

Feldenpflanz made a supreme effort of will. The darkness seemed to shake— and his eyes were open! Above him he saw six faces in a frozen tableau.

Father Josef wore a look of utmost horror and shock.

The tailor's face, long and pale and drawn, wore an expression of fear and shocked suspicion.

The butcher opened eyes and mouth wide.

The grocer crossed himself again and again, his lips moving in frantic prayer.

The blacksmith, more afraid of the supernatural than the rest, closed his eyes, gasped, and staggered back.

The mayor stared for a moment with bulging eyes, then bawled out a single word:

"Vampire!"

Then there came the sound of running and shouting, and Feldenpflanz saw the faces disappear from above his prostrate form, except for that of Father Josef, who was reading a Latin invocation from his prayerbook.

The cataleptic victim, now desperate, heard the noise of many feet running toward him, and the faces of the blacksmith and the butcher burst into view above him. There was a sound of fumbling at the side of the coffin, and then— the lid was raised. He was saved!

But what was this? The butcher had placed a knife against his left side, and the blacksmith raised a hammer high. There came to his ears the monotone of Father Josef's Latin prayer.

Feldenpflanz made inarticulate sounds.

"No, n', huh, huh, help, no!"

The hammer rose and fell. One! Two! Three!

Herr Feldenpflanz ceased to think of escape.

ISLE OF THE UNDEAD

LLOYD ARTHUR ESHBACH

The vampire story was no different from any other type of pulp fantasy, insofar as readers expected it to deliver its share of thrills and chills. Lloyd Arthur Eshbach's "Isle of the Undead" is so full of lurid adventure that it nearly tips over into shudder-pulp territory. The story may hold the record for the number of times a pulp hero faints at the most inopportune moments.

1. A Horror from the Past

A DRAB GRAY SHEET of cloud slipped stealthily from the moon's round face, like a shroud slipping from the face of one long dead, a coldly phosphorescent face from which the eyes had been plucked. Yellow radiance fell toward a calm, oily sea, seeking a narrow bank of fog lying low on the water, penetrating its somber mass like frozen yellow fingers.

Vilma Bradley shuddered and shrank against Clifford Darrell's brawny form. "It's—it's ghastly, Cliff!" she said.

"Ghastly?" Darrell leaned against the railing, laughing softly. "One cocktail too many—that's the answer. It's given you the jitters. Listen!" Faintly from the salon came strains of dance music and the rhythmic shuffle of feet. "A nifty yacht, a South Sea moon, a radio dance orchestra, dancers—and little Clifford! And you call it ghastly!" Almost savagely his arms tightened about her, and the bantering note left his voice. "I'm crazy about you, Vilma."

She tried to laugh, but it was an unconvincing sound. "It's the moon, Cliff—I guess. I never saw it like that before. Something's going to happen—something dreadful. I just *know* it!"

"Oh—be sensible, Vilma!" There was a hint of impatience in Cliff's deep voice. A gorgeous girl in his arms—dark-haired, dark-eyed, made for love—and she talked of dreadful things which were going to happen because the moon looked screwy.

She released herself and glanced out over the sea. "I know I'm silly, but— Her voice froze and her slender body stiffened. "Cliff—look!"

Darrel spun around, and as he stared, he felt a dryness seeping into his throat, choking him. . . .

Out of the winding sheet of fog into the moonlight crept a strange, strange craft, her crumbling timbers blackened and rotted with incredible age. The corpse of a ship, she seemed, resurrected from the grave of the sea. Her prow thrust upward like a simitar bent backward, hovering over the gaunt ruin of the cabin whose seaward sides were formed by port and starboard bows. From a shallow pit amidships jutted the broken arm of a mast, its splintered tip pointing toward the blindly watching moon. The stern, thickly covered with the moldering encrustations of age, curved inward above the strange high poop, beneath which lay another cabin. And along either side of her worm-eaten freeboard ran a row of apertures like oblong portholes. Out of these projected great oars, long, unwieldy, as somberly black as the rest of the ancient hulk.

Now a sound drifted across the waters, the steady, rhythmic *br-rr-oom, br-rr-oom, br-rr-oom* of a drum beating time for the rowers. Its hollow thud checked the heart, set it to throbbing in tempo with its own weary pulse. Ghostly fingers, dripping dread, crawled up Darrell's spine.

Stiff-lipped, Vilma gasped: "What—what is it?"

Cliff answered in a dry husky voice, the words seeming to trip over an awkward tongue. "It's—it's—it *can't* be, damn it!—but it's a galley, a ship from the days of Alexander the Great! What's it doing—here—*now*?"

Closer she came through the moonpath, a frothing lip of brine curling away from her swelling prow. Closer—her course crossing that of the *Ariel*—and the watchers saw her crew! They gasped, and the blood ebbed from their faces.

Men of ancient Persia, clad in leather kirtles and rusted armor, and they were hideous! In the yellow moon-glow Cliff could see them clearly now—a lookout standing motionless in the stem, the steersman on the poop-deck, the drummer squatting beside the broken mast, the rowers in the pit—and all, *all* were a bloodless white, the skin of their faces puffed and bloated and horribly wrinkled, like flesh that had been under water a long time.

Dead men . . . men whose movements were stiffly wooden . . . as dead as their faces. But most horrible was the fact that they were there, that they moved at all!

"A queer mirage, isn't it?" A hollow voice spoke suavely behind them. Vilma gasped at the sudden sound, and they whirled. A foot away stood the tall, lean figure of the *Ariel*'s captain, Leon Corio. A queer smile twisted his thin lips.

"What's the idea—sneaking up on us?" Darrell demanded angrily. He didn't like this man, hadn't liked him from the moment he had approached Cliff to sell him the yacht. But Cliff had bought the craft because she was a bargain, and in accordance with their agreement he had hired Corio as captain.

The tall man's smile remained fixed, and he bowed gravely. "Sorry, sir. I always walk softly. A habit, I suppose." He gestured toward the galley. "It looks quite lifelike, don't you think so?"

"Lifelike?" Cliff spoke between his teeth as he again faced the black ship. "It looks *dead* to me!"

The galley had almost reached them now, veering sharply to draw up beside the *Ariel*. The drum quieted, and the oars trailed in the water, motionless except for the swaying imparted by the waves. A musty, age-old odor filtered through the air like a breath from a grave. The music and dancing had stopped. A fear-filled hush shrouded the yacht.

Vilma drew Cliff's arm about her shoulder. He glanced back at the motionless captain.

"*Do* something, Corio!" he rasped. "Don't stand there like a dummy!"

Corio nodded with his same queer smile. His hand darted to an inside pocket, came out bearing a curious instrument like four twisted cones of silver bound together with silver thongs. As he raised this to his mouth, his eyelids were slits behind which burned the embers of his eyes.

Out over the sea crept a single note, deep, hollow, laden with eery minor wailings—a sound that summoned imperatively, yet a sound that repelled. It was a moan, hideous as the moan of a dying demon. It raked the heart with fear-tipped claws. It rose, and fell, and rose again, and as it died, it awakened the crew of the ancient galley to motion, sweeping them in a horde to the rail of the yacht.

Cliff swung toward Corio in bursting fury, fury mingled with dread. His fist lashed out at that glittering silver instrument and the face behind it, but Corio avoided him like a wraith, still smiling fixedly, the horn again at his lips. Cliff cursed, and hurled himself through the air. One hand caught a bony shoulder; he felt fingers like hooks close on his own throat. He wrenched free, landing a stunning blow on Corio's face—saw him reel and crash to the deck—and then he heard Vilma scream!

He whirled. She was struggling between two of the flabby-faced things from the galley! In an instant he was upon them, his fist thudding against icy flesh, burying itself in something horribly soft and yielding. Startled, Cliff swung a second blow; and an arm, tomb-cold and strong as the tentacle of an octopus, wrapped itself around him—a vise of thin-covered bone! A dead, drowned face peered over his shoulder, staring blankly. Other arms seized his legs, and though he struggled and writhed with the strength of a mounting fear, he was borne to the rail. Over they went, and dropped to the rotting deck of the galley.

A numbness was creeping through him like a contagion, spreading from those crushing hands of ice. His struggles ceased. With eyes that turned stiffly in their sockets he looked for Vilma, saw her raised high above the heads of two other pallid creatures, saw them climb over the rail. Then the blackness of a dank and musty cabin enveloped him; and he was dropped with jarring force. His captors bulked black against the moonlit doorway, treading soundlessly, and were gone.

Cliff lay in a rigid paralysis, every sense keenly alive, his mind striving to clutch a single spar of reason in this chaotic whirlpool of the incredible. This *couldn't* be! Soon he'd awaken to laugh at his absurd nightmare. . . . Yet it seemed horribly real . . . It *was* real!

From the *Ariel* boiled a fearful bedlam. Screams of terror. Curses. Then other shadows loomed in the doorway, and Vilma, motionless and rigid, was dropped brutally beside him on the spongy floor.

Furiously Cliff struggled against the maddening restraint of paralysis. He couldn't lie here helpless! Vilma needed him! He'd—he'd *have* to do something. With an effort that studded his forehead with rounded drops of sweat and sent the blood throbbing through the distended veins of his neck, he sought to move. And like a cord snapping, his invisible bonds fell from him.

He was crouching over Vilma, rubbing her wrists, calling to her, when again he heard the silver horn of Corio. A low droning utterly unlike the note that had awakened the galley's crew, it drifted languidly along a channel of endless sleep. It seeped through the eardrums, touching every nerve-tip with resistless lassitude. Doggedly Cliff fought against the sound, pressing his hands over his ears, gritting his teeth, holding his eyelids wide. Yet he felt his muscles weaken, began to relax, knew dimly that his mind, sodden with drowsiness, was creeping toward the pits of slumber—and the vibrant drone ended!

His head cleared rapidly, and he bent over Vilma. As he touched a limp arm, he knew she had passed from paralysis into a deep, quiet sleep. He shook her. It was useless. He listened, heard her steady breathing; and at that instant realized that the noises from the yacht had ceased.

Rising, he strode toward the square of chalky moonlight. A foot away he halted, fell back. He had heard a faint footfall, had seen an armor-clad figure climbing over the rail! With silent haste he flung himself down beside Vilma.

And there he lay while the crew of the galley carried his friends from the *Ariel*, all slumped in that unnatural sleep, and stretched them out on the floor of the black cabin. Unmoving, he watched through narrow lids till all save Corio had been carried aboard, and the drowned things had gone back to their places in the rowers' pit. Again the hollow voice of the drum began throbbing through the silence, and the oars creaked a faint accompaniment. He could feel the galley cleaving the oily sea.

On his feet, he peered through the doorway. The backs of the rowers rose and fell with stiff, mechanical rhythm. Beyond the galley's stern came the yacht, slinking along like a thief, only one dim light showing, her diesel engines purring almost soundlessly.

He turned and bent over Vilma, still in thrall to that strange deep slumber. As he traced the delicate outlines of her lovely face, now so lifeless and pale, bitter wrath flared within him, wrath and hatred for Leon Corio. But as he thought of the ghastly *undead* things out there in the galley pit, thought of this water-soaked anachronism which had no right to be afloat, his skin crisped with a sense of foreboding, a fear of what was yet to come. He must do something!

Stepping over the still forms of his friends, he moved to the forward wall where a beam of radiance crept fearfully through a gap between two boards. His hands touched the hull—and he jerked them away. Rotten, clammy, like a decayed corpse, partly frozen. Crouching, he peered through.

Far ahead, a blotch of evil blackness squatted on the horizon, an island crouching low like a black beast ready to spring. Around it the moonlight seemed to dim, as though it were striving to hide some nameless horror. Interminably Cliff watched while the shadowed mass drew closer . . . closer. . . .

They were headed for a towering wall of black basalt; and as the galley neared it, Cliff saw that it bore striking resemblance to a gigantic human skull, its rounded surface broken by caves that the sea had carved into hollow eye-sockets and an empty nasal cavity. The rock wall ended high above the water; beneath it lay a gaping chasm of pitchy darkness. And the galley, drum silenced, oars at rest, slid under the ledge, into the mouth of the skull!

Just before total blackness fell, Cliff sprang to Vilma's side and raised her in his arms. If he hoped to do anything, he must do it now! He groped his way to the starboard bow and moved one hand along the dank timbers, searching. He found what he sought, a wide gap at the edge of a board. Gently lowering Vilma to the floor, he gripped the slimy wood with both hands and thrust outward mightily. A wide strip of decayed timber burst free. He dropped it into the sea and attacked the next board. In moments a wide irregular opening yawned in the galley's hull.

Leaning out, Cliff looked down. He could see nothing. Then suddenly a faint light appeared, and he heard the hum of the *Ariel*'s motors as she entered the cave. The humming ceased instantly, but the faint light persisted.

Now he could see the blackness of waters, a rock wall beyond. He drew back—and as he did so, he heard movements on deck! At any moment the rowers might enter! He'd have to risk a drop into the water with Vilma—there was nothing else to do. If only she were conscious!

He stooped and raised her, holding her firmly with one arm. Gripping the hull with the other, he climbed through the opening, inhaled deeply, and dropped! A heart-stopping plunge—and cold water closed over them. Down, down—then they shot upward, reached the surface; and even as Cliff gulped a single gasping breath, something struck his skull a blinding, stunning blow! The oars!

With rapidly numbing arms and legs Cliff kicked and flailed the water, striving for land. Dimly he knew he no longer held Vilma; dimly he visioned her as were those ghastly undead; then his body scraped on something hard, and a blackness that was not physical blotted out consciousness.

2. The Dreadful Isle

RED HOT HAMMERS pounding against his temples wakened Cliff Darrell. He opened his eyes to stare into total darkness crawling with mental monsters spawned by his pain-stabbed brain. He lay half immersed in shallow brine, his head resting on a jagged stone just above the surface. Struggling to his hands and knees, he shook his head from side to side, dumbly, like an animal in pain. Something had hit him—and now he was in water—and there was no light. What had happened? Where was Vilma?

Vilma! He groaned. He remembered now. They had dropped—and his head had struck something—and—and—maybe she was floating out there even now, dead eyes staring upward.

"Vilma!" he cried, his voice pleading. "Vilma!"

Only a mocking echo answered him. There was no other sound, not even the whisper of waves swishing among the rocks.

Cliff pressed his hands fiercely against his throbbing head. The pain had become a madness, matched only by the agony of his own helplessness. He felt his reason reeling; he fought an insane desire to fling himself shrieking into that silent expanse of water to search for Vilma; then with a tremendous physical effort he jarred himself back to sanity.

He staggered to his feet, groped stumblingly over the rocks away from the water. His hand touched a rock wall broken and pitted by the action of the sea; and he crept slowly inland, feeling his way, like a blind man. As he plodded on his thoughts blended into one fixed idea: He must get to light, must get light to search for Vilma.

Gradually the insensate pounding in his head abated, and strength returned to his body. When at last he saw light beyond a narrow fissure around an angle in the cavern, he had almost recovered. In moments he was gazing out over a plain bathed in the glow of a leprous moon. As he stared, he shivered; and it was not because of the cold draft drawing through the fissure, fanning his brine-drenched body.

Grim and starkly forbidding the plain lay before him, dead as the frozen landscape of the moon. Once there had been life there, but now only the skeletons of trees remained, lifting their wasted limbs in rigid pleading to an unresponsive sky. Some, there were, that had fallen, uprooted by the fury of passing hurricanes; these lay like the scattered bones of a dismembered giant, age-blackened, and painted with hoarfrost by the brushes of moonlight. Feebly the dead forest stirred under the touch of a moaning wind, and the gaunt shadows cast by the trees seemed to be multiarmed monsters slithering over the rocky earth.

He looked beyond the trees, and he saw light. Little squares of pale radiance cut high in the walls of an ancient black castle. Castle? Cliff frowned. He could liken it to nothing else, though he could not recall ever having seen a castle which thrust curving, needle-thin spires into the sky like a devil's horns.

Impatiently Cliff stepped from the wall of rock and glanced along a path that writhed through the forest; glanced—and crouched swiftly, a low cry escaping him. A single spot of water on a smooth, flat stone! A spot shaped like a woman's shoe! Vilma had passed this way!

But—might it not have been some other woman from the *Ariel*? No! They had been carried—and even if they had walked, their feet were dry!

Like a hound on the scent, Cliff Darrell sped along the serpentine path. The wind moaned above him, and the soughing branches seemed to whisper croaking warnings, but he ran on, his eyes constantly seeking signs of Vilma's course. Here a drop of water shaken from her drenched skirt, there another; and Cliff blessed the full moon whose light made possible his trailing of the almost invisible spoor.

Now he had passed beyond the dead forest and was moving toward the castle. The trail had been growing steadily fainter, but he managed to follow it. It led him toward a narrow stone stairway climbing crookedly to a misshapen opening in the wall. Light glowed faintly lurid somewhere deep within; and now Cliff heard a blasphemous sound belch from the depths of the castle—a wheezing, sardonic croaking like the moan of a demoniac organ, rumbling an obscene dirge. His hair bristled, and he stopped short.

He looked at the steps, searching for the fading trail—and he stiffened. There on the second step was an irregular blotch of moisture! What did it mean? Had Vilma crouched there? Had she ascended those steps? Entered?

With drawn face he began to skirt the base of the black building, searching every nook and cranny, scanning the bare walls. His heart lay like ballast in his breast. If—if something had lured Vilma into that demon-infested vault . . . he checked the thought.

Suddenly he cursed. Mechanically he had begun to measure his stride in time with the doleful dirge from the castle. He stalked on with altered pace. As he rounded the corner at the rear of the structure, he saw a shadow outlined against the sky, crouching on a ledge below one of the little windows. He looked again—cried:

"Vilma!"

The figure above him stirred, looked down, then climbed hastily earthward. It was Vilma . . . Vilma, with black hair hanging stringily about her head, face pale, eyes fixed in the wideness of fear . . . Vilma, with her wet clothing clinging to the lovely contours of her symmetrical body.

"Oh, Cliff!" she gasped, a dry sob choking her. "Thank God—thank God!"

She clung to him, her face hidden against his shoulder, quivering uncontrollably. Then tears came, saving tears, relieving her pent-up emotions.

Cliff said nothing, only held her close, strongly protective. And gradually he felt the tempest of terror subside. At last she looked up. Some of the dread had gone from her face, and she tried to smile.

"I guess—I can't take it," she said.

Cliff shook his head solemnly. "You're a game girl, Vilma! You've nerve enough for two men. If you can, tell me what happened. Or if you'd rather let it wait, just say so."

"I'll feel better if I get it off my chest," she said. "You probably saw those—things—carry me from the yacht." Cliff nodded. "Well, I was just about paralyzed when they dropped me in their terrible boat. I remember, you tried to arouse me; then that horn blew, and I just seemed to float away in an ocean of sleep.

"After that I can remember nothing till I awoke with water filling my eyes and nose and mouth, choking me. Someone's arms were around me—it must have been you, Cliff—and then they weren't there anymore, and I struggled wildly, out of my wits. I don't know how I got to shore, but I did, and I lay there in the shadow of the galley, choking and gagging, but afraid to cough. It wasn't altogether dark, and I could see those dreadful things with people hanging over their shoulders, carrying them along a narrow ledge close to the water's edge, heading inland. I thought maybe you were one of those limp bodies; and I—I almost died of fright. After a while the last one had gone, and the light went out. Then I heard another pair of feet moving over the rocks. Corio, I suppose. The sound died—and I was alone.

"That place was awful, Cliff. The blackness almost drove me mad. I wanted to scream, but I was afraid to. Some terrible weight seemed to be crushing my lungs. If I followed those undead things, they might capture me, but it seemed worse to stay there in that dreadful dark.

"I got out of there somehow, though it seemed to take hours. Then I didn't know what to do. I stood at the edge of the dead forest trying to decide; trying, too, to keep myself from shrieking and running—anywhere. Then Corio's horn blew again—a sound, Cliff, worse than anything I've ever heard. It—it was a wicked sound, promising to fulfill every foul desire that ever tainted a human mind. It repelled, yet it lured irresistibly. And—I answered!"

She stopped, and buried her face in her hands. After a moment she went on. "The sound stopped just as I found myself crawling on hands and knees up the stone stairway on the other side. Another started—that awful groaning—music— but it didn't draw me. I ran down the steps and scurried away like a rabbit trying to find a place to hide.

"After a while I came back—I thought you must be in there—and I climbed up to the window. And—and—Cliff, it's hellish!"

Her eyes, boring into his, widened in the same rigid terror he had seen in them when he joined her.

"We could go back to the cove and get away on the *Ariel*, Vilma," Cliff said stonily. "And if you think we should, we will. But—I brought our friends here, and—well, I want to get them out if I can."

With an effort Vilma nodded. "Of course. We can't do anything else."

He released her and stepped up to the wall.

"I'm going to see what's going on in there," he said. "You wait here till I come down."

In sudden dread Vilma seized his arm. "No, Cliff. I couldn't stand waiting here alone. I'll go with you."

He nodded understandingly. And together they began climbing the precipitous wall, fitting hands and feet in steplike crevices that made progress fairly rapid. Soon they were crouching on a wide stone ledge, clinging to thin, rusted bars, staring into the black castle.

3. The Steps of Torture

A GIGANTIC HALL lay before them, a single chamber whose walls were the walls of the castle, whose arched ceiling rose far above them. Directly below their window a stone platform jutted from the wall, spreading entirely across the chamber. A stone altar squatted in the center of the platform, a strangely phosphorescent fire smoldering on its top. And from the altar descended a wide, wide stairway ending in the middle of the hall. All this Cliff saw in a single sweeping glance; afterward he had eyes for nothing save the lethal horror of a mad, mad scene, revealed by the dim radiance of the altar fire.

Behind the altar stood five huge figures clad in long, hooded cloaks of scarlet. The central figure had arms raised wide, his cloak spread like the wings of some bloody bird of prey; and from his lips came a guttural incantation, a blasphemous chant in archaic Latin, in time with the wheeze of the buried organ. Now his arms dropped, and he was silent.

From the room below came a concerted whine of ceremonial devotion, a hollow, hungry wail. It rose from the bloodless lips of strangely assorted human figures ranging down the center of the long stairway in two facing columns. A hundred or more there must have been, representing half as many periods and countries, according to their strange and ancient costumes. Men in the armor of medieval Persia—the crew of the black galley; yellow-haired Vikings; hawk-faced Egyptians with leather-brown skin; half-naked islanders; red-sashed pirates from the Spanish main; men of today! And about all, like the dampness that clings to a tombstone, hovered a cloud of—death! The undead!

Cliff's gaze roved over the tensely waiting columns, then leaped to the foot of the stairs. There, cowering dumbly like sheep in a slaughter-pen, were his friends from the *Ariel*. All clothing had been stripped from them, and they stood waiting in waxen, statuesque stiffness. He saw then that three others lay prone before the stone altar, naked and ominously still.

And far down at the very end of the hall stood Leon Corio, draped in a hooded cape of unbroken black, a glint of silver in his hand—his horn of drugging sounds.

Now, as though at a silent command, a girl left the group and began to mount the stairs, as those motionless three must have mounted! Vivacious Ann—she had been the life of Cliff's yacht party; but now she was—changed. Her blanched face was rigid with inexpressible terror despite the semi-stupor which numbed her senses. Her nude body glowed like marble in the dim light. Horribly, her feet began their climb with a little catch step suggested by the moaning chant of that cracked organ note.

She reached the first of the undead, and Cliff saw light glint on a knife-blade. A crimson gash appeared in the flesh of her thigh; and dead lips touched that wound, drank thirstily. The girl strode on, blood gleaming darkly on the white skin. A second drank of the crimson flow—a third—and the blood ceased gushing forth.

Another knife flashed—and lips closed again and again on the redly dripping wound. And the girl with the unchanging pace of a robot climbed the stairway to its very top—climbed while fiendish corpses drank her life's blood—climbed, to sink down on the altar.

One of the red-clad figures stooped over her, lifted her, buried long teeth in her throat—and Cliff saw his face. . . . His own face paled, and talons of fear raked his brain. Those others on the stairs—they were abhorrent, zombies freed from the grave. But this monster! A vampire vested with the lust and cruelty and power of hell!

He lowered her, finally, and she sank down, lay still, beside the other three.

Another began the hellish climb, a giant of a man with a thickly muscled torso. Cliff knew him instantly; and his heart seemed to stop. Leslie Starke! They'd played football together. A brave man—a fighter. He mounted the stairway with the same little catch step, the same plodding stiffness. No resistance, no struggle—only a hell of fear on his face.

The marrow melted from Cliff Darrell's bones. What—what could he do against a power that did *that* to Les Starke? He tried to swallow, but the saliva had dried on his tongue. He wanted to turn to Vilma, but he could not wrench his eyes from the frightful spectacle.

Up the stone steps Starke strode. And no blade leaped toward him; no thirsty lips closed on his flesh! In an unwavering line he mounted toward the cowled monster in the center of the dais, like a puppet on the end of a string; mounted to pause before the stone altar, to lie on it, head bent back, throat bared. . . . Mercifully Cliff regained enough control to close his eyes.

He opened them at a gasp from Vilma; saw the vampire raise the flaccid body of Les Starke and hurl it far from him, to crash to the stone steps, to roll and thud and tumble, down and down, sickeningly, to lie awkwardly twisted on the floor before his companions!

And another began to climb the long stone steps. . . .

All through the interminable night Cliff and Vilma crouched on the ledge, staring through the barred window. A hundred times they would have fled to escape the maddening scene, but they could not move. Senses reeled before the awful monotony of the ceaseless climbing, their eyes smarted with fixed staring, their tongues and throats were parched to desert dryness; yet only after hours of endless watching, only after the last victim had climbed the steps, did the edge of terror dull, and a modicum of control return to their bodies.

Stiffly Cliff looked over his shoulder. A faint tinge of gray rimmed the sea on the eastern horizon.

"Almost daylight," he whispered hoarsely.

Vilma nodded, her gaze still held by that chamber of horror. Cliff followed the direction of her eyes; and saw Corio standing like a great bat in his hooded cape close to the far wall. He raised his four-piped horn to his lips. And the instrument's fourth note crept through the room.

It was a doleful sound, a cry like the cry Death itself might possess; yet oddly—and horribly—it was soothing, promising the peace of endless sleep. And touched by its power, the columns of undead stiffened, thinned to wraiths, flowed as water flows down the stone steps, vanished!

The dead-alive—those five vampires in crimson cowls—looked upward uneasily. The shadows under the roof were graying with the light of dawn. Cliff could sense their thought. Before sunrise they must be in their tombs under the castle, to sleep until another night. With one accord they strode down the stairs, past Corio who had prostrated himself, and entered a black opening in the wall. With their departure the altar fire dimmed to a sullen ember.

Corio arose. He was alone in the chamber save for that dead, broken body lying in a twisted heap at the foot of the stairs, and those other half-alive wretches stretched out before the altar. Now, Cliff told himself, was the time for him to get in there at Corio; now was the time to rescue his friends—but he continued to crouch, unmoving.

Again Corio blew on his silver horn, and a faint cry leaped from Vilma's tensed lips. The luring note that had drawn her, Cliff thought hazily; then he thought of nothing save the sound, the sound that promised him all he could desire. Earth and its dominion, his for the taking—if he answered that call! . . . Then even the sound eluded his senses, and he heard only the promise. . . . He must answer, must claim what was rightfully his!

But those half-dead creatures—sight of their stirring steadied his staggering sanity. Here and there heads lifted and bloodless husks of bodies tried to rise. In the pallid light they seemed like corpses, freed from newly opened graves. Some could only reach their knees; others rose to uncertain limbs. And all moved down the stairway toward Corio, answering his summons; followed as he made his slow way toward the opening in the wall, still blowing the single note—the note that promised Earth and all it held. . . .

Cliff glanced toward Vilma—and she was not there. He looked down, saw her far below, dropping from crack to crevice with amazing speed and daring, hastening toward—Corio!

The thought jarred any lingering taint of allurement from Cliff's mind. He must stop her. He swung around, ignoring the cramped stiffness of his legs, and started down the steep wall. Down, down, recklessly, with Corio's horn-note only a faintly heard sound fading behind him.

Now he saw Vilma reach the rocks below and dash around the corner of the castle, and he cursed, redoubling his speed. Down—down—and suddenly the ancient rock crumbled underfoot. For an instant he hung from straining finger-tips—then dropped.

A smashing impact—a stone that slid beneath him—and his head crashed against the castle wall. Through a fiery mist of pain he pictured Vilma in the grasp of Corio. The mist thickened—grew black—engulfed him.

4. In Corio's Hands

CLIFF AWOKE with the sun glaring down on his face. He opened his eyes, and stabbing lances of light pierced his eyeballs. Momentarily blinded, he pressed his hands across his face and struggled erect. There was a sick feeling in his stomach, and the back of his head throbbed incessantly. He touched the aching area, and winced. A lump like an egg thrust out his scalp; it was sticky with blood. He stood there, weaving from side to side, trying to recall some-thing. . . .

As memory came, he groaned. Vilma! He had last seen her racing madly toward Corio, lured by his damned horn. It was daylight now; the sun had risen at least an hour ago. An hour—with Vilma gone!

Shaking his head to clear it, and gritting his teeth at the pain, he stalked along the wall. Turning the corner he strode on toward the crooked steps. The lifeless terrain reeled dizzily, but he went on resolutely. The pain in his head was fading to a dull ache; and as he mounted the steps, strength seemed to flow back into his legs. With every sense taut he passed into the gloom of the castle.

A quick glance he cast about—saw the body of Starke lying where it had fallen. No use to examine it; there was no life there. His gaze swept up the slope of the stairway to the altar at its head, lingering on the phosphorescent eye of light still glowing there. Then he shrugged grimly and moved on to the doorway in the wall. Warily he peered in.

As his eyes adjusted themselves to the greater darkness, he saw a narrow stairway leading downward into a shadowy corridor. Somewhere in the tunnel's depths a faint light shone. He could see nothing more. He moved stealthily down the damp, dank stairs.

At the bottom he paused, listening. He could hear nothing. A hundred feet ahead, the corridor divided in two; a burning torch was thrust in the wall at the junction. Cliff nodded with satisfaction. Corio *must* be somewhere nearby; for only a human needed light.

Silently Cliff strode along the corridor. At the fork he hesitated, then chose the right branch, for light glowed faintly along the passageway. The other led downward, black as the pits of hell.

A doorway appeared in the wall ahead, and he moved warily, his fists clenched. Flickering torchlight filtered into the corridor. There was no audible sound. Now Cliff peered into a small chamber, and gasped in sudden horror, his eyes staring unwinkingly at a spectacle incredibly pitiful.

Here were the passengers of the *Ariel*, whitely naked, and lying in little groups on the cold stone floor, huddled together for warmth. Their faces turned toward Darrell as he stood in the doorway, but there was no recognition in the vacuous eyes, no thought, no intelligence, and little life in the wide-mouthed stares. It seemed as though their souls had been drained from their bodies with their blood.

Sickened, Cliff turned away, cursing his own helplessness to aid them, cursing Leon Corio who was responsible for their plight. Black wrath gripped him as he moved on.

Again the corridor branched, and again he kept to the right. Suddenly he halted, ears straining. He heard the sound of a voice—the hollow voice of Corio! It came faintly but clearly from a room at the end of the passageway. Cliff went forward slowly.

"And so, my dear," Corio was saying, "we entered into a pact with the— Master, a pact sealed with blood. In exchange for our lives we three were to bring other humans to this island for the feasting of the dead-alive. Every third month each of must return with our cargo when the moon is full; and since we come back on alternating months, they have a constant supply of fresh blood. Usually some of our captives live from full moon to full moon before they become like those of the galley—the undead. Some of these we waken when it suits our fancy; they are not like the Masters; they awaken only when we call them—we three or the Masters.

"More than life they give us for what we do. Centuries ago pirates used this island for refuge. They—died—and they left their treasure in this castle. It lies in the room where the Masters lie; and we three receive payment in gold and gems. Tonight I receive my pay, and tomorrow I leave on the *Ariel*—and you go with me!"

Cliff heard Vilma answer, and even while his heart leaped with relief, he marveled at the cool scorn in her voice.

"So I go with you, do I? I'd rather climb the stairs with the rest of your victims than have anything to do with you—you monster! When Cliff Darrell finds you—"

"Darrell!" Corio's voice was a frozen sneer. "He'll do nothing! I'll find *him*—and he'll wish he could climb the stairs of blood! As for you, you'll go with me, and like it! A drop of my blood in your veins, and you will belong to the Master, as I do. We shall attend to that; but first there is something else—more pleasant." His words fell to an indistinguishable purr.

Still moving stealthily, Cliff hastened forward. Suddenly Vilma screamed; and he launched himself madly across the remaining distance, stood crouching at the threshold.

Vilma lay on an ancient bed, her wrists and ankles bound with leather thongs drawn about the four tall bedposts. Only the torn remnants of her undergarments covered the rounded contours of her body, and Corio crouched over her, caressing the pink flesh. Vilma writhed beneath his touch.

Cliff growled deep in his throat as he sprang. Corio spun around and leaped aside, but he was too slow to escape Cliff's powerful lunge. One hand closed on his thin neck, and the other, a rocklike fist, made a bloody ruin of his mouth. Howling with pain, Corio tried to sink his teeth in Cliff's arm.

Cliff flung him aside, following with the easy glide of a boxer. Corio crawled to his feet, cringing, dodging before the nemesis that stalked him. Again Cliff leaped, and Corio, yellow with fear, darted around the bed and ran wildly into the hallway. At the door Cliff checked himself, reason holding him. Corio could elude him with ease in this labyrinth of passages; and his first concern was Vilma's safety.

He returned to the bed. Vilma looked up at him with such relief and thankfulness on her face that Cliff, with a little choked cry, flung himself to his knees beside the bed and kissed her hungrily. For moments their lips clung; then Cliff straightened shakily, trying to laugh.

"We've got to get out of here, sweetheart," he said. "I'm not afraid of Corio, but he knows things about this place that we don't know. After you're safe on the yacht, I'll come back and get him."

He looked around for something with which to cut her bonds. On the wall above the bed were crossed a pair of murderous-looking cutlases. Seizing one of these, Cliff wrenched it from its fastenings and drew it through the cords. . . . She stood beside him, free.

"Your clothing—" Cliff began, his eyes on her almost-nude body.

She blushed and pointed mutely to a heap of rags on the floor. Her eyes flamed wrathfully. "He—he ripped them from me!"

The muscles of Cliff's jaws knotted, and he scowled as he surveyed the room for a drape or hanging to cover her. For the first time he really saw the place. All the lavish splendor of royalty had been expended on this chamber. It might have been the bedroom of a king, except that the ancient furnishings belonged to no particular period; were, in fact, the loot of raids extended over centuries. Yet despite its splendor, everything was repulsive, cloaked with the same air of unearthly gloom that hovered about the galley.

He moved toward an intricately woven tapestry; but Vilma checked him, shuddering with revulsion.

"No, Cliff—it's too much like grave clothes. Everything about this place makes my flesh crawl. I'd rather stay as I am than touch any of it!"

Cliff nodded slowly. "Let's go then."

They hurried through the corridors toward the stairway, with Cliff holding the cutlas in readiness. As they passed the room in which lay the *Ariel*'s passengers, he tried to divert Vilma's attention, but she looked in as though hypnotized.

"I saw them before," she whispered. "It's awful."

As they started up the stairway to the great hall, Cliff took the lead. He moved with utmost caution.

"It doesn't seem right," he said uneasily. "We should hear from Corio."

At that moment they did hear from him—literally. From somewhere in the maze of tunnels came the sound of his accursed horn—the note of sleep! It swirled insidiously about their heads, numbing their senses. Cliff felt his stride falter, saw Vilma stumble, and he hurled himself forward furiously, gripping her arm.

"Hurry!" he shouted, striving to pierce the fog of sleep. "We've *got* to get out! Damn him!"

Vilma rallied for an instant, and they reached the top of the stairs. On—across that wide, wide room, each step a struggle. . . . On while the droning sound floated languidly through every nerve cell. . . . On—till their muscles could no longer move, and they sagged to the hard stone, asleep.

Moments later Cliff opened his eyes to meet the hellish glare of Leon Corio. Corio smiled thinly.

"So—you awaken. Good! I would have you know the fate I had planned for you. You see this?" He held the cutlas high above Darrell's throat like the blade of a guillotine. "With this I could end your life quite painlessly and quickly. It really would prove entertaining for Miss Bradley, I'm sure." He chuckled faintly behind bruised and swollen lips.

Cliff squirmed, striving to rise, then subsided instantly. He was bound hand and foot.

"I *could* kill you," Corio repeated musingly, "but that would lack finesse." His teeth bared in a feline smile. "And it would be such a waste—of blood! Instead, I'll take you out to the galley and let you lie there till her crew awakens tonight. They have tasted blood, and after tonight will taste none again for another month. I imagine they'll—drain you dry!" The last phrase was a vicious snarl.

Cliff heard Vilma utter a suppressed sob, and he turned his head. She lay close by, bound like him with strips of leather. Furiously Cliff strained at his fetters, but they held.

"And while you wait for those gentle Persians to awaken," Corio continued in tones caressingly soft, "you can think of your sweetheart in my arms! It may teach you not to strike your betters—though you can never profit by your lesson."

Stooping, he raised Cliff's powerful form and managed to fling him over one shoulder. Then he moved from the great hall, down the stone steps, and across the dead plain with its sighing skeleton trees. He was panting jerkily by the time he came to the fissure leading to the cove, but he reached it, despite Cliff's two hundred pounds. Without pausing, he went on into the cavern, along the rock ledge, to step at last upon the deck of the black galley.

"Pleasant thoughts," he said gently as he dropped Cliff to the spongy boards. "You have only to wait till dark!"

Cliff listened to his rapid footfalls till they died in distance; then there was no sound save his own breathing.

Gradually his eyes became accustomed to the heavy gloom, and he saw that Corio had dropped him just at the edge of the rowers' pit. There were white things down there—bones, pale as marble, scattered about aimlessly. Could—could those bones join to make the rowers who would arise with the night? It seemed absurd—*was* absurd—yet he knew it was so! He had seen too much to doubt it.

He rolled over on his back and stared upward into the shadows. He must lie here helpless while Corio returned to Vilma—did with her as he pleased! Perhaps he might even transform her into a blood-tainted monster like himself! He saw her again in that room of ancient splendor, spread-eagled to the bed; and the muscles corded in his arms, and his lips strained white in a futile effort to break free.

Interminably he lay there waiting. The galley was damp with the chilling dampness of a sepulcher, and the dampness penetrated deeper and deeper. Clamping his jaws together to prevent their quivering, he struggled against the rising tide of madness which gnawed at his reason. His mind began to crunch and jangle like a machine out of gear, threatening to destroy itself.

On and on in plodding indifference the stolid moments passed, till at last Cliff realized that it was growing darker. He rolled over on his side and stared into the galley pit, eyes fixed on the inert masses of white. Soon they would move! Soon the undead would rise! His thoughts, touched by the whips of dread, sped about like slaves seeking escape from a torture pit. And abruptly out of the welter of chaotic ideas came one straw of sanity; he seized it, his heart hammering with hope.

Those Persian sailors were armed! Their swords and knives were real, for they cut flesh! Somewhere among their bones must lie sharp-edged blades!

He struggled to the edge of the pit, let his feet drop over. As they touched, he balanced precariously for an instant, then fell to his knees. He peered feverishly about among white bones, moldering garments, and rusted armor—and saw a faint glimmer of light on pointed steel. He sank forward on his face in the direction of the gleam, turned over, squirmed and writhed till he felt the cold blade against his hands. He caught it between his fingers and began sawing back and forth.

It was heartbreaking work. Age had dulled the weapon, and long slivers of rust flaked off, but the leather which bound him was also ancient. Though progress was slow, and the effort laborious, Cliff knew his bonds were weakening.

But it was growing darker. Even now he could see only a suggestion of gray among the shadows. If those undead things materialized while he lay among them! . . . Sweat stood out on his forehead and he redoubled his efforts, straining at the leather as he sawed.

With a snap the cords parted and his hands were free. A single slash severed the thongs about his ankles, and he stood up, leaped to the deck. Not an instant too soon! There was movement in the pit—a hideous crawling of bones assembling themselves into skeletal form. . . .

Cliff waited to see no more. There were limits to what one could see and remain sane. With a bound he crossed the rotting deck, and sprang ashore. Despite the dark, he almost ran from the madness of that cave, ran till he passed through the wall of rock, till he saw the rim of the moon gleaming behind the castle.

5. The End of the Island

OUT ON THE plain he sprinted through the ghostly forest. He knew he had no time to spare—knew that soon the march of torture would begin—knew that if Vilma were within the castle, she must answer the summons of Corio's horn. Even now light glowed faintly in the high, square windows.

That horn! At the foot of the steps he stopped short. If *he* heard the horn, he too must answer! He dared not risk it. With impatient fingers he tore a strip of cloth from his shirt, rolled it into a cylinder, and thrust it into his ear. Another for the other ear—and he darted up to the castle.

A sweeping glance revealed no one, only the murky glow of the altar fire, and the wraiths of smoke pluming upward toward the shadowed roof. Wishing now that he had brought a weapon from the galley, Cliff crossed to the opening in the wall. He stood at the top of the steps, listening, then cursed silently as he remembered that he could hear none but very loud sounds. He saw nothing; so he hastened down into the corridor. His steps were swiftly stealthy as he moved toward Corio's room.

He was past the first branching passage, when a sixth sense warned him of someone's approach. He ran swiftly to the next fork, then paused within its shelter and glanced back, saw five red-cowled figures glide along the tunnel and vanish up the stairway. Cliff frowned. With the vampires in the great hall, Corio must soon follow, leading his victims to the blood-feast. He drew back deeper into the shadows.

His groping hands touched something in the dark—round and hard—like a keg. Curiously he investigated. It *was* a keg, and there were others. A sandy powder trailed to the floor from a crack in one of them. Thoughtfully Cliff let it run through his fingers. Gunpowder! Of course—he had heard Corio mention pirates and their treasure, and this had been their cache of explosive. An idea was forming. . . .

He looked up to see a shadow pass the mouth of the tunnel; he crept forward and peered out. He saw the black-hooded figure of Leon Corio striding along, saw him enter the room where the passengers of the *Ariel* lay. In a breath Cliff was down the corridor to Corio's room. A tarnished silver candelabrum shed faint light through the chamber, and by its flickering glow he searched for Vilma, thoroughly, painstakingly—futilely.

He stood in the center of the room in indecision, his forehead creased with anxiety. If only he could find her, he'd know how to plan! He ran his hand through his hair helplessly, then heard very faintly the luring note of Corio's horn. She must answer that summons, unless Corio had her tied somewhere. His best chance of finding her lay in the hall above.

On the wall still hung the mate of the cutlas he had used to free Vilma; he wrenched it down and ran out into the corridor. The last of the naked marchers was disappearing up the stairway. Now the horn-note died, and he could feel more than hear the rumbling bass of the dirge from the depths below him.

He ran the rest of the distance along the passageway and mounted the steps two at a stride. He looked into the torture hall. As on the previous night, Corio stood far back, close to the wall in which Cliff crouched. The arms of the Master were raised high; raised, Cliff knew though he could not hear it, in a blasphemous incantation. And then he saw something that sent a crimson lance of fury crashing through his brain.

Vilma, stripped like the rest, stood with the other victims at the foot of the long steps! Her body gleamed pinkly, in contrast to the pallid drabness of the half-dead automatons, and she held her head proudly erect. But from where he stood Cliff could see the side of her face, and it bore a look of terror.

He could see Corio's face, too, and he was looking at the girl, baffled fury glaring from his eyes—as though she were there against his will.

Cliff's first impulse was to fling himself out there with his cutlas and hack a way to freedom for Vilma and himself, but cold reason checked this folly. Such a course could end only in death. Motionless he watched the scene before him, his brain frantically seeking a plan with even a ghost of a chance of succeeding.

The gunpowder! There was enough of the stuff below to blast this entire castle into the hell where it belonged! Hastily he retraced his steps to the tunnel in which he had found the kegs, plucking the torch from its niche in the wall as he passed it. He held it high above his head as he examined the contents of the broken keg. Unmistakably gunpowder!

Thrusting the cutlas beneath his belt, he clutched a handful of the black dust. Then, crouching close to the floor, he drew an irregular thread through the passageway toward the stairs. Once he returned for more powder, but in a few minutes the job was done. At the foot of the steps where the trail ended, he touched his torch to the black line and watched a hissing spark snake its white-smoked way back toward the powder kegs. An instant he watched it, then sprang up the stairs. He'd have to move fast!

With a hideous howl he darted into the hall, his cutlas above his head. Corio spun about—and it was his last living act. A single sweep of the great blade sheared his head from his neck, sent it rolling grotesquely along the floor. For three heart-beats the body stood with a fountain of blood spurting from severed arteries; then it crashed.

Coolly Cliff leaned over the twitching cadaver, ignoring the bedlam on the stairs, the horde sweeping down toward him, hurling aside the waiting humans. He pried open the clutching fingers, seized a twisted silver instrument, and raised it to his lips.

The mass of undead were almost upon him, the murky light glinting on menacing blades, when Cliff blew the first note. The note of sleep! He tried again, hastily. And it was the right one!

At the doleful, soothing sound the undead halted in their tracks; halted—and melted into nothingness before his eyes!

But now those other five in their robes of bloody red—they were charging, and even though they were unarmed, Cliff felt a stab of fear. They possessed powers beyond the human, powers a mortal could not combat. He braced himself and waited.

At the bottom of the steps they stopped, ranging in a wide half-circle. The central monster—the Master—flung up his arms in a strangely terrifying gesture, and Cliff saw his carmine lips move in a chant which he could not hear. Something, a chilling Presence, hovered about him, seemed to settle upon him, cloaking him with the might of the devil himself. That unheard incantation continued, and Cliff felt a cold rigidity creeping over every fiber, slowly freezing his limbs into columns of ice.

With a mighty effort of will he flung himself toward that accursed drinker of blood—and at that instant a terrific detonation rocked the ancient building, and a cloud of smoke and flame burst from the opening in the wall. Cliff was hurled from his feet, rolled over and over, and crashed against the wall by the awful concussion, the cutlas and silver horn sent whirling through the air.

Dizzily he staggered to his feet, crouching defensively. Sounds came to him clearly now; the explosion must have jarred the plugs from his ears. He scanned the room; saw the unclad humans scattered everywhere, most of them lying still and unconscious. He saw Vilma rising slowly; then he looked for the monsters in red. Startled, he saw them rushing toward the opening in the wall, to vanish in its smoke-filled interior. Why did they—? Then he knew. Down there somewhere were their graves—graves rent and broken by the explosion—graves threatened by flames—and panic had seized the vampires, fear of the death which would result with exile from their tombs!

Unsteadily Cliff crossed to Vilma. She saw him coming and flung herself sobbing into his arms. He crushed her lithe form close—and another explosion, more violent than the first, sent a section of the stone floor leaping upward as though with life of its own. Clinging to Vilma, Cliff managed to maintain his footing, though the floor bucked and heaved. A snapping, booming roar—and a great chasm opened in the floor. A breathless instant—and a segment of the stone stairs, rumbling thunderously, dropped out of sight into a newly formed pit! With it went the blasphemous altar and its phosphorescent fire.

Deafened, stunned, momentarily powerless to move, Cliff's mind groped for an explanation. It seemed incredible that gunpowder could cause such havoc. And the swaying of the floor continued; the thick stone walls shook alarmingly. Suddenly he understood. An earthquake! The explosions had jarred the none-too-stable understrata of rock into spasmodic motion that must grind everything to bits! The island was doomed! And Earth would be better without it.

If only they could reach the *Ariel* first!

New strength flowed through him, and hugging Vilma close, he staggered toward the spot where he knew the door must be. Somehow he reached it, and reeled down the broken stone steps.

The plain of dead trees swayed like the deck of a ship in a storm as Cliff started across it. A gale had arisen and swept in from the sea, ripping dry branches from the skeleton growths and whirling them about like straws. Yet somehow Cliff reached the crevice in the rock wall with his burden, reached the deck of the galley, crossed it, and won to the safety of the *Ariel*. Minutes later, with diesel engines purring, they crept out through the narrow channel into the open sea.

Ten minutes later the Isle of the Undead lay safely behind them. Vilma had dressed; and now they sat together in the pilot house. Cliff had one arm about her, and one hand on the wheel.

"And so," the girl was saying, "while Corio carried you to that terrible old boat, I got loose. He hadn't tied me very tightly, and I slipped my hands free. I had to hide, and I could think of only one place that might be safe, where he wouldn't think to look for me. I ran down to the room where those—those others lay; I undressed, and buried myself among them. It was horrible—the way they sucked each other's wounds. . . ."

Cliff pressed a hand across her lips. "Forget that!" he said almost fiercely. "Forget all of it—d'you hear?"

She looked up at him and said simply: "I'll try."

They glanced back toward the black blotch on the horizon. The seismic disturbances continued unabated. At that moment they saw the barrier of rock like a skull split and sink into the sea. Beyond, cleansing tongues of flame licked the sky. They saw a single jagged wall of the castle still standing, one window glowing in its black expanse like a square, bloody moon against a bloody sky. It crumbled.

They turned away, and Cliff's arm circled the girl he loved. Their lips met and clung. . . . And the *Ariel* plowed on through the frothing brine, bearing them toward safety and forgetfulness. . . . Together.

DOOM OF THE HOUSE OF DURYEA

EARL PEIRCE, JR.

As pulp writers sought new ways to render the vampire theme, many steered further and further away from the traditional portrayal of vampirism as an affliction passed on through a bite. In "The Doom of the House of Duryea," midwestern writer Earl Peirce, Jr., presents vampiric immortality as a curse passed down from generation to generation within a family. Here, the inevitability of fate turns the vampire into a sympathetic victim of circumstance.

1

ARTHUR DURYEA, a young, handsome man, came to meet his father for the first time in twenty years. As he strode into the hotel lobby—long strides which had the spring of elastic in them—idle eyes lifted to appraise him, for he was an impressive figure, somehow grim with exaltation.

The desk clerk looked up with his habitual smile of expectation—how-do-you-do-Mr.-So-and-So—and his fingers strayed to the green fountain pen which stood in a holder on the desk.

Arthur Duryea cleared his throat, but still his voice was clogged and unsteady. To the clerk he said:

"I'm looking for my father, Doctor Henry Duryea. I understand he is registered here. He has recently arrived from Paris."

The clerk lowered his glance to a list of names. "Doctor Duryea is in suite 600, sixth floor." He looked up, his eyebrows arched questioningly. "Are you staying too, sir, Mr. Duryea?"

Arthur took the pen and scribbled his name rapidly. Without a further word, neglecting even to get his key and own room number, he turned and walked to the elevators. Not until he reached his father's suite on the sixth floor did he make an audible noise, and this was a mere sigh which fell from his lips like a prayer.

The man who opened the door was unusually tall, his slender frame clothed in tight-fitting black. He hardly dared to smile. His clean-shaven face was pale, an almost livid whiteness against the sparkle in his eyes. His jaw had a bluish luster.

"Arthur!" The word was scarcely a whisper. It seemed choked up quietly, as if it had been repeated time and again on his thin lips.

Arthur Duryea felt the kindliness of those eyes go through him, and then he was in his father's embrace.

Later, when these two grown men had regained their outer calm, they closed the door and went into the drawing room. The elder Duryea held out a humidor of fine cigars, and his hand shook so hard when he held the match that his son was forced to cup his own hands about the flame. They both had tears in their eyes, but their eyes were smiling.

Henry Duryea placed a hand on his son's shoulder. "This is the happiest day of my life," he said. "You can never know how much I have longed for this moment."

Arthur, looking into that glance, realized, with growing pride, that he had loved his father all his life, despite any of those things which had been cursed against him. He sat down on the edge of a chair.

"I—I don't know how to act," he confessed. "You surprised me, Dad. You're so different from what I had expected."

A cloud came over Doctor Duryea's features. "What *did* you expect, Arthur?" he demanded quickly. "An evil eye? A shaved head and knotted jowls?"

"Please, Dad—no!" Arthur's words clipped short. "I don't think I ever really visualized you. I knew you would be a splendid man. But I thought you'd look older, more like a man who has really suffered."

"I have suffered, more than I can ever describe. But seeing you again, and the prospect of spending the rest of my life with you, has more than compensated for my sorrows. Even during the twenty years we were apart I found an ironic joy in learning of your progress in college, and in your American game of football."

"Then you've been following my work?"

"Yes, Arthur; I've received monthly reports ever since you left me. From my study in Paris I've been really close to you, working out your problems as if they were my own. And now that the twenty years are completed, the ban which kept us apart is lifted forever. From now on, son, we shall be the closest of companions—unless your Aunt Cecilia has succeeded in her terrible mission."

The mention of that name caused an unfamiliar chill to come between the two men. It stood for something, in each of them, which gnawed their minds like a malignancy. But to the younger Duryea, in his intense effort to forget the awful past, her name as well as her madness must be forgotten.

He had no wish to carry on this subject of conversation, for it betrayed an internal weakness which he hated. With forced determination, and a ludicrous lift of his eyebrows, he said,

"Cecilia is dead, and her silly superstition is dead also. From now on, Dad, we're going to enjoy life as we should. Bygones are really bygones in this case."

Doctor Duryea closed his eyes slowly, as though an exquisite pain had gone through him.

"Then you have no indignation?" he questioned. "You have none of your aunt's hatred?"

"Indignation? Hatred?" Arthur laughed aloud. "Ever since I was twelve years old I have disbelieved Cecilia's stories. I have known that those horrible things were impossible, that they belonged to the ancient category of mythology and tradition. How, then, can I be indignant, and how can I hate you? How can I do anything but recognize Cecilia for what she was—a mean, frustrated woman, cursed with an insane grudge against you and your family? I tell you, Dad, that nothing she has ever said can possibly come between us again."

Henry Duryea nodded his head. His lips were tight together, and the muscles in his throat held back a cry. In that same soft tone of defense he spoke further, doubting words.

"Are you so sure of your subconscious mind, Arthur? Can you be so certain that you are free from all suspicion, however vague? Is there not a lingering premonition—a premonition which warns of peril?"

"No, Dad—no!" Arthur shot to his feet. "I don't believe it. I've never believed it. I know, as any sane man would know, that you are neither a vampire nor a murderer. You know it, too; and Cecilia knew it, only she was mad.

"That family rot is dispelled, Father. This is a civilized century. Belief in vampirism is sheer lunacy. Wh-why, it's too absurd even to think about!"

"You have the enthusiasm of youth," said his father, in a rather tired voice. "But have you not heard the legend?"

Arthur stepped back instinctively. He moistened his lips, for their dryness might crack them. "The—legend?"

He said the word in a curious hush of awed softness, as he had heard his Aunt Cecilia say it many times.

"That awful legend that you—"

"That I *eat* my children?"

"Oh, God, Father!" Arthur went to his knees as a cry burst through his lips. "Dad, that—that's ghastly! We must forget Cecilia's ravings."

"You are affected, then?" asked Doctor Duryea bitterly.

"Affected? Certainly I'm affected, but only as I should be at such an accusation. Cecilia was mad, I tell you. Those books she showed me years ago, and those folktales of vampires and ghouls—they burned into my infantile mind like acid. They haunted me day and night in my youth, and caused me to hate you worse than death itself."

"But in Heaven's name, Father, I've outgrown those things as I have outgrown my clothes. I'm a man now; do you understand that? A man, with a man's sense of logic."

"Yes, I understand." Henry Duryea threw his cigar into the fireplace, and placed a hand on his son's shoulder.

"We shall forget Cecilia," he said. "As I told you in my letter, I have rented a lodge in Maine where we can go to be alone for the rest of the summer. We'll get in some fishing and hiking and perhaps some hunting. But first, Arthur, I must be sure in my own mind that you are sure in yours. I must be sure you won't bar your door against me at night, and sleep with a loaded revolver at your elbow. I must be sure that you're not afraid of going up there alone with me, and dying—"

His voice ended abruptly, as if an age-long dread had taken hold of it. His son's face was waxen, with sweat standing out like pearls on his brow. He said nothing, but his eyes were filled with questions which his lips could not put into words. His own hand touched his father's and tightened over it.

Henry Duryea drew his hand away.

"I'm sorry," he said, and his eyes looked straight over Arthur's lowered head. "This thing must be thrashed out now. I believe you when you say that you discredit Cecilia's stories, but for a sake greater than sanity I must tell you the truth behind the legend—and believe me, Arthur; there is a truth!"

He climbed to his feet and walked to the window which looked out over the street below. For a moment he gazed into space, silent. Then he turned and looked down at his son.

"You have heard only your aunt's version of the legend, Arthur. Doubtless it was warped into a thing far more hideous than it actually was—if that is possible! Doubtless she spoke to you of the Inquisitorial stake in Carcassonne where one of my ancestors perished. Also she may have mentioned that book, *Vampyrs,* which a former Duryea is supposed to have written. Then certainly she told you about your two younger brothers—my own poor, motherless children— who were sucked bloodless in their cradles. . . ."

Arthur Duryea passed a hand across his aching eyes. Those words, so often repeated by that witch of an aunt, stirred up the same visions which had made his childhood nights sleepless with terror. He could hardly bear to hear them again— and from the very man to whom they were accredited.

"Listen, Arthur," the elder Duryea went on quickly, his voice low with the pain it gave him. "You must know that true basis of your aunt's hatred. You must know of that curse—that curse of vampirism which is supposed to have followed the Duryeas through five centuries of French history, but which we can dispel as pure superstition, so often connected with ancient families. But I must tell you that this part of the legend is true:

"Your two young brothers actually died in their cradles, bloodless. And I stood trial in France for their murder, and my name was smirched throughout all of Europe with such an inhuman damnation that it drove your aunt and you to America, and has left me childless, hated, and ostracized from society the world over.

"I must tell you that on that terrible night in Duryea Castle I had been working late on historic volumes of Crespet and Prinn, and on that loathsome tome, *Vampyrs*. I must tell you of the soreness that was in my throat and of the heaviness of the blood which coursed through my veins. . . . And of that *presence,* which was neither man nor animal, but which I knew was some place near me, yet neither within the castle nor outside of it, and which was closer to me than my heart and more terrible to me than the touch of the grave. . . .

"I was at the desk in my library, my head swimming in delirium which left me senseless until dawn. There were nightmares that frightened me—frightened *me,* Arthur, a grown man who had dissected countless cadavers in morgues and medical schools. I know that my tongue was swollen in my mouth and that brine moistened my lips, and that a rottenness pervaded my body like a fever.

"I can make no recollection of sanity or of consciousness. That night remains vivid, unforgettable, yet somehow completely in shadows. When I had fallen asleep—if in God's name it *was* sleep—I was slumped across my desk. But when I awoke in the morning I was lying face down on my couch. So you see, Arthur, I *had* moved during that night, *and I had never known it!*

"What I'd done and where I'd gone during those dark hours will always remain an impenetrable mystery. But I do know this. On the morrow I was torn from my sleep by the shrieks of maids and butlers, and by that mad wailing of your aunt. I stumbled through the open door of my study, and in the nursery I saw those two babies there—lifeless, white and dry like mummies, and with twin holes in their necks that were caked black with their own blood. . . .

"Oh, I don't blame you for your incredulousness, Arthur. I cannot believe it yet myself, nor shall I ever believe it. The belief of it would drive me to suicide; and still the doubting of it drives me mad with horror.

"All of France was doubtful, and even the savants who defended my name at the trial found that they could not explain it nor disbelieve it. The case was quieted by the Republic, for it might have shaken science to its very foundation and split the pedestals of religion and logic. I was released from the charge of murder; but the actual murder has hung about me like a stench.

"The coroners who examined those tiny cadavers found them both dry of all their blood, but could find no blood on the floor of the nursery nor in the cradles. Something from hell stalked the halls of Duryea that night—and I should blow my brains out if I dared to think deeply of who that was. You, too, my son, would have been dead and bloodless if you hadn't been sleeping in a separate room with your door barred on the inside.

"You were a timid child, Arthur. You were only seven years old, but you were filled with the folklore of those mad Lombards and the decadent poetry of your aunt. On that same night, while I was some place between heaven and hell, you, also, heard the padded footsteps on the stone corridor and heard the tugging at your door handle, for in the morning you complained of a chill and of terrible nightmares which frightened you in your sleep. . . . I only thank God that your door was barred!"

Henry Duryea's voice choked into a sob which brought the stinging tears back into his eyes. He paused to wipe his face, and to dig his fingers into his palm.

"You understand, Arthur, that for twenty years, under my sworn oath at the Palace of Justice, I could neither see you nor write to you. Twenty years, my son, while all of that time you had grown to hate me and to spit at my name. Not until your aunt's death have you called yourself a Duryea. . . . And now you come to me at my bidding, and say you love me as a son should love his father.

"Perhaps it is God's forgiveness for everything. Now, at last, we shall be together, and that terrible, unexplainable past will be buried forever. . . ."

He put his handkerchief back into his pocket and walked slowly to his son. He dropped to one knee, and his hands gripped Arthur's arms.

"My son, I can say no more to you. I have told the truth as I alone know it. I may be, by all accounts, some ghoulish creation of Satan on earth. I may be a child-killer, a vampire, some morbidly diseased specimen of *vrykolakas*—things which science cannot explain.

"Perhaps the dreaded legend of the Duryeas is true. Autiel Duryea was convicted of murdering his brother in that same monstrous fashion in the year 1576, and he died in flames at the stake. François Duryea, in 1802, blew his head apart with a blunderbuss on the morning after his youngest son was found dead, apparently from anemia. And there are others, of whom I cannot bear to speak, that would chill your soul if you were to hear them.

"So you see, Arthur, there is a hellish tradition behind our family. There is a heritage which no sane God would ever have allowed. The future of the Duryeas lies in you, for you are the last of the race. I pray with all of my heart that providence will permit you to live your full share of years, and to leave other Duryeas behind you. And so if ever again I feel that presence as I did in Duryea Castle, I am going to die as François Duryea died, over a hundred years ago. . . ."

He stood up, and his son stood up at his side.

"If you are willing to forget, Arthur, we shall go up to that lodge in Maine. There is a life we've never known awaiting us. We must find that life, and we must find the happiness which a curious fate snatched from us on those Lombard sourlands, twenty years ago. . . ."

2

HENRY DURYEA'S tall stature, coupled with a slenderness of frame and a sleekness of muscle, gave him an appearance that was unusually *gaunt*. His son couldn't help thinking of that word as he sat on the rustic porch of the lodge, watching his father sunning himself at the lake's edge.

Henry Duryea had a kindliness in his face, at times an almost sublime kindliness which great prophets often possess. But when his face was partly in shadows, particularly about his brow, there was a frightening tone which came into his features; for it was a tone of farness, of mysticism and conjuration. Somehow, in the late evenings, he assumed the unapproachable mantle of a dreamer and sat silently before the fire, his mind ever off in unknown places.

In that little lodge there was no electricity, and the glow of the oil lamps played curious tricks with the human expression which frequently resulted in something unhuman. It may have been the dusk of night, the flickering of the lamps, but Arthur Duryea had certainly noticed how his father's eyes had sunken further into his head, and how his cheeks were tighter, and the outline of his teeth pressed into the skin about his lips.

It was nearing sundown on the second day of their stay at Timber Lake. Six miles away the dirt road wound on toward Houtlon, near the Canadian border. So it was lonely there, on a solitary little lake hemmed in closely with dark evergreens and a sky which drooped low over dusty-summited mountains.

Within the lodge was a homy fireplace, and a glossy elk's head which peered out above the mantel. There were guns and fishing tackle on the walls, shelves of reliable American fiction—Mark Twain, Melville, Stockton, and a well-worn edition of Bret Harte.

A fully supplied kitchen and a wood stove furnished them with hearty meals which were welcome after a whole day's tramp in the woods. On that evening Henry Duryea prepared a select French stew out of every available vegetable, and a can of soup. They ate well, then stretched out before the fire for a smoke. They were outlining a trip to the Orient together, when the back door blew open with a terrific bang, and a wind swept into the lodge with a coldness which chilled them both.

"A storm," Henry Duryea said, rising to his feet. "Sometimes they have them up here, and they're pretty bad. The roof might leak over your bedroom. Perhaps you'd like to sleep down here with me." His finger strayed playfully over his son's head as he went out into the kitchen to bar the swinging door.

Arthur's room was upstairs, next to a spare room filled with extra furniture. He'd chosen it because he liked the altitude, and because the only other bedroom was occupied. . . .

He went upstairs swiftly and silently. His roof didn't leak; it was absurd even to think it might. It had been his father again, suggesting that they sleep together. He had done it before, in a jesting, whispering way—as if to challenge them both if they *dared* to sleep together.

Arthur came back downstairs dressed in his bathrobe and slippers. He stood on the fifth stair, rubbing a two-day's growth of beard. "I think I'll shave tonight," he said to his father. "May I use your razor?"

Henry Duryea, draped in a black raincoat and with his face haloed in the brim of a rain hat, looked up from the hall. A frown glided obscurely from his features. "Not at all, son. Sleeping upstairs?"

Arthur nodded, and quickly said, "Are you—going out?"

"Yes, I'm going to tie the boats up tighter. I'm afraid the lake will rough it up a bit."

Duryea jerked back the door and stepped outside. The door slammed shut, and his footsteps sounded on the wood flooring of the porch.

Arthur came slowly down the remaining steps. He saw his father's figure pass across the dark rectangle of a window, saw the flash of lightning that suddenly printed his grim silhouette against the glass.

He sighed deeply, a sigh which burned in his throat, for his throat was sore and aching. Then he went into the bedroom, found the razor lying in plain view on a birch table-top.

As he reached for it, his glance fell upon his father's open Gladstone bag which rested at the foot of the bed. There was a book resting there, half hidden by a gray flannel shirt. It was a narrow, yellow-bound book, oddly out of place.

Frowning, he bent down and lifted it from the bag. It was surprisingly heavy in his hands, and he noticed a faintly sickening odor of decay which drifted from it like a perfume. The title of the volume had been thumbed away into an indecipherable blur of gold letters. But pasted across the front cover was a white strip of paper, on which was typewritten the word—INFANTIPHAGI.

He flipped back the cover and ran his eyes over the title page. The book was printed in French—an early French—yet to him wholly comprehensible. The publication date was 1580, in Caen.

Breathlessly he turned back a second page, saw a chapter headed, *Vampires.*

He slumped to one elbow across the bed. His eyes were four inches from those mildewed pages, his nostrils reeked with the stench of them.

He skipped long paragraphs of pedantic jargon on theology, he scanned brief accounts of strange, blood-eating monsters, *vrykolakas,* and leprechauns. He read of Jeanne d'Arc, of Ludvig Prinn, and muttered aloud the Latin snatches from *Episcopi.*

He passed pages in quick succession, his fingers shaking with the fear of it and his eyes hanging heavily in their sockets. He saw vague reference to "Enoch," and saw the terrible drawings by an ancient Dominican of Rome. . . .

Paragraph after paragraph he read: the horror-striking testimony of Nider's *Ant-Hill,* the testimony of people who died shrieking at the stake; the recitals of grave-tenders, of jurists and hangmen. Then unexpectedly, among all of this munimental vestige, there appeared before his eyes the name of—*Autiel Duryea;* and he stopped reading as though invisibly struck.

Thunder clapped near the lodge and rattled the windowpanes. The deep rolling of bursting clouds echoed over the valley. But he heard none of it. His eyes were on those two short sentences which his father—someone—had underlined with dark red crayon.

. . . The execution, four years ago, of Autiel Duryea does not end the Duryea controversy. Time alone can decide whether the Demon has claimed that family from its beginning to its end. . . .

Arthur read on about the trial of Autiel Duryea before Veniti, the Carcassonnean Inquisitor-General; read, with mounting horror, the evidence which had sent that far-gone Duryea to the pillar—the evidence of a bloodless corpse who had been Autiel Duryea's young brother.

Unmindful now of the tremendous storm which had centered over Timber Lake, unheeding the clatter of windows and the swish of pines on the roof—even of his father who worked down on the lake's edge in a drenching rain—Arthur fastened his glance to the blurred print of those pages, sinking deeper and deeper into the garbled legends of a dark age. . . .

On the last page of the chapter he again saw the name of his ancestor, Autiel Duryea. He traced a shaking finger over the narrow lines of words, and when he finished reading them he rolled sideways on the bed, and from his lips came a sobbing, mumbling prayer.

"God, oh God in Heaven protect me. . . ."

For he had read:

As in the case of Autiel Duryea we observe that this specimen of *vrykolakas* preys only upon the blood of its own family. It possesses none of the characteristics of the undead vampire, being usually a living male person of otherwise normal appearance, unsuspecting its inherent demonism.

But this *vrykolakas* cannot act according to its demoniacal possession unless it is in the presence of a second member of the same family, who acts as a medium between the man and its demon. This medium has none of the traits of the vampire, but it senses the being of this creature (when the metamorphosis is about to occur) by reason of intense pains in the head and throat. Both the vampire and the medium undergo similar reactions, involving nausea, nocturnal visions, and physical disquietude.

When these two outcasts are within a certain distance of each other, the coalescence of inherent demonism is completed, and the vampire is subject to its attacks, demanding blood for its sustenance. No member of the family is safe at these times, for the *vrykolakas,* acting in its true agency on earth, will unerringly seek out the blood. In rare cases, where other victims are unavailable, *the vampire will even take the blood from the very medium which made it possible*.

This vampire is born into certain aged families, and naught but death can destroy it. It is not conscious of its blood-madness, and acts only in a psychic state. The medium, also, is unaware of its terrible role; and when these two are together, despite any lapse of years, the fusion of inheritance is so violent that no power known on earth can turn it back.

3

THE LODGE DOOR slammed shut with a sudden, interrupting bang. The lock grated, and Henry Duryea's footsteps sounded on the planked floor.

Arthur shook himself from the bed. He had only time to fling that haunting book into the Gladstone bag before he sensed his father standing in the doorway.

"You—you're not shaving, Arthur." Duryea's words, spliced hesitantly, were toneless. He glanced from the table-top to the Gladstone, and to his son. He said nothing for a moment, his glance inscrutable.

Then, "It's blowing up quite a storm outside."

Arthur swallowed the first words which had come into his throat, nodded quickly. "Yes, isn't it? Quite a storm." He met his father's gaze, his face burning. "I—I don't think I'll shave, Dad. My head aches."

Duryea came swiftly into the room and pinned Arthur's arms in his grasp. "What do you mean—your head aches? How? Does your throat—"

"No!" Arthur jerked himself away. He laughed. "It's that French stew of yours! It's hit me in the stomach!" He stepped past his father and started up the stairs.

"The stew?" Duryea pivoted on his heel. "Possibly. I think I feel it myself." Arthur stopped, his face suddenly white. "You—too?"

The words were hardly audible. Their glances met—clashed like dueling swords.

For ten seconds neither of them said a word or moved a muscle: Arthur, from the stairs, looking down; his father below, gazing up at him. In Henry Duryea the blood drained slowly from his face and left a purple etching across the bridge of his nose and above his eyes. He looked like a death's head.

Arthur winced at the sight and twisted his eyes away. He turned to go up the remaining stairs.

"Son!"

He stopped again; his hand tightening on the banister.

"Yes, Dad?"

Duryea put his foot on the first stair. "I want you to lock your door tonight. The wind would keep it banging!"

"Yes," breathed Arthur, and pushed up the stairs to his room.

Doctor Duryea's hollow footsteps sounded in steady, unhesitant beats across the floor of Timber Lake Lodge. Sometimes they stopped, and the crackling hiss of a sulfur match took their place, then perhaps a distended sigh, and, again, footsteps. . . .

Arthur crouched at the open door of his room. His head was cocked for those noises from below. In his hands was a double-barrel shotgun of violent gage.

. . . Thud . . . thud . . . thud . . .

Then a pause, the clinking of a glass and the gurgling of liquid. The sigh, the tread of his feet over the floor. . . .

He's thirsty, Arthur thought—*Thirsty!*

Outside, the storm had grown into fury. Lightning zigzagged between the mountains, filling the valley with weird phosphorescence. Thunder, like drums, rolled incessantly.

Within the lodge the heat of the fireplace piled the atmosphere thick with stagnation. All the doors and windows were locked shut, the oil-lamps glowed weakly—a pale, anemic light.

Henry Duryea walked to the foot of the stairs and stood looking up.

Arthur sensed his movements and ducked back into his room, the gun gripped in his shaking fingers.

Then Henry Duryea's footstep sounded on the first stair.

Arthur slumped to one knee. He buckled a fist against his teeth as a prayer tumbled through them.

Duryea climbed a second step . . . and another . . . and still one more. On the fourth stair he stopped.

"Arthur!" His voice cut into the silence like the crack of a whip. "Arthur! Will you come down here?"

"Yes, Dad." Bedraggled, his body hanging like cloth, young Duryea took five steps to the landing.

"We can't be zanies!" cried Henry Duryea. "My soul is sick with dread. Tomorrow we're going back to New York. I'm going to get the first boat to open sea. . . . Please come down here." He turned about and descended the stairs to his room.

Arthur choked back the words which had lumped in his mouth. Half dazed, he followed. . . .

In the bedroom he saw his father stretched face-up along the bed. He saw a pile of rope at his father's feet.

"Tie me to the bedposts, Arthur," came the command. "Tie both my hands and both my feet."

Arthur stood gaping.

"Do as I tell you!"

"Dad, what hor—"

"Don't be a fool! You read that book! You know what relation you are to me! I'd always hoped it was Cecilia, but now I know it's you. I should have known it on that night twenty years ago when you complained of a headache and nightmares. . . . Quickly, my head rocks with pain. *Tie me!*"

Speechless, his own pain piercing him with agony, Arthur fell to that grisly task. Both hands he tied—and both feet . . . tied them so firmly to the iron posts that his father could not lift himself an inch off the bed.

Then he blew out the lamps, and without a further glance at that Prometheus, he reascended the stairs to his room, and slammed and locked his door behind him.

He looked once at the breech of his gun, and set it against a chair by his bed. He flung off his robe and slippers, and within five minutes he was senseless in slumber.

4

HE SLEPT LATE, and when he awakened his muscles were as stiff as boards, and the lingering visions of a nightmare clung before his eyes. He pushed his way out of bed, stood dazedly on the floor.

A dull, numbing cruciation circulated through his head. He felt bloated . . . coarse and running with internal mucus. His mouth was dry, his gums sore and stinging.

He tightened his hands as he lunged for the door. "Dad," he cried, and he heard his voice breaking in his throat.

Sunlight filtered through the window at the top of the stairs. The air was hot and dry, and carried in it a mild odor of decay.

Arthur suddenly drew back at that odor—drew back with a gasp of awful fear. For he recognized it—that stench, the heaviness of his blood, the rawness of his tongue and gums. . . . Age-long it seemed, yet rising like a spirit in his memory. All of these things he had known and felt before.

He leaned against the banister, and half slid, half stumbled down the stairs. . . .

His father had died during the night. He lay like a waxen figure tied to his bed, his face done up in knots.

Arthur stood dumbly at the foot of the bed for only a few seconds; then he went back upstairs to his room.

Almost immediately he emptied both barrels of the shotgun into his head.

The tragedy at Timber Lake was discovered accidentally three days later. A party of fishermen, upon finding the two bodies, notified state authorities, and an investigation was directly under way.

Arthur Duryea had undoubtedly met death at his own hands. The condition of his wounds, and the manner with which he held the lethal weapon, at once foreclosed the suspicion of any foul play.

But the death of Doctor Henry Duryea confronted the police with an inexplicable mystery; for his trussed-up body, unscathed except for two jagged holes over the jugular vein, *had been drained of all its blood.*

The autopsy protocol of Henry Duryea laid death to "undetermined causes," and it was not until the yellowish tabloids commenced an investigation into the Duryea family history that the incredible and fantastic explanations were offered to the public.

Obviously such talk was held in popular contempt; yet in view of the controversial war which followed, the authorities considered it expedient to consign both Duryeas to the crematory. . . .

I, THE VAMPIRE

HENRY KUTTNER

Before he became one of the most important writers of science fiction's Golden Age, Henry Kuttner brought quirky twists to classic supernatural themes in the pages of Weird Tales *and* Unknown Worlds. *His 1937 story, "I, the Vampire," with its cinematic take on the superstition that vampires cast no reflection, could only have been written after 1931 and the enormous popularity of Tod Browning's film* Dracula. *Indeed, with his exotic European background and suave lady-killing ways, there is more than a hint of Bela Lugosi in Kuttner's tragic Chevalier Futaine.*

1. The Chevalier Futaine

THE PARTY was dull. I had come too early. There was a preview that night at Grauman's Chinese, and few of the important guests would arrive until it was over. Indeed, Jack Hardy, ace director at Summit Pictures, where I worked as assistant director, hadn't arrived—yet—and he was the host. But Hardy had never been noted for punctuality.

I went out on the porch and leaned against a pillar, sipping a cocktail and looking down at the lights of Hollywood. Hardy's place was on the summit of a hill overlooking the film capital, near Falcon Lair, Valentino's famous turreted castle. I shivered a little. Fog was sweeping in from Santa Monica, blotting out the lights to the west.

Jean Hubbard, who was an ingenue at Summit, came up beside me and took the glass out of my hand.

"Hello, Mart," she said, sipping the liquor. "Where've you been?"

"Down with the *Murder Desert* troupe, on location in the Mojave," I said. "Miss me, honey?" I drew her close.

She smiled up at me, her tilted eyebrows lending a touch of diablerie to the tanned, lovely face. I was going to marry Jean, but I wasn't sure just when.

"Missed you lots," she said, and held up her lips. I responded.

After a moment I said, "What's this about the vampire man?"

She chuckled. "Oh, the Chevalier Futaine. Didn't you read Lolly Parsons's write-up in *Script?* Jack Hardy picked him up last month in Europe. Silly rot. But it's good publicity."

"Three cheers for publicity," I said. "Look what it did for *Birth of a Nation*. But where does the vampire angle come in?"

"Mystery man. Nobody can take a picture of him, scarcely anybody can see him. Weird tales are told about his former life in Paris. Going to play in Jack's *Red Thirst*. The kind of build-up Universal gave Karloff for *Frankenstein*. The Chevalier Futaine"—she rolled out the words with amused relish—"is probably a singing waiter from a Paris café. I haven't seen him—but the deuce with him, anyway. Mart, I want you to do something for me. For Deming."

"Hess Deming?" I raised my eyebrows in astonishment. Hess Deming, Summit's biggest box-office star, whose wife, Sandra Colter, had died two days before. She, too, had been an actress, although never the great star her husband was. Hess loved her, I knew—and now I guessed what the trouble was. I said, "I noticed he was a bit wobbly."

"He'll kill himself," Jean said, looking worried. "I—I feel responsible for him somehow, Mart. After all, he gave me my start at Summit. And he's due for the DTs any time now."

"Well, I'll do what I can," I told her. "But that isn't a great deal. After all, getting tight is probably the best thing he could do. I know if I lost you, Jean—"

I stopped. I didn't like to think of it.

Jean nodded. "See what you can do for him, anyway. Losing Sandra that way was—pretty terrible."

"What way?" I asked. "I've been away, remember. I read something about it, but—"

"She just died," Jean said. "Pernicious anemia, they said. But Hess told me the doctor really didn't know what it was. She just seemed to grow weaker and weaker until—she passed away."

I nodded, gave Jean a hasty kiss, and went back into the house. I had just seen Hess Deming walk past, a glass in his hand.

He turned as I tapped his shoulder.

"Oh, Mart," he said, his voice just a bit fuzzy. He could hold his liquor, but

I could tell by his bloodshot eyes that he was almost at the end of his rope. He was a handsome devil, all right, well-built, strong-featured, with level gray eyes and a broad mouth that was usually smiling. It wasn't smiling now. It was slack, and his face was bedewed with perspiration.

"You know about Sandra?" he asked.

"Yeah," I said. "I'm sorry, Hess."

He drank deeply from the glass, wiped his mouth with a grimace of distaste.

"I'm drunk, Mart," he confided. "I had to get drunk. It was awful—those last few days. I've got to burn her up."

I didn't say anything.

"Burn her up. Oh, my God, Mart—that beautiful body of hers, crumbling to dust—and I've got to watch it! She made me promise I'd watch to make sure they burned her."

I said, "Cremation's a clean ending, Hess. And Sandra was a clean girl, and a damned good actress."

He put his flushed face close to mine. "Yeah—but I've got to burn her up. It'll kill me, Mart. Oh, God!" He put the empty glass down on a table and looked around dazedly.

I was wondering why Sandra had insisted on cremation. She'd given an interview once in which she stressed her dread of fire. Most write-ups of stars are applesauce, but I happened to know that Sandra did dread fire. Once, on the set, I'd seen her go into hysterics when her leading man lit his pipe too near her face.

"Excuse me, Mart," Hess said. "I've got to get another drink."

"Wait a minute," I said, holding him. "You want to watch yourself, Hess. You've had too much already."

"It still hurts," he said. "Just a little more and maybe it won't hurt so much." But he didn't pull away. Instead he stared at me with the dullness of intoxication in his eyes. "Clean," he said presently. "She said that too, Mart. She said burning was a clean death. But, God, that beautiful white body of hers—I can't stand it, Mart! I'm going crazy, I think. Get me a drink, like a good fellow."

I said, "Wait here, Hess. I'll get you one." I didn't add that it would be watered—considerably.

He sank down in a chair, mumbling thanks. As I went off I felt sick. I'd seen too many actors going on the rocks to mistake Hess's symptoms. I knew that his box-office days were over. There would be longer and longer waits between pictures, and then personal appearances, and finally Poverty Row and serials. And in the end maybe a man found dead in a cheap hall bedroom on Main Street, with the gas on.

There was a crowd around the bar. Somebody said, "Here's Mart. Hey, come over and meet the vampire."

Then I got a shock. I saw Jack Hardy, my host, the director with whom I'd worked on many a hit. He looked like a corpse. And I'd seen him looking plenty bad before. A man with a hangover or a marijuana jag isn't a pretty sight, but I'd never seen Hardy like this. He looked as though he was keeping going on his nerve alone. There was no blood in the man.

I'd last seen him as a stocky, ruddy blond, who looked like nothing so much as a wrestler, with his huge biceps, his ugly, good-natured face, and his bristling crop of yellow hair. Now he looked like a skeleton, with skin hanging loosely on the big frame. His face was a network of sagging wrinkles. Pouches bagged beneath his eyes, and those eyes were dull and glazed. About his neck a black silk scarf was knotted tightly.

"Good God, Jack!" I exclaimed. "What have you done to yourself?"

He looked away quickly. "Nothing," he said brusquely. "I'm all right. I want you to meet the Chevalier Futaine—this is Mart Prescott."

"Pierre," a voice said. "Hollywood is no place for titles. Mart Prescott—the pleasure is mine."

I faced the Chevalier Pierre Futaine.

We shook hands. My first impression was of icy cold, and a slick kind of dryness—and I let go of his hand too quickly to be polite. He smiled at me.

A charming man, the chevalier. Or so he seemed. Slender, below medium height, his bland, round face seemed incongruously youthful. Blond hair was plastered close to his scalp. I saw that his cheeks were rouged—very deftly, but I know something about makeup. And under the rouge I read a curious, deathly pallor that would have made him a marked man had he not disguised it. Some disease, perhaps, had blanched his skin—but his lips were not artificially reddened. And they were as crimson as blood.

He was clean-shaved, wore impeccable evening clothes, and his eyes were black pools of ink.

"Glad to know you," I said. "You're the vampire, eh?"

He smiled. "So they tell me. But we all serve the dark god of publicity, eh, Mr. Prescott? Or—is it Mart?"

"It's Mart," I said, still staring at him. I saw his eyes go past me, and an extraordinary expression appeared on his face—an expression of amazement, disbelief. Swiftly it was gone.

I turned. Jean was approaching, was at my side as I moved. She said, "Is this the chevalier?"

Pierre Futaine was staring at her, his lips parted a little. Almost inaudibly he murmured, "Sonya." And then, on a note of interrogation, "Sonya?"

I introduced the two. Jean said, "You see, my name isn't Sonya."

The chevalier shook his head, an odd look in his black eyes.

"I once knew a girl like you," he said softly. "Very much like you. It is strange."

"Will you excuse me?" I broke in. Jack Hardy was leaving the bar. Quickly I followed him.

I touched his shoulder as he went out the French windows. He jerked out a startled oath, turned a white death-mask of a face to me.

"Damn you, Mart," he snarled. "Keep your hands to yourself."

I put my hands on his shoulders and swung him around.

"What the devil has happened to you?" I asked. "Listen, Jack, you can't bluff me or lie to me. You know that. I've straightened you out enough times in the past, and I can do it again. Let me in on it."

His ruined face softened. He reached up and took away my hands. His own were ice-cold, like the hands of the Chevalier Futaine.

"No," he said. "No use, Mart. There's nothing you can do. I'm all right, really. Just—overstrain. I had too good a time in Paris."

I was up against a blank wall. Suddenly, without volition, a thought popped into my mind and out of my mouth before I knew it.

"What's the matter with your neck?" I asked abruptly.

He didn't answer. He just frowned and shook his head.

"I've a throat infection," he told me. "Caught it on the steamer."

His hand went up and touched the black scarf.

There was a croaking, harsh sound from behind us—a sound that didn't seem quite human. I turned. It was Hess Deming. He was swaying in the portal, his eyes glaring and bloodshot, a little trickle of saliva running down his chin.

He said in a dead, expressionless voice that was somehow dreadful, "Sandra died of a throat infection, Hardy."

Jack didn't answer. He stumbled back a step. Hess went on dully.

"She got all white and died. And the doctor didn't know what it was, although the death certificate said anemia. Did you bring back some filthy disease with you, Hardy? Because if you did I'm going to kill you."

"Wait a minute," I said. "A throat infection? I didn't know—"

"There was a wound on her throat—two little marks, close together. That couldn't have killed her, unless some loathsome disease—"

"You're crazy, Hess," I said. "You know you're drunk. Listen to me: Jack couldn't have had anything to do with—that."

Hess didn't look at me. He watched Jack Hardy out of his bloodshot eyes. He went on in that low, deadly monotone:

"Will you swear Mart's right, Hardy? Will you?"

Jack's lips were twisted by some inner agony. I said, "Go on, Jack. Tell him he's wrong."

Hardy burst out, "I haven't been near your wife! I haven't seen her since I got back. There's—"

"That's not the answer I want," Hess whispered. And he sprang for the other man—reeled forward, rather.

Hess was too drunk, and Jack too weak, for them to do each other any harm, but there was a nasty scuffle for a moment before I separated them. As I pulled them apart, Hess's hand clutched the scarf about Jack's neck, ripped it away.

And I saw the marks on Jack Hardy's throat. Two red, angry little pits, white-rimmed, just over the left jugular.

2. The Cremation of Sandra

IT WAS the next day that Jean telephoned me.

"Mart," she said, "we're going to run over a scene for *Red Thirst* tonight at the studio—Stage 6. You've been assigned as assistant director for the pic, so you should be there. And—I had an idea Jack might not tell you. He's been—so odd lately."

"Thanks, honey," I said. "I'll be there. But I didn't know you were in the flicker."

"Neither did I, but there's been some wire-pulling. Somebody wanted me in it—the chevalier, I think—and the big boss phoned me this morning and let me in on the secret. I don't feel up to it, though. Had a bad night."

"Sorry," I sympathized. "You were okay when I left you."

"I had a—nightmare," she said slowly. "It was rather frightful, Mart. It's funny, though, I can't remember what it was about. Well—you'll be there tonight?"

I said I would, but as it happened I was unable to keep my promise. Hess Deming telephoned me, asking if I'd come out to his Malibu place and drive him into town. He was too shaky to handle a car himself, he said, and Sandra's cremation was to take place that afternoon. I got out my roadster and sent it spinning west on Sunset. In twenty minutes I was at Deming's beach house.

The houseboy let me in, shaking his head gravely as he recognized me.

"Mist' Deming pretty bad," he told me. "All morning drinking gin straight—"

From upstairs Hess shouted, "That you, Mart? Okay—I'll be down right away. Come up here, Jim!"

The Japanese, with a meaningful glance at me, pattered upstairs.

I wandered over to a table, examining the magazines upon it. A little breath of wind came through the half-open window, fluttering a scrap of paper. A word on it caught my eye, and I picked up the note. For that's what it was. It was addressed to Hess, and after one glance I had no compunction about scanning it.

"Hess dear," the message read. "I feel I'm going to die very soon. And I want you to do something for me. I've been out of my head, I know, saying things I didn't mean. Don't cremate me, Hess. Even though I were dead I'd feel the fire—I know it. Bury me in a vault in Forest Lawn—and don't embalm me. I shall be dead when you find this, but I know you'll do as I wish, dear. And, alive or dead, I'll always love you."

The note was signed by Sandra Colter, Hess's wife. This was odd. I wondered whether Hess had seen it yet.

There was a little hiss of indrawn breath from behind me. It was Jim, the houseboy. He said, "Mist' Prescott—I find that note last night. Mist' Hess not seen it. It Mis' Colter's writing."

He hesitated, and I read fear in his eyes—sheer, unashamed fear. He put a brown forefinger on the note.

"See that, Mist' Prescott?"

He was pointing to a smudge of ink that half obscured the signature. I said, "Well?"

"I do that, Mist' Prescott. When I pick up the note. The ink—not dry."

I stared at him. He turned hastily at the sound of footsteps on the stairs. Hess Deming was coming down, rather shakily.

I think it was then that I first realized the horrible truth. I didn't believe it, though—not then. It was too fantastic, too incredible; yet something of the truth must have crept into my mind, for there was no other explanation for what I did then.

Hess said, "What have you got there, Mart?"

"Nothing," I said quietly. I crumpled the note and thrust it into my pocket. "Nothing important, anyway. Ready to go?"

He nodded, and we went to the door. I caught a glimpse of Jim staring after us, an expression of—was it relief?—in his dark, wizened face.

The crematory was in Pasadena, and I left Hess there. I would have stayed with him, but he wouldn't have it. I knew he didn't want anyone to be watching him when Sandra's body was being incinerated. And I knew it would be easier for him that way. I took a short cut through the Hollywood hills, and that's where the trouble started.

I broke an axle. Recent rains had gullied the road, and I barely saved the car from turning over. After that I had to hike miles to the nearest telephone, and then I wasted more time waiting for a taxi to pick me up. It was nearly eight o'clock when I arrived at the studio.

The gateman let me in, and I hurried to Stage 6. It was dark. Cursing under my breath, I turned away, and almost collided with a small figure. It was Forrest, one of the cameramen. He let out a curious squeal, and clutched my arm.

"That you, Mart? Listen, will you do me a favor? I want you to watch a print—"

"Haven't time," I said. "Seen Jean around here? I was to—"

"It's about that," Forrest said. He was a shriveled, monkey-faced little chap, but a mighty good cameraman. "They've gone—Jean and Hardy and the chevalier. There's something funny about that guy."

"Think so? Well, I'll phone Jean. I'll look at your rushes tomorrow."

"She won't be home," he told me. "The chevalier took her over to the Grove. Listen, Mart, you've got to watch this. Either I don't know how to handle a grinder any more, or that Frenchman is the damnedest thing I've ever shot. Come over to the theater, Mart—I've got the reel ready to run. Just developed the rough print myself."

"Oh, all right," I assented, and followed Forrest to the theater.

I found a seat in the dark little auditorium, and listened to Forrest moving about in the projection booth. He clicked on the amplifier and said, "Hardy didn't want any pictures taken—insisted on it, you know. But the boss told me to leave one of the automatic cameras going—not to bother with the sound—just to get an idea how the French guy would screen. Lucky it wasn't one of the old rattler cameras, or Hardy would have caught on. Here it comes, Mart!"

I heard a click as the amplifier was switched off. White light flared on the screen. It faded, gave place to a picture—the interior of Stage 6. The set was incongruous—a mid-Victorian parlor, with overstuffed plush chairs, gilt-edged paintings, even a particularly hideous what-not. Jack Hardy moved into the range of the camera. On the screen his face seemed to leap out at me like a death's-head, covered with sagging, wrinkled skin. Following him came Jean, wearing a tailored suit—no one dresses for rehearsals—and behind her—

I blinked, thinking that my eyes were tricking me. Something like a glowing fog—oval, tall as a man—was moving across the screen. You've seen the nimbus of light on the screen when a flashlight is turned directly on the camera? Well—it was like that, except that its source was not traceable. And, horribly, it moved forward at about the pace a man would walk.

The amplifier clicked again. Forrest said, "When I saw it on the negative I thought I was screwy, Mart. I saw the take—there wasn't any funny light there. Look—" The oval, glowing haze was motionless beside Jean, and she was looking directly at it, a smile on her lips. "Mart, when that was taken, Jean was looking right at the French guy!"

I said, somewhat hoarsely, "Hold it, Forrest. Right there."

The images slowed down, became motionless. Jean's profile was toward the camera. I leaned forward, staring at something I had glimpsed on the girl's neck. It was scarcely visible save as a tiny, discolored mark on Jean's throat, above the jugular—but unmistakably the same wound I had seen on the throat of Jack Hardy the night before!

I heard the amplifier click off. Suddenly the screen showed blindingly white, and then when black.

I waited a moment, but there was no sound from the booth.

"Forrest," I called. "You okay?"

There was no sound. The faint whirring of the projector had died. I got up quickly and went to the back of the theater. There were two entrances to the booth, a door which opened on stairs leading down to the alley outside, and a hole in the floor reached by means of a metal ladder. I went up this swiftly, an ominous apprehension mounting within me.

Forrest was still there. But he was no longer alive. He lay sprawled on his back, his wizened face staring up blindly, his head twisted at an impossible angle. It was quite apparent that his neck had been broken almost instantly.

I sent a hasty glance at the projector. The can of film was gone! And the door opening on the stairway was ajar a few inches.

I stepped out on the stairs, although I knew I would see no one. The white-lit broad alley between Stages 6 and 4 was silent and empty.

The sound of running feet came to me, steadily growing louder. A man came racing into view. I recognized him as one of the publicity gang. I hailed him.

"Can't wait," he gasped, but slowed down nevertheless.

I said, "Have you seen anyone around here just now? The—Chevalier Futaine?"

He shook his head. "No, but—" His face was white as he looked up at me. "Hess Deming's gone crazy. I've got to contact the papers."

Ice gripped me. I raced down the stairs, clutched his arm.

"What do you mean?" I snapped. "Hess was all right when I left him. A bit tight, that's all."

His face was glistening with sweat. "It's awful—I'm not sure yet what happened. His wife—Sandra Colter—came to life while they were cremating her. They saw her through the window, you know—screaming and pounding at the glass while she was being burned alive. Hess got her out too late. He went stark, raving mad. Suspended animation, they say—I've got to get to a phone, Mr. Prescott!"

He tore himself away, sprinted in the direction of the administration buildings.

I put my hand in my pocket and pulled out a scrap of paper. It was the note I had found in Hess Deming's house. The words danced and wavered before my eyes. Over and over I was telling myself, "It can't be true! Such things can't happen!"

I didn't mean Sandra Colter's terrible resurrection during the cremation. That, alone, might be plausibly explained—catalepsy, perhaps. But taken in conjunction with certain other occurrences, it led to one definite conclusion—and it was a conclusion I dared not face.

What had poor Forrest said? That the chevalier was taking Jean to the Cocoanut Grove? Well—

The taxi was still waiting. I got in.

"The Ambassador," I told the driver grimly. "Twenty bucks if you hit the green lights all the way."

3. The Black Coffin

ALL night I had been combing Hollywood—without success. Neither the Chevalier Futaine nor Jean had been to the Grove, I discovered. And no one knew the Chevalier's address. A telephone call to the studio, now ablaze with the excitement over the Hess Deming disaster and the Forrest killing, netted me exactly nothing. I went the rounds of Hollywood night life vainly. The Trocadero, Sardi's, all three of the Brown Derbies, the smart, notorious clubs of the Sunset eighties—nowhere could I find my quarry. I telephoned Jack Hardy a dozen times, but got no answer. Finally, in a "private club" in Culver City, I met with my first stroke of good luck.

"Mr. Hardy's upstairs," the proprietor told me, looking anxious. "Nothing wrong, I hope, Mr. Prescott? I heard about Deming."

"Nothing," I said. "Take me up to him."

"He's sleeping it off," the man admitted. "Tried to drink the place dry, and I put him upstairs where he'd be safe."

"Not the first time, eh?" I said, with an assumption of lightness. "Well, bring up some coffee, will you? Black. I've got to—talk to him."

But it was half an hour before Hardy was in any shape to understand what I was saying. At last he sat up on the couch, blinking, and a gleam of realization came into his sunken eyes.

"Prescott," he said, "can't you leave me alone?"

I leaned close to him, articulating carefully so he would be sure to understand me. "I know what the Chevalier Futaine is," I said.

And I waited for the dreadful, impossible confirmation, or for the words which would convince me that I was an insane fool.

Hardy looked at me dully. "How did you find out?" he whispered.

An icy shock went through me. Up to that moment I had not really believed, in spite of all the evidence. But now Hardy was confirming the suspicions which I had not let myself believe.

I didn't answer his question. Instead, I said, "Do you know about Hess?"

He nodded, and at sight of the agony in his face I almost pitied him. Then the thought of Jean steadied me.

"Do you know where he is now?" I asked.

"No. What are you talking about?" he flared suddenly. "Are you mad, Mart? Do you—"

"I'm not mad. But Hess Deming is."

He looked at me like a cowering, whipped dog.

I went on grimly: "Are you going to tell me the truth? How you got those marks on your throat? How you met this—creature? And where he's taken Jean?"

"Jean!" He looked genuinely startled. "Has he got—I didn't know that, Mart—I swear I didn't. You—you've been a good friend to me, and—and I'll tell you the truth—for your sake and Jean's—although now it may be too late—"

My involuntary movement made him glance at me quickly. Then he went on.

"I met him in Paris. I was out after new sensations—but I didn't expect anything like that. A Satanist club—devil-worshippers, they were. The ordinary stuff—cheap, furtive blasphemy. But it was there that I met—him.

"He can be a fascinating chap when he tries. He drew me out, made me tell him about Hollywood—about the women we have here. I bragged a little. He asked me about the stars, whether they were really as beautiful as they seemed. His eyes were hungry as he listened to me, Mart.

"Then one night I had a fearful nightmare. A monstrous, black horror crept in through my window and attacked me—bit me in the throat, I dreamed, or thought I did. After that—

"I was in his power. He told me the truth. He made me his slave, and I could do nothing. His powers—are not human."

I licked dry lips.

Hardy continued: "He made me bring him here, introducing him as a new discovery to be starred in *Red Thirst*—I'd mentioned the picture to him, before I—knew. How he must have laughed at me! He made me serve him, keeping away photographers, making sure that there were no cameras, no mirrors near him. And for a reward—he let me live."

I knew I should feel contempt for Hardy, panderer to such a loathsome evil. But somehow I couldn't.

I said quietly, "What about Jean? Where does the chevalier live?"

He told me. "But you can't do anything, Mart. There's a vault under the house, where he stays during the day. It can't be opened, except with a key he always keeps with him—a silver key. He had a door specially made, and then did something to it so that nothing can open it but that key. Even dynamite wouldn't do it, he told me."

I said, "Such things—can be killed."

"Not easily. Sandra Colter was a victim of his. After death she, too, became a vampire, sleeping by day and living only at night. The fire destroyed her, but there's no way to get into the vault under Futaine's house."

"I wasn't thinking of fire," I said. "A knife—"

"Through the heart," Hardy interrupted almost eagerly. "Yes—and decapitation. I've thought of it myself, but I can do nothing. I—am his slave, Mart."

I said nothing, but pressed the bell. Presently the proprietor appeared.

"Can you get me a butcher knife?" I measured with my hands. "About so long? A sharp one?"

Accustomed to strange requests, he nodded. "Right away, Mr. Prescott."

As I followed him out, Hardy said weakly, "Mart."

I turned.

"Good luck," he said. The look on his wrecked face robbed the words of their pathos.

"Thanks," I forced myself to say. "I don't blame you, Jack, for what's happened. I—I'd have done the same."

I left him there, slumped on the couch, staring after me with eyes that had looked into hell.

It was past daylight when I drove out of Culver City, a long, razor-edged knife hidden securely inside my coat. And the day went past all too quickly. A telephone call told me that Jean had not yet returned home. It took me more than an hour to locate a certain man I wanted—a man who had worked for the studio before on certain delicate jobs. There was little about locks he did not know, as the police had sometimes ruefully admitted.

218   HENRY KUTTNER

His name was Axel Ferguson, a bulky, good-natured Swede, whose thick fingers seemed more adapted to handling a shovel than the mechanisms of locks. Yet he was as expert as Houdini—indeed, he had at one time been a professional magician.

The front door of Futaine's isolated canyon home proved no bar to Ferguson's fingers and the tiny sliver of steel he used. The house, a modern two-story place, seemed deserted. But Hardy had said *below* the house.

We went down the cellar stairs and found ourselves in a concrete-lined passage that ran down at a slight angle for perhaps thirty feet. There the corridor ended in what seemed to be a blank wall of bluish steel. The glossy surface of the door was unbroken, save for a single keyhole.

Ferguson set to work. At first he hummed under his breath, but after a time he worked in silence. Sweat began to glisten on his face. Trepidation assailed me as I watched.

The flashlight he had placed beside him grew dim. He inserted another battery, got out unfamiliar-looking apparatus. He buckled on dark goggles, and handed me a pair. A blue, intensely brilliant flame began to play on the door.

It was useless. The torch was discarded after a time, and Ferguson returned to his tools. He was using a stethoscope, taking infinite pains in the delicate movements of his hands.

It was fascinating to watch him. But all the time I realized that the night was coming, that presently the sun would go down, and that the life of the vampire lasts from sunset to sunrise.

At last Ferguson gave up. "I can't do it," he told me, panting as though from a hard race. "And if I can't, nobody can. Even Houdini couldn't have broken this lock. The only thing that'll open it is the key."

"All right, Axel," I said dully. "Here's your money."

He hesitated, watching me. "You going to stay here, Mr. Prescott?"

"Yeah," I said. "You can find your way out. I'll—wait awhile."

"Well, I'll leave the light with you," he said. "You can let me have it sometime, eh?"

He waited, and, as I made no answer, he departed, shaking his head.

Then utter silence closed around me. I took the knife out of my coat, tested its edge against my thumb, and settled back to wait.

Less than half an hour later the steel door began to swing open. I stood up. Through the widening crack I saw a bare, steel-lined chamber, empty save for a long, black object that rested on the floor. It was a coffin.

The door was wide. Into view moved a white, slender figure—Jean, clad in a diaphanous, silken robe. Her eyes were wide, fixed and staring. She looked like a sleepwalker.

A man followed her—a man wearing impeccable evening clothes. Not a hair was out of place on his sleek blond head, and he was touching his lips delicately with a handkerchief as he came out of the vault.

There was a little crimson stain on the white linen where his lips had brushed.

4. I, the Vampire

JEAN walked past me as though I didn't exist. But the Chevalier Futaine paused, his eyebrows lifted. His black eyes pierced through me.

The handle of the knife was hot in my hand. I moved aside to block Futaine's way. Behind me came a rustle of silk, and from the corner of my eye I saw Jean pause hesitatingly.

The chevalier eyed me, toying negligently with his handkerchief. "Mart," he said slowly. "Mart Prescott." His eyes flickered toward the knife, and a little smile touched his lips.

I said, "You know why I'm here, don't you?"

"Yes," he said. "I—heard you. I was not disturbed. Only one thing can open this door."

From his pocket he drew a key, shining with a dull silver sheen.

"Only this," he finished, replacing it. "Your knife is useless, Mart Prescott."

"Maybe," I said, edging forward very slightly. "What have you done to Jean?"

A curious expression, almost of pain, flashed into his eyes. "She is mine," he shot out half angrily. "You can do nothing, for—"

I sprang then, or, at least, I tried to. The blade of the knife sheared down straight for Futaine's white shirtfront. It was arrested in midair. Yet he had not moved. His eyes had bored into mine, suddenly, terribly, and it seemed as though a wave of fearful energy had blasted out at me—paralyzing me, rendering me helpless. I stood rigid. Veins throbbed in my temples as I tried to move—to bring down the knife. It was useless. I stood as immovable as a statue.

The chevalier brushed past me.

"Follow," he said almost casually, and like an automaton I swung about, began to move along the passage. What hellish hypnotic power was this that held me helpless?

Futaine led the way upstairs. It was not yet dark, although the sun had gone down. I followed him into a room, and at his gesture dropped into a chair. At my side was a small table. The chevalier touched my arm gently, and something like a mild electric shock went through me. The knife dropped from my fingers, clattering to the table.

Jean was standing rigidly nearby, her eyes dull and expressionless. Futaine moved to her side, put an arm about her waist. My mouth felt as though it were filled with mud, but somehow I managed to croak out articulate words.

"Damn you, Futaine! Leave her alone!"

He released her, and came toward me, his face dark with anger.

"You fool, I could kill you now, very easily. I could make you go down to the busiest corner of Hollywood and slit your throat with that knife. I have the power. You have found out much, apparently. Then you know—my power.''

"Yes," I muttered thickly. "I know that. You devil—Jean is mine!"

The face of a beast looking into mine. He snarled, "She is not yours. Nor is she—*Jean*. She is Sonya.''

I remembered what Futaine had murmured when he had first seen Jean. He read the question in my eyes.

"I knew a girl like that once, very long ago. That was Sonya. They killed her—put a stake through her heart, long ago in Thurn. Now that I've found this girl, who might be a reincarnation of Sonya—they are so alike—I shall not give her up. Nor can anyone force me.''

"You've made her a devil like yourself," I said through half-paralyzed lips. "I'd rather kill her—"

Futaine turned to watch Jean. "Not yet," he said softly. "She is mine—yes. She bears the stigmata. But she is still—alive. She will not become—*wampyr*—until she has died, or until she has tasted the red milk. She shall do that tonight.''

I cursed him bitterly, foully. He touched my lips, and I could utter no sound. Then they left me—Jean and her master. I heard a door close quietly.

The night dragged on. Futile struggles had convinced me that it was useless to attempt escape—I could not even force a whisper through my lips. More than once I felt myself on the verge of madness—thinking of Jean, and remembering Futaine's ominous words. Eventually agony brought its own surcease, and I fell into a kind of coma, lasting for how long I could not guess. Many hours had passed, I knew, before I heard footsteps coming toward my prison.

Jean moved into my range of vision. I searched her face with my eyes, seeking for some mark of a dreadful metamorphosis. I could find none. Her beauty was unmarred, save for the terrible little wounds on her throat. She went to a couch and quietly lay down. Her eyes closed.

The chevalier came past me and went to Jean's side. He stood looking down at her. I have mentioned before the incongruous youthfulness of his face. That was gone now. He looked old—old beyond imagination.

At last he shrugged and turned to me. His fingers brushed my lips again, and I found that I could speak. Life flooded back into my veins, benign lancing twinges of pain. I moved an arm experimentally. The paralysis was leaving me.

The chevalier said, "She is still—clean. I could not do it.''

Amazement flooded me. My eyes widened in disbelief.

Futaine smiled wryly. "It is quite true. I could have made her as myself—undead. But at the last moment I forbade her." He looked toward the windows. "It will be dawn soon.''

I glanced at the knife on the table beside me. The chevalier put out a hand and drew it away.

"Wait," he said. "There is something I must tell you, Mart Prescott. You say that you know who and what I am.''

I nodded.

"Yet you cannot know," he went on. "Something you have learned, and something you have guessed, but you can never know me. You are human, and I am—the undead.

"Through the ages I have come, since first I fell victim to another vampire—for thus is the evil spread. Deathless and not alive, bringing fear and sorrow always, knowing the bitter agony of Tantalus, I have gone down through the weary centuries. I have known Richard and Henry and Elizabeth of England, and ever have I brought terror and destruction in the night, for I am an alien thing, I am the undead."

The quiet voice went on, holding me motionless in its weird spell.

"I, the vampire. I, the accursed, the shining evil, *negotium perambulans in tenebris* . . . but I was not always thus. Long ago in Thurn, before the shadow fell upon me, I loved a girl—Sonya. But the vampire visited me, and I sickened and died—and awoke. Then I arose.

"It is the curse of the undead to prey upon those they love. I visited Sonya. I made her my own. She, too, died, and for a brief while we walked the earth together, neither alive nor dead. But that was not Sonya. It was her body, yes, but I had not loved her body alone. I realized too late that I had destroyed her utterly."

"One day they opened her grave, and the priest drove a stake through her heart, and gave her rest. Me they could not find, for my coffin was hidden too well. I put love behind me then, knowing that there was none for such as I."

"Hope came to me when I found—Jean. Hundreds of years have passed since Sonya crumbled to dust, but I thought I had found her again. And—I took her. Nothing human could prevent me."

The chevalier's eyelids sagged. He looked infinitely old.

"Nothing human. Yet in the end I found that I could not condemn her to the hell that is mine. I thought I had forgotten love. But, long and long ago, I loved Sonya. And, because of her, and because I know that I would only destroy, as I did once before, I shall not work my will on this girl."

I turned to watch the still figure on the couch. The chevalier followed my gaze and nodded slowly.

"Yes, she bears the stigmata. She will die, unless"—he met my gaze un-flinchingly—"unless I die. If you had broken into the vault yesterday, if you had sunk that knife into my heart, she would be free now." He glanced at the windows again. "The sun will rise soon."

Then he went quickly to Jean's side. He looked down at her for a moment.

"She is very beautiful," he murmured. "Too beautiful for hell."

The chevalier swung about, went toward the door. As he passed me he threw something carelessly on the table, something that tinkled as it fell. In the portal he paused, and a little smile twisted the scarlet lips. I remembered him thus, framed against the black background of the doorway, his sleek blond head erect and unafraid. He lifted his arm in a gesture that should have been theatrical, but, somehow, wasn't.

"And so farewell. I who am about to die—"

He did not finish. In the faint grayness of dawn I saw him striding away, heard his footsteps on the stairs, receding and faint—heard a muffled clang as of a great door closing. The paralysis had left me. I was trembling a little, for I realized what I must do soon. But I knew I would not fail.

I glanced down at the table. Even before I saw what lay beside the knife, I knew what would be there. A silver key . . .

THE SILVER COFFIN

ROBERT BARBOUR JOHNSON

*Robert Barbour Johnson is remembered almost exclusively today for "Far
Below," his immensely popular story of creatures who lurk in the depths of the
New York City subway system. Among his five other* Weird Tales *contributions
was "The Silver Coffin," a sort of vampire hunter's guide to building a better
mousetrap.*

"CAREFUL, sir!" the old man warned me. "Tread cautiously, for these old
stairs are worn away and slippery here. And the tunnel itself is very low
and narrow. 'Tis better so, of course, for 'tis less conspicuous. Only a couple of
the cemetery men know that it's down here at all, sir, below the other vaults.
And neither of them knows where it leads to, nor what lies down here in the old
crypt."

He lifted his lantern. I saw a vast stone chamber ahead, the walls dank with
moisture and covered with strange lichens that were like a pale leprosy over
everything. The silence of death was about us as we stood there.

"Here we are, sir," the old man said. "Here's the spot where I've kept vigil
all these years. How've I stood it? 'Tis a question I've often asked myself, sir.
But I guess what we must do we'll find the strength to do, hard though it be. And
then, ye see, I'm what ye might call *bred* to the thing. 'Twas me father's task
before me, and he did it well! It makes a sort of tradition in the family, ye see,
a legacy we daren't relinquish.

"There's my own son, sir. Paul (he's just turned twenty this year), he'll have

223

to take me place down here in the crypt when I'm too old to carry on. He knows about it already, and he's resigned. But sometimes I can see the shadow of the future on his young face, and it troubles me, sir, troubles me more than I can say. But then he could be worse off, ye know. He'll have a sure job and good wages throughout his life, just as I've had, and all just for watchin' down here at night. In these evil times a man could be much worse off. The Holt trust fund takes care of the pay, guarantees it through all time. And as for a raise—why, bless ye, sir, I could ask for ten times the money I'm getting now, and there'd never be a question. Why don't I, then? Well, it's like I said, sir. I feel that this thing is a duty and not a job. Somehow even talking about more money for doing it seems—ye know, sir, I was about to say 'sacrilege'! Funny, isn't it? For the good Lord knows there's nothing sacred about this business. It savors more of the Other Place, if ye take my meaning!''

The shadows crawled like crippled rats about us.

''Ye see, sir,'' the croaking voice went on, ''there must be always a guard down here. Someone has to watch, night after night, someone who had discretion and patience and—courage, if I do say it meself as shouldn't! Those were me father's virtues before me, and I've copied them as best I could. And ye know, sir, a man just wouldn't *last* down here unless he was fairly steady! Ye get the strangest thoughts sometimes in the long hours before dawn, when there's no sound but the drip, drip of moisture from the old arches and that other sound that ye'll be hearing in just a moment, sir, that sound that hasn't ceased in half a century, and that may never cease until Judgment's trumpet sounds to end the horror along with all else.

''You understand, of course, that the Holts aren't just another family. They are the best, if ye know what I mean, sir. They're proud, and they've a right to be proud. They were nobility back in England, sir, and they've been noble folk here, too, since Virginia was still a royal fief. There was General Ebenezer Holt, who fought beside Washington all through the Revolution, and Abijah Holt, him as was with Perry on Lake Erie, and—oh, a lot of others just as distinguished. The Holts are a mighty line, sir. Stiff-necked, some call them, but 'tis their blood that makes them so.

''And so, of course, this stain has to be kept a secret, at all costs. There's even some of the family that don't know; they have just heard that something queer was amiss. Only the 'Head' of each generation ever comes down in the vault, and then only on occasional inspection tours to be sure that all's well. Young Mr. Gerald Holt—though he's not so young by now, I reckon; time gets away from ye down here—Mr. Gerald had his hair turn gray at the temples the first time he saw the vault! So I guess I've naught to complain of, at that. I'm not touched personally by the thing, ye see. It's only objective horror to me, of course, just as 'twill be only objective to my son when I'm gone. But the horror that waits for each young Holt when he comes of age—why, it turns ye sick just thinking about it, sir!

''Of course, the whole secret has been well kept all these years. The Holts themselves own this cemetery. I'm supposed to be just one of the regular guards. I wear the uniform and I help out a bit at grave-digging and funerals now and then, so that there'll be no suspicion of me. 'Tis generally believed that I'm watching this place because of the silver casket. *That* would be a prize to robbers—now wouldn't it, sir?—although of course there's no danger of robbery now. 'Tis for quite a different purpose I watch down here from dusk till dawn, sir—not to keep something out, but to keep something *in,* if ye take my meaning!

"Ye didn't know about the silver coffin? Why, yes sir! It's the only one ever made, so far's I know. The old man ordered it made himself, in his will. He'd great faith in it, they say. Ye see, silver has always figured strong in the legends about Them, sir. Silver bullets was the only things potent against their unholy lives. And this, sir—this was a silver bullet seven feet long, welded into a solid mass! I've never seen a sight so amazing as that coffin was. I used to raise the pall sometimes at night and look at it. It'd make me feel safer to see that gleaming surface between me and the Horror through long night watches. . . .

"They say, sir, 'twas old Andrew Holt himself who collected the silver that went into it. He was abroad for many years on his smuggling trips, and he picked up a lot of foreign stuff, candlesticks and vases and even silver crucifixes, they say, that he melted down into ingots. But thousands and thousands of silver dollars went into the ingots, too. They found a fortune in metal bricks in the old man's room when he died, hidden under a cloth. That's how they knew the curse was on him, you see—by that and by the will he left, providing for the making of the coffin and for the preparation of this crypt and for the trust fund for perpetual care—which is me now, sir, and which was my father—Old Andrew's butler he was in his youth, you see—and which will be my son who comes after me. And his son, too, I suppose, unless the blight be lifted by then. . . .

" 'I shall rest quietly in a silver coffin,' my father told me Old Holt said in his will. 'There will be no need to fear, so long as there be no chink or rift in the metal. I have conned well the lore of these things, and I know. So it is my final prayer that no stake through the heart, no mutilation or ceremonial wounding shall desecrate my body after it be interred. So let my unnatural enduring go on until the taint that is in me shall perish through lack of nourishment for its unholy life. For without the blood there surely must be eventually a death even for the Undying!'

"The Holts carried out his wishes to the letter. They built his vault for him and set my father to watch over him in his silver casket. And the years went by without incident of any kind. Throughout my father's lifetime Old Andrew's grave was just another grave by day; though God alone knows what went on down here during the long night watches. My father's hair turned white long before his time. But he lived to be more than seventy, sir, and died at last peacefully in his bed. The Holts had him buried in their own plot, and put a headstone at his grave that reads: 'Well done, thou good and faithful servant!' I shall sleep there beside him when my turn comes to go, Mr. Gerald tells me, 'for the debt my family owes to you and yours,' he says, 'can never be repaid.'

"He was referring, of course, to that business of a few years ago, when the Horror sort of boiled over, you know. And it was me alone that first found out about it. Of course that's my job to watch for just such things. That's why I'm down here in the night. But strangely enough, 'twas not by being on duty in the vault that I learned about it. 'Twas by reading local newspapers at my home uptown, during the day!

"I don't know yet why I should have been so interested in those children and their mysterious 'disease.' Just a presentiment, I suppose. All my life I'd been fearful that such a thing might happen, even though the coffin seemed a safe-guard. And after all those long years of safety! But I realized at once the significance of that epidemic that broke out among the poor wretched little brats in the Minsport tenements scarcely a mile away from here. 'Pernicious anemia' the doctors insisted it was. Child after child sickened and wasted away, their little bodies growing each day more pallid and bloodless and wan until finally death ended their sufferings. One—two—three—a dozen of them all taken the same way in so many days, or rather nights, crying out to their parents of queer, wild dreams, complaining of pains in their little throats each morning on awak-ening from troubled sleep; but dying, sir, slowly dying despite everything that science could do to save them! Wasting away to little cold corpses that were dumped like sacks into the potter's field in this very cemetery.

"God knows how long it had been going on before it came to my notice. But when at last I knew, I went at once to Mr. Gerald with the story. 'It's come at last,' I told him, 'The horror that we've been dreading all these years.' I showed him the items in the papers. 'You recognize the symptoms, sir?' I asked.

"For a moment I thought he was going to faint. It's no joke, sir, seeing a healthy man's face go white as marble and his breath cut off by sheer, over-whelming shock.

" 'But—but,' he stammered at last, 'it can't be true! It can't be! You've been there watching every night! You would have seen—'

"I shook my head. 'You don't see Them if they will it otherwise, sir!' I told him. 'That's what all the books I've ever read agree on. They come and go like ghosts; only They aren't ghosts, but something far, far worse! The silver in that casket must have cracked, Mr. Gerald. Some flaw has come in it. You'll see!'

"He didn't want to believe me, of course. But I finally persuaded him to go and look at one of the poor little victims laid out for burial in the local morgue. And there could be no doubting the truth then. No doubt at all! Blind or mad the doctors must have been to prate of 'anemia' and to overlook those marks that were so plain on the dead babe's white throat; the swollen livid marks where needle-sharp teeth had pressed home to drain away the life-blood and leave the little form so wasted and thin that it might almost have been some grotesque rag doll that lay there before us on the slab.

" 'Nosferatu! the master muttered as he turned away. 'Nosferatu, the undy-ing! Somehow I never really believed it until now. I've carried out Grandfather's wishes because it was his will that I do so. But my sanity always clung to the hope that it was all only madness of a childish old man, out of his head with the wild tales and superstitions he'd picked up in his Balkan wanderings. I read in his will of the Thing he said had bitten him in the night, had sucked his blood and made him into—well, into what he said he was! But I never really believed.'

"I shook my head sadly. 'Ye'd believe,' I told him, 'if ye could be down here in the vault with me at night, sir—if ye could hear what I've heard and see what I've seen. But until now I believed that no harm could come to anyone, that the casket was proof—but now, don't ye see, sir? We daren't trust it longer. We must act, at once! The Thing gains strength and cunning with each little life it takes. We must lay it once and for all. I know how 'its done; I've read the olden rituals for laying them a thousand times over. And I've had all the needful things ready for just such an emergency.'

"But poor Mr. Gerald held back. 'No stake through the heart,' he quoted to me, 'no mutilation or ceremonial wounding shall desecrate my body after it be interred. Our pledge to poor Grandfather has been carried out all these years. Your family as well as mine has served in it. Must all our efforts go for nothing now, just because of one little rift in the coffin? Surely we can find that crack, seal it up—'

"'But in time there'd be another, sir,' I reminded him. 'And another! Even the silver is not strong enough to hold against the eternal struggling of that which never dies, which never ceases in its blind efforts to escape and find its unholy nourishment!'

"And then suddenly Mr. Gerald's face lit up. 'Strength!' he gasped. 'That's it! More strength! The silver's potency is unimpaired. All it needs is support, the reinforcement of something harder! Man alive, there are other metals harder than silver nowadays! We've the resources of modern science to pit against this horror out of the past. I tell you, we may yet be able to seal it up for all eternity. Wait and see!'

"The very next day the workmen came, sir, from Bessemer—came with their weird apparatus and their scaffoldings and blowtorches. For days this old vault was lit with hissing blue flame like a spot in Hell, sir, and resounded with such hammering and pounding as quite to drown out—well, whatever other sounds there might have been. And when the men had done their job and gone away again—look, sir! That's what they left behind!"

He held the lantern high. What was that vast black shape its rays lit lambently at the vault's far end?—that monstrous gleaming shape on stone trestles? A coffin? But surely it was larger than any coffin ever shaped by the hand of man.

"They tell me it's a new alloy they use for battleships, sir!" the old man said proudly. "An outer casting of stainless steel welded solidly to the silver coffin itself. Soldered, the outer and the inner layers, so that the magic power of the white metal, whatever queer potency it has to hold evil at bay, will be eternally supported by the strongest steel on earth! I doubt that a bolt of lightning could so much as dent that shining surface, sir. Seamless and air-tight, it'll endure a thousand years, even with what still struggled inside it.

"Yes, sir! I heard it too, sir. Of course I heard it. 'Tis no novelty to me, ye know. All these long dragging years I've been hearing it, down here in the night's hush. But I was wondering when *you'd* first notice it, sir. 'Tis plain enough when your attention is called to it, for all 'tis so muffled it might be coming from miles off. But it's right here in the crypt with us, that sound, only filtered through the silver and the steel.

"There's really nothing at all human about it, is there, sir? It might be the howling of a wolf, or almost anything savage and bestial. And yet sometimes there's such a note of human misery and despair in it as to fair bring tears to your eyes, sir. Only tonight there's more of menace in it somehow, sir, more than I've ever heard in all these years. You know, sir, I'm wondering if—good God, sir! Look! Look there!

"The coffin! It moved! I know ye think me mad—that thing weighs a score of tons. Your strength and mine united could not as much as tip it. And yet I saw it move a bit. There! Again! Ye see, sir? 'Tis not just the wavering of the lantern-light. Can't ye feel the vibrations of it in the very walls about us, in the very stones about us as it shakes? Oh God, sir! It's all my fault. I should never have fetched ye down here. I never thought—it's your blood, of course, that maddens him—the smell of your blood! He's used to mine, from all these years of familiarity. But you, young and strong—he'd burst himself to bits to get at you, sir. All these long years he's had no slaking for his hideous thirst. He's dying, sir, of a starvation so slow and so hideous it don't bear even thinking about. And now, fresh blood . . . your blood. . . ."

"No, sir, we daren't flee from him. There's no running from things quicker than light, swifter than an adder's pounce. We must fight him, sir! Here, take this. I know 'tis but an aspen stake, well sharpened, but a better weapon ye'll find it than any gun against what no gun could ever hit, sir! And here! Wind this string of garlic about your throat. Now stand, sir, and we'll defy him together We'll fight all Hell, if need be. . . . Oh heavens, sir! how that coffin does shake! How it rocks and lurches on its stone trestles! All those tons of weight quivering like a jelly—I tell you, sir I never saw the like of it before. The blind fury and malignity—can he break out? Oh, God, sir! I don't know! I don't know! I never saw him like this before. We can only pray. . . .

"Crash! And that awful sound of rocks splintering to powder, those clouds of dust arising to choke us—that was the coffin falling, sir. I saw it teetering just at the very edge of the trestles. Then it toppled—but now you can't see anything, sir, not even your hand before your eyes! And this dust gets in a man's nostrils, cuts off his breath. And all the while that howling and screeching rises to a very devil's pæan of triumph in our ears. Stand firm, sir! Pray to whatever God ye believe in, and be ready. We've our stakes here, and we'll strike with them at the heart of anything we see in the dust-cloud—the evil heart that only an aspen stake can pierce; that an aspen stake should have pierced long ago. . . . We'll defy him together. D'ye hear. Hell-thing that was once old Andrew Holt! *We defy ye . . .*

"Take it easy, sir. Don't try to get up yet. Just rest there for a moment. I guess ye must have fainted, sir. I caught ye as ye fell!

"Ye must forgive an old man's nerves, sir! It's these long years of solitude and long night vigils. I'm not the man I was once, and the shock of the thing— but of course there never was any actual *danger!* How could there be? Did I not say that nothing could possibly damage that coffin, sir? See, there it lies, still there on the floor's cracked old slabs, safe and sound, for all its battering; though the Lord knows how we'll ever get it back on those trestles, sir. It may be that it will have to stay always half propped like that, for I doubt that twenty men could lift it. Sure, the struggle with it exhausted even him, sir. There's been no sound from him, no movement since that last frenzied effort. I wonder, sir. . . . Of course there must be natural laws governing these things, just as governs ourselves, sir. And too much effort may be—well, fatal to them, as to us!

"Perhaps ye've seen the last dying struggle of That which should never have lived at all, sir. Perhaps ye've seen peace come at last to the soul of old Andrew Holt!

"And if not now, surely it must come at last, sir, mayhap not in my time, or even in my son's time. But in the end—steady, sir. We'll go this way."

He helped me stagger toward the old stairs, through the leprous dark.

CROSS OF FIRE

LESTER DEL REY

In the pages of Astounding Science-Fiction *and* Unknown Worlds, *Lester del Rey proved a master at retelling fairy tales and legends for the modern age, often with a humorous slant. His sole* Weird Tales *story, "Cross of Fire," is a straightforward tale of horror, told uniquely from the vampire's point of view. Here, del Rey speculates what might happen if one of the most remorseless figures of Gothic horror were suddenly to develop a conscience.*

THAT RAIN! Will it never stop? My clothes are soaked, my body frozen. But at least the lightning is gone. Strange; I haven't seen it since I awoke. There was lightning, I think. I can't seem to remember anything clearly, yet I am sure there was a fork of light in the sky; no, not a fork, it was like a cross.

That's silly, of course. Lightning can't form a cross. It must have been a dream while I was lying there in the mud. I don't recall how I came there, either. Perhaps I was ambushed and robbed, then left lying there until the rain brought me to. But my head doesn't hurt; the pain is in my shoulder, a sharp, jabbing ache. No, I couldn't have been robbed; I still have my ring, and there is money in my pocket.

I wish I could remember what happened. When I try to think, my brain refuses. There is some part of it that doesn't want to remember. Now why should that be? There. . . . No, it's gone again. It must have been another dream; it had to be. Horrible!

Now I must find shelter from the rain. I'll make a fire when I get home and stop trying to think until my mind is rested. Ah, I know where home is. This can't be so terrible if I know that. . . .

There, I have made a fire and my clothes are drying before it. I was right; this is my home. And I'm Karl Hahrhöffer. Tomorrow I'll ask in the village how I came here. The people in Altdorf are my friends. Altdorf! When I am not trying to think, things come back a little. Yes, I'll go to the village tomorrow. I'll need food, anyway, and there are no provisions in the house.

But that is not strange. When I arrived here, it was boarded and nailed shut, and I spent nearly an hour trying to get in. Then my feet guided me to the cellar, and it was not locked. My muscles sometimes know better than my brain. And sometimes they trick me. They would have led me deeper into the cellar instead of up the steps to this room.

Dust and dirt are everywhere, and the furniture seems about to fall apart. One might think no one had lived here for a century. Perhaps I have been away from Altdorf a long time, but surely I can't have lived away while all this happened. I find a mirror. There should be one over there, but it's gone. No matter, a tin pan of water will serve.

Not a mirror in the house. I used to like my reflection, and found my face fine and aristocratic. I've changed. My face is but little older, but the eyes are hard, the lips thin and red, and there is something unpleasant about my expression. When I smile, the muscles twist crookedly before they attempt my old cockiness. Sister Flämchen used to love my smile.

There is a bright red wound on my shoulder, like a burn. It must have been the lightning, after all. Perhaps it was that cross of fire in the sky I seem to remember. It shocked my brain badly, then left me on the soggy earth until the cold revived me.

But that does not explain the condition of the house, nor where old Fritz has gone. Flämchen may have married and gone away, but Fritz would have stayed with me. I may have taken him to America with me, but what became of him then? Yes, I was going to America before . . . before something happened. I must have gone and been away longer than I look to have been. In ten years much might happen to a deserted house. And Fritz was old. Did I bury him in America?

They may know in Altdorf. The rain has stopped and there is a flush of dawn in the sky. I'll go down soon. But now I am growing sleepy. Small wonder, with all I have been through. I'll go upstairs and sleep for a little while before going to the village. The sun will be up in a few minutes.

No, fool legs, to the left! The right leads back to the cellar, not the bedroom. Up! The bed may not be the best now, but the linens should keep well, and I should be able to sleep there. I can hardly keep my eyes open long enough to reach it.

I must have been more tired than I thought, since it's dark again. Extreme fatigue always brings nightmares, too. They've faded out, as dreams do, but they must have been rather gruesome, from the expression left behind. And I woke up ravenously hungry.

It is good that my pockets are well filled with money. It would take a long time to go to Eldeldorf where the bank is. Now it won't be necessary for some time. This money seems odd, but I suppose the coinage has changed while I was gone. How long have I been away?

The air is cool and sweet after yesterday's rain, but the moon is hidden. I've picked up an aversion to cloudy nights. And something seems wrong with the road to the village. Of course it would change, but it seems to have been an unusually great change for ten years or so.

Ah, Altdorf! Where the Burgermeister's house was, there is now some shop with a queer pump in front of it—gasoline. Much that I cannot recall ever seeing before, my mind seems to recognize, even to expect. Changes all around me, yet Altdorf has not changed as greatly as I feared. There is the tavern, beyond is the food store, and down the street is the wine shop. Excellent!

No, I was wrong; Altdorf has not changed, but the people have. I don't recognize any of them, and they stare at me most unpleasantly. They should be my friends; the children should run after me for sweets. Why should they fear me? Why should that old woman cry out and draw her children into the house as I pass? Why are the lights turned out as I approach and the streets deserted? Could I have become a criminal in America? I had no leaning toward crime. They must mistake me for someone else; I do look greatly different.

The storekeeper seems familiar, but younger and altered in subtle ways from the one I remember. A brother, perhaps. "Don't run away, you fool! I won't hurt you. I only wish to purchase some vegetables and provisions. Let me see—no, no beef. I am no robber, I will pay you. See, I have money."

His face is white, his hands tremble. Why does he stare at me when I order such common things? "For myself, of course. For whom else should I buy these? My larder is empty. Yes, that will do nicely."

If he would stop shaking; must he look back to that door so furtively? Now his back is turned, and his hands grope up as if he were crossing himself. Does he think one sells one's soul to the devil by going to America?

"No, not that, storekeeper. Its color is the most nauseous red I've seen. And some coffee and cream, some sugar, some—yes, some liverwurst and some of that brown sausage. I'd like some bacon, but cut out the lean—I want only the fat. Blutwurst? No, never. What a thought! Yes, I'll take it myself, if your boy is sick. It *is* a long walk to my place. If you'll lend me that wagon, I'll return it tomorrow. . . . All right, I'll buy it.

"How much? No, of course I'll pay. This should cover it, if you won't name a price. Do I have to throw it at you? Here, I'll leave it on the counter. Yes, you can go."

Now why should the fool scuttle off as if I had the plague?

That might be it. They would avoid me, of course, if I had had some contagious disease. Yet surely I couldn't have returned here alone, if I had been sick. No, that doesn't explain it.

Now the wine dealer. He is a young man, very self-satisfied. Perhaps he will act sensibly. At least he doesn't run, though his skin blanches. "Yes, some wine."

He isn't surprised as much as the storekeeper; wine seems a more normal request than groceries. "No, white port, not the red. Don't look so surprised, man. White port and light tokay. Yes, that brand will do if you haven't the other. And a little cognac. These evenings are so cool. Your money. . . . Very well."

He doesn't refuse the money, nor hesitate to charge double for his goods. But he picks it up with a hesitant gesture and then dumps the change into my hand without counting it out. There must be something in my looks that the water did not reveal last night. He stands staring at me so fixedly as I draw my wagon away. Next time I shall buy a good mirror, but I have had enough of this village for the time.

Night again. This morning I lay down before sunrise, expecting to catch a little sleep before exploring the house, but again it was dark before I awoke. Well, I have candles enough; it makes little difference whether I explore the place by day or night.

Hungry as I am, it seems an effort to swallow the food, and the taste is odd and unfamiliar, as if I had eaten none of it for a long time. But then, naturally the foods in America would not be the same. I am beginning to believe that I was away longer than I thought. The wine is good, though. It courses through my veins like new life.

And the wine dispels the lurking queerness of the nightmares. I had hoped that my sleep would be dreamless, but they came again, this time stronger. Some I half remember. Flämchen was in one, Fritz in several.

That is due to my being back in the old house. And because the house has changed so unpleasantly, Fritz and Flämchen have altered into the horrible travesties I see in my dreams.

Now to look over the house. First the attic, then the cellar. The rest of it I have seen, and it is little different except for its anachronistic appearance of age. Probably the attic will be the same, though curiosity and idleness urge me to see.

These stairs must be fixed; the ladder looks too shaky to risk. It seems solid enough, though. Now the trapdoor—ah, it opens easily. But what is that odor? Garlic—or the age-worn ghost of garlic. The place reeks of it; there are little withered bunches of it tied everywhere.

Someone must have lived up here once. There is a bed and a table, with a few soiled dishes. That refuse might have been food once. And that old hat was one that Fritz always wore. The cross on the wall and the Bible on the table were Flämchen's. My sister and Fritz must have shut themselves up here after I was gone. More mysteries. If that is true, they may have died here. The villagers must know of them. Perhaps there is one who will tell me. That wine dealer might, for a price.

There is little to hold me here, unless the table drawer has secrets it will surrender. Stuck! The rust and rotten wood cannot be wrong. I must have been away more years than I thought. Ah, there it comes. Yes, there is something here, a book of some sort. *Diary of Fritz August Schmidt*. This should give me a clue, if I can break the clasp. There should be tools in the workroom.

But first I must explore the cellar. It seems strange that the door should have been open there when all the rest were so carefully nailed shut. If I could only remember how long I've been gone!

How easily my feet lead me down into the cellar! Well, let them have their way this once. Perhaps they know more than my memory tells. They guided me here well enough before. Tracks in the dust! A man's shoe print. Wait. . . . Yes, they match perfectly; they are mine. Then I came down here before the shock. Ah, that explains the door. I came here, opened that, and walked about. Probably I was on my way to the village when the storm came up. Yes, that must be it. And that explains why my legs moved so surely to the cellar entrance. Muscular habits are hard to break.

But why should I have stayed here so long? The tracks go in all directions, and they cover the floor. Surely there is nothing to hold my interest here. The walls are bare, the shelves crumbling to pieces, and not a sign of anything unusual anywhere. No, there is something; that board shouldn't be loose, where the tracks all meet again. How easily it comes away in my hand!

Now why should there be a pit dug out behind the wall, when the cellar is still empty? Perhaps something is hidden here. The air is moldy and sickening inside. Somewhere I've smelled it before, and the association is not pleasant. Ah, now I can see. There's a box there, a large one, and heavy. Inside. . . . A coffin, open and empty!

Someone buried here? But that is senseless; it is empty. Too, the earth would have been filled in. No, there is something wrong here. Strange things have gone on in this house while I have been away. The house is too old, the villagers fear me, Fritz shut himself up in the attic, this coffin is hidden here; somehow they must be connected. And I must find that connection.

This was an unusually fine coffin once; the satin lining is still scarcely soiled, except for those odd brown blotches. Mold, perhaps, though I've never seen it harden the cloth before; it looks more like blood. Evidently I'll not find my connection here. But there still remains the diary. Somewhere there has to be an answer. I'll break that clasp at once, and see if my questions are settled there.

This time, reading and working have given me no chance to sleep through the day as before. It is almost night again, and I am still awake.

Yes, the diary held the answer. I have burned it now, but I could recite it from memory. Memory! How I hate that word! Mercifully, some things are still only half clear; my hope now is that I may never remember fully. How I have remained sane this long is a miracle beyond comprehension. If I had not found the diary, things might . . . but better this way.

The story is complete now. At first as I read Fritz's scrawl it was all strange and unbelievable; but the names and events jogged my memory until I was living again the nightmare I read. I should have guessed before. The sleeping by day, the age of the house, the lack of mirrors, the action of the villagers, my appearance—a hundred things—all should have told me what I had been. The story is told all too clearly by the words Fritz wrote before he left the attic.

My plans had been made, and I was to leave for America in three days when I met a stranger the villagers called the Night Lady. Evil things had been whispered of her, and they feared and despised her, but I would have none of their superstition. For me she had an uncanny fascination. My journey was forgotten, and I was seen with her at night until even my priest turned against me. Only Fritz and Flämchen stayed with me.

When I "died," the doctors called it anemia, but the villagers knew better. They banded together and hunted until they found the body of the woman. On her they used a hartshorn stake and fire. But my coffin had been moved; though they knew I had become a monster, they could not find my body.

Fritz knew what would happen. The old servant sealed himself and Flämchen in the attic away from me. He could not give up hopes for me, though. He had a theory of his own about the Undead. "It is not death," he wrote, "but a possession. The true soul sleeps, while the demon who has entered the body rules instead. There must be some way to drive out the fiend without killing the real person, as our Lord did to the man possessed. Somehow, I must find that method."

That was before I returned and lured Flämchen to me. Why is it that we—such as I was—must prey always on those whom we loved? Is it not enough to lie writhing in the hell the usurper has made of our body without the added agonies of seeing one's friends its victims?

When Flämchen joined me in Undeath, Fritz came down from his retreat. He came willingly if not happily to join us. Such loyalty deserved a better reward. Wretched Flämchen, miserable Fritz!

They came here last night, but it was almost dawn, and they had to go back. Poor, lustful faces, pressed against the broken windows, calling me to them! Since they have found me, they will surely be back. It is night again, and they should be here any moment now. Let them come. My preparations are made, and I am ready. We have stayed together before, and will vanish together tonight.

A torch is lit and within reach, and the dry old floor is covered with rags and oil to fire the place. On the table I have had a gun loaded with three bullets. Two of them are of silver, and on each a cross is cut deeply. If Fritz were right, only such bullets may kill a vampire, and in all other things he has proved correct.

Once I, too, should have needed the argent metal, but now this simple bit of lead will serve well. Fritz's theory was correct.

That cross of lightning, which drove away the demon possessing my body, brought my real soul back to life; once a vampire, again I became a man. But almost I should prefer the curse to the memories it has left.

Ah, they have returned. They are tapping at the door I have unfastened, moaning, their blood lust as of old.

"Come in, come in. It is not locked. See, I am ready for you. No, don't draw back from the gun. Fritz, Flämchen, you should welcome this. . . ."

How peaceful they look now! Real death is so clean. But I'll drop the torch on the tinder, to make doubly sure. Fire is cleanest of all things. Then I shall join them. . . . This gun against my heart seems like an old friend; the pull of the trigger is like a soft caress.

Strange. The pistol flame looks like a cross. . . . Flämchen . . . the cross . . . so clean!

RETURN OF THE UNDEAD

FRANK BELKNAP LONG AND OTIS ADELBERT KLINE

Frank Belknap Long was a distinguished poet and disciple of H. P. Lovecraft. Otis Adelbert Kline was a pulpsmith and literary agent best remembered for his pastiches of the work of Edgar Rice Burroughs. In their sole collaboration, these two writers produced a vampire story unlike anything they had written individually, one that combines graveyard humor with gruesome subject matter.

The Grave Robbers

TERENCE O'ROURKE was frightened. There was a strained horror in his gaze as he stood staring down at old Simeon Hodges lying still and pale in his coffin.

The tall young man beside him was grinning derisively. "What's the matter, Terry? Scared of your own shadow?"

O'Rourke drew in his breath sharply. "I can't understand it," he muttered. "He's been dead nearly a month, but he—he still looks *spruced up!*"

Marvin Cummings shifted his spade and spat down into the empty grave. "Pull yourself together, Terry," he gibed. "He's been shot full of arsenic. You ought to know that a well-preserved corpse can take it."

Harsh laughter came from both sides of him. O'Rourke's three companions were trying hard to be hard. Tall, blue-eyed M. T. (Empty) Cummings, his straw-colored hair blowing in the night wind. Little John Slater, his shoulders hunched and his hands thrust deep into his pockets—to hide their trembling. Lanky, freckled-faced Clarence Limerick, looking even younger than his nineteen years.

Only O'Rourke wasn't pretending. "All right," he muttered. "Laugh your heads off. Digging that poor old fellow up and robbing him of the peace he's entitled to isn't *my* idea of a joke."

"The joke won't be on him," said Cummings, ghoulishly. "His sense of humor has atrophied—along with his heart, lungs, and liver."

"That's right," said little Slater. "The joke will be on Freddy. He'll hit the ceiling when he sees a corpse in his bed."

"It's a mean, malicious trick," said O'Rourke. "I'm ashamed of myself. We're grave robbers. We're worse than—"

"Aw, stow it, Terry," rapped Limerick. "You weren't so thin-skinned this morning. You agreed with us that Freddy needed hardening. He's so damned nervous and excitable that a dead fly on his undershirt would scare the pants off him."

"Yeah, something has got to be done about Freddy," agreed Cummings. "If he wants to be a sawbones he'll have to stop yelling for his mama every time he sees a calvaria chiseled off, and a nice, juicy brain exposed. It's a wonder Nancy has any respect for him."

"That's what gets me down," grunted Limerick. "He faints in the dissecting room and what happens? She goes out with him on a date. With nail-hard material to choose from why did she have to go soft on a weak-kneed freshman squirt?"

"Oh, Freddy's all right," grunted Cummings, charitably. "All he needs is a jolt. We're doing everything possible for the lad. Digging up Hodges is no crime because the old fellow was a nonentity plus."

"We couldn't have picked a lonelier corpse," chimed in Slater. "He lived like an animal, alone in the woods. There'll be no mourners coming to *his* grave."

"Yeah, that's the beauty of it," agreed Limerick. "When we put him back no one will be the wiser—except Freddy."

O'Rourke scarcely heard him. He was staring at Cummings as though unable to believe his eyes. Cummings had ceased to grin. The revulsion in his mind had at last undermined his bravado. His face was twitching and he was staring down at the dead man as though transfixed.

It wasn't to be wondered at, really. The yawning grave, the smell of tainted, moldy earth, and the shadowy outlines of tombstones had alone sufficed to terrify O'Rourke. Cummings was made of sterner stuff, but the pinched and sallow face of old Hodges would have struck terror to the heart of a ghoul.

In his cheap, pineboard coffin under the moon he commanded more respect than he had ever commanded in life. His clawlike hands folded limply on his chest, the charity clothes in which he had been buried and the rough stubble on his cheeks seemed somehow pathetic, horrible—dragging him forth to meet the light worse than a desecration.

Cummings took a cigarette out of his pocket and stuck it in his pale, twitching mouth. "We've got to work fast," he muttered. "Nancy has to be in by ten. Freddy will waste maybe fifteen minutes billing and cooing with her in the vestibule of the femme dorm, but we can't count on it."

He lit the cigarette with trembling fingers. "Terry, you and Limerick take hold of his shoulders. Slats and I will lift his legs."

It was a gruesome undertaking. O'Rourke was shaking like a leaf when they rolled the corpse into a tarpaulin, and loaded it on a carry-cot from the college supply room.

The cadaver was limp, flaccid, but remarkably well-preserved. Simeon Hodges had looked cadaverous in life and death had not changed him.

"Well, well," rapped Cummings. "What are we waiting for?"

"My legs," croaked O'Rourke.

"Damn your legs. Get going."

Out of the moonlit cemetery they plodded, four frightened medical students carrying a gruesome burden. Down a narrow dirt road to Miller's junction, and then east between lonely farmhouses to the dormitories, halls and grounds of Carlton Medical School.

Frederick Simpson was a fresh-air fiend. He had gone off with Nancy Summers and left the window of his room on the ground floor of the men's dormitory open to the warm September night. Removing the wing fasteners on the outside of the screen and passing Simeon Hodges across the sill was as simpler matter.

Slater and Cummings climbed into the room while O'Rourke and Limerick remained on the lawn with the carry-cot, hoisting the body up and sighing with relief when it was seized from above and dragged into blackness.

Slater and Cummings gripped the corpse in a sort of half-Nelson and staggered with it to Freddy's bed. It took them scarcely five minutes to accomplish their grisly task. They descended breathlessly, their faces wan in the moonlight.

"Did you tuck him in for the night?" whispered Limerick, hoarsely.

"You bet we did. We propped him right up in Freddy's bed, and put a book in his hands. Babcock's Post-Mortem Appearances."

A gruesome smile creased Limerick's thin, bloodless lips. "A living case book, eh?"

"We shouldn't be standing here chinning," interposed O'Rourke. "Freddy'll be back any minute now."

Cummings nodded, rotated the wing fastener till it overlapped the screen and screwed it into place.

"You'd better return that cot to the supply room, Slats," he said. "Keep out of the moonlight and tiptoe when you hit the corridor. You'll find us in Terry's room."

Terry's room was three windows further along, at the southern extremity of

242   FRANK BELKNAP LONG AND OTIS ADELBERT KLINE

the dormitory. Terry was not a fresh-air fanatic, but he had left his window open on purpose to the warm autumn night.

The three conspirators climbed in hastily, leaving the screen fastener ajar. They sank into chairs by the window in darkness, and mopped sweat from their brows. O'Rourke had set four wicker chairs in a semicircle close to the window in preparation for just such an event.

The session of watchful waiting which ensued dragged like a dead eternity. Every once in a while O'Rourke peered out, craning his thin neck and humming to keep his courage up.

Finally he saw it. A wide swath of radiance on the trampled lawn immediately beneath Freddy's window. He withdrew his head with a jerk.

"Freddy's back," he whispered, hoarsely.

There was a scraping of chair legs, followed by a muffled oath and Cummings and Limerick collided a foot from the sill. Ruthlessly Cummings elbowed the younger student aside.

"Yeah, he's standing right by the window," he confirmed. "I can see his shadow on the lawn."

"*You* can see! How about me?"

"Pipe down, Limerick. Keep back. We don't want him to hear us."

"He'll yell out in a second," O'Rourke murmured. "He hasn't seen it yet."

Breathlessly the three students waited for a blood-curdling scream to echo across the campus. They *hoped* it would be blood-curdling. What was the good of frightening Freddy if he didn't go all to pieces and cry out in abject terror.

For five full minutes they waited, cursing Freddy inwardly. Finally Cummings jumped up, and started pacing the room like a caged orang-outang.

"Something's wrong," he muttered. "He's either drunk, or we've underestimated him. A lad who can—"

His speech congealed. From beyond the window there had come an unutterably terrifying sound—a metallic screeching and rasping which wrenched a cry from Limerick and jelled the blood in O'Rourke's veins.

This time Cummings and Limerick reached the window simultaneously. Together they stared out, their view-hogging impulses forgotten.

The sound was not repeated. But streaking across the campus in the moonlight was a tall and quaking figure, its arms crooked sharply at the elbows, and its coat-tails flying.

"Freddy!" gasped Cummings. "Just look at him go!"

"As though the Devil were after him," chuckled Limerick. "That sound we heard must have been the screen ripping. He frightens slow, but boy, does it take!"

Cummings sighed with relief. "So that's what it was. I thought for a minute it was a banshee on a tear."

The three students sank down in their chairs and exchanged significant glances. They had put it over. Freddy had had the scare of his life.

They were having a quiet laugh together when there came a knock at the door.

Cummings' grin vanished. "That you, Slats?" he called.

Through the thin panel came the rasping voice of Dr. Amos Harlow, the professor in charge of the men's dormitory. "Your door is bolted on the inside, Mr. O'Rourke. Open it immediately."

Cummings jumped up, swung his chair into the middle of the room and grabbed a book.

Limerick threw himself down on O'Rourke's bed and whipped out a pipe.

O'Rourke crossed swiftly to the door and threw it open. "Sorry, sir," he apologized.

Dr. Harlow was a wiry little man with snow-white hair and a skin as smooth as a baby's. He fairly stormed into the room, his eyes blazing.

"You know damn well it's an infraction to keep your door bolted after ten-thirty," he rapped.

"Baloney," Cummings murmured.

Dr. Harlow swung on him. "What was that?"

Cummings grimaced. "I said it was *only* an accident, sir. Mr. O'Rourke snapped the bolt absent-mindedly, without thinking."

"Well, all right. But think next time—all of you. You'll turn the dormitory into a fire-trap."

He cleared his throat. "A moment ago I heard a very strange noise on your side of the hall—a sort of tearing sound. It seemed to come from this room. Did you gentlemen—"

"We heard it," said Limerick.

"You did? Then perhaps you can tell me what caused it."

"I—I think it came from outside," stammered O'Rourke. "We heard it through the window."

"Nonsense," snapped Harlow. "How could I hear an outside noise from my side of the hall. Gentlemen, I intend to find out where that sound came from."

He wheeled and walked out of the room. Fearfully, their hearts in their throats, O'Rourke, Cummings and Limerick followed him. "Play innocent and dumb," cautioned Cummings.

Harlow tapped on a dozen doors up and down the corridor before he came to Freddy's room. At Freddy's room he tapped again and again.

"Mr. Simpson," he called. "I wish to speak to you. Are you awake, Simpson?"

There was no reply.

"Better open it, sir," whispered O'Rourke. He knew that Harlow intended to do that very thing, so what was the use of stalling? Harlow would step into the room and run smack into the horror.

It couldn't be avoided now. Harlow had questioned every student on the ground floor with the exception of Freddy and Freddy didn't answer. Harlow would get a jolt too. But *he* wouldn't plunge shrieking through what was left of the screen. He'd swing around and start asking questions.

It would mean expulsion, but it had to be faced. They would have to take their medicine like men.

Harlow's face was purpling when he pushed into the room. "No student could sleep *that* soundly," he muttered.

Tremulously the guilty three piled in after him.

The light was still on in Freddy's room. It flooded over the crumpled bed and the still, white form lying there. Not sitting with a book gruesomely propped up before it, but lying with its head dangling over the foot of the bed and its arms rigidly outflung.

For an instant they thought that Simeon Hodges had simply toppled over. Passing from the darkness of the corridor into the brightly lighted room and seeing what looked like a corpse such a first impression was unavoidable.

For a merciful instant their minds envisaged simply expulsion, disgrace and the difficulty of explaining it to the home folks. Then real horror gripped them, shook them and left them as limp as rags.

Hideously the truth dawned. It wasn't old Hodges lying there. It was Freddy Simpson and he looked—ghastly. Freddy had red hair and a fresh, boyish complexion, but now his face was corpse pale and the blood on his throat was such a bright, glaring red that his hair seemed drab by contrast.

The blood had come from two tiny cuts immediately above Freddy's Adam's apple. One on each side of his throat—two tiny punctures oozing bright blood.

The reactions of O'Rourke, Limerick and Cummings were as divergent as their personalities.

Cummings said: "My God!" and turned as white as a sheet.

Limerick swore lustily.

O'Rourke said nothing at all. He didn't even cry out. All he did was reel back against the wall and slump to the floor in a dead faint.

Let's Bury Him

IT WAS past midnight when they reassembled in O'Rourke's room to talk it over in hushed whispers. Slater had rejoined them and was adding his voice to the discussions, his hands in his pockets, his shoulders hunched.

"We ought to be thankful he's rallying," he muttered. "I was afraid his overtaxed heart couldn't stand anything but a saline infusion."

"I'd have given him the hemorrhage emergency treatment," agreed Cummings. "Fifty grains of sodium chloride and sodium sulphate in boiling water by hypodermoclysis. Pumping all that blood into him was risky as hell. But I suppose heroic measures are sometimes justified."

"Stockwell says he was almost *drained*—and Stockwell ought to know. He's stained more leukocytes than any bloodhound in America."

"Stow the shop talk," interjected Limerick. "We're facing a grim situation. I don't believe Simeon Hodges came to life and broke through that screen. I don't believe it was him we saw streaking it across the campus. O'Rourke thinks it was. Okay, O'Rourke believes in vampires. If we want to grovel we couldn't ask for a better explanation.

"Old Simeon was a vampire. We dug up a vampire. He attacked Freddy, bit into his neck and sucked him dry. You saw the teeth marks on Freddy's throat. Blood all over poor Freddy, and we're to blame. We dug up a limp, blood-hungry vampire.''

Limerick's lips were twisting in a sneer. "Okay, if you want it that way. We'll put our brains in hock and throw away the loan ticket.''

"Limerick,'' said O'Rourke, his voice strained. "You've got to listen. I'm appealing to you not as a student of medicine, remember. I'm just a run-of-the-mill guy who has done a lot of reading on his own.

"I've read books you've never head about, by writers with a lot of sound scholarship behind them. Plenty of educated people believe in vampires today. There's an English scholar named Summers who cites hundreds of cases of vampirism in the twentieth century. A few of them have come under his own personal observation.

"He believes in vampires, ghouls, werewolves, and incubi. You can't laugh away the findings of a man like that. He's got more on the ball than any prof in this college. When I read his six-hundred page books for the first time it was as though a hundred ton weight had descended on my brain.''

"Yeah, and crushed it,'' sneered Limerick. "What do you take us for? It's easy to understand why that sort of tripe was taken seriously in the Middle Ages—people had nothing better to do than sit around and wait for something to happen.''

"Perhaps someone was spying on us when we dug Simeon up,'' hazarded Cummings. "Perhaps he tried to scare hell out of us by stealing the corpse and turning our little joke against us. I wouldn't put it past a couple of seniors I know.''

"That wouldn't account for Freddy's loss of blood or the cuts in his throat,'' objected Slater.

"Stockwell says that Freddy was anaemic,'' buttressed Limerick. "He was treating Freddy for mild oligocythemia. How do we know he lost so much blood? Maybe he cut himself while shaving, or something.''

Cummings was pacing the room. "All this is getting us nowhere,'' he muttered. "It isn't far to the cemetery. I move we adjourn to Simeon Hodges's grave.''

There was a chorus of assents.

"Maybe Simeon has come home to roost.''

"Yeah. Whoever snatched him may have put him back.''

"We'd better take our spades along—just in case.''

Returning to the cemetery was a nightmare ordeal to O'Rourke. His companions seemed to share his forebodings, for they approached Simeon Hodges's grave in complete silence.

Their heavy brogues made a crunching sound as they plodded over the black, mouldy earth. Between the wind-stirred branches of tall, thick-boled trees they caught occasional glimpses of a moon that seemed to be swimming in a sea of blood.

The illusion chilled O'Rourke more than the huge, misshapen shadows which crouched at the base of the tombstones and slumbered on the neglected graves. He knew that it wasn't the redness of approaching dawn which glimmered between the branches but that mysterious, inexplicable ruddiness which the sky sometimes assumes in the small hours when the moon is gibbous and the night wanes.

Their thoughts were sloping down into terror-haunted depths when they arrived at the grave and halted before Simeon Hodges's coffin. The coffin was still standing beside the grave where they had left it, but it was no longer open, and it was no longer empty!

Protruding from one corner of the stained, pine-board casket was a pale, clawlike hand.

"God!" shrieked O'Rourke, his neckhairs raising in terror.

Limerick dropped his spade and took a swift step backwards. Slater and Cummings stood rooted, their eyes wide and staring.

The coffin was unevenly sprinkled with fresh earth. A crude mound had been built up on one side of it, and part of the heaped earth had spilled over on the closed lid.

O'Rourke was ghastly pale. "He—he must have crawled back himself," he moaned.

Cummings' hands had gone to his face as though to shut out the sight. Now they dropped to reveal a countenance of haggard concern.

"What in hell do you mean?"

"It's as plain as the nose on your face. He clawed up all that earth and climbed back inside before he let the lid fall. He knew that the jar would scatter dirt on the coffin."

It was an ingenious explanation, but Limerick didn't like it. "Why should he do that?" he sneered.

"For protection after sunrise," said O'Rourke. "An unburied vampire endures the most horrible torments. He's buried now—symbolically."

"It looks like a one-man job, all right," muttered Slater, awe and terror in his voice.

Limerick wheeled on him.

"Don't be a fool, Slats. This could have been the work of a dozen persons."

"I'll soon find out whether he's a vampire or not," muttered Cummings. "If he has blood-stains on his mouth—"

He was reaching for the coffin lid when O'Rourke grabbed his wrist. "Don't raise that lid, Empty."

Cummings straightened, his lips twitching. "Why—why not?"

"It's dangerous to look at a vampire right after it has *feasted*. We've got to drive a wooden stake through the coffin, Empty. We've got to destroy him tonight. Summers says—"

"To hell with your bogey books," rasped Limerick. "We'll look at him and *then we'll bury him.*"

"All right," said O'Rourke. "Raise the lid then, Limerick. Go on, raise it." Limerick hesitated, bit his lips.

"Maybe we better just bury him," Cummings said.

Limerick and O'Rourke grasped one end of the coffin and Cummings and Slater the other. They lowered it into the grave and covered it swiftly with earth. O'Rourke shuddered when a spadeful of dirt descended on the protruding hand, but he went right on shoveling.

The grave looked fine when they had finished with it. Not so O'Rourke. He stood for a moment leaning on his spade, his eyes closed and a terrified expressions on his face.

Suddenly he shuddered and stared across the grave at Cummings. "We're standing on the grave of a sated vampire," he said. "I can feel it tugging at my heart. There is a coldness under my heart and—"

"Oh, nuts," sneered Limerick. "I'm going to hit the hay. I'm not afraid of little boy things that go boop in the night."

"We should have driven a stake through the coffin," said O'Rourke grimly. "We'll be sorry we didn't. We'll be sorry, Limerick."

Attack on the Campus

IT DIDN'T seem as though he could be right. Freddy Simpson was sitting up in bed, and Nancy Summers was holding his hand, and because it was another day entirely and the sunlight was flooding into the hospital room old Simeon Hodges's corpse seemed unreal, remote.

The four students had trooped in to see Freddy, but Nancy was getting most of the attention. Nancy was a very intelligent, red-headed girl with a willowy figure and a face which was just right. The four students were badly smitten.

They tried to hide their real feelings from one another, but Nancy was aware of how they felt. "You boys have been swell," she said. "Freddy seems to have a gift for friendship."

"You bet he has," agreed Cummings. "We think a lot of Freddy. I guess he knows that."

Freddy smiled wanly. His thin, freckled face was still abnormally pale.

"I can't understand it," he said. "I had a dizzy spell. Naw, I didn't see anything. As soon as I stepped into the room things began to swim and I went out like a light."

"You didn't cut yourself while shaving, Freddy?" asked O'Rourke.

Freddy shook his head. "Of course not. I use an electric razor, except when I'm in a hurry."

"Freddy, there's a big hole in your window screen. Know anything about that?"

O'Rourke was holding his breath. He hoped that Freddy was telling the truth.

"Not a thing, Terry. You say there were footsteps on the soft earth under my window. Maybe a burglar was hiding in my room. Maybe he socked me from behind with a lead pipe or something. Maybe the blow stunned me, so that I just folded without feeling it."

"Yeah," agreed Limerick. "That would account for it."

"Doctor Harlow thinks Freddy scratched his throat without noticing it," Nancy said. "He thinks he fainted when he saw the blood. Freddy says that's ridiculous, but some people do faint at the sight of blood. Perhaps Freddy saw the blood and it registered in his subconscious—"

"Now, Nancy, you know that's farfetched," muttered Freddy, blushing slightly despite his pallor. "Blood doesn't affect me like that. If if did, would I be studying medicine?"

"You're just a little boy in some respects, Freddy," said Nancy, maternally. "If you've a psychological handicap you should own up to it."

"He fainted yesterday in the dissecting room," said Limerick, flashing a glance at Nancy which said as plain as words: "Why don't you ditch the kid and take up with a real he-guy, Nancy?"

Freddy glared at him. "It was just biliousness," he said. "I've been studying too hard and I allow myself to get run down."

"It occurred at a funny time," gibed Limerick, mercilessly.

"Maybe he had another bilious attack last night," prompted Cummings.

"That could be," admitted Freddy. "I'm subject to them."

When the four students left the hospital building they exchanged meaningful glances.

"We're in the clear," said Limerick. "He didn't even catch a glimpse of Simeon."

"And where does that leave us?" retorted Cummings. "Someone knows, someone is in on it. Who returned Simeon to the cemetery? It's blackmail I'm worrying about."

"Who would want to blackmail us?"

"I don't know. But someone pulled off a complicated body-snatching stunt. Did he do it for his health?"

"I've warned you," said O'Rourke. "Simeon Hodges is a vampire. He attacked Freddy, sucked his blood, and fled back to the cemetery."

Three scornful medical students, their skepticism restored by the sunlight, parted on the campus from one whom they considered a craven, superstitious fool, going their separate ways in silence.

Limerick and Slater had lectures to attend, and O'Rourke a gymnasium workout. Cummings headed for the school library. He wasn't *quite* as skeptical as Limerick and Slater.

The small, dark girl at the withdrawal desk was Cummings' consolation date. Her name was Sally Sherwin and she was almost as good-looking as Nancy.

"What do you want with all these scary books, Empty?" she murmured, as she passed over the counter Merrick's *Vampirism in Europe*, Dwight's *The Vampire*, Dunn's *Superstitions of the Dark Ages*, Aldrich's *The Witch Cult*, Street's *Magic Talisman*, and Wayne's *Hungarian Legends*.

"Just amusing myself, Sally," Cummings said. "Sometimes I enjoy that sort of reading. Deep inside me there is a repressed Edgar Allan Poe."

"Well! I didn't know you had literary talents, Empty."

"I have many talents," said Cummings. He put his arm about Sally Sherwin and kissed her till she gasped. Fortunately the library was deserted.

"Now why did I do that?" he asked himself as he carried the books into a secluded alcove. "I'm not in love with her. There is supposed to be some connection between fear and amorous impulses. Perhaps I'm more frightened than I suspect. I wish to hell O'Rourke had kept his trap shut."

The books were horribly depressing. Merrick, Street and Wayne professed to disbelieve in vampires, but *something* had unquestionably scared them. Every page he turned carried shrill and hysterical admonitions. Dwight refused to commit himself. Dunn wavered between belief and skepticism.

The most reassuring sentences were in *Superstitions of the Dark Ages:*

It was commonly believed that no vampire would attack a man or woman bearing a cross and protected by a necklace of garlic. It was also believed that no vampire could leave its grave before sundown.

Ambrose Pere observes, however, that heavily overcast skies often lure vampires from the earth and that during thunderstorms they range the countryside with a hellish and illicit greediness.

It was also believed that vampires could imitate the voices of the living, and insinuate themselves with diabolical cunning into the domiciles of maidens.

Cummings was so absorbed in the Middle Ages that he scarcely noticed how dismal the library had become. Hunched and purplish shadows clustered about the deserted book racks and the sunlight which had been pouring down through the tall windows behind him had ceased to warm the back of his neck.

He closed the book at last, stacked it with the others and returned the entire pile to the desk. "I'll call for you at eighty-thirty, Sally," he said.

Sally Sherwin scowled. "You know what happened the last time we went stepping. You kept me out so late I lost my date privileges for two weeks."

"I'm sorry about that Sally," said Cummings, contritely. "It won't happen again."

"I'll say it won't. You've seen to it that I can't walk out of the dorm with you like a decent girl. I have to sneak out by the window."

"It's more romantic that way," said Cummings. "I'll be under your window at eight-thirty sharp."

Sally sighed. "All right, heart-throb. But if it rains the date is off."

"If it *rains?* Why should it rain? There wasn't a cloud in the sky when I—"

His speech jelled. The dismalness which had crept over the library could mean only one thing. During his researches the sun had ceased to bathe the campus in a warm and mellow glow!

Turning from the desk he hurried along the deserted corridors of the library building, and out onto the campus. The campus was bathed in an ominous *negation* of light which struck a chill to his heart.

The ivy-draped quadrangle of dormitories and lecture halls loomed eerily through the murk, their Gothic outlines reminding him of something out of Sir Walter Scott.

He stood before the library building staring in amusement at a running figure. The figure had emerged from the Hall of Pharmacy, and was running straight toward him. A slim, pale girl running. He recognized her instantly despite the darkness.

"Nancy!" he exclaimed, and strode forward to meet her.

She swayed when she saw him and tottered forward until she was in his arms. "Nancy, what is it?"

Sobbingly she clung to him, her whole body trembling.

"It's Slats," she moaned. "They've taken him into the pharmacy building, Oh, it's horrible, Empty. His throat is torn, *mangled*. He's drenched with blood. He's dying, Empty—there's nothing they can do for him."

Cummings turned deathly pale. He stared at her aghast, cold perspiration breaking out all over him. "When—when did this happen, Nancy?"

"They found him in Norwood Lane about ten minutes ago. You know how dark it is there, even when the sun is shining."

Cummings knew. Norwood Lane ran between the Hall of Pharmacy and the Hospital Unit. It was simply a narrow alleyway between the two buildings, a sort of lover's lane where students petted in shadows on their way to the lecture rooms. Brick-walled and ivy-festooned, it offered a seclusion for furtive embraces at high noon and for more leisurely love-making after dark.

"You mean—you were there with him, Nancy?"

Nancy Summers shook her head. "I was coming out of Doc Whitehead's classroom when they brought him into the hall. I was so sickened I—I just ran, Empty."

"I know it was cowardly, Empty, but I couldn't help it. My stomach twisted and I had to get out fast."

Cummings nodded. "I understand, Nancy. It was perfectly natural. We knew Slats, loved him. He was a great little guy. He had his faults, but there'll never be another Slats."

"I just ran, Empty. I wasn't looking for you or anybody. I just wanted to get as far as I could away."

"Sure, sure, Nancy, I understand," Cummings soothed.

"Empty, his throat was horribly torn. Do you think it was an animal, Empty? A rabid dog?"

"There are no blood-sucking dogs, Nancy."

"A bat then? Empty, isn't there a huge, South American vampire bat which attacks men? Perhaps one of those bats was shipped north in a crate of oranges or bananas, and has escaped and crawled into a hollow tree somewhere on the campus.''

Cummings' face was grim. ''No, Nancy. The blood-sucking bat of South America has a wing span of scarcely three inches. It couldn't tear a man's throat or suck more than a thimbleful of blood. The *big* South American bats are fruit-eaters—perfectly harmless.''

''But something fiendish attacked Freddy last night and now Slats. Oh, Empty, I'm frightened!''

Night Visit

CUMMINGS was frightened, too, but he kept his emotions to himself. Only Limerick and O'Rourke knew. A half hour later they were at Simeon Hodges's grave again. The sun was westering rapidly and the sloping tomb-stones now seemed drenched with blood. On all sides of them were tumbled mounds of freshly upturned earth.

They were digging like mad. Sweat was streaming from them and they were wearing necklaces of garlic which O'Rourke had bought at the village Italian fruit store. They were getting down to the coffin as far as they could.

''I can't understand it,'' muttered Cummings. ''How did he get back in without disturbing the earth?''

''A vampire can turn into a thin mist and filter through a screen, a keyhole, under a door or down through the earth,'' panted O'Rourke. ''The last time *we* left the coffin above ground and he had to bury himself. Now the coffin's under four feet of earth. He simply seeped back.''

''I don't know why I'm doing this,'' grumbled Limerick. ''You're both as mad as March hares. There's nothing but a dried-up old guy in that coffin named Simeon Hodges. He's been out and around, sure. But that's because we took him out and somebody with a rotten sense of humor put him back.''

''You're wearing a necklace of garlic, Limerick,'' said O'Rourke. ''Why don't you take it off?''

Limerick grunted. ''When you're with fools do as fools do. Why should I make myself conspicuous?''

There was a dull, heavy thud. ''Careful,'' warned Cummings. ''We don't want to smash the coffin.''

''We made our big mistake when we brought him into the dormitory,'' muttered O'Rourke. ''Once you bring a vampire into your home or invite him in he can flow back anytime. You might as well try to keep out smoke, or running water.''

''He had to break the screen to get out,'' said Cummings. ''That proves he could not—''

''It doesn't prove a thing. He simply wanted to get out quickly. I'm telling you, Empty, he can seep in and out now by simply changing himself into a puff of vapor. By driving this stake through his heart we'll be saving three lives. Important lives, Empty—our own.''

He patted the long, wooden stake which protruded from his hip pocket. ''We should have destroyed him last night when he was glutted and rosy from the blood that came out of poor Freddy.''

''He'll still be rosy,'' said Cummings, grimly.

They were breast-deep in the grave now and rapidly uncovering the horror. Spadefuls of dirt went flying out over the grave, to the accompaniment of hollow thumpings as their spades grazed the half-exposed coffin.

''There are three different ways of destroying a vampire,'' said O'Rourke. ''You can pour vinegar and boiling water into the grave, you can cut off his head, or use a stake, as we are doing. In the Ukraine they—''

''Get the hell up out of there!''

The voice was harsh, menacing and came from directly above them. Cummings gasped and stared up blinking. O'Rourke and Limerick stood rooted, their spades arrested in mid-air.

Standing at the edge of the grave was a sandy-haired little man around fifty years old, armed with a sawed-off shotgun. His eyes were frosty.

''I said, climb up out of there, the three of you.''

O'Rourke and Cummings lost no time in complying. Sexton William Sharp was reputed to be a good shot and a very hot-tempered man when crossed. Limerick hesitated an instant but clambered up fast enough when the gun barrel started sloping down into the grave.

''I've heard tell of such outrages, but I never thought I'd live to—medical students, eh?''

Cummings caught O'Rourke's eye and inclined his head the fraction of an inch. ''He was just a nobody, Mr. Sharp,'' he said. ''He had no relatives or friends. We needed a subject and we thought—''

''You thought you'd rob a poor dead man of his repose. It's a burning shame. You were going to dissect him, I suppose?''

''That was our intention, Mr. Sharp,'' said Cummings, looking contrite.

''Well, you're going to put all that earth back,'' stormed Sharp. ''Otherwise I'll report you and have you expelled. I ought to report you anyway. You're just a bunch of young hyenas.''

Refilling the grave under Sharp's supervision was a back-breaking task. The sexton stood over them and gave them no respite. They were still at it when the sun passed from view below the horizon and darkness settled down over the cemetery.

Limerick had started muttering to himself. ''I'm getting fed up with this. Digging him up, putting him back. Of all the fool—''

He stiffened suddenly. Beneath his spade the earth was stirring, heaving. A chill of horror passed over him. His eyes went wide and his throat became as dry as death.

Simeon Hodges was pushing up through the loose, dark earth with loathsome writhings. His pale, clawlike hands emerged first; then the bulge of his shoulders, and finally, his head. The upper portion of his body shot up straight.

Like a leprous gargoyle he swayed rigid in the moonlight, his gore-caked, tattered garments flapping in the night wind, his face contorted in a malign and hideous mask.

O'Rourke and Cummings saw it simultaneously. O'Rourke let loose a wild shriek, dropped his spade and went staggering backwards. Cummings stood as though turned to stone. He stood staring with wide eyes and gaping jaw, his Adam's apple bobbing up and down.

The vampire was staring up at Sexton Sharp, its dead, white eyes fastened on his throat. Even in the midst of his terror Limerick found himself wondering whether the foul thing was not some sort of hoax.

But when it leapt soundlessly from the grave, flung itself on the cemetery guardian and bore him to the earth his last doubts were dispelled.

He turned and fled in terror from a greedily feasting vampire crouching above its victim, hideous, sucking sounds coming from its mouth. Fled across country, between lonely farmhouses, stumbling in blind panic over fallen branches and bruising his shins on stone fences and ramshackle stiles.

He was halfway to the college when he became aware of footsteps pounding at his heels. Reluctantly he slowed up, allowing Cummings and O'Rourke to overtake him.

O'Rourke was out of breath from running. "The garlic worked," he panted. "It protected us. But we've got to rouse the dormitory and distribute necklaces to all the students. It's loose for the night! That ghastly thing is loose!"

"Sharp's dead," contributed Cummings, his face ghastly white. "The vampire slashed open his throat and then tried to attack us. But the garlic hurled it back. The last we saw of it it had turned into a bat. It was circling upward *and heading for the college, Limerick.*"

Limerick muttered: "I don't see how in hell a little sprig of garlic could do that."

Sally Sherwin was powdering her nose when she heard the tapping. Unmistakably it was coming from just outside her window—a persistent tapping on the screen.

An irritable frown creased her attractive features. She was sitting before her dresser with her back to the screen. Her coiffure was flawless, but there were still some things she wanted to do to her face. She needed at least ten more minutes to transform herself into a really glamorous person.

It was very annoying. Why couldn't Cummings wait? He was always ahead of time.

He just didn't seem to realize that no girl likes to be rushed into keeping a date. Especially a furtive, against-the-rules date which included descending from the window into the arms of a man.

She said without turning around: "All right, Empty. Don't be impatient."

The tapping ceased abruptly. There was an instant of silence and then a faint whisper drifted into the room.

"Why can't I come in, Sally? It's chilly out here."

Sally straightened in indignation. She wasn't conventional or prudish, but she bridled at the thought that perhaps Cummings didn't respect her. He had kept her out late, scandalously late, and now he was urging her to risk expulsion by inviting a man into the girl's dormitory.

"No, you can't come in," she said. "You'll have to wait. Take a walk around the campus, if you're cold."

"Be reasonable, Sally. You've finished dressing. I'll climb in without making a sound."

"No, go away. You ought to be ashamed to even suggest such a thing."

"If I go away, Sally, I may not come back."

Sally Sherwin bit her lip. She was just crazy enough about the big, handsome, athletic Cummings not to want to lose him.

"All right," she said. "You can come in. But you'll have to wait a minute."

Hastily she rouged her lips, an angry flush stealing up over her face. The concessions which a girl had to make merely to hold a man were outrageous. It was a man's world entirely. A girl had no rights, no—

"It was kind of you to invite me in," said a deep, sepulchral voice behind her.

Terrified, she whirled about. The vampire was advancing toward her with bared teeth, its dead, white eyes roaming all over her. There was blood on its clawlike hands and its tattered clothes were drenched, sodden.

About its hunched shoulders swirled a grayish mist which slowly dissolved as it advanced, the last dispersing wisps of its de-materialized state.

The gray, mottled flesh of Simeon Hodges was all compact again after its brief percolation through the screen, a shambling horror that advanced soullessly upon the terrified girl and cackled in hellish mirth.

An Arrow for the Restless Dead

IN ANOTHER second the distance between the girl and the hideous thing had been bridged, and Sally Sherwin was screaming in its embrace.

Frantically she struggled to free herself. She jerked her shoulders back and beat with clenched fists upon its boardlike chest, her breath coming in heaving gasps.

The horror's breath was fetid, its squirming body reeking with the odors of the grave. Mercilessly its long, dirt-encrusted fingernails raked her flesh, inflicting deep gashes on her bared back and heaving bosom.

For five full minutes Sally fought with every ounce of her strength. So frenzied were her struggles that she did not hear the door open or see Nancy

Summers advancing into the room, a look of unutterable horror on her face.

Nancy Summers was clutching a four-foot wooden bow and a gleaming bob-tailed arrow. When Nancy Summers had borrowed Sally's bow-and-arrow set to practice with on the school archery range she had never dreamed that returning it would expose her to the most ghastly peril she had ever known. She stood now white and shaken, her mouth as dry as death.

She could hear the pounding of her own heart above the vampire's harsh breathing.

"Don't touch me! No, no!" There was a strangling horror in Sally's voice. the vampire had seized her dark hair in one scrawny hand and was fastening its greedy lips on her throat.

Nancy Summers nocked her bow with automatic fingers, her gaze riveted on the cadaver's squirming back. The room and Sally seemed to recede as she stared. She had eyes only for that ghastly twisting lich—a shape more foul and terrifying than all the sensations of nightmare.

She knew that she must kill it. Swiftly, remorselessly, or Sally would be lost. Her eyes did not waver as she raised the bow and took deliberate aim.

There was a sharp twang. Screeching, the thing that had been Simeon Hodges twisted about and tugged frantically at the long, barbed shaft which was quivering between its shoulder blades.

Nancy shrank back against the wall and stared wide-eyed at the petrifying sight of blood gushing from the horror's mouth and spattering on walls which were spinning and heaving sickeningly.

The vampire had turned and was stumbling straight toward her across the room, its gray face twisting in anguish, the arrow still vibrating in its flesh.

Its eyes were glazed, but it seemed to sense that Nancy was responsible for its plight. Nancy's head was spinning madly. She feared that she was going to faint. She saw Sally Sherwin sway, clutch at the dresser and slump with delirious babblings to her knees, her hair falling over her face. She saw the vampire's arms go out—

She could smell the taint of it now. It was very near and reaching for her and she could not move at all. She stood as though paralyzed, terror beating into her brain.

An instant of sickening unreality followed. She thought the vampire was already upon her and then she wasn't sure and then an awful coldness seemed to sweep over her.

Then—oh, merciful God—came the sound of a familiar voice. "Get her out of here, Limerick. Damn it, man, take over."

Strong, muscular hands descended on her shoulders and pulled her toward the door. She shuddered convulsively, but offered no resistance. Dimly she sensed that Limerick was too terrified to realize how cruelly he was bruising her flesh. Through the door he dragged her, his breath rattling in his throat.

"His number is up, Nancy," he wheezed. "Empty is putting the squeeze on him."

Nancy's lips twisted but no sound came from them. She had caught a brief, hideous glimpse of the vampire writhing beneath Cummings on the floor. Cummings had pinned the foul thing down with his knees and was driving the long, wooden arrow deep, *deep* into its quivering body.

For an instant through the doorway she saw its dark blood gushing out over Cummings' hands. Then the merciful dimness of the corridor enveloped her, blotting out the sight.

Briefly she saw crude wooden crosses waving in the dim corridor light and smelt the sickening odor of garlic. Then the white, terror-convulsed faces of milling students swam close to her and coalesced into an enormous gray smudge which swooped and swirled and spilled over her until she went utterly limp in Limerick's arms.

It was curious how seldom a girl fainted in just the right pair of arms. When awareness came sweeping back the first person she thought of was Freddy.

She felt very sorry for Freddy—poor kid. She had foolishly imagined that she was in love with him. It was just her maternal instinct running away with her, she realized that now.

Lying on a sofa in the reception room of the girls' dormitory, staring up into Cummings' anxious blue eyes, she realized that there was only one man for her in all the world.

"Thank God we heard you scream in time, Nancy," Cummings said. "We never thought it would try to get into the femme dorm."

Nancy smiled wanly. "I'd rather not talk about it, darling," she said. "Not just now."

"Darling!"

"I *said* darling."

For an instant she thought that Cummings was going to pass out from shock. She had to reach up and pull his head down and kiss him on the mouth to bring back even a little color to his face.

"I don't think so much of your bedside manner, darling," she said.

THE ANTIMACASSAR

GREYE LA SPINA

The vampires of pulp fiction were almost invariably portrayed as unsympathetic villains. Greye La Spina broke with this tradition as early as 1926 with her novella Fettered, *the poignant tale of a man who knowingly marries a vampire to help her curb her bloodthirsty habits. "The Antimacassar," written twenty-three years later, is another sympathetic portrait of the vampire, as well as a grim twist on the adage, Children should be seen and not heard.*

"S HE didn't last very long," said Mrs. Renner's resentful voice.

Lucy Butterfield turned her head on the pillow so that she might hear better the whisperings outside her bedroom door. She was not loath to eavesdrop in that house of secret happenings, if by listening she might find some clue to Cora Kent's mysterious disappearance.

"Because she was not a well woman, missus. It was just too much for her. You should've knowed it, if Kathy didn't."

That, Lucy knew, was the voice of Aaron Gross, the ancient pauper whom her landlady explained she had taken from the county poor-farm to do her outdoor chores. It was a high, cackling voice quite in character with the dried-up little man to whom it belonged.

"Sh-sh-sh! Want to wake her up?"

Lucy sat upright in bed, now keenly attuned to those low voices in the corridor outside her room. The knowledge that she was not supposed to hear what her landlady and the hired man were discussing lent a certain allure—half mischievous, half serious—to her almost involuntary eavesdropping.

"Kathy had to be fed," said Mrs. Renner's sharp whisper. "Listen at her now! How'm I going to put her off? Tell me that!"

Lucy, too, listened. From one of the locked rooms along the corridor she heard a soft moaning and knew that what she had been hearing for several nights was not a dream. Twelve-year-old Kathy Renner, confined to her bed with rheumatic fever and denied the solace of sympathetic company for fear the excitement might bring on a heart attack, was wailing softly.

"Mom! I'm hungry! Mom! I'm hungry!"

Why, the poor kid! Lying there alone all day with no one to talk to, and crying all night with hunger. Lucy's gorge rose against the hard efficiency of Mrs. Renner. How could a mother bear hearing that pitiful pleading? As if some relentless intuition pushed her into explanation, Mrs. Renner's voice came huskily.

"Listen at her! Oh, my little Kathy! I just can't bear it. I can't get at them tonight but tomorrow I'm going to take out that honeysuckle!"

Lucy's gray eyes roved across the room to rest with puzzlement upon a tall vase of yellow-blossomed honeysuckle dimly seen in the half light on one shelf of the old bureau between the two south windows. She had thought it pleasant that her landlady brought them in fresh daily, for their high perfume was sweet and they seemed part of the country life to which she had given herself for a two-week vacation from her new and responsible buyer's position in the linen department of Munger Brothers in Philadelphia.

"Don't do it, missus. You'll just be sorry if you do. Don't do it!" Sharp protest in old Aaron's querulous voice. "You know what happened with that other gal. You can't keep that up, missus. If this one goes, it won't be like the first one and then you'll have double trouble, missus, mark my words. Don't do it! Accidents are one thing; on purpose is another. Let me get a sharp stake, missus—?"

"Hush! Get back to bed, Aaron. Leave this to me. After all, I'm Kathy's mother. You're not going to stop me. I'm not going to let her go hungry. Get back to bed, I tell you."

"Well, her door's locked and there's honeysuckle inside. You can't do anything tonight," grudgingly acceded Aaron.

Footsteps receded softly down the corridor. The old Pennsylvania Dutch farmhouse out in the Haycock sank into silence, save only for that plaintive moaning from the child's room.

"Mom! I'm hungry! Mom!"

Lucy lay long awake. She could not compose herself to sleep while that unhappy whimper continued. Against its eerie background her thoughts went to the reason for her stay at Mrs. Renner's out-of-the-way farmhouse in Bucks County. It had begun with the non-appearance of Cora Kent, Lucy's immediate superior in Munger Brother's linen department. Cora had not returned to work at the expiration of her vacation period and inquiries only emphasized the fact of her disappearance. She had left for the country in her coupe, taking a small table loom and boxes of colored thread.

Lucy had liked Miss Kent as a business associate and felt reluctant at taking over her job. Somebody had had to assume the responsibility and Lucy stood next in line. Her vacation had come three weeks after Miss Kent's and she had insisted upon taking it as a partial preparation for taking over the job. In her heart she determined to scout about the country side to find if she could find some clue to Cora Kent's mysterious disappearance. She felt that Cora would not have gone far afield and so she took up her headquarters in Doylestown, county seat of Bucks, while she carried on her self-imposed detective work.

In the Haycock region outside Quakertown, where many isolated farms were located, she came upon a clue. She had learned that at the Doylestown Museum the names of weavers and inquiries had taken her to Mrs. Renner's farm. On the third day of her vacation Lucy had come to an agreement with Mrs. Renner for a week's board and weaving lessons. In the upstairs front room that was to be hers, Lucy exclaimed with enthusiasm over the coverlet on the old spool bed, at the runners on the washstand and the antique bureau with its tall shelves and drawers on either side of the high mirror. A stuffed chair upholstered in material that Mrs. Renner said was woven by herself caught Lucy's attention and the antimacassar pinned on the back caught her eye particularly. Mrs. Renner said with a certain uneasiness that she hadn't woven it herself and her eyes evaded Lucy's shiftily. Lucy offered to buy it and Mrs. Renner at once unpinned it.

She said shortly: "Take it. I never did like it. Glad to be shut of it."

When Lucy went back to Doylestown to pick up her belongings, she wrote a brief note to Stan's mother and enclosed the weaving. She gave her prospective mother-in-law Mrs. Renner's address. Lucy knew that Stan's mother, with whom she was on exceptionally good terms, would be pleased with the odd bit of weaving and was sure it would be shown to Stan when he came home over the weekend from his senior medical course studies.

The antimacassar wasn't as crazy-looking as she had at first imagined. It was a neat piece of work, even if the central design was loosely haphazard. The decorative blocks at the corners and center top and bottom weren't so poorly designed and the irregular markings through the center were amusing; they looked like some kind of ancient symbols. Mrs. Brunner would be charmed to receive an authentic piece of obviously original weaving. Lucy promised herself to find out about the weaver, once she had gained her landlady's confidence.

She had asked Mrs. Renner outright if ever a Miss Cora Kent had been at the Renner place and her landlady had eyed her strangely and denied ever having heard the name, even. On Friday morning, her second day on the Renner Farm, Aaron Gross brought Lucy a package from the Doylestown laundry, where she had left lingerie. He acted so suspicious and fearful that she was puzzled. When she stripped the covering from the package, he took it and crumpled it as if he were afraid someone would know she had given her address freely before going to the farm. Lucy counted the small pieces; there were eleven instead of ten.

There was an extra handkerchief and it was initialed. It was then that Lucy received the first impact of ominous intuition. The handkerchief carried the initials *C. K.* Cora Kent must have lived somewhere in the vicinity.

There was a penciled note from the laundry. The handkerchief had been mistakenly delivered to another customer and was now being returned apologetically to its owner's address. Cora Kent had been to the Renner farm. Mrs. Renner had lied deliberately when she said she had never heard the name.

Lucy looked up at the sound of a rustling starched skirt, to find Mrs. Renner staring down at Cora's handkerchief, sallow brow furrowed, lips a straight line, black eyes narrowed. Mrs. Renner said nothing; she only stared. Then she turned suddenly on her heel and marched into the house. Lucy was disturbed without actually knowing why, yet Mrs. Renner's deliberate lie was in itself a puzzle.

This was only one of the small things that began to trouble her, like the locked door that confined Kathy Renner. Mrs. Renner had said definitely that she didn't want people barging in on Kathy, perhaps getting her all excited, what with the danger of heart trouble on account of the rheumatic fever. Kathy, it would appear, slept all day for Lucy was asked to be very quiet about the house in daytime. At might noise didn't disturb the little sick girl because then she would be awake anyway.

Lucy sat up in bed now and listened to the child's whining complaint. Why didn't Kathy's mother give the poor child something to eat? Surely starvation was not included in a regimen for rheumatic fever? There was the faint sound of a door opening and the wails subsided. Lucy lay down then and slipped comfortably off to sleep, feeling that Kathy's needs had been met.

Mrs. Renner's enigmatic remarks and Aaron's peevish disapproval of his employer's behavior on some former occasion dimmed as sleep stilled Lucy's active mind. It was not until afternoon of the following day that Lucy, entering her room to get her scissors so that she might use them when weaving, noticed with sudden sharp recollection of her landlady's whispered words of the previous night that the vase of honeysuckle was conspicuous by its absence. She asked herself vainly what connection had honeysuckle to do with Kathy's wailing cry of hunger? Or, for that matter, with herself.

With the vague idea of blocking Mrs. Renner's contemplated design hinted to Aaron Friday night, Lucy managed to pluck several sprays of lilac and honeysuckle from her open window, smartly avoiding carrying them through the house. She put them into the heavy stonewear tooth-mug that stood on the washstand. To remove these flowers, Mrs. Renner must come out into the open and explain her reason for taking them away, thought Lucy mischievously.

In the big downstairs living room where Mrs. Renner's enormous lofty loom occupied space, the landlady had cleared a table and upon it stood a small loom about fifteen inches wide. Lucy examined this with interest for she recognized it at once as a model carried in the store where she worked. She said nothing of this but eyed Mrs. Renner surreptitiously when the lady explained that it was an old machine given her years ago by a former student who had no need for it. There was a white warp threaded in twill, for a plain weave, Mrs. Renner explained.

"What kind of weaving can you do on twill?" Lucy queried, thinking of the antimacassar she had sent to Stan's mother, the piece with the queer little hand-inlaid figures woven into it.

"All manner of things," Mrs. Renner said. "On a twill, you can do almost anything, Miss. Mostly hand work." She manipulated the levers in illustration as she talked. "You'd better stick to plain weaving at first. Hand work isn't so easy and takes a heap more time."

"That antimacassar you let me have is hand work, isn't it?" Lucy probed.

Mrs. Renner flung her an oddly veiled look.

"Tomorrow you can weave a white cotton towel with colored borders," she said abruptly. "No use starting tonight. Hard to work with kerosene lamps."

Lucy opined that she could hardly wait. It seemed incredible that she was actually to manufacture the fabric of a towel with her own hands and within the brief limits of a day. She went up to her room fairly early, as she had done from the first, locked her door, a habit acquired from living in city boarding houses. From deep sleep she stirred once into half waking at the sound of a cautious turning of the doorknob and retreating footsteps and the moaning plaint of the little sick girl's "Mom, I'm hungry!" which seemed so close that for a moment she could have believed the child to be standing closely without her locked door. She thought she heard the child say, "Mom, I can't get in! I can't get in!"

Mrs. Renner was obviously feeling far from well the following morning. Her eyes were ringed by dark circles and she wore a loosely knotted kerchief about her neck, although the sweltering heat would have seemed sufficient to have made her discard rather than wear any superfluous article of clothing. When Lucy was seated at the loom, she showed her how to change the sheds and throw the shuttle for a plain weave, then left her working there while she went upstairs to tidy her guest's room. When she came down a few moments later, she walked up to Lucy, her face dark and grim, her lips a hard uncompromising line.

"Did you put those flowers up in your room?" she demanded.

Lucy stopped weaving and turned her face to Mrs. Renner in feigned surprise but her intuition told her that there was more to the inquiry than was apparent on the surface.

"I love flowers so much," she murmured, deprecatorily.

"Not in a room at night," snapped Mrs. Renner. "They're unhealthy at night. That's why I took out the others. I don't want flowers in my bedrooms at night."

The tone was that of an order and Lucy's natural resentment, as well as her heightened curiosity, made her rebel.

"I'm not afraid of having flowers in my room at night, Mrs. Renner," she persisted stubbornly.

"Well, I won't have it," said her landlady with determined voice and air.

Lucy raised her eyebrows.

"I see no good reason to make an issue of a few flowers, Mrs. Renner."

"I've thrown those flowers out, Miss. You needn't bring any more, for I'll just throw them out, too. If you want to stay in my house, you'll have to get along without flowers in your room."

"If you feel so strongly about it, of course I won't bring flowers inside. But I must say frankly that it sounds silly to me, their being unhealthful."

Mrs. Renner stalked away. She appeared satisfied at the assertion of her authority as hostess and the balance of Sunday was spent initiating Lucy into the intricacies of decorative twill weaves, to such good effect that by the time evening came Lucy had completed a small towel in white cotton with striped twill borders in color.

Lucy fell half asleep in the hammock that evening. The fresh country air and the lavish supply of good country food combined to bring early drowsiness to her eyes. She came awake when a small mongrel dog she had seen from time to time in and out of the Renner barn began to dig furiously around the roots of a nearby shrub, unearthing eventually a small blue bottle half filled with white tablets. She pushed the dog away and picked up the bottle. She looked at it curiously. A shiver of apprehension went over her body. She had seen just such a container on Cora Kent's office desk and Cora had said something about garlic being good for tubercular-inclined people. Lucy unscrewed the bottle cap and sniffed at the contents. The odor was unmistakable. She quickly slipped the bottle inside her blouse. She knew now beyond the shadow of a doubt that Cora Kent had preceded her as a guest in the Renner household. She knew now that the small loom must have been Cora's. The initialed handkerchief was yet another silent witness.

Lucy crept up to her room and again locked the door. She slipped the back of the chair under the knob as a further precaution. For the first time, she began to sense some threat to her own safety. Her thoughts flew to the flowers Mrs. Renner had tossed from the window. Why should her landlady take such a stand? Why had she told old Aaron that she was going to "take out the honeysuckle?" What was there about honeysuckle that made Mrs. Renner wish to remove it from her guest's room, as if it had something to do with Kathy Renner's plaintive, "Mom, I'm hungry!"

Lucy could not fit the pieces of the puzzle together properly. But the outstanding mention of honeysuckle determined her to pull several more sprays from the vine clambering up the wall outside her window. If Mrs. Renner did not want them in the room, then Lucy was determined to have them there. She removed the screen quietly and leaned out. It struck her with a shock. Every spray of flowering honeysuckle within reaching distance had been rudely broken off and dropped to the ground below. Somebody had foreseen her reaction. She replaced the screen and sat down on the edge of the bed, puzzled and disturbed. If Mrs. Renner was entertaining nefarious designs that mysteriously involved the absence of honeysuckle, then Lucy knew she would be unable to meet the situation suitably.

It might have been amusing in broad daylight. She could just walk away to the shed where her car was garaged. Even if "they" had done something to it, Lucy

figured that she could walk or run until she reached the main road where there
ought to be trucks and passenger cars, not the solitude of the secluded Renner
farm, hidden behind thickly wooded slopes.

She told herself sharply that she was just being an imaginative goose, just
being silly and over-suspicious. What could honeysuckle have to do with her
personal security? She got ready for bed, resolutely turned out the kerosene
lamp. Drowsiness overcame her and she sank into heavy sleep.

She did not hear Mrs. Renner's sibilant whisper: "Sh-sh-sh! Kathy! You can
come now, Kathy. She's sound asleep. Mother took out the honeysuckle. You
can get in now. Sh-sh-sh!"

She did not hear old Aaron's querulous protest: "You can't do this, missus.
Let me get the stake, missus. It'd be better than way. Missus . . .''

To Lucy, soundly sleeping within her locked room no sound penetrated. Her
dreams were strangely vivid and when she finally wakened Monday morning she
lay languidly recalling that final dream wherein a white-clad child had approached her bed timidly, had crept in beside her until her arms had embraced the
small, shy intruder. The child had put small warm lips against her throat in what
Lucy felt was a kiss, but a kiss such as she had never in her life experienced. It
stung cruelly. But when she yielded to the child's caress, a complete relaxation
of mind and muscle fell upon her and it was as if all of herself were being drawn
up to meet those childish lips that clung close to her neck. It was a disturbing
dream and even the memory of it held something of mingled antipathy and
allure.

Lucy knew it was time to rise and she sat up, feeling tired, almost weak, and
somehow disinclined to make the slightest physical effort. It was as if something
had gone out of her, she thought exhaustedly. She lifted one hand involuntarily
to her neck. Her fingers sensed a small roughness, like two pin pricks, where the
dream child had kissed her so strangely, so poignantly. Lucy got out of bed then
and went to the mirror. Clear on her neck were those two marks, as if a great
beetle had clipped the soft flesh with sharp mandibles. She cried out softly at the
sight of those ruddy punctures.

That there was something wrong, she was now convinced. That it also concerned herself, she felt certain. She was unable to analyze the precise nature of
the wrongness but knew that it held something inimical in the very atmosphere
of the Renner farmhouse and unreasoning terror mounted within her. Could she
get to her car and escape? *Escape* . . . ? She stared at her neck in the mirrored
reflection and fingered the red marks gingerly. Her thoughts could not be mar-
shalled into coherence and she found herself thinking of but one thing—flight.
She could not have put into words just what it was from which she ought to flee
but that she must leave the Renner farmhouse at the earliest possible moment
became a stronger conviction with every passing moment. In her mind one ugly,
incontrovertible fact stood out only too clearly: Cora Kent had visited the Renner
farm and had not been seen since.

Lucy dressed hastily and managed to slip out of the house without encountering her landlady. She found her car under the shed in the rear of the barn, where she had left it. It looked all right but when she got closer, she saw to her dismay that it had two flats. She had, as was usual, but one spare tire. She did not know how to take off or put on even that one spare tire, let alone manage to repair the second flat. She would be unable to drive away from the Renner farm in her car. She stood staring in dismay at the useless vehicle.

Aaron Gross's whining voice came softly to her ear. She whirled to confront him accusingly.

"What happened to my car? Who—?"

"You can't be using it right away, miss, with them two tires flat," Aaron volunteered, whiningly. "Want I should take them down to a service station for you?"

She cried with relief: "That would be splendid, Aaron. But I don't know how to get them off."

"Neither do I, miss. I dunno nothing about machines."

Impatience and apprehension mingled in the girl's voice. She threw open the luggage compartment and began to pull out the tools.

"I think I can jack up the car, Aaron. I've never done it before, but I do want the car so that I can get to town. Shopping," she added quickly, trying to smile carelessly.

Aaron made no comment. He stood at the end of the shed watching her as she managed to get the jack under the rear axle and began to pump the car off the ground.

"I'll need a box to hold this up when I put the jack under that other tire," she suggested.

Aaron shuffled away.

Lucy managed to pry off the hub cap but with all her feverish attempts at the nuts and bolts, she could stir nothing. She stopped in despair, waiting for Aaron to return with the box. She thought she might get him to have a mechanic come up from town. Panting and disheveled, she walked out of the shed to look for him. As she emerged, Mrs. Renner confronted her, grim-lipped, narrow-eyed.

"Anything wrong?" inquired Mrs. Renner, both fat hands smoothing down a blue checkered apron over ample hips.

"My car has two flats. I can't understand why," blurted Lucy.

Mrs. Renner's face remained impassive. She stated rather than asked, "You don't need to go into town. Aaron can do your errands."

"Oh, but I do want to get to town," insisted Lucy with vehemence.

"You don't need your car until you're leaving here," said Mrs. Renner coldly. She regarded Lucy with an impassive face, then turned her back and walked toward the house without another word.

Lucy called: "Mrs. Renner! Mrs. Renner! I'd like to have Aaron take these two wheels into town to be repaired but I can't get them off."

Mrs. Renner continued on her way and disappeared into the house without turning or giving the least sign that she had heard a word.

From the interior of the barn Aaron's querulous voice issued cautiously.

"Miss, want I should ask the mechanic to come out here?"

"Oh, Aaron, that would be wonderful! I'd be glad to pay him—and you—well. Tell him I just can't get those tires off by myself."

That would do it, she told herself. Once the mechanic was there, she would bring down her suitcase and manage to get into town and have him send someone to bring out her car when the tires were repaired. She would manage to leave before night. While Aaron was away, she would work on the loom that she was convinced had been Cora Kent's property. That might disarm Mrs. Renner's suspicions.

She walked slowly back to the house. She was thankful that Mrs. Renner was upstairs tidying the bedroom; Lucy could hear her steps as she walked from one side to the other of the big bed. Lucy sat down at the loom and began to experiment with a colored thread, to see if she could make an ornamental border like that of the antimacassar she had sent to Stan's mother. It was not as difficult as she had thought it might be and went faster than she believed possible; it was almost as if other fingers laid the threads in place for her. She began to build up the border emblems with growing excitement. The corner inserts looked for all the world like curving serpents standing upright on their tails and the center one was like a snake with its tail in its mouth. Time passed. The weaving grew under what she felt were guided fingers.

"Why," she said aloud, amazed at what she had woven in so short a time. "It looks like SOS!"

"So?" hissed Mrs. Renner significantly.

She was standing directly behind Lucy, staring at the woven symbols with narrowed eyes and grim mouth. She picked up the scissors lying on the table and slashed across the weaving with deliberate intent. In a moment it had been utterly destroyed.

"So!" she said with dark finality.

Lucy's hands had flown to her mouth to shut off horrified protest. She could not for a moment utter a word. The significance of that action was all too clear. She knew suddenly who had woven the antimacassar. She knew why the adaptable serpents had been chosen for decor. She looked at Mrs. Renner, all this knowledge clear on her startled face, and met the grim determination with all the opposing courage and strength of purpose she could muster.

"What happened to Cora Kent?" she demanded point-blank, her head high, her eyes wide with horror. "She was here. I know she was here. What did you do to her?" As if the words had been thrust up on her, she continued: "Did you take the honeysuckle from *her* room?"

Amazingly, Mrs. Renner seemed to be breaking down. She began to wring her hands with futile gestures of despair. Her air of indomitable determination dissipated as she bent her body from one side to the other like an automaton.

"She didn't last long, did she?" Lucy pursued with cruel relentlessness, as the recollection of that overheard conversation pushed to the foreground of her thoughts.

Mrs. Renner stumbled backward and fell crumpled shapelessly into a chair.

"How did you know that?" she whispered hoarsely. And then, "I didn't know she was sick. I had to feed Kathy, didn't I? I thought—"

"You thought she'd last longer, missus, didn't you? You didn't really mean to let Kathy kill her, did you?"

Aaron was standing in the kitchen doorway. One gnarled hand held a stout stick, whittled into a sharp point at one end. A heavy wooden mallet weighed down his other hand.

Mrs. Renner's eyes fastened on the pointed stick. She cried out weakly.

Aaron shuffled back into the kitchen and Lucy heard his footsteps going up the stairs.

Mrs. Renner was sobbing and crying frantically: "No! No!"

She seemed entirely bereft of physical stamina, unable to lift herself from the chair into which her body had sunk weakly. She only continued to cry out pitifully in protest against something which made Lucy's dizzy surmises could not shape into tangibility.

A door opened upstairs. Aaron's footsteps paused. For a long terrible moment silence prevailed. Even Mrs. Renner's cries ceased. It was as if the house and all in it were awaiting an irrevocable event.

Then there sailed out upon that sea of silence a long quavering shriek of tormented, protesting agony that died away in spreading ripples of sound, ebbing into the finality of deep stillness as if the silence had absorbed them.

Mrs. Renner slipped unconscious to the floor. She said one word only as her body went from chair to floor. "Kathy!" Her lips pushed apart sluggishly to permit the escape of that sound.

Lucy stood without moving beside the loom with its slashed and ruined web. It was as if she were unable to initiate the next scene in the drama and were obliged to await her cue. It came with the sound of wheels and a brake and a voice that repeatedly called her name.

"Lucy! Lucy!"

Why, it was Stan. How was it that Stan had come to her? How was it that his arms were about her shelteringly? She found her own voice then.

"Aaron has killed Kathy with a sharp stick and a mallet," she accused sickly.

Stan's voice was full of quiet reassurance.

"Aaron hasn't killed Kathy. Kathy has been dead for many weeks."

"Impossible," whispered Lucy. "I've heard her calling for food, night after night."

"Food, Lucy? All Kathy wanted was blood. Her mother tried to satisfy her and couldn't, so Kathy took what Cora Kent could give and Cora couldn't stand the drain."

"Mrs. Renner said Cora didn't last long—"

Stan held her closer, comfortingly safe within his man's protective strength.

"Lucy, did she—"

Lucy touched her neck. Incomprehensibly, the red points had smoothed away.

She said uncertainly: "I think she came once, Stan. But I thought it was a dream. Now the red marks are gone."

"For that you can thank Aaron's action, Lucy. He has put an end to Kathy's vampirism."

He bent over the prostrate woman. "Nothing but a faint," he said briefly.

"Aaron—?"

"He's perfectly sane, and he won't hurt anybody, Lucy. What he's done won't be understood by the authorities, but I doubt it they do more than call him insane, for an examination will prove that Kathy was long dead before he drove that wooden stake into her heart."

"How did you know about her, Stan?"

"From the antimacassar you sent Mother."

"With the SOS worked into the border?" Lucy ventured.

"So you found that, too, Lucy? Did you know that poor girl had woven shorthand symbols all over the piece? As soon as I realized that they stood for 'Vampire, danger, death, Cora Kent', I came for you."

"What will happen to Mrs. Renner, Stan?"

"That's hard to say. But she may be charged with murder if they ever find Cora's body."

Lucy shuddered.

"The likelihood is that she is mentally unsound, dear. She probably never realized that Kathy was dead. Her punishment may not be too severe.

"But come on, Lucy, and pack up your things. You're going back to town with me and we'll inform the authorities of what's happened."

ASYLUM

A. E. VAN VOGT

When looking for a good pulp vampire story, one did not turn to the pages of Astounding Science-Fiction, *the magazine that helped to establish science fiction as a mythology for the age of modern technology. For this reason A. E. van Vogt's "Asylum," with its incorporation of blood lust into the character of an alien species, was considered something of a breakthrough story. Here, though, van Vogt subordinates the horror of the vampire menace to tell one of his trademark tales of alien intelligence battling human supermen.*

I

INDECISION WAS DARK in the man's thoughts as he walked across the spaceship control room to the cot where the woman lay so taut and so still. He bent over her; he said in his deep voice:

"We're slowing down, Merla."

No answer, no movement, not a quiver in her delicate, abnormally blanched cheeks. Her fine nostrils dilated ever so slightly with each measured breath. That was all.

The Dreegh lifted her arm, then let it go. It dropped to her lap like a piece of lifeless wood, and her body remained rigid and unnatural. Carefully, he put his fingers to one eye, raised the lid, peered into it. It stared back at him, a clouded, sightless blue.

He straightened, and stood very still there in the utter silence of the hurtling ship. For a moment, then, in the intensity of his posture and in the dark ruthlessness of his lean, hard features, he seemed the veritable embodiment of grim, icy calculation.

He thought grayly: "If I revived her now, she'd have more time to attack me, and more strength. If I wait, she'd be weaker—"

Slowly, he relaxed. Some of the weariness of the years he and this woman had spent together in the dark vastness of space came to shatter his abnormal logic. Bleak sympathy touched him—and the decision was made.

He prepared an injection, and fed it into her arm. His gray eyes held a steely brightness as he put his lips near the woman's ear; in a ringing, resonant voice he said: "We're near a star system. There'll be blood, Merla! And life!"

The woman stirred; momentarily, she seemed like a golden-haired doll come alive. No color touched her perfectly formed cheeks, but alertness crept into her eyes. She stared up at him with a hardening hostility, half questioning.

"I've been chemical," she said—and abruptly the doll-like effect was gone. Her gaze tightened on him, and some of the prettiness vanished from her face. Her lips twisted into words:

"It's damned funny, Jeel, that you're still O.K. If I thought—"

He was cold, watchful. "Forget it," he said curtly. "You're an energy waster, and you know it. Anyway, we're going to land."

The flamelike tenseness of her faded. She sat up painfully, but there was a thoughtful look on her face as she said:

"I'm interested in the risks. This is not a Galactic planet, is it?"

"There are no Galactics out here. But there is an Observer. I've been catching the secret *ultra* signals for the last two hours"—a sardonic note entered his voice—"warning all ships to stay clear because the system isn't ready for any kind of contact with Galactic planets."

Some of the diabolic glee that was in his thoughts must have communicated through his tone. The woman stared at him, and slowly her eyes widened. She half whispered:

"You mean—"

He shrugged. "The signals ought to be registering full blast now. We'll see what degree system this is. But you can start hoping hard right now."

At the control board, he cautiously manipulated the room into darkness and set the automatics—a picture took form on a screen on the opposite wall.

At first there was only a point of light in the middle of a starry sky, then a planet floating brightly in the dark space, continents and oceans plainly visible. A voice came out of the screen: "This star system contains one inhabited planet, the third from the Sun, called Earth by its inhabitants. It was colonized by Galactics about seven thousand years ago in the usual manner. It is now in the third degree of development, having attained a limited form of space travel little more than a hundred years ago. It—"

With a swift movement, the man cut off the picture and turned on the light, then looked across at the woman in blank, triumphant silence.

"Third degree!" he said softly, and there was an almost incredulous note in his voice. "Only third degree. Merla, do you realize what this means? This is the opportunity of the ages. I'm going to call the Dreegh tribe. If we can't get away with several tankers of blood and a whole battery of 'life,' we don't deserve to be immortal. We—"

He turned toward the communicator, and for that exultant moment caution was a dim thing in the back of his mind. From the corner of his eye, he saw the woman flow from the edge of the cot. Too late he twisted aside. The frantic jerk saved him only partially; it was their cheeks, not their lips that met.

Blue flame flashed from him to her. The burning energy seared his cheek to instant, bleeding rawness. He half fell to the floor from the shock; and then, furious with the intense agony, he fought free.

"I'll break your bones!" he raged.

Her laughter, unlovely with her own suppressed fury, floated up at him from the floor, where he had flung her. She snarled: "So you did have a secret supply of 'life' for yourself. You damned double-crosser!"

His black mortification dimmed before the stark realization that anger was useless. Tense with the weakness that was already a weight on his muscles, he whirled toward the control board and began feverishly to make the adjustments that would pull the ship back into normal space and time.

The body urge grew in him swiftly, a dark, remorseless need. Twice, black nausea sent him reeling to the cot; but each time he fought back to the control board. He sat there finally at the controls, head drooping, conscious of the numbing tautness that crept deeper, deeper—

Almost, he drove the ship too fast. It turned a blazing white when at last it struck the atmosphere of the third planet. But those hard metals held their shape; and the terrible speeds yielded to the fury of the reversers and to the pressures of the air that thickened with every receding mile.

It was the woman who helped his faltering form into the tiny lifeboat. He lay there, gathering strength, staring with tense eagerness down at the blazing sea of lights that was the first city he had seen on the night side of this strange world.

Dully, he watched as the woman carefully eased the small ship into the darkness behind a shed in a little back alley; and, because succor seemed suddenly near, sheer hope enabled him to walk beside her to the dimly lighted residential street nearby.

He would have walked on blankly into the street, but the woman's fingers held him back into the shadows of the alleyway.

"Are you mad?" she whispered. "Lie down. We'll stay right here till someone comes."

The cement was hard beneath his body, but after a moment of the painful rest it brought, he felt a faint surge of energy; and he was able to voice his bitter thought:

"If you hadn't stolen most of my carefully saved 'life,' we wouldn't be in this desperate position. You know well that it's more important that I remain at full power.''

In the dark beside him, the woman lay quiet for a while; then her defiant whisper came:

"We both need a change of blood and a new charge of 'life.' Perhaps I did take a little too much out of you, but that was because I had to steal it. You wouldn't have given it to me of your own free will, and you know it.''

For a time, the futility of argument held him silent, but, as the minutes dragged, that dreadful physical urgency once more tainted his thoughts, he said heavily: "You realize of course that we've revealed our presence. We should have waited for the others to come. There's no doubt at all that our ship was spotted by the Galactic Observer in this system before we reached the outer planets. They'll have tracers on us wherever we go, and, no matter where we bury our machine, they'll know its exact location. It is impossible to hide the interstellar drive energies, and, since they wouldn't make the mistake of bringing such energies to a third-degree planet, we can't hope to locate them in that fashion.

"But we must expect an attack of some kind. I only hope one of the great Galactics doesn't take part in it.''

"One of them!'' Her whisper was a gasp, then she snapped irritably, ''Don't try to scare me. You've told me time and again that—''

"All right, all right!'' He spoke grudgingly, wearily. ''A million years have proven that they consider us beneath their personal attention. And''—in spite of his appalling weakness, scorn came—''let any of the kind of agents they have in these lower-category planets try to stop us.''

"Hush!'' Her whisper was tense. ''Footsteps! Quick, get to your feet!''

He was aware of the shadowed form of her rising; then her hands were tugging at him. Dizzily, he stood up.

"I don't think,'' he began wanly, ''that I can—''

"Jeel!'' Her whisper beat at him; her hands shook him. ''It's a man and a woman. They're 'life,' Jeel, 'life'!''

Life!

He straightened with a terrible effort. A spark of the unquenchable will to live that had brought him across the black miles and the blacker years, burst into flames inside him. Lightly, swiftly, he fell into step beside Merla, and strode beside her into the open. He saw the shapes of the man and the woman.

In the half-night under the trees of that street, the couple came toward them, drawing aside to let them pass; first the woman came, then the man—and it was as simple as if all his strength had been there in his muscles.

He saw Merla launch herself at the man; and then he was grabbing the woman, his head bending instantly for that abnormal kiss—

Afterward—after they had taken the blood, too—grimness came to the man, a hard fabric of thought and counterthought, that slowly formed into purpose; he said: ''We'll leave the bodies here.''

Her startled whisper rose in objection, but he cut her short harshly: "Let me handle this. These dead bodies will draw to this city news gatherers, news reporters or whatever their breed are called on this planet; and we need such a person now. Somewhere in the reservoir of facts possessed by a person of this type must be clues, meaningless to him, but by which we can discover the secret base of the Galactic Observer in this system. We must find that base, discover its strength, and destroy it if necessary when the tribe comes."

His voice took on a steely note: "And now, we've got to explore this city, find a much frequented building under which we can bury our ship, learn the language, replenish our own vital supplies—and capture that reporter.

"After I'm through with him"—his tone became silk smooth—"he will undoubtedly provide you with that physical diversion which you apparently crave when you have been particularly chemical."

He laughed gently, as her fingers gripped his arm in the darkness, a convulsive gesture; her voice came: "Thank you, Jeel. You do understand, don't you?"

II

BEHIND LEIGH, a door opened. Instantly the clatter of voices in the room faded to a murmur. He turned alertly, tossing his cigarette onto the marble floor, and stepping on it, all in one motion.

Overhead, the lights brightened to daylight intensity; and in that blaze he saw what the other eyes were already staring at: the two bodies, the man's and the woman's, as they were wheeled in.

The dead couple lay side by side on the flat, gleaming top of the carrier. Their bodies were rigid, their eyes closed; they looked as dead as they were, and not at all, Leigh thought, as if they were sleeping.

He caught himself making a mental note of that fact—and felt abruptly shocked.

The first murders on the North American continent in twenty-seven years. And it was only another job. By Heaven, he was tougher than he'd ever believed.

He grew aware that the voices had stopped completely. The only sound was the hoarse breathing of the man nearest him—and then the scrape of his own shoes as he went forward.

His movements acted like a signal on that tense group of men. There was a general pressing forward. Leigh had a moment of hard anxiety; and then his bigger, harder muscles brought him where he wanted to be, opposite the two heads.

He leaned forward in dark absorption. His finger probed gingerly the neck of the woman, where the incisions showed. He did not look up at the attendant, as he said softly:

"This is where the blood was drained?"

"Yes."

Before he could speak again, another reporter interjected: "Any special comment from the police scientists? The murders are more than a day old now. There ought to be something new."

Leigh scarcely heard. The woman's body, electrically warmed for embalming, felt eerily lifelike to his touch. It was only after a long moment that he noticed her lips were badly, almost brutally bruised.

His gaze flicked to the man, and there were the same neck cuts, the same torn lips. He looked up, questions quivered on his tongue—and remained unspoken as realization came that the calm-voiced attendant was still talking. The man was saying:

"—normally, when the electric embalmers are applied, there is resistance from the static electricity of the body. Curiously, that resistance was not present in either body."

Somebody said: "Just what does that mean?"

"This static force is actually a form of life force, which usually trickles out of a corpse over a period of a month. We know of no way to hasten the process, but the bruises on the lips show distinct burns, which are suggestive."

There was a craning of necks, a crowding forward, and Leigh allowed himself to be pushed aside. He stopped attentively, as the attendant said: "Presumably, a pervert could have kissed with such violence."

"I thought," Leigh called distinctly, "there were no more perverts since Professor Ungarn persuaded the government to institute his brand of mechanical psychology in all schools, thus ending murder, theft, war and all unsocial perversions."

The attendant in his black frock coat hesitated; then: "A very bad one seems to have been missed."

He finished: "That's all, gentlemen. No clues, no promise of an early capture, and only this final fact: We've wirelessed Professor Ungarn and, by great good fortune, we caught him on his way to Earth from his meteorite retreat near Jupiter. He'll be landing shortly after dark, in a few hours now."

The lights dimmed. As Leigh stood frowning, watching the bodies being wheeled out, a phrase floated out of the gathering chorus of voices:

"—The kiss of death—"

"I tell you," another voice said, "the captain of this space liner swears it happened—the spaceship came past him at a million miles an hour, and it was slowing down, get that, slowing down—two days ago."

"—The vampire case! That's what I'm going to call it—"

That's what Leigh called it, too, as he talked briefly into his wrist communicator. He finished: "I'm going to supper now, Jim."

"O.K., Bill." The local editor's voice came metallically. "And say, I'm supposed to commend you. Nine thousand papers took the Planetarian Service on this story, as compared with about forty-seven hundred who bought from Universal, who got the second largest coverage.

"And I think you've got the right angle for today also. Husband and wife, ordinary young couple, taking an evening's walk. Some devil hauls up alongside them, drains their blood into a tank, their life energy onto a wire or something— people will believe that, I guess. Anyway, you suggest it could happen to anybody; so be careful, folks. And you warn that, in these days of interplanetary speeds, he could be anywhere tonight for his next murder.

"As I said before, good stuff. That'll keep the story frying hard for tonight. Oh, by the way—"

"Shoot!"

"A kid called half an hour ago to see you. Said you expected him."

"A kid?" Leigh frowned to himself.

"Name of Patrick. High school age, about sixteen. No, come to think of it, that was only my first impression. Eighteen, maybe twenty, very bright, confi- dent, proud."

"I remember now," said Leigh, "college student. Interview for a college paper. Called me up this afternoon. One of those damned persuasive talkers. before I knew it, I was signed up for supper at Constantine's."

"That's right. I was supposed to remind you. O.K.?"

Leigh shrugged. "I promised," he said.

Actually, as he went out into the blaze of late afternoon, sunlit street, there was not a thought in his head. Nor a premonition.

Around him, the swarm of humankind began to thicken. Vast buildings dis- charged the first surge of the five o'clock tidal wave—and twice Leigh felt the tug at his arm before it struck him that someone was not just bumping him.

He turned, and stared down at a pair of dark, eager eyes set in a brown, wizened face. The little man waved a sheaf of papers at him. Leigh caught a glimpse of writing in longhand on the papers. Then the fellow was babbling:

"Mr. Leigh, hundred dollars for these . . . biggest story—"

"Oh," said Leigh. His interest collapsed: then his mind roused itself from its almost blank state, and pure politeness made him say: "Take it up to the Plan- etarian office. Jim Brian will pay you what the story is worth."

He walked on, the vague conviction in his mind that the matter was settled. Then, abruptly, there was the tugging at his arm again.

"Scoop!" the little man was muttering. "Professor Ungarn's log, all about a spaceship that came from the stars. Devils in it who drink blood and kiss people to death!"

"See here!" Leigh began, irritated; and then he stopped physically and men- tally. A strange ugly chill swept through him. He stood there, swaying a little from the shock of the thought that was frozen in his brain:

The newspapers with those details of "blood" and "kiss" were not on the street yet, wouldn't be for another five minutes.

The man was saying: "Look, it's got Professor Ungarn's name printed in gold on the top of each sheet, and it's all about how he first spotted the ship eighteen light-years out, and how it came all that distance in a few hours . . . and he knows where it is now and—"

Leigh heard, but that was all. His reporter's brain, that special, highly developed department, was whirling with a little swarm of thoughts that suddenly straightened into a hard, bright pattern; and in that tightly built design, there was no room for any such brazen coincidence as this man coming to him here in this crowded street.

He said: "Let me see those!" And reached as he spoke.

The papers came free from the other's fingers into his hands, but Leigh did not even glance at them. His brain was crystal-clear, his eyes cold; he snapped: "I don't know what game you're trying to pull. I want to know three things, and make your answers damned fast! One: How did you pick me out, name and job and all, here in this packed street of a city I haven't been in for a year?"

He was vaguely aware of the little man trying to speak, stammering incomprehensible words. But he paid no attention. Remorselessly, he pounded on: "Two: Professor Ungarn is arriving from Jupiter in three hours. How do you explain your possession of papers he must have written less than two days ago?"

"Look, boss," the man chattered, "you've got me all wrong—"

"My third question," Leigh said grimly, "is how are you going to explain to the police your pre-knowledge of the details of—murder?"

"Huh!" The little man's eyes were glassy, and for the first time pity came to Leigh. He said almost softly: "All right, fellah, start talking."

The words came swiftly, and at first they were simply senseless sounds; only gradually did coherence come.

"—And that's the way it was, boss. I'm standing there, and this kid comes up to me and points you out, and gives me five bucks and those papers you've got, and tells me what I'm supposed to say to you and—"

"Kid!" said Leigh; and the first shock was already in him.

"Yeah, kid about sixteen; no, more like eighteen or twenty . . . and he gives me the papers and—"

"This kid," said Leigh, "would you say he was of college age?"

"That's it, boss; you've got it. That's just what he was. You know him, eh? OK. That leaves me in the clear, and I'll be going—"

"Wait!" Leigh called, but the little man seemed suddenly to realize that he need only run, for he jerked into a mad pace; and people stared, and that was all. He vanished around a corner, and was gone forever.

Leigh stood, frowning, reading the thin sheaf of papers. And there was nothing beyond what the little man had already conveyed by his incoherent word of mouth, simply a vague series of entries on sheets from a looseleaf notebook.

Written down, the tale about the spaceship and its occupants lacked depth, and seemed more unconvincing each passing second. True, there was the single word "Ungarn" inscribed in gold on the top of each sheet but—

Leigh shook himself. The sense of silly hoax grew so violently that he thought with abrupt anger: If that damned fool college kid really pulled a stunt like—

The thought ended; for the idea was as senseless as everything that had happened.

And still there was no real tension in him. He was only going to a restaurant.

He turned into the splendid foyer that was the beginning of the vast and wonderful Constantine's. In the great doorway, he paused for a moment to survey the expansive glitter of tables, the hanging garden tearooms; and it was all there.

Brilliant Constantine's, famous the world over—but not much changed from his last visit.

Leigh gave his name, and began: "A Mr. Patrick made reservations, I understand—"

The girl cut him short. "Oh, yes, Mr. Leigh. Mr. Patrick reserved Private 3 for you. He just now phoned to say he'd be along in a few minutes. Our premier will escort you."

Leigh was turning away, a vague puzzled thought in his mind at the way the girl had gushed, when a flamelike thought struck him: "Just a minute, did you say *Private 3*? Who's paying for this?"

The girl glowed at him: "It was paid by phone. Forty-five hundred dollars!"

Leigh stood very still. In a single, flashing moment, this meeting that, even after what had happened on the street, had seemed scarcely more than an irritation to be gotten over with, was becoming a fantastic, abnormal thing.

Forty-five—hundred—dollars! Could it be some damned fool rich kid sent by a college paper, but who had pulled this whole affair because he was determined to make a strong, personal impression?

Coldly, alertly, his brain rejected the solution. Humanity produced egoists on an elephantine scale, but not one who would order a feast like that to impress a reporter.

His eyes narrowed on an idea: "Where's your registered phone?" he asked curtly.

A minute later, he was saying into the mouthpiece: "Is that the Amalgamated Universities Secretariat? . . . I want to find out if there is a Mr. Patrick registered at any of your local colleges, and, if there is, whether or not he has been authorized by any college paper to interview William Leigh of the Planetarian News Service. This is Leigh calling."

It took six minutes, and then the answer came back, brisk, tremendous and final: "There are three Mr. Patricks in our seventeen units. All are at present having supper at their various official residences. There are four Miss Patricks similarly accounted for by our staff of secretaries. None of these seven is in any way connected with the university paper. Do you wish any assistance in dealing with the imposter?"

Leigh hesitated, and when he finally spoke, it was with the queer, dark realization that he was committing himself. "No," he said, and hung up.

He came out of the phone box, shaken by his own thoughts. There was only one reason why he was in this city at this time. Murder! And he knew scarcely a soul. Therefore—

It was absolutely incredible that any stranger would want to see him for a reason not connected with his own purpose. He shook the ugly thrill out of his system; he said: "To Private 3, please—"

Tensed but cool, he examined the apartment that was Private 3. Actually that was all it was, a splendidly furnished apartment with a palacelike dining salon dominating the five rooms, and one entire wall of the salon was lined with decorated mirror facings, behind which glittered hundreds of bottles of liquors.

The brands were strange to his inexpensive tastes, the scent of several that he opened heady and quite uninviting. In the ladies' dressing room was a long showcase displaying a gleaming array of jewelry—several hundred thousand dollars' worth, if it was genuine, he estimated swiftly.

Leigh whistled softly to himself. On the surface, Constantine's appeared to supply good rental value for the money they charged.

"I'm glad you're physically big," said a cool voice behind him. "So many reporters are thin and small."

It was the voice that did it, subtly, differently toned than it had been over the phone in the early afternoon. Deliberately different.

The difference, he noted as he turned, was in the body, too, the difference in the shape of a woman from a boy, skillfully but not perfectly concealed under the well-tailored man's suit—actually, of course, she was quite boyish in build, young, finely molded.

And, actually, he would never have suspected if she had not allowed her voice to be so purposefully womanish. She echoed his thought coolly:

"Yes, I wanted you to know. But now, there's no use wasting words. You know as much as you need to know. Here's a gun. The spaceship is buried below this building."

Leigh made no effort to take the weapon, nor did he even glance at it. Instead, cool now, that the first shock was over, he seated himself on the silk-yielding chair of the vanity dresser in one corner, leaned heavily back against the vanity itself, raised his eyebrows, and said: "Consider me a slow-witted lunk who's got to know what it's all about. Why so much preliminary hocus-pocus?"

He thought deliberately: He had never in his adult life allowed himself to be rushed into anything. He was not going to start now.

III

THE GIRL, he saw after a moment, was small of build. Which was odd, he decided carefully. Because his first impression had been of reasonable length of body. Or perhaps—he considered the possibility unhurriedly—this second effect was a more considered result of her male disguise.

He dismissed that particular problem as temporarily insoluble, and because actually—it struck him abruptly—this girl's size was unimportant. She had long, black lashes and dark eyes that glowed at him from a proud, almost haughty face. And that was it; quite definitely that was the essence of her blazing, powerful personality.

Pride was in the way she held her head. It was in the poised easiness of every movement, the natural shift from grace to grace as she walked slowly toward him. Not conscious pride here, but an awareness of superiority that affected every movement of her muscles, and came vibrantly into her voice, as she said scathingly: "I picked you because every newspaper I've read today carried your account of the murders, and because it seemed to me that somebody who already was actively working on the case would be reasonably quick at grasping essentials. As for the dramatic preparation, I considered that would be more convincing than drab explanation. I see I was mistaken in all these assumptions."

She was quite close to him now. She leaned over, laid her revolver on the vanity beside his arm, and finished almost indifferently: "Here's an effective weapon. It doesn't shoot bullets, but it has a trigger and you aim it like any gun. In the event you develop the beginning of courage, come down the tunnel after me as quickly as possible, but don't blunder in on me and the people I shall be talking to. Stay hidden! Act only if I'm threatened."

Tunnel, Leigh thought stolidly, as she walked with a free, swift stride out of the room—tunnel here in this apartment called Private 3. Either he was crazy, or she was.

Quite suddenly, realization came that he ought to be offended at the way she had spoken. And that insultingly simple come-on trick of hers, leaving the room, leaving him to develop curiosity—he smiled ruefully; if he hadn't been a reporter, he'd show her that such a second-rate psychology didn't work on him.

Still annoyed, he climbed to his feet, took the gun, and then paused briefly as the odd, muffled sound came of a door opening reluctantly—

He found her in the bedroom to the left of the dining salon; and because his mind was still in that state of pure receptiveness, which, for him, replaced indecisiveness, he felt only the vaguest surprise to see that she had the end of a lush green rug rolled back, and that there was a hole in the floor at her feet.

The gleaming square of floor that must have covered the opening, lay back neatly, pinned to position by a single, glitteringly complicated hinge. But Leigh scarcely noticed that.

His gaze reached beyond that—tunnel—to the girl; and, in that moment, just before she became aware of him, there was the barest suggestion of uncertainty about her. And her right profile, half turned away from him, showed pursed lips, a strained whiteness, as if—

The impression he received was of indecisiveness. He had the subtle sense of observing a young woman who, briefly, had lost her superb confidence. Then she saw him; and his whole emotion picture twisted.

She didn't seem to stiffen in any way. Paying no attention to him at all, she stepped down to the first stair of the little stairway that led down into the hole, and began to descend without a quiver of hesitation. And yet—

Yet his first conviction that she had faltered brought him forward with narrowed eyes. And, suddenly, that certainty of her brief fear made this whole madness real. He plunged forward, down the steep stairway, and pulled up only when he saw that he was actually in a smooth, dimly lighted tunnel and that the girl had paused, one finger to her lips.

"*Sssshh!*" she said. "The door of the ship may be open."

Irritation struck Leigh, a hard trickle of anger. Now that he had committed himself, he felt automatically the leader of this fantastic expedition; and that girl's pretensions, the devastating haughtiness of her merely produced his first real impatience.

"Don't '*ssshh*' me!" he whispered sharply. "Just give me the facts, and I'll do the rest."

He stopped. For the first time the meaning of all the words she had spoken penetrated. His anger collapsed like a plane in a crash landing.

"Ship!" he said incredulously. "Are you trying to tell me there's actually a spaceship buried here under Constantine's?"

The girl seemed not to hear, and Leigh saw that they were at the end of a short passageway. Metal gleamed dully just ahead. Then the girl was saying:

"Here's the door. Now, remember, you act as guard. Stay hidden, ready to shoot. And if I yell 'Shoot,' you shoot!"

She bent forward. There was the tiniest scarlet flash. The door opened, revealing a second door just beyond. Again that minute, intense blaze of red; and that door too swung open.

It was swiftly done, too swiftly. Before Leigh could more than grasp that the crisis was come, the girl stepped coolly into the brilliantly lighted room beyond the second door.

There was a shadow where Leigh stood half-paralyzed by the girl's action. There was deeper shadow against the metal wall toward which he pressed himself in one instinctive move. He froze there, cursing silently at a stupid young woman who actually walked into a den of enemies of unknown numbers without a genuine plan of self-protection.

Or did she know how many there were? And who?

The questions made twisting paths in his mind down, down to a thrall of blankness—that ended only when an entirely different thought replaced it: At least he was out here with a gun, unnoticed—or was he?

He waited tensely. But the door remained open, and there was no apparent movement towards it. Slowly, Leigh let himself relax, and allowed his straining mind to absorb its first considered impressions.

The portion of underground room that he could see showed one end of what seemed to be a control board, a metal wall that blinked with tiny lights, the edge of a rather sumptuous cot—and the whole was actually so suggestive of a spaceship that Leigh's logic-resistance collapsed.

Incredibly, here under the ground, actually *under* Constantine's was a small spaceship and—

That thought ended, too, as the silence beyond the open door, the curiously long silence, was broken by a man's cool voice: "I wouldn't even try to raise that gun if I were you. The fact that you have said nothing since entering shows how enormously different we are to what you expected."

He laughed gently, an unhurried, deep-throated derisive laughter that came clearly to Leigh.

The man said: "Merla, what would you say is the psychology behind this young lady's action? You have of course noticed that she is a young lady, and not a boy."

A richly toned woman's voice replied: "She was born here, Jeel. She has none of the normal characteristics of a Klugg, but she is a Galactic, though definitely not the Galactic Observer. Probably, she's not alone. Shall I investigate?"

"No!" The man sounded indifferent to the tensing Leigh. "We don't have to worry about a Klugg's assistant."

Leigh relaxed slowly, but there was a vast uneasiness in his solar nerves, a sense of emptiness, the first realization of how great a part the calm assurance of the young woman had played in the fabricating of his own basic confidence.

Shattered now! Before the enormous certainties of these two, and in the face of their instant penetration of her male disguise, the effects of the girl's rather wonderful personality seemed a remote pattern, secondary, definitely over-whelmed.

He forced the fear from him, as the girl spoke; forced his courage to grow with each word she uttered, feeding on the haughty and immense confidence that was there. It didn't matter whether she was simulating or not, because they were in this now, he as deep as she; and only the utmost boldness could hope to draw a fraction of victory from the defeat that loomed so starkly.

With genuine admiration, he noted the glowing intensity of her speech, as she said:

"My silence had its origin in the fact that you are the first Dreeghs I have ever seen. Naturally, I studied you with some curiosity, but I can assure you I am not impressed.

"However, in view of your extraordinary opinions on the matter, I shall come to the point at once: I have been instructed by the Galactic Observer of this system to inform you to be gone by morning. Our sole reason for giving you that much leeway is that we don't wish to bring the truth of all this into the open.

"But don't count on that. Earth is on the verge of being given fourth-degree rating; and, as you probably know, in emergencies fourths are given Galactic knowledge. That emergency we will consider to have arrived tomorrow at dawn."

"Well, well"—the man was laughing gently, satirically—"a pretty speech, powerfully spoken, but meaningless for us who can analyze its pretensions, however sincere, back to the Klugg origin."

"What do you intend to do with her, Jeel?"

The man was cold, deadly, utterly sure. "There's no reason why she should escape. She had blood and more than normal life. It will convey to the Observer with clarity our contempt for his ultimatum."

He finished with a slow, surprisingly rich laughter: "We shall now enact a simple drama. The young lady will attempt to jerk up her gun and shoot me with it. Before she can even begin to succeed, I shall have my own weapon out and firing. The whole thing, as she will discover, is a matter of nervous coordination. And Kluggs are chronically almost as slow-moving as human beings."

His voice stopped. His laughter trickled away.

Silence.

In all his alert years, Leigh had never felt more indecisive. His emotions said—*now*; surely, she'd call now. And even if she didn't, he must act on his own. Rush in! Shoot!

But his mind was cold with an awful dread. There was something about the man's voice, a surging power, a blazing, incredible certainty. Abnormal, savage strength was here; and if this was really a spaceship from the stars—

His brain wouldn't follow that flashing, terrible thought. He crouched, fingering the gun she had given him, dimly conscious for the first time that it felt queer, unlike any revolver he'd ever had.

He crouched stiffly, waiting—and the silence from the spaceship control room, from the tensed figures that must be there just beyond his line of vision, continued. The same curious silence that had followed the girl's entrance short minutes before. Only this time it was the girl who broke it, her voice faintly breathless but withal cool, vibrant, unafraid: "I'm here to warn, not to force issues. And unless you're charged with the life energy of fifteen men, I wouldn't advise you to try anything either. After all, I came here knowing what you were."

"What do you think, Merla? Can we be sure she's a Klugg? Could she possibly be of the higher Lennel type?"

It was the man, his tone conceding her point, but the derision was still there, the implacable purpose, the high, tremendous confidence.

And yet, in spite of that unrelenting sense of imminent violence, Leigh felt himself torn from the thought of her danger—and his. His reporter's brain twisted irresistibly to the fantastic meaning of what was taking place: —*Life energy of fifteen men*—

It was all there; in a monstrous way it all fitted. The two dead bodies he had seen drained of blood and *life energy*, the repeated reference to a Galactic Observer, with whom the girl was connected.

Leigh thought almost blankly: Galactic meant—well—Galactic; and that was so terrific that—

He grew aware that the woman was speaking: "Klugg!" she said positively. "Pay no attention to her protestations, Jeel. You know, I'm sensitive when it comes to women. She's lying. She's just a little fool who walked in here expecting us to be frightened of her. Destroy her at your pleasure."

"I'm not given to waiting," said the man. "So—"

Quite automatically, Leigh leaped for the open doorway. He had a flashing glimpse of a man and woman, dressed in evening clothes, the man standing, the woman seated. There was awareness of a gleaming, metallic background, the control board, part of which he had already seen, now revealed as a massive thing of glowing instruments; and then all that blotted out as he snapped: "That will do. Put up your hands."

For a long, dazzling moment he had the impression that his entry was a complete surprise; and that he dominated the situation. None of the three people in the room was turned toward him. The man, Jeel, and the girl were standing, facing each other; the woman, Merla, sat in a deep chair, her fine profile to him, her golden head flung back.

It was she who, still without looking at him, sneered visibly—and spoke the words that ended his brief conviction of triumph. She said to the disguised girl: "You certainly travel in low company, a stupid human being. Tell him to go away before he's damaged."

The girl said: "Leigh, I'm sorry I brought you into this. Every move you made in entering was heard, observed, and dismissed before you could even adjust your mind to the scene."

"Is his name Leigh?" said the woman sharply. "I thought I recognized him as he entered. He's very like his photograph over his newspaper column." Her voice grew strangely tense: "Jeel, a newspaper reporter!"

"We don't need him now," the man said. "We know who the Galactic Observer is."

"Eh?" said Leigh; his mind fastened hard on those amazing words. "Who? How did you find out? What—"

"The information," said the woman, and it struck him suddenly that the strange quality in her voice was eagerness, "will be of no use to you. Regardless of what happens to the girl, you're staying."

She glanced swiftly at the man, as if seeking his sanction. "Remember, Jeel, you promised."

It was all quite senseless, so meaningless that Leigh had no sense of personal danger. His mind scarcely more than passed the words; his eyes concentrated tautly on a reality that had, until that moment, escaped his awareness. He said softly: "Just now you used the phrase, 'Regardless of what happens to the girl.' When I came in, you said, 'Tell him to go away before he's damaged.' " Leigh smiled grimly. "I need hardly say this is a far cry from the threat of immediate death that hung over us a few seconds ago. And I have just now noticed the reason.

"A little while ago, I heard our pal, Jeel, dare my little girl friend here to raise her gun. I notice now that *she has it raised*. My entrance did have an effect." He addressed himself to the girl, finished swiftly: "Shall we shoot—or withdraw?"

It was the man who answered: "I would advise withdrawal. I could still win, but I am not the heroic type who takes the risk of what might well be a close call."

He added, in an aside to the woman: "Merla, we can always catch this man, Leigh, now that we know who he is."

The girl said: "You first, Mr. Leigh." And Leigh did not stop to argue.

Metal doors clanged behind him, as he charged along the tunnel. After a moment, he was aware of the girl running lightly beside him.

The strangely unreal, the unbelievably murderous little drama was over, finished as fantastically as it had begun.

IV

Outside constantine's a gray light gathered around them. A twilight side street it was, and people hurried past them with the strange, anxious look of the late for supper. Night was falling.

Leigh stared at his companion; in the dimness of the deep dusk, she seemed all boy, slightly, lithely built, striding along boldly. He laughed a little, huskily, then more grimly:

"Just what was all that? Did we escape by the skin of our teeth? Or did we win? What made you think you could act like God and give those tough eggs twelve hours to get out of the Solar System?"

The girl was silent after he had spoken. She walked just ahead of him, head bent into the gloom. Abruptly, she turned; she said: "I hope you will have no nonsensical idea of telling what you've seen or heard."

Leigh said: "This is the biggest story since—"

"Look"—the girl's voice was pitying—"you're not going to print a word because in about ten seconds you'll see that no one in the world would believe the first paragraph."

In the darkness, Leigh smiled tightly: "The mechanical psychologist will verify every syllable."

"I came prepared for that, too!" said the vibrant voice. Her hand swung up, toward his face. Too late, he jerked back.

Light flared in his eyes, a dazzling, blinding force that exploded into his sensitive optic nerves with all the agonizing power of intolerable brightness. Leigh cursed aloud, wildly, and snatched forward toward his tormentor. His right hand grazed a shoulder. He lashed out violently with his left, and tantalizingly caught only the edge of a sleeve that instantly jerked away.

"You little devil!" he raged futilely. "You've blinded me."

"You'll be all right," came the cool answer, "but you'll find that the mechanical psychologist will report anything you say as the purest imagination. In view of your threat to publish, I had to do that. Now, give me my gun."

The first glimmer of sight was returning. Leigh could see her body—a dim, wavering shape in the night. In spite of the continuing pain, Leigh smiled grimly. He said softly: "I've just now remembered you said this gun didn't shoot bullets.

Even the *feel* of it suggests that it'll make an interesting proof of anything I say. So—''

His smile faded abruptly. For the girl stepped forward. The metal that jabbed into his ribs was so hardly thrust, it made him grunt.

"Give me that gun!"

"Like fun I will," Leigh snapped. "You ungrateful little ruffian, how dare you treat me so shoddily after I saved your life? I ought to knock you one right on the jaw for—"

He stopped—stopped because with staggering suddenness the hard, hard realization struck that she meant it. This was no girl raised in a refined school who wouldn't dare to shoot, but a cold-blooded young creature, who had already proved the metalliclike fabric of which her courage was made.

He had never had any notions about the superiority of man over woman; and he felt none now. Without a single word, almost hastily, he handed the weapon over.

The girl took it and said coldly: "You seem to be laboring under the illusion that your entry into the spaceship enabled me to raise my weapon. You're quite mistaken. What you did was to provide me with the opportunity to let them think that that was the situation, and that they dominated it. But I assure you, that is the extent of your assistance, almost valueless."

Leigh laughed out loud, a pitying, ridiculing laugh.

"In my admittedly short life," he said laconically, "I've learned to recognize a quality of personality and magnetism in human beings. You've got it, a lot of it, but not a fraction of what either of those two had, particularly the man. He was terrible. He was absolutely the most abnormally magnetic human being I've ever run across. Lady, I can only guess what all this is about, but I'd advise you"— Leigh paused, then finished slashingly—"you and all the other Kluggs to stay away from that couple."

"Personally, I'm going to get the police in on this, and there's going to be a raid on Private 3. I didn't like that odd threat that they could capture me any time. Why me—" He broke off hastily: "Hey, where are you going? I want to know your name. I want to know what made you think you could order those two around. *Who did you think you were?*"

He said no more, his whole effort concentrated on running. He could see her for a moment, a hazy, boyish figure against a dim corner light. Then she was around the corner.

His only point of contact with all this, and if she got away—

Sweating, he rounded the corner, and at first the street seemed dark and empty of life. Then he saw the car.

A normal-looking, high-hooded coupe, long, low-built, that began to move forward noiselessly and—quite normally.

It became abnormal. It lifted. Amazingly, it lifted from the ground. He had a swift glimpse of white rubber wheels folding out of sight. Streamlined, almost cigar-shaped now, the spaceship that had been a car darted at a steep angle into the sky.

Instantly it was gone.

Above Leigh, the gathering night towered, a strange, bright blue. In spite of the brilliant lights of the city glaring into the sky, one or two stars showed. He stared up at them, empty inside, thinking: "It was like a dream. Those— Dreeghs—coming out of space—bloodsuckers, vampires."

Suddenly hungry, he bought a chocolate from a sidewalk stand, and stood munching it.

He began to feel better. He walked over to a nearby wall socket, and plugged in his wrist radio.

"Jim" he said. "I've got some stuff, not for publication, but maybe we can get some police action on it. Then I want you to have a mechanical psychologist sent to my hotel room. There must be some memory that can be salvaged from my brain—"

He went on briskly. His sense of inadequacy waned notably. Reporter Leigh was himself again.

V

THE LITTLE GLISTENING balls of the mechanical psychologist were whirring faster, faster. They became a single, glowing circle in the darkness. And not till then did the first, delicious whiff of psychogas touch his nostrils. He felt himself drifting, slipping—

A voice began to speak in the dim distance, so far away that not a word came through. There was only the sound, the faint, curious sound, and the feeling, stronger every instant, that he would soon be able to hear the fascinating things it seemed to be saying.

The longing to hear, to become a part of the swelling, murmuring sound drew his whole being in little rhythmical, wavelike surges. And still the promise of meaning was unfulfilled.

Other, private thoughts ended utterly. Only the mindless chant remained, and the pleasing gas holding him so close to sleep, its flow nevertheless so delicately adjusted that his mind hovered minute after minute on the ultimate abyss of consciousness.

He lay, finally, still partially awake, but even the voice was merging now into blackness. It clung for a while, a gentle, friendly, melodious sound in the remote background of his brain, becoming more remote with each passing instant. He slept, a deep, hypnotic sleep, as the machine purred on—

When Leigh opened his eyes, the bedroom was dark except for the floor lamp beside a corner chair. It illuminated the darkly dressed woman who sat there, all except her face, which was in shadow above the circle of light.

He must have moved, for the shadowed head suddenly looked up from some sheets of typewriter-size paper. The voice of Merla, the Dreegh, said: "The girl did a very good job of erasing your subconscious memories. There's only one possible clue to her identity and—''

Her words went on, but his brain jangled them to senselessness in that first horrible shock of recognition. It was too much, too much fear in too short a time. For a brief, terrible moment, he was like a child, and strange, cunning, *intense* thoughts of escape came: If he could slide to the side of the bed, away from where she was sitting, and run for the bathroom door—

''Surely, Mr. Leigh,'' the woman's voice reached toward him, ''you know better than to try anything foolish. And, surely, if I had intended to kill you, I would have done it much more easily while you were asleep.''

Leigh lay very still, gathering his mind back into his head, licking dry lips. Her words were utterly unreassuring. ''What—do—you—want?'' he managed finally.

''Information!'' Laconically. ''What was that girl?''

''I don't know.'' He stared into the half gloom, where her face was. His eyes were more accustomed to the light now, and he could catch the faint, golden glint of her hair. ''I thought—you knew.''

He went on more swiftly: ''I thought you knew the Galactic Observer, and that implied the girl could be identified any time.''

He had the impression she was smiling. She said: ''Our statement to that effect was designed to throw both you and the girl off guard, and constituted the partial victory we snatched from what had become an impossible situation.''

The body sickness was still upon Leigh, but the desperate fear that had produced it was fading before the implications of her confession of weakness, the realization that these Dreeghs were not so superhuman as he had thought. Relief was followed by caution. Careful, he warned himself, it wouldn't be wise to underestimate. But he couldn't help saying:

''So you weren't so smart. And I'd like to point out that even your so-called snatching of victory from defeat was not so well done. Your husband's statement that you could pick me up any time could easily have spoiled the picking.''

The woman's voice was cool, faintly contemptuous. ''If you knew anything of psychology, you would realize that the vague phrasing of the threat actually lulled you. Certainly, you failed to take even minimum precautions. And the girl has definitely not made any effort to protect you.''

The suggestion of deliberately subtle tactics brought to Leigh a twinge of returning alarm. Deep, deep inside him was the thought: What ending did the Dreegh woman plan for this strange meeting?

''You realize, of course,'' the Dreegh said softly, ''that you will either be of value to us alive—or dead. There are no easy alternatives. I would advise alertness and utmost sincerity in your cooperation. You are in this affair without limit.''

So that was the plan. A thin bead of perspiration trickled down Leigh's cheek. And his fingers trembled as he reached for a cigarette on the table beside the bed.

He was shakily lighting the cigarette when his gaze fastened on the window.

That brought a faint shock, for it was raining, a furious rain that hammered soundlessly against the noise-proof glass.

He pictured the bleak, empty streets, their brilliance dulled by the black, rain-filled night; and, strangely, the mind picture unnerved him.

Deserted streets—deserted Leigh. For he was deserted here; all the friends he had, scattered over the great reaches of the earth, couldn't add one ounce of strength, or bring one real ray of hope to him in this darkened room, against this woman who sat so calmly under the light, studying him from shadowed eyes.

With a sharp effort, Leigh steadied himself. He said: "I gather that's my psychograph report you have in your hand. What does it say?"

"Very disappointing." Her voice seemed far away. "There's a warning in it about your diet. It seems your meals are irregular."

She was playing with him. The heavy attempt at humor made her seem more inhuman, not less; for, somehow, the words clashed unbearably with the reality of her, the dark immensity of space across which she had come, the unnatural lusts that had brought her and the man to this literally unprotected Earth.

Leigh shivered. Then he thought fiercely: Damn it, I'm scaring myself. So long as she stays in her chair, she can't pull the vampire on me.

The harder thought came that it was no use being frightened. He'd better simply be himself, and await events. Aloud, he said: "If there's nothing in the psychograph, then I'm afraid I can't help you. You might as well leave. Your presence isn't making me any happier."

In a dim way, he hoped she'd laugh. But she didn't. She sat there, her eyes glinting dully out of the gloom. At last, she said: "We'll go through this report together. I think we can safely omit the references to your health as being irrelevant. But there are a number of factors that I want developed. Who is Professor Ungarn?"

"A scientist." Leigh spoke frankly. "He invented this system of mechanical hypnosis, and he was called in when the dead bodies were found because the killings seemed to have been done by perverts."

"Have you any knowledge of his physical appearance?"

"I've never seen him," Leigh said more slowly. "He never gives interviews, and his photograph is not available now. I've heard stories, but—"

He hesitated. It wasn't, he thought frowning, as if he was giving what was not general knowledge. What was the woman getting at, anyway? Ungarn—

"These stories," she said, "do they give the impression that he's a man of inordinate magnetic force, but with lines of mental suffering etched in his face, and a sort of resignation?"

"Resignation to what?" Leigh exclaimed sharply. "I haven't the faintest idea what you're talking about. I've only seen photographs, and they show a fine, rather sensitive, tired face."

She said: "There would be more information in any library?"

"Or in the Planetarian Service morgue," Leigh said and could have bitten off his tongue for that bit of gratuitous information.

"Morgue?" said the woman.

Leigh explained, but his voice was trembling with self-rage. For seconds now the feeling had been growing on him: Was it possible this devilish woman was on the right track? And getting damaging answers out of him because he dared not stop and organize for lying?

Even as savage anxiety came, he had an incongruous sense of the unfairness of the abnormally swift way she had solved the Observer's identity because, damn it, damn it, it could be Professor Ungarn.

Ungarn, the mystery scientist, great inventor in a dozen highly complicated, widely separated fields, and there was that mysterious meteorite home near one of Jupiter's moons and he had a daughter named Patricia. Good heavens, Patrick—Patricia—

His shaky stream of thoughts ended, as the woman said: "Can you have your office send the information to your recorder here?"

"Y-yes!" His reluctance was so obvious that the woman bent into the light. For a moment, her golden hair glittered; her pale blue eyes glowed at him in a strangely humorless, satanic amusement.

"Ah!" she said, "you think so, too?"

She laughed, an odd, musical laugh—odd in that it was at once so curt and so pleasant. The laugh ended abruptly, unnaturally, on a high note. And then—although he had not seen her move—there was a metal thing in her hand, pointing at him. Her voice came at him, with a brittle, jarring command: "You will climb out of the bed, operate the recorder, and naturally you will do nothing, say nothing but what is necessary."

Leigh felt genuinely dizzy. The room swayed, and he thought sickly: If he could only faint.

But he recognized dismally that that was beyond the power of his tough body. It was sheer mental dismay that made his nerves so shivery. And even that faded like fog in strong sunlight, as he walked to the recorder. For the first time in his life, he hated the resilience of strength that made his voice steady as a rock, as, after setting the machine, he said: "This is William Leigh. Give me all the dope you've got on Professor Garret Ungarn."

There was a pause, during which he thought hopelessly: It wasn't as if he was giving information not otherwise accessible. Only—

There was a click in the machine; then a brisk voice: "You've got it. Sign the form."

Leigh signed, and watched the signature dissolve into the machine. It was then, as he was straightening, that the woman said:

"Shall I read it here, Jeel, or shall we take the machine along?"

That was mind-wrecking. Like a man possessed, Leigh whirled, and then, very carefully, he sat down on the bed.

The Dreegh Jeel was leaning idly against the jamb of the bathroom door, a dark, malignantly handsome man, with a faint, unpleasant smile on his lips. Behind him—incredibly, behind him, through the open bathroom door was, not the gleaming bath, but another door, and beyond that door still another door, and beyond that—

The control room of the Dreegh spaceship!

There it was, exactly as he had seen it in the solid ground under Constantine's. He had the same partial view of the sumptuous cot, the imposing section of instrument board, the tastefully padded floor—

In his bathroom!

The insane thought came to Leigh: Oh, yes, I keep my spaceship in my bathroom and—

It was the Dreegh's voice that drew his brain from its dizzy contemplation, the Dreegh saying: "I think we'd better leave. I'm having difficulty holding the ship on the alternation of space-time planes. Bring the man and the machine and—"

Leigh didn't hear the last word. He jerked his mind all the way out of the—bathroom. "You're—taking—me?"

"Why, of course." It was the woman who spoke. "You've been promised to me, and, besides, we'll need your help in finding Ungarn's meteorite."

Leigh sat very still. The unnatural thought came: He was glad that he had in the past proven to himself that he was not a coward.

For here was certainty of death.

He saw after a moment that the rain was still beating against the glass, great, sparkling drops that washed murkily down the broad panes. And he saw that the night was dark.

Dark night, dark rain, dark destiny—they fitted his dark, grim thoughts. With an effort he forced his body, his mind, into greater stiffness. Automatically, he shifted his position so that the weight of muscles would draw a tight band over the hollowness that he felt in his stomach. When at last he faced his alien captors again, Reporter Leigh was cold with acceptance of his fate—and prepared to fight for his life.

"I can't think of a single reason," he said, "why I should go with you. And if you think I'm going to help you destroy the Observer, you're crazy."

The woman said matter-of-factly: "There was a passing reference in your psychograph to a Mrs. Henry Leigh, who lives in a village called Relton, on the Pacific coast. We could be there in half an hour, your mother and her home destroyed within a minute after that. Or, perhaps, we could add her blood to our reserves."

"She would be too old," the man said in a chill tone. "We do not want the blood of old people."

It was the icy objection that brought horror to Leigh. He had a brief, terrible picture of a silent, immensely swift ship sweeping out of the Eastern night, over the peaceful hamlet, and then unearthly energies would reach down in a blaze of fury.

One second of slashing fire, and the ship would sweep on over the long, dark waters to the west.

The deadly picture faded. The woman was saying, gently: "Jeel and I have evolved an interesting little system of interviewing human beings of the lower order. For some reason, he frightens people merely by his presence. Similarly, people develop an unnatural fear of me when they see me clearly in a strong light. So we have always tried to arrange our meetings with human beings with me sitting in semidarkness and Jeel very much in the background. It has proved very effective.''

She stood up, a tall, lithely built, shadowed figure in a rather tight-fitting skirt and a dark blouse. She finished: "But now, shall we go? You bring the machine, Mr. Leigh.''

"I'll take it,'' said the Dreegh.

Leigh glanced sharply at the lean, sinewed face of the terrible man, startled at the instant, accurate suspicion of the desperate intention that had formed in his mind.

The Dreegh loomed over the small machine, where it stood on a corner desk. "How does it work?'' he asked almost mildly.

Trembling, Leigh stepped forward. There was still a chance that he could manage this without additional danger to anyone. Not that it would be more than a vexation, unless—as their suggestion about finding the Ungarn meteorite indicated—they headed straight out to space. Then, why, it might actually cause real delay. He began swiftly: "Press the key marked Titles, and the machine will type all the main headings.''

"That sounds reasonable.'' The long, grim-faced head nodded. The Dreegh reached forward, pressed the button. The recorder hummed softly, and a section of it lit up, showing typed lines under a transparent covering. There were several headings.

"—'His Meteorite Home,' '' the Dreegh read. "That's what I want. What is the next step?''

"Press the key marked Subheads.''

Leigh was suddenly shaky. He groaned inwardly. Was it possible this creature-man was going to obtain the information he wanted? Certainly, such a tremendous intelligence would not easily be led away from logical sequence.

He forced himself to grimness. He'd have to take a chance.

"The subhead I desire,'' said the Dreegh, "is marked Location. And there is a number, one, in front of it. What next?''

"Press key no. 1,'' Leigh said, "then press the key lettered General Release.''

The moment he had spoken, he grew taut. If this worked—and it should—there was no reason why it shouldn't—key no. 1 would impart all the information under that heading. And surely the man would not want more until later. After all, this was only a test. They were in a hurry.

And later, when the Dreegh discovered that the General Release key had dissolved all the other information—it would be too late.

The thought dimmed. Leigh started. The Dreegh was staring at him with a bleak sardonicism. The man said: "Your voice has been like an organ, each word uttered full of subtle shadings that mean much to the sensitive ear. Accordingly''—a steely, ferocious smile twisted that lean and deadly face—"I shall press key no 1. But not General Release. And as soon as I've examined the little story on the recorder, I shall attend to you for that attempted trick. The sentence is—death.''

"Jeel!"

"Death!" reiterated the man flatly. And the woman was silent.

There was silence, then, except for the subdued humming of the recorder. Leigh's mind was almost without thought. He felt fleshless, a strange, disembodied soul; and only gradually did a curious realization grow that he was waiting here on the brink of a night darker than the black wastes of space from which these monster humans had come.

Consciousness came of kinship with the black rain that poured with such solid, noiseless power against the glinting panes. For soon he would be part of the inorganic darkness, a shadowed figure sprawling sightlessly in this dim room.

His aimless gaze returned to the recorder machine and to the grim man who stood so thoughtfully, staring down at the words it was unfolding.

His thought quickened. His life, that had been pressed so shockingly out of his system by the sentence of death, quivered forth. He straightened, physically and mentally. And, suddenly, there was purpose in him.

If death was inescapable, at least he could try again, somehow, to knock down that General Release key. He stared at the key, measuring the distance and the gray thought came: What incredible irony that he should die, that he should waste his effort, to prevent the Dreeghs from having *this minute* information that was available from ten thousand sources. And yet—

The purpose remained. Three feet, he thought carefully, perhaps four. If he should fling himself toward it, how could even a Dreegh prevent the dead weight of his body and his extended fingers from accomplishing such a simple, straightforward mission?

After all, his sudden action had once before frustrated the Dreeghs, permitting the Ungarn girl—in spite of her denials—to get her gun into position for firing. And—

He grew rigid as he saw that the Dreegh was turning away from the machine. The man pursed his lips, but it was the woman, Merla, who spoke from where she stood in the gloom: "Well?"

The man frowned. "The exact location is nowhere on record. Apparently, there has been no development of meteorites in this system. I suspected as much. After all, space travel has only existed a hundred years, and the new planets and the moons of Jupiter have absorbed all the energies of exploring, exploiting man."

"I could have told you that," said Leigh.

If he could move a little to one side of the recorder, so that the Dreegh would have to do more than simply put his arm out—

The man was saying: "There is, however, a reference to some man who transports food and merchandise from the moon Europa to the Ungarns. We will . . . er . . . persuade this man to show us the way."

"One of these days," said Leigh, "you're going to discover that all human beings cannot be persuaded. What pressure are you going to put on this chap? Suppose he hasn't got a mother."

"He has—life!" said the woman softly.

"One look at you," Leigh snapped, "and he'd know that he'd lose that, anyway."

As he spoke, he stepped with enormous casualness to the left, one short step. He had a violent impulse to say something, anything to cover the action. But his voice had betrayed him once. And actually it might already have done so again. The cold face of the man was almost too enigmatic.

"We could," said the woman, "use William Leigh to persuade him."

The words were softly spoken but they shocked Leigh to his bones. For they offered a distorted hope. And that shattered his will to action. His purpose faded into remoteness. Almost grimly, he fought to draw that hard determination back into his consciousness.

He concentrated his gaze on the recorder machine but the woman was speaking again, and his mind wouldn't hold anything except the urgent meaning of her words: "He is too valuable a slave to destroy. We can always take his blood and energy, but now we must send him to Europa, there to find the freighter pilot of the Ungarns and actually accompany him to the Ungarn meteorite. If he could investigate the interior, our attack might conceivably be simplified, and there is just a possibility that there might be new weapons, of which we should be informed. We must not underestimate the science of the great Galactics."

"Naturally, before we allowed Leigh his freedom, we would do a little tampering with his mind and so blot out from his conscious mind all that has happened in this hotel room.

"The identification of Professor Ungarn as the Galactic Observer we would make plausible for Leigh by a little rewriting of his psychograph report, and tomorrow he will waken in his bed with a new purpose, based on some simple human impulse such as love of the girl."

The very fact that the Dreegh Jeel was allowing her to go on, brought the first, faint color to Leigh's cheeks, a thin flush at the enormous series of betrayals she was so passionately expecting of him. Nevertheless, so weak was his resistance to the idea of continued life, that he could only snap: "If you think I'm going to fall in love with a dame who's got twice my I.Q., you're—"

The woman cut him off. "Shut up, you fool! Can't you see I've saved your life?"

The man was cold, ice-cold. "Yes, we shall use him, not because he is essential, but because we have time to search for easier victories. The first members of the Dreegh tribe will not arrive for a month and a half, and it will take Mr. Leigh a month of that to get to the moon, Europa, by one of Earth's primitive passenger liners. Fortunately, the nearest Galactic military base is well over three months distant—by Galactic ship speeds.''

"Finally"—with a disconcerting, tigerish swiftness, the Dreegh whirled full from Leigh, eyes that were like pools of black fire measured his own startled stare—"finally, as a notable reminder to your subconscious of the error of trickery, and as complete punishment for past and—intended—offenses, *this!*''

Despairingly, Leigh twisted away from the metal that glowed at him. His muscles tried horribly to carry out the purpose that had been working to a crisis inside him. He lunged for the recorder—but *something* caught his body. Something—not physical. But the very pain seemed mortal.

There was no visible flame of energy, only that glow at the metal source. But his nerve writhed; enormous forces contorted his throat muscles, froze the scream that quivered there, hideously.

His whole being welcomed the blackness that came mercifully to blot out the hellish pain.

VI

ON THE THIRD DAY, Europa began to give up some of the sky to the vast mass of Jupiter behind it. The engines that so imperfectly transformed magnetic attraction to a half-hearted repulsion functioned more and more smoothly as the infinite complication of pull and counterpull yielded to distance.

The old, slow, small freighter scurried on into the immense, enveloping night; and the days dragged into weeks, the weeks crawled their drab course toward the full month.

On the thirty-seventh day, the sense of slowing up was so distinct that Leigh crept dully out of his bunk, and croaked: "How much farther?"

He was aware of the stolid-faced space trucker grinning at him. The man's name was Hanardy, and he said now matter-of-factly: "We're just pulling in. See that spot of light over to the left? It's moving this way."

He ended with a rough sympathy. "Been a tough trip, eh? Tougher'n you figgered when you offered to write up my little route for your big syndicate."

Leigh scarcely heard. He was clawing at the porthole, straining to penetrate the blackness. At first his eyes kept blinking on him, and nothing came. Stars were out there, but it was long seconds before his bleary gaze made out moving lights. He counted them with sluggish puzzlement: "One, two, three—seven—" he counted. "And all that traveling together."

"What's that?" Hanardy bent beside him. "Seven?"

There was a brief silence between them, as the lights grew visibly dim with distance, and winked out.

"Too bad," Leigh ventured, "that Jupiter's behind us. They mightn't fade out like that in silhouette. Which one was Ungarn's meteorite?"

With a shock, he grew aware that Hanardy was standing. The man's heavy face was dark with frown. Hanardy said slowly: "Those were ships. I never saw ships go so fast before. They were out of sight in less than a minute."

The frown faded from his stolid face. He shrugged. "Some of those new police ships, I guess. And we must have seen them from a funny angle for them to disappear so fast."

Leigh half sat, half knelt, frozen into immobility. And after that one swift glance at the pilot's rough face, he averted his own. For a moment, the black fear was in him that his wild thoughts would blaze from his eyes.

Dreeghs! Two and a half months had wound their appalling slow course since the murders. More than a month to get from Earth to Europa, and now this miserable, lonely journey with Hanardy, the man who trucked for the Ungarns.

Every day of that time, he had known with an inner certainty that none of this incredible business had gone backward. That it could only have assumed a hidden, more dangerous form. The one fortunate reality in the whole mad affair was that he had wakened on the morning after the mechanical psychologist test from a dreamless sleep, and there in the psychograph report was the identification of Ungarn as the Observer, and the statement, borne out by an all too familiar emotional tension that he was in love with the girl.

Now this! His mind flared. Dreeghs in seven ships. That meant the first had been reinforced by—many. And perhaps the seven were only a reconnaissance group, withdrawing at Hanardy's approach.

Or perhaps those fantastic murderers had already attacked the Observer's base. Perhaps the girl—

He fought the desperate thought out of his consciousness, and watched, frowning, as the Ungarn meteorite made a dark, glinting path in the blackness to one side. The two objects, the ship and the bleak, rough-shaped mass of metallic stone drew together in the night, the ship slightly behind.

A great steel door slid open in the rock. Skillfully, the ship glided into the chasm. There was a noisy clicking. Hanardy came out of the control room, his face dark with puzzlement.

"Those damn ships are out there again," he said. "I've closed the big steel locks, but I'd better tell the professor and—"

Crash! The world jiggled. The floor came up and hit Leigh a violent blow. He lay there, cold in spite of the thoughts that burned at fire heat in his mind: For some reason, the vampires had waited until the freighter was inside. Then instantly, ferociously, attacked.

In packs!

"Hanardy!" A vibrant girl's voice blared from one of the loudspeakers.

The pilot sat up shakily on the floor, where he had fallen, near Leigh. "Yes, Miss Patricia."

"You dared to bring a stranger with you!"

"It's only a reporter, miss; he's writing up my route for me."

"You conceited fool! That's William Leigh. He's a hypnotized spy of those

A. E. VAN VOGT

devils who are attacking us. Bring him immediately to my apartment. He must be killed at once.''

"Huh!" Leigh began and then slowly he began to stiffen. For the pilot was staring at him from narrowing eyes, all the friendliness gone from his rough, heavy face. Finally, Leigh laughed curtly.

"Don't you be a fool, too, Hanardy. I made the mistake once of saving that young lady's life, and she's hated me ever since.''

The heavy face scowled at him. "So you knew her before, eh? You didn't tell me that. You'd better come along before I sock you one.''

Almost awkwardly, he drew the gun from his side holster, and pointed its ugly snout at Leigh.

"Get along!" he said.

Hanardy reached toward a tiny arrangement of lights beside the paneled door of Patricia Ungarn's apartment—and Leigh gave one leap, one blow. He caught the short, heavy body as it fell, grabbed the sagging gun, lowered the dead weight to the floor of the corridor, and then, for a grim, tense moment, he stood like a great animal, straining for sound.

Silence! He studied the bland panels of the doorway to the apartment, as if by sheer, savage intentness he would penetrate their golden, beautiful grained opaqueness.

It was the silence that struck him again after a moment, the emptiness of the long, tunnellike corridors. He thought, amazed: Was it possible father and daughter actually lived here without companions or servants or any human association? And that they had some idea that they could withstand the attack of the mighty and terrible Dreeghs?

They had a lot of stuff here, of course: Earthlike gravity and—and, by Heaven, he'd better get going before the girl acquired impatience and came out with one of her fancy weapons. What he must do was quite simple, unconnected with any nonsense of spying, hypnotic or otherwise.

He must find the combination automobile-spaceship in which—Mr. Patrick—had escaped him that night after they left Constantine's. And with that tiny ship, he must try to slip out of Ungarn's meteorite, sneak through the Dreegh line, and so head back for Earth.

What a fool he had been, a mediocre human being, mixing in such fast, brainy company. The world was full of more normal, thoroughly dumb girls. Why in hell wasn't he safely married to one of them and—and damn it, it was time he got busy.

He began laboriously to drag Hanardy along the smooth flooring. Halfway to the nearest corner, the man stirred. Instantly, quite coolly, Leigh struck him with the revolver butt, hard. This was not time for squeamishness.

The pilot dropped and the rest was simple. He deserted the body as soon as he had pulled it out of sight behind the corner, and raced along the hallway, trying doors. The first four wouldn't open. At the fifth, he pulled up in a dark consideration.

It was impossible that the whole place was locked up. Two people in an isolated meteorite wouldn't go around perpetually locking and unlocking doors. There must be a trick catch.

There was. The fifth door yielded to a simple pressure on a tiny, half-hidden push button, that had seemed an integral part of the design of the latch. He stepped through the entrance, then started back in brief, terrible shock.

The room had no ceiling. Above him was—space. An ice-cold blast of air swept at him.

He had a flashing glimpse of gigantic machines in the room, machines that dimly resembled the ultramodern astronomical observatory on the moon that he had visited on opening day two days before. That one swift look was all Leigh allowed himself. Then he stepped back into the hallway. The door of the observatory closed automatically in his face.

He stood there, chagrined. Silly fool! The very fact that cold air had blown at him showed that the open effect of the ceiling was only an illusion of invisible glass. Good Lord, in that room might be wizard telescopes that could see to the stars. Or—an ugly thrill raced along his spine—he might have seen the Dreeghs attacking.

He shook out of his system the brief, abnormal desire to look again. This was no time for distractions. For, by now, the girl must know that something was wrong.

At top speed, Leigh ran to the sixth door. It opened into a little cubbyhole. A blank moment passed before he recognized what it was.

An elevator!

He scrambled in. The farther he got away from the residential floor, the less the likelihood of quick discovery.

He turned to close the door, and saw that it was shutting automatically. It clicked softly; the elevator immediately began to go up. Piercingly sharp doubt came to Leigh. The machine was apparently geared to go to some definite point. And that could be very bad.

His eyes searched hastily for controls. But nothing was visible. Gun poised, he stood grim and alert, as the elevator stopped. The door slid open.

Leigh stared. There was no room. The door opened—onto blackness.

Not the blackness of space with its stars. Or a dark room, half revealed by the light from the elevator. But—blackness!

Impenetrable.

Leigh put a tentative hand forward, half expecting to feel a solid object. But as his hand entered the black area, it vanished. He jerked it back, and stared at it, dismayed. It shone with a light of its own, all the bones plainly visible.

Swiftly, the light faded, the skin became opaque, but his whole arm pulsed with a pattern of pain.

The stark, terrible thought came that this could be a death chamber. After all, the elevator had deliberately brought him here; it might not have been automatic. Outside forces could have directed it. True, he had stepped in of his own free will, but—

Fool, fool!

He laughed bitterly, braced himself—and then it happened.

There was a flash out of the blackness. Something that sparkled vividly, something material that blazed a brilliant path to his forehead—and drew itself inside his head. And then—

He was no longer in the elevator. On either side of him stretched a long corridor. The stocky Hanardy was just reaching for some tiny lights beside the door of Patricia Ungarn's apartment.

The man's fingers touched one of the lights. It dimmed. Softly, the door opened. A young woman with proud, insolent eyes and a queenlike bearing stood there.

"Father wants you down on Level 4," she said to Hanardy. "One of the energy screens has gone down; and he needs some machine before he can put up another."

She turned to Leigh; her voice took on metallic overtones as she said: "*Mr. Leigh, you can come in!*"

The crazy part of it was that he walked in with scarcely a physical tremor. A cool breeze caressed his cheeks; and there was the liltingly sweet sound of birds singing in the distance. Leigh stood stockstill for a moment after he had entered, dazed partly by the wonders of the room and the unbelievable sunlit garden beyond the French windows, partly by—what?

What had happened to him?

Gingerly, he put his hands to his head, and felt his forehead, then his whole head. But nothing was wrong, not a contusion, not a pain. He grew aware of the girl staring at him, and realization came that his actions must seem unutterably queer.

"What is the matter with you?" the girl asked.

Leigh looked at her with abrupt, grim suspicion. He snapped harshly: "Don't pull that innocent stuff. I've been up in the blackness room, and all I've got to say is, if you're going to kill me, don't skulk behind artificial night and other trickery."

The girl's eyes, he saw, were narrowed, unpleasantly cold. "I don't know what you're trying to pretend," she said icily. "I assure you it will not postpone the death we have to deal you." She hesitated, then finished sharply: "The *what* room?"

Leigh explained grimly, puzzled by her puzzlement, then annoyed by the contemptuous smile that grew into her face. She cut him off curtly: "I've never heard a less balanced story. If your intention was to astound me and delay your death with that improbable tale, it has failed. You must be mad. You didn't knock out Hanardy, because when I opened the door, Hanardy was there, and I sent him down to father."

"See here!" Leigh began. He stopped wildly. By Heaven, Hanardy had been there as she opened the door!

And yet earlier—

WHEN?

Doggedly, Leigh pushed the thought on: Earlier, he had attacked Hanardy. And then he—Leigh—had gone up in an elevator, and then, somehow, back and—

Shakily, he felt his head again. And it was absolutely normal. Only, he thought, there was something inside it that sparkled.

Something—

With a start, he grew aware that the girl was quite deliberately drawing a gun from a pocket of her simple white dress. He stared at the weapon, and before its gleaming menace, his thoughts faded, all except the deadly consciousness that what he had said had delayed her several minutes now. It was the only thing that could delay her further until, somehow—

The vague hope wouldn't finish. Urgently, he said: 'I'm going to assume you're genuinely puzzled by my words. Let's begin at the beginning. There is such a room, is there not?''

"Please," said the girl wearily, "let us not have any of your logic. My I.Q. is 243, yours is 112. So I assure you I am quite capable of reasoning from any beginning you can think of."

She went on, her low voice as curt as the sound of struck steel: "There is no 'blackness' room, as you call it, no sparkling thing that crawls inside a human head. There is but one fact: The Dreeghs in their visit to your hotel room, hypnotized you, and this curious mind illusion can only be a result of that hypnotism—don't argue with me—"

With a savage gesture of her gun, she cut off his attempt to speak. "There's no time. For some reason, the Dreeghs did something to you. Why? What did you see in those rooms?"

Even as he explained and described, Leigh was thinking chilly: He'd have to catch hold of himself, get a plan, however risky, and carry it through. The purpose was tight and cold in his mind as he obeyed her motion, and went ahead of her into the corridor. It was there, an icy determination, as he counted the doors from the corner where he had left the unconscious Hanardy.

"One, two, three, four, five. This door!" he said.

"Open it!" the girl gestured.

He did so; and his lower jaw sagged. He was staring into a fine, cozy room filled with shelf on shelf of beautifully bound books. There were comfortable chairs, a magnificent rag rug and—

It was the girl who closed the door firmly and—he trembled with a tremendousness of the opportunity—she walked ahead of him to the sixth door.

"And is this your elevator?"

Leigh nodded mutely, and because his whole body was shaking, he was only dimly surprise that there was no elevator, but a long, empty, silent corridor.

The girl was standing with her back partly to him; and if he hit her, it would knock her hard against the door jamb and—

The sheer brutality of the thought was what stopped him, held him for the barest second—as the girl whirled, and looked straight into his eyes.

Her gun was up, pointing steadily. "Not that way," she said quietly. "For a moment I was wishing you would have the nerve to try it. But, after all, that would be the weak way for me."

Her eyes glowed with a fierce pride. "After all, I've killed before through necessity, and hated it. You can see yourself that, because of what the Dreeghs have done to you, it is necessary. So—"

Her voice took on a whiplash quality. "So back to my rooms. I have a space lock there to get rid of your body. Get going!"

It was the emptiness, the silence except for the faint click of their shoes that caught Leigh's nerves, as he walked hopelessly back to the apartment. This meteorite hurtling darkly through the remote wastes of the Solar System, pursued and attacked by deadly ships from the fixed stars, and himself inside it, under sentence of death, the executioner to be a girl—

And that was the devastating part. He couldn't begin to argue with this damnable young woman, for every word would sound like pleading. The very thought of mentally getting down on the knees to any woman was paralyzing.

The singing of the birds, as he entered the apartment, perked him violently out of his black passion. Abruptly marveling, he walked to the stately French windows, and stared at the glorious summery garden.

At least two acres of green wonder spread before him, a blaze of flowers, trees where gorgeously colored birds fluttered and trilled, a wide, deep pool of green, green water, and over all, the glory of brilliant sunshine.

It was the sunshine that held Leigh finally; and he stood almost breathless for a long minute before it seemed that he had the solution. He said in a hushed voice, without turning:

"The roof—is an arrangement—of magnifying glass. It makes the Sun as big as on Earth. Is that the—"

"You'd better turn around," came the hostile, vibrant voice from behind him. "I don't shoot people in the back. And I want to get this over with."

It was the moralistic smugness of her words that shook every muscle in Leigh's body. He whirled, and raged: "You damned little Klugg. You can't shoot me in the back, eh? Oh, no! And you couldn't possibly shoot me while I was attacking you because that would be the weak way. It's all got to be made right with your conscience."

He stopped so short that, if he had been running instead of talking, he would have stumbled. Figuratively, almost literally, he saw Patricia Ungarn for the first time since his arrival. His mind had been so concentrated, so absorbed by deadly things that—

—For the first time as a woman.

Leigh drew a long breath. Dressed a man, she had been darkly handsome in an extremely youthful fashion. Now she wore a simple, snow-white sports dress. It was scarcely more than a tunic, and came well above her knees.

Her hair shone with a brilliant brownness, and cascaded down to her shoulders. Her bare arms and legs gleamed a deep, healthy tan. Sandals pure white graced her feet. Her face—

The impression of extraordinary beauty yielded to the amazing fact that her perfect cheeks were flushing vividly. The girl snapped: "Don't you dare use that word to me."

She must have been utterly beside herself. Her fury was an enormous fact that Leigh gasped, and he couldn't have stopped himself from saying what he did, if the salvation of his soul had depended on it.

"Klugg!" he said, "Klugg, Klugg, Klugg! So you realize now that the Dreeghs had you down pat, that all your mighty pretensions was simply your Klugg mind demanding pretentious compensation for a dreary, lonely life. You had to think you were somebody, and yet all the time you must have known they'd only ship the tenth-raters to these remote posts. Klugg, not even Lennel; the Dreegh woman wouldn't even grant you Lennel status, whatever that is. And she'd know. Because if your I.Q. were 243, the Dreeghs were 400. You've realized that, too, haven't you?"

"Shut up! Or I'll kill you by inches!" said Patricia Ungarn; and Leigh was amazed to see that she was as white as a sheet. The astounded realization came that he had struck, not only the emotional Achilles heel of this strange and terrible young woman, but the very vital roots of her mental existence.

"So," he said deliberately, "the high morality is growing dim. Now you can torture me to death without a qualm. And to think that I came here to ask you to marry me because I thought a Klugg and a human being might get along."

"You what?" said the girl. Then she sneered. "So that was the form of their hypnotism. They would use some simple impulse for a simple human mind.

"But now I think we've had just about enough. I know just the type of thoughts that come to a male human in love; and even the realization that you're not responsible makes the very idea none the less bearable. I feel sickened, utterly insulted. Know, please, that my future husband is arriving with the reinforcements three weeks from now. He will be trained to take over father's work—"

"Another Klugg!" said Leigh, and the girl turned shades whiter.

Leigh stood utterly thunderstruck. In all his life, he had never gotten anybody going the way he had this young girl. The intellectual mask was off, and underneath was a seething mass of emotions bitter beyond the power of words to express. Here was evidence of a life so lonely that it strained his imagination. Her every word showed an incredible pent-up masochism as well as sadism, for she was torturing herself as well as him.

And he couldn't stop now to feel sorry for her. His life was at stake, and only more words could postpone death—or bring the swift and bearable surcease of a gun fired in sudden passion. He hammered on grimly: "I'd like to ask one question. How did you find out my I.Q. was 112? What special interest made you inquire about that? Is it possible that, all by yourself here, you, too, had a special type of thought, and that, though your intellect rejected the very idea of such lowly love, its existence is the mainspring behind your fantastic determination to kill rather than cure me? I—"

"That will do," interrupted Patricia Ungarn.

It required one lengthy moment for Leigh to realize that in those few short seconds she had pulled herself completely together.

He stared in gathering alarm, as her gun motioned toward a door he had not seen before.

She said curtly: "I suppose there is a solution other than death. That is, immediate death. And I have decided to accept the resultant loss of my spaceship." She nodded at the door: "It's there in the air lock. It works very simply. The steering wheel pulls up or down or sideways, and that's the way the ship will go. Just step on the accelerator, and the machine will go forward. The decelerator is the left pedal. The automobile wheels fold in automatically as soon as they lift from the floor.

"Now, get going. I need hardly tell you that the Dreeghs will probably catch you. But you can't stay here. That's obvious."

"Thanks!" That was all Leigh allowed himself to say. He had exploded an emotional powder keg, and he dared not tamper even a single word further. There was a tremendous psychological mystery here, but it was not for him to solve.

Suddenly shaky from realization of what was still ahead of him, he walked gingerly toward the air lock. And then—

It happened!

He had a sense of unutterable nausea. There was a wild swaying through blackness and—

He was standing at the paneled doorway leading from the corridor to Patricia Ungarn's apartment. Beside him stood Hanardy. The door opened. The young woman who stood there said strangely familiar words to Hanardy, about going down to the fourth level to fix an energy screen. Then she turned to Leigh, and in a voice hard and metallic said: "*Mr.* Leigh, you can come in."

VII

THE CRAZY PART of it was that he walked in with scarcely a physical tremor. A cool breeze caressed his cheeks, and there was the liltingly sweet sound of birds singing in the distance. Leigh stood stockstill for a moment after he had entered; by sheer will power he emptied the terrible daze out of his mind, and bent, mentally, into the cyclone path of complete memory. Everything was there suddenly, the way the Dreeghs had come to his hotel apartment and ruthlessly forced him to their will, the way the "blackness" room had affected him, and how the girl had spared his life.

For some reason, the whole scene with the girl had been unsatisfactory to— Jeel, and it was now, fantastically, to be repeated.

That thought ended. The entire, tremendous reality of what had happened yielded to a vastly greater fact: There was—something—inside his head, a distinctly physical something; and in a queer, horrible, inexperienced way, his mind was instinctively fighting—it. The result was ghastly confusion. Which hurt him, not the thing.

Whatever it was, rested inside his head, unaffected by his brain's feverish contortions, cold, aloof, watching.

Watching.

Madly, then, he realized what it was. Another mind. Leigh shrank from the thought as from the purest destroying fire. He tensed his brain. For a moment the frenzy of his horror was so great that his face twisted with the anguish of his efforts. And everything blurred.

Exhausted finally, he simply stood there. And the thing-mind was still inside his head.

Untouched.

What had happened to him?

Shakily, Leigh put his hands up to his forehead; then he felt his whole head. There was a vague idea in him that if he pressed—

He jerked his hands down with an unspoken curse. Damnation on damnation, he was even repeating the actions of this scene. He grew aware of the girl staring at him. He heard her say: "What is the matter with you?"

It was the sound of the words, exactly the same words, that did it. He smiled wryly. His mind drew back from the abyss, where it had teetered.

He was sane again.

Gloomy recognition came then that his brain was still a long way down; sane yes, but dispirited. It was only too obvious that the girl had no memory of the previous scene, or she wouldn't be parroting. She'd—

That thought stopped, too. Because a strange thing was happening. The mind inside him stirred, and looked through his—Leigh's—eyes. Looked intently.

Intently.

The room and the girl in it changed, not physically, but subjectively, in what he saw, in the—details.

Details burned at him; furniture and design that a moment before had seemed a flowing, artistic whole, abruptly showed flaws, hideous errors in taste and arrangement and structure.

His gaze flashed out to the garden, and in instants tore it to mental shreds. Never in all his existence had he seen or felt criticism on such a high, devastating scale. Only—

Only it wasn't criticism. Actually. The mind was indifferent. It saw things. Automatically, it saw some of the possibilities, and by comparison the reality suffered.

It was not a matter of anything being hopelessly bad. The wrongness was frequently a subtle thing. Birds not suited, for a dozen reasons, to their environment. Shrubs that added infinitesimal discord not harmony to the superb garden.

The mind flashed back from the garden, and this time, for the first time, studied the girl.

On all Earth, no woman had ever been so piercingly examined. The structure of her body and her face, to Leigh, so finely, proudly shaped, so gloriously patrician—found low grade now.

An excellent example of low-grade development in isolation.

That was the thought, not contemptuous, not derogatory, simply an impression by an appallingly direct mind that saw—overtones, realities behind realities, a thousand facts where one showed.

There followed crystal-clear awareness of the girl's psychology, objective admiration for the system of isolated upbringing that made Klugg girls such fine breeders, and then—

Purpose!

Instantly carried out. Leigh took three swift steps toward the girl. He was aware of her snatching the gun in her pocket, and there was the sheerest startled amazement on her face. Then he had her.

Her muscles writhed like steel springs. But they were hopeless against his superstrength, his superspeed. He tied her with some wire he had noticed in a half-opened clothes closet.

Then he stepped back, and to Leigh came the shocked personal thought of the incredible thing that had happened, comprehension that all this, which seemed so normal, was actually so devastatingly superhuman, so swift that—seconds only had passed since he came into the room.

Private thought ended. He grew aware of the mind, contemplating what it had done, and what it must do before the meteorite would be completely under control.

Vampire victory was near.

There was a phase of walking along empty corridors, down several flights of stairs. The vague, dull thought came to Leigh, his own personal thought, that the Dreegh seemed to know completely the interior of the meteorite.

Somehow, during the periods of—transition, of time manipulation, the creature-mind must have used his, Leigh's, body to explore the vast tomb of a place *thoroughly*. And now, with utter simplicity of purpose—*he* was heading for the machine shops of the fourth level, where Professor Ungarn and Hanardy labored to put up another energy defense screen.

He found Hanardy alone, working at a lathe that throbbed—and the sound made it easy to sneak up—

The professor was in a vast room, where great engines hummed a strange, deep tune of titanic power. He was a tall man, and his back was turned to the door as Leigh entered.

But he was immeasurably quicker than Hanardy, quicker even than the girl. He sensed danger. He whirled with catlike agility. Literally. And succumbed instantly to muscles that could have torn him limb from limb. It was during the binding of the man's hands that Leigh had time for an impression.

In the photographs that Leigh had seen, as he had told the Dreegh, Merla, in the hotel, the professor's face had been sensitive, tired-looking, withal noble. He was more than that, tremendously more.

The man radiated power, as no photograph could show it, *good* power in contrast to the savage, malignant, immensely greater power of the Dreegh.

The sense of power faded before the aura of—weariness. Cosmic weariness. It was a lined, an amazingly lined face. In a flash, Leigh remembered what the Dreegh woman had said, and it was all there: deep-graven lines of tragedy and untold mental suffering, interlaced with a curious peacefulness, like resignation.

On that night months ago, he had asked the Dreegh woman: Resignation to what? And now, here in this tortured, kindly face was the answer: *Resignation to hell.*

Queerly, an unexpected second answer trickled in his mind: Morons; they're Galactic morons. Kluggs.

The thought seemed to have no source; but it gathered with all the fury of a storm. Professor Ungarn and his daughter were Kluggs, *morons* in the incredible Galactic sense. No wonder the girl had reacted like a crazy person. Obviously born here, she must have only guessed the truth in the last two months.

The I.Q. of human morons wavered between seventy-five and ninety, of Kluggs possibly between two hundred and twenty-five and, say, two hundred and forty-three.

Two hundred and forty-three. What kind of civilization was this Galactic—if Dreeghs were four hundred and—

Somebody, of course, had to do the dreary, routine work of civilization; and Kluggs and Lennels and their kind were obviously elected. No wonder they looked like morons with that weight of inferiority to influence their very nerve and muscle structure. No wonder whole planets were kept in ignorance—

Leigh left the professor tied hand and foot, and began to turn off power switches. Some of the great motors were slowing noticeably as he went out of that mighty engine room; the potent hum of power dimmed.

Back in the girl's room, he entered the air lock, climbed into the small automobile spaceship—and launched into the night.

Instantly, the gleaming mass of meteorite receded into the darkness behind him. Instantly, magnetic force rays caught his tiny craft, and drew it remorselessly toward the hundred and fifty foot, cigar-shaped machine that flashed out of the darkness.

He felt the spy rays, and he must have been recognized. For another ship flashed up to claim him.

Air locks opened noiselessly—and shut. Sickly, Leigh stared at the two Dreeghs, the tall man and the tall woman, and, as from a great distance, heard himself explaining what he had done.

Dimly, hopelessly, he wondered why he should have to explain. Then he heard Jeel say: "Merla, this is the most astoundingly successful case of hypnotism in our existence. He's done everything. Even the tiniest thoughts we put into his mind have been carried out to the letter. And the proof is, the screens are going down. With the control of this station, we can hold out even after the Galactic warships arrive—and fill our tankers and our energy reservoirs for ten thousand years. Do you hear, *ten thousand years?*''

His excitement died. He smiled with sudden, dry understanding as he looked at the woman. Then he said laconically: ''My dear, the reward is all yours. We could have broken down those screens in another twelve hours, but it would have meant the destruction of the meteorite. This victory is so much greater. Take your reporter. Satisfy your craving—while the rest of us prepare for the occupation. Meanwhile, I'll tie him up for you.''

Leigh thought, a cold, remote thought: The kiss of death—

He shivered in sudden, appalled realization of what he had done.

He lay on the couch where Jeel had tied him. He was surprised, after a moment, to notice that, though *the* mind had withdrawn into the background of his brain—it was still there, cold, steely, abnormally conscious.

The wonder came: what possible satisfaction could Jeel obtain from experiencing the mortal thrill of death with him? These people were utterly abnormal, of course, but—

The wonder died like dry grass under a heat ray, as the woman came into the room, and glided toward him. She smiled. She sat down on the edge of the couch.

''So here you are,'' she said.

She was, Leigh thought, like a tigress. There was a purpose in every cunning muscle of her long body. In surprise he saw that she had changed her dress. She wore a sleek, flimsy, sheeny, tight-fitting gown that set off in startling fashion her golden hair and starkly white face. Utterly fascinated, he watched her. Almost automatically, he said: ''Yes, I'm here.''

Silly words. But he didn't feel silly. Tenseness came the moment he had spoken. It was her eyes that did it. For the first time since he had first seen her, her eyes struck him like a blow. Blue eyes, and steady. So steady. Not the steady frankness of honesty. But steady—like dead eyes.

A chill grew on Leigh, a special, extra chill, adding to the ice that was already there inside him; and the unholy thought came that this was a dead woman— artificially kept alive by the blood and *life* of dead men and women.

She smiled, but the bleakness remained in those cold fish eyes. No smile, no warmth could ever bring light to that chill, beautiful countenance. But she smiled the form of a smile, and she said:

''We Dreeghs live a hard, lonely life. So lonely that sometimes I cannot help thinking our struggle to remain alive is a blind, mad thing. We're what we are through no fault of our own. It happened during an interstellar flight that took place a million years ago.''

She stopped, almost hopelessly. ''It seems longer. It must be longer. I've really lost track.''

She went on, suddenly grim, as if the memory, the very telling, brought a return of horror: "We were among several thousand holidayers who were caught in the gravitational pull of a sun, afterward called the Dreegh sun.

"Its rays, immensely dangerous to human life, infected us all. It was discovered that only continuous blood transfusions, and the life force of other human beings, could save us. For a while we received donations; then the government decided to have us destroyed as hopeless incurables.

"We were all young, terribly young and in love with life; some hundreds of us had been expecting the sentence, and we still had friends in the beginning. We escaped, and we've been fighting ever since to stay alive."

And still he could feel no sympathy. It was odd, for all the thoughts she undoubtedly wanted him to have, came. Picture of a bleak, endless existence in spaceships, staring out into the perpetual night; all life circumscribed by the tireless, abnormal needs of bodies gone mad from ravenous disease.

It was all there, all the emotional pictures. But no emotions came. She was too cold; the years and the devil's hunt had stamped her soul and her eyes and her face.

And besides, her body seemed tenser now, leaning toward him, bending forward closer, closer, till he could hear her slow, measured breathing. Even her eyes suddenly held the vaguest inner light—her whole being quivered with the chill tensity of her purpose; when she spoke, she almost breathed the words: "I want you to kiss me, and don't be afraid. I shall keep you alive for days, but I must have response, not passivity. You're a bachelor, at least thirty. You won't have any more morals about the matter than I. But you must let your whole body yield."

He didn't believe it. Her face hovered six inches about his, and there was such ferocity of suppressed eagerness in her that it could only mean death.

Her lips were pursed, as if to suck, and they quivered with a strange, tense, trembling desire, utterly unnatural, almost obscene. Her nostrils dilated at every breath—and no normal woman who had kissed as often as she must have in all her years could feel like that, if that was all she expected to get.

"Quick!" she said breathlessly. "Yield, yield!"

Leigh scarcely heard; for that other mind that had been lingering in his brain, surged forward in its incredible way. He heard himself say: "I'll trust your promise because I can't resist such an appeal. You can kiss your head off. I guess I can stand it—"

There was a blue flash, an agonizing burning sensation that spread in a flash to every nerve of his body.

The anguish became a series of tiny pains, like small needles piercing a thousand bits of his flesh. Tingling, writhing a little, amazed that he was still alive, Leigh opened his eyes.

He felt a wave of purely personal surprise.

The woman lay slumped, lips half twisted off of his, body collapsed hard across his chest. And the mind, that blazing mind was there, watching—as the tall figure of the Dreegh man sauntered into the room, stiffened, and then darted forward.

He jerked her limp form into his arms. There was the same kind of blue flash as their lips met, from the man to the woman. She stirred finally, moaning. He shook her brutally.

"You wretched fool!" he raged. "How did you let a thing like that happen? You would have been dead in another minute, if I hadn't come along."

"I—don't—know." Her voice was thin and old. She sank down to the floor at his feet, and slumped there like a tired old woman. Her blond hair straggled, and looked curiously faded. "I don't know, Jeel. I tried to get his life force, and he got mine instead. He—"

She stopped. Her blue eyes widened. She staggered to her feet. "Jeel, he must be a spy. No human being could do a thing like that to me."

"Jeel"—there was sudden terror in her voice—"Jeel, get out of this room. Don't you realize? He's got my energy in him. He's lying there now, and whatever has control of him has my energy to work with—"

"All right, all right." He patted her fingers. "I assure you he's only a human being. And he's got your energy. You made a mistake, and the flow went the wrong way. But it would take much more than that for *anyone* to use a human body successfully against us. So—"

"You don't understand!" Her voice shook. "Jeel, I've been cheating. I don't know what got into me, but I couldn't get enough life force. Every time I was able, during the four times we stayed on Earth, I sneaked out.

"I caught men on the street. I don't know exactly how many because I dissolved their bodies after I was through with them. But there were dozens. And he's got all the energy I collected, enough for scores of years, enough for—don't you see?—enough for *them*."

"My dear!" The Dreegh shook her violently, as a doctor would an hysterical woman. "For a million years, the great ones of Galactic have ignored us and—"

He paused. A black frown twisted his long face. He whirled like the tiger man he was, snatching at his gun—as Leigh stood up.

The man Leigh was no longer surprised at anything. At the way the hard cords fell rotted from his wrists and legs. At the way the Dreegh froze rigid after one look into his eyes. For the first shock of the tremendous, the almost cataclysmic, truth was already in him.

"There is only one difference," said Leigh in a voice so vibrant that the top of his head shivered from the unaccustomed violence of sound. "This time there are two hundred and twenty-seven Dreegh ships gathered in one concentrated area. The rest—and our records show only a dozen others—we can safely leave to our police patrols."

The Great Galactic, who had been William Leigh, smiled darkly and walked toward his captives. "It has been a most interesting experiment in deliberate splitting of personality. Three years ago, our time manipulators showed this opportunity of destroying the Dreeghs, who hitherto had escaped by reason of the vastness of our galaxy.

"And so I came to Earth, and here built up the character of William Leigh, reporter, complete with family and past history. It was necessary to withdraw into a special compartment of the brain some nine-tenths of my mind, and to drain completely an equal percentage of life energy.

"That was the difficulty. How to replace that energy in sufficient degree at the proper time, without playing the role of vampire. I constructed a number of energy caches, but naturally at no time had we been able to see all the future. We could not see the details of what was to transpire aboard this ship, or in my hotel room that night you came, or under Constantine's restaurant.

"Besides, if I had possessed full energy as I approached this ship, your spy ray would have registered it; and you would instantly have destroyed my small automobile-spaceship.

"My first necessity, accordingly, was to come to the meteorite, and obtain an initial control over my own body through the medium of what my Earth personality called the 'blackness' room.

"That Earth personality offered unexpected difficulties. In three years it had gathered momentum *as* a personality, and that impetus made it necessary to repeat a scene with Patricia Ungarn, and to appear directly as another conscious mind, in order to convince Leigh that he must yield. The rest, of course, was a matter of gaining additional energy after boarding your ship, which''—he bowed slightly at the muscularly congealed body of the woman—"which she supplied me.

"I have explained all this because of the fact that a mind will accept complete control only if full understanding of—defeat—is present. I must finally inform you, therefore, that you are to remain alive for the next few days, during which time you will assist me in making personal contact with your friends.''

He made a gesture of dismissal: "Return to your normal existence. I have still to coordinate my two personalities completely, and that does not require your presence.''

The Dreeghs went out blank-eyed, almost briskly, and the two minds in one body were—alone!

For Leigh, the Leigh of Earth, the first desperate shock was past. The room was curiously dim, as if he was staring out through eyes that were no longer—his!

He thought, with a horrible effort at self-control: "I've got to fight. Some *thing* is trying to possess my body. All the rest is lie.''

A soothing, mind-pulsation stole into the shadowed chamber where his—self—was cornered: No lie, but wondrous truth. You have not seen what the Dreeghs saw and felt, for you are inside this body, and know not that it has come marvelously *alive,* unlike anything that your petty dreams on Earth could begin to conceive. You must accept your high destiny, else the sight of your own body will be a terrible thing to you. Be calm, be braver than you've ever been, and pain will turn to joy.

Calm came out. His mind quivered in its dark corner, abnormally conscious of strange and unnatural pressures that pushed in at it like winds out of unearthly night. For a moment of terrible fear, it funked that pressing night, then forced back to sanity, and had another thought of its own, a grimly cunning thought: The devilish interloper was arguing. Could that mean—his mind rocked with hope—that coordination was impossible without *his* yielding to clever persuasion?

Never would he yield.

"Think," whispered the alien mind, "think of being one valuable facet of a mind with an I.Q. of twelve hundred, think of yourself as having played a role; and now you are returning to normalcy, a normalcy of unlimited power. You have been an actor completely absorbed in your role, but the play is over; you are alone in your dressing room removing the grease paint; your mood of the play is fading, fading, fading—"

"Go to hell!" said William Leigh, loudly. "I'm William Leigh, I.Q. one hundred and twelve, satisfied to be just what I am. I don't give a damn whether you built me up from the component elements of your brain, or whether I was born normally. I can just see what you're trying to do with that hypnotic suggestion stuff, but it isn't working. I'm here, I'm myself, and I stay myself. Go find yourself another body, if you're so smart."

Silence settled where his voice had been, and the emptiness, the utter lack of sound brought a sharp twinge of fear greater than that which he had before he spoke.

He was so intent on that inner struggle that he was not aware of outer movement until—

With a start he grew aware that he was staring out of a port window. Night spread there, the living night of space.

A trick, he thought in an agony of fear, a trick somehow designed to add to the corroding power of hypnotism.

A trick! He tried to jerk back—and, terrifyingly, couldn't. His body wouldn't move. Instantly, then, he tried to speak, to crash through that enveloping blanket of unholy silence. But no sound came.

Not a muscle, not a finger stirred; not a single nerve so much as trembled.

He was alone.

Cut off in his little corner of brain.

Lost.

Yes, lost, came a strangely pitying sibilation of thought, lost to a cheap, sordid existence, lost to a life whose end is visible from the hour of birth, lost to a civilization that has already had to be saved from itself a thousand times. Even you, I think, can see that all this is lost to you forever—

Leigh thought starkly: The *thing* was trying by a repetition of ideas, by showing evidence of defeat, to lay the foundation of further defeat. It was the oldest trick of simple hypnotism for simple people. And he couldn't let it work—

You have, urged the mind inexorably, accepted the fact that you were playing a role; and now you have recognized our oneness, and are giving up the role. The proof of this recognition on your part is that you have yielded control of—our—body.

—Our body, *our* body, OUR body—

The word re-echoed like some Gargantuan sound through his brain, then merged swiftly into that calm, other-mind pulsation: —Concentration. All intellect derives from the capacity to concentrate, and, progressively, the body itself shows *life,* reflects and focuses that gathering, vaulting power.

—One more step remains: You must see—

Amazingly, then, he was staring into a mirror. Where it had come from, he had no memory. It was there in front of him, where, an instant before, had been a black porthole—and there was an image in the mirror, shapeless at first to his blurred vision.

Deliberately—he felt the enormous deliberateness—the vision was cleared for him. He *saw*—and then he didn't.

His brain wouldn't look. It twisted in a mad desperation, like a body buried alive, and briefly, horrendously conscious of its fate. Insanely, it fought away from the blazing thing in the mirror. So awful was the effort, so titanic the fear, that it began to gibber mentally, its consciousness to whirl dizzily, like a wheel spinning faster, faster—

The wheel shattered into ten thousand aching fragments. Darkness came, blacker than Galactic night. And there was—

Oneness!

THE DARK CASTLE

MARION BRANDON

Marion Brandon's "The Dark Castle" appeared in the debut issue of Strange Tales *in 1931, at a time when the vampire story was just beginning to develop in the pages of American popular fiction magazines. One of only two contributions Brandon made to the pulps, its traditional setting and near-reportorial style reflect how little readers demanded from such stories at the time.*

L OST ON A mountain road—and out of gas!
    That worst possible combination of misfortunes for the tourist had overtaken us; worse than ever, with night now fallen on the unknown countryside around us, wrapping it in darkness, veiling the simplest objects in mystery, and endowing the most commonplace of sounds with sinister meaning. But there was no getting around the fact that the tank was on dry as the proverbial bone, and that no matter how Arescu and I cursed our luck, our car would never stir again until something could be procured to fill the empty gasoline tank.

Nor was there any telling when that might be, for in the mountain districts of Central Europe sources of supply are few and far between. Wrong directions had been given us somewhere on the way from the little city which we had left at noon, and instead of reaching the town that was our destination before sundown, here we were, hours later, nowhere—and unable to move.

I was touring these remote regions with but one companion, a most likable young fellow, a Romanian, who had graduated that June from the college where I was an instructor. We had formed one of the peculiar friendships that sometimes occur between an older man and a younger, and when the time came for him to return to his native country, he had suggested that I accompany him and make up a party of two for a summer of leisurely travel in such unfamiliar countries as Serbia, Bulgaria, and his own Romania—where we were at the moment when our engine died on that tortuous road.

It was very cold in the high, clear atmosphere, for it was late in August and autumn was approaching. Not a sound to break the silence but the eery screech of an owl and the faint rustle of the night wind in the undergrowth by the roadside, like the stealthy prowling of some hostile animal. Though the entire day had been heavily overcast and dull, the night was clear and starry, but black as the pit, for the moon had not yet risen, and beyond the small range of our headlights we could see not a thing.

"Well," I said resignedly as I sat down on the running-board, and filled my pipe, "this may be very romantic, but it's cold, too, and I'd give a good deal at this minute to be on a prosaic, concrete state highway, with a red gas pump sure to turn up within half a mile!"

Arescu seated himself beside me. "It's only about an hour till moonrise," he said. "We can perhaps get some idea of where we are then. There must be a village somewhere. . . . Hear that dog that's just begun to howl? Wonder whose death *he's* heralding."

I have never blamed the originator of the superstition that the repeated howling of a dog means impending death, for it is the most depressing and ominous of sounds—doubly so at night—and it was beginning to get on my nerves when Arescu said in surprise, "We're looking for the moon in the wrong direction! I had expected it to come up on the right, behind us. . . . Look the other way."

I obeyed. To the left, the sky was softly golden, proclaiming the approach of the hidden moon, and throwing into bold relief the turrets and peaked roofs of a building.

Not a light in it anywhere, not a sound, not a sign of life. But at least it promised some degree of protection from the penetrating mountain wind which was by this time going through our clothing as if it were made of paper. Releasing the brakes of our useless car, we rolled it backward down the slight decline of the road for the few hundred feet that lay between us and the tall open gates, sagging heavily on their hinges. With a final effort, we pushed it through them, that the headlights might illumine the scene before us.

The building was, as we had already surmised, a ruin, a small castle, or very large house, its paneless windows staring like hostile eyes from the embrasures of the rough stone walls. Some of its turrets were broken, like jagged teeth, others seemingly intact—all darkly outlined against the rapidly brightening sky. As we gazed, the golden rim of the moon rose above it; the shivering screech of the owl trembled through the chilly air, answered by the dismal howl of the distant dog. A scene of such unearthly desolation may I never behold again!

"Looks pretty solid at the righthand end," Arescu remarked after we had examined it as fully as was possible from the distance at which we stood. And arming ourselves, each with an electric torch, we approached the building.

The huge iron-bound door sagged open like the gate, and passing in, we found ourselves in a great stone-floored hall, roofless and chill and forbidding. At the right, however, a doorway opened, beyond which we discovered a smaller room in fair condition. It was but a single story high. The strong black beams that supported the ceiling were all in place and looked as if they would stay there. Boards had been pushed against the paneless windows; half-burned logs lay in the gaping stone fireplace, and in a corner of the room was a pile of dry wood.

"Not at all bad!" said Arescu, surveying the scene approvingly. "Others have camped here like ourselves. Made arrangements for a longer stay though, and apparently changed their minds. But the wood they didn't burn up will come in nicely for us!

"I'll build up the fire," he went on, "while you start carrying in the rugs and food."

The moon had by this time risen high enough to render a torch unnecessary out of doors, its greenish silver radiance making the world almost as light as day. We were well prepared for camping out, with plenty of warm rugs, cans of soup, coffee, bread, bacon, and, fortunately, candles.

As I went out for my last load, I was startled to find, standing by the car and gazing toward me, a woman. She was enveloped in a long, dark, hooded cloak which so shrouded her form and shadowed her face that I could form no idea of her age, though the voice in which she addressed me, in German, had the clear vigorous ring of youth. I could see only that her eyes were very bright, and her teeth remarkably fine and white between the scarlet lips that parted with her smile.

"Pardon," she said, "if I have startled you. But I live nearby, and strangers seldom come this way."

I expressed my surprise that people lived near, since I had seen no lights and suggested that she could perhaps find us a warmer lodging for the night.

"My home is hardly large enough," she replied with that flashing, brilliant smile. "I came only to look—*this* time, but I shall perhaps see you—later." And as I gathered a few more articles from the back of the car, she wished me good night, and hurried away with sure steps down the dark road.

"Fine!" Arescu exclaimed when I reported the encounter. "Perhaps they have a small farm where we can get eggs for breakfast, and something on four legs to hunt gas with!"

Arescu was of a decidedly domestic turn, and by the time that he had spread a couple of our heavy traveling rugs on the floor by the roaring fire which he had built, and which was already having an effect upon the chilly atmosphere, stuck a candle at each end of the heavy stone chimneypiece, and set our camp coffee pot on a brick to boil—he had found a well just outside—the ruined room looked almost cozy!

Yet, for some unfathomable reason, I felt nervous and edgy. I would gladly have strangled the distant owl and the more distant dog, each of which, at irregular intervals, continued to emit its eldritch lament. Just as I would think that they had knocked off for good, one or the other of the eery sounds would break out through the night. And the miserable dog seemed to be coming gradually nearer! A couple of bats flitted blunderingly about the room; the night wind prowled uneasily outside.

"I've always heard that you Central Europeans were a superstitious lot," I remarked as Arescu, whistling cheerfully, set the finished coffee aside to keep hot, and placed over the fire a generous pan of bacon; "but here we are in what might be the setting for all sorts of horrors. It gives even me the creeps, and for all the effect it has on you, you might be fixing up a midnight mess in a college dormitory!"

Arescu sat back on his heels. "I'm just as superstitious as the next person—when I have reason to be," he replied in a perfectly matter-of-fact manner. "But plain creepy surroundings don't disturb me in the least when I know there's nothing wrong."

"How do you know there's nothing wrong with this place?" I asked curiously. "You never saw it before, did you?"

"Never." Arescu placidly arranged the crisp, hot bacon between slices of bread, and poured the coffee into enamel cups. "But there is only one haunted place—a vampire castle—in this entire region, and it's on a road leading out of the other side of Koslo from the direction we took this noon. There's nothing else within a hundred miles that's credited with even the mildest of specters!"

"And you really do believe in the supernatural?" I demanded incredulously. "You wouldn't sleep here if the place were called haunted?"

"My good friend," said Arescu, for the moment unwontedly serious, as he turned his dark eyes on mine. "It seems strange, I know, to a native of the great supercivilized United States that supposedly intelligent people can believe the unbelievable—that is, unbelievable from *your* point of view. But, after all, the powers of darkness love—the dark, and isn't it only reasonable to think that they shun the more civilized and populous regions of the earth, and cling to the remote and little-known places? Granted that the idea of a specter or spirit seems preposterous to one sitting comfortably in his modern well-lighted home, or driving along a traveled highway. But, if you were told that *this* was haunted, would it seem so ridiculous?"

The sinister howl of the dog, nearer beyond all question, answered him.

"Knowing that it isn't," he added, "I'm as happy as I'd be in the finest of hotels. But if this were Archenfels, you may be certain that I shouldn't be here!"

And as we devoured our hot supper, this astonishing young man whose American education had not shaken one whit his belief in supernatural manifestations told me the story of the Vampire Castle.

"It's twenty miles out in the mountains, to the west of Koslo," he said. "Hasn't been lived in for over a century. It had been for hundreds of years the perfectly peaceful home of a noble family, who had to abandon it a hundred and twenty years or so ago, when it suddenly became vampire-haunted, for no reason that anyone could think of. First the eldest son and heir was found dead in his bed, then his brothers, one after the other, at considerable intervals. After the original owners got out in despair, a few attempts at living in it were made by others who hoped to get a fine estate at little cost, but it was just the same: a series of mysterious deaths. Always men, too—young men, never a woman. Grin as much as you like,'' he reproved me, ''but in every case, the same little sharp wound was to be found in the throat of the victim!

''Nobody has knowingly spent a night there in over a century, as I have said,'' he went on. ''But now and again a traveler has done so—as we are doing here—and always with the same dire result: the finding of his body, sometimes long afterward; the throat marked by that cruel little wound. No one lives near it anymore; its only neighbors are the dead in the churchyard of an old ruined church.

''No, Professor,'' he finished with his engaging young smile, ''if this were Archenfels, I should be running now with a speed that would surprise you! As it is, in our cosy spot, with neighbors not far, I shall sleep soundly, and I wish you the same.''

With that, he wrapped himself in one of our extra rugs, lay down by the fire, and with his coat for a pillow, fell asleep almost immediately. I suddenly felt very lonely.

But though I tried my best to follow his example, it was of no use. The fire was burning low. The bats, joined by others, still blundered among the wavering shadows. The rising wind moaned outside, as it tried one window after another. The last howl of the accursed dog was surely much nearer! I shouldn't have drunk that coffee so late at night, shouldn't let my mind play with the boy's ghastly tale of the ruined castle, haunted by those hideous visitants who are said to feed upon the blood of their living victims. . . .

Suddenly, as I lay staring at the dying fire, my heart seemed actually to stop—then to race thundering in my ears. Icy sweat crept out upon my body. Though I had heard nothing, I *knew* that someone—*something*—was in the room, advancing soundlessly upon us from the doorway behind me!

With a desperate effort, I fought down the engulfing terror that had laid hold on me, and turned my head.

Coming slowly toward me across the room, in the fitful glow of the failing fire, was the woman who had spoken to me at the gate. But how terribly, how awesomely, changed! The long cloak had been cast aside, revealing a white gown of olden fashion; the face, shadowed before by the dark hood, exhibited a strangely bright pink-and-white quality that was not human. The lips, red as blood, were parted in a mocking smile. Her fingers were clawlike, and suggested the talons of a bird of prey.

And the eyes! I could not—heaven help me—remove my own from the baleful gaze with which they fixed on me. They fascinated me, like the eyes of some deadly serpent. I could neither move nor speak. I lay inert, paralyzed, and cold.

''Welcome to Archenfels!'' she said, smiling a terrible smile of derisive triumph. ''It has long lain untenanted, and I have had to go far afield.''

Archenfels! The castle of dread repute! Paralyzed as my body had become, my brain was clear as I groped frantically for an explanation of the horror.

Archenfels, Arescu had said, was to the west of the city; we had gone east. Impossible! . . . Yet as I stared into the narrowed cruel eyes of the scarlet-mouthed creature whose sharp teeth shone white in the flickering light of the fire, I knew that it was not impossible; knew that there are indeed more terrible things in the world than man dare dream of. . . . Some of the country people of whom we had asked directions had doubtless given wrong ones, and with the sun overcast as it had been all day, it had been easy enough to lose our sense of direction and circle around. Simple enough to understand—*now,* when it was too late!

Frantically I struggled to break the hold of those awful eyes. Sweat streamed from every pore, yet I lay inert as a log. Not a movement could I make; not a finger could I lift. Nor could I, by the most desperate striving, remove my gaze from hers. If I could do that, something told me, the spell would dissolve. I might attack her and perhaps save our lives. . . . But can the sparrow look away from the beady eyes of the snake gliding toward it?

All this time, Arescu lay sleeping as quietly as a baby, one arm over his heart, the other thrown out upon the coverlet, his slow, regular breathing the only sound in the room. A heavy graveyard odor of damp earth and decay stifled me as the creature came closer—*closer!* Stepped past me but always facing me, never taking those terrible eyes from mine. . . . Knelt by Arescu, and, gathering his slumbering form into her arms, bared her shining teeth. . . .

As she paused, still holding me chained by that unwavering gaze, I thought in blind revulsion, of a tiger crouching over its prey, glaring jealously lest another beast interfere.

Disturbed from the deep sleep of youth and health, Arescu opened his eyes. For an instant he stared, blankly and uncomprehendingly, as if in a nightmare. Then over his handsome young face swept a look of stark frozen horror that I shall see in my dreams till my last day. Under the very window the dog suddenly howled, long and despairingly.

I think that the boy died at once from shock. I hope he did. For when I realized to the full the appalling thing that was about to occur, a thing which I cannot even now put into words, I felt that I, too, was dying—and merciful unconsciousness overcame me. . . .

After what seemed an eternity of struggling, submerged in blackness, I won back to consciousness, confusedly aware of a white form slipping out through the door. Weak and dizzy, I sat up. The room was still. The fire had sunk to a few sullen embers. Even the wind had died, and I, thank heaven, was no longer in the grip of that nefarious gaze!

Snatching the torch that lay beside me, I turned its beam upon the crumpled young figure by the hearth.

No need to look a second time; to feel the pulseless wrist! The terribly unearthly pallor of the boyish face, the ghastly, drained grayness, was enough.

Boiling rage seized upon me. Where had the foul creature gone? To find others of her kind and tell them that a living man still survived in the accursed castle, material for another grim feast?

Demented and without plan, I rushed out into the night. Across the lawn, plain in the clear green moonlight, a white form was passing through the great gate. I dashed after it in mad pursuit as, realizing that it was followed, it fled, fleet as the wind itself, down the rough mountain road.

Never once did I raise my eyes from the level of its feet as, with bursting lungs, I labored after the flying shape. Not again would I fall a victim to that dread gaze!

I was almost upon it when it suddenly veered to the left. Unable to check myself, I ran past the little gate in the stone wall, thus permitting the monster to gain time. Halting as quickly as possible, I turned and rushed through the gate—into a graveyard. . . . Yes, there were the fluttering robes before me, silver in the moonlight, the streaming golden hair. With a final mighty effort, temples pounding, pulses throbbing, I gained upon my quarry. No more than twenty feet separated us when it suddenly stopped, laid hold upon an ancient slanting tombstone—and vanished into the earth. . . .

Sick with horror and utterly exhausted, I dropped beside the grave, and for a second time that night—and the second in all my life—a wave of unconsciousness swept over me. . . .

When I came to myself, the stars were paling before the rosy light in the east; cocks crowed in the distance; birds twittered in the trees. Lame and stiff, I struggled to my feet.

I was standing in an old cemetery, disused, apparently, for many years. The aged lichened tombstones were canted drunkenly this way and that; the ruined little church was half-hidden in overgrown shrubbery. All as poor Arescu had described the fateful region, had we but been able to see! For some reason, I drove a little stick into the grave at my feet—her home was indeed small!—and hastened back along the road to the dire castle of Archenfels.

Here I found many people grouped around our car, all talking excitedly, but in hushed tones, and pale with fear. Others were within. As I entered the room of death, a tall old priest rose from his knees beside the body of Arescu, now decently arranged, with eyes closed and hands crossed.

We both spoke German, and the priest told his story. A small farmer, living across the valley from Archenfels, had seen our lights in the night, and had, at first peep of dawn, hastened to the village to report what could mean but one thing—another tragedy. Practically the entire population had accompanied him to the castle, to find what they had feared, a new victim of the vampire. They had deduced that two people had occupied the room; and upon my explaining where I had been, the priest's dark eyes lighted strangely.

"Sir," he inquired eagerly, "do you *know* where she disappeared?"

"I do, indeed!" I answered. "I marked the spot."

An incomprehensible look flashed from face to face among the listeners as the priest translated my reply, and one woman, with tears streaming down her cheeks, knelt and kissed my hand.

"I think, sir," said the priest slowly, after he had given some directions in his own tongue to several of the men present, "that, shocking as this experience has been for you, you have been the instrument for saving the countryside from a great fear. I will explain to you as we return to the graveyard."

The priest's story tallied closely with Arescu's—with a grim addition. The victims of the attacks, as the boy had said, always men, young men, a fact which doubtless accounted for my own survival. But during the hundred years that the castle had stood untenanted, the number of young men who by chance spent a night there had been insufficient to satisfy the creature's blood lust; and now and again, some village lad would be found, dead in his bed, a sharp little wound plain in his throat. The last victim, two years before, had been a son of the woman who had kissed my hand, and as she had two other living sons, her fear had been great.

None but the dead had ever seen the destroyer; no description had ever been given; no theory could be formed as to its sudden origin in so peaceful a district. The village had taken such steps as it could. The few graves of suicides, and others who had died violent deaths, situated outside the graveyard wall beyond the consecrated area, had been opened long ago, for such unfortunates were said sometimes to become vampires. But the rotting coffins had contained nothing suspicious; only the moldering bones that would be natural. And one cannot open all the graves in an old cemetery with no clues to go on!

Long beams of morning sunlight were stretching across the dewy grass when we arrived at the one that I had marked. "Helena Barrientos," read the almost obliterated inscription upon the stone. "Died August 5, 1799, aged twenty years."

For a time we waited there, the people behind us, all silent under the solemn spell of impending strange events, until the men to whom the priest had spoken his orders returned, some with picks, shovels and ropes, and one with a long strong stake, sharpened at one end. A lad carried the processional cross from the village church.

Amid a deep strained silence, they set to work, the pile of fresh black clods rising rapidly beside the excavation. Then came the dull sound of blows upon rotting wood. The hole was made wide and deep enough to permit the workers to descend into it, the earth carefully cleared from around the coffin, too frail with age to bear removal from its place. The lid was loosened, lifted off. . . .

Cries of horror rose from those crowding around the grave. As for me, my brain reeled. Even then, I could not believe my own eyes.

Lying before us, in the decayed old coffin, with the fresh rosy coloring and scarlet lips of a child asleep, was the terrible visitant of the night before! But now, everything terrible about her was gone. The eyes which had exercised their dread power of fascination were quietly closed, the red lips pressed together. . . .
A corpse, fresh and bright as the living, where should lie a heap of disintegrating bones!

"You see!" said the old priest simply.

A little metal box lay beside the body, and this he opened, disclosing a letter written in faded, but still legible, ink. Slowly and solemnly he read it aloud:

"I confess to God—but not to man—that this, my daughter, met her death by her own hand. I wish that my child, wronged and mistaken though she has been, shall lie in consecrated ground, for I fear that she will not rest outside. For a day after her death I told others that she was grievously ill, then, that she had died. I prepared her for the grave myself, and none suspect. May God forgive her. She had much provocation, having been heartlessly betrayed by the young lord of Archenfels, though I alone know. May God forgive me, too, her mother."

Amid a profound hush the priest folded up the tragic message from a long-gone day, and let himself down into the grave. The sharpened stake was passed to him. Grasping it in his right hand, he received in his left the shining brass cross. Even I, stranger and skeptic though I had been, had heard tales of the grim method of exorcising vampires, and I held my breath with the rest as we watched.

Murmuring a Latin sentence, he raised the sharpened stake.

"May God have mercy on your soul!" he said. And plunged the point into the heart of the body before him.

A gasp of mingled relief and horror rose from all who could see into the grave. In the winking of an eyelid, the corpse vanished. Only a disintegrating skeleton lay in the coffin in a pool of bright red blood that was running rapidly out through the cracks, and soaking into the rich black earth.

"May God have mercy!" said the priest once more, in the sonorous rolling Latin of the Church, and with infinite compassion in his tone.

"Amen!" answered the people. And went their ways.

That is all.

I remember but little of the trip back to the ancient city of Koslo where I spent nearly a month in the hospital, delirious much of the time.

When I had recovered enough to study a map of the region, it was easy to see how we had wandered into the fatal neighborhood. The road on which Archenfels stood left the city in a westerly direction, it is true, but soon bore decidedly south, while ours, going east at first, also bent south before very long. The wrong direction given us had put us on a road that joined the two, and our own wanderings had done the rest.

If only the sun had not been hidden! If only we had reached the dread spot before night veiled the scene.

The college granted me leave of absence for a year, and I am somewhat better now. But my hair is white at forty, and I know that never again shall I have the nervous balance of a normal human being.

The doctors said that it might help me to write it all out—"get it off my mind," in a measure. I think that it has helped. And I feel too that if the recital of my experience brings others to the realization that there are still dark and terrible things to be encountered in this commonplace world of today, and restrains them from speaking—or even thinking—lightly of them, I shall at least have accomplished something of good.

STRAGELLA

HUGH B. CAVE

The prolific and multi-talented Hugh Cave wrote four stories for Strange Tales, *two of which were concerned with vampires. In "Stragella," he devised a unique strategy by which vampires might protect themselves from vengeful mortals during the daylight hours. The story's original use of the cross to repel the vampire anticipates his landmark short vampire novel* Murgunstrumm.

NIGHT, BLACK AS PITCH and filled with the wailing of a dead wind, sank like a shapeless specter into the oily waters of the Indian Ocean, leaving a great gray expanse of sullen sea, empty except for a solitary speck that rose and dropped in the long swell.

The forlorn thing was a ship's boat. For seven days and seven nights it had drifted through the waste, bearing its ghastly burden. Now, groping to his knees, one of the two survivors peered away into the East, where the first glare of a red sun filtered over the rim of the world.

Within arm's reach, in the bottom of the boat, lay a second figure, face down. All night long he had lain there. Even the torrential shower, descending in the dark hours and flooding the dory with life-giving water, had failed to move him.

The first man crawled forward. Scooping water out of the tarpaulin with a battered tin cup, he turned his companion over and forced the stuff through receded lips.

"Miggs!" The voice was a cracked whisper. "Miggs! Good God, you ain't dead, Miggs? I ain't left all alone out here—"

John Miggs opened his eyes feebly.

"What's—what's wrong?" he muttered.

"We got water, Miggs! Water!"

"You're dreamin' again, Yancy. It—it ain't water. It's nuthin' but sea—"

"It rained!" Yancy screeched. "Last night it rained. I stretched the tarpaulin. All night long I been lyin' face up, lettin' it rain in my mouth!"

Miggs touched the tin cup to his tongue and lapped its contents suspiciously. With a mumbled cry he gulped the water down. Then, gibbering like a monkey, he was crawling toward the tarpaulin.

Yancy flung him back, snarling.

"No you won't!" Yancy rasped. "We got to save it, see? We got to get out of here."

Miggs glowered at him from the opposite end of the dory. Yancy sprawled down beside the tarpaulin and stared once again over the abandoned sea, struggling to reason things out.

They were somewhere in the Bay of Bengal. A week ago they had been on board the *Cardigan,* a tiny tramp freighter carrying its handful of passengers from Maulmain to Georgetown. The *Cardigan* had foundered in the typhoon off the Mergui Archipelago. For twelve hours she had heaved and groaned through an inferno of swirling seas. Then she had gone under.

Yancy's memory of the succeeding events was a twisted, unreal parade of horrors. At first there had been five men in the little boat. Four days of terrific heat, no water, no food, had driven the little Persian priest mad, and he had jumped overboard. The other two had drunk salt water and died in agony. Now he and Miggs were alone.

The sun was incandescent in a white hot sky. The sea was calm, greasy, unbroken except for the slow, patient black fins that had been following the boat for days. But something else, during the night, had joined the sharks in their hellish pursuit. Sea snakes, hydrophiinae, wriggling out of nowhere, had come to haunt the dory, gliding in circles round and round, venomous, vivid, vindictive. And overhead were gulls wheeling, swooping in erratic arcs, cackling fiendishly and watching the two men with relentless eyes.

Yancy glanced up at them. Gulls and snakes could mean only one thing—land! He supposed they had come from the Andamans, the prison isles of India. It didn't much matter. They were here. Hideous, menacing harbingers of hope!

His shirt, filthy and ragged, hung open to the belt, revealing a lean chest tattooed with grotesque figures. A long time ago—too long to remember—he had gone on a drunken binge in Goa. Jap rum had done it. In company with two others of the *Cardigan*'s crew he had shambled into a tattooing establishment and ordered the Jap, in a bloated voice, to "paint anything you damned well like, professor. Anything at all!" And the Jap, being of a religious mind and sentimental, had decorated Yancy's chest with a most beautiful crucifix, large, ornate, and colorful.

It brought a grim smile to Yancy's lips as he peered down at it. But presently his attention was centered on something else—something unnatural, bewildering, on the horizon. The thing was a narrow bank of fog lying low on the water, as if a distorted cloud had sunk out of the sky and was floating heavily, half submerged in the sea. And the small boat was drifting toward it.

In a little while the fog bank hung dense on all sides. Yancy groped to his feet, gazing about him. John Miggs muttered something beneath his breath and crossed himself.

The thing was shapeless, grayish-white, clammy. It reeked—not with the dank smell of sea fog, but with the sickly, pungent stench of a buried jungle or a subterranean mushroom cellar. The sun seemed unable to penetrate it. Yancy could see the red ball above him, a feeble, smothered eye of crimson fire, blotted by swirling vapor.

"The gulls," mumbled Miggs. "They're gone."

"I know it. The sharks, too—and the snakes. We're all alone, Miggs."

An eternity passed, while the dory drifted deeper and deeper into the cone. And then there was something else—something that came like a moaning voice out of the fog. The muted, irregular, sing-song clangor of a ship's bell!

"Listen!" Miggs cackled. "You hear—"

But Yancy's trembling arm had come up abruptly, pointing ahead.

"By God, Miggs! Look!"

Miggs scrambled up, rocking the boat beneath him. His bony fingers gripped Yancy's arm. They stood there, the two of them, staring at the massive black shape that loomed up, like an ethereal phantom of another world, a hundred feet before them.

"We're saved," Miggs said incoherently. "Thank God, Nels—"

Yancy called out shrilly. His voice rang through the fog with a hoarse jangle, like the scream of a caged tiger. It choked into silence. And there was no answer, no responsive outcry—nothing so much as a whisper.

The dory drifted closer. No sound came from the lips of the two men as they drew alongside. There was nothing—nothing but the intermittent tolling of that mysterious, muted bell.

Then they realized the truth—a truth that brought a moan from Miggs' lips. The thing was a derelict, frowning out of the water, inanimate, sullen, buried in its winding sheet of unearthly fog. Its stern was high, exposing a propeller red with rust and matted with clinging weeds. Across the bow, nearly obliterated by age, appeared the words: *Golconda—Cardiff.*

"Yancy, it ain't no real ship! It ain't of this world—"

Yancy stooped with a snarl, and picked up the oar in the bottom of the dory. A rope dangled within reach, hanging like a black serpent over the scarred hull. With clumsy strokes he drove the small boat beneath it; then, reaching up, he seized the line and made the boat fast.

"You're—goin' aboard?" Miggs said fearfully.

Yancy hesitated, staring up with bleary eyes. He was afraid, without knowing why. The *Golconda* frightened him. The mist clung to her tenaciously. She rolled heavily, ponderously in the long swell, and the bell was still tolling softly somewhere within the lost vessel.

"Well, why not?" Yancy growled. "There may be food aboard. What's there to be afraid of?"

Miggs was silent. Grasping the ropes, Yancy clambered up them. His body swung like a gibbet-corpse against the side. Clutching the rail, he heaved himself over, then stood there, peering into the layers of thick fog, as Miggs climbed up and dropped down beside him.

"I—don't like it," Miggs whispered. "It ain't—"

Yancy groped forward. The deck planks creaked dismally under him. With Miggs clinging close, he led the way into the waist, then into the bow. The cold fog seemed to have accumulated here in a sluggish mass, as if some magnetic force had drawn it. Through it, with arms outheld in front of him, Yancy moved with shuffling steps, a blind man in a strange world.

Suddenly he stopped—stopped so abruptly that Miggs lurched headlong into him. Yancy's body stiffened. His eyes were wide, glaring at the deck before him. A hollow, unintelligible sound parted his lips.

Miggs cringed back with a livid screech, clawing at his shoulder.

"What—what is it?" he said thickly.

At their feet were bones. Skeletons—lying there in the swirl of vapor. Yancy shuddered as he examined them. Dead things they were, dead and harmless, yet they were given new life by the motion of the mist. They seemed to crawl, to wriggle, to slither toward him and away from him.

He recognized some of them as portions of human frames. Others were weird, unshapely things. A tiger skull grinned up at him with jaws that seemed to widen hungrily. The vertebrae of a huge python lay in disjointed coils on the planks, twisted as if in agony. He discerned the skeletonic remains of tigers, tapirs, and jungle beasts of unknown identity. And human heads, many of them, scattered about like an assembly of mocking, dead-alive faces, leering at him, watching him with hellish anticipation. The place was a morgue—a charnel house!

Yancy fell back, stumbling. His terror had returned with triple intensity. He felt cold perspiration forming on his forehead, on his chest, trickling down the tattooed crucifix.

Frantically he swung about in his tracks and made for the welcome solitude of the stern deck, only to have Miggs clutch feverishly at his arm.

"I'm goin' to get out of here, Nels! That damned bell—these here things—"

Yancy flung the groping hands away. He tried to control his terror. This ship—this *Golconda*—was nothing but a tramp trader. She'd been carrying a cargo of jungle animals for some expedition. The beasts had got loose, gone amuck, in a storm. There was nothing fantastic about it!

In answer, came the intermittent clang of the hidden bell below decks and the soft lapping sound of the water swishing through the thick weeds which clung to the ship's bottom.

"Come on," Yancy said grimly. "I'm goin' to have a look around. We need food."

He strode back through the waist of the ship, with Miggs shuffling behind. Feeling his way to the towering stern, he found the fog thinner, less pungent.

The hatch leading down into the stern hold was open. It hung before his face like an uplifted hand, scarred, bloated, as if in mute warning. And out of the aperture at its base straggled a spidery thing that was strangely out of place here on this abandoned derelict—a curious, menacing, crawling vine with mottled triangular leaves and immense orange-hued blossoms. Like a living snake, intertwined about itself, it coiled out of the hold and wormed over the deck.

Yancy stepped closer, hesitantly. Bending down, he reached to grasp one of the blooms, only to turn his face away and fall back with an involuntary mutter. The flowers were sickly sweet, nauseating. They repelled him with their savage odor.

"Somethin'—" Miggs whispered sibilantly, "is watchin' us, Nels! I can feel it!"

Yancy peered all about him. He, too, felt a third presence close at hand. Something malignant, evil, unearthly. He could not name it.

"It's your imagination," he snapped. "Shut up, will you?"

"We ain't alone, Nels. This ain't no ship at all!"

"Shut *up*!"

"But the flowers there—they ain't right. Flowers don't grow aboard a Christian ship, Nels!"

"This hulk's been here long enough for trees to grow on it," Yancy said curtly. "The seeds probably took root in the filth below."

"Well, I don't like it."

"Go forward and see what you can find. I'm goin' below to look around."

Miggs shrugged helplessly and moved away. Alone, Yancy descended to the lower levels. It was dark down here, full of shadows and huge gaunt forms that lost their substance in the coils of thick, sinuous fog. He felt his way along the passage, pawing the wall with both hands. Deeper and deeper into the labyrinth he went, until he found the galley.

The galley was a dungeon, reeking of dead, decayed food, as if the stench had hung there for an eternity without being molested; as if the entire ship lay in an atmosphere of its own—an atmosphere of the grave—through which the clean outer air never broke.

But there was food here, canned food that stared down at him from the rotted shelves. The labels were blurred, illegible. Some of the cans crumbled in Yancy's fingers as he seized them—disintegrated into brown, dry dust and trickled to the floor. Others were in fair condition, airtight. He stuffed four of them into his pockets and turned away.

Eagerly now, he stumbled back along the passage. The prospects of food took some of those other thoughts out of his mind, and he was in better humor when he finally found the captain's cabin.

Here, too, the evident age of the place gripped him. The walls were gray with mold, falling into a broken, warped floor. A single table stood on the far side near the bunk, a blackened, grimy table bearing an upright oil lamp and a single black book.

He picked the lamp up timidly and shook it. The circular base was yet half full of oil, and he set it down carefully. It would come in handy later. Frowning, he peered at the book beside it.

It was a seaman's Bible, a small one, lying there, coated with cracked dust, dismal with age. Around it, as if some crawling slug had examined it on all sides, leaving a trail of excretion, lay a peculiar line of black pitch, irregular but unbroken.

Yancy picked the book up and flipped it open. The pages slid under his fingers, allowing a scrap of loose paper to flutter to the floor. He stooped to retrieve it, then, seeing that it bore a line of penciled script, he peered closely at it.

The writing was an apparently irrelevant scrawl—a meaningless memorandum which said crudely:

It's the bats and the crates. I know it now, but it is too late. God help me!

With a shrug, he replaced it and thrust the Bible into his belt, where it pressed comfortingly against his body. Then he continued his exploration.

In the wall cupboard he found two full bottles of liquor, which proved to be brandy. Leaving them there, he groped out of the cabin and returned to the upper deck in search of Miggs.

Miggs was leaning on the rail, watching something below. Yancy trudged toward him, calling out shrilly:

"Say, I got food, Miggs! Food and brand—"

He did not finish. Mechanically his eyes followed the direction of Miggs's stare, and he recoiled involuntarily as his words clipped into stifled silence. On the surface of the oily water below, huge sea snakes paddled against the ship's side—enormous slithering shapes, banded with streaks of black and red and yellow, vicious and repulsive.

"They're back," Miggs said quickly. "They know this ain't no proper ship. They come here out of their hell-hole, to wait for us."

Yancy glanced at him curiously. The inflection of Miggs' voice was peculiar—not at all the phlegmatic, gutteral tone that usually grumbled through the little man's lips. It was almost eager!

"What did you find?" Yancy faltered.

"Nothin'. All the ship's boats are hangin' in their davits. Never been touched."

"I found food," Yancy said abruptly, gripping his arm. "We'll eat, then we'll feel better. What the hell are we, anyhow—a couple of fools? Soon as we eat, we'll stock the dory and get off this blasted death ship and clear out of this stinkin' fog. We got water in the tarpaulin."

"We'll clear out? Will we, Nels?"

"Yah. Let's eat."

Once again, Yancy led the way below decks to the galley. There, after a twenty-minute effort in building a fire in the rusty stove, he and Miggs prepared a meal, carrying the food into the captain's cabin, where Yancy lighted the lamp.

They ate slowly, sucking the taste hungrily out of every mouthful, reluctant to finish. The lamplight, flickering in their faces, made gaunt masks of features that were already haggard and full of anticipation.

The brandy, which Yancy fetched out of the cupboard, brought back strength and reason—and confidence. It brought back, too, that unnatural sheen to Miggs' twitching eyes.

"We'd be damned fools to clear out of here right off," Miggs said suddenly. "The fog's got to lift sooner or later. I ain't trustin' myself to no small boat again. Nels—not when we don't know where we're at."

Yancy looked at him sharply. The little man turned away with a guilty shrug. Then hesitantly:

"I—I kinda like it here, Nels."

Yancy caught the odd gleam in those small eyes. He bent forward quickly.

"Where'd you go when I left you alone?" he demanded.

"Me? I didn't go nowhere. I—I just looked around a bit, and I picked a couple of them flowers. See."

Miggs groped in his shirt pocket and held up one of the livid, orange-colored blooms. His face took on an unholy brilliance as he held the thing close to his lips and inhaled its deadly aroma. His eyes, glittering across the table, were on fire with sudden fanatic lust.

For an instant Yancy did not move. Then, with a savage oath, he lurched up and snatched the flower out of Miggs's fingers. Whirling, he flung it to the floor and ground it under his boot.

"You damned thick-headed fool!" he screeched. "You— God help you!"

Then he went limp, muttering incoherently. With faltering steps he stumbled out of the cabin and along the black passageway, and up on the abandoned deck. He staggered to the rail and stood there, holding himself erect with nerveless hands.

"God!" he whispered hoarsely. "God—what did I do that for? Am I goin' crazy?"

No answer came out of the silence. But he knew the answer. The thing he had done down there in the skipper's cabin—those mad words that had spewed from his mouth—had been involuntary. Something inside him, some sense of danger that was all about him, had hurled the words out of his mouth before he could control them. And his nerves were on edge, too. They felt as though they were ready to crack.

But he knew instinctively that Miggs had made a terrible mistake. There was something unearthly and wicked about those sickly sweet flowers. Flowers didn't grow aboard ship. Not real flowers. Real flowers had to take root somewhere, and, besides, they didn't have that drunken, etherish odor. Miggs should have left the vine alone. Clinging at the rail there, Yancy *knew* it, without knowing why.

He stayed there for a long time, trying to think and get his nerves back again. In a little while he began to feel frightened, being alone, and he returned below-decks to the cabin.

He stopped in the doorway, and stared.

Miggs was still there, slumped grotesquely over the table. The bottle was empty. Miggs was drunk, unconscious, mercifully oblivious of his surroundings.

For a moment Yancy glared at him morosely. For a moment, too, a new fear tugged at Yancy's heart—fear of being left alone through the coming night. He yanked Miggs' arm and shook him savagely; but there was no response. It would be hours, long, dreary, sinister hours, before Miggs regained his senses.

Bitterly Yancy took the lamp and set about exploring the rest of the ship. If he could find the ship's papers, he considered, they might dispel his terror. He might learn the truth.

With this in mind, he sought the mate's quarters. The papers had not been in the captain's cabin where they belonged; therefore they might be here.

But they were not. There was nothing—nothing but a chronometer, sextant, and other nautical instruments lying in curious positions on the mate's table, rusted beyond repair. And there were flags, signal flags, thrown down as if they had been used at the last moment. And, lying in a distorted heap on the floor, was a human skeleton.

Avoiding this last horror, Yancy searched the room thoroughly. Evidently, he reasoned, the captain had died early in the *Golconda*'s unknown plague. The mate had brought these instruments, these flags, to his own cabin, only to succumb before he could use them.

Only one thing Yancy took with him when he went out: a lantern, rusty and brittle, but still serviceable. It was empty, but he poured oil into it from the lamp. Then, returning the lamp to the captain's quarters where Miggs lay unconscious, he went on deck.

He climbed the bridge and set the lantern beside him. Night was coming. Already the fog was lifting, allowing darkness to creep in beneath it. And so Yancy stood there, alone and helpless, while blackness settled with uncanny quickness over the entire ship.

He was being watched. He felt it. Invisible eyes, hungry and menacing, were keeping check on his movements. On the deck beneath him were those inexplicable flowers, trailing out of the unexplored hold, glowing like phosphorescent faces in the gloom.

"By God," Yancy mumbled, "I'm goin' to get out of here!"

His own voice startled him and caused him to stiffen and peer about him, as if someone else had uttered the words. And then, very suddenly, his eyes became fixed on the far horizon to starboard. His lips twitched open, spitting out a shrill cry.

"Miggs! Miggs! A light! Look, Miggs—"

Frantically he stumbled down from the bridge and clawed his way below decks to the mate's cabin. Feverishly he seized the signal flags. Then, clutching them in his hand, he moaned helplessly and let them fall. He realized that they were no good, no good in the dark. Gibbering to himself, he searched for rockets. There were none.

Suddenly he remembered the lantern. Back again he raced through the passage, on deck, up on the bridge. In another moment, with the lantern dangling from his arm, he was clambering higher and higher into the black spars of the mainmast. Again and again he slipped and caught himself with outflung hands. And at length he stood high above the deck, feet braced, swinging the lantern back and forth. . . .

Below him the deck was no longer silent, no longer abandoned. From bow to stern it was trembling, creaking, whispering up at him. He peered down fearfully. Blurred shadows seemed to be prowling through the darkness, coming out of nowhere, pacing dolefully back and forth through the gloom. They were watching him with a furtive interest.

He called out feebly. The muted echo of his own voice came back up to him. He was aware that the bell was tolling again, and the swish of the sea was louder, more persistent.

With an effort he caught a grip on himself.

"Damned fool," he rasped. "Drivin' yourself crazy—"

The moon was rising. It blurred the blinking light on the horizon and penetrated the darkness like a livid yellow finger. Yancy lowered the lantern with a sob. It was no good now. In the glare of the moonlight, this puny flame would be invisible to the men aboard that other ship. Slowly, cautiously, he climbed down to the deck.

He tried to think of something to do, to take his mind off the fear. Striding to the rail, he hauled up the water butts from the dory. Then he stretched the tarpaulin to catch the precipitation of the night dew. No telling how long he and Miggs would be forced to remain aboard the hulk.

He turned, then, to explore the forecastle. On his way across the deck, he stopped and held the light over the creeping vine. The curious flowers had become fragrant, heady, with the fumes of an intoxicating drug. He followed the coils to where they vanished into the hold, and he looked down. He saw only a tumbled pile of boxes and crates—barred boxes, which must have been cages at one time.

Again he turned away. The ship was trying to tell him something. He felt it—felt the movements of the deck planks beneath his feet. The moonlight, too, had made hideous white things of the scattered bones in the bow. Yancy stared at them with a shiver. He stared again, and grotesque thoughts obtruded into his consciousness. The bones were moving. Slithering, sliding over the deck, assembling themselves, gathering into definite shapes. He could have sworn it!

Cursing, he wrenched his eyes away. Damned fool, thinking such thoughts! With clenched fists he advanced to the forecastle; but before he reached it, he stopped again.

It was the sound of flapping wings that brought him about. Turning quickly, with a jerk, he was aware that the sound emanated from the open hold. Hesitantly he stepped forward—and stood rigid with an involuntary scream.

Out of the aperture came two horrible shapes—two inhuman things with immense, clapping wings and glittering eyes. Hideous; enormous. *Bats!*

Instinctively he flung his arm up to protect himself. But the creatures did not attack. They hung for an instant, poised over the hatch, eyeing him with something that was fiendishly like intelligence. Then they flapped over the deck, over the rail, and away into the night. As they sped away towards the west, where he had seen the light of the other ship twinkling, they clung together like witches hell-bent on some evil mission. And below them, in the bloated sea, huge snakes weaved smoky, golden patterns—waiting! . . .

He stood fast, squinting after the bats. Like two hellish black eyes they grew smaller and smaller, became pinpoints in the moon-glow, and finally vanished. Still he did not stir. His lips were dry, his body stiff and unnatural. He licked his mouth. Then he was conscious of something more. From somewhere behind him came a thin, throbbing threat of harmony—a lovely, utterly sweet musical note that fascinated him.

He turned slowly. His heart was hammering, surging. His eyes went suddenly wide.

There, not five feet from him, stood a human form. Not his imagination. Real!

But he had never seen a girl like her before. She was too beautiful.She was wild, almost savage, with her great dark eyes boring into him. Her skin was white, smooth as alabaster. Her hair was jet black; and a waving coil of it, like a broken cobweb of pitch strings, framed her face. Grotesque hoops of gold dangled from her ears. In her hair, above them, gleamed two of those sinister flowers from the straggling vine.

He did not speak; he simply gaped. The girl was barefoot, bare-legged. A short, dark skirt covered her slender thighs. A ragged white waist, open at the throat, revealed the full curve of her breast. In one hand she held a long wooden reed, a flutelike instrument fashioned out of crude wood. And about her middle, dangling almost to the deck, twined a scarlet, silken sash, brilliant as the sun, but not so scarlet as her lips, which were parted in a faint, suggestive smile, showing teeth of marble whiteness!

"Who—who are you?" Yancy mumbled.

She shook her head. Yet she smiled with her eyes, and he felt, somehow, that she understood him. He tried again, in such tongues as he knew. Still, she shook her head, and still he felt that she was mocking him. Not until he chanced upon a scattered, faltering greeting in Serbian, did she nod her head.

"Dobra!" she replied, in a husky, rich voice which sounded, somehow, as if it were rarely used.

He stepped closer then. She was a gipsy evidently. A Tzany of the Serbian hills. She moved very close to him with a floating, almost ethereal movement of her slender body. Peering into his face, flashing her haunting smile at him, she lifted the flutelike instrument and, as if it were nothing at all unnatural or out of place, began to play again the song which had first attracted his attention.

He listened in silence until she had finished. Then, with a cunning smile, she touched her fingers to her lips and whispered softly:

"You—mine. Yes?"

He did not understand. She clutched his arm and glanced fearfully toward the west, out over the sea.

"You—mine!" she said again, fiercely. "Papa Bocito—Seraphino—they no have you. You—not go—to them!"

He thought he understood then. She turned away from him and went silently across the deck. He watched her disappear into the forecastle, and would have followed her, but once again the ship—the whole ship—seemed to be struggling to whisper a warning.

Presently she returned, holding in her white hand a battered silver goblet, very old and very tarnished, brimming with scarlet fluid. He took it silently. It was impossible to refuse her. Her eyes had grown into lakes of night, lit by the burning moon. Her lips were soft, searching, undeniable.

"Who are you?" he whispered.

"Stragella," she smiled.

"Stragella . . . Stragella . . ."

The name itself was compelling. He drank the liquid slowly, without taking his eyes from her lovely face. The stuff had the taste of wine—strong, sweet wine. It was intoxicating, with the same weird effect that was contained in the orange blooms which she wore in her hair and which groveled over the deck behind her.

Yancy's hands groped up weakly. He rubbed his eyes, feeling suddenly weak, powerless, as if the very blood had been drained from his veins. Struggling futilely, he staggered back, moaning half inaudibly.

Stragella's arms went about him, caressing him with sensuous touch. He felt them, and they were powerful, irresistible. The girl's smile maddened him. Her crimson lips hung before his face, drawing nearer, mocking him. Then, all at once, she was seeking his throat. Those warm, passionate, deliriously pleasant lips were searching to touch him.

He sensed his danger. Frantically he strove to lift his arms and push her away. Deep in his mind some struggling intuition, some half-alive idea, warned him that he was in terrible peril. This girl, Stragella, was not of his kind; she was a creature of the darkness, a denizen of a different, frightful world of her own! Those lips, wanting his flesh, were inhuman, too fervid—

Suddenly she shrank away from him, releasing him with a jerk. A snarling animal-like sound surged through her flaming mouth. Her hand lashed out, rigid, pointing to the thing that hung in his belt. Talonic fingers pointed to the Bible that defied her!

But the scarlet fluid had taken its full effect. Yancy slumped down, unable to cry out. In a heap he lay there, paralyzed, powerless to stir.

He knew that she was commanding him to rise. Her lips, moving in panto-mime, forming soundless words. Her glittering eyes were fixed upon him, hyp-notic. The Bible—she wanted him to cast it over the rail! She wanted him to stand up and go into her arms. Then her lips would find a hold. . . .

But he could not obey. He could not raise his arms to support himself. She, in turn, stood at bay and refused to advance. Then, whirling about, her lips drawn into a diabolical curve, beautiful but bestial, she retreated. He saw her dart back, saw her tapering body whip about, with the crimson sash outflung behind her as she raced across the deck.

Yancy closed his eyes to blot out the sight. When he opened them again, they opened to a new, more intense horror. On the *Golconda*'s deck, Stragella was darting erratically among those piles of gleaming bones. But they were bones no longer. They had gathered into shapes, taken on flesh, blood. Before his very eyes they assumed substance, men and beasts alike. And then began an orgy such as Nels Yancy had never before looked upon—an orgy of the undead.

Monkeys, giant apes, lunged about the deck. A huge python reared its sinuous head to glare. On the hatch cover a snow-leopard, snarling furiously, crouched to spring. Tigers, tapirs, crocodiles—fought together in the bow. A great brown bear, of the type found in the lofty plateaus of the Pamirs, clawed at the rail.

And the men! Most of them were dark-skinned—dark enough to have come from the same region, from Madras. With them crouched Chinamen, and some Anglo-Saxons. Starved, all of them. Lean, gaunt, mad!

Pandemonium raged then. Animals and men alike were insane with hunger. In a little struggling knot, the men were gathered about the number-two hatch, defending themselves. They were wielding firearms—firing point-blank with desperation into the writhing mass that confronted them. And always, between them and around them and among, darted the girl who called herself Stragella.

They cast no shadows, those ghost shapes. Not even the girl, whose arms he had felt about him only a moment ago. There was nothing real in the scene, nothing human. Even the sounds of the shots and the screams of the cornered men, even the roaring growls of the big cats, were smothered as if they came to him through heavy glass windows, from a sealed chamber.

He was powerless to move. He lay in a cataleptic condition, conscious of the entire pantomime, yet unable to flee from it. And his senses were horribly acute—so acute that he turned his eyes upward with an abrupt twitch, instinc-tively, and then shrank into himself with a new fear as he discerned the two huge bats which had winged their way across the sea. . . .

They were returning now. Circling above him, they flapped down one after the other and settled with heavy, sullen thuds upon the hatch, close to that weird vine of flowers. They seemed to have lost their shape, these nocturnal monstros-ities, to have become fantastic blurs, enveloped in an unearthly bluish radiance. Even as he stared at them, they vanished altogether for a moment; and then the strange vapor cleared to reveal the two creatures who stood there!

Not bats! Humans! Inhumans! They were gipsies, attired in moldy, decayed garments which stamped them as Balkans. Man and woman. Lean, emaciated, ancient man with fierce white mustache, plump old woman with black, rat-like eyes that seemed unused to the light of day. And they spoke to Stragella—spoke to her eagerly. She, in turn, swung about with enraged face and pointed to the Bible in Yancy's belt.

But the pantomime was not finished. On the deck the men and animals lay moaning, sobbing. Stragella turned noiselessly, calling the old man and woman after her. Calling them by name.

"Come—Papa Bocito, Seraphino!"

The tragedy of the ghost ship was being reenacted. Yancy knew it, and shuddered at the thought. Starvation, cholera had driven the *Golconda*'s crew mad. The jungle beasts, unfed, hideously savage, had escaped out of their confinement. And now—now that the final conflict was over—Stragella and Papa Bocito and Seraphino were proceeding about their ghastly work.

Stragella was leading them. Her charm, her beauty, gave her a hold on the men. They were in love with her. She had *made* them love her, madly and without reason. Now she was moving from one to another, loving them and holding them close to her. And as she stepped away from each man, he went limp, faint, while she laughed terribly and passed on to the next. Her lips were parted. She licked them hungrily—licked the blood from them with a sharp, crimson tongue.

How long it lasted, Yancy did not know. Hours, hours on end. He was aware, suddenly, that a high wind was screeching and wailing in the upper reaches of the ship; and, peering up, he saw that the spars were no longer bare and rotten with age. Great gray sails stood out against the black sky—fantastic things without any definite form or outline. And the moon above them had vanished utterly. The howling wind was bringing a storm with it, filling the sails to bulging proportions. Beneath the decks the ship was groaning like a creature in agony. The seas were lashing her, slashing her, carrying her forward with amazing speed.

Of a sudden came a mighty grinding sound. The *Golconda* hurtled back, as if a huge, jagged reef of submerged rock had bored into her bottom. She listed. Her stern rose high in the air. And Stragella, with her two fellow fiends, was standing in the bow, screaming in mad laughter in the teeth of the wind. The other two laughed with her.

Yancy saw them turn toward him, but they did not stop. Somehow, he did not expect them to stop. This scene, this mad pantomime, was not the present; it was the past. He was not here at all. All this had happened years ago! Forgotten, buried in the past!

But he heard them talking, in a mongrel dialect full of Serbian words.

"It is done, Papa Bocito! We shall stay here forever now. There is land within an hour's flight, where fresh blood abounds and will always abound. And here, on this wretched hulk, they will never find our graves to destroy us!"

The horrible trio passed close. Stragella turned, to stare out across the water, and raised her hand in silent warning. Yancy, turning wearily to stare in the same direction, saw that the first streaks of daylight were beginning to filter over the sea.

With a curious floating, drifting movement the three undead creatures moved toward the open hatch. They descended out of sight. Yancy, jerking himself erect and surprised to find that the effects of the drug had worn off with the coming of dawn, crept to the hatch and peered down—in time to see those fiendish forms enter their coffins. He knew then what the crates were. In the dim light, now that he was staring directly into the aperture, he saw what he had not noticed before. Three of those oblong boxes were filled with dank grave-earth!

He knew then the secret of the unnatural flowers. They *had* roots! They were rooted in the soil which harbored those undead bodies!

Then, like a groping finger, the dawn came out of the sea. Yancy walked to the rail, dazed. It was over now—all over. The orgy was ended. The *Golconda* was once more an abandoned, rotted hulk.

For an hour he stood at the rail, sucking in the warmth and glory of the sunlight. Once again that wall of unsightly mist was rising out of the water on all sides. Presently it would bury the ship, and Yancy shuddered.

He thought of Miggs. With quick steps he paced to the companionway and descended to the lower passage. Hesitantly he prowled through the thickening layers of dank fog. A queer sense of foreboding crept over him.

He called out even before he reached the door. There was no answer. Thrusting the barrier open, he stepped across the sill—and then he stood still while a sudden harsh cry broke from his lips.

Miggs was lying there, half across the table, his arms flung out, his head turned grotesquely on its side, staring up at the ceiling.

"Miggs! Miggs!" The sound came choking through Yancy's lips. "Oh, God, Miggs—what's happened?"

He reeled forward. Miggs was cold and stiff, and quite dead. All the blood was gone out of his face and arms. His eyes were glassy, wide open. He was as white as marble, shrunken horribly. In his throat were two parallel marks, as if a sharp-pointed staple had been hammered into the flesh and then withdrawn. The marks of the vampire.

For a long time Yancy did not retreat. The room swayed and lurched before him. He was alone. Alone! The whole ghastly thing was too sudden, too unexpected.

Then he stumbled forward and went down on his knees, clawing at Miggs' dangling arm.

"Oh God, Miggs," he mumbled incoherently. "You got to help me. I can't stand it!"

He clung there, white-faced, staring, sobbing thickly—and presently slumped in a pitiful heap, dragging Miggs over on top of him.

It was late afternoon when he regained consciousness. He stood up, fighting away the fear that overwhelmed him. He had to get away, get away! The thought hammered into his head with monotonous force. Get away!

He found his way to the upper deck. There was nothing he could do for Miggs. He would have to leave him here. Stumbling, he moved along the rail and reached down to draw the small boat closer, where he could provision it and make it ready for his departure.

His fingers clutched emptiness. The ropes were gone. The dory was gone. He hung limp, staring down at a flat expanse of oily sea.

For an hour he did not move. He fought to throw off his fear long enough to think of a way out. Then he stiffened with a sudden jerk and pushed himself away from the rail.

The ship's boats offered the only chance. He groped to the nearest one and labored feverishly over it.

But the task was hopeless. The life boats were of metal, rusted through and through, wedged in their davits. The wire cables were knotted and immovable. He tore his hands on them, wringing blood from his scarred fingers. Even while he worked, he knew that the boats would not float. They were rotten, through and through.

He had to stop, at last, from exhaustion.

After that, knowing that there was no escape, he had to do something, anything, to keep sane. First he would clear those horrible bones from the deck, then explore the rest of the ship. . . .

It was a repulsive task, but he drove himself to it. If he could get rid of the bones, perhaps Stragella and the other two creatures would not return. He did not know. It was merely a faint hope, something to cling to.

With grim, tight-pressed lips he dragged the bleached skeletons over the deck and kicked them over the side, and stood watching them as they sank from sight. Then he went to the hold, smothering his terror, and descended into the gloomy belly of the vessel. He avoided the crates with a shudder of revulsion. Ripping up that evil vine-thing by the roots, he carried it to the rail and flung it away, with the mold of grave earth still clinging to it.

After that he went over the entire ship, end to end, but found nothing.

He slipped the anchor chains then, in the hopes that the ship would drift away from that vindictive bank of fog. Then he paced back and forth, muttering to himself and trying to force courage for the most hideous task of all.

The sea was growing dark, and with dusk came increasing terror. He knew the *Golconda* was drifting. Knew, too, that the undead inhabitants of the vessel were furious with him for allowing the boat to drift away from their source of food. Or they *would* be furious when they came alive again after their interim of forced sleep.

And there was only one method of defeating them. It was a horrible method, and he was already frightened. Nevertheless he searched the deck for a marlin spike and found one; and, turning sluggishly, he went back to the hold.

A stake, driven through the heart of each of the horrible trio. . . .

The rickety stairs were steep in shadow. Already the dying sun, buried behind its wreath of evil fog, was a ring of bloody mist. He glanced at it and realized that he must hurry. He cursed himself for having waited so long.

It was hard, lowering himself into the pitch-black hold when he could only feel his footing and trust to fate. His boots scraped ominously on the steps. He held his hands above him, gripping the deck timbers.

And suddenly he slipped.

His foot caught on the edge of a lower step, twisted abruptly, and pitched him forward. He cried out. The marlin spike dropped from his hand and clattered on one of the crates below. He tumbled in a heap, clawing for support. The impact knocked something out of his belt. And he realized, even as his head came in sharp contact with the foremost oblong box, that the Bible, which had heretofore protected him, was no longer a part of him.

He did not lose complete control of his senses. Frantically he sought to regain his knees and grope for the black book in the gloom of the hold. A sobbing, choking sound came pitifully from his lips.

A soft, triumphant laugh came out of the darkness close to him. He swung about heavily—so heavily that the movement sent him sprawling again in an inert heap.

He was too late. She was already there on her knees, glaring at him hungrily. A peculiar bluish glow welled about her face. She was ghastly beautiful as she reached behind her into the oblong crate and began to trace a circle about the Bible with a chunk of soft, tarry, pitch-like substance clutched in her white fingers.

Yancy stumbled toward her, finding strength in desperation. She straightened to meet him. Her lips, curled back, exposed white teeth. Her arms coiled out, enveloping him, stifling his struggles. God, they were strong. He could not resist them. The same languid, resigned feeling came over him. He would have fallen, but she held him erect.

She did not touch him with her lips. Behind her he saw two other shapes take form in the darkness. The savage features of Papa Bocito glowered at him; and Seraphino's ratty, smoldering eyes, full of hunger, bored into him. Stragella was obviously afraid of them.

Yancy was lifted from his feet. He was carried out on deck and borne swiftly, easily, down the companionway, along the lower passage, through a swirling blanket of hellish fog and darkness, to the cabin where Miggs lay dead. And he lost consciousness while they carried him.

He could not tell, when he opened his eyes, how long he had been asleep. It seemed a long, long interlude. Stragella was sitting beside him. He lay on the bunk in the cabin, and the lamp was burning on the table, revealing Miggs's limp body in full detail.

Yancy reached up fearfully to touch his throat. There were no marks there, not yet.

He was aware of voices, then. Papa Bocito and the ferret-faced woman were arguing with the girl beside him. The savage old man in particular was being angered by her cool, possessive smile.

"We are drifting away from the prison isles," Papa Bocito snarled, glancing at Yancy with unmasked hate. "It is his work, lifting the anchor. Unless you share him with us until we drift ashore, we shall perish!"

"He is mine," Stragella shrugged, modulating her voice to a persuasive whisper. "You had the other. This one is mine. I shall have him!"

"He belongs to us all!"

"Why?" Stragella smiled. "Because he has looked upon the resurrection night? Ah, he is the first to learn our secret."

Seraphino's eyes narrowed at that, almost to pinpoints. She jerked forward, clutching the girl's shoulder.

"We have quarreled enough," she hissed. "Soon it will be daylight. He belongs to us all because he has taken us away from the isles and learned our secrets."

The words drilled their way into Yancy's brain. "The resurrection night!" There was an ominous significance in it, and he thought he knew its meaning. His eyes, or his face, must have revealed his thoughts, for Papa Bocito drew near to him and pointed into his face with a long, bony forefinger, muttering triumphantly.

"You have seen what no other eyes have seen," the ancient man growled bitterly. "Now, for that, you shall become one of us. Stragella wants you. She shall have you for eternity—for a life without death. Do you know what that means?"

Yancy shook his head dumbly, fearfully.

"We are the undead," Bocito leered. "Our victims become creatures of the blood, like us. At night we are free. During the day we must return to our graves. That is why"—he cast his arm toward the upper deck in a hideous gesture—"those other victims of ours have not yet become like us. They were never buried; they have no graves to return to. Each night we give them life for our own amusement, but they are not of the brotherhood—yet."

Yancy licked his lips and said nothing. He understood then. Every night it happened. A nightly pantomime, when the dead became alive again, reenacting the events of the night when the *Golconda* had become a ship of hell.

"We are gipsies," the old man gloated. "Once we were human, living in our pleasant little camp in the shadow of Pobyezdin Potok's crusty peaks, in the Morava Valley of Serbia. That was in the time of Milutin, six hundreds of years ago. Then the vampires of the hills came for us and took us to them. We lived the undead life until there was no more blood in the valley. So we went to the coast, we three, transporting our grave earth with us. And we lived there, alive by night and dead by day, in the coastal villages of the Black Sea, until the time came when we wished to go to the far places."

Seraphino's guttural voice interrupted him, saying harshly:

"Hurry. It is nearly dawn!"

"And we obtained passage on this *Golconda,* arranging to have our crates of grave earth carried secretly to the hold. And the ship fell into cholera and starvation and storm. She went aground. And—here we are. Ah, but there is blood upon the islands, my pretty one, and so we anchored the *Golconda* on the reef, where life was close at hand!''

Yancy closed his eyes with a shudder. He did not understand all of the words. They were a jargon of gipsy tongue. But he knew enough to horrify him.

Then the old man ceased gloating. He fell back, glowering at Stragella. And the girl laughed, a mad, cackling, triumphant laugh of possession. She leaned forward, and the movement brought her out of the line of the lamplight, so that the feeble glow fell full over Yancy's prostrate body.

At that, with an angry snarl, she recoiled. Her eyes went wide with abhorrence. Upon his chest gleamed the crucifix—the tattooed cross and savior which had been indelibly printed there. Stragella held her face away, shielding her eyes. She cursed him horribly. Backing away, she seized the arms of her companions and pointed with trembling finger to the thing which had repulsed her.

The fog seemed to seep deeper and deeper into the cabin during the ensuing silence. Yancy struggled to a sitting posture and cringed back against the wall, waiting for them to attack him. It would be finished in a moment, he knew. Then he would join Miggs, with those awful marks on his throat and Stragella's lips crimson with his sucked blood.

But they held their distance. The fog enveloped them, made them almost indistinct. He could see only three pairs of glaring, staring, phosphorescent eyes that grew larger and wider and more intensely terrible.

He buried his face in his hands, waiting. They did not come. He heard them mumbling, whispering. Vaguely he was conscious of another sound, far off and barely audible. The howl of wolves.

Beneath him the bunk was swaying from side to side with the movement of the ship. The *Golconda* was drifting swiftly. A storm had risen out of nowhere, and the wind was singing its dead dirge in the rotten spars high above decks. He could hear it moaning, wheezing, like a human being in torment.

Then the three pairs of glittering orbs moved nearer. The whispered voices ceased, and a cunning smile passed over Stragella's features. Yancy screamed, and flattened against the wall. He watched her in fascination as she crept upon him. One arm was flung across her eyes to protect them from the sight of the Crucifix. In the other hand, outstretched, groping ever nearer, she clutched that hellish chunk of pitchlike substance with which she had encircled the Bible!

He knew what she would do. The thought struck him like an icy blast, full of fear and madness. She would slink closer, closer, until her hand touched his flesh. Then she would place the black substance around the tattooed cross and kill its powers. His defense would be gone. Then—those cruel lips on his throat. . . .

There was no avenue of escape. Papa Bocito and the plump old woman, grinning malignantly, had slid to one side, between him and the doorway. And Stragella writhed forward with one alabaster arm feeling . . . feeling. . . .

He was conscious of the roar of surf, very close, very loud, outside the walls of the fog-filled enclosure. The ship was lurching, reeling heavily, pitching in the swell. Hours must have passed. Hours and hours of darkness and horror.

Then she touched him. The sticky stuff was hot on his chest, moving in a slow circle. He hurled himself back, stumbled, went down, and she fell upon him.

Under his tormented body the floor of the cabin split asunder. The ship buckled from top to bottom with a grinding, roaring impact. A terrific shock burst through the ancient hulk, shattering its rotted timbers.

The lamp caromed off the table, plunging the cabin in semi-darkness. Through the port-holes filtered a gray glare. Stragella's face, thrust into Yancy's, became a mask of beautiful fury. She whirled back. She stood rigid, screaming lividly to Papa Bocito and the old hag.

"Go back! Go back!" she riled. "We have waited too long! It is dawn!"

She ran across the floor, grappling with them. Her lips were distorted. Her body trembled. She hurled her companions to the door. Then, as she followed them into the gloom of the passage, she turned upon Yancy with a last unholy snarl of defeated rage. And she was gone.

Yancy lay limp. When he struggled to his feet at last and went on deck, the sun was high in the sky, bloated and crimson, struggling to penetrate the cone of fog which swirled about the ship.

The ship lay far over, careened on her side. A hundred yards distant over the port rail lay the heaven-sent sight of land—a bleak, vacant expanse of jungle-rimmed shore line.

He went deliberately to work—a task that had to be finished quickly, lest he be discovered by the inhabitants of the shore and be considered stark mad. Returning to the cabin, he took the oil lamp and carried it to the open hold. There, sprinkling the liquid over the ancient wood, he set fire to it.

Turning, he stepped to the rail. A scream of agony, unearthly and prolonged, rose up behind him. Then he was over the rail, battling in the surf.

When he staggered up on the beach, twenty minutes later, the *Golconda* was a roaring furnace. On all sides of her the flames snarled skyward, spewing through that hellish cone of vapor. Grimly Yancy turned away and trudged along the beach.

He looked back after an hour of steady plodding. The lagoon was empty. The fog had vanished. The sun gleamed down with warm brilliance on a broad, empty expanse of sea.

Hours later he reached a settlement. Men came and talked to him, and asked curious questions. They pointed to his hair, which was stark white. They told him he had reached Port Blair, on the southern island of the Andamans. After that, noticing the peculiar gleam of his blood-shot eyes, they took him to the home of the governor.

There he told his story—told it hesitantly, because he expected to be disbelieved, mocked.

The governor looked at him critically.

"You don't expect me to understand?" the governor said. "I am not so sure, sir. This is a penal colony, a prison isle. During the past few years, more than two hundred of our convicts have died in the most curious way. Two tiny punctures in the throat. Loss of blood.''

"You—you must destroy the graves," Yancy muttered.

The governor nodded silently, significantly.

After that, Yancy returned to the world, alone. Always alone. Men peered into his face and shrank away from the haunted stare of his eyes. They saw the crucifix upon his chest and wondered why, day and night, he wore his shirt flapping open, so that the brilliant design glared forth.

But their curiosity was never appeased. Only Yancy knew; and Yancy was silent.

THE THIRSTY DEAD

RAYMOND WHETSTONE

Typical shudder-pulp stories worked out elaborate if farfetched rationales to show how events of seemingly supernatural origin were merely devious subterfuges masterminded by mad scientists or perverted powermongers. The best of these tales, however, left open to speculation whether a supernatural explanation could be dismissed entirely. "The Thirsty Dead," with its suggestion that the vampire-haunted narrator may not be entirely reliable, is such a story.

I HAD SEEN HIM a number of times before, that little spiderlike old man, but never at such close range. Previously I had contented myself with peering through a spyglass at his house, squatting like a leprous toad in its setting of withered, dying maples. Sometimes he would come out on the porch, a tiny black figure, moving about restlessly as though he knew I was watching him, and at those times his appearance always aroused in me a strange, crawling feeling of dread. Nor was that feeling due entirely to the half fearsome whispers about him, hushed words more awful in their implications than in their actual meaning. Even from a distance I could tell there was something wrong with him—something almost unthinkable. Could it be that those ghastly hints about him were true?

Although he lived but a stone's throw from Willoughby, he never came to the village. Once a week Helga, his housekeeper, hobbled into the general store to buy supplies. She was a hideous old hag with a perpetual sneer on her pock-marked face and a body bent and twisted like a solitary, wind-tortured tree.

Needless to say, the villagers feared her almost as much as they feared her master. "She, too, has the evil eye," they would mutter darkly. "She, too, has given her soul to the devil!" And they would hastily make the sign of the cross every time they caught a glimpse of her.

I had gone out for a walk early that autumn afternoon, wishing to take a vacation from the novel I was writing. The forest fires were beginning to blaze in the woods through which I passed. Crimson oaks vied with yellow maples in brilliance. Along the stream bank I followed flamed a scarlet line of cat-briers, while in the distance towered a single white ash whose leaves were turning a golden bronze. I strode along, exulting in this lavish display of beauty, filling my lungs with the clean sharp air, taking no thought of time.

Gradually the hours slipped by. The sun sunk lower, winked out behind a violet line of hills. Darkness impalpable as fine dust sifted about me. Realizing how late it was getting, I started back toward Willoughby. I knew that my landlady, a motherly old creature, would become worried about me if I stayed away too long.

It was impossible for him to have known that I was coming. I had made no noise as I emerged from the woods. And yet he was waiting for me beside the road, a dusty lantern swinging from his arm. A cold wind seemed to blow through me as I caught sight of that misshapen figure and stared into those gleaming eyes.

"Well?" The word seemed to burst from my lips.

"My name's Moore—Philip Moore. You've probably heard of me." His voice had the reedy pitch of senility, unpleasant yet pathetic. "I—I was wondering whether you'd care to visit me this evening. My house is only a short distance away."

"I'm sorry, but I can't, Mr. Moore. It's getting late and I'm due at my boardinghouse right now. Some other time, perhaps." I had drawn back sharply as he came closer to me. I'm not exactly squeamish about such things, but the very air about him seemed to reek with contamination. Then, too, that queer, unaccountable feeling that he was horribly abnormal—unhuman in some way— intensified my uneasiness. I began to walk away.

"Don't go. Please don't go." His bony fingers plucked at my sleeve, his thin face thrust close to mine. "Don't believe the awful things they've been saying about me," he quavered. "They're lies! Monstrous lies! You know I couldn't harm you, even if I wanted to. Look how weak and old I am. Be my guest, if only for an hour. I've been so lonely with nobody but that stupid housekeeper to talk to. It's such a little thing I'm asking of you—just an hour of your company. You—you'll do it, won't you?"

I hesitated, pity and curiosity struggling with my sense of dread and loathing. After all, what was there to be afraid of? The man didn't look capable of hurting a fly. And he was so eager for my companionship that I felt sorry for him. I knew what terrible things loneliness could do to one. Besides, I was anxious to see what that house of his looked like from the inside. There had been as many strange tales told about it as about its owner.

"Very well," I agreed reluctantly. "But I warn you, I can't stay more than an hour."

A light seemed to flash across his countenance, bringing every sharp feature into relief. I glimpsed two blazing hypnotic eyes, a hawklike nose with distended nostrils, and parchment-thin lips drawn back. . . . The effect was only momentary, but it turned the blood to ice in my veins.

"You will come, then?" he shrilled in triumph, like that of a deformed, incredibly ancient child. "You will come? Ah, my friend, how good you are to me! You are young. You have the joy of life in you—a joy that I have almost forgotten. Perhaps you will help me to taste the zest of life again—to grow young. . . . Perhaps."

And even then I did not know. I did not understand what he meant. I followed him blindly, stupidly—as a sheep follows a butcher.

We went up a winding path and through a weed-grown yard. Before us loomed the house, gloomy and forbidding, its dark windows staring vacantly like sightless eyes. Swiftly my host led the way across the rotting front porch and threw open the door. Air, dank and cold, rushed out, enveloping me like a suffocating blanket. I coughed once, felt irritated when the old man chuckled mirthlessly.

Revealed by the light from the lantern, the room we entered was dim and ghostly and seemed extraordinarily large. Many chairs and tables dotted the floor, while along one wall ran a massive fireplace flanked by empty shelves which once might have contained books. A film of dust lay over everything and cobwebs hung in festoons from windows and ceiling. The odor of decay was strong in my nostrils.

"I seldom use it," the old man whispered, evidently guessing what was in my mind. "I keep it closed, except when I entertain guests."

"And do you have many of them?" I could not help asking.

"You are the first . . . in a long time." Once more his face underwent that metamorphosis which had startled me so while we were along the road. I felt his hand on my arm, and I jerked away as though from the touch of reptilian scales.

"But I am forgetting my duties as a host." Slowly that gleam of obscene triumph went out of his eyes. Beyond a slight twitching of his mouth, his features were composed again. "Make yourself at home while I get some wood," he told me softly. "It's too chilly in here to do without a fire."

I sank into a chair, not realizing until that moment my overpowering fatigue. Setting the lantern on a nearby table, he glided across the floor and disappeared through a door in the other side of the room. I heard a feminine voice, quickly hushed by a muttered word or two from the old man. Then the door swung shut.

I was alone in that shadowy, mysterious room. Alone, and suddenly filled with a ghastly fear that choked the breath in my throat, squeezed my heart with its skeleton hands. I knew intuitively I was in horrible danger, knew I should escape while there was still time. Why I was so cold with terror I did not even try to discover. I only knew that this fear was real, almost a physical thing. Yet I couldn't. Some power—that weird sense of fatigue—stronger than my own will, kept me from moving, bound me as though by invisible chains to the chair in which I sat. Unable to help myself, I awaited whatever was to come.

The old man returned, carrying a heavy load of wood. Deftly he arranged the fuel in the fireplace, struck a match. Soon flames were darting up the black maw of the chimney and throwing waves of heat into the room. I leaned forward, forgetful of my fear, of that strange, heavy lassitude, my chilled body eagerly absorbing the warmth. I could feel the old man watching me, knew he was smiling, even though his face was in shadow.

For some time neither of us moved or said a word. Then the old man walked over to a tall cabinet that stood in one corner of the room and took out a worn violin case. Bringing it back to the fireplace, he opened the lid reverently. Inside on a bed of blue velvet lay a magnificent Stradivarius, its polished wood gleaming in the firelight. I gasped as I realized its value.

"It was Paganini's instrument—Paganini, the greatest violinist of all time!" The old man spoke dreamily, his eyes on the priceless thing in his hands. "He himself gave it to me before he died."

"Before he died?" I echoed in amazement. "But Paganini has been dead— for almost a hundred years!"

He paid no attention to my words. "Some say Paganini learned his technique from the devil," he went on, speaking more to himself than to me. "But who should know that better than I? Did not the same master teach us both?"

There was no doubt about it. The man was mad. Raving mad. Shuddering, I attempted to rise from my chair. But he motioned me to sit still. "I will play for you!" he cried fiercely. "I will play as Paganini might play—were he alive tonight!"

How can I tell of his music? How can one describe color to a blind man? The flame of his genius brought vital, throbbing life to the instrument in his hands. He swept his bow across the strings and a slow, seductive melody filled that shadow-haunted room. There was something hypnotic about its steady, unchanging rhythm—something which gave me a false sense of peace and security. Mesmerized by that clear stream of sound, I leaned back, surrendering myself to an overpowering lassitude, a glorious crowd of visions pouring through my mind.

Gradually, almost imperceptibly, the music changed. A minor strain crept into it, defiling its purity. It was sinister and threatening now, a rushing flood of discordant sounds. The visions, too, were different. Hideous faces leered at me, clawed at me with fleshless hands. Grinning skulls floated around me, mouthing horrible obscenities. A screaming horde fought for a rotting shroud. That clear, limpid stream had become a foul muddy torrent from hell!

He had put down the violin and was slowly approaching me. Still under the spell of his diabolical music, unable to move a muscle, I saw the gloating look in his eyes, saw his lips writhe back from his sharp teeth. Saliva trickled from one corner of his mouth. . . .

"I have waited long . . . so long!" he mumbled, bending over me. "But now . . . now I can drink until I am satisfied!"

Then, like a ravenous beast he tore at my shirt, ripped it open. Clammy lips fastened on my throat, clung there. Pointed teeth sought my jugular vein! Sweat pricked through my skin as I strove to release myself from the awful paralysis which gripped me. It was useless. I could not so much as lift a finger to protect my body—*my soul*—from the malevolent Thing which had attacked me.

Suddenly Helga, the witchlike housekeeper, was in the room, her eyes blazing insanely, her skinny fist clutching a gleaming knife. "You child of Hell!" she shrieked. "Did you not promise to share him with me?" And a flood of vile curses spewed from her twisted mouth.

The Thing raised dripping jaws and lunged at her. Biting, clawing, they went down in a furious tangle of squirming bodies. Again and again Helga stabbed at the old man. But either she did not reach a vital spot or else he could not be harmed by an ordinary weapon, for the knife thrusts seemed to have no effect on him. The fight raged on, rendered more horrible by acts of sadistic hate.

And then—crowning horror—the room began to fill with weird and terrible shapes! I knew that hellish music had summoned them, knew, too, the reason for their coming. Vague and amorphous they were, twisting and curling, hardly more tangible than smoke or fog. But each one of them had a cruel, hungry mouth and eyes which were bright with blood lust! Slowly, inexorably, they drew nearer . . . ever nearer.

Sheer terror, then, must have snapped the invisible bond inside my brain. I was free, miraculously free, of the hypnotic spell which had held me a prisoner. Screaming like a lost soul, I raced for the door, flung it open. Behind me rose a fiendish clamor. I stumbled down the steps, the pack of hell-hounds close at my heels. A dozen yards away gurgled the little stream along which I had walked that afternoon. Desperately I strove to reach and cross it, to lose myself in the clean, dark, friendly woods beyond.

I was almost there when my foot caught in a root. I fell to the ground with stunning force. Before I could rise they were swarming over me, their slobbering ice-cold lips glued to my quivering flesh. Merciful oblivion descended upon me, blotting out my horror and agony. . . .

I have been here for a long time now. The doctor pays me a visit every day. He is very patient and kind, but he keeps insisting that I had an attack of brain fever up there in the woods. He laughs at me when I tell him what actually happened. Damn him! Does he think he can fool me? Why can't he explain the unaccountable lengthening and sharpening of my canine teeth? Why does he turn his head away when I ask him what caused those wounds in my neck?

The nurse, too, is kind. She is a pretty girl with a long smooth throat in which a tiny pulse beats. That pulse fascinates me. I have an insane desire to press my mouth to it, to tear and rend—Oh, God! Oh, merciless God! Is there no hope? Is there nothing that can save me? Am I one of them already?

I am told that the old man and his housekeeper have disappeared. The house is no longer occupied. I can well believe that, for every night I can see their evil faces outside the window, gloating over me. Every night I can hear the hellish strains of the violin, calling to me, commanding me to come!

How can I fight against them any longer? I am so tired—so very tired. How long must I wait before I join them?

MURDER BRIDES

ARTHUR J. BURKS

Arthur J. Burks was the quintessential pulpsmith, a writer who knew how to tailor his fiction for any market. "Murder Brides," one of his typical contributions to Horror Stories, *was standard shudder-pulp fare, with a healthy dose of erotic suggestion, a perfectly logical explanation for its bizarre events, and just the slightest suggestion that its characters might really be immortal vampires.*

CHAPTER ONE
The Beginning

THE FEELING of strangeness, of unreality, which sent fear crawling along my spine like speeding termites, came to me when I swung into the narrow path which ran beside the Swamp of Hawkwold, two miles from my residence in Georgeville, a remote little country village. I seldom walked, being a bit lazy, but my car was in the shop for repairs, so I did the next best thing: I took the Hawkwold shortcut. I didn't believe, never had, the wild, eerie stories which were told of the place. I was a gross materialist.

It was said that peculiar cries were sometimes heard in the dead of night, among the gloomy trees which bordered the Hawkwold. Some said the sounds were the wails of women in mortal agony. Others believed they were the moan-ings of lost souls, ghosts of people who could not find their way out of the bogs in the swamp where they had died, down the years.

I did know that it was an unhealthy place, where mosquitoes bred in summer, a silent place where wind seldom was able to blow away the miasmatic vapors. The water was black as midnight, perhaps because of decayed matter far below. There was quicksand, of course. The trees, even in midsummer green, had a dead look. That sounds peculiar, I am sure, but it was the truth. If I had had it to do over again, I would have taken the long way around, by the main-traveled road. But there was another reason for the shortcut: I had cussed out too many pedestrians, when driving my own car, to tempt other motorists to the same blasphemy by walking.

All of which is very prosaic. I was just a lazy man walking cross-lots, and wishing I didn't have to walk at all, with perhaps a little tremor of doubt when I thought of the swamp, so close at hand. I had but to jump off the trail at my right, to vanish from the face of the earth forever, and not a living soul would be the wiser. Not that it would have mattered in my case, for I was not only alone in the world, but liked being alone. I had fled from Greenwich Village, in New York City, to escape people—all sorts of people, especially peculiar people.

A chill caressed me as I took the first turn, and moonlight glowed fleetingly upon the black water. There was something menacing about that black expanse with black ferns dotting it like voodoo islands. It made me think of some ebon monster, getting set to spring at my throat, clutch me, drag me to its depths.

"Nonsense!" I told myself. "You're letting the stories of the ignorant get the best of you."

But the feeling kept growing, reminding me of something which had been told me by the only psychometrist I had ever visited.

"You, Claude Dern, are one of the most psychic of men ever to visit me."

He had almost sold me on the idea, so much so, in fact, that after I thought it over a bit I resolved never to go back to the fellow.

Now I remembered. Memory came roaring back like a tidal wave, whose waters were as black as Hawkwold. I hunched my neck deeper into my shoulders, like a turtle. In spite of myself my eyes began to search the gloom for monsters of nightmare, fully expecting to find them. I remembered dreams of my youth, when shapeless black creatures out of the unwritten past had silently thronged my bedchamber, and I had pulled the covers over my head, almost smothering, to escape them.

The limbs of trees raked my face, and they were like skeleton hands, clutching. They were, it seemed to me, in league with Hawkwold, to capture me for the maw of some black monster. I was working myself into a blue funk, which was unusual for me, and all the more frightening because it *was* unusual. I wanted to blame it on indigestion—but it wasn't that. There *were* monsters in the swamp, and the trees were their servitors, grasping for the unwary! I didn't run, though I wanted to, for a strange reason: By running I would make more noise with my feet and bring the monsters faster.

"Ho-ho," I laughed to myself, without conviction. "I'll pretend that all the stories I've heard are true—and get myself a new thrill."

I was, you see, suddenly the small boy whistling in the dark to keep up his courage.

By the time I had traversed half that portion of the shortcut, which paralleled the black shore of the ebon swamp—my shoes oozing in and out of the slime when I missed brief turns on the trail—I was in a mental condition bordering almost on hysteria. For all the way, so far, the feeling of something impending, something shocking, terrifying, grew upon me.

"If anything is going to break, Claude my boy," I told myself, "it's going to happen right now, or you are going to explode, start screaming and running with all your might!"

It was then that it happened, and I'm not exaggerating when I say that my spine went cold and the hair bristled at the nape of my neck. I was *scared*! And that cry in the night, in the heart of the woods, beside fearful Hawkwold, would have frightened anybody with the slightest imagination.

It was a moaning cry, as though the victim of some torture had started crying at the first touch of hurt, and increased the volume as the torture grew intense. I had heard things like it in my time, the cry a woman utters in the painful throes of a certain depraved ecstasy, the cry of a wildcat under the moon, the baying of a coyote who seeks his mate—a number of other things. . . .

This was the cry of a woman. It came from the woods to my left, as though whoever cried out expected me to reach this exact spot at exactly this time, to render assistance.

I stood stockstill, and caught the hint of fearsome sobbing in the cry, which was the sobbing, lip-biting terror of a woman gripped by fear she cannot control, caused by a menace she both fears and courts. That is strange. But it was true.

I took more caution after I banged my whole body against a tree as I cut automatically toward the sound, without stopping to heed where I was going in the semi-darkness of the dimly moonlit night. I had left the trail without intending to, and could not go back without admitting—to myself, at least—that I was afraid. There was one thing of which I had always stood in deadly fear: fear itself!

The sound was dying away, but I had the location in mind. I rubbed my face with my right hand, and knew that it came away wet with blood. The limb of an overhanging tree, like the hand of a skeleton, had raked my face. That was simple and understandable. But that moaning cry?

I did something, on a hunch, never realizing into what horror I was precipitating myself. I took out my long-bladed pocket knife, shot it open by pressing a spring on the handle, and was ready for anything. If the threat, whatever it was, were human, I could handle it. If it were supernatural—something in which I did not believe—a weapon would make no difference, either way.

I saw a splotch of white, and again almost froze in my tracks. The moonlight which flickered through the trees must be playing tricks with my eyes, I thought, for I couldn't really be seeing what I thought I saw: a nude woman, supine upon a pile of leafy branches, with a black shadow hovering over her. The shadow, I was sure, was that of a man.

I pictured a fiend, tearing a woman's clothing from her in a frenzy of desire. A fiend like that, I believed, would take some handling. The knife might come in handy.

I stood there for a moment, staring, almost rubbing my eyes. I caught the white flash of writhing limbs. The shadow of the man was moving. I heard a snarl, somehow wolfish, and thought of werewolves. The ignorant natives hereabouts *had* hinted of werewolves. But they had hinted of everything else, vampires, ghosts, and the like.

I saw the black shadow bend, snarling, again over the white splotch, which I had seen as a supine woman—the woman who moaned and cried out in pain.

Then I hurled myself forward.

"Take your dirty hands off her, you rotten—!" I yelled.

I reached the spot, and for a moment the moon looked down upon the three of us. Yes, the woman—young and girlish—*was* nude. She was unconscious, with her head rolling from side to side on the leafy pallet. Her hair, black as the wings of a crow, was like a cloud about her head and fell in shiny jet cascades that partly draped her snowy shoulders. Her face had been bleeding.

The shadow whirled toward me, showing a white face with mouth black— black. I knew—knew that blood in the dark seems black.

The shadow had been tasting the blood on the girl's face! So I thought at the moment.

The shadow snarled, spat out words: "Attend to your own affairs, meddler, or something will happen to you, and Hawkwold will—"

I think the monster meant to say that Hawkwold would claim another victim, but the words never came out, for it leaped, and we grappled. I wouldn't have used the knife if the other person hadn't used one first. A slash from his knife slit my coat sleeve and blood spurted from my arm. The shadow grabbed that arm, sank its teeth into the flesh. I felt it suck, drink of my blood, and horror such as I had never expected to experience, flooded me. The stories of vampires, then, were true, at least in part!

I struck the creature in the face. Its right hand, looking small for a man, struck back, still holding the knife, and I knew I fought for two lives, that of the moaning woman, and my own. There was nothing else for it, so I closed in, battling with all my might, and the other fought back like a tiger.

I struggled harder, amazed that one so slight should be able to give such hardy account of himself. I knew from the first that I would have to kill to keep from being killed.

I grasped a warm throat, under a mouth smeared with blood, and drove the knife to its hilt in the left breast of my adversary. I was amazed that the breast of so doughty a fighter should be so soft.

My assailant sank down, moaning a little, and expired at my feet. I considered a moment. I bent to examine my victim, glad that I had won, panting with my exertions. And I almost had heart failure when I knocked off the cap on the head of the opponent I had just stabbed.

Hair as black and as long as that of the unconscious moaning woman, spilled about this white face! No wonder the breast of the "man" had been soft, for the man was a woman, garbed in male clothing. I had slain a woman. It had been a fair fight, yes, but what country jury would believe that any fight between a man and a woman could have been fair? None!

If I told what I had seen, it would be even worse for me—a story cooked up to save my life from the law.

I saw one certainty facing me if this were ever known—lynching! In fancy I saw the marching mob with its flaming torches, riding me on a rail through the darkness to this very spot, perhaps even to the tree under which I was then standing, there to loop the lethal rope and swing me, so that my twisted neck turned my dead face to the moon.

I began to plan what every killer plans to save himself in his terror: disposal of the body.

There was the Hawkwold Swamp, ready at hand. The woman was no woman I had ever seen anywhere in the countryside. If any woman, anywhere hereabouts, paraded in man's clothing, I had never heard of her. The woman, I argued, was a stranger. My one chance for life depended on none of her friends knowing where she had gone.

But what sort of friends would a woman like this one have?

It was fear—*fear,* I tell you!—which drove me to what I did.

I flung the dead woman's body into the black water of the swamp, watched it close sullenly over her and gurgle a murmur of hellish thanks.

I went back to the supine woman who still moaned. I looked all about the place for her clothing and could not find any. I came to the conclusion that she had been stripped before she had been brought here, moreover, that she had been unconscious for a long time. Well, the woman I had killed had been strong enough to carry the one I now lifted tenderly in my arms, to bear along the trail.

I knew, even as I carried her along, that more than the hurt of her wound, inflicted by a living vampire tasting of her blood, was what she had been forced to surrender to by ungodly desire of the woman in man's clothing.

The girl moaned as I tried to carry her comfortably.

"Take her away from me! Don't let them have me! Oh, my God! Oh, my God! Oh, my God. . . ."

She kept saying that over and over again: "Oh, my God! Oh, my God!"

Finally, bloody and perspiring, I broke out of the woods along Hawkwold, and looked back at them, fear mounting in me when it should have left me as I quit the woods. For back of me the black trees seemed to be swaying long arms at me, and sighing:

"This is not the end, Claude Dern, but the beginning!"

Against the shadow of the woods I thought I saw yet other shadows moving.

I wondered if they were of people who had seen me drop the corpse of that she-devil into Hawkwold Swamp.

I hurried, almost running in spite of my burden, over the rise of the hill, to the door of my white house, entered, switched on the lights, and placed the girl on a sofa. Then, in sudden, unreasoning terror, I snapped the lights off again.

CHAPTER TWO
Challenge of the Undead

I HAD to be able to look through my own windows, into the darkness beyond, to see what, or who, might approach the house. I couldn't explain my fright, for it was inexplicable. I thought of the potential lynching, but it wasn't that I feared, it was something deeper, worse—though I knew not what.

I covered the girl with a blanket and sat down in an easy chair for a moment. But creeping terror mounted in me—for no reason I could even guess at, I rose, pushed my chair into a corner, so that nothing whatever could reach me from behind, and sat there motionless, in silence. From where I sat I could see the face of the girl on the couch, with her black hair all about her. She moved her head limply from side to side, as though she had had a broken neck, and kept on murmuring:

"Oh, God, oh, God, oh, God!"

Moonlight played over her. The shadow of her head, her bosom, her torso, was on the floor beside the couch—a black woman sleeping, save that her head moved from side to side. Chills played along my spine, and I hated myself because this was so. I was in deadly fear, and knew now that it was not from the rope of the lynchers, or from any material thing, but from the unknown, which now was bestial, unnatural.

After a long time, she ceased from her ritual of calling upon her God. I heard things from her lips which brought the sweat forth all over my body. Hideous things. I remembered something a doctor had once told me about an aged spinster who had never had a lover undergoing an operation in middle age and saying things while she was coming out of the anesthetic—awful things, things which, if they had been repeated to her in her normal existence, would have driven her to shameful suicide.

Things one does not mention, does not even dare to think about, things which bring the horror closer and closer. . . .

I could, of course, have called in some neighbor, but I knew little of them. I was a recluse by choice and the nearest of my few neighbors lived a mile away—and all left me alone because they guessed that I did not care for company. I could expect neither help nor sympathy from them.

I forced brandy between the girl's lips. I chafed her hands. Her pulse was almost normal, so I knew she was in no immediate danger. Only time would heal her hurts. Maybe her clouded mind never would heal.

Then, too, she was . . . God, she was beautiful! And a sweet, childlike expression of fretful hurt, playing about the corners of her pretty mouth, pulled at my heartstrings.

I drank in her beauty like rare wine when I began to realize its extent. I could well understand why she spoke, in her delirium, of the things she did. She was young, rampant with life—all the things a man sought for in woman.

I thought my feeling for her was merely one of sympathy—but I would have given my life for her. I hadn't the slightest idea what to do with her when she regained consciousness, if she ever did. Tomorrow I must get a doctor—one whom I could trust.

Tonight I must take care of her, and her secrets would be shared by God and myself. I swore, even then, that none other should ever know them, unless she told. I pictured her shame, her horror, when she should regain consciousness. I must find a way to show my sympathy—totally impersonal, I told myself—so that she would not be afraid to trust me.

I couldn't spend much time beside her because a fear of things behind me— always behind me!—kept driving me back to my chair, to a nerve-wracking vigil. I almost ran back to it and, sitting down, stared through every window I could see, at the moonlight landscape outside, expecting—I didn't know what to expect—that something hellish would come to me out of Hawkwold.

The girl changed the tenor of her delirious utterance.

"They're coming for me again! They're coming, I tell you! I can *feel* them!"

What the devil did she mean? I couldn't even guess, and because I couldn't I was more afraid than ever—though now my fear was for her instead of for myself. If she sensed the approach of unnamed and unnameable menace, she probably was correct—for who can say what power of telepathy is possessed by the delirious, the hypnotized, the dying?

There was nothing by which to identify her. I remembered someone telling me once that one can converse with a sleep-talker. I decided to try it out. Bending over her, I asked: "What is your name?"

I put all of my sympathy into the question, seeking to penetrate her subconscious. Even as I stooped over her, I felt eyes boring into my back—some menace spying upon us both. . . .

She answered: "Marna! Marna Shattuck!"

She broke off in the midst of the next repetition of her name to say, almost to scream: *"They're coming, I tell you! They're coming for me again!"*

I went scurrying back to my chair, where I sat like a statue, frozen in my place, with only my eyes alive. When sweat came forth on my forehead I did not wipe it away, waited for its own weight to send it cascading down my chin to drop upon my coat. If I lifted my arm its shadow might hide some nameless enemy.

It was in the midst of all this that I heard the rustling sound. Outside it was, outside the door by which I had brought Marna Shattuck into my cabin. It was as though a cat rubbed its back against the screen, as though a dog scratched with its blunted paws, as though . . .

I stared through the darkness at the door I could not see, wishing I had left the light on over it, knowing now that it was too late. I would have been able to see at least the form of whatever it was that now tried the knob of the door. I wished I had locked it, but it was too late for that now.

Beyond that door, the back one, the trail led over the hill, down through growing shadows to the edge of the woods which bordered black Hawkwold!

I didn't rush to the door, I merely sat. And presently I saw the door swing slowly open. A whispering came in, a whispering that was, in part, a strange and terrifying laughter—*whispered* laughter! I saw, in the shadow of the open door, another shadow forming, flowing into the room.

If, then, I had tried to scream, no sound would have come forth, because my vocal cords would have refused to make a sound at all. I could only watch, like one paralyzed, the creeping crawl of doom.

Now the girl on the couch was still. I saw that her eyes were open, staring at the ceiling, as though she tried to guess where she was. Then, ever so slowly, she turned her head, to look toward that door where the shadow slowly formed.

She did not cry out. She merely looked. I saw her lips part as though she would scream, but she did not.

I swung my eyes back to the shadow, and now, without command from my brain, my hand was bringing forth the knife with which, once tonight, I had taken the life—of a woman!

The shadow glided into the moonlight beside the bed. It glided, paused, and soundless screams leaped from my throat. I had been right, in my intuitive fear of pursuit by some ghastly creature of unplumbed horror! The screams came, sped from my lips, but totally without sound.

I heard a husky voice say: *"You could never escape us so easily, Marna!* You know what I, what we, can do. So you'll believe me now when I say I have nine lives. He can't kill me that many times!"

And then I saw the shadow fully, standing beside the couch, with a hand reaching forth, a slender white hand. I saw red lips part to show white teeth, as the hand closed over the coverlet which hid the form of Marna Shattuck. The hand twitched the coverlet onto the floor, and again I saw that matchless beauty. . . .

But I had no eyes for the smooth white contours of the breasts, the torso, and fulsome thighs. . . . I was staring in close-throated horror at the thing above the bed. For I recognized the thing. . . . It was the woman I had already slain! There was no mistaking her. . . .

I had slain this woman. I had driven a knife through her heart. I had, moreover, thrown her into Hawkwold, and the black water had murmured its thanks as it took her.

I had stabbed her, she had bled—and died!

Now she lifted the other hand and took off her cap, to show the same hair. Water from the swamp dripped from her clothing.

"It is not murder to slay the dead!"

I screamed it, screamed it like a raving madman, as I hurled myself to my feet, flung myself upon the woman I had slain, lunging again at her breast with the point of my knife.

She laughed in my face. She spoke through her laughter: "Hawkwold will yet claim you, meddler! Remember, Marna, nine lives!"

But as I extended a hand to grasp at her throat, she whirled to the open door, stood for a moment on the threshold, looking back, laughing. And in her glittering eyes, full upon mine—for now we both stood in moonlight—I read invitation, ghastly invitation as no woman's invitation ever came to me, in silent telepathy.

Invitation—and challenge!

The woman closed the door as softly as she had opened it, and I heard her footfalls go quietly, hesitantly—as though she listened to know whether I followed—along the path toward Hawkwold.

I stood there, moveless, until my brain began to react to the *new,* delirious words of Marna Shattuck: *The cat also has nine lives! The cat also has nine lives! The cat also has nine lives!"*

I didn't stop to analyze her words, which nevertheless sent superstitious terror plumbing the very roots of my being. There was a ghastly, though as yet incomprehensible meaning, in them. I had slain a woman. She had come back to challenge me—to what?

I knew, for my own peace of mind, that I must pursue her to the very woods of Hawkwold to find the answer.

As I hurried to the door, when all my soul kept bidding me stay and bar the door, or shriek aloud for the comfort of some distant neighbors' presence, Marna's delirious cries rang in my ears:

"The cat also has nine lives! The cat also. . . ."

I slammed the door behind me as I rushed outside, and stared into the moonlight across the countryside, along the trail which led to Hawkwold.

Swiftly moving down that trail, toward the woods, was the woman I had slain.

She looked back, her face like a splotch of snow in the moonlight.

Terror was a giant hand against my chest as I took up swift pursuit. . . .

CHAPTER THREE

The Swamp Feasts Once More

BUT IF I DID NOT follow, I told myself, I would be forever disgraced in my own eyes. I tried not to believe that this was the same woman I had slain. But it *was*! There could be no mistake about it. Yet I knew it *couldn't* be. Such things didn't happen. . . .

The woman again looked back, and slowed her pace a little, as though to encourage in me a hope of catching her, before the shadows of Hawkwold swallowed her. I knew that I would never have the courage to enter Hawkwold again tonight, unless I closed my heart to fear—when fear already was a pair of black hands closing on my hammering heart.

"You can't kill the already-dead!" I kept telling myself.

Even as I ran I thought of the girl, Marna Shattuck, back there alone, mumbling on my couch.

I hadn't locked her in. What if she opened the door and sped into the night? What would happen to her? Would she, like the she-monster ahead of me, speed after us to Hawkwold? God only knew. . . .

I was torn two ways: whether to follow the woman ahead of me to fresh, unnameable fears, or to return to Marna Shattuck, and know myself, forever, a coward afraid of shadows. But no, that fleeting, ghoulish creature ahead of me was no shadow—for she *cast* a shadow! That somehow comforted me. Vampires cast no shadows. . . .

I ran faster, but as the woman paused at the very edge of Hawkwold, I slowed my steps, because I could not help it, and from the murdered woman, in a voice peculiarly throaty, like that of a man, came the challenge:

"Are you afraid to follow? Whether you follow or not, the girl returns to Hawkwold before you can return to her, even though you go back this instant! And I shall bring her again to that from which you think you have released her!"

"Not if I kill you! Not if you are never out of my sight!"

She laughed, with a note of knowledge beyond my ken in her laughter.

I forced myself to go closer, heard her say:

"What use to slay one who will not die!"

"It's a trick!" I shouted. "A trick!"

Throaty laughter was my answer. It angered me beyond all power to control myself. To slay this monster in feminine form and masculine garb was not murder, but justice—a vast service to society.

I had the knife in my hand again, and its blade glittered in the moonlight, save where it was red with the blood—*of that woman ahead of me!*

It should be dyed again. And what had Marna kept saying?

"The cat has nine lives!"

Had she meant that this woman must be slain nine times to really die? She couldn't have meant anything so preposterous. She couldn't have meant anything at all. She had been out of her head because of what she had experienced—if other babblings of her delirium had been true—and the words had been just that: words!

And yet, I couldn't keep those words out of my mind, or forget the girl back there, moaning them, rolling from side to side, speaking now to the empty room:

"They're coming for me again! They're coming for me again!"

Was it true? Would this woman go back for Marna Shattuck, as she had promised? Not if I slew her, and this time made *sure* of her death!

I dashed after her, conscious the minute I entered the woods, that she followed a path I would never forget—straight back to the bed of leafy limbs where I had come upon her crouched over Marna Shattuck. It was as though I had committed murder, and gone away, and fate had sent me backward through the time of the murder and the flight, like a motion picture in reverse. If this were to be like that, would I go back, replace Marna on the leaves, go to the swamp, bring the body of the woman out of the depths, stand her beside Marna, and go on back the way I had come, back to my friend's house, to appear at the door raving, my face as white as a sheet?

I was going crazy to think of such a thing. But if she were a ghost—and how could she come back otherwise?—what could be more natural than that her restless spirit challenge me to return, even to the shore of Hawkwold Swamp, there to destroy me as she had promised, before my knife had plunged to the hilt in her left breast?

But nothing of the sort happened. She kept to the trail, did not swerve aside toward the pallet of leafy boughs.

And I was gaining on her. I overtook her. She whirled on me like a panther. Her teeth were bared. Her eyes were wild, terrifying. Her cap had been dragged from her head by a tree limb. Her hair was a black fury about her head and shoulders. My whole soul cringed as I reached for her shoulders, with some idea of holding her off, shaking her until her white teeth rattled, and forcing from her some explanation of the inexplicable.

I caught her, and held her at arms' length, so that her fingernails could not reach me—and the slimy water of the swamp came off her clothing onto my hands and the pungent odor of blood from her bosom stung my nostrils. I shook her, hating the touch of her, and spoke to her like a man who could not cease from stammering, telling her of what the girl had said in her delirium—the unnameable things, which to this woman might be named.

She laughed in my face.

"All true!" she said. "You and your world do not know us; do not know that our world is richer. . . ."

"Our world," I interrupted her, "is cleaner without you! It is an act of mercy to you, and blessing to the world, to destroy you. And I'm going to do that!"

And she laughed at me.

"Slay me," she answered, "and hurl my body again into the swamp of Hawkwold, and I shall return to your cabin, as I did a while ago, to the body of Marna, whom you are growing to love—you fool!—before you could fly there, even if you had the wings of an eagle!"

Could she make good her threat? Of one thing I was sure—my own sincerity. To slay this woman would not be murder. I told her so. She answered me in words which might never be spoken, save under a dark moon in the silence of Satan's woods, beside a swamp like Hawkwold.

Might never be written anywhere! Even the forbidden, ancient books of Egypt had not held such words up to the eyes of men. I hurled her from me, and leaped after her with the speed of an attacking serpent.

My knife was lifted to strike. She whirled to her back as I plunged at her. Her head was back, her beady eyes staring into mine as she said:

"It is *we* who are masterful. You only *try* to be! If you really were, there would be none of us upon the earth!"

Her throat was bared to the knife. I thought, as I struck at it with my blade, that she welcomed it, that she had bared her throat for the thrust—that she *yearned* for it as surcease from the inner fires of a hell beyond normal ken.

Off to my left was the shore of Hawkwold.

I dropped upon the woman, and she flung powerful, muscular arms about me! She fastened her teeth in my throat. Her body was against mine. It was a woman's body—of that I was sure—yet a man's embrace could not have been more repugnant to me! She said things to me—even as I drove the knife home, again and again—which reached deeply into my soul, as though seeking there for the souls of any of my forbears to whom she might claim kinship.

And all the time, as I stabbed at her, she moaned as though in ecstasy, though her moans were dying in a gurgle, as she gurgled lifeblood and died.

Thus the woman I had slain was slain again, by the same knife, and by the same hand. I thought of cutting off her head—make sure—but I was too revolted at the thought. I could not do it, and yet the urge was there, not from fear for myself, or for Marna, but to prove my mastery of this monster. Mastery had been that which had driven her, had been her guiding beacon in a hell on earth. . . .

Quickly, and with furtive speed, I fastened a heavy stone about her legs with strips torn from her own clothing, and with the man's belt she wore. I studied her breast, which I bared for a moment, to see whether there actually *had* been a previous stab-wound in her heart. But it was no use. In my latest frenzy I had stabbed her there so many times that one wound was like any other wound.

I flung her into Hawkwold, where once before I had tonight thrown her.

I raced from the woods, as though all of Satan's friends pursued me, inspired by just one urge: to reach the crest of the hill and look down upon my home, where I had left Marna Shattuck.

I reached the crest, stood stockstill.

Behind me Hawkwold whispered, jeering, repeating exactly what it had seemed to say when I had left it before, with Marna Shattuck in my arms.

It was the wind among the trees, nothing more, I told myself—and knew I lied.

Maybe what I saw at my white home—or *didn't* see—was part of the proof that I lied.

I had snapped on a light in my living room, over the couch of Marna Shattuck, so that she would not be frightened if she regained consciousness in a strange place. Now there was no light. Just the windows in the moonlight, like sightless, yet all-seeing eyes of dreadful meaning.

I ran, and sobbed as I ran, and hated myself for sobbing.

My fear was an incubus upon my shoulders, my body, my heart, my very soul. It was like fleeing with the world upon my shoulders, like trying to run away from danger in a nightmare, with the feet rooted to the black ground.

Behind me, like a jeering wind pursuing, I seemed to hear the laughter of the woman I had slain—and slain again. . . .

Like a thunderbolt I crashed through the front door, into my living room, to look down at an empty couch!

CHAPTER FOUR
Murder Brides

GREAT GOD! Had the woman I had twice killed made good her boast—risen from the dead, returned and spirited Marna Shattuck away, before I could return to her? Utterly impossible! Yet Marna Shattuck was gone. The coverlet was thrown back. There were no women's clothes in the room. So, then, she had gone forth as I had brought her . . . mumbling, perhaps, as I had last heard her—a delirious woman going out to a grisly, unnamable rendezvous.

"Marna! Marna!" I whispered her name, over and over again. The syllables of it, as they came from my mouth which was stiff with my terror, told me the dreadful truth—that I loved this woman whose lips had never, during my knowledge of her, spoken a word, except in the mad unconsciousness.

I loved a madwoman!

What if, when she regained consciousness, she should be a woman whom no man could love, somehow akin to the woman I had twice slain? It would have killed *me* to find that out, yet I am sure I would still have loved her.

I learned then, standing there in the moonlight which now reached somewhat farther into my living room, the horror of being alone—I who had courted solitude. It was agony itself to be alone, shut out, when outside somewhere my beloved wandered in mind and body, lured to some gruesome end by the whispers of hellish women. Yes, women. It could not have been just one, I kept telling myself. There were no such things as vampires, and only the ignorant believed in them.

What should I do? Silence answered the question as I whispered, over and over again, the name of Marna Shattuck. The night seemed to whisper it with me—night that was filled with horror. The clock on my mantlepiece struck the hour: two o'clock in the morning. Good Lord, it would be four hours more until dawn. I had slain twice since midnight. How many times would I yet slay, before I myself died?

Had grisly fate set me some impossible task? Was I doomed to fight until dawn against a woman who . . . I shuttered violently.

The silence was far more horrible than screams in the night would have been. I think, then, that had the scream of Marna Shattuck come at that moment, out of the very heart of ebon Hawkwold, it would have been a relief. But there was nothing but silence. I thought that perhaps Marna had risen, gone upstairs to the bedroom.

I took time to dash all through the house—and as I did I could hear in my mind the chuckles of the evil woman, laughing at me for a fool. I did not find Marna.

What should I do? There were no marks upon the floor, except the splotches the evil woman had made when she had stood beside Marna's couch, dripping the slime of Hawkwold—dark and evil as her own soul—upon the boards.

I turned on the light in every room—and that did no good whatever. For beyond the windows, each and every one of them, I fancied I could see a face—and every face at every window was the face of the woman I had killed and cast into the swamp.

I counted those faces, for some strange, ghastly reason, and my heart almost stood still. There were seven faces of evil, all of them the same. That, of course, could have been explained by the fact that unreality, my own imagination perhaps, made them all seem the same. Naturally they could not have been.

But *seven* faces!

"Every cat has nine lives! Every cat . . ."

God! Must I, between now and morning, slay the other seven whose faces looked gloatingly, triumphantly, in at my window? How could I know, if I did, but that I must do it again tomorrow night, and the night following, on and on without end? I felt that I had to do something, or die.

I went out the door of my house, the door which faced toward Hawkwold, and walked into the night far enough so that the lights behind me did not blind my eyes. I stood for a long moment with my eyes closed, *because I was afraid to open them,* afraid of what I might see at black Hawkwold.

Then—and it required all my power of will—I opened my eyes, which seemed to be held down by leaden weights.

I don't know what I expected to see, exactly. Certainly not what I did see—a white shape against the woods, just off the trail, seeming almost to float there, above the ground. It was a woman who wore no clothing. She stood, with her long black hair about her shoulders, looking at me. For a long moment I thought she was a statue, so moveless was she.

Slowly, leadenly, her every move causing the chills to race anew along my spine, she lifted her right hand above her head, the fingers extended like the talons of a bird of prey—and beckoned to me!

I could see now that she was Marna Shattuck—whom I would have sworn would never, even in delirium, have beckoned a man to her so wantonly—who was bidding me go to her at the edge of Hawkwold. Every curve of her body as she stood there was an invitation. What sort of woman was this, who urged a man to an after-midnight rendezvous among the skeletal growths of trees about the black swamp?

I hesitated, and found the answer. Her soul and her body called to me across the moonlit distance which separated us, and I knew one thing: that where Marna beckoned I would follow, even into the slime if, in the end, I could clasp her in my arms, feel her lips against mine, her body against mine, her arms strong with response to my yearning. I would follow her anywhere. . . .

I broke into a run toward her, sobbing: "Marna! Marna!"

My very voice was filled with desire. I wanted her to hear it, know the depths of it. I wanted Marna! I would have sworn it *was* Marna, *did* swear that to myself.

I stumbled, almost fell, and even those few seconds lost were eons out of eternity—when I wanted all eternity in which to take and hold the woman who beckoned.

I staggered up, running, my arms outstretched. I heard again the guttural voice of the woman I had slain, calling me a fool for falling in love with Marna. She had known it, then, before knowledge had come to me. She was calling me a fool now, when I knew she was at the bottom of Hawkwold. I knew, myself, that I was a fool, but it didn't matter. I wanted to be a fool for Marna's sake.

The white figure was still all invitation, but as I came closer it retreated into the deeper shadows of the woods, so that her form was dim. But a feminine form dimly veiled in shadows holds even greater promise to a man. . . .

She stood again, waiting. I stopped, wondering, in deadly fear of Hawkwold which had held for me already so much horror. As I halted she faced me, and beckoned once more.

"Marna! Marna!"

I stepped into the woods, flung myself forward. She moved backward away from me, still beckoning. I fancied, so close was I now, that I could hear the escape of her panting breath—as though she could scarcely wait the mad embrace every bit of my being cried out to give. Yet the place was not here, her attitude seemed to say, the time not yet. Soon, very soon, but not yet. . . .

I moved deeper into the woods. I had forgotten the woman I had slain. I had forgotten the horror of my first meeting with Marna Shattuck, the horror of what had happened in my cabin. I had forgotten everything but the alluring woman ahead of me.

Again she moved backward. And then . . . the *whispered* laughter! The woman I had slain was there, standing between me and my beloved, laughing! Her lips were drawn back from her teeth, and holding a gleaming knife in her hand, she had glided toward us from the direction of Hawkwold Swamp, to my left. Her lips were black in the night, but I knew how red they really were. Her cap was gone. Her clothing showed the tears, where I had ripped parts of it away, to fasten her limbs and weight her down, so that she would not escape from Hawkwold.

Her face went into shadow a little as I recognized her. Maybe the moon was darkened for a moment, as though Luna hid her face in shame. Maybe the woman tried to hide from me the evil she intended. Maybe—I didn't know what to think, save this: Over behind the woman I had stabbed was the woman for whom I had slain her. I must have that woman, and nothing that lived—or died and could rise again—would keep me from her.

"Back!" I heard myself say hoarsely, and realized that I again held the knife in my hand. "Back! Nothing, even you, shall keep me from Marna Shattuck!"

She laughed, answered: "Nothing can give her to you, passion-sick fool! She belongs to us! Only over my dead body shall you have her."

I saw the swamp water dripping from her, the marks on her body of the wounds from my knife. Moving forward a little, my knife-hand was swinging into position. I thought, dimly: "I slay her again and there will be six deaths still for her to die!"

About the words there was a strange memory of something I had heard or read somewhere: ". . . and those who live more lives than one, more deaths than one must die!"

More deaths? In God's name how many deaths could this unnatural creature die? No matter, if she must die again at my hand, so be it. Let her die. I would forget her, knowing it wasn't really murder, when my arms would be about Marna Shattuck.

I hurled myself at her.

She returned to the attack, as always, but stronger than before, with a strength that was almost the strength of a man. She fought like a tigress. I didn't mind striking her with the knife because she was a woman, for I knew, deep in my heart, whatever the form of her earthly casement, that she was no woman—really.

Not a woman, nor yet a man . . . something grisly, ghastly, in between. . . .

Why prolong it? I slew her. Over her dying body I hurled myself forward, forgetting the creature as my strides carried me past her, as though she had never existed. Marna now was in shadow that clothed her with a dark allure which I could not resist. I must . . .

But now she no longer denied me. She came to meet me, with her arms out. I flung myself into the shadows to grasp her, to clutch her. My voice spoke endearments that were sobs of agony. She answered me likewise, with no hint of delirium remaining.

I pressed her closer to me. Her arms about me were strong to hold me, to make answer to my urge, and for a brief space, while worlds tumbled upon worlds, and time stood still, there was nothing that mattered—nothing but she and I.

And then—a hoarse voice said: "Now I would die! I do not care to live longer! I have had granted a wish that never before seemed possible, and in so much have made myself different from my companions of Hawkwold. Slay me, man, while I know myself like other women!"

Great God in Heaven! That voice! It was not the voice of Marna Shattuck that came from her lips!

I knew it the second she spoke, for when would I ever forget that voice in this life? A voice that might have been a man's voice, or a woman's voice, or either, or both. . . . That other woman had taken Marna's place in the shadows!

Savagely I caught her up, bore her into a patch of moonlight, where I could see her face—be sure.

It was not the face of Marna Shattuck, not her form. . . . And her eyes were filled with mockery as she said: "Slay me, man, while I know myself a *woman*!"

Amazingly, without wounding either of us, I had retained the knife which had so often slain tonight. While I stared, and coldness of horror possessed, obsessed me, she clutched at the knife with both hands.

Her eyes never left mine. Her lips were parted in a half-smile of unearthly triumph as, with both those small hands which had so recently caressed me, she drove the knife to the hilt under her left breast. . . .

Where was Marna? Where was she, O God?

Three shadows, mouthing evil words, and crying out: "Betrayer! Betrayer! Betrayer!" dashed at me from three sides, wielding knives, attacking like furies.

A thin cry, from somewhere to the left, in a voice I would never forget, this side the grave, was my answer. Somewhere, there, was Marna. She needed me, called me, though she did not know my name, or what I had already done for her. And between Marna and me were the three furies who attacked me.

But not three, nor five, nor seven, furies, could have stopped me when my beloved called in such a voice of pain.

Hawkwold became a shambles, and I was a man clothed in red blood drawn by slashing knives, when I was finally free to follow the eerie cry from somewhere near the swamp.

"A cat also has nine lives! A cat also has nine lives!"

It was a litany, beating in my soul as I crashed through the woods. How many of those lives had I taken? I had lost count of them. I knew, only, that some still remained, and that these, too, must be taken, before I could hold Marna Shattuck—the real Marna—in my arms and keep her safe against them.

There were three of the shadows, this time, looming over my beloved. One was saying: "She is mine, for I saw her first!" Another said: "She belongs to one as much as to the others." The third said: "There are no others now, only ourselves!"

"You," I gasped, "shall not have her! In God's Name what *are* you?"

For I knew, should have known all along, that not just one woman had been slain tonight, but many.

Where had they been hiding in Hawkwold? They had been here a long time, else the wild stories I had heard would never have been told of Hawkwold. They had been. . . .

They whirled, teeth bared, to face me, and one of them said: "Is this the end? Or a new beginning?"

"It is the end of your sisterhood!" My voice was like a croak of doubting despair. But I knew what I had to do. If I failed, Marna Shattuck would never escape them. I saw her now, plainly, leaning against a tree. She still suffered delirium, which was merciful for her.

If I failed, no power on earth could save her, for nobody would ever come to this place at night.

I had slain. I would slay again, and again, and yet again, to save one normal woman from women who were monsters unnameable.

"Perhaps," said one, "you are a creature of mercy."

"Fool, Margot!" said the other. "Let the pact be broken here and now. I for one am satisfied for things to continue as they were before we made it."

Of what were they hinting? What dreadful thing would I know before the end?

I closed with them. My whole body, my very soul, revolted at the touch of them, the feel of their hands, their bodies straining against mine, and as we fought Marna Shattuck kept saying: *"The cat also has nine lives! The cat also . . ."*

It was a senseless, unaccented monotone that would drive me mad unless I held her in my arms, and soothed her until she forgot to say it.

I fought. They fought back. Their knives madly slashing at me. Finally the last one was supine at my feet, not dead, but dying, and she looked up into my eyes—and in her beady black ones there were hints of a strange gratitude.

"You know us?" she whispered.

"Yes," I answered.

"We were four—all of us together, in a city. Never mind which. We were shunned by *your* kind. We made a pact, a pact of suicide. One of us knew of Hawkwold. She told. We came here. Then, despairing further, we planned, one at a time, to drown ourselves in the swamp, when we had the courage, to blot our unholy selves out forever—so that we should be free from the averted glances of *your* kind. We lacked the courage, postponed the end, each as her turn came. And then, tonight, we saw a girl, alone, entering Hawkwold, fearfully, forcing herself to the path, because she feared it . . . and were, all of us, ourselves again.

"Here was beauty, innocence. And when you came to take it from us, we would not be mastered. We, who regarded ourselves as masterly beyond the mastery of men! And when you destroyed the first of us we felt that you were our answer, that if we fought you, and lost, and died, we would not have to die at our own choosing—kill ourselves—which we found we had not the courage to do for ourselves. .

"It was easy," she went on, "to fool you into thinking there was but one, who returned again and again. We took the girl, and she saw us, and I suggested to her, in your house, the symbol of the cat—about which she now mumbles. Listen—for I am dying—and you can save yourself, as it is just that you should—for to destroy our kind is not murder, in the eyes of your kind. We came for the solace of black Hawkwold. Let Hawkwold swallow our secret, which to you must be a dreadful . . ."

I gave her my promise, before she died. Then, shuddering, I threw the bodies of those terrible, suffering women into the dark waters of Hawkwold Swamp, which seemed to have been waiting for them all this time, with an eerie, knowing patience. And I realized it was better so. Their souls might now be purged of their frightful malady. Also, I breathed more freely, as I remembered having been told that the depths of the swamp had never been plumbed; that it was bottomless. At any rate, I felt that this fact—if it were true—or the mire and quicksand, would hide the ghastly secret of those corpses forever.

Unafraid, believing in my heart that the future would keep Marna safe in my arms, I carried her home, to care for her hurts, and comfort her. In a few days—thank God!—she was well enough to tell me about herself. For I would not let her talk about the horrors she had undergone until I was sure she had regained her strength.

She was an artist, just commencing her career, and to the isolated, unusual country surrounding Hawkwold Swamp she had come in search of eerie atmosphere for her paintings.

We did not stay there. We left hurriedly, thankful for our escape from a tenfold hideous doom at the hands of those goulish creatures I had slain. And in our new home, in a pleasant country valley that is free from swamps and gloomy trees, we are striving with the help of our newborn happiness together—to forget that gruesome night at Hawkwold. . . .

THE CLOAK

ROBERT BLOCH

Under the editorship of John W. Campbell, Unknown Worlds *was renowned for shedding the light of the modern age on the darkest themes of horror and fantasy. Robert Bloch's "The Cloak" appeared in the magazine's third issue and helped set the tone of whimsical fantasy for which the magazine is remembered today. Bloch, who hitherto had been known as the author of many gruesome horror stories written under the influence of H. P. Lovecraft, may have been the first writer to suggest that the best defense against a vampire is a good sense of humor.*

T HE SUN WAS DYING, and its blood spattered the sky as it crept into its sepulcher behind the hills. The keening wind sent the dry, fallen leaves scurrying toward the west, as though hastening them to the funeral of the sun.

"Nuts!" said Henderson to himself and stopped thinking.

The sun was setting in a dingy red sky, and a dirty raw wind was kicking up the half-rotten leaves in a filthy gutter. Why should he waste time with cheap imagery?

"Nuts!" said Henderson, again.

It was probably a mood evoked by the day, he mused. After all, this was the sunset of Halloween. Tonight was the dreaded All Hallows Eve, when spirits walked and skulls cried out from their graves beneath the earth.

Either that, or tonight was just another rotten cold fall day. Henderson sighed. There was a time, he reflected, when the coming of this night meant something. A dark Europe, groaning in superstitious terror, dedicated this eve to the grinning

369

Unknown. A million doors had once been barred against the evil visitants, a million prayers mumbled, a million candles lit. There was something majestic about the idea, Henderson reflected. Life had been an adventure in those times, and men walked in terror of what the next turn of a midnight road might bring. They had lived in a world of demons and ghouls and elementals who sought their souls—and by Heaven, in those days a man's soul meant something. This new skepticism had taken a profound meaning away from life. Men no longer revered their souls.

"Nuts!" said Henderson again, quite automatically. There was something crude and twentieth-century about the coarse expression which always checked his introspective flights of fancy.

The voice in his brain that said "nuts" took the place of humanity to Henderson—common humanity which would voice the same sentiment if they heard his secret thoughts. So now Henderson uttered the word and endeavored to forget problems and purple patches alike.

He was walking down this street at sunset to buy a costume for the masquerade party tonight, and he had much better concentrate on finding the costumer's before it closed than waste his time daydreaming about Halloween.

His eyes searched the darkening shadows of the dingy buildings lining the narrow thoroughfare. Once again he peered at the address he had scribbled down after finding it in the phone book.

Why the devil didn't they light up the shops when it got dark? He couldn't make out numbers. This was a poor, run-down neighborhood, but after all—

Abruptly, Henderson spied the place across the street and started over. He passed the window and glanced in. The last rays of the sun slanted over the top of the building across the way and fell directly on the window and its display. Henderson drew a sharp intake of breath.

He was staring at a costumer's window—not looking through a fissure into hell. Then why was it all red fire, lighting the grinning visages of fiends?

"Sunset," Henderson muttered aloud. Of course it was, and the faces were merely clever masks such as would be displayed in this sort of place. Still, it gave the imaginative man a start. He opened the door and entered.

The place was dark and still. There was a smell of loneliness in the air—the smell that haunts all places long undisturbed; tombs, and graves in deep woods, and caverns in the earth, and—

"Nuts."

What the devil was wrong with him, anyway? Henderson smiled apologetically at the empty darkness. This was the smell of the costumer's shop, and it carried him back to college days of amateur theatricals. Henderson had known this smell of mothballs, decayed furs, grease paint and oils. He had played amateur Hamlet and in his hands he had held a smirking skull that hid all knowledge in its empty eyes—a skull, from the costumer's.

Well, here he was again, and the skull gave him the idea. After all, Halloween night it was. Certainly in this mood of his he didn't want to go as a rajah, or a

Turk, or a pirate—they all did that. Why not go as a fiend, or a warlock, or a werewolf? He could see Lindstrom's face when he walked into the elegant penthouse wearing rags of some sort. The fellow would have a fit, with society crowds wearing their expensive Elsa Maxwell take-offs. Henderson didn't greatly care for Lindstrom's sophisticated friends anyway; a gang of amateur Noel Cowards and horsy women wearing harnesses of jewels. Why not carry out the spirit of Halloween and go as a monster?

Henderson stood there in the dusk, waiting for someone to turn on the lights, come out from the back room, and serve him. After a minute or so he grew impatient and rapped sharply on the counter.

"Say in there! Service!"

Silence. And a shuffling noise from the rear, then—an unpleasant noise to hear in the gloom. There was a banging from downstairs and then the heavy clump of footsteps. Suddenly Henderson gasped. A black bulk was rising from the floor!

It was, of course, only the opening of the trapdoor from the basement. A man shuffled behind the counter, carrying a lamp. In that light his eyes blinked drowsily.

The man's yellowish face crinkled into a smile.

"I was sleeping, I'm afraid," said the man, softly. "Can I serve you, sir?"

"I was looking for a Halloween costume."

"Oh, yes. And what was it you had in mind?"

The voice was weary, infinitely weary. The eyes continued to blink in the flabby yellow face.

"Nothing usual, I'm afraid. You see, I rather fancied some sort of monster getup for a par—Don't suppose you carry anything in that line?"

"I could show you masks."

"No. I mean, werewolf outfits, something of that sort. More of the authentic."

"So. The *authentic.*"

"Yes." Why did this old dunce stress the word?

"I might—yes, I might have just the thing for you, sir." The eyes blinked, but the thin mouth pursed in a smile. "Just the thing for Halloween."

"What's that?"

"Have you ever considered the possibility of being a vampire?"

"Like Dracula?"

"Ah—yes, I suppose—Dracula."

"Not a bad idea. Do you think I'm the type for that, though?"

The man appraised him with that tight smile. "Vampires are of all types, I understand. You would do nicely."

"Hardly a compliment," Henderson chuckled. "But why not? What's the outfit?"

"Outfit? Merely evening clothes, or what you wear. I will furnish you with the authentic cloak."

"Just a cloak—is that all?"

"Just a cloak. But it is worn like a shroud. It is shroud-cloth, you know. Wait, I'll get it for you."

The shuffling feet carried the man into the rear of the shop again. Down the trapdoor entrance he went, and Henderson waited. There was more banging, and presently the old man reappeared carrying the cloak. He was shaking dust from it in the darkness.

"Here it is—the genuine cloak."

"Genuine?"

"Allow me to adjust it for you—it will work wonders, I'm sure."

The cold, heavy cloth hung draped about Henderson's shoulders. The faint odor rose mustily in his nostrils as he stepped back and surveyed himself in the mirror. The light was poor, but Henderson saw that the cloak effected a striking transformation in his appearance. His long face seemed thinner, his eyes were accentuated in the facial pallor heightened by the somber cloak he wore. It was a big, black shroud.

"Genuine," murmured the old man. He must have come up suddenly, for Henderson hadn't noticed him in the glass.

"I'll take it," Henderson said. "How much?"

"You'll find it quite entertaining, I'm sure."

"How much?"

"Oh. Shall we say five dollars?"

"Here."

The old man took the money, blinking, and drew the cloak from Henderson's shoulders. When it slid away he felt suddenly warm again. It must be cold in the basement—the cloth was icy.

The old man wrapped the garment, smiling, and handed it over.

"I'll have it back tomorrow," Henderson promised.

"No need. You purchased it. It is yours."

"But—"

"I am leaving business shortly. Keep it. You will find more use for it than I, surely."

"But—"

"A pleasant evening to you."

Henderson made his way to the door in confusion, then turned to salute the blinking old man in the dimness.

Two eyes were burning at him from across the counter—two eyes that did not blink.

"Good night," said Henderson, and closed the door quickly. He wondered if he were going just a trifle mad.

At eight, Henderson nearly called up Lindstrom to tell him he couldn't make it. The cold chills came the minute he put on the cloak, and when he looked at himself in the mirror his blurred eyes could scarcely make out the reflection.

But after a few drinks he felt better about it. He hadn't eaten, and the liquor warmed his blood. He paced the floor, attitudinizing with the cloak—sweeping it about him and scowling in what he thought was a ferocious manner. He was going to be a vampire all right! He called a cab, went down to the lobby. The driver came in, and Henderson was waiting, black cloak furled.

"I wish you to drive me," he said, in a low voice.

The cabman took one look at him in the cloak and turned pale.

"Whazzat?"

"I ordered you to come," said Henderson gutturally, while he quaked with inner mirth. He leered ferociously and swept the cloak back.

"Yeah, yeah. O.K."

The driver almost ran outside. Henderson stalked after him.

"Where to, boss—I mean, sir?"

The frightened face didn't turn as Henderson intoned the address and sat back.

The cab started with a lurch that set Henderson to chuckling deeply, in character. At the sound of the laughter the driver got panicky and raced his engine up to the limit set by the governor. Henderson laughed loudly, and the impressionable driver fairly quivered in his seat. It was quite a ride, but Henderson was entirely unprepared to open the door and find it slammed after him as the cabman drove hastily away without collecting a fare.

"I must look the part," he thought complacently, as he took the elevator up to the penthouse apartment.

There were three or four others in the elevator; Henderson had seen them before at other affairs Lindstrom had invited him to attend, but nobody seemed to recognize him. It rather pleased him to think how his wearing of an unfamiliar cloak and an unfamiliar scowl seemed to change his entire personality and appearance. Here the other guests had donned elaborate disguises—one woman wore the costume of a Watteau shepherdess, another was attired as a Spanish ballerina, a tall man dressed as Pagliacci, and his companion had donned a toreador outfit. Yet Henderson recognized them all, knew that their expansive habiliments were not truly disguises at all, but merely elaborations calculated to enhance their appearance. Most people at costume parties gave vent to suppressed desires. The women showed off their figures, the men either accentuated their masculinity as the toreador did, or clowned it. Such things were pitiful; these conventional fools eagerly doffing their dismal business suits and rushing off to a lodge, or amateur theatrical, or masked ball in order to satisfy their starving imaginations. Why didn't they dress in garish colors on the street? Henderson often pondered the question.

Surely, these society folk in the elevator were fine-looking men and women in their outfits—so healthy, so red-faced, and full of vitality. They had such robust throats and necks. Henderson looked at the plump arms of the woman next to him. He stared, without realizing it, for a long moment. And then, he saw that the occupants of the car had drawn away from him. They were standing in the corner, as though they feared his cloak and scowl, and his eyes fixed on the woman. Their chatter had ceased abruptly. The woman looked at him, as though she were about to speak, when the elevator doors opened and afforded Henderson a welcome respite.

What the devil was wrong? First the cab driver, then the woman. Had he drunk too much?

Well, no chance to consider that. Here was Marcus Lindstrom, and he was thrusting a glass into Henderson's hand.

"What have we here? Ah, a bogeyman!" It needed no second glance to perceive that Lindstrom, as usual at such affairs, was already quite bottle-dizzy. The fat host was positively swimming in alcohol.

"Have a drink, Henderson, my lad! I'll take mine from the bottle. That outfit of yours gave me a shock. Where'd you get the makeup?"

"Makeup? I'm not wearing any makeup."

"Oh. So you're not. How . . . silly of me."

Henderson wondered if he were crazy. Had Lindstrom really drawn back? Were his eyes actually filled with a certain dismay?

"I'll . . . I'll see you later," babbled Lindstrom, edging away and quickly turning to the other arrivals. Henderson watched the back of Lindstrom's neck. It was fat and white. It bulged over the collar of his costume and there was a vein in it. A vein in Lindstrom's fat neck. Frightened Lindstrom.

Henderson stood alone in the anteroom. From the parlor beyond came the sound of music and laughter, party noises. Henderson hesitated before entering. He drank from the glass in his hand—Bacardi rum, and powerful. On top of his other drinks it almost made the man reel. But he drank, wondering. What was wrong with him and his costume? Why did he frighten people? Was he unconsciously acting his vampire role? That crack of Lindstrom's about makeup, now—

Acting on impulse, Henderson stepped over to the long panel mirror in the hall. He lurched a little, then stood in the harsh light before it. He faced the glass, stared into the mirror, and saw nothing.

He looked at himself in the mirror, and there was no one there!

Henderson began to laugh softly, evilly, deep in his throat. And as he gazed into the empty, unreflecting glass, his laughter rose in black glee.

"I'm drunk," he whispered. "I must be drunk. Mirror in my apartment made me blurred. Now I'm so far gone I can't see straight. Sure I'm drunk. Been acting ridiculously, scaring people. Now I'm seeing hallucinations—or not seeing them, rather. Visions. Angels."

His voice lowered. "Sure, angels. Standing right in back of me, now, Hello, angel."

"Hello."

Henderson whirled. There she stood, in the dark cloak, her hair a shimmering halo above her white, proud face; her eyes celestial blue, and her lips infernal red.

"Are you real?" asked Henderson, gently. "Or am I a fool to believe in miracles?"

"This miracle's name is Sheila Darrly, and it would like to powder its nose if you please."

"Kindly use this mirror through the courtesy of Stephen Henderson," replied the cloaked man, with a grin. He stepped back a ways, eyes intent.

The girl turned her head and favored him with a slow, impish smile. "Haven't you ever seen powder used before?" she asked.

"Didn't know angels indulged in cosmetics," Henderson replied. "But then there's a lot I don't know about angels. From now on I shall make them a special study of mine. There's so much I want to find out. So you'll probably find me following you around with a notebook all evening."

"Notebooks for a vampire?"

"Oh, but I'm a very intelligent vampire—not one of those backwoods Transylvanian types. You'll find me charming, I'm sure."

"Yes, you look like the sure type," the girl mocked. "But an angel and a vampire—that's a queer combination."

"We can reform one another," Henderson pointed out. "Besides, I have a suspicion that there's a bit of the devil in you. That dark cloak over your angel costume; dark angel, you know. Instead of heaven you might hail from my home town."

Henderson was flippant, but, underneath his banter, cyclonic thoughts whirled. He recalled discussions in the past, cynical observations he had made and believed.

Once, Henderson had declared that there was no such thing as love at first sight, save in books or plays where such a dramatic device served to speed up action. He asserted that people learned about romance from books and plays and accordingly adopted a belief in love at first sight when all one could possibly feel was desire.

And now this Sheila—this blond angel—had to come along and drive out all thoughts of morbidity, all thoughts of drunkenness and foolish gazings into mirrors, from his mind, had to send him badly plunging into dreams of red lips, ethereal blue eyes and slim white arms.

Something of his feelings had swept into his eyes, and as the girl gazed up at him she felt the truth.

"Well," she breathed, "I hope the inspection pleases."

"A miracle of understatement, that. But there was something I wanted to find out particularly about divinity. Do angels dance?"

"Tactful vampire! The next room?"

Arm in arm they entered the parlor. The merrymakers were in full swing. Liquor had already pitched gaiety at its height, but there was no dancing any longer. Boisterous little grouped couples laughed arm in arm about the room. The usual party gagsters were performing their antics in corners. The superficial atmosphere, which Henderson detested, was fully in evidence.

It was reaction which made Henderson draw himself up to full height and sweep the cloak about his shoulders. Reaction brought the scowl to his pale face, caused him to stalk along in brooding silence. Sheila seemed to regard this as a great joke.

"Pull a vampire act on them," she giggled, clutching his arm. Henderson accordingly scowled at the couples, sneered horrendously at the women. And his progress was marked by the turning of heads, the abrupt cessation of chatter. He walked through the long room like Red Death incarnate. Whispers trailed in his wake.

"Who is that man?"

"We came up with him in the elevator, and he—"

"His eyes—"

"Vampire!"

"Hello, Dracula!" It was Marcus Lindstrom and a sullen-looking brunette in Cleopatra costume who lurched toward Henderson. Host Lindstrom could scarcely stand, and his companion in cups was equally at a loss. Henderson liked the man when sober at the club, but his behavior at parties had always irritated him. Lindstrom was particularly objectionable in his present condition—it made him boorish.

"M'dear, I want you t'meet a very dear friend of mine. Yessir, it being Halloween and all, I invited Count Dracula here, t'gether with his daughter. Asked his grandmother, but she's busy tonight at a Black Sabbath—along with Aunt Jemima. Ha! Count, meet my little playmate."

The woman leered up at Henderson.

"Oooh Dracula, what big eyes you have! Oooh, what big teeth you have! Ooooh—"

"Really, Marcus," Henderson protested. But the host had turned and shouted to the room.

"Folks, meet the real goods—only genuine living vampire in captivity! Dracula Henderson, only existing vampire with false teeth."

In any other circumstances Henderson would have given Lindstrom a quick, efficient punch on the jaw. But Sheila was at his side, it was a public gathering; better to humor the man's clumsy jest. Why not be a vampire?

Smiling quickly at the girl, Henderson drew himself erect, faced the crowd, and frowned. His hands brushed the cloak. Funny, it still felt cold. Looking down he noticed for the first time that it was a little dirty at the edges; muddy or dusty. But the cold silk slid through his fingers as he drew it across his breast with one long hand. The feeling seemed to inspire him. He opened his eyes wide and let them blaze. His mouth opened. A sense of dramatic power filled him. And he looked at Marcus Lindstrom's soft, fat neck with the vein standing in the whiteness. He looked at the neck, saw the crowd watching him, and then the impulse seized him. He turned, eyes on that creasy neck—that wabbling, creasy neck of the fat man.

Hands darted out. Lindstrom squeaked like a frightened rat. He was a plump, sleek white rat, bursting with blood. Vampires liked blood. Blood from the rat, from the neck of the rat, from the vein in the neck of the squeaking rat.

"Warm blood."

The deep voice was Henderson's own.

The hands were Henderson's own.

The hands that went around Lindstrom's neck as he spoke, the hands that felt the warmth, that searched out the vein. Henderson's face was bending for the neck, and, as Lindstrom struggled, his grip tightened. Lindstrom's face was turning purple. Blood was rushing to his head. That was good. Blood!

Henderson's mouth opened. He felt the air on his teeth. He bent down toward that fat neck, and then—

"Stop! That's plenty!"

The voice, the cooling voice of Sheila. Her fingers on his arm. Henderson looked up, startled. He released Lindstrom, who sagged with open mouth.

The crowd was staring, and their mouths were all shaped in the instinctive O of amazement.

Sheila whispered, "Bravo! Served him right—but you frightened him!"

Henderson struggled a moment to collect himself. Then he smiled and turned.

"Ladies and gentlemen," he said, "I have just given a slight demonstration to prove to you what our host said of me was entirely correct. I *am* a vampire. Now that you have been given fair warning, I am sure you will be in no further danger. If there is a doctor in the house I can, perhaps, arrange for a blood transfusion."

The O's relaxed and laughter came from startled throats. Hysterical laughter, in part, then genuine. Henderson had carried it off. Marcus Lindstrom alone still stared with eyes that held utter fear. *He* knew.

And then the moment broke, for one of the gagsters ran into the room from the elevator. He had gone downstairs and borrowed the apron and cap of a newsboy. Now he raced through the crowd with a bundle of papers under his arm.

"Extra! Extra! Read all about it. Big Halloween Horror! Extra!"

Laughing guests purchased papers. A woman approached Sheila, and Henderson watched the girl walk away in a daze.

"See you later," she called, and her glance sent fire through his veins. Still, he could not forget the terrible feeling that came over him when he had seized Lindstrom. Why?

Automatically, he accepted a paper from the shouting pseudo-newsboy. "Big Halloween Horror," he had shouted. What was that?

Blurred eyes searched the paper.

Then Henderson reeled back. That headline! It was an *Extra* after all. Henderson scanned the columns with mounting dread.

"Fire in costumer's . . . shortly after 8 P.M. firemen were summoned to the shop of . . . flames beyond control . . . completely demolished . . . damage estimated at . . . peculiarly enough, name of proprietor unknown . . . skeleton found in—"

"No!" gasped Henderson aloud.

He read, reread *that* closely. The skeleton had been found in a box of earth in the cellar beneath the shop. The box was a coffin. There had been two other boxes, empty. The skeleton had been wrapped in a cloak, undamaged by the flames—

And in the hastily penned box at the bottom of the column were eyewitness comments, written up under scareheads of heavy black type. Neighbors had feared the place. Hungarian neighborhood, hints of vampirism, of strangers who entered the shop. One man spoke of a cult believed to have held meetings in the place. Superstition about things sold there—love philters, outlandish charms and weird disguises.

Weird disguises—vampires—cloaks—his eyes!

"This is an authentic cloak."

"I will not be using this much longer. Keep it."

Memories of these words screamed through Henderson's brain. He plunged out of the room and rushed to the panel mirror.

A moment, then he flung one arm before his face to shield his eyes from the image that was not there—the missing reflection. *Vampires have no reflections.*

No wonder he looked strange. No wonder arms and necks invited him. He had wanted Lindstrom. Good God!

The cloak had done that, the dark cloak with the stains. The stains of earth, grave-earth. The wearing of the cloak, the cold cloak, had given him the feelings of a true vampire. It was a garment accursed, a thing that had lain on the body of one undead. The rusty stain along one sleeve was blood.

Blood. It would be nice to see blood. To taste its warmth, its red life, flowing.

No. That was insane. He was drunk, crazy.

"Ah! My pale friend the vampire."

It was Sheila again. And above all horror rose the beating of Henderson's heart. As he looked at her shining eyes, her warm mouth shaped in red invitation, Henderson felt a wave of warmth. He looked at her white throat rising above her dark, shimmering cloak, and another kind of warmth arose. Love, desire, and a—hunger.

She must have seen it in his eyes, but she did not flinch. Instead her own gaze burned in return.

Sheila loved him, too!

With an impulsive gesture, Henderson ripped the cloak from about his throat. The icy weight lifted. He was free. Somehow, he hadn't wanted to take the cloak off, but he had to. It was a cursed thing, and in another minute he might have taken the girl in his arms, taken her for a kiss and remained to—

But he dared not think of that.

"Tired of masquerading?" she asked. With a similar gesture she, too, removed her cloak and stood revealed in the glory of her angel robe. Her blond, statuesque perfection forced a gasp to Henderson's throat.

"Angel," he whispered.

"Devil," she mocked.

And suddenly they were embracing. Henderson had taken her cloak in his arm with his own. They stood with lips seeking rapture until Lindstrom and a group moved noisily into the anteroom.

At the sight of Henderson the fat host recoiled.

"You—" he whispered. "You are—"

"Just leaving," Henderson smiled. Grasping the girl's arm, he drew her toward the empty elevator. The door shut on Lindstrom's pale, fear-filled face.

"Were we leaving?" Sheila whispered, snuggling against his shoulder.

"We were. But not for earth. We do not go down into my realm, but up—into yours."

"The roof garden?"

"Exactly, my angelic one. I want to talk to you against the background of your own heavens, kiss you amidst the clouds, and—"

Her lips found his as the car rose.

"Angel and devil. What a match!"

"I thought so, too," the girl confessed. "Will our children have halos or horns?"

"Both, I'm sure."

They stepped out onto the deserted rooftop. And once again it was Halloween.

Henderson felt it. Downstairs it was Lindstrom and his society friends, in a drunken costume party. Here it was night, silence, gloom. No light, no music, no drinking, no chatter which made one party identical with another, one night like all the rest. This night was individual here.

The sky was not blue, but black. Clouds hung like the gray beards of hovering giants peering at the round orange globe of the moon. A cold wind blew from the sea, and filled the air with tiny murmurings from afar.

It was also quite cold.

"Give me my cloak," Sheila whispered. Automatically, Henderson extended the garment, and the girl's body swirled under the dark splendor of the cloth. Her eyes burned up at Henderson with a call he could not resist. He kissed her, trembling.

"You're cold," the girl said. "Put on your cloak."

Yes, Henderson, he thought to himself. Put on your cloak while you stare at her throat. Then, the next time you kiss her you will want her throat and she will give it in love and you will take it in—hunger.

"Put it on, darling—I insist," the girl whispered. Her eyes were impatient, burning with an eagerness to match his own.

Henderson trembled.

Put on the cloak of darkness? The cloak of the grave, the cloak of death, the cloak of the vampire? The evil cloak, filled with a cold life of its own that transformed his face, transformed his mind?

"Here."

The girl's slim arms were about him, pushing the cloak onto his shoulders. Her fingers brushed his neck, caressingly, as she linked the cloak about his throat.

Then he felt it—through him—that icy coldness turning to a more dreadful heat. He felt himself expanded, felt the sneer across his face. This was Power!

And the girl before him, her eyes taunting, inviting. He saw her ivory neck, her warm slim neck, waiting. It was waiting for him, for his lips.

For his teeth.

No—it couldn't be. He loved her. His love must conquer this madness. Yes, wear the cloak, defy its power, and take her in his arms as a man, not as a fiend. He must. It was the test.

"Sheila, I must tell you this."

Her eyes—so alluring. It would be easy!

"Sheila, please. You read the paper tonight."

"Yes."

"I . . . I got my cloak there. I can't explain it. You saw how I took Lindstrom. I wanted to go through with it. Do you understand me? I meant to . . . to bite him. Wearing this thing makes me feel like one of those creatures. But I love you, Sheila."

"I know." Her eyes gleamed in the moonlight.

"I want to test it. I want to kiss you, wearing this cloak. I want to feel that my love is stronger than this—thing. If I weaken, promise me you'll break away and run, quickly. But don't misunderstand. I must face this feeling and fight it; I want my love for you to be that pure, that secure. Are you afraid?"

"No." Still she stared at him, just as he stared at her throat. If she knew what was in his mind!

"You don't think I'm crazy? I went to this costumer's—he was a horrible little old man—and he gave me the cloak. Actually told me it was a real vampire's. I thought he was joking, but tonight I didn't see myself in the mirror, and I wanted Lindstrom's neck, and I want you. But I must test it."

The girl's face mocked. Henderson summoned his strength. He bent forward, his impulses battling. For a moment he stood there under the ghastly orange moon, and his face was twisted in struggle.

And the girl lured.

Her odd, incredibly red lips parted in a silvery, chuckly laugh as her white arms rose from the black cloak she wore to circle his neck gently. "I know—I knew when I looked in the mirror. I knew you had a cloak like mine—got yours where I got mine—"

Queerly, her lips seemed to elude his as he stood frozen for an instant of shock. Then he felt the icy hardness of her sharp little teeth on his throat, a strangely soothing sting, and an engulfing blackness rising over him.

WHEN IT WAS MOONLIGHT

MANLY WADE WELLMAN

In his long writing career, Manly Wade Wellman was responsible for a number of vampire stories, many of which appeared in the pages of Weird Tales *and* The Magazine of Fantasy and Science Fiction. *Though Wellman was partial to incorporating folk legends from the American South into his fiction, the two vampire stories he wrote for* Unknown Worlds *took a completely different approach: "The Devil Is Not Mocked" mused about the fate of the Nazis in Transylvania, while "When It Was Moonlight" suggested a possible "real-life" basis for some of Edgar Allan Poe's tales.*

> Let my heart be still a moment, and this mystery explore.
> —"The Raven"

His hand, as slim as a white claw, dipped a quillful of ink and wrote in one corner of the page the date—March 3, 1842. Then:

THE PREMATURE BURIAL
By Edgar A. Poe

He hated his middle name, the name of his miserly and spiteful stepfather. For a moment he considered crossing out even the initial, then he told himself that he was only wool-gathering, putting off the drudgery of writing. And write he must, or starve—the Philadelphia *Dollar Newspaper* was clamoring for the story

he had promised. Well, today he had heard a tag of gossip—his mother-in-law
had it from a neighbor—that revived in his mind a subject always fascinating.

He began rapidly to write, in a fine copperplate hand:

There are certain themes of which the interest is all-absorbing, but which are
entirely too horrible for the purposes of legitimate fiction—

This would really be an essay, not a tale, and he could do it justice. Often he
thought of the whole world as a vast fat cemetery, close set with tombs in which
not all the occupants were at rest—too many struggled unavailingly against their
smothering shrouds, their locked and weighted coffin lids. What were his own
literary labors, he mused, but a struggle against being shut down and throttled by
a society as heavy and grim and senseless as clods heaped by a sexton's spade?

He paused, and went to the slate mantelshelf for a candle. His kerosene lamp
had long ago been pawned, and it was dark for midafternoon, even in March.
Elsewhere in the house his mother-in-law swept busily, and in the room next to
his sounded the quiet breathing of his invalid wife. Poor Virginia slept, and for
the moment knew no pain. Returning with his light, he dipped more ink and
continued down the sheet:

To be buried while alive is, beyond question, the most terrific of these extremes
which has ever fallen to the lot of mere mortality. That it has frequently, very
frequently, fallen will scarcely be denied—

Again his dark imagination savored the tale he had heard that day. It had
happened here in Philadelphia, in this very quarter, less than a month ago. A
widower had gone, after weeks of mourning, to his wife's tomb, with flowers.
Stooping to place them on the marble slab, he had heard noise beneath. At once
joyful and aghast, he fetched men and crowbars, and recovered the body, all
untouched by decay. At home that night, the woman returned to consciousness.

So said the gossip, perhaps exaggerated, perhaps not. And the house was only
six blocks away from Spring Garden Street, where he sat.

Poe fetched out his notebooks and began to marshal bits of narrative for his
composition—a gloomy tale of resurrection in Baltimore, another from France,
a genuinely creepy citation from the *Chirurgical Journal* of Leipzig; a sworn
case of revival, by electric impulses, of a dead man in London. Then he added
an experience of his own, romantically embellished, a dream adventure of his
boyhood in Virginia. Just as he thought to make an end, he had a new inspiration.

Why not learn more about that reputed Philadelphia burial and the one who
rose from seeming death? It would point up his piece, give it a timely local
climax, ensure acceptance—he could hardly risk a rejection. Too, it would
satisfy his own curiosity. Laying down the pen, Poe got up. From a peg he took
his wide black hat, his old military cloak that he had worn since his ill-fated cadet

days at West Point. Huddling it round his slim little body, he opened the front door and went out.

March had come in like a lion and, lionlike, roared and rampaged over Philadelphia. Dry, cold dust blew up into Poe's full gray eyes, and he hardened his mouth under the gay dark mustache. His shins felt goosefleshy; his striped trousers were unseasonably thin and his shoes badly needed mending. Which way lay his journey?

He remembered the name of the street, and something about a ruined garden. Eventually he came to the place, or what must be the place—the garden was certainly ruined, full of dry, hardy weeds that still stood in great ragged clumps after the hard winter. Poe forced open the creaky gate, went up the rough-flagged path to the stoop. He saw a bronzed nameplate—"Gauber," it said. Yes, that was the name he had heard. He swung the knocker loudly, and thought he caught a whisper of movement inside. But the door did not open.

"Nobody lives there, Mr. Poe," said someone from the street. It was a grocery boy, with a heavy basket on his arm. Poe left the doorstep. He knew the lad; indeed he owed the grocer eleven dollars.

"Are you sure?" Poe prompted.

"Well"—and the boy shifted the weight of his burden—"if anybody lived here, they'd buy from our shop, wouldn't they? And I'd deliver, wouldn't I? But I've had this job for six months, and never set foot inside that door."

Poe thanked him and walked down the street, but did not take the turn that would lead home. Instead he sought the shop of one Pemberton, a printer and a friend, to pass the time of day and ask for a loan.

Pemberton could not lend even one dollar—times were hard—but he offered a drink of Monongahela whiskey, which Poe forced himself to refuse; then a supper of crackers, cheese and garlic sausage, which Poe thankfully shared. At home, unless his mother-in-law had begged or borrowed from the neighbors, would be only bread and molasses. It was past sundown when the writer shook hands with Pemberton, thanked him with warm courtesy for his hospitality, and ventured into the evening.

Thank Heaven, it did not rain. Poe was saddened by storms. The wind had abated and the March sky was clear save for a tiny fluff of scudding cloud and a banked dark line at the horizon, while up rose a full moon the color of frozen cream. Poe squinted from under his hat brim at the shadow-pattern on the disk. Might he not write another story of a lunar voyage—like the one about Hans Pfaal, but dead serious this time? Musing thus, he walked along the dusk-filling street until he came again opposite the ruined garden, the creaky gate, and the house with the doorplate marked: "Gauber."

Hello, the grocery boy had been wrong. There was light inside the front window, water-blue light—or was there? Anyway, motion—yes, a figure stooped there, as if to peer out at him.

Poe turned in at the gate, and knocked at the door once again.

Four or five moments of silence; then he heard the old lock grating. The door moved inward, slowly and noisily. Poe fancied that he had been wrong about the blue light, for he saw only darkness inside. A voice spoke: "Well, sir?"

The two words came huskily but softly, as though the door-opener scarcely breathed. Poe swept off his broad black hat and made one of his graceful bows.

"If you will pardon me—" He paused, not knowing whether he addressed man or woman. "This is the Gauber residence?"

"It is," was the reply, soft, hoarse and sexless. "Your business, sir?"

Poe spoke with official crispness; he had been a sergeant-major of artillery before he was twenty-one, and knew how to inject the proper note. "I am here on public duty," he announced. "I am a journalist, tracing a strange report."

"Journalist?" repeated his interrogator. "Strange report? Come in, sir."

Poe complied, and the door closed abruptly behind him, with a rusty snick of the lock. He remembered being in jail once, and how the door of his cell had slammed just so. It was not a pleasant memory. But he saw more clearly, now he was inside—his eyes got used to the tiny trickle of moonlight.

He stood in a dark hallway, all paneled in wood, with no furniture, drapes or pictures. With him was a woman, in full skirt and down-drawn lace cap, a woman as tall as he and with intent eyes that glowed as from within. She neither moved nor spoke, but waited for him to tell her more of his errand.

Poe did so, giving his name and, stretching a point, claiming to be a subeditor of the *Dollar Newspaper,* definitely assigned to the interview. "And now, madam, concerning this story that is rife concerning a premature burial—"

She had moved very close, but as his face turned toward her she drew back. Poe fancied that his breath had blown her away like a feather; then, remembering Pemberton's garlic sausage, he was chagrined. To confirm his new thought, the woman was offering him wine—to sweeten his breath.

"Would you take a glass of canary, Mr. Poe?" she invited, and opened a side door. He followed her into a room papered in pale blue. Moonglow, drenching it, reflected from that paper and seemed an artificial light. That was what he had seen from outside. From an undraped table his hostess lifted a bottle, poured wine into a metal goblet and offered it.

Poe wanted that wine, but he had recently promised his sick wife, solemnly and honestly, to abstain from even a sip of the drink that so easily upset him. Through thirsty lips he said: "I thank you kindly, but I am a temperance man."

"Oh," and she smiled. Poe saw white teeth. Then: "I am Elva Gauber—Mrs. John Gauber. The matter of which you ask I cannot explain clearly, but it is true. My husband was buried, in the Eastman Lutheran Churchyard—"

"I had heard, Mrs. Gauber, that the burial concerned a woman."

"No, my husband. He had been ill. He felt cold and quiet. A physician, a Dr. Mechem, pronounced him dead, and he was interred beneath a marble slab in his family vault." She sounded weary, but her voice was calm. "This happened shortly after the New Year. On Valentine's Day, I brought flowers. Beneath his slab he stirred and struggled. I had him brought forth. And he lives—after a fashion—today."

"Lives today?" repeated Poe. "In this house?"

"Would you care to see him? Interview him?"

Poe's heart raced, his spine chilled. It was his peculiarity that such sensations gave him pleasure. "I would like nothing better," he assured her, and she went to another door, an inner one.

Opening it, she paused on the threshold, as though summoning her resolution for a plunge into cold, swift water. Then she started down a flight of steps.

Poe followed, unconsciously drawing the door shut behind him.

The gloom of midnight, of prison—yes, of the tomb—fell at once upon those stairs. He heard Elva Gauber gasp: "No—the moonlight—let it in—" And then she fell, heavily and limply, rolling downstairs.

Aghast, Poe quickly groped his way after her. She lay against a door at the foot of the flight, wedged against the panel. He touched her—she was cool and rigid, without motion or elasticity of life. His thin hand groped for and found the knob of the lower door, flung it open. More dim reflected moonlight, and he made shift to drag the woman into it.

Almost at once she sighed heavily, lifted her head, and rose. "How stupid of me," she apologized hoarsely.

"The fault was mine," protested Poe. "Your nerves, your health, have naturally suffered. The sudden dark—the closeness—overcame you." He fumbled in his pocket for a tinderbox. "Suffer me to strike a light."

But she held out a hand to stop him. "No, no. The moon is sufficient." She walked to a small, oblong pane set in the wall. Her hands, thin as Poe's own, with long grubby nails, hooked on the sill. Her face, bathed in the full light of the moon, strengthened and grew calm. She breathed deeply, almost voluptuously. "I am quite recovered," she said. "Do not fear for me. You need not stand so near, sir."

He had forgotten that garlic odor, and drew back contritely. She must be as sensitive to the smell as . . . as . . . what was it that was sickened and driven away by garlic? Poe could not remember, and took time to note that they were in a basement, stone-walled and with a floor of dirt. In one corner water seemed to drip, forming a dank pool of mud. Close to this, set into the wall, showed a latched trapdoor of planks, thick and wide, cleated crosswise, as though to cover a window. But no window would be set so low. Everything smelt earthy and close, as though fresh air had been shut out for decades.

"Your husband is here?" he inquired.

"Yes." She walked to the shutterlike trap, unlatched it and drew it open.

The recess beyond was as black as ink, and from it came a feeble mutter. Poe followed Elva Gauber, and strained his eyes. In a little stone-flagged nook a bed had been made up. Upon it lay a man, stripped almost naked. His skin was as white as dead bone, and only his eyes, now opening, had life. He gazed at Elva Gauber, and past her at Poe.

"Go away," he mumbled.

"Sir," ventured Poe formally, "I have come to hear of how you came to life in the grave—"

"It's a lie," broke in the man on the pallet. He writhed halfway to a sitting posture, laboring upward as against a crushing weight. The wash of moonlight showed how wasted and fragile he was. His face stared and snarled bare-toothed, like a skull. "A lie, I say!" he cried, with a sudden strength that might well have been his last. "Told by this monster who is not—my wife—"

The shutter-trap slammed upon his cries. Elva Gauber faced Poe, withdrawing a pace to avoid his garlic breath.

"You have seen my husband," she said. "Was it a pretty sight, sir?"

He did not answer, and she moved across the dirt to the stair doorway. "Will you go up first?" she asked. "At the top, hold the door open, that I may have—" She said "life," or, perhaps, "light." Poe could not be sure which.

Plainly she, who had almost welcomed his intrusion at first, now sought to lead him away. Her eyes, compelling as shouted commands, were fixed upon him. He felt their power, and bowed to it.

Obediently he mounted the stairs, and stood with the upper door wide. Elva Gauber came up after him. At the top her eyes again seized his. Suddenly Poe knew more than ever before about the mesmeric impulses he loved to write about.

"I hope," she said measuredly, "that you have not found your visit fruitless. I live here alone—seeing nobody, caring for the poor thing that was once my husband, John Gauber. My mind is not clear. Perhaps my manners are not good. Forgive me, and good night."

Poe found himself ushered from the house, and outside the wind was howling once again. The front door closed behind him, and the lock grated.

The fresh air, the whip of gale in his face, and the absence of Elva Gauber's impelling gaze suddenly brought him back, as though from sleep, to a realization of what had happened—or what had not happened.

He had come out, on this uncomfortable March evening, to investigate the report of a premature burial. He had seen a ghastly sick thing, that had called the gossip a lie. Somehow, then, he had been drawn abruptly away—stopped from full study of what might be one of the strangest adventures it was ever a writer's good fortune to know. Why was he letting things drop at this stage?

He decided not to let them drop. That would be worse than staying away altogether.

He made up his mind, formed quickly a plan. Leaving the doorstep, he turned from the gate, slipped quickly around the house. He knelt by the foundation at the side, just where a small oblong pane was set flush with the ground.

Bending his head, he found that he could see plainly inside, by reason of the flood of moonlight—a phenomenon, he realized, for generally an apartment was disclosed only by light within. The open doorway to the stairs, the swamp mess of mud in the corner, the out-flung trapdoor, were discernible. And something stood or huddled at the exposed niche—something that bent itself upon and above the frail white body of John Gauber.

Full skirt, white cap—it was Elva Gauber. She bent herself down, her face was touching the face or shoulder of her husband.

Poe's heart, never the healthiest of organs, began to drum and race. He pressed closer to the pane, for a better glimpse of what went on in the cellar. His shadow cut away some of the light. Elva Gauber turned to look.

Her face was as pale as the moon itself. Like the moon, it was shadowed in irregular patches. She came quickly, almost running, toward the pane where Poe crouched. He saw her, plainly and at close hand.

Dark, wet, sticky stains lay upon her mouth and cheeks. Her tongue roved out, licking at the stains—

Blood!

Poe sprang up and ran to the front of the house. He forced his thin, trembling fingers to seize the knocker, to swing it heavily again and again. When there was no answer, he pushed heavily against the door itself—it did not give. He moved to a window, rapped on it, pried at the sill, lifted his fist to smash the glass.

A silhouette moved beyond the pane, and threw it up. Something shot out at him like a pale snake striking—before he could move back, fingers had twisted in the front of his coat. Elva Gauber's eyes glared into his.

Her cap was off, her dark hair fallen in disorder. Blood still smeared and dewed her mouth and jowls.

"You have pried too far," she said, in a voice as measured and cold as the drip from icicles. "I was going to spare you, because of the odor about you that repelled me—the garlic. I showed you a little, enough to warn any wise person, and let you go. Now—"

Poe struggled to free himself. Her grip was immovable, like the clutch of a steel trap. She grimaced in triumph, yet she could not quite face him—the garlic still clung to his breath.

"Look in my eyes," she bade him. "Look—you cannot refuse, you cannot escape. You will die, with John—and the two of you, dying, shall rise again like me. I'll have two fountains of life while you remain—two companions after you die."

"Woman," said Poe, fighting against her stabbing gaze, "you are mad."

She snickered gustily. "I am sane, and so are you. We both know that I speak the truth. We both know the futility of your struggle." Her voice rose a little. "Through a chink in the tomb, as I lay dead, a ray of moonlight streamed and struck my eyes. I woke. I struggled. I was set free. Now at night, when the moon shines— *Ugh!* Don't breathe that herb in my face!"

She turned her head away. At that instant it seemed to Poe that a curtain of utter darkness fell, and with it sank down the form of Elva Gauber.

He peered in the sudden gloom. She was collapsed across the window sill, like a discarded puppet in its booth. Her hand still twisted in the bosom of his coat, and he pried himself loose from it, finger by steely, cold finger. Then he turned to flee from this place of shadowed peril to body and soul.

As he turned, he saw whence had come the dark. A cloud had come up from its place on the horizon—the fat, sooty bank he had noted there at sundown—and now it obscured the moon. Poe paused, in midretreat, gazing.

His thoughtful eye gauged the speed and size of the cloud. It curtained the moon, would continue to curtain it for—well, ten minutes. And for that ten minutes, Elva Gauber would lie motionless, lifeless. She had told the truth about the moon giving her life. Hadn't she fallen like one slain on the stairs when they were darkened. Poe began grimly to string the evidence together.

It was Elva Gauber, not her husband, who had died and gone to the family vault. She had come back to life, or a mockery of life, by touch of the moon's rays. Such light was an unpredictable force—it made dogs howl, it flogged madmen to violence, it brought fear, or black sorrow, or ecstasy. Old legends said that it was the birth of fairies, the transformation of werewolves, the motive power of broom-riding witches. It was surely the source of the strength and evil animating what had been the corpse of Elva Gauber—and he, Poe, must not stand there dreaming.

He summoned all the courage that was his, and scrambled in at the window through which slumped the woman's form. He groped across the room to the cellar door, opened it and went down the stairs, through the door at the bottom, and into the stone-walled basement.

It was dark, moonless still. Poe paused only to bring forth his tinder box, strike a light and kindle the end of a tightly twisted linen rag. It gave a feeble steady light, and he found his way to the shutter, opened it and touched the naked, wasted shoulder of John Gauber.

"Get up," he said. "I've come to save you."

The skullface feebly lifted its position to meet his gaze. The man managed to speak, moaningly: "Useless. I can't move—unless she lets me. Her eyes keep me here—half alive. I'd have died long ago, but somehow—"

Poe thought of a wretched spider, paralyzed by the sting of a mudwasp, lying helpless in its captive's close den until the hour of feeding comes. He bent down, holding his blazing tinder close. He could see Gauber's neck, and it was a mass of tiny puncture wounds, some of them still beaded with blood drops fresh or dried. He winced, but bode firm in his purpose.

"Let me guess the truth," he said quickly. "Your wife was brought home from the grave, came back to a seeming of life. She put a spell on you, or played a trick—made you a helpless prisoner. That isn't contrary to nature, that last. I've studied mesmerism."

"It's true," John Gauber mumbled.

"And nightly she comes to drink your blood?"

Gauber weakly nodded. "Yes. She was beginning just now, but ran upstairs. She will be coming back."

"Good," said Poe bleakly. "Perhaps she will come back to more than she expects. Have you ever heard of vampires? Probably not, but I have studied them, too. I began to guess, I think, when first she was so repelled by the odor of garlic. Vampires lie motionless by day, and walk and feed at night. They are creatures of the moon—their food is blood. Come."

Poe broke off, put out his light, and lifted the man in his arms. Gauber was as light as a child. The writer carried him to the slanting shelter of the closed-in staircase, and there set him against the wall. Over him Poe spread his old cadet cloak. In the gloom, the gray of the cloak harmonized with the gray of the wall stones. The poor fellow would be well hidden.

Next Poe flung off his coat, waistcoat and shirt. Heaping his clothing in a deeper shadow of the stairway, he stood up, stripped to the waist. His skin was almost as bloodlessly pale as Gauber's, his chest and arms almost as gaunt. He dared believe that he might pass momentarily for the unfortunate man.

The cellar sprang full of light again. The cloud must be passing from the moon. Poe listened. There was a dragging sound above, then footsteps.

Elva Gauber, the blood drinker by night, had revived.

Now for it. Poe hurried to the niche, thrust himself in and pulled the trapdoor shut after him.

He grinned, sharing a horrid paradox with the blackness around him. He had heard all the fabled ways of destroying vampires—transfixing stakes, holy water, prayer, fire. But he, Edgar Allan Poe, had evolved a new way. Myriads of tales whispered frighteningly of fiends lying in wait for normal men, but who ever heard of a normal man lying in wait for a fiend? Well, he had never considered himself normal, in spirit, or brain, or taste.

He stretched out, feet together, hands crossed on his bare midriff. Thus it would be in the tomb, he found himself thinking. To his mind came a snatch of poetry by a man named Bryant, published long ago in a New England review— *"Breathless darkness, and the narrow house."* It was breathless and dark enough in this hole, Heaven knew, and narrow as well. He rejected, almost hysterically, the implication of being buried. To break the ugly spell, that daunted him where thought of Elva Gauber failed, he turned sideways to face the wall, his naked arm lying across his cheek and temple.

As his ear touched the musty bedding, it brought to him once again the echo of footsteps, footsteps descending stairs. They were rhythmic, confident. They were eager.

Elva Gauber was coming to seek again her interrupted repast.

Now she was crossing the floor. She did not pause or turn aside—she had not noticed her husband, lying under the cadet cloak in the shadow of the stairs. The noise came straight to the trapdoor, and he heard her fumbling for the latch.

Light, blue as skimmed milk, poured into his nook. A shadow fell in the midst of it, full upon him. His imagination, ever outstripping reality, whispered that the shadow had weight, like lead—oppressive, baleful.

"John," said the voice of Elva Gauber in his ear, "I've come back. You know why—you know what for." Her voice sounded greedy, as though it came through loose, trembling lips. "You're my only source of strength now. I thought tonight, that a stranger—but he got away. He had a cursed odor about him, anyway."

Her hand touched the skin of his neck. She was prodding him, like a butcher fingering a doomed beast.

"Don't hold yourself away from me, John," she was commanding, in a voice of harsh mockery. "You know it won't do any good. This is the night of the full moon, and I have power for anything, anything!" She was trying to drag his arm away from his face. "You won't gain by—" She broke off, aghast. Then, in a wild-dry-throated scream:

"You're not John!"

Poe whipped over on his back, and his bird-claw hands shot out and seized her—one hand clinching upon her snaky disorder of dark hair, the other digging its fingertips into the chill flesh of her arm.

The scream quivered away into a horrible breathless rattle. Poe dragged his captive violently inward, throwing all his collected strength into the effort. Her feet were jerked from the floor and she flew into the recess, hurtling above and beyond Poe's recumbent body. She struck the inner stones with a crashing force that might break bones, and would have collapsed upon Poe; but, at the same moment, he had released her and slid swiftly out upon the floor of the cellar.

With frantic haste he seized the edge of the back-flung trapdoor. Elva Gauber struggled up on hands and knees, among the tumbled bedclothes in the niche; then Poe had slammed the panel shut.

She threw herself against it from within, yammering and wailing like an animal in a trap. She was almost as strong as he, and for a moment he thought that she would win out of the niche. But, sweating and wheezing, he bore against the planks with his shoulder, bracing his feet against the earth. His fingers found the latch, lifted it, forced it into place.

"Dark," moaned Elva Gauber from inside. "Dark—no moon—" Her voice trailed off.

Poe went to the muddy pool in the corner, thrust in his hands. The muck was slimy but workable. He pushed a double handful of it against the trapdoor, sealing cracks and edges. Another handful, another. Using his palms like trowels, he coated the boards with thick mud.

"Gauber," he said breathlessly, "how are you?"

"All right—I think." The voice was strangely strong and clear. Looking over his shoulder, Poe saw that Gauber had come upright of himself, still pale but apparently steady. "What are you doing?" Gauber asked.

"Walling her up," jerked out Poe, scooping still more mud. "Walling her up forever, with her devil."

He had a momentary flash of inspiration, a symbolic germ of a story; in it a man sealed a woman into such a nook of the wall, and with her an embodiment of active evil—perhaps in the form of a black cat.

Pausing at last to breathe deeply, he smiled to himself. Even in the direst of danger, the most heartbreaking moment of toil and fear, he must ever be coining new plots for stories.

"I cannot thank you enough," Gauber was saying to him. "I feel that all will be well—if only she stays there."

Poe put his ear to the wall. "Not a whisper of motion, sir. She's shut off from moonlight—from life and power. Can you help me with my clothes? I feel terribly chilled."

His mother-in-law met him on the threshold when he returned to the house in Spring Garden Street. Under the white widow's cap, her strong-boned face was drawn with worry.

"Eddie, are you ill?" She was really asking if he had been drinking. A look reassured her. "No," she answered herself, "but you've been away from home so long. And you're dirty, Eddie—filthy. You must wash."

He let her lead him in, pour hot water into a basin. As he scrubbed himself, he formed excuses, a banal lie about a long walk for inspiration, a moment of dizzy weariness, a stumble into a mud puddle.

"I'll make you some nice hot coffee, Eddie," his mother-in-law offered.

"Please," he responded, and went back to his room with the slate mantelpiece. Again he lighted the candle, sat down and took up his pen.

His mind was embellishing the story inspiration that had come to him at such a black moment, in the cellar of the Gauber house. He'd work on that tomorrow. The *United States Saturday Post* would take it, he hoped. Title? He would call it simply "The Black Cat."

But to finish the present task! He dipped his pen in ink. How to begin? How to end? How, after writing and publishing such an account, to defend himself against the growing whisper of his insanity?

He decided to forget it, if he could—at least to seek healthy company, comfort, quiet—perhaps even to write some light verse, some humorous articles and stories. For the first time in his life, he had had enough of the macabre.

Quickly he wrote a final paragraph:

> There are moments when, even to the sober eye of Reason, the world of our sad Humanity may assume the semblance of a Hell—but the imagination of man is no Carathis, to explore with impunity its every cavern. Alas! The grim legion of sepulchral terrors cannot be regarded as altogether fanciful—but, like the Demons in whose company Afrasiab made his voyage down the Oxus, they must sleep, or they will devour us—they must be suffered to slumber, or we will perish.

That would do for the public, decided Edgar Allan Poe. In any case, it would do for the Philadelphia *Dollar Newspaper*.

His mother-in-law brought in the coffee.

"WHO SHALL I SAY IS CALLING?"

AUGUST DERLETH

August Derleth's first professional sale, the 1926 story "Bat's Belfry," was a vampire tale. Over the next forty-five years, Derleth wrote numerous other vampire stories for a variety of pulp magazines, but none so engaging as the satirical "Who Shall I Say Is Calling?" Reflecting the light tone of much horror fiction written in the postwar years, the tale suggests that proper social graces might be as critical as blood for a vampire's survival.

MY SISTER SAW the place first—one of those fine old houses bought up by someone newly rich and rehabilitated. It was set back a little way from the road, and now, in mid-evening, it was ablaze with lights.

"A party," she whispered. "A masquerade!"

We could see people in costume gliding back and forth across the windows.

"Let's crash it," she said.

I was game. "Who shall we be?"

She looked at me judiciously, her head cocked to one side, and her eyes shone, as always, in the darkness. "You could be the Admirable Crichton and I could go as I am for Lady Windermere."

She raced ahead of me and rang the bell.

The fellow who answered the door was in costume, too—Jeeves to the life. He was correct, austere, but with a twinkle. "Who shall I say is calling?" he asked.

"The Admirable Crichton," I said. "And Lady Windermere."

He chuckled admonitorily and shook his head. "I'm sorry," he said. "We already have an Admirable Crichton. The rule was no duplications."

Maryla snapped her fingers impatiently. "Make it Count and Lady Dracula," she said.

Jeeves made a low bow and swept us in.

Maryla put a hand on my arm and held me back until Jeeves caught up and led us to our host and hostess.

"Robespierre and Madame de Maintenon," he said. "The Count and Lady Dracula."

"We are just in from Orleans," said Madame de Maintenon, acting her part. "And you?"

I hesitated. Was I now Crichton or Count Dracula, by Maryla's impetuous decision?

"From Castle Dracula, near Bistritz, Transylvania," said Maryla, making a curtsy.

They were trying to figure out who we were. They looked puzzled. I could see that we had a familiar appearance for them, particularly me. I turned to our hostess and offered her my arm.

"May I have the honor of this dance?" I asked.

She nodded, took my arm, and we swung away. Maryla fairly fell into Robespierre's arms, and away they went. We danced among other maskers, some with dominoes, some with false faces, some without anything but makeup. Frankenstein, Hamlet, Lady Macbeth, Peter the Hermit, Landru, Marie Antoinette, Carmen, the Admirable Crichton, Psmith, Major Barbara, Lord Jim, Captain Bligh, Pearl White, Cleopatra—they were all there. It was quite a party; evidently our host and hostess had wangled every worthwhile costume from the nearby city.

I caught Maryla's eye. She winked and ran her tongue quickly out over her lower lip.

"Who are you?" asked my partner at last.

"Is it fair to tell?" I asked. "I could have been the Admirable Crichton. But you have one. I could have passed for the Duke of Gloucester—without his medals and ribbons, of course—but that's a little prosaic. Dukes, you know. Aren't you traditional? Unmask at midnight."

She nodded. "Count Dracula," she mused. "You do remind me of Bela Lugosi. I know you. I've met you somewhere."

"I see you have Frankenstein and Boris Karloff. I'm in good company."

"Yes, and Dr. Fu Manchu, too." She looked at me closely through her domino. "I know I've seen you somewhere. Don't tell me. Let me guess. Was it on the stage? Were you in *Arsenic and Old Lace*?"

"No, and I'm not Monty Woolley, either," I said. "Though I confess I like to stay for dinner."

She laughed. She was not so young as I had thought at first. If you stay out of circulation long enough you find your judgment a little warped. But her makeup was heavy, very heavy. I wanted to dance with someone younger.

"How is it?" Maryla asked, when we got together after that first dance.

"It goes," I answered. "What about you?"

"He bored me. A little fresh. Couldn't dance, either."

"Maybe you were the stiff one," I said. "After all . . ."

"Take a look at that boy over there," Maryla said.

I did. Apollo. "Watch yourself," I said.

She smiled and darted into the crowd, straight for Apollo. I gazed past Sherlock Holmes and Professor Moriarty and picked out Cinderella. She looked good—flushed with youth and vibrant. She was pink and white and too pretty to hide it behind anything more than a domino on a stick, which she held up dowagerlike as a lorgnette. Just at the moment she did not appear to be engaged. I walked over.

"May I?" I said, leering and showing my teeth. "Count Dracula, at your service."

She squealed and giggled. "My, what pointed teeth you have, Dracula!" she said.

"The better to bite you with, my dear," I answered.

She gave me her arm. "If you promise not to bite you may have this dance."

"I promise," I said. "It's too early, anyway. I've just had supper."

She laughed.

She danced well, but there was something about her that repelled me.

Maryla had had luck, too. "That was a good dance," she said. "Who are these people, anyway?"

"Don't ask me. Are you beginning to feel there's something queer here, too?"

"Yes, a tension or something."

"Sure, I noticed it right away."

Had I? I wondered. But it was there—a strange, intense sense of waiting, as if they all expected something to happen, or were waiting for someone who was late.

"Could it be that couple we met four or five miles down the road?" asked Maryla. "You did think they were oddly dressed."

"Of course," I said. "That's it. They were coming here. Reverend Dimmesdale and Hester Prynne. I knew they reminded me of someone."

"Car trouble," said Maryla.

"We won't say anything about it," I said. "There's something more. It makes me uneasy."

"Oh, we can't back out now," she cried.

"No. Just the same, they may suspect we're gate-crashers."

"They couldn't tell among all these people." She laughed. "Our host even thought I was wearing one of those new skintight rubber masks. I told him they didn't make them that close to the life."

The orchestra struck up another number.

"What time is it?" asked Maryla.

"There's a clock over there. Almost eleven."

"We can dance some more."

I had the next dance with a little beauty, as light as a feather on her feet. It was a pleasure to dance with her, though I felt awkward. She seemed to know her way about, and she knew a great many people.

"I don't know you," she confessed.

"I don't even know who you're supposed to be," I said.

"I'm Bluebeard's tenth wife," she said.

That puzzled me for a moment. "Did he have ten?" I asked cautiously.

"No. That's just the point. Since he didn't have ten nobody could say just what she looked like, could he? So I'm safe."

I laughed.

She looked preoccupied, and kept gazing over my shoulder toward the door to the ballroom.

"Are they waiting for someone?" I asked.

"Oh, you noticed it, too," she said.

"It's in the air."

"Something is, yes. I don't know what. I know they're expecting Arthur Porefoy and his wife, Ardeth; they're late. But it isn't that. They're usually late. It's fashionable, you see; so they come late."

"How do you know they're not here? Or do you know all the maskers?" I asked.

She shook her head. "I happen to know how they're masking. They're coming as Dimmesdale and Hester Prynne; there's no one here who looks remotely like either one of them. So they're late. Oh, they'll come before twelve; they always do. But it isn't the Porefoys; it's something else. I can feel it."

"What do you mean?" I asked.

"Do you believe in the psychic?" she countered.

"Yes and no," I answered.

"Ah, you're playing it on the safe side. Now, I'm psychic. I'm uneasy because I know there's something wrong, something very much wrong about Hartson's party, and I can't put my finger on it."

"I think we all have feelings like that from time to time," I said. "That's no proof of the psychic. The scientists have shown—"

"Oh, they're so glib, so smooth, so sure of themselves!" she protested impatiently.

"Aren't they!" I agreed.

There was something in what she said, just the same. The air of the masquerade was thickening, the feeling of strangeness was deepening. I could see the maskers looking uneasily about. A new mask had joined the throng, in fire-red; he was the Mask of the Red Death, and he certainly caught the eyes of most of the dancers, for he was tall and terrible and impressive—his was a wonderfully effective costume!

"My God!" whispered Bluebeard's tenth wife, "that's Johnny Deakin—and isn't he exciting!"

"Isn't he a little tall for Deakin?" I asked.

She looked again, anxiously. "He *is* a little tall," she conceded. "But he might be wearing something on his feet to make him look taller."

"Half a foot?" I asked.

"Oh, no—three or four inches."

"It could be his costume."

"It's his build, though; you can see that through all the flummery."

The dance came to an end and Maryla joined me as soon as Bluebeard's tenth wife walked away. The Mask of the Red Death stalked grandly and menacingly among the dancers; people looked after him, some of them in puzzlement, some with what seemed to be recognition.

"What a creation!" said Maryla.

"It must have taken him half the evening to get into that costume," I said.

"Listen, I hope you don't mind, but I've smitten Apollo."

"Oh, congratulations," I said. "I've made quite an impression on Cinderella, too."

"Oh, that one. I thought it was this last one. I would have preferred her," Maryla said, a little coldly.

"Darling, you don't mind?"

"Of course not. I'm dancing again with Apollo. I think I might go outside with him."

I looked at the clock. "Probably that would be a good idea. We ought to get away before the unmasking takes place. That would be midnight; these dances are long. Can you manage? I'll try to make it at about the same time. Meet you somewhere outside."

"All right."

I looked over at Apollo. He had his eye on Maryla, undoubtedly. He had a magnificent physique, though he was only of medium height, and not as tall as Maryla usually liked men to be.

"You certainly can pick them," I murmured.

"Listen," she said again, urgently. "Don't you feel this choking queerness in the room?"

"Yes. I've felt it all along. The rest of them are beginning to feel it, too. They're waiting for the Porefoys, for one thing."

"Who are they?"

"That couple we met."

"Oh, yes—Dimmesdale and Hester. Older people."

The music struck up again. We found partners and danced.

I took a turn with my hostess once more, then another woman, and finally took Cinderella out again.

"It's close to midnight," she said, teasingly. "Are you getting ready to bite?"

"Darling, I've been whetting my teeth all evening," I said.

"Oh, you're funny!" she said giggling. "I'll bet you say that to all the girls."

I laughed. "How did you know?" I asked. "But they never believe me; I'm losing my touch."

"Do you know, you're cold," she said.

"Oh, I might be—here. I don't like crowds. But if we were alone, I rather think I wouldn't be so cold."

She giggled again. It had an almost nasty sound.

"Where's your Prince?" I asked.

"I left him at home," she answered.

"It's getting uncommonly warm and uncomfortable in this room," I said then, having just seen Maryla slip away with Apollo, out of a back door.

Cinderella gave me an arch look. "The French windows are just over there. We could step outside for a moment. It's warm there, too."

"But it wouldn't be stuffy."

"We could walk in the gardens."

"Could we?"

"If you liked. You make me very curious. I'm going to hang on to you until midnight and find out who you are."

"Oh, we came as ourselves," I said. "Or didn't I tell you?"

We slipped out through the partly open French windows and found ourselves on a wide verandah. One or two other couples were there, too. I looked quickly around, just in time to see Maryla and her Apollo vanishing into the shrubbery of the well-appointed garden that stretched away beyond the house.

"The gardens are that way," whispered Cinderella.

Behind us the music ceased suddenly, and a hubbub of conversation rose, mingled with cries of consternation and horror.

"Something happened," I said.

"Just a moment. I'll see."

Cinderella joined the other dancers crowding back into the room from the verandah, but in a few moments she was back at my side, taking my hand confidently in hers, and leading the way to the gardens, rapidly, before anyone could catch us moving away from the house. She must have had some relative among the dancers or someone who might have followed, and she did not intend that we should be followed.

"What was it?" I asked.

"Oh, some ghastly joke," she answered. "It's just like Arthur Porefoy; he's always doing things like that. He sent three people masquerading as policemen to tell the Hartsons that he and his wife had been murdered down the road a little way, and they're spreading a wild story about how they stopped because they apparently had motor trouble and were killed by animals or something of that kind. Porefoy always has had bad taste."

"Yes," I agreed. "A bad taste and thinned blood. Both of them."

"My God! they're the tightest people I know. It must have cost them something to do a stunt like this one—unless the policemen owed him money."

We were in the gardens now, and just ahead of us we could see Maryla and her Apollo. They were languid. She was leaning on his arm, and he was acting possessive and proud. He was definitely on the make, and Maryla was leading him on, just as she always does.

Looking at them, I was aware once more of that curiously tense anxiety I had known throughout the evening. "Do you know Apollo?" I asked.

"Sure," she answered. "He's my cousin, Dick Girdler."

Let them get ahead, I thought. I deliberately held back, moving closer to Cinderella.

"That's a lovely locket," I said.

I reached out to touch it, but something happened. I couldn't reach it. Something like a wall stood between me and the locket. It felt warm, hot—hot as the center of that revulsion I had experienced dancing with her.

"Oh, that," she said, and laughed. "It's an heirloom—and so old! I couldn't begin to tell you how old. It's supposed to contain a fragment of the true cross." She laughed again. "But nobody believes in superstitions like that any more, do they?"

"No," I said, "of course not."

I stopped. The locket burned on her throat; it burned in my sight.

"What's the matter?" she asked, smiling flirtatiously. "Have you lost your yen to bite?"

"I've been thinking of your cousin. After all, I know my sister. Maryla can be unpleasant."

"I don't doubt it. I must confess I don't like her looks."

"Do you mind very much if I just run forward and see that everything's all right?"

She shook her head. "Not at all. I had no idea you were so—shall we say, old-fashioned?"

"Oh, I am, I am," I said.

I hurried down the garden. Tension and unease flowed out behind me. That confounded locket! I should have known.

Maryla was in his arms, teasing him.

"Maryla," I said.

She broke free of him, her eyes blazing with anger. "Go away."

"Look," I said, making a signal of danger she understood. "Come."

"Go away," she said again, furiously. "Can't you see?"

I could see plainly enough. Hunger took precedence over all else. Gluttony, rather. After the Reverend Dimmesdale and Hester Prynne, even Apollo could hardly be more than an anti-climax.

"Your husband?" asked Apollo, holding on to her.

"Absurd," said Maryla. "He interferes."

"It would be better to come at once," I said, nettled.

"Look, brother," said Apollo aggressively. "Take a powder, can't you?"

"I won't be long," said Maryla.

I could believe that. I said, "Now."

"Maybe I could persuade you," said Apollo.

I looked at him. He had clenched one fist suggestively. It would serve him right, I thought. But Maryla vexed me. She knew that her obedience was mandatory, but this exposure to American freedom for her sex had gone to her head.

"Why don't you go back to your castle or your coffin or wherever you came from," said Apollo.

"Thanks," I said.

I turned and went back to where Cinderella was waiting.

"Look," I said. "Your cousin's in danger."

"What danger?"

"Must you ask?" I cried. "Her teeth are sharper than mine."

"Claws, more likely," she said.

"Will you do something? It might sound foolish, but—"

Her eyes gleamed. "What is it?"

"Will you go down there where they are and go up to them and just take your locket and touch her with it?"

She looked at me open-mouthed. "Are you serious?"

"Perfectly. You'll surprise her. You'll really surprise her. She'll hardly be able to bear it."

She cradled the locket in her hand and looked at it. "This locket?" she said wonderingly.

I nodded. "She has an allergy to crosses—especially true crosses."

"Oh, I get it," she said. "Her cross is the double-cross." She laughed immoderately.

That, in addition to her locket! I gritted my teeth as much as I was able and held myself in. "Please, will you?" I said.

"Will she jump?" she asked.

"She certainly will." I smiled.

She made a curious figure O with her thumb and index finger and said, "You're in. I'm on."

And away she went.

That will teach Maryla, I thought. If I have to go without dinner, by Hell! so will she! I moved away into the shadows to wait for her. She would be coming in a hurry, smarting and furious.

I heard her scream. It gave me a great deal of satisfaction.

In a moment she came running out, almost carelessly fast. She saw me and came at me in a direct line.

"Beast!" she cried.

"I warned you," I said.

"He was so pliable, so strong; he would have been so *good*! We could have shared him."

"Is it too late?" I asked. "Look. Or does she know?"

Cinderella sped toward the house, one hand clapped to her mouth.

"Ridiculous. She thought it was a game."

"And now he comes. He's really smitten."

Apollo came out, looking this way and that, calling softly.

"Ass," I whispered.

"I'm here," Maryla called.

"Hurry," I said.

She moved toward him, and I edged around to be ready on the other side. There was so little time. But I could count on Maryla. She is always so anxious, so voracious, so ravenously hungry, and she works so fast, so cleanly! She was right about him, too. It would have been a mistake to leave him.

SHE ONLY GOES OUT AT NIGHT

WILLIAM TENN

William Tenn was one of the handful of truly original science fiction writers to emerge from the glut of science fiction magazines published in the postwar years. Occasionally, he wrote fantasy and horror for such magazines as Weird Tales *and* Famous Fantastic Mysteries, *where his famous vampire tale "The Human Angle" appeared.* Fantastic Universe *allowed him to apply the principles of science fiction to a traditional weird fiction theme in "She Only Goes Out at Night," a story that promotes a scientifically feasible means for vampires to coexist with mortals.*

IN THIS PART of the country, folks think that Doc Judd carries magic in his black leather satchel. He's *that* good.

Ever since I lost my leg in the sawmill, I've been all-around handyman at the Judd place. Lots of times when Doc gets a night call after a real hard day, he's too tired to drive, so he hunts me up and I become a chauffeur too. With the shiny plastic leg that Doc got me at a discount, I can stamp the gas pedal with the best of them.

We roar up to the farmhouse and, while Doc goes inside to deliver a baby or swab grandma's throat, I sit in the car and listen to them talk about what a ball of fire the old Doc is. In Groppa County, they'll tell you Doc Judd can handle *anything*. And I nod and listen, nod and listen.

But all the time I'm wondering what they'd think of the way he handled his only son falling in love with a vampire. . . .

It was a terrifically hot summer when Steve came home on vacation—real blister weather. He wanted to drive his father around and kind of help with the chores, but Doc said that after the first tough year of medical school anyone deserved a vacation.

"Summer's a pretty quiet time in our line," he told the boy. "Nothing but poison ivy and such until we hit the polio season in August. Besides, you wouldn't want to shove old Tom out of his job, would you? No, Stevie you just bounce around the countryside in your jalopy and enjoy yourself."

Steve nodded and took off. And I mean took off. About a week later, he started coming home five or six o'clock in the morning. He'd sleep till about three in the afternoon, laze around for a couple of hours and, come eight thirty, off he'd rattle in his little hotrod. Road-houses, we figured, or maybe some girl . . .

Doc didn't like it, but he'd brought up the boy with a nice easy hand and he didn't feel like saying anything just yet. Old buttinsky Tom, though—I was different. I'd helped raise the kid since his mother died, and I'd walloped him when I caught him raiding the icebox.

So I dropped a hint now and then, kind of asking him, like, not to go too far off the deep end. I could have been talking to a stone fence for all the good it did. Not that Steve was rude. He was just too far gone in whatever it was to pay attention to me.

And then the other stuff started and Doc and I forgot about Steve.

Some kind of weird epidemic hit the kids of Groppa County and knocked twenty, thirty of them flat on their backs.

"It's almost got me beat, Tom," Doc would confide in me as we bump-bump-bumped over dirty back-country roads. "It acts like a bad fever, yet the rise in temperature is hardly noticeable. But the kids get very weak and their blood count goes way down. And it stays that way, no matter what I do. Only good thing, it doesn't seem to be fatal—so far."

Every time he talked about it, I felt a funny twinge in my stump where it was attached to the plastic leg. I got so uncomfortable that I tried to change the subject, but that didn't go with Doc. He'd gotten used to thinking out his problems by talking to me, and this epidemic thing was pretty heavy on his mind.

He'd written to a couple of universities for advice, but they didn't seem to be of much help. And all the time, the parents of the kids stood around waiting for him to pull a cellophane-wrapped miracle out of his little black bag, because, as they said in Groppa County, there was nothing could go wrong with a human body that Doc Judd couldn't take care of some way or other. And all the time, the kids got weaker and weaker.

Doc got big, bleary bags under his eyes from sitting up nights going over the latest books and medical magazines he'd ordered from the city. Near as I could tell he'd find nothing even though lots of times he'd get to bed almost as late as Steve.

And then he brought home the handkerchief. Soon as I saw it, my stump gave a good, hard, extra twinge and I wanted to walk out of the kitchen. Tiny, fancy handkerchief, it was, all embroidered linen and lace edges.

"What do you think, Tom? Found this on the floor of the bedroom of the Stopes' kids. Neither Betty nor Willy have any idea where it came from. For a bit, I thought I might have a way of tracing the source of infection, but those kids wouldn't lie. If they say they never saw it before, then that's the way it is." He dropped the handkerchief on the kitchen table that I was clearing up, stood there sighing. "Betty's anemia is beginning to look serious. I wish I knew . . . I wish . . . Oh, well." He walked out to the study, his shoulders bent like they were under a sack of cement.

I was still staring at the handkerchief, chewing on a fingernail, when Steve bounced in. He poured himself a cup of coffee, plumped it down on the table, and saw the handkerchief.

"Hey," he said. "That's Tatiana's. How did it get here?"

I swallowed what was left of the fingernail and sat down very carefully opposite him. "Steve," I asked, and then stopped because I had to massage my aching stump. "Steve, you know a girl who owns that handkerchief? A girl named Tatiana?"

"Sure. Tatiana Latianu. See, there are her initials embroidered in the corner—T. L. She's descended from the Romanian nobility; family goes back about five hundred years. I'm going to marry her."

"She the girl you've been seeing every night for the past month?"

He nodded. "She only goes out at night. Hates the glare of the sun. You know, poetic kind of girl. And Tom, she's so *beautiful*. . . ."

For the next hour, I just sat there and listened to him. And I felt sicker and sicker. Because I'm Romanian myself, on my mother's side. And I knew why I'd been getting those twinges in my stump.

She lived in Brasket Township, about twelve miles away. Steve had run into her late one night on the road when her convertible had broken down. He'd given her a lift to her house—she'd just rented the old Mead mansion—and he'd fallen for her, hook, line, and whole darn fishing rod.

Lots of times, when he arrived for a date, she'd be out driving around the countryside in the cool night air, and he'd have to play cribbage with her maid, an old beak-faced Romanian biddy, until she got back. Once or twice he'd tried to go after her in his hotrod, but that had led to trouble. When she wanted to be alone, she had told him she wanted to be *alone*. So that was that. He waited for her night after night. But when she got back, according to Steve, she really made up for everything. They listened to music and talked and danced and ate strange Romanian dishes that the maid whipped up. Until dawn. Then he came home.

Steve put his hand on my arm. "Tom, you know that poem, "The Owl and the Pussycat"? I've always thought the last line was beautiful. 'They danced by the light of the moon, the moon, the moon. They danced by the light of the moon.' That's what my life will be like with Tatiana. If only she'll have me. I'm still having trouble talking her into it."

He let out a long breath. "The first good thing I've heard," I said without thinking. "Marriage to *that* girl—"

When I saw Steve's eyes, I broke off. But it was too late.

"What the hell do you mean, Tom; *that* girl? You've never even met her."

I tried to twist out of it, but Steve wouldn't let me. He was real sore. So I figured the best thing was to tell him the truth.

"Stevie. Listen. Don't laugh. Your girl friend is a vampire."

He opened his mouth slowly. "Tom, you're off your—"

"No, I'm not." And I told him about vampires. What I'd heard from my mother who'd come over from the old country, from Transylvania, when she was twenty. How they can live and have all sorts of strange powers—just so long as they have a feast of human blood once in a while. How the vampire taint is inherited, usually just one child in the family getting it. And how they go out only at night, because sunlight is one of the things that can destroy them.

Steve turned pale at this point. But I went on. I told him about the mysterious epidemic that had hit the kids of Groppa County—and made them anemic. I told him about his father finding the handkerchief in the Stopes' house, near two of the sickest kids. And I told him—but all of a sudden I was talking to myself. Steve tore out of the kitchen. A second or two later, he was off in the hotrod.

He came back about eleven thirty, looking old as his father. I was right, all right. When he'd wakened Tatiana and asked her straight, she'd broken down and wept a couple of buckets-full. Yes, she was a vampire, but she'd only got the urge a couple of months ago. She'd fought it until her mind began to break when the craving hit her. She'd only touched kids, because she was afraid of grown-ups—they might wake up and be able to catch her. But she'd kind of worked on a lot of kids at one time, so that no one kid would lose too much blood. Only the craving had been getting stronger. . . .

And still Steve had asked her to marry him! "There must be a way of curing it," he said. "It's a sickness like any other sickness." But she, and—believe me—I thanked God, had said no. She'd pushed him out and made him leave. "Where's Dad?" he asked. "He might know."

I told him that his father must have left at the same time he did, and hadn't come back yet. So the two of us sat and thought. *And thought.*

When the telephone rang, we both almost fell out of our seats. Steve answered it, and I heard him yelling into the mouthpiece.

He ran into the kitchen, grabbed me by the arm and hauled me out into his hotrod. "That was Tatiana's maid, Magda," he told me as we went blasting down the highway. "She says Tatiana got hysterical after I left, and a few minutes ago she drove away in her convertible. She wouldn't say where she was going. Magda says she thinks Tatiana is going to do away with herself."

"*Suicide?* But if she's a vampire, how—" And all of a sudden I knew just how. I looked at my watch. "Stevie," I said, "drive to Crispin Junction. And drive like holy hell!"

He opened that hotrod all the way. It looked as if the motor was going to tear itself right off the car. I remember we went around curves just barely touching the road with the rim of one tire.

We saw the convertible as soon as we entered Crispin Junction. It was parked by the side of one of the three roads that cross the town. There was a tiny figure in a flimsy nightdress standing in the middle of the deserted street. My leg stump felt like it was being hit with a hammer.

The church clock started to toll midnight just as we reached her. Steve leaped out and knocked the pointed piece of wood out of her hands. He pulled her into his arms and let her cry.

I was feeling pretty bad at this point. Because all I'd been thinking of was how Steve was in love with a vampire. I hadn't looked at it from her side. She'd been enough in love with him to try to kill herself the *only* way a vampire could be killed—by driving a stake through her heart on a crossroads at midnight.

And she was a pretty little creature. I'd pictured one of these siren dames: you know, tall, slinky, with a tight dress. A witch. But this was a very frightened, very upset young lady who got in the car and cuddled up in Steve's free arm like she'd taken a lease on it. And I could tell she was even younger than Steve.

So, all the time we were driving back, I was thinking to myself *these kids have got plenty trouble*. Bad enough to be in love with a vampire, but to be a vampire in love with a normal human being. . . .

"But how *can* I marry you?" Tatiana wailed. "What kind of home life would we have? And Steve, one night I might even get hungry enough to attack *you*!"

The only thing none of us counted on was Doc. Not enough, that is.

Once he'd been introduced to Tatiana and heard her story, his shoulders straightened and the lights came back on in his eyes. The sick children would be all right now. That was most important. And as for Tatiana—

"Nonsense," he told her. "Vampirism might have been an incurable disease in the fifteenth century, but I'm sure it can be handled in the twentieth. First, this nocturnal living points to a possible allergy involving sunlight and perhaps a touch of photophobia. You'll wear tinted glasses for a bit, my girl, and we'll see what we can do with hormone injections. The need for consuming blood, however presents a somewhat greater problem."

But he solved it.

They make blood in a dehydrated, crystalline form these days. So every night before Mrs. Steven Judd goes to sleep, she shakes some powder into a tall glass of water, drops in an ice cube or two and has her daily blood toddy. Far as I know, she and her husband are living happily ever after.

THE MINDWORM

CYRIL M. KORNBLUTH

In the postwar years, science fiction and fantasy alike had to adapt to accommodate the new imaginative needs of the technological era. One of science fiction's more perceptive thinkers, Cyril M. Kornbluth, helped revitalize the vampire story for the nuclear age with ''The Mindworm,'' which appeared in the first issue of the short-lived Worlds Beyond. *Here, Kornbluth suggests both a strikingly original origin for vampires and a unique new form of sustenance.*

THE HANDSOME j. g. and the pretty nurse held out against it as long as they reasonably could, but blue Pacific water, languid tropical nights, the low atoll dreaming on the horizon—and the complete absence of any other nice young people for company on the small, uncomfortable parts boat—did their work. On June 30th they watched through dark glasses as the dazzling thing burst over the fleet and the atoll. Her manicured hand gripped his arm in excitement and terror. Unfelt radiation sleeted through their loins.

A storekeeper-third-class named Bielaski watched the young couple with more interest than he showed in Test Able. After all, he had twenty-five dollars riding on the nurse. That night he lost it to a chief bosun's mate who had backed the j. g.

In the course of time, the careless nurse was discharged under conditions other than honorable. The j. g., who didn't like to put things in writing, phoned her all the way from Manila to say it was a damned shame. When her gratitude gave way to specific inquiry, their overseas connection went bad and he had to hang up.

She had a child, a boy, turned it over to a foundling home, and vanished from his life into a series of good jobs and finally marriage.

The boy grew up stupid, puny, and stubborn, greedy and miserable. To the home's hilarious young athletics director he suddenly said: "You hate me. You think I make the rest of the boys look bad."

The athletics director blustered and laughed, and later told the doctor over coffee: "I watch myself around the kids. They're sharp—they catch a look or a gesture and it's like a blow in the face to them, I know that, so I watch myself. So how did he know?"

The doctor told the boy: "Three pounds more this month isn't bad, but how about you pitch in and clean up your plate *every* day? Can't live on meat and water; those vegetables make you big and strong."

The boy said: "What's 'neurasthenic' mean?"

The doctor later said to the director: "It made my flesh creep. I was looking at his little spindling body and dishing out the old pep talk about growing big and strong, and inside my head I was thinking 'we'd call him neurasthenic in the old days' and then out he popped with it. What should we do? Should we do anything? Maybe it'll go away. I don't know anything about these things. I don't know whether anybody does."

"Reads minds, does he?" asked the director. *Be damned if he's going to read my mind about Schultz Meat Market's ten percent.* "Doctor, I think I'm going to take my vacation a little early this year. Has anybody shown any interest in adopting the child?"

"Not him. He wasn't a baby doll when we got him, and at present he's an exceptionally unattractive-looking kid. You know how people don't give a damn about anything but their looks."

"*Some* couples would take anything, or so they tell me."

"Unapproved for foster parenthood, you mean?"

"Red tape and arbitrary classifications sometimes limit us too severely in our adoptions."

"If you're going to wish him on some screwball couple that the courts turned down as unfit, I want no part of it."

"You don't have to have any part of it, doctor. By the way, which dorm does he sleep in?"

"West," grunted the doctor, leaving the office.

The director called a few friends—a judge, a couple the judge referred him to, a court clerk. Then he left by way of the east wing of the building.

The boy survived three months with the Berrymans. Hard-drinking Mimi alternately caressed and shrieked at him; Edward W. tried to be a good scout and just gradually lost interest, looking clean through him. He hit the road in June and got by with it for a while. He wore a Boy Scout uniform, and Boy Scouts can turn up anywhere, any time. The money he had taken with him lasted a month. When the last penny of the last dollar was three days spent, he was adrift on a Nebraska prairie. He had walked out of the last small town because the constable was beginning to wonder what on earth he was hanging around for and who he belonged to. The town was miles behind on the two-lane highway; the infrequent cars did not stop.

One of Nebraska's "rivers," a dry bed at this time of year, lay ahead, spanned by a railroad culvert. There were some men in its shade, and he was hungry.

They were ugly, dirty men, and their thoughts were muddled and stupid. They called him Shorty and gave him a little dirty bread and some stinking sardines from a can. The thoughts of one of them became less muddled and uglier. He talked to the rest out of the boy's hearing, and they whooped with laughter. The boy got ready to run, but his legs wouldn't hold him up.

He could read the thoughts of the men quite clearly as they headed for him. Outrage, fear, and disgust blended in him and somehow turned inside-out and one of the men was dead on the dry ground, grasshoppers vaulting onto his flannel shirt, the others backing away, frightened now, not frightening.

He wasn't hungry anymore; he felt quite comfortable and satisfied. He got up and headed for the other men, who ran. The rearmost of them was thinking *Jeez he folded up the evil eye we was only gonna—*

Again the boy let the thoughts flow into his head and again he flipped his own thoughts around them; it was quite easy to do. It was different—this man's terror from the other's lustful anticipation. But both had their points. . . .

At his leisure, he robbed the bodies of three dollars and twenty-four cents.

Thereafter his fame preceded him like a death wind. Two years on the road and he had his growth and his fill of the dull and stupid minds he met there. He moved to northern cities, a year here, a year there, quiet, unobtrusive, prudent, an epicure.

Sebastian Long woke suddenly, with something on his mind. As night fog cleared away he remembered, happily. Today he started the Demeter Bowl! At last there was time, at last there was money—six hundred and twenty-three dollars in the bank. He had packed and shipped the three dozen cocktail glasses last night, engraved with Mrs. Klausman's initials—his last commercial order for as many months as the bowl would take.

He shifted from nightshirt to denims, gulped coffee, boiled an egg but was too excited to eat it. He went to the front of his shop-workroom-apartment, checked the lock, waved at neighbors' children on their way to school, and ceremoniously set a sign in the cluttered window.

It said: NO COMMERCIAL ORDERS TAKEN UNTIL FURTHER NOTICE

From a closet he tenderly carried a shrouded object that made a double armful and laid it on his workbench. Unshrouded, it was a glass bowl—*what* a glass bowl! The clearest Swedish lead glass, the purest lines he had ever seen, his secret treasure since the crazy day he had bought it, long ago, for six months' earnings. His wife had given him hell for that until the day she died. From the closet he brought a portfolio filled with sketches and designs dating back to the day he had bought the bowl. He smiled over the first, excitedly scrawled—a florid, rococo conception, unsuited to the classicism of the lines and the serenity of the perfect glass.

Through many years and hundreds of sketches he had refined his conception to the point where it was, he humbly felt, not unsuited to the medium. A strongly molded Demeter was to dominate the piece, a matron as serene as the glass, and all the fruits of the earth would flow from her gravely outstretched arms.

Suddenly and surely, he began to work. With a candle he thinly smoked an oval area on the outside of the bowl. Two steady fingers clipped the Demeter drawing against the carbon black; a hair-fine needle in his other hand traced her lines. When the transfer of the design was done, Sebastian Long readied his lathe. He fitted a small copper wheel, slightly worn as he liked them, into the chuck and with his fingers charged it with the finest rouge from Rouen. He took an ashtray cracked in delivery and held it against the spinning disk. It bit in smoothly, with the *wiping* feel to it that was exactly right.

Holding out his hands, seeing that the fingers did not tremble with excitement, he eased the great bowl to the lathe and was about to make the first tiny cut of the millions that would go into the masterpiece.

Somebody knocked on his door and rattled the doorknob.

Sebastian Long did not move or look toward the door. Soon the busybody would read the sign and go away. But the pounding and the rattling of the knob went on. He eased down the bowl and angrily went to the window, picked up the sign, and shook it at whoever it was—he couldn't make out the face very well. But the idiot wouldn't go away.

The engraver unlocked the door, opened it a bit, and snapped: "The shop is closed. I shall not be taking any orders for several months. Please don't bother me now."

"It's about the Demeter Bowl," said the intruder.

Sebastian Long stared at him. "What the devil do you know about my Demeter Bowl?" He saw the man was a stranger, undersized by a little, middle-aged . . .

"Just let me in please," urged the man. "It's important. Please!"

"I don't know what you're talking about," said the engraver. "But what do you know about my Demeter Bowl?" He hooked his thumbs pugnaciously over the waistband of his denims and glowered at the stranger. The stranger promptly took advantage of his hand being removed from the door and glided in.

Sebastian Long thought briefly that it might be a nightmare as the man darted quickly about his shop, picking up a graver and throwing it down, picking up a wire scratch-wheel and throwing it down. "Here, you!" he roared, as the stranger picked up a crescent wrench which he did not throw down.

As Long started for him, the stranger darted to the workbench and brought the crescent wrench down shatteringly on the bowl.

Sebastian Long's heart was bursting with sorrow and rage; such a storm of emotions as he never had known thundered through him. Paralyzed, he saw the stranger smile with anticipation.

The engraver's legs folded under him and he fell to the floor, drained and dead.

The Mindworm, locked in the bedroom of his brownstone front, smiled again, reminiscently.

Smiling, he checked the day on a wall calendar.

"Dolores!" yelled her mother in Spanish. "Are you going to pass the whole day in there?"

She had been practicing low-lidded, sexy half-smiles like Lauren Bacall in the bathroom mirror. She stormed out and yelled in English: "I don't know how many times I tell you not to call me that Spick name no more!"

"Dolly!" sneered her mother. "Dah-lee! When was there a Saint Dah-lee that you call yourself after, eh?"

The girl snarled a Spanish obscenity at her mother and ran down the tenement stairs. Jeez, she was gonna be late for sure!

Held up by a stream of traffic between her and her streetcar, she danced with impatience. Then the miracle happened. Just like in the movies, a big convertible pulled up before her and its lounging driver said, opening the door: "You seem to be in a hurry. Could I drop you somewhere?"

Dazed at the sudden realization of a hundred daydreams, she did not fail to give the driver a low-lidded, sexy smile as she said: "Why, *thanks!*" and climbed in. He wasn't no Cary Grant, but he had all his hair . . . kind of small, but so was she . . . and jeez, the convertible had *leopard-skin seat covers!*

The car was in the stream of traffic, purring down the avenue. "It's a lovely day," she said. "Really too nice to work."

The driver smiled shyly, kind of like Jimmy Stewart but of course not so tall, and said: "I feel like playing hooky myself. How would you like a spin down Long Island?"

"Be wonderful!" The convertible cut left on an odd-numbered street.

"Play hooky, you said. What do you do?"

"Advertising."

"*Advertising!*" Dolly wanted to kick herself for ever having doubted, for ever having thought in low, self-loathing moments that it wouldn't work out, that she'd marry a grocer or a mechanic and live forever after in a smelly tenement and grow old and sick and stooped. She felt vaguely in her happy daze that it might have been cuter, she might have accidentally pushed him into a pond or something, but this was cute enough. An advertising man, leopard-skin seat covers. . . . What more could a girl with a sexy smile and a nice little figure want?

Speeding down the South Shore she learned that his name was Michael Brent, exactly as it ought to be. She wished she could tell him she was Jennifer Brown or one of those real cute names they had nowadays, but was reassured when he told her he thought Dolly Gonzalez was a beautiful name. He didn't, and she noticed that omission, add: "It's the most beautiful name I ever heard!" That, she comfortably thought as she settled herself against the cushions, would come later.

They stopped at Medford for lunch, a wonderful lunch in a little restaurant where you went down some steps and there were candles on the table. She called him Michael and he called her Dolly. She learned that he liked dark girls and thought the stories in *True Story* really were true, and that he thought she was just tall enough, and that Greer Garson was wonderful, but not the way she was, and that he thought her dress was just wonderful.

They drove slowly after Medford, and Michael Brent did most of the talking. He had traveled all over the world. He had been in the war and wounded—just a flesh wound. He was thirty-eight, and had been married once, but she died. There were no children. He was alone in the world. He had nobody to share his town house in the fifties, his country place in Westchester, his lodge in the Maine woods. Every word sent the girl floating higher and higher on a tide of happiness; the signs were unmistakable.

When they reached Montauk Point, the last sandy bit of the continent before blue water and Europe, it was sunset, with a great wrinkled sheet of purple and rose stretching half across the sky and the first stars appearing above the dark horizon of the water.

The two of them walked from the parked car out onto the sand, alone, bathed in glorious Technicolor. Her heart was nearly bursting with joy as she heard Michael Brent say, his arms tightening around her: "Darling, will you marry me?"

"Oh, *yes*, Michael!" she breathed, dying.

The Mindworm, drowsing, suddenly felt the sharp sting of danger. He cast out through the great city, dragging tentacles of thought:

". . . die if she don't let me . . ."

". . . six an' six is twelve an' carry one an' three is four . . ."

". . . gobblegobble *madre de dios pero soy* gobblegobble . . ."

". . . parlay Domino an' Missab and shoot the roll on Duchess Peg in the feature . . ."

". . . melt resin add the silver chloride and dissolve in oil of lavender stand and decant and fire to cone zero twelve give you shimmering streaks of luster down the walls . . ."

". . . moiderin' square-headed gobblegobble tried ta poke his eye out wassamatta witta ref . . ."

". . . O God I am most heartily sorry I have offended Thee in . . ."

". . . talk like a commie . . ."

". . . gobblegobblegobble two dolla twenny-fi' cents gobble . . ."

". . . just a nip and fill it up with water and brush my teeth . . ."

". . . really know I'm God but fear to confess their sins . . ."

". . . dirty lousy rock-headed claw-handed paddle-footed goggle-eyed snot-nosed hunch-backed feeble-minded pot-bellied son of . . ."

". . . write on the wall alfie is a stunkur and then . . ."

". . . thinks I believe it's a television set but I know he's got a bomb in there but who can I tell who can help so alone . . ."

". . . gabble *was ich weiss nicht* gabble geh bei Broadvay gabble . . ."

". . . *habt mein* daughter Rosie such a fella gobblegobble . . ."

". . . wonder if that's one didn't look back . . ."

". . . seen with her in the Medford restaurant . . ."

The Mindworm struck into that thought.

". . . not a mark on her but the M. E.s have been wrong before and heart failure don't mean a thing anyway try to talk to her old lady authorize an autopsy get Pancho little guy talks Spanish be best . . ."

The Mindworm knew he would have to be moving again—soon. He was sorry; some of the thoughts he had tapped indicated good . . . hunting?

Regretfully, he again dragged his net:

". . . with chartreuse drinks I mean drapes could use a drink come to think of it . . ."

". . . reep-beep-reep-beep reepiddy-beepiddy-beep bop man wadda beat . . ."

$$`` \sum_{r-l+1}^{a} \phi(a_x, a_r) - \sum_{g-l}^{l} \phi(a_x, a_s). \textit{ What the hell was that?''}$$

The Mindworm withdrew, in frantic haste. The intelligence was massive, its overtones those of a vigorous adult. He had learned from certain dangerous children that there was peril of a leveling flow. Shaken and scared, he contemplated traveling. He would need more than that wretched girl had supplied, and it would not be epicurean. There would be no time to find individuals at a ripe emotional crisis, or goad them to one. It would be plain—munching. The Mindworm drank a glass of water, also necessary to his metabolism.

EIGHT FOUND DEAD
IN UPTOWN MOVIE;
"MOLESTER" SOUGHT

Eight persons, including three women, were found dead Wednesday night of unknown causes in widely separated seats in the balcony of the Odeon Theater at 117th St. and Broadway. Police are seeking a man described by the balcony usher, Michael Fenelly, 18, as "acting like a woman-molester."

Fenelly discovered the first of the fatalities after seeing the man "moving from one empty seat to another several times." He went to ask a woman in a seat next to one the man had just vacated whether he had annoyed her. She was dead.

Almost at once, a scream rang out. In another part of the balcony Mrs. Sadie Rabinowitz, 40, uttered the cry when another victim toppled from his seat next to her.

Theater manager I. J. Marcusohn stopped the show and turned on the house lights. He tried to instruct his staff to keep the audience from leaving before the police arrived. He failed to get word to them in time, however, and most of the audience was gone when a detail from the 24th Pct. and an ambulance from Harlem hospital took over at the scene of the tragedy.

The Medical Examiner's office has not yet made a report as to the causes of death. A spokesman said the victims showed no signs of poisoning or violence. He added that it "was inconceivable that it could be a coincidence."

Lt. John Braidwood of the 24th Pct. said of the alleged molester: "We got a fair description of him and naturally we will try to bring him in for questioning."

Clickety-click, clickety-click, clickety-click sang the rails as the Mindworm drowsed in his coach seat.

Some people were walking forward from the diner. One was thinking: "Different-looking fellow. (a) he's aberrant. (b) he's nonaberrant and ill. Cancel (b)—respiration normal, skin smooth and healthy, no tremor of limbs, well-groomed. Is aberrant (1) trivially. (2) significantly. Cancel (1)—displayed no involuntary interest when . . . odd! *Running* for the washroom! Unexpected because (a) neat grooming indicates amour propre inconsistent with amusing others; (b) evident health inconsistent with . . ." It had taken one second, was fully detailed.

The Mindworm, locked in the toilet of the coach, wondered what the next stop was. He was getting off at it—not frightened, just careful. Dodge them, keep dodging them and everything would be all right. Send out no mental taps until the train was far away and everything would be all right.

He got off at a West Virginia coal and iron town surrounded by ruined mountains and filled with the offscourings of Eastern Europe. Serbs, Albanians, Croats, Hungarians, Slovenes, Bulgarians, and all possible combinations and permutations thereof. He walked slowly from the smoke-stained, brownstone passenger station. The train had roared on its way.

". . . ain' no gemmum that's fo sho', fi-cen' tip fo' a good shine lak ah give um . . ."

". . . dumb bassar don't know how to make out a billa lading yet he ain't never gonna know so fire him get it over with . . ."

". . . gabblegabblegabble . . ." Not a word he recognized in it.

". . . gobblegobble dat tam vooman I brek she nack . . ."

". . . gobble trink visky chin glassabeer gobblegobblegobble . . ."

". . . gabblegabblegabble . . ."

". . . makes me so gobblegobble mad little no-good tramp no she ain' but I don' like no standup from no dame . . ."

A blond, square-headed boy fuming under a street light.

". . . out wit' Casey Osiak I could kill that dumb bohunk alla time trine ta paw her . . ."

It was a possibility. The Mindworm drew near.

". . . stand me up for that gobblegobble bohunk I oughtta slap her inna mush like my ole man says . . ."

"Hello," said the Mindworm.

"Waddaya wan'?"

"Casey Oswiak told me to tell you not to wait up for your girl. He's taking her out tonight."

The blond boy's rage boiled into his face and shot from his eyes. He was about to swing when the Mindworm began to feed. It was like pheasant after chicken, venison after beef. The coarseness of the environment, or the ancient strain? The Mindworm wondered as he strolled down the street. A girl passed him:

". . . oh but he's gonna be mad like last time wish I came right away so jealous kinda nice but he might bust me one some day be nice to him tonight there he is lam'post leaning on it looks kinda funny gawd I hope he ain't drunk looks kinda funny sleeping sick or bozhe moi gabblegabblegabble . . ."

Her thoughts trailed into a foreign language of which the Mindworm knew not a word. After hysteria had gone she recalled, in the foreign language, that she had passed him.

The Mindworm, stimulated by the unfamiliar quality of the last feeding, determined to stay for some days. He checked in at a Main Street hotel.

Musing, he dragged his net:

". . . gobblegobblewhompyeargobblecheskygobblegabblechyesh . . ."

". . . take him down cellar beat the can off the damn chesky thief put the fear of god into him teach him can't bust into no boxcars in *mah* parta the caounty . . ."

". . . gabblegabble . . ."

". . . phone ole Mister Ryan in She-cawgo and he'll tell them three-card monte grifters who got the horse-room rights in this necka the woods by damn don't pay protection money for no protection . . ."

The Mindworm followed that one further; it sounded as though it could lead to some money if he wanted to stay in the town long enough.

The Eastern Europeans of the town, he mistakenly thought, were like the tramps and bums he had known and fed on during his years on the road—stupid and safe, safe and stupid, quite the same thing.

In the morning he found no mention of the square-headed boy's death in the town's paper and thought it had gone practically unnoticed. It had—by the paper, which was of, by, and for the coal and iron company and its native-American bosses and straw bosses. The other town, the one without a charter or police force, with only an imported weekly newspaper or two from the nearest city, noticed it. The other town had roots more than two thousand years deep, which are hard to pull up. But the Mindworm didn't know it was there.

He fed again that night, on a giddy young streetwalker in her room. He had astounded and delighted her with a fistful of ten-dollar bills before he began to gorge. Again the delightful difference from city-bred folk was there. . . .

Again in the morning he had been unnoticed, he thought. The chartered town, unwilling to admit that there were streetwalkers or that they were found dead, wiped the slate clean; its only member who really cared was the native American cop on the beat who had collected weekly from the dead girl.

The other town, unknown to the Mindworm, buzzed with it. A delegation went to the other town's only public officer. Unfortunately he was young, American-trained, perhaps even ignorant about some important things. For what he told them was: "My children, that is foolish superstition. Go home."

The Mindworm, through the day, roiled the surface of the town proper by allowing himself to be roped into a poker game in a parlor of the hotel. He wasn't good at it, he didn't like it, and he quit with relief when he had cleaned six shifty-eyed, hard-drinking loafers out of about three hundred dollars. One of them went straight to the police station and accused the unknown of being a sharper. A humorous sergeant, the Mindworm was pleased to note, joshed the loafer out of his temper.

Nightfall again, hunger again . . .

He walked the streets of the town and found them empty. It was strange. The native American citizens were out, tending bar, walking their beats, locking up their newspaper on the stones, collecting their rents, managing their movies—but where were the others? He cast his net:

". . . gobblegobblegobble whomp year gobble . . ."

". . . crazy old Polack mama of mine try to lock me in with Errol Flynn at the Majestic never know the difference if I sneak out the back . . ."

That was near. He crossed the street and it was nearer. He homed on the thought:

". . . jeez he's a hunka man like Stanley but he never looks at me that Vera Kowalik I'd like to kick her just once in the gobblegobblegobble crazy old mama won't be American so ashamed . . ."

It was half a block, no more, down a side street. Brick houses, two stories, with back yards on an alley. She was going out the back way.

How strangely quiet it was in the alley.

". . . ea-sy down them steps fix that damn board that's how she caught me last time what the hell are they all so scared of went to see Father Drugas won't talk bet somebody got it again that Vera Kowalik and her big . . ."

". . . gobble bozhe gobble whomp year gobble . . ."

She was closer; she was closer.

"All think I'm a kid show them who's a kid bet if Stanley caught me all alone out here in the alley dark and all he wouldn't think I was a kid that damn Vera Kowalik her folks don't think she's a kid . . ."

For all her bravado she was stark terrified when he said: "Hello."

"Who—who—who—?" she stammered.

Quick, before she screamed. Her terror was delightful.

Not too replete to be alert, he cast about, questing.

". . . gobblegobblegobble whomp year."

The countless eyes of the other town, with more than two thousand years of experience in such things, had been following him. What he had sensed as a meaningless hash of noise was actually an impassioned outburst in a nearby darkened house.

"Fools! fools! Now he has taken a virgin! I said not to wait. What will we say to her mother?"

An old man with handlebar mustache and, in spite of the heat, his shirt sleeves decently rolled down and buttoned at the cuffs, evenly replied: "My heart in me died with hers, Casimir, but one must be sure. It would be a terrible thing to make a mistake in such an affair."

The weight of conservative elder opinion was with him. Other old men with mustaches, some perhaps remembering mistakes long ago, nodded and said: "A terrible thing. A terrible thing."

The Mindworm strolled back to his hotel and napped on the made bed briefly. A tingle of danger awakened him. Instantly he cast out:

". . . gobblegobble whompyear."

". . . whampyir."

"WAMPYIR!"

Close! Close and deadly!

The door of his room burst open, and mustached old men with their shirt sleeves rolled down and decently buttoned at the cuffs unhesitatingly marched in, their thoughts a turmoil of alien noises, foreign gibberish that he could not wrap his mind around, disconcerting, from every direction.

The sharpened stake was through his heart and the scythe blade through his throat before he could realize that he had not been the first of his kind, and that what clever people have not yet learned, some quite ordinary people have not yet entirely forgotten.

SHARE ALIKE

JEROME BIXBY AND JOE E. DEAN

Like its prototype Unknown Worlds, Beyond Fantasy Fiction *sought original ways to express fantasy themes for readers sated with the cliches of gothic horror. "Share Alike," from the first issue, was a good example. The only collaboration between Jerome Bixby (author of the fantasy classic, "It's a Good Life") and Joe E. Dean, it remains both an intriguing survival story and a fascinating variation on the traditional parasitic relationship between vampire and victim.*

THEY SPREAD-EAGLED themselves in the lifeboat, bracing hands and feet against the gunwales.

Above them, the pitted and barnacled stern of the *S. S. Luciano,* two days out of Palermo and now headed for hell, reared up hugely into the overcast of oily black smoke that boiled from ports and superstructure. Craig had time to note that the screws were still slowly turning, and that a woman was screaming from the crazily tilted afterdeck. Then the smoke intervened—a dark pall that lowered about the lifeboat as the wind shifted, blotting out the sky, the ship.

Fire met water. One roared; the other hissed. Gouts of blazing gasoline flared through the smoke like flame demons dancing on the waves.

Groaning, shuddering, complaining with extreme bitterness, the ship plunged.

Sky and smoke became a sickening whirl, as the lifeboat tore into the churning water in a suicidal effort to follow the parent ship to the bottom. Spray flew; waves loomed, broke, fell away; the lifeboat shipped water. Craig cursed aloud, making rage a substitute for terror. Facing him, Hofmanstahal grinned sourly.

421

The small boat righted itself. It was still in violent motion, lurching aimlessly across a sea jagged with whitecaps; but Craig knew that the crisis was past. He lifted his face into the cold wind, pulling himself up from the water-slopping bottom of the boat until his chin rested on the gunwale.

A wide patch of brownish foam and oil-scum spread slowly from the vortex of exploding bubbles that rose from the vanished ship.

The sea quieted. A gull swooped down and lit on an orange crate that had bobbed to the surface.

"Well," said Craig. "Well. That's that."

Hofmanstahal peeled off his shirt, wrung it out over the side. The hair that matted his thick chest and peeped from his armpits had a golden sheen that was highlighted by the sun. A small cut was under his left eye, a streak of oil across his forehead.

"You were of the crew?" he asked.

"Yes."

"But not an A. B. You are too spindly for that."

"I was navigator."

Hofmanstahal chuckled, a deep sound that told of large lungs. "Do you think you can navigate us out of this, my friend?"

"I won't have to. We're in a well-traveled shipping lane. We'll be picked up soon enough."

"How soon might that be?"

"I don't know. I don't even know if we got an SOS out; it all happened so fast." Craig sighed, rolled over so that he sat with his back curved against the side of the boat. "I doubt if we did, though. The tanks right under the radio shack were the first to go. I wonder who got careless with a ciagrette. . . ."

"M'm. So we'll eventually be picked up. And in the meantime, do we starve?"

Craig got up tiredly. "You underestimate the merchant marine." He sloshed to the stern of the lifeboat, threw open the food locker. They saw kegs of water, tins of biscuits and salt meat, canned juices, a first-aid kit.

"More than enough," Craig said. He turned, searched the surrounding swells. "I wonder if any others survived. . . ."

Hofmanstahal shook his head. "I have been looking too. No others. All were sucked down with the ship."

Craig kept looking. Smoke, heaving stained water, debris, a few dying gasoline flames—that was all.

Hofmanstahal said, "At least we shall be well fed. Did you have any close friends aboard?"

"No." Craig sat down, pushed wet hair back from his forehead, let his hands fall to his lap. "And you?"

"Me? No one. I have outlived all my friends. I content myself with being a man of the crowd. a select group of *bon vivants* for drinking and conversation. . . . It is enough."

*   *   *

Sitting with a seat between them, as if each somehow wanted to be alone, the men exchanged backgrounds. By his own account, Hofmanstahal was an adventurer. No locality could hold him for long, and he seldom revisited a place he already knew. He had been secretary to a former Resident in Malaya, and concerned himself with gems in Borneo, with teak in China; a few of his paintings had been displayed in the *Galerie des Arts* in Paris. He had been en route to Damascus to examine some old manuscripts which he believed might contain references to one of his ancestors.

"Although I was born in Brashov," he said, "family records indicate that we had our beginnings elsewhere. You may think it snobbish, this delving into my background, but it is a hobby which has absorbed me for many years. I am not looking for glory, only for facts."

"Nothing wrong with that," Craig said. "I envy you your colorful past."

"Is yours so dull, then?"

"Not dull . . . the colors just aren't so nice. I grew up in the Atlanta slums. Things were pretty rough when I was a kid—"

"You weren't big enough to be tough."

Craig nodded, wondering why he didn't resent this second reference to his small size. He decided that it was because he liked the big man. Hofmanstahal wasn't insolent, just candid and direct.

"I read a lot," Craig went on. "My interest in astronomy led me into navigation while I was in the navy. After I was mustered out I stayed at sea rather than go back to what I'd left."

They continued to converse in low, earnest voices for the remainder of the afternoon. Always above them the white gulls circled.

"Beautiful, aren't they?" asked Craig.

Hofmanstahal looked up. His pale eyes narrowed. "Scavengers! See the wicked eyes, the cruel beaks! Pah!"

Craig shrugged. "Let's eat. And hadn't you better do something for that cut under your eye?"

Hofmanstahal shook his massive head. "You eat, if you wish. I am not hungry." He touched his tongue to the dribble of blood that ran down his cheek.

They kept track of the days by cutting notches in the gunwale. There were two notches when Craig first began to wonder about Hofmanstahal.

They had arranged a system of rationing for food and water. It was far from being a strict ration, for there was plenty for both of them.

But Craig never saw Hofmanstahal eat.

The Romanian, Craig thought, was a big man, he should certainly have an equally big appetite.

"I prefer," said Hofmanstahal, when Craig asked about it, "to take my meals at night."

Craig let it pass, assuming that the big man had a digestive disorder, or perhaps was one of those unfortunates who possess inhibitions about eating in front of others. Not that the latter seemed likely, considering Hofmanstahal's amiably aggressive personality and the present unusual circumstances but, on the other hand, what did it matter? Let him eat standing on his head if he wanted to.

Next morning, when Craig opened the food locker to eat his share, the food supply was apparently undiminished.

The morning after that, the same thing.

Another notch. Five days, now. And Craig found something else to puzzle about. He was eating well; yet he felt himself sinking deeper and deeper into a strange, uncaring lethargy, as if he were well on his way toward starvation.

He took advantage of the abundance of food to eat more than was his wont. It didn't help.

Hofmanstahal, on the other hand, greeted each day with a sparkling eye and a spate of good-humored talk.

Both men by now had beards. Craig detested his, for it itched. Hofmanstahal was favoring his, combing it with his fingers, already training the mustache with insistent twiddlings of thumb and forefinger.

Craig lay wearily in the bow and watched.

"Hofmanstahal," he said. "You're not starving yourself on my account, are you? It isn't necessary, you know."

"No, my friend. I have never eaten better."

"But you've hardly touched the stores."

"Ah!" Hofmanstahal flexed his big muscles. Sunlight flickered along the golden hair that fuzzed his torso. "It is the inactivity. My appetite suffers."

Another notch. Craig continued to wonder. Each day, each hour, found him weaker, more listless. He lay in the bow of the boat, soaking in the warmth of the sun, his eyes opaque, his body limp. Sometimes he let one hand dangle in the cool water, but the appearance of ugly, triangular shark fins put a stop to that.

"They are like all of nature, the sharks," Hofmanstahal said. "They rend and kill, and give nothing in return for the food they so brutally take. They can offer only their very bodies, which are in turn devoured by larger creatures. And on and on. The world is not a pretty place, my friend."

"Are men so different?"

"Men are the worst of all."

Seven notches, now. Craig was growing weaker. He was positive by now that Hofmanstahal was simply not eating.

There were nine notches on the gunwale when Craig found that Hofmanstahal *was* eating, after all.

It was night, and the sea was rougher than it had been. The *slap-slap* of waves against the hull wakened Craig from a deep, trancelike sleep. That, and the oppressive feeling of a nearby presence.

He stirred, felt the presence withdraw. Through half-shut eyes he saw Hofmanstahal, darkly silhouetted against a sky ablaze with stars.

"You were crying out in your sleep, my friend." The big man's voice was solicitous. "Nightmare?"

"My throat . . . stinging, burning. I . . ."

"The salt air. You will be all right in the morning."

Craig's face felt like a numb mask of clay. It was an effort to move his lips. "I think—I think I'm going—to die."

"No. You are not going to die. You must not. If you die, I die."

Craig thought about that. The rocking of the boat was gentle, soothing. A warmth stole over him, though the night was cool. He was weak, but comfortable; fearful, yet content. Head back, breathing easily, he let himself become aware of the glory of the heavens.

The constellation Perseus was slanting toward the western horizon, and Craig noted almost unconsciously, with the skill of long practice, that the variable star Algol was at its maximum brilliancy. Algol—the ghoul.

The thought lingered. It turned over and over in his mind, as his unconscious seemed to examine it for some hidden meaning.

Then, abruptly, the thought surged up into his conscious mind.

And he knew.

He lifted himself up to his elbows, supporting himself weakly.

"Hofmanstahal," he said, "you're a vampire, aren't you?"

The other's chuckle was deep and melodious in the darkness.

"Answer me, Hofmanstahal. Are you a vampire?"

"Yes."

Craig had fainted. Now it was as if layer after layer of blackness were being removed, bringing him closer to the light with every moment. A tiny sullen orange disk glowed in the darkness, expanding, increasing in brightness until it filled the world.

The blackness was gone, and he was staring up into the blinding, brassy heart of the sun.

He gasped and turned his head away.

There was music. Someone whistling a German folk tune.

Hofmanstahal . . .

Hofmanstahal sat in the stern, his brawny gold-fuzzed forearms resting on his knees.

The whistling stopped.

"Good morning, my friend. You have had a good, long rest."

Craig stared, his lips working.

Far above a gull called harshly, and was answered by one skimming at water level.

Hofmanstahal smiled. "You mustn't look at me that way. I'm almost harmless, I assure you." He laughed gently. "Things could be much worse, you know. Suppose, for example, I had been a werewolf. Eh?"

He waited a moment.

"Oh, yes, Lycanthropy is real—as real as those gulls out there. Or—more fitting, perhaps—as real as those sharks. Once, in Paris, I lived for three months with a young woman who was a public bath attendant by day and a werewolf by night. She would choose her victims by their—"

Craig listened numbly, aware that Hofmanstahal was merely making idle talk. The story of the female werewolf turned into an anecdote, patently untrue. Hofmanstahal chuckled at it, and seemed disappointed when Craig did not. There was a certain sensitive shyness about the big Romanian, Craig thought . . . a sensitive vampire! Aware of Craig's revulsion, he was camouflaging the situation with a flood of words.

"—And when the gendarme saw that the bullet which had killed her was an ordinary lead one, he said, 'Messieurs, you have done this *pauvre jeune fille* a grave injustice.' Ha! The moment was a sad one for me, but—"

"Stop it!" Craig gasped. "Go turn yourself into a bat or something and fly away. Just get out of my sight . . . my blood in your stomach . . ."

He tried to turn away, and his elbows slipped. His shoulderblades thumped the bottom of the boat. He lay there, eyes closed, and his throat thickened as if he wanted to laugh and vomit at the same time.

"I cannot turn myself into a bat, my friend. Ugly little creatures—" Hofmanstahal sighed heavily. "Nor do I sleep in a coffin. Nor does daylight kill me, as you can see. All that is superstition. Superstition! Do you know that my grandfather died with a white ash stake through his heart?" His beard tilted angrily. "Believe me, we variants have more to fear from the ignorant and superstitious than they from us. There are so many of them, and so few of us."

Craig said, "You won't touch me again!"

"Ah, but I must."

"I'm still strong enough to fight you off."

"But not strong enough to get at the food if I choose to prevent you."

Craig shook his head. "I'll throw myself overboard!"

"That I cannot permit. Now, why not submit to the inevitable? Each day, I will supply you with your ration of food; each night, you will supply me with mine. A symbiotic relationship. What could be fairer?"

"Beast! Monster! *I will not*—"

Hofmanstahal sighed and looked out over the tossing sea. "Monster. Always they say that of us; they, who feed off the burned flesh of living creatures."

It was the face of his father, stern and reproving, that Craig always saw before him during those long nights in the lifeboat. His father, who had been a Baptist minister. When the lifeboat drifted on a sea that was like glass, reflecting the stars with such clarity that the boat might have been suspended n a vast star-filled sphere, and Craig felt the warm, moist lips of the vampire at his throat—then conscience arose in the form of his father.

Well . . . he wasn't submitting willingly. Not at first. But the food had been withheld until his belly twisted with hunger and he cried out with parched lips for water. Then, shudderingly, he had allowed the vampire to feed.

It was not as bad as he had expected. An acute, stinging sensation as the sharp canines pricked the flesh (strange, that he had not noticed before how *sharp* they were); then numbness as the anesthetic venom did its work. The venom must have been a hypnotic. As the numbness spread toward his face, and his lips and cheeks became chill, strange colors danced before his eyes, blending and twining in cloudy patterns that sent his thoughts wandering down incomprehensible byways. He was part of Hofmanstahal. Hofmanstahal was part of him. The feeling was almost lascivious.

And each time it was less painful, less shocking, till finally it was mere routine.

Strangely, his conscience did not torment him during the day. The comfortable warmth and lassitude that before had only touched him now enveloped him completely. His thoughts were vague; memory tended to slip away from what had gone before, and to evade what was to come. The sea, the sky, the wheeling gulls were beautiful. And Hofmanstahal, vampire or not, was an interesting conversationalist.

"You are pale, friend Craig," he would say. "Perhaps I have been too greedy. Do you know, with that wan face and the beard, you remind me of a poet I knew in Austria. For a long time he was one of my favorite companions. But perhaps you did not know that we prefer certain donors to others. Believe me, we are not the indiscriminate gluttons that literature would have you think."

"How—did you become as you are?"

"How did I, Eric Hofmanstahal, become a vampire? That is a question with broad implications. I can tell you that my people were vampires, but that leaves unanswered the question of our origin. This I cannot tell you, though I have searched deeply into the matter. There are legends, of course, but they are contradictory." Hofmanstahal stroked his beard and seemed lost in thought.

"Some say," he went on, after a moment, "that when *Homo sapiens* and the ape branched from a common ancestor, there was a third strain which was so despised by both that it was driven into obscurity. Others maintain that we came to Earth from another planet, in prehistoric times. There is even mention of a species which was quite different from man but which, because of man's dominance over the earth, imitated him until it developed a physical likeness to him. Then there is the fanciful notion that we are servants of the Devil—one battalion among his legions, created by him to spread sorrow and misery throughout the ages of the world.

"Legends! We have been persecuted, imprisoned, burned alive; we have been classified as maniacs and perverts—all because our body chemistry is unlike that of man. We drink from the fountain of life while man feasts at the fleshpots of the dead, yet we are called monsters." He crumpled a biscuit in his powerful hand and cast the pieces upon the water, which immediately boiled with sharks.

"Man!" he said softly.

Life went on. Craig ate. Hofmanstahal fed. And horror diminished with familiarity.

There were only the two of them, under the vast sky, rising and falling gently to the whim of the sea. The horizon was the edge of their world. No other existed. Night and day merged into gray sameness. Sea and sky were vague, warm reflections; the motion of the boat soothed. This was peace. There was no thought of resistance left in Craig. Hofmanstahal's symbiosis became a way of life, then life itself.

There was time in plenty to gaze up at the stars, a pleasure which everyday exigencies had so often denied him. And there was strange, dark companionship: lips that sought his throat and drained away all thoughts of urgency or violent action, leaving him exhausted and somehow thrilled. It was peace. It was satisfaction. It was fulfillment.

Fear was lost in stupor; revulsion, in a certain sensuality. Hofmanstahal's nightly visit was no longer a thing of horror, but the soft arrival of a friend whom he wanted to help with all his being, and who was in turn helping him. Night and day they exchanged life, and the life they nurture became a single flow and purpose between them. Craig was the quiescent vessel of life, which Hofmanstahal filled every day, so that life might build itself against the coming of night and the return of its essence to Hofmanstahal.

Day and night marched above them toward the pale horizon that circumscribed their world. In their world values had changed, and the fact of change been forgotten.

Still, deep in his mind, Craig's conscience wailed. Legend, history, the church, all at one time or another had said that vampires were evil. He was submitting to a vampire; therefore, he was submitting to evil. Food or no food, the Reverend Craig would never have submitted. He would have sharpened a stake or cast a silver bullet—

But there were no such things here. His father's face rose before him to tell him that this did not matter. He sought to drive it away, but it remained. During the moments of nightly meeting, of warmth and strange intimacy, it glared down upon them brighter than the moon. But Hofmanstahal's back was always turned to it, and Craig, in all his weakness and agony and ecstasy and indecision, did not mention it.

They had forgotten to carve the notches on the gunwale. Neither was certain now how long they had been adrift.

There came a day, however, when Hofmanstahal was forced to cut down Craig's ration of food.

"I am sorry," he said, "but you can see for yourself that it is necessary."

"We're so near the end of our supplies, then?"

"I am sorry," Hofmanstahal repeated, "Yes, we are nearing the end of your supplies . . . and if yours end, so will mine eventually."

"I don't really mind," Craig whispered, "I'm seldom really hungry now. At first, even the full rations left me unsatisfied, but now I don't even like the taste of the food. I suppose it's because I'm getting no exercise.''

Hofmanstahal's smile was gentle. ''Perhaps. Perhaps not. We must keep a sharp lookout for ships. If one does not come soon, we will starve, though, of course, I will now cut down my own rations as well as yours.''

''I don't care.''

''My poor Craig, when you regain your strength you will care very much. Like me, you will want to live and go on living.''

''Maybe. But now I feel that dying would be easy and pleasant. Better, maybe, than going back to the world.''

''The world is evil, yes; but the will to live in it drives all of us.''

Craig lay motionless and wondered, with a clarity of mind he had not experienced in many, many days, whether he dreaded going back to the world because the world was evil, or whether it was because he felt that he himself was tainted, unfit to mix with human beings again.

. . . And Hofmanstahal might be a problem. Should he be reported to the authorities? No, for then they would know about Craig.

But was all that had happened so disgraceful, so reprehensible? Had Craig had any other choice but to do what he had done?

None.

His conscience, in the form of his father, screamed agony.

Well, then perhaps Hofmanstahal would try to force him to continue the relationship. Had he—*pleased* the Romanian? He felt that he had. . . .

But surely gentle, considerate Hofmanstahal, the sensitive vampire, would not try to force—

Craig's mind rebelled against such practical thoughts. They required too much effort. It was easier not to think at all—to lie as he had lain for so many days, peaceful, relaxed, uncaring.

Clarity of mind faded into the gray sameness of day and night. He ate. Hofmanstahal fed.

He was scarcely conscious when Hofmanstahal spotted the smoke on the horizon. The big man lifted him up so that he could see it. It was a ship, and it was coming in their direction.

''So—now it is over.'' Hofmanstahal's voice was soft, his hands were warm on Craig's shoulders. ''So it ends—our little idyll.'' The hands tightened. ''My friend . . . my friend, before the ship comes, the men and the noise, the work and the worry and all that goes with it, let us for the last time—''

His head bent, his lips found Craig's throat with their almost sexual avidity.

Craig shivered. Over the Romanian's shoulder he could see the ship approaching, a dot on the horizon. There would be men aboard.

Men! Normalcy and sanity, cities and machines and half-forgotten values, coming nearer and nearer over the tossing sea, beneath the brassy sky, from the real world of men that lay somewhere beyond the horizon. . . .

Men! Like himself, like his father, who hovered shouting his disgust.

And he, lying in the arms of—

God, God, *what if they should see him!*

He kicked. He threw his arms about. He found strength he hadn't known he had, and threshed and flailed and shrieked with it.

The lifeboat rocked. A foot caught Hofmanstahal in the midriff. The vampire's arms flew wide and he staggered back with a cry: *"Craig—"*

The backs of his knees struck the gunwale—the one with meaningless notches carved in it. His arms lashed as he strove to regain his balance. His eyes locked with Craig's, shock in them. Then he plunged backward into the sea.

The sharks rejected him as food, but not before they had killed him.

Craig found himself weeping in the bottom of the boat, his face in slime. And saying hoarsely again and again, "Eric, I'm sorry—"

It seemed a very long time before the ship came close enough for him to make out the moving figures on the deck. It seemed so long because of the thoughts and half-formed images that were racing through his brain.

A new awareness was coming over him in a hot flood, an awareness of—

Of the one thing popularly believed about vampires that must have solid foundation in fact.

Had the venom done it? He didn't know. He didn't care.

He lay weakly, watching the steamer through half-closed eyes. Sailors lined the rails, their field glasses trained on him.

He wondered if they could see his father. No, of course not—that had all been hallucination. Besides, a moment ago his father had fled.

It was a navy ship, a destroyer. He was glad of that. He knew the navy. The men would be healthy. Strenuous duty would make them sleep soundly.

And at the end of its voyage lay the whole pulsing world.

Craig licked his lips.

AND NOT QUITE HUMAN

JOE L. HENSLEY

The tale of interplanetary invasion proliferated in science fiction magazines as America slid from the technocratic self-assurance of the early postwar years into the paranoia of the McCarthy era. But though marauding aliens were always presented as intellectually aloof and technologically superior to humans, they were not without some vital flaw that ultimately proved their undoing. In "And Not Quite Human," Joe L. Hensley suggests that one such weak spot might be the rigid skepticism necessary to achieve scientific sophistication.

THEY WON of course. One ship against a world, but they won easily.

The Regents would be pleased. Another planet for colonization—even a few specimens for the labs: Earthmen, who had incredibly lived through the attack.

Forward, in a part of the great ship where the complex control panels whirred and clicked, two of the Arcturians conferred together.

"How are the Earth specimens, Doctor?" the older one asked, his voice indifferent. He touched his splendid purple pants, straightening the already precise creases.

"They stare at the walls, Captain. They do not eat what we give them. They seem to look through the guards, say very little and use their bodies feebly. I do not think that all of them will live through the trip."

"They are weak. It only shows the laboratories are wrong. Our people are *not* related to them despite the similarity in appearance. No, we are cast in a stronger

431

mold than that.'' He drummed his desk with impatient fingers. ''Well—we can't let them die. Force-feed them if necessary. Our scientists demand specimens; we are lucky that some of them lived through the attack. I don't see how it was possible—it was such a splendid attack.''

''They have no real sickness, not even a radiation burn in the lot of them,'' the doctor said. ''But they are weak and morose.''

''Keep them alive and well, Doctor.''

The doctor searched the captain's metallic face. ''Captain, do you ever have dreams?''

''Eh—dreams?'' It took the captain a moment to comprehend. ''Dreams are forbidden by the Regents! They show instability.''

''The men, Sir . . . some of the crew have been complaining.''

''Complaining! Complaining's expressly forbidden in the rules. You know that, Doctor. Why haven't I been informed?''

''It was such a little thing, something psychological, I think. I've had a few in who've had nightmares.'' The doctor made a deprecatory gesture. ''Space fear, I think. Most of the men complained were first trippers.''

''Make a list of the names and submit it to me. We have to eliminate such types, as you should know.''

''Yes sir.'' The doctor got up to leave.

''Uh—Doctor—did they tell you what the dreams were about?''

''Blood, Sir.'' The doctor shook his head and clenched his antiseptic, scoured hands. ''Skulls and bats and old women around a bubbling pot, bony shadows that trapped them when they ran.''

''Rot.''

''Yes sir.''

The doctor walked down the gleaming passageway, seeing the men like well-oiled machines; the talented men, each in his own technical job, each uniform precisely the same, the teeth, clean and white, each face and body cut from the same matrix, even the boots alike, dark shiny mirrors. Unlined faces—young, unlike the skeleton faces in the hold.

The first guard brought hand to forehead in a snappy salute. ''Yes sir?''

''Prisoner inspection.''

The door whined open and the doctor started through.

''Sir!'' The urgency in the guard's voice detained him.

''Yes?'' He remembered the man as one of the ones who had been at sick call that morning.

''May I be relieved? I feel ill. I've been sick since—since last sleep period.''

The doctor looked impassively at the too-white eyes. *Better not let it start,* he thought.

''Stand your duty. I can't have you relieved. You know the rules.''

''But sir!''

''Report to sickbay after you are relieved. For psychoanalysis—and I mean after you are *regularly* relieved!'' The doctor again looked into the frightened eyes and considered making an exception this one time. *No, there'll be more, then,* he thought.

The automatic salute reassured him. ''Yes sir.''

''Your name?'' He wrote it in his prescription book and walked on.

First cell, second cell, the fifteenth—all the same. The listless faces, the hungry dead men's eyes watching him. Eyes cut from coffins. Twenty-two cells—two to a cell, women segregated as they should be. Forty-four prisoners in all.

Eighty-eight eyes watching him. He shivered inwardly.

How many were there? he thought. *Forty-four individuals left out of a billion or two?*

He read the guards' notebooks. ''Man in cell fourteen, Name: Alexander Green. Was observed drawing strange patterns on the deck with chalk. Chalk taken away from him. No resistance.''

''Woman in cell three, Name: Elizabeth Gout. Talking to herself and to the walls. Was quieted by her cellmate, Meg Newcomb, on orders of corporal of the guard.''

The shadows were thick in the prisoners' hold; the lights dim, the only sounds were the thrum of the rhythmic atomic engines and the click of the guards' heels as each one came to attention and presented his book for inspection.

The corporal of the guard walked silently behind him and took the orders down at the end of the cell block.

''Force-feed them. Bring the vitamin lights down here. Give them injections.'' The doctor paused and stared coldly. ''The guard at cell four was inept in his salute. Place him on report.''

''Yes sir.''

''Anything else to report, Corporal?''

The man hesitated; then said, ''Some of the guards are jumpy.''

''And the prisoners?'' the doctor asked caustically.

The corporal was flustered. ''They seem stronger, sir.''

''They're getting acclimated to the conditions of the trip.''

''They still haven't eaten anything.''

''I said—in case you misunderstood me, Corporal—that they are getting acclimated to the trip. You may consider yourself on report too.'' The doctor enunciated each word savagely.

The corporal clicked his heels and the doctor went quickly back up the line of cells. He averted his head, not looking into the cells. An electronic device scanned him and opened the door as it read his identity.

He went through the hatch, felt it close quickly behind him, and disregarded the guard who had wanted to be relieved. He went on to his own office in the small, efficient sickbay. He slumped over his desk exhausted.

There was a sound of running feet outside. Then the door to his office was almost torn from its hinges as a soundless blast of energy struck it. The doctor leaped to his feet and flung open the metal door.

The sick guard stood there, weaving drunkenly on boneless legs. "Stand back, Doctor. I see one over by the wall. See it over there?" the man screamed. "It's coming for me. Can't get away—can't." He raised the pistol as the doctor watched.

"Stop—you damned fool!"

The man lay on the floor, gun pointed at his own shapeless body, his torso a mass of torn, charred tissue. His eyes were still open and they stared sightlessly at the small porthole, beyond which the luminous stars reeled.

The sight was not revolting to the doctor, but the implications were. He had seen too many dead, both of his own race and others, to care particularly about one more. It was what this death might mean to him personally that worried him—what the Regents might say.

He called the guard on watch and gave orders automatically until the task of examining and disposing was done. There were necessary papers to fill out and sign, the personal effects to be inventoried—and the report to the captain. And all the time he was engaged in the routine, his mind flashed the question: *I wonder what it will mean to me when we get back? The Regents will want to examine me. They'll say it was my fault.* He felt the panic begin to rise, but his body made the necessary responses and his face was imperturbable.

He went to the captain's office.

"Why did he do it, Doctor?" The captain was more perplexed than angry.

The doctor stonily replied, "We're in space."

"We have a hundred million men in space!" the captain exclaimed. "Few of them ever commit suicide. It's been bred out of the race. It just doesn't happen." He pounded his hand against his plastic desk, the almost muted sound incongruous with the angry gesture. "I want to know why. It's against the rules—*you* know that."

The doctor did not flinch. "He was a first tripper. First time away from home. A guard? No—a farmboy in uniform, that's what he was." The doctor found himself almost homicidally angry at the dead guard. *What right does he have to cause me all this trouble?*

The captain watched him strangely. "That's what most of our men are—men from farms. I'm from a farm myself." The captain eyed him dubiously while the insidious sounds of the machines rocked and jolted around them. "You're tired, Doctor. You need some rest."

The doctor ignored the remark. "Maybe it's the prisoners. All the guards who have complained have been standing prisoner watches."

"I've seen the prisoners." The barking voice was contemptuous.

Have you seen them? Have you seen the way they look at you? the doctor thought, but aloud he said, through regulated teeth: "Yes sir."

"Find out what's wrong."

"Yes sir. I'll do my best." Spit and polish and everything according to the rules.

"Report to me on everything."

"Of course, Captain."

"Do an autopsy—look at his brain."

"I did, sir." He fought to keep his voice rational. "We kept his head. We always do in a case like this."

"Do it again." The captain stared penetratingly at him. "Find out what was wrong with his head, so that we can eliminate it from the race. Something was wrong with his head—that was it. Find out!"

"Yes sir!" *Feet together, salute, turn—keep your back straight. Be a soldier, be a spaceman, be an Arcturian, be strong—be a conqueror.*

The doctor went back to his own office and sat down shakily at his plastic desk. Then he fought his way upright again and looked in the room's small mirror.

Still the same. I'm still the same—but so tired—why am I so tired?

He touched his face. "Same face." *But it was more deeply marked and harsh now.*

His hair: "Like always." *Is that a streak of gray?*

His eyes: "They see." *What do they see? What? What?*

And then, for the first time, his tightly held mind barrier let down and he admitted the dreams and the long sleepless periods to himself. Remembered them for what they were. Knew he could no longer fool himself.

Insects crawling on him; a great gray rat with canine teeth at his throat, while bats eyed him evilly—and curious women who plied their trade around a bubbling pot, their thin-edged voices plotting more horrors. And always the shadows, shadows that leaped and tore at his unprotected body, shadows that had a definite form—shadows which faded disconcertingly just as he seemed to be able to make out the faces that were sickeningly familiar.

The nightmares became real to him.

Quite suddenly, the nightmares came close to him as he sat at the plastic desk and together they planned the ghastly joke, while they laughed together. He nicked, with surgical care, the arteries in his wrists and groins and smiled as he bubbled away on the metal desk.

"Goodby, Doctor," said a voice.

Goodby, Voice. And the sound echoed while the uniform became discolored, the boots greasy with death, the face too white—smiling and staring.

And the others—the many others—soon.

For three sleep periods the machines sighed as the carnage went on. The captain put out directives and took the guns away. After that they found other ways. Crewmen jumped out the escape hatches and into the atomic convertors—or smashed their heads against the steel bulkheads.

For three sleep periods.

Each time he heard the clicking of the guard's heels, the captain almost screamed. In his imagination, he was seeing the Arcturian Regents. They were pointing accusing fingers at him, while the extermination chambers waited.

"Your ship," they said.

"My ship," he admitted.

"The doctor, half of your crew dead. How—why did they die?"

"Suicide." He trembled under the blanket.

"It's against the rules, Captain," the voices said calmly, convincing him.

"I told them."

"But you are the captain. The captain is responsible. The rule says that."

"Yes—the doctor said it was the prisoners."

The Regents laughed. "For the good of the race, we have no choice but . . ."

The captain pulled the covers tighter over his aching head and lay stiffly on his cot. He drowned the voices in a sea of his own making, smiling as he saw each hand disappear under the stormy waves. For a while he lay that way, while the juggernaut shadows slippered carefully about the room, hovering and watchful.

And then, once again, he could hear the whine of the great engines. He sat up.

The old man—the one listed on the rolls as Adam Manning, one of the specimen Earthmen—sat on one of the stiff chairs by the captain's desk.

"Hello," the old man said.

"Guards!" screamed the captain.

But no one answered. Only the machines roared on, replying softly in their unhearing way.

"Guards!" the captain screamed again as he watched the old man's face.

"They can't hear you," the old man said.

The captain knew instinctively that it was true. "You did it!" He strained to leap from his cot at the old man. He could not move. His hands clenched as he fought against invisible bonds.

He began to cry. But the Regents' voices came, stopping it. "Crying's against the rules," they said stiffly, without pity.

The old man smiled at him from the chair. The shadows murmured softly, conferring in myriad groups, dirtying the aseptic bulkheads. They drew closer to captain and he could only half stifle a scream.

"What are you?" he managed.

"Something you've trained out of your people. You wouldn't understand even if we told you, because you don't believe that there ever was anything like us." The old man smiled. "We're your new Regents." The shadows smiled hideously, agreeing, and revealing their long, canine teeth.

"It was a wonderful attack, Captain," the old man said softly. The shadows nodded as they formed and faded. "Nothing human could have lived through it—nothing human did. Some of us were deep underground where they'd buried us long ago—the stakes through our hearts—they knew how to deal with us. But your fire burned the stakes away."

He waved a scaly hand at the shadows. They came down upon the captain relentlessly.

The captain began to scream.

Then, there was only the automatic sound of the machines.

The ship roared on through space.

PLACE OF MEETING

CHARLES BEAUMONT

Like his colleagues Ray Bradbury, Richard Matheson, and William F. Nolan, Charles Beaumont often wrote science fiction founded on horror themes. "Place of Meeting" was written in the aftermath of nuclear war, a theme that dominated science fiction in the 1950s and early 1960s. Implicit in this reworking of the vampire legend is the belief that man's superstitions will persist as long as human folly endures.

IT SWEPT DOWN from the mountains, a loose, crystal-smelling wind, an autumn chill of moving wetness. Down from the mountains and into the town, where it set the dead trees hissing and the signboards creaking. And it even went into the church, because the bell was ringing and there was no one to ring the bell.

The people in the yard stopped their talk and listened to the rusty music.

Big Jim Kroner listened too. Then he cleared his throat and clapped his hands—thick hands, calloused and work-dirtied.

"All right," he said loudly. "All right, let's us settle down now." He walked out from the group and turned. "Who's got the list?"

"Got it right here, Jim," a woman said, coming forward with a looseleaf folder.

"All present?"

"Everybody except that there German, Mr. Grunin—Grunger—"

Kroner smiled; he made a megaphone of his hands. "Grüninger—Barthold Grüninger?"

A small man with a mustache called out excitedly, *"Ja, ja! . . . s'war schwer den Friedhof zu finden."*

"All right. That's all we wanted to know, whether you was here or not." Kroner studied the pages carefully. Then he reached into the back pocket of his overalls and withdrew a stub of pencil and put the tip to his mouth.

"Now, before we start off," he said to the group, "I want to know is there anybody here that's got a question or anything to ask?" He looked over the crowd of silent faces. "Anybody don't know who I am? No?"

It came another wind then, mountain-scattered and fast: It billowed dresses, set damp hair moving; it pushed over pewter vases, and smashed dead roses and hydrangeas to swirling dust against the gritty tombstones. Its clean rain smell was gone now, though, for it had passed over the fields with the odors of rotting life.

Kroner made a check mark in the notebook. "Anderson," he shouted. "Edward L."

A man in overalls like Kroner's stepped forward.

"Andy, you covered Skagit valley, Snohomish and King counties, as well as Seattle and the rest?"

"Yes, sir."

"What you got to report?"

"They're all dead," Anderson said.

"You looked everywhere? You was real careful?"

"Yes, sir. Ain't nobody alive in the whole state."

Kroner nodded and made another check mark. "That's all, Andy. Next: Avakian, Katina."

A woman in a wool skirt and gray blouse walked up from the back, waving her arms. She started to speak.

Kroner tapped his stick. "Listen here for a second, folks," he said. "For those that don't know how to talk English, you know what this is all about—so when I ask my question, you just nod up and down for yes (like this) and sideways (like this) for no. Makes it a lot easier for those of us as don't remember too good. All right?"

There were murmurings and whispered consultations and for a little while the yard was full of noise. The woman called Avakian kept nodding.

"Fine," Kroner said. "Now, Miss Avakian. You covered what? . . . Iran, Iraq, Turkey, Syria. Did you—find—an-ybody a-live?"

The woman stopped nodding. "No," she said. "No, no."

Kroner checked the name. "Let's see here. Boleslavsky, Peter. You go on back, Miss Avakian."

A man in bright city clothes walked briskly to the tree clearing. "Yes, sir," he said.

"What have you got for us?"

The man shrugged. 'Well, I tell you; I went over New York with a fine-tooth comb. Then I hit Brooklyn and Jersey. Nothin', man. Nothin' nowhere."

"He is right," a dark-faced woman said in a tremulous voice. "I was there too. Only the dead in the streets, all over, all over the city; in the cars I looked even, in the *offices*. Everywhere is people dead."

"Chavez, Pietro. Baja California."

"All dead, señor chief."

"Ciodo, Ruggiero. Capri."

The man from Capri shook his head violently.

"Denman, Charlotte. Southern United States."

"Dead as doornails . . ."

"Elgar, David S. . . .

"Ferrazio, lgnatz . . .

"Goldfarb, Bernard . . .

"Halpern . . .

"Ives . . . Kranek . . . O'Brian . . ."

The names exploded in the pale evening air like deep gunshots; there was much head-shaking, many people saying, "No. No."

At last Kroner stopped marking. He closed the notebook and spread his big workman's hands. He saw the round eyes, the trembling mouths, the young faces; he saw all the frightened people.

A girl began to cry. She sank to the damp ground, and covered her face and made these crying sounds. An elderly man put his hand on her head. The elderly man looked sad. But not afraid. Only the young ones seemed afraid.

"Settle down now," Kroner said firmly. "Settle on down. Now, listen to me. I'm going to ask you all the same question one more time, because we got to be sure." He waited for them to grow quiet. "All right. This here is all of us, every one. We've covered all the spots. Did anybody here find one single solitary sign of life?"

The people were silent. The wind had died again, so there was no sound at all. Across the corroded wire fence the gray meadows lay strewn with the carcasses of cows and horses and, in one of the fields, sheep. No flies buzzed near the dead animals; there were no maggots burrowing. No vultures; the sky was clean of birds. And in all the untended rolling hills of grass and weeds which had once sung and pulsed with a million voices, in all the land there was only this immense stillness now, still as years, still as the unheard motion of the stars.

Kroner watched the people. The young woman in the gay print dress; the tall African with his bright paint and cultivated scars; the fierce-looking Swede looking not so fierce now in this graying twilight. He watched all the tall and short and old and young people from all over the world, pressed together now, a vast silent polyglot in this country meeting place, this always lonely and long-deserted spot—deserted even before the gas bombs and the disease and the flying pestilences that had covered the earth in three days and three nights. Deserted. Forgotten.

"Talk to us, Jim," the woman who had handed him the notebook said. She was new.

Kroner put the list inside his big overalls pocket.

"Tell us," someone else said. "How shall we be nourished? What will we do?"

"The world's all dead," a child moaned. "Dead as dead, the whole world . . ."

"Todo el mund—"

"Monsieur Kroner, Monsieur Kroner, what will we do?"

Kroner smiled. "Do?" He looked up through the still-hanging poison cloud, the dun blanket, up to where the moon was now risen in full coldness. His voice was steady, but it lacked life. "What some of us have done before," he said. "We'll go back and wait. It ain't the first time. It ain't the last."

A little fat bald man with old eyes sighed and began to waver in the October dusk. The outline of his form wavered and disappeared in the shadows under the trees where the moonlight did not reach. Others followed him as Kroner talked.

"Same thing we'll do again and likely keep on doing. We'll go back and— sleep. And we'll wait. Then it'll start all over again and folks'll build their cities—new folks with new blood—and then we'll wake up. Maybe a long time yet. But it ain't so bad; it's quiet, and time passes." He lifted a small girl of fifteen or sixteen with pale cheeks and red lips. "Come on, now! Why, just think of the appetite you'll have all built up!"

The girl smiled. Kroner faced the crowd and waved his hands, large hands, rough from the stone of midnight pyramids and the feel of muskets, boil-speckled from night hours in packing plants and trucking lines; broken by the impact of a tomahawk and a machine-gun bullet, but white where the dirt was not caked, and bloodless. Old hands, old beyond years.

As he waved, the wind came limping back from the mountains. It blew the heavy iron bell high in the steepled white barn, and set the signboards creaking, and lifted ancient dusts and hissed again through the dead trees.

Kroner watched the air turn black. He listened to it fill with the flappings and the flutterings and the squeakings. He waited. Then he stopped waving and sighed and began to walk.

He walked to a place of vines and heavy brush. Here he paused for a moment and looked out at the silent place of high dark grass, of hidden huddled tombs, of scrolls and stone-frozen children stained silver in the night's wet darkness; at the crosses he did not look. The people were gone; the place was empty.

Kroner kicked away the foliage. Then he got into the coffin and closed the lid.

Soon he was asleep.